PRAISE FOR *THEY KNOW NOT WHAT THEY DO*

'A hugely ambitious book. Literary fiction meets sci-fi meets thriller in a gripping exploration of animal rights, the light and dark of new technologies, international academia, and the dynamics within modern families. Excellent.'   Will Dean, author of *Dark Pines*

'Classy and engrossing drama.'   *Daily Mail*

'Smart, slightly futuristic, nicely plotted.'   *Mail on Sunday*

'An engaging and fascinating exploration of the difficulties of modern parenting in the face of social media and technological advancements.'
Guy Bolton, author of *The Pictures*

'A contemporary novel that doesn't lose sight of perennial dilemmas.'
Kirkus

'Remarkable... Valtonen's grip on plot and character is so masterful that his storytelling easily contains his restless speculation about influences on how we live now and where we might end up as our old value systems begin to crumble.'   *World Literature Today*

'*They Know Not What They Do*...charts its own course toward an understanding of contemporary society and the importance of perspective. And a page turner to boot – huzzah!'   *Words Without Borders*

'This Scandinavian thriller is the perfect read for long winter nights. Winner of the 2014 Finlandia Prize, *They Know Not What They Do* weaves family drama and high stakes with chilling results.'
Paste

'This hugely ambitious work of contemporary realism offers a dramatic warning about the influence of digital culture.'   *Booklist*

THEY
KNOW
NOT
WHAT
THEY
DO

JUSSI VALTONEN

Translated by
Kristian London

ONEWORLD

A Oneworld Book

First published in North America, Great Britain and Australia
by Oneworld Publications, 2017
This paperback edition published 2018
Originally published in Finnish as *He eivät tiedä mitä tekevät* by
Tammi Publishers, 2014

English edition published by agreement with Jussi Valtonen
and Elina Ahlback Literary Agency, Helsinki, Finland

ISBN 978-1-78607-353-2
ISBN 978-1-78074-965-5 (eBook)

Work published with the support of the Finnish Literature Exchange

FILI   FINNISH
LITERATURE
EXCHANGE

Printed and bound in Great Britain by Clays Ltd, St Ives plc

Oneworld Publications
10 Bloomsbury Street
London WC1B 3SR
England

FSC
www.fsc.org
MIX
Paper from
responsible sources
FSC® C018072

For Lasse, Marianne, Colin and Andy

He stared at the television, hypnotized by the noise they made: the unrelenting sound. The old house screeched and thrummed with it. He felt as if they were inside with him, despite the width of the continent dividing them.

The cicadas were singing.

He had never even heard of them before. But they had been there in the soil the whole time, unseen, leaching nutrients from the roots of plants, waiting for the right time to emerge.

They'd been featured on the news, too. One of the Portland activists padded in from the kitchen carrying a mug of kombucha, passed a joint around, and said it was only a matter of time before they showed up here. Not this cycle, of course, maybe not even the next, but eventually genetic adaptation would enable them to spread from the East Coast. The others didn't buy it, there was definitely a reason you only encountered them back east; but the guy from Portland said the only surprising thing was that they hadn't got this far yet.

He turned back to the screen: the wings of a nymph glistened in the sun, picked out against a Japanese maple. Its milky body was maggot-like against the leaves' vivid green. It was waiting for its shell to harden. According to the scientist on TV, they didn't sting, bite, or spread disease, posed no threat to humans, animals, or even plants, really. The reason accidents happened, the guy from Portland said, taking a long drag from the joint, was because people panicked: closed their eyes at the wheel, started swatting at them in intersections and on freeway ramps. Everything would be fine, the scientist on television confirmed, if folks would just stay calm.

There was something awe-inspiring about it, he reflected, lying back against the recliner's ripped upholstery: they had been waiting out of sight this whole time, almost twenty years.

This was what they were watching in the living room, some of them sprawled on the floor, others on the sofa, when they suddenly heard it through the cicadas' incessant drone: a pounding on the house's heavy wooden door, as if someone was trying to knock it off its hinges.

They glanced at each other. Had there been a softer knock they'd missed, drowned out by the television? The thump of booted feet on the floor of the porch told them their visitor was not alone.

The television was still blaring when one of the guys from Eugene got up to answer. Coming! You don't have to kick the fucking door down.

Before it opened and he was the first to register the looks of stunned disbelief on the others' faces, he caught the scientist on TV saying it helped if you remembered that they were nature's creations, just like us: they were a miracle.

THE OTHER WOMAN

HELSINKI, FINLAND 1994

It was supposed to be temporary: everything would gradually return to normal.

According to the pamphlet from the maternity clinic, you couldn't put an exact time frame on it – which it then, ignoring its own advice, proceeded to do: three months, give or take, for over fifty percent of couples. But you had to bear in mind that every couple was different; this was a tricky time.

You shouldn't think there was anything wrong with either of you.

It had been a week since Alina left the pamphlet on the nightstand. She wasn't sure what she'd expected, but when she saw it still lying there, untouched, she felt something inside her sink.

After the break had lasted another three months, Alina raised the issue.

Joe seemed surprised. 'I thought it would still be too...' He searched for the right word. 'Complicated.'

'I don't think so.'

'Really? Hmm.' Then: 'OK.'

They'd tried the first time three months after Samuel's birth, and the experience had been an unexpected return to adolescence. It was like having to start all over again, concentrate on technique rather than content, guess how things would feel, what might work. Maybe this was what it was like, Alina reflected, for people with brain damage who had to learn how to walk again.

There were articles about it in the baby magazines at the library. Low estrogen levels meant it was natural if she didn't feel like having sex.

Did she? Her entire body had started feeling foreign to her, fickle. They were going to have to try again, but would it go any more smoothly? Maybe it wouldn't work this time either, which would raise the bar that much higher.

That evening, after Samuel was asleep, Joe climbed into bed in his flannel pajamas and picked up *Masters of Chess*. He read about the game's world champions every night before turning off the light. Sometimes he would set out the chess things on his nightstand, move one of the pieces according to the diagrams in the book, and stare at the board, lips pursed, as if waiting for the pawns or knights to speak.

They used to kiss before turning in; sometimes it had led to sex, sometimes not.

She waited. Joe's eyes skipped eagerly across the pages.

Eventually he became aware of her gaze. 'What?'

'I thought we… talked about—'

Joe's eyes were blank.

'Earlier today.'

'Oh, yeah,' he said, looking like he still didn't quite remember. 'That's right.'

He set aside the book. They cautiously turned towards each other and lay there, each waiting for a sign from the other, as if the situation and all that it entailed were completely foreign. Joe gingerly reached out and touched her side. As if afraid his touch would hurt, Alina thought.

Joe's mouth was familiar and felt right, but there was something mechanical about the whole thing. Is this what sex would be like with someone you didn't love? But then she felt Joe's warm hand on her skin and allowed it to rove at will, and it instantly remembered the route, the familiar contours.

Then the hand paused, made a minute change of course, and continued, but in an unaccustomed way. Alina monitored Joe's movements and felt something was missing. And she saw that Joe knew it, too.

'Would you like me to…' he said. She knew what Joe meant; it's what she had been hoping for.

'Mm-hm.' She nodded, not opening her eyes. 'Yes.'

Then she saw the girl: sitting on the edge of the bed, gazing at them blank-faced, as if she'd always been there.

Alina whimpered and pulled back.

'Did I hurt you?' Joe asked, concerned.

'No, but… maybe it's still too soon.''

'Hmm,' Joe said. 'OK.'

She thought she caught a hint of relief in his tone; they wouldn't have to try after all.

They looked at each other. She had always liked Joe's eyes. They were the eyes of a kind man. He stroked her hair. 'It's going to be fine.'

'Yeah.'

'Let's not rush it.'

'OK.'

They turned away from each other, and a little while later she could hear that he had fallen asleep.

The girl had started in the fall.

Alina had seen her staring at her computer screen in Joe's office, next to the door where there didn't used to be a desk. She was sitting with one leg folded under her. The position looked uncomfortable, as if she hadn't been able to decide whether to slump into a normal office slouch or arch over her computer like a cat. She had bobbed coal-black hair and a forehead furrowed in concentration, her lips lightly parted.

As she waited for her to acknowledge the presence of a visitor, Alina's eyes fixed on the fat silver bracelet on the girl's slender wrist. You get to spend all day here, she thought, and then pop into cute boutiques after work to pick out jewelry.

'Excuse me,' Alina finally said. The girl turned languidly, as if she'd been aware of her presence the whole time.

'I was supposed to...' Alina began. 'Joe and I...'

The girl raised an eyebrow as if in disbelief. Then she nodded towards the far wall. 'That's his desk over there.'

'I know.' Alina's voice sounded more clipped than she'd meant.

'He should be back soon.'

Alina wasn't sure if the girl didn't know where Joe was or if she didn't want to say. She stood in the doorway with the stroller, and the girl kept sitting in her peculiar position in Alina's husband's tiny office.

'If Joe comes back, tell him I went to the bathroom,' Alina said, turning away.

She pushed the stroller back down the hallway, overly conscious of seeming like a frumpy housewife – probably because, she thought, that's what I am – and of the girl's direct view of her as she retreated.

She would have dressed differently if she'd known about the girl… The thought immediately irked her, the need to impress a complete stranger.

But who did the girl think she was? Of course Alina knew which desk was Joe's. Alina had first brought him here and shown him around, they'd been here for ages, she and Joe; the girl was the interloper, the one who should have been asking Alina for advice.

Samuel stirred in his sleep and made a little noise, and her coming here with her son in his stroller suddenly struck Alina as embarrassing. Distracted, she walked too fast, and the stroller bumped into the corner of a table in the hallway. She tried to hum cheerfully and stand up straighter, but her cheeks were on fire. Once she had the stroller moving again, she glanced back; the girl in Joe's office was concentrating on her screen as if Alina and the child did not exist.

She had wanted to mention the girl to Joe. Just remark in passing that she'd noticed a new face at the department, someone who'd been assigned her own niche. In such a small unit, it made a difference who you bumped into in the hallways. Maybe they'd even see the girl socially at some point, say at the party they were going to throw?

The party, she thought: Joe had suggested it several times, but Alina was afraid of feeling like she was on display. People wandering around, inspecting their apartment, eyeing the food, Samuel and his clothes, toys, and crib, the record shelf, the living-room rug: so *this* is how Joe's wife likes things.

When she looked around, she didn't see much she liked or wanted. There was no light in the living room, because the switch on the lamp had been shorting out; Joe had promised to have it fixed and then forgotten. The switch and the wire were probably still traveling back and forth to the university every day in his satchel. She'd asked about it, but always at the wrong moment, and she didn't want to make a big deal about something so trivial. The most prominent element of the décor was the drying rack filled with Samuel's clothing: some of it from the maternity package given free to all expecting mothers in Finland, some hand-me-downs from Julia's sister, yet others from the flea market. The very thought of people from the department in their home, surrounded by the smell of milk and heaps of food-stained laundry, was embarrassing.

'It's not very common to invite your coworkers over in Finland,' she'd said, when Joe had asked again about hosting a party.

'It is in the States.'

'Yes. I'm just saying—'

'I know, I know,' Joe said and went to change into his squash gear, and Alina was never sure if he did know.

More than anything, she wanted to repaint the living room, correct her mistake. The walls had turned out too white. On the sample card the color had seemed fresh, but on a big surface it made other colors look harsh. The tiniest smudges stood out.

But Joe didn't think it was a good idea to redecorate *until things were clearer.*

Alina's heart skipped a beat.

'What things?'

'You know, like… where we're going to settle down and…'

She waited for him to continue, and then realized that the sentence had come to its end. It wasn't like they were going to live here for the rest of their lives, he finally said.

'No, probably not for the rest of our lives. But for now,' she said.

'Couldn't we just wait and see?'

'See what?'

'If we might find something…' Joe said. 'Maybe some opportunities back home.'

Back home. How easy it was to use the term in passing, *home*, its soft sounds, so natural and warm, as if it meant the same regardless of speaker or place. She stared at him, gulped and turned away.

'Come on, Alina,' Joe said, touching her arm, but she yanked it free.

He tried again: *Come on, Alina.* The way Joe pronounced her name, the stress fell on the second syllable and left the initial vowel silent: *Leena.* She'd liked it when they met; she'd wanted to be a person who needed a new, international version of her name.

'*We*,' she said. 'Did you really say we?'

'You know what I mean.'

'Actually, I don't.'

That evening, without being asked, Joe changed Samuel's diaper, fed him his bedtime oatmeal, and put him in his pajamas, all without saying a word.

After breastfeeding Samuel, Alina lay quietly in bed, her back to Joe. She didn't know if he could tell she was crying.

'Were you thinking we'd live in Finland for the rest of our lives?' he asked eventually.

Alina tried to think of the right question to ask back, equally obvious, supposedly neutral, but all she could feel was the tidal wave of unprocessed emotion crashing through her. A long time later, she heard him sigh, lower his glasses to the nightstand, and click off his reading lamp.

'When were you planning on telling me?' she said into the darkness.

'We've talked about various options,' he said.

Alina was dumbfounded. She was supposed to take that seriously? They'd played at making a list of all the countries they'd consider moving to; this had taken place in that little hotel room off Piccadilly Circus, before reality intervened. The list had included Poland and Ghana.

'Is this because you didn't get that job?' she asked. 'I thought you said you didn't want it.'

Joe was instantly irritated. Alina's stomach clenched; she wished she'd chosen her words more wisely.

'Tell me,' she said, caressing his cheek.

Joe looked at the ceiling, ignoring the brush of her hand. 'I feel like I'm surrounded by an invisible wall.'

'Socially or professionally?'

'Both.'

Joe felt like Finns didn't want to let strangers in. No one asked him out for coffee or invited him over. In their professional and personal lives, Finns seemed to close their social circles to outsiders. 'Especially if you have no free evenings,' he added.

Especially since I can't spend evenings away from home. I'm not keeping you here, Alina thought. You should have said something if you didn't want a baby.

Joe definitely didn't want a second baby. Alina wanted three. They'd tried discussing the matter on a few occasions, but the conversation grew strained, and Alina felt like she was demanding something her husband was incapable of giving.

'What are you thinking?' he asked. 'Say something.'

She thought about her father, who needed her help on a more or less weekly basis, dealing with the social security office or the bank. Dad hadn't ever learned to use the bill payment terminals in the bank's vestibule, although Alina had taken him there what seemed like a dozen times and held his hand through the process. How was she going to do that from the States? What if something happened to him? What if Dad got sick and needed help going to the store or reading the directions on his medication? Ever since Mom had died, Dad had become absent-minded and listless. It still seemed unreal to Alina that a woman who had radiated vigor and health could die a few months after the cancer diagnosis.

'Have you felt this way the whole time?' Alina said. 'You should have said something.'

'I didn't want to worry you,' Joe told her.

He stroked her hand and spoke in a low, steady voice. If anything came up, he explained, they could both think it over, decide then how they'd feel about a short stint in the States. What if Joe just kept an eye out on the off chance a suitable opportunity arose?

'But only if it's OK with you,' he added.

Alina thought about her father, about who he would spend Christmas with, and felt a lump in her throat. She turned away. She didn't want Joe to see her cry, she wasn't sure why.

'Does a short stint mean a short stint or a short stint that gradually turns into a long one?' she finally said.

'You can't always plan out everything in advance,' he said, and his tone made her feel like a petulant child.

'We're moving to the States,' she told her friend Julia, as the babies crawled around on the carpet at their feet. The lights were bright in Julia's living room, and the television was on low. They were eating cookies and mostly ignoring the movie playing on the VCR, where a single woman and single man refused to see they were meant for each other.

When? Julia wanted to know. Where? For good? Would Alina work there? What kind of school would Samuel attend?

'I don't know,' Alina said, blushing when Julia looked at her. Every day she expected Joe to come home and announce something had turned up in San Diego or Austin or Santa Barbara or Albuquerque and needed a yes or a no. She dreaded the conversation that would ensue, the arguments required of her and the barrage of counterarguments Joe would rain down in response, the war of attrition, the bargaining that would define their marriage and their life, Samuel's school years and language, how everything would take shape.

'Everything's still up in the air,' Alina said, turning away. She was sure things would work out for the best, she added.

Julia nodded. Her son Jimi, a dead ringer for Alfred Hitchcock, was already on his third diaper-change of the movie. 'Things always do.'

'It all depends on Joe's work, really.'

Julia said she admired Alina, about to fly off to a foreign country, game enough to start all over again. As she listened to Julia, Alina saw herself through her friend's eyes and was suddenly pleased to be going, to be the adventurous woman living life on her own terms. Moving began to sound intriguing, even enviable, and when Julia didn't seem to question it, Alina gradually managed to convince herself that this was the way things were now, and this was, if not optimal, then at least tolerable. This was her life, and she had chosen it, and there was a price to pay for every decision, as well as for not doing, not going and not agreeing to anything. And the price for that was often the highest.

It had been a challenge for Alina getting the stroller into the bathroom. After working it in through the narrow doorway, she stood in the fluorescent glare, unsure of what to do with herself, then washed her hands and waited. A little later, when she thought she heard the girl's footsteps in the corridor, she laboriously maneuvered the stroller back out.

Joe was alone in his office. They embraced tentatively; Alina got the impression that he didn't feel comfortable hugging in his professional persona, even with no one around to see. The building felt as deserted as a shuttered factory.

She looked around. Except for the girl's side of the room, Joe's office was exactly the same, which suddenly struck Alina as incomprehensible. Their home had undergone a complete transformation. The crib had taken over the bedroom's lone unoccupied wall, their bed had moved from its former place, a diaper table had been drilled in where the second bathroom cabinet used to be. The basket of toys and baby bouncer formed an encampment – evidently a permanent one, although that hadn't been the intention – in the middle of the living room. The girl had claimed half of Joe's office and the baby half their home, but Joe's desk, bulletin board, and bookshelf appeared untouched.

'What are you looking at?' he asked.

'I just forgot what it looked like in here.'

Joe hitched his trousers and lined up the pens on his desk as if he found the slightest disorder disturbing. Alina was struck by the sensation that they were meeting to discuss some unavoidable but unpleasant arrangement.

She'd been a student here too once upon a time. It seemed hard to believe now. She tried to recall the material from her textbooks that had seemed so essential then, the minutiae that pretentious boys in ponytails had argued about in the cafeteria that had been of zero relevance since.

'Well,' she said, after they had sat in silence for some time. Joe looked at her and smiled.

'Yes?'

'Um… are we just going to stay here?' Alina said, meaning his office.

'Where would you like to go?' Joe asked.

'Go?'

Alina blinked. She'd imagined that he would want to show Samuel to his colleagues, some of whom she knew too, or at least had known. Hadn't that been the point of the visit? Did Joe think she didn't have anything better to do with her day than kill time in her husband's office? Or was he waiting for Samuel to wake up? Alina started to wonder if she was perpetually leaving the most important part of what she wanted to convey unsaid.

Suddenly something indescribable and heavy washed over her and she had to sit down, but the only chair free was the girl's.

'What's wrong?' Joe asked.

'I just feel a little dizzy.'

It's probably dehydration on account of the breastfeeding, she was on the verge of saying, but then the office door opened.

The girl was standing by the open door. She was twirling an unlit cigarette between her forefinger and middle finger as if trying to signal something to Joe. Alina thought, Is she going to smoke in a room where there's a baby?

'Oh. I'm sorry,' the girl said in English, and the twirling stopped. 'I didn't realize you were still here,' she added to Alina in Finnish, somehow managing to avoid her gaze. 'I was just heading out for a smoke,' she said to Joe, and shot a quick glance at her cigarette, as if it had appeared there of its own accord.

The girl's lips were red, freshly painted.

'But you don't smoke,' Alina commented to her husband.

The girl raised her artfully plucked eyebrows at Joe: really? For a second, Alina thought she would burst out laughing.

'To keep me company,' the girl explained to Alina, in a mocking tone, it seemed.

'I'm kind of busy today,' Joe said in an unfamiliar, formal voice.

The girl raised her eyebrows again as if to say: let's get back to this once that woman is gone, spun on her heel, and left.

Alina looked at Joe inquiringly.

'I go along sometimes to stretch my legs,' he said, and coughed. 'If I have the time.'

'You can smoke for all I care,' she told him. 'I'm just surprised.'

'I don't smoke.'

'I meant that if you did, I wouldn't mind.' She tried to smile and lighten her voice. 'What's her name?'

Joe's expression remained serious.

'Aleksandra.'

Alina had only gone to Italy because she felt guilty. The memory of it, though, still set her heart hammering. She would let her thoughts wander back to the trip whenever she felt like she hadn't experienced anything in life.

She had been so young. It had only been a year and a half ago, but still: she had been so young.

She hadn't wanted anyone else to learn about her abominable master's thesis, let alone give a presentation on it. But Wallenberg had implied it was part of the deal.

'P. Wallenberg would be pleased to welcome you to his team,' he had announced, which would mean her doing a dissertation. Even at his most casual, Wallenberg spoke in a formal register. It was an attempt at humor, which Alina found touching: a sixty-year-old professor, still so inept. There was no one else on Wallenberg's team. The students knew that he tried to lure someone from every cohort into continuing his work, his unique line of research in danger of dying with him.

In a way, the trip was Alina's apology for not having the nerve to say she had no interest in writing a dissertation or rescuing Wallenberg's life's work from extinction; for even implying she was still giving the matter serious consideration.

As hundreds of conference participants surged into the main exhibition hall to meander through the poster presentations, Alina stood alone in front of her poster, praying no one would stop. They could all tell she was a fraud. She was ashamed of her study, its results, and the last-minute way she'd thrown the thesis together. The poster's dimensions had been specified by the organizers but struck her as brazen. She still found it hard to believe that the university press had printed the big, black and white announcement just for her, for this. It must have cost hundreds of marks.

She did her best to look preoccupied and lost in thought, and to her relief everyone stepped briskly past. The people around her were discussing their research; she melted into her bland poster and felt her pulse rate gradually normalize.

Only fifteen more minutes, Alina thought, trying not to glance at her watch. She could hear the Spanish girl at the next stand explain her research for the thirtieth time. She repeated her spiel word for word for every new listener, down to the jokes Alina now knew by heart. *I can cover for you if you need a bathroom break*, she thought as she looked over at the approachable girl people liked listening to, laughing politely at the appropriate moments.

Suddenly Alina envied the girl everything: her research design, less sophisticated than Alina's; her conclusions, over-confident in light of the data; her English, clumsier than Alina's; the ease with which she presented her work. An audience had gathered around her, and the men in particular looked as if they had been waiting their entire lives for this encounter.

Alina snapped out of it when she realized someone was studying her poster. A brown-eyed, friendly-looking, non-Finnish man had stopped and asked her to describe her research to him. *Walk me through it*, he said. There was something touching about the expression, and suddenly Alina felt exhausted and bored of being so repressed and uptight and taking her ridiculous thesis and everything else so seriously, and so she briefly reported what she'd done and what she thought about it, as if the impression the man formed of her and losing her final shot at academic credibility didn't matter – and, astonishingly, at that moment they didn't. To cut him off before he could point out all of the study's flaws, which made it impossible to draw any conclusions from it, Alina wrapped up by insisting how poorly the whole thing had been done from start to finish.

But the man frowned in disagreement. *But listen*: those were the words he'd used. And just like that, the moment was the opposite of what she'd envisioned: she was critiquing her own study, while a credible – that is, *real* – researcher who was not from Finland was defending it, as though it made perfect sense.

The most important thing is to ask the right questions, the man said, sounding so convinced that Alina wanted to believe him. Behind them, a group of distinguished-looking middle-aged men in sport coats were laughing at the beautiful Spanish girl's joke, the one Alina had heard thirty-one times now and the brown-eyed man twice, and they looked at each other and could tell that they'd both picked up on this. They suppressed smiles, and the man rolled his eyes up to the ceiling to indicate he thought the joke was lame, too, and Alina started hoping he wouldn't leave just yet.

The man thanked her and continued on to the next person – a pudgy, wheezy kid so poorly dressed he must have been some sort of child prodigy – and once the man was gone, Alina realized she was standing in front of her poster in a different way than before. Now when someone walked past, she looked them in the eye and smiled, and people paused and scanned her poster, which meant more and more people paused, and Alina described her conclusions to all of them as if they were valid and she justifiably proud of them, and to her surprise none of the people who stopped questioned this. *Interesting*, they said, and: *Thank you*. And: *Are you planning on publishing the results? Could you send me the paper?* And Alina was annoyed that she didn't have a one-sheeter, the kind everyone else was handing out and that people were suddenly asking her for. She caught herself hoping that the time allocated wasn't about to run out because she was just getting started. For the first time, the idea of *joining Wallenberg's team* seemed viable, and she found herself momentarily envisaging a new life for herself.

As the session ended and she removed the thumbtacks from the easel, she thought about the brown-eyed man and his friendly smile, remembered the words he'd used to describe her study: *methodologically sound*. She wondered if he'd meant what he said or if that was just the way Americans talked, saying something nice to everyone even when it wasn't true. She thought about the man's name, Joe, and that of the university where he worked in the United States, which Alina recognized from the newspapers and the movies. She tried to imagine what his life must be like, and felt a momentary sadness that she wouldn't be starting a dissertation, or coming to conferences like these and meeting polite, intelligent foreign men like Joe, ever again.

She rolled up her poster, slid it back into the cardboard tube she'd bought at the art supply store, and tossed the strap over her shoulder. Then she saw the man walk back into the exhibition hall: he seemed disoriented, but a second later noticed her and looked pleased.

She never did find out if Joe had returned because of her or for some other reason, but when he asked her to dinner, she accepted gladly.

I have to bring it up again, she thought, two weeks after the previous attempt. Maybe things would go better this time. Regardless of what happened, they needed to try.

But in the evenings, when it crossed Alina's mind and the moment was right, the girl would be lying in their bed, smoking a cigarette. She'd offer one to Joe, and he would set aside his *Masters of Chess* and take it, and then the girl would pull back the covers, lean languorously on her elbows, and offer herself.

Alina would close her eyes and try to sleep, but she couldn't help hearing the silver bracelet bang rhythmically against the headboard with every moan. The girl was lying beneath Joe in a studio apartment where the tables weren't covered in baby clothes but glossy interior design magazines; he was lifting the girl's firm buttocks against the wall of a filthy service station bathroom, or an empty lecture hall late at night, after everyone else had left. The girl was sitting, bare-breasted, on Joe in a musty hotel room or their darkened office, and she moaned and moved in a way he had always hoped Alina would but had never asked her to: like a cat.

Occasionally the girl would show up in the middle of the day; one time, she arrived dressed in an evening gown. Open to the small of her back, it revealed a small, tasteful tattoo on the girl's shoulder blade. Alina had never seen a tattoo on a young woman before, only on sailors and convicted criminals. The girl took a seat next to her while Samuel was napping and Alina was watching a television series set in a British hospital, where the doctors didn't tend to patients but lovesick nurses. The girl glanced at the television screen and then at Alina. *Good, you think?* the scornful look said.

Joe and I have so much to talk about, the girl's arrogant body language signaled. Her victorious eyes demonstrated that the deal was sealed; the practical arrangements were just lagging a little behind, the way they always did.

Alina felt a constriction in her heart.

The girl already viewed herself as Joe's true partner, imagined she'd rescued him from cosmic loneliness. You could see it in her serene, sated bearing; I wonder if you fully grasp what you look like, the girl's raised eyebrows had asked that time Alina visited the office. I'm the only one Joe can discuss his work with, her judgmental eyes had said, challenge himself with: *share his life with*.

That's why he doesn't want to leave Finland anymore, the girl's quivering lashes had telegraphed, although Alina hadn't been able to interpret this message correctly back then.

Things are going so well for us.

Before long, Alina started to see the girl outside the house, too, while walking down the street with Samuel in his stroller, at a trendy restaurant with another childless, carefree friend.

Why did the girl always have to show up and spoil things? Alina would have done anything to get rid of her, anything at all.

This is absurd, she thought, as she pushed the stroller into motion again and the girl waved to her cheerfully through the restaurant window, smiled with her perfect, plump lips, revealing flawless, beautiful teeth. I need help, Alina thought, psychoanalysis, the longest and most miserable kind.

Initially she'd held back. You were supposed to say no, at least at first. And that's what she'd done, too, in her mind – up until the moment the waiter refilled their glasses and asked if they'd care for dessert. The longer they sat in the restaurant, the harder it became to resist the dim lighting, the wine's warmth, Joe's attentive questions that demonstrated how highly he thought of her.

In contrast to everything she'd imagined about herself, she mentally succumbed during the cab ride. She knew exactly what she was doing when, after that one last late-night glass of Calvados, she summoned up an innocent tone of voice and, heart pounding, asked Joe in the hotel hallway if he wanted to come to her room for a nightcap.

The next morning, when she told Julia over the phone, cheeks blazing, about the American and insisted there was no way she would ever do anything with him – only a few hours after the wine-mellowed early morning when she'd rolled a condom onto him with a surreal naturalness – Julia had said: everyone should have at least one vacation romance during their lifetime.

Alina had spent the last two nights of the conference in Joe's bed. Italy in September had been so hot that they'd had to sleep with the windows open, the crickets' chirping outside soft and foreign-sounding. Early in the morning, she'd scampered barefoot down the carpeted corridor, on the off chance Wallenberg knocked on her door before breakfast.

During the return flight, he had asked Alina if she was happy she'd come. Alina's cheeks grew hot as she thought about what had happened, and that she was the one it had happened to; this time, she wasn't the one hearing about it.

Alina had never had a one-night stand before, but she knew what was expected of her and was proud she'd been able to act appropriately. She knew she'd never see Joe again. You were supposed to let the other person go, disappear. That was part of the excitement, what men craved.

But when he suggested it, she'd agreed to a long weekend that fall in London, where he was attending another conference. '*Again?*' Alina had blurted into the phone, and Joe had laughed heartily at the joke, although she had asked the question in all seriousness.

To pay for the trip, she had taken out her first and only student loan – and, to her surprise, without the slightest hesitation. Initially she didn't even tell Julia, to whom she told everything, because her going would reveal who she'd always been, deep down inside: openly naïve, secretly slutty, or both. She was surprised, eventually, when on confessing she didn't encounter the faintest trace of disapproval; instead, her friend's voice echoed with surprised delight, like a mother whose toddler has finally dared to dip her toe in the water. For a fleeting moment Alina wondered if that's the way things had always been, that you really could do whatever you wanted with your life. Her exhilaration was short-lived, however, stifled by the suspicion that Julia had, for as long as they'd been friends, seen Alina as repressing her womanhood.

But in London Joe was considerate and affectionate, and Alina envied herself, a woman who, without asking permission, flew off to London for four days to have sex with an American she barely knew because she felt like it. And the sex with Joe was bolder than with her ex-boyfriend, Joni Hakalainen. The things Joni had wanted in bed had made her feel uncomfortable and acutely aware of every unerotic detail the situation entailed, but somehow in London it felt possible to do many of these exact same things, even initiate them, and with Joe they didn't feel awkward but lovely, which reinforced the growing impression that, without realizing it, she had spent her life to date driving down some peculiar side-road in too low a gear.

When Joe made vague murmurs about Finland she didn't believe him, but as the automatic doors at Helsinki-Vantaa International Airport parted a few days before Christmas and Joe strode into the arrivals hall with his two suitcases to give her a long, possessive kiss, everything felt natural and as if they'd known exactly what they were doing all along. Natural was also how things felt as the snow fell in the darkness outside her studio apartment on those unhurried, lazy late-December afternoons when Samuel must have been conceived. The pregnancy came as a surprise, even to her. Could it be that easy? And although things hadn't, perhaps, been thought all the way through on those December nights, and neither of them had envisioned that one unprotected, reckless weekend would lead to this, they had still done it together, and if this was the result, perhaps it was meant to be.

The long, lonely spring that followed Joe's post-New Year's return to the States didn't bother Alina, either. She took pleasure in observing the changes in her body – her swelling breasts, the belly that felt like hers, yet unfamiliar. Never before had she stepped onto a tram, her entire body signaling *look at me*! Nor, oddly enough, did it feel the least bit wrong – even when Alina had always hated calling attention to herself. In a strange way, this wasn't about her, but about something bigger, as if her body were radiating some infinite, transcendental truth. An essential element of the pleasure lay in the sensation of coming fulfillment, of the lovely summer with Joe that drew closer with every week. This allowed her to react with an amused tranquility to the maternity clinic staff's concerned questions about her spouse, to their acquaintances' pointed glances at her growing, unacknowledged belly, because she knew when Joe moved to Finland that summer things would be settled finally, permanently, and entirely.

Now Alina wished she could go back and change everything: the memories of Italy and London, the crickets, her poster and the Spanish girl's accent, the hotel room near Piccadilly Circus, how it had all begun.

The hazy, unreal start, the things that sent her breath racing and made the moments electric and full, she didn't want to think about them anymore. Remembering the hotel room and the crickets no longer set her heart hammering; it made her weak, as if she hadn't eaten properly.

She was a woman who'd made love to a stranger her first night abroad, consented to everything, gotten involved in a long-distance relationship that had no guarantee of success. Worse, she'd gotten involved in a relationship that meant another relationship, somewhere far away, had fallen apart.

She wasn't like that.

She wished she could change the past to correspond to who she was, and who he was, who they were: a married couple, a family. Sincere, trustworthy people with hearts and souls.

At night, as she soothed the crying Samuel in her arms, she'd look at Joe sleeping on his own side of the bed. Joe wasn't the sort of man, she thought to herself, who would do something like that: go to bed with someone he'd just met, risk everything, leave his partner and turn his whole life upside down for a woman he knew nothing about. He wasn't like that.

But that's exactly what Joe was like.

How could Alina have known? Joe hadn't said a word about the girlfriend before London. *From a certain tone of voice*, something inside her instantly replied. From the momentary silence when she'd asked about his previous relationships. And sure enough, she recalled a casualness in his courtship of her, a certain detachment she'd wanted to interpret as self-confidence but that someone else would have seen through in a heartbeat. Later, when she'd asked, Joe had finally, as if it were some trivial detail, remarked in passing that he'd been dating someone, been engaged, as a matter of fact, and the relationship hadn't ended until after the trip to London.

The entire weekend, the whole time in that hotel room in London, someone named Hannah waiting in the United States had been engaged to Joe.

At the Vietnamese restaurant, following their first meeting, Joe had asked Alina which year she was in in her PhD program. She stammered before saying first, because she felt embarrassed to explain that she wasn't a PhD student at all, just a master's student, a gatecrasher at a conference for real academics.

She didn't even know if their department had a PhD program the way they did at schools in other countries. People just did a thesis and vanished. There was a researcher who had an office along the same corridor as Wallenberg, but Alina had only seen him once. He carried tattered plastic bags and looked like he hadn't bathed in months. Was Plastic Bag Man a doctoral student? She wasn't sure.

'First year?' Joe looked at her in admiration. 'You Europeans are light-years ahead of us. There's no way our first-year students would be able to conduct an entire study on their own. None of them would be capable of doing what you just did. Not to mention the undergrads, in the States – they're basically children.'

Alina was ashamed of having lied; now Joe was paying her compliments that didn't have a shred of justification to them. Her cheeks flushed, and she had to excuse herself to go powder her nose. She was flattered by being thought of as European, as a forerunner. When she came back to the table, she had to concentrate so hard on her fat cao lau noodles it made her head ache; she'd never used chopsticks before, yet for some reason had claimed she knew how when Joe asked. But the fresh mint and some other herb she didn't recognize, cinnamony, mingled tart and sweet in her mouth, and her heart leaped when she thought about where she was and with whom, how much life had to offer if you opened up to it.

Joe talked about the European mentality and how, since the 1950s, Americans had gradually been losing their souls. Alina listened and hoped it wouldn't be obvious to him how little she knew about what he was saying. She made a mental note of the phrases he used so she wouldn't embarrass herself if she needed them later: *keep an eye on the job market, do a postdoc, do your undergrad.*

Joe explained he used to think he'd like to do a postdoc in Europe if he didn't get a job right away, it's good to broaden your horizons. But when the postdoc at Harvard was offered, it had felt like too good an opportunity to turn down.

'Idiot.' He smiled to himself. Alina wasn't sure why.

There wasn't anything keeping him on the East Coast, Joe contin-ued, especially now that he was probably going to have to move from Boston anyway. He could easily imagine himself living in Europe, at least for a while.

With some beautiful, intelligent woman, Alina thought, and was sad: Joe would pick some other, more attractive woman, move to a more interesting country, the Netherlands or Spain. Even Sweden.

Now his postdoc was coming to an end, and he was looking for a job. *A job?* Alina asked, and Joe looked perplexed. It took a while for Alina to realize that by 'a job', he meant a professorship. At the age of twenty-eight? There was clearly something about all this Alina wasn't getting, but she was embarrassed to ask.

Joe told her that he'd looked at open positions all over the place. It gradually became clear to Alina that *all over the place* meant the United States, both East and West Coasts. Joe's parents and almost all of his siblings lived in Boston or New York, he explained. It would be a long way from Europe at Thanksgiving.

'But I guess I applied in California, too,' he said. 'It's twenty-five hundred miles from Boston to LA. Helsinki's not that much further.'

After moving to Finland, Joe lived in another time zone. For weeks he'd go to bed at four in the morning and get up at noon, boyishly enthusiastic about how light it had been outside all night. He wanted to get to work the instant he woke up. The leisurely morning cups of coffee Alina had been so looking forward to sharing with him never materialized, even on weekends, because he was always working.

In the evening, they'd walk down to the early-summer seashore, where the gulls guarded their nests – 'What's this river called?' Joe asked – and when they got home they'd make love, and Alina would think: I have an American husband. She'd hold Joe's hand as they walked around town, the baby contorting itself into absurd positions under her lightweight maternity dress, and she could see in Joe's eyes how proud he was of the child that was on the way. People looked at them, and Alina could tell they saw she had a foreign spouse.

It wasn't until later that she learned he had been offered a tenure-track position at UCLA. Joe listed the faculty members and told her their interests and at which conference he'd met them and where they'd done their doctoral work. This aroused a mystified admiration in Alina. She couldn't have named more than a handful of researchers aside from Wallenberg, and those by last name only, from the bibliography of her thesis: she had no idea who they were, where they worked, or if they were even alive; she had never thought of the names in the studies she cited as real, living people with jobs and homes and relationships, not to mention that they could be her colleagues.

Alina asked Joe if he was disappointed he hadn't taken the job. Summer had just begun, and Helsinki was lovely and warm; they sat at the hilltop café at Linnunlaulu, eating ice cream and enjoying the view across the bay. Lush swathes of nettles grew beyond the picket fence; sparrows hopped under the tables, ready to pounce on any stray crumbs.

Alina heard a tinge of something she'd never heard before in his voice and felt a painful pang above her big, new belly.

'Argh,' he said, waving dismissively. 'Work is work.'

But later, she'd heard him on the phone, sounding agitated: *How many offers like that do you get?* And Alina remembered Joe's brother

David at the wedding, asking him in a low, serious voice, thinking she couldn't hear: *What are you doing?*

Which meant: making a big, fat mistake.

After that phone call, Joe had looked pensive. Later, he asked in passing if Alina could imagine living in the United States.

'I don't know,' she had said, and Joe had let the matter drop.

On Sunday evenings, he phoned the States. During those calls he laughed differently, used unfamiliar expressions, and mentioned about people she didn't know. After the calls, he spoke more quickly, in a sharper, sterner tone.

'Matt got an NIH grant.'

Or: 'Jean-Marie got tenure at Northwestern.'

Or: 'Maura Tumulty was asked to give a keynote at BU.'

And: 'Danny had to settle for adjuncting.'

And she was supposed to understand the importance – or tragedy, in Danny's case – of the event in question.

Alina had checked; Joe was wrong. It was much further from Helsinki to Boston than it was to Boston from Los Angeles: almost four thousand miles, over six thousand kilometers.

Joe had wanted to go into the department his very first morning in Finland. Alina admired his dedication. He wanted to start taking Finnish classes and asked if the departmental secretary spoke English. When they got to the university, he stopped to admire the marbled walls, asked questions about the buildings Alina didn't have the faintest clue how to answer.

Everywhere they went, he said hello to people who had nothing to do with the department and looked back at him, flustered. When he was introduced to someone, he immediately parroted the name back to them. He would repeat the names to Alina later, check if he was remembering them correctly: Jah-koh? Hey-key? Su-zah-nah?

The secretary who was supposed to give Joe his keys didn't show up all day; they waited in the dimly lit, deserted corridor.

'Is today a holiday?' he asked – and Alina suddenly realized that he had pictured the department and the entire university totally differently.

Even Wallenberg didn't know where the office assigned to Joe was

located. When, after some sleuthing, they found it the following week,
it turned out to be a tiny cubbyhole with no desk or computer, on a
different floor than the rest of the department. In the bright summer
sun, the window looked like it had been rinsed with dirty dishwater.
A layer of dust drifted in the corners, along with a sheaf of dirty
photocopies, stamped with black footprints.

Joe needed to make revisions to a manuscript that had just been
accepted for publication, but none of the three books the reviewers
asked him to cite were available at the university library. One he had
to order through the Academic Bookstore, pay a hundred marks in
postage and wait two months for it to arrive from the United States.
For the second, his friend at Princeton reviewed the most germane
points and summarized them over the phone. Joe looked discouraged
after the call. When Alina asked if everything was OK, he smiled as if
having stomach cramps and said: 'Yeah! 'Course. I just took up a lot
of Bob's time. It might not be something I want to do every week.'
And Alina felt his smile prick her belly like a thorn.

Joe was forced to leave the third required book uncited, which didn't
prevent the article from being published, but Alina could see he wasn't
used to making compromises, no matter how minor.

'Things are always tough in the beginning,' he said, and: 'The work
is the same, no matter where you do it.'

In the evenings, when Alina announced she was going to bed, Joe
would cheerfully reply OK and return to his laptop. Alina realized
she'd been expecting something she wasn't getting. When the baby's
kicks woke her up, she'd hear the keyboard and see the blue glow of
the screen in the living room late into the night.

Until she met Joe, she'd never known anyone her age who owned
a laptop. Her father had had a Mikro-Mikko the size of a television,
and she'd grown used to the green dot-matrix letters flashing across
the screen. Luckily Joe didn't have a mobile phone; that would have
been mortifying.

She tried to ignore the impression that there was something pompous, something American, about Joe. A little like Alina's high-school
classmate Karri, whom she'd run into on the street. Karri had boasted
that he'd founded a company that was going to start publishing
internet guides – thick printed catalogs of internet addresses, like
phone books. A few years from now the whole world was going to be

using the internet, Karri raved, and when that happened, the catalogs would be a must-have, as necessary as a normal phone book. Maybe they could even be delivered automatically to every doorstep! Karri was going to be rich.

Alina hadn't dared to say what she really thought. The idea of the catalog might have made some sense, if the internet itself were the slightest use to anyone. On a few occasions, she had heard the internet being talked about at the university in the hushed tones that technology-loving boys used to demonstrate their advanced degree of solitary superiority. When the department, in a fit of technological bravura, acquired a brand-new 386 computer that came equipped with the internet – apparently it was something you could buy from the computer store – she had asked a cute, fit tech boy to show her how it worked; initiating something with him had been the real impetus rather than the World Wide Web. Alina could still remember her own plunging sense of disappointment. The boy didn't respond to her advances, and she didn't get what anyone saw in this internet everyone was talking about. It was like a Potemkin village from a communist country, a deserted mud-puddle of artificial techno-hubris lacking any signs of life; you couldn't get anyone to visit even if you forced them.

Email could have been a useful invention, in theory – if anyone ever used it. But the mailbox that the university's over-eager computing department had, without asking, set up for her and everyone else was always empty, and she didn't know anyone who would have emailed her in any case. She could have sent messages to her friends at school, but in order for them to realize they'd received anything, she'd have had to call each of them individually by phone and tell them to make the trek to campus to check their mail.

June had been warm and sunny that year. The air smelled of sand, the wind rustled in the pale-green birches. Joe oohed over Topelius Park and wanted to sit on café patios and eat smoked herring ('if that's what a Finn would order in a place like this').

He found it amusing and admirable that whoever designed the toilet in Finland had included two flush buttons, to conserve water. He told all his friends about it, and his friends also found it amusing.

During his Sunday evening phone calls, Joe listed facts about Europe to his mother: even the dingiest dive bars didn't throw beer bottles in the trash. The university canteens had porcelain plates, for students! Baked salmon and salad for a couple of bucks. Imagine that, the state subsidized students' meals! The climate wasn't as bad as you'd think, either, surprisingly similar to New England. They even grew apples.

The apples in particular no one seemed to believe.

Alina hadn't wanted to admit it at first, but something about Joe's attitude bothered her. It took her a while to figure out it was his sales-pitch tone; when Joe talked about Finland, he sounded like a real estate agent. She grasped this at David and Marnie's Long Island wedding, which, because of her big belly, she needed her doctor's permission to fly to. Joe would tell his relatives about the public libraries that let you take home LPs, or even laser discs, and Alina thought: he has to sell each one of them on Finland individually.

Alina had hoped the wedding would be an opportunity to grow closer to her mother-in-law. But as she listened to the Hebrew ceremony, she felt like she started to understand Joe's mother, who kept Alina at a distance. The instant Alina rested her hands on the magnificent hump that was her belly, Joe's mother would shift her stern gaze elsewhere. As she observed the wedding couple under the chuppah, the guests in their yarmulkes, Joe's mother beaming as Joe stomped on the glass, the guests shouting *Mazel tov*!, as she watched the arms lift the newlyweds overhead in their chairs, as she listened to the words of the wistful songs, Alina felt like she gradually understood. Joe would never be able to give this to his mother, even if Alina converted, even if they arranged a similar ceremony, which was no longer possible, and even if they did everything else in life the same way, which was also no longer possible. The best she could be for Joe's mother was a foreign, hard-working substitute.

Did it make things better or worse that she was Christian? Alina couldn't say. When Joe's mother asked out of the blue at the wedding table what Alina believed in, she'd been forced to confess she didn't know. In hindsight, she'd tried to imagine that the question hadn't been intended as criticism. She'd had her hands full trying to make out what Joe's mother was saying to her in English while the music played and the baby pressed on her bladder; she'd been waiting for an appropriate lull in the conversation so she could excuse herself to visit the ladies'. After this embarrassing exchange, Alina had come up with a religious position she could present when asked: *I believe there's some incomprehensible power that different religions refer to by different names.* This she could stand behind. But no one ever asked again.

At Joe's mother's request, Samuel would be raised attending a Jewish school and congregation, so he could join the congregation at his bar mitzvah if he later chose. Alina hadn't been opposed; just the opposite, it felt natural and important. Yet in retrospect, she'd started wondering if she should have had stronger views: would she have better earned the respect of Joe's mother and family by standing up for something, anything, even militant atheism?

'Argh,' Joe said, when Alina shared her doubts with him. 'It's nice to have some traditions, but...'

When they filled out their son's birth certificate, Joe wanted to put down *scientist* for father's religion and *the closed system of the laws of physics* for parish.

Someone had said it at David and Marnie's wedding: Joe suffered from HS, Harvard Syndrome. For the too highly educated, life was a series of disappointments and the vague sensation that the future hadn't opened up the way it should have, that the rest of the world was perpetually in their debt.

Alina didn't know what Joe was telling his family about Finland these days, but at home he wasn't raving about nine-month maternity leave anymore; instead he complained incessantly about the weather, about how it was never sunny in Finland, even in the summertime. He criticized Finnish academics, who were superficial and lazy, students who took exams without having studied and never graduated. How was a country like this ever going to pull itself out of the economic doldrums? The grants and funding decisions were like something out of Ceausescu-era Romania. Why couldn't Joe apply for a grant intended for Swedish-speaking Finns? Alina tried to explain that the system was set up to protect the rights of minorities, sort of like for the Native Americans, but as she said the words, Alina could hear herself how hollow the comparison rang. 'Hadn't Swedish-speaking Finns historically been privileged rather than marginalized?' Joe asked. And a private foundation that disbursed research grants only to those who had been born in Savo province? Such a tiny country – but academics received funding on their place of birth, not merits or talent?

Things probably would have turned out differently, Alina thought, if Joe's own research hadn't proved so problematic. The idea had been to conduct experiments on primates, which was how he'd justified the move to himself in the first place. The department of animal physiology had a macaque population that, through significant effort, had been bred for alcoholism. Alcohol had nothing to do with Joe's prior work, but he had said that with a sufficiently successful set of experiments, he'd be able to justify it to himself and his future employers.

When he applied for real jobs, as Joe had started to say. Which meant: in a different country.

But of the two PhD students Joe had expected to run his experiments, one was pregnant and had a full-time job and, over the course of the fall, dropped out. The other one started, but stopped showing up at meetings without any explanation. (*Lab meetings*, as Joe called them, although Alina had tried to warn him that it would sound ridiculous to Finns.) Joe couldn't get hold of them no matter how hard he tried. Eventually someone told him that the non-pregnant student had ended up in the psychiatric ward at Hesperia Hospital.

'How does anyone ever get anything done in this country?' Joe asked, when the ground was covered in frost and the main topic of conversation at the department was the date of the upcoming Little Christmas party. Alina was holding Samuel in a nursing pillow, sitting on their couch, where a hollow the shape of her backside had formed. The monkeys had been drinking the sugar-ethanol solution for months, but because there was no way Joe could single-handedly keep up with a series of experiments designed for three full-time researchers, the monkeys developed alcoholism isolated in their cages, for no reason, and he raged to Alina about the thousands of marks this was costing every day and why didn't anyone seem to care?

'Maybe you shouldn't have designed such an ambitious study,' she made the mistake of suggesting. She was irritated that everything seemed to be Finland's fault, even though the work was Joe's. Not to mention that they'd just had a baby in September, and as tender and loving as Joe could be with Samuel in the evenings, it still felt like he was some sort of footnote penciled into the margins of Joe's life.

'Ambitious?' Joe stared at her as if she were an imbecile. 'This is the most ridiculous, piddliest, smallest, simplest thing I've ever come up with, because I thought that, OK, this should be doable in a developing country. But evidently even this was asking too much. Even this!'

'Maybe it'll just take longer to finish than you thought.'

'I'm not going to be able to finish it all! It's too late to measure the baselines! The whole project, down the tubes!'

'So why didn't you measure them, then? What are you shouting at me for?'

'I would have measured them, goddammit, if I'd have known I was going to have to do the whole thing myself! How come you can't rely on anyone around here, how come no one is held accountable for anything?'

A week later, Joe still hadn't calmed down. He said living in Finland was like having dementia: you lost more brain cells with every month that passed. He needed to be in an environment where he'd be challenged to think more critically, do more and better; to be somewhere he just *might* learn something new. Now he was regressing alone in his cubbyhole, forgetting things he used to know, growing accustomed to nothing being expected of anyone and falling further and further behind in the race. He was never going to publish again, never speak at a conference. How was he going to find a job?

And again: Joe meant a *real* job, an American one.

'Oh, for God's sakes,' Alina said. 'A few years isn't going to ruin your career.'

Joe looked at her. His eyes were red.

'How would you know?' he said.

And despite the words' sting, Alina realized she wouldn't.

As she stepped down from the tram, Alina tried to gauge how she felt. It was supposed to feel as if you were suddenly missing a limb, or as if you'd headed out of the house without remembering to dress, the first time you were separated from your newborn.

The city admittedly looked different without Samuel along. She watched the women hurry past, bundled in their parkas against the

February cold, and wondered if they were mothers, and if so, where their children were. Or hadn't they wanted children? When she saw a stroller, she caught herself smiling at the woman pushing it and feeling vaguely offended when the woman didn't notice her the way other mothers did when she had a stroller, too.

After a little while, she realized she'd completely forgotten Samuel, had found herself preoccupied with things that had nothing to do with her son or motherhood. She was momentarily alarmed – had she forgotten her baby somewhere? – and had a remarkably bad conscience, even though he was safely in Julia's care.

The sidewalk was uneven and slippery despite being sanded. Yesterday had been warm; the snow had melted from the rooftops and the road-sides and re-frozen during the night. Alina glanced at her watch as she rounded the corner where the entrance to the department came into view. She paused and looked around. It was only twenty to. She'd gotten in the habit of leaving the house early on account of Samuel's clothing and diaper changes, and she'd done it again today, even though Samuel wasn't along. Joe might be trying to wrap something up before he ended his day.

She walked slowly to kill time, the dirty sand at the curb rasping under her shoes. The sky stretched out overhead, an unbroken expanse of gray. People swathed in black winter-wear weaved their way through the cold current of cars. She felt like she understood Joe. Finland wasn't the easiest place in the world. But was life really that different anywhere else? Besides, soon it would be spring again, and after that summer, short but ravishing, and Joe would enjoy that, too.

They needed a breather. A day in Nuuksio, she thought, would that help? The woods, the peace and quiet, the fresh air. At least it couldn't hurt. She'd look up the trails, get a proper baby pack to carry Samuel in, big enough for him in his snowsuit. They'd cook sausages on the shores of a wilderness lake, Joe would love that there was a stockpile of firewood for day-hikers, that no one needed to guard it or sell it, that people could be trusted to only use as much as required for their own needs and not steal.

Alina walked up the stairs to the department and headed towards Joe's office. He'd be pleased she'd been thinking about him, about what might cheer him up. Maybe they could go this upcoming weekend. The hike might also help with what they still hadn't tried again. As she knocked on his door, she remembered she'd decided she wouldn't disturb him just yet.

The idea of slipping away before he answered crossed her mind, but then the door opened. Joe looked at her, for a fraction of a second as if he didn't know who she was.

'I'm sorry. I guess I'm a little early.'

'Hi.'

'I have a fun idea,' Alina said. 'I was thinking you might think it's fun, too.'

Joe looked at her as if his mind were still somewhere totally different.

'But we can talk about that in a sec.'

'OK.' Joe looked irritated. 'I'm still kind of in the middle of something.'

'Take your time. Come down when you're ready. I'll go for a little walk.'

He doesn't even care, Alina found herself thinking as she backtracked to the stairwell. Exiting the building, she thought about Nuuksio and what national parks were like in the United States: the giant sequoias and the seeds Joe had sent her from San Francisco, the eagles he had photographed from the bluffs of the Potomac and the Shenandoah. Would Nuuksio be a disappointment for him, too small and unimpressive, like everything else in Finland?

It wasn't long before she'd walked around the block and was standing in front of Joe's building again. Only a few minutes had passed.

She needed to waste another fifteen.

Lost in thought, she meandered back inside and past the elevator. The door to the courtyard stood behind it and down a short flight of steps. Alina happened to glance out through the glass in this door and was surprised – at first happily so, but then her heart skipped a beat.

Joe was standing in the courtyard with the girl. Both of them were in shirt-sleeves, even though it was almost ten below. The girl was smoking and telling Joe something; they were hunching in towards each other. Joe's expression was carefree and light-hearted, the one Alina realized she hadn't seen in ages. The girl's final words were lost in a burst of shared laughter that carried in faintly from the far side of the courtyard.

Alina waited for them to go inside. Instead, the girl lit another cigarette, Joe jumped in place like an athlete warming up, and they continued chatting.

She watched this from the echoing corridor, could hear the sound of her own breathing in the darkness.

By the time Joe emerged from the front door with his bags, he was fifteen minutes late.

'Did you get your work finished?' Alina asked, and Joe said: 'Yes.'

The auditorium smelled of smoke. A fire, evidently a real one, had been lit in the iron stove on the stage.

Alina tried to sit still. She had promised herself she wouldn't eavesdrop on the conversation. She was missing the whole performance, when for once she could have enjoyed a two-hour break, live a scintilla of her former, pre-baby life, one that had included cultural interests.

She'd caught the first snippets back in the cab. She and Joe had been sitting in silence, and the girl had immediately slipped in between them. Alina had a hard time hearing their low-pitched conversation over the radio and the engine noise.

'...*the baby changed... relationship?*' the girl asked.

Joe's amused grunt, which meant: *You'd better believe it.*

'*In what way?*' the girl asked.

Alina pricked up her ears. She considered asking Joe to repeat himself, to insert herself into their conversation. The thought set her heart pounding; she could feel her forehead grow damp.

'*Well, of course... we don't... which makes it that much... harder.*'

'*It's important to talk.*'

The girl wanted to lend a sympathetic ear, hear all sides of the story. She knew how to tamp down her own enthusiasm, not to frighten away the skittish feelings she was coaxing out of Joe.

'*As a matter of fact, I haven't really talked about this with anyone until just now.*' His tone was soft, confiding.

'*Wow, that must ... hard. Doesn't your wife want to...?*'

'*Things between us... where we come from... kind of changed... so that I don't even really think about her that way anymore.*'

Alina heard Joe sigh. When she involuntarily looked over, the girl was tenderly caressing his cheek. Joe lowered his head onto her shoulder, burdened with care.

A sudden torrent of cursing and banging roused Alina from her reverie. She saw the actors running and bellowing in their military uniforms, chins covered in spittle, remembered she was still sitting in the theater. One of the actors was whacking a hockey stick against the stage.

The performance seemed to amuse Joe, which was surprising, considering he couldn't understand the dialogue. The girl was sitting on his other side, holding his hand; she pointed at the stage and whispered something in Joe's ear. He nodded and they smiled, enjoying the performance and each other's company. The girl was dressed in low-slung trousers and a slinky knit top that skimmed her breasts with a lack of restraint Alina would have found embarrassing.

The girl had it so easy: she didn't have to pick her outfits based on which two she could fit into after childbirth. The girl probably had a membership at an expensive gym-slash-spa, where she wrapped herself in plush bathrobes and sipped tea.

Alina thought about tomorrow and the Tunes for Tots class she'd be taking Samuel to at the park again, unless budget cuts had forced it to close. Her son was too small to do anything except sit in her lap, so she'd be singing children's songs along with the other mothers as if she couldn't think of anything she'd rather do with her day: three little ducklings went off to play, over the hills and far away. But when the three little ducklings refused to return, Daddy Drake flew over the lake and shouted: *QUACK!*

It was only then that the three little ducklings came hurrying back.

After squirming in her seat for a while, Alina let out an audible sigh. The middle-aged man sitting on her other side glanced at her, but Joe's eyes stayed glued to the stage. She coughed. Joe continued watching the play, his hand in the girl's. Alina looked at her watch; still an hour left.

Fuck this.

She grabbed her purse.

Excuse me. Excuse me. Excuse me. Excuse me. She didn't turn to see the expression on Joe's face as she fought her way over people's legs in the cramped space.

He caught up to her at the coat check.

'What happened?'

'I'm just not interested in watching potty humor.'

'I thought it was surprisingly funny.'

She stalked off without waiting for him to get his coat; her ankle folded as she hurried down the stairs. Alina was sure the girl never forgot how to walk in high heels. She felt the urge to pick up a big cobblestone and hurl it through the window of one of the expensive Jugendstil apartments lining the street.

She was at the end of the block before Joe emerged from the theater's doors and shouted to her to wait. She continued up the icy pavement as briskly as she could in her heels without turning around.

Joe had to run to catch up to her.

'What's going on? You just leave without saying anything?'

'If these two hours are all the free time I'm going to have for the next six months, this is not how I'm going to spend them.'

'Baby,' Joe said softly, wrapping his arms around her. They stood there. 'This was supposed to be our night out together.'

He peered into her face. Alina felt the tears an instant before they flooded over her cheeks, and thought: I'm being unreasonable. Why am I behaving this way?

'I'm sorry,' she said, wiping her eyes. 'I'm just tired.'

'It's OK,' he said. 'Things have been hard on you with the baby.'

Which was true: Samuel had slept poorly all week, or all month, she couldn't keep track anymore.

'Should we grab a drink?' Joe asked. He led her to the door of a small wine bar.

He ordered a big glass of red wine for her and a beer for himself, pulled up a chair, and spoke in a soothing voice. She listened to the steady, low stream of talk coming from his mouth as if it were a hypnotist's suggestion. She felt the warmth of the wine and looked out at the people heading, without the slightest hesitation, exactly where they were supposed to be going.

Alina found herself returning to Joe's mother's question. That it kept nagging at her must have had something to do with her own instability, her problems with Joe, as well as Joe's family's connection to its roots. And yet as she sat breastfeeding, the ever-present water bottle and women's magazine at her side, she felt something important was missing. Maybe this was what Joe's mother had tried to hint at; maybe this was why Alina was acting so crazy with her husband right now. Or was she still so offended by Joe's mother she couldn't shake the question? Maybe both.

What did she believe in? Since Samuel's birth, she'd found herself contemplating God relatively often, considering she didn't think she believed in one. Her ponderings did not take the form of deliberate searching of an individual with a propensity for religious or philosophical reflection, but more the haphazard staggering of a drunk towards any door where whoever answered wouldn't spit in her face.

Once again, she felt a pang of envy for Joe's Judaism. She hadn't been to church more than a handful of times since Confirmation camp. Once or twice, maybe, at Christmas?

She remembered the pastor having talked about longing. That she could relate to – if the longing she felt was the same thing. Her heart burned, constantly and for no discernible reason, kind of like being offended or having lost something. But was this what the pastor meant?

She tried to remember the pastor's name, but she only remembered his baleful air, the black beard and a sort of imperviousness, something she'd think about in bed at night but couldn't quite put her finger on. She remembered the pastor having listened in silence as some of the girls had talked about Olympic gold medal winner Lasse Virén, about how success had gone to his head, and that's why he couldn't run anymore. The pastor had suddenly looked at them and said: 'You girls have no idea what you're talking about.'

That's what he'd say during lessons, too: you're talking without any understanding of what you're saying. There was a seriousness to the pastor's tone that made it impossible not to believe him. After Confirmation camp, Alina had never dared voice an opinion about Lasse Virén ever again, or running in general.

Alina remembered what the pastor had told her about God on the last day, after quizzing her on her memorization: *you can always turn to Him.*

Especially on those still blue winter afternoons when a cranky baby felt impossible and the days so crushingly lonely that life was reducible to restrained tears, on those days in particular she found herself thinking about Confirmation camp and what the pastor had said. One time she went so far as to pick up the phone, look up the parish numbers in the phone book, and pick one to call based on the gender and sound of the name. But she had no connection to that parish. She lowered the receiver and didn't make the call, knew she never would.

Once the receiver was lowered she remembered how she'd wanted to talk to the pastor about God on the last day of Confirmation camp. She'd decided she wanted to be one of those kids who goes to counselor training and helps the pastor pick the songs for youth night. But there outside the church, after the bus had pulled out, when she approached the pastor to ask him about counselor training, he said: 'All the best,' and Alina had only been able to reply: 'Thanks, you too.'

She hadn't meant to look.

But Joe's bulky laptop was in the same room as the cupboard where they kept the iron. It was the only place with a free phone jack to plug in the squealing modem, with its robotic squawks and rumbles. Alina thought it was crazy to pay higher phone bills for a computer – who needed an email connection at home? And *why*?

As she went in to get the iron, she thought about the coming evening. They hadn't made love a single time since Samuel's birth, and again tonight they would each climb in on their own side of the bed and go to sleep. Joe would delve into *Masters of Chess*; she would turn off the light and think it was still too soon and that she shouldn't dwell on things.

Then she saw the computer screen.

Joe was working, his back to her, and at first she just happened to notice the list over Joe's shoulder, saw that it was formed of many of the same words over and over, and her curiosity was piqued.

Aleksandra Viitasalo, it read on the screen. It took a second for Alina's mind to make the connection to black, blunt-cut hair and comic-book eyebrows.

Aleksandra Viitasalo Re: thingies
Aleksandra Viitasalo Re: Vs: Re: thingies

Interspersed with the odd *David Chayefski* or *Pertti Wallenberg*, and then:

Aleksandra Viitasalo Re: Vs: Re: Vs: Re: thingies
Aleksandra Viitasalo Re: Vs: Re: Vs: Re: Vs: Re: thingies
Aleksandra Viitasalo Re: Vs: Re: Vs: Re: Vs: Re: Vs: Re: thingies
Aleksandra Viitasalo Re: Vs: Re: Vs: Re: Vs: Re: Vs: Re: Vs:
Re: thingies

Alina could feel her pulse throbbing as she bent over to get the iron from the bottom shelf, where it lay wrapped in its soft cord. Dozens of e-mails… over several days? Or all on one day?

She had fed and dressed the baby, put him down for his nap, washed the dishes, vacuumed, ironed: *because Joe needed to work.*

Didn't he see enough of the girl at the office? What was so important that it required this fusillade of messages? Didn't he want to spend his free time with them, his wife and child?

Joe had never said a word about the girl.

Joe had 'needed to work.'

But as it turned out, what Joe needed to do was take care of thingies.

The baby monitor clicked on, screeched with Samuel's howling. The wail penetrated the white noise of the transmitter as if her son were crying from outer space. Alina rushed out onto the balcony, brought the carrier inside, and started undressing Samuel. She could hear Joe tapping away at the computer, tap tap.

Alina hadn't read the messages. She had just caught a glimpse of one. At most a couple.

She would definitely not read her husband's email.

Samuel was bawling his lungs out, tiny face distorted and bright red. Alina heard his voice giving out. Had he been crying for a long time? Hadn't she heard, or hadn't the alarm been tripped immediately?

Joe tapped out his emails. So that was more important? Evidently. Left bootie, waaaah! OK, Samuel, calm down now, tap tap tap. Right bootie, waaah! Everything's fine, Samuel, tap tap tap. Right hand through the sleeve of the padded overalls, waaah! Tap tap, left hand, waaah!

Samuel was undressed and shrieking in her arms when she heard Joe go into the kitchen and open the fridge.

'Do we have plans for Saturday?' he asked.

'How should I know?'

Joe stood at the bedroom door and tried to make eye contact with her.

'Is something wrong?'

'You tell me.'

Joe's face was blank.

'Did something happen?'

'You tell me.'

'Hey,' he said, and circled around in front of Alina so she wouldn't be able to avoid his gaze.

'You could help out, too, sometimes, goddammit!' she suddenly shouted.

She was being unreasonable, she thought, as she flung Samuel's booties to the floor, hysterical. *It's the hormones, the breastfeeding, I'm not really like this: always some crisis or other.* Samuel had stopped crying, but now he started bawling again and tried to corkscrew out of her arms.

Joe looked at her in disbelief. Without saying anything, he took the baby, lowered him to the bed, and started removing the clothes Alina hadn't gotten to yet. *It's all right*, Joe said to his son in a soft, low voice, *everything's all right*. He took a clean diaper out of the drawer, picked up his son, and headed for the bathroom. Alina followed, wiping her wet cheeks and looking on as Joe washed Samuel's bottom and dried their son tenderly with a towel.

Joe seemed offended, justifiably so, Alina thought: she was a madwoman. Why couldn't she be normal, sensible, stable? But at the same time, she heard another voice rebutting every argument she presented: she had been far too patient, too accommodating.

Too much of a nobody: that's why people walked all over her.

'I'm sorry,' she said quietly.

'You could have told me you needed help,' Joe said. 'Of course I'll help. I just didn't know.'

'And you could have told me you had twenty more emails to write to that girl.'

Joe froze. Alina was no longer agitated; her voice was calm. Did I really just say that? she thought in disbelief. Suddenly she felt strong.

Joe turned to her. 'Excuse me?'

'That girl.'

'Who are you talking about?'

'Come on, Joe. A second ago, when I came in for the iron… Your email was up on the screen. I just happened to see.'

'You read my emails?'

'Of course not! But you spend more time with that girl than you do with us! You were supposed to be working, but all the time you were sending messages to her.'

Joe stared at his wife. Then, without saying a word, turned back to Samuel.

'Listen,' Alina began, 'I think there are all sorts of things we should tell each other.'

Joe rocked Samuel in his arms, refusing to look at her. 'Like what?'

'I'm not saying there's anything specific. I just mean maybe we should tell each other things that don't mean anything... maybe especially those. Things that haven't happened, at least not yet.'

Joe looked like he still didn't understand, but he kept listening.

'Like the girl,' Alina said, and explained how she'd spent far too much time thinking about Aleksandra, the girl from the department, for no good reason. 'I keep imagining,' she said, 'that you're having an affair. And if you are, now would be a good time to tell me.'

Joe stayed silent.

The same with the plan to move to America, she continued, and what customs and traditions they'd observe. She and Joe and the girl and going to America and country music and Christianity and the Eppu Normaali album *Valkoinen kupla* – which was important to her but meaningless to Joe – were suddenly distinct and clear in their own places in her mind. She wanted to know about the girl, but to her surprise she wasn't angry or jealous, at least not at the moment.

And she shared how she'd been thinking about moving to America and preparing for it but still wasn't clear as to what Joe was intending or doing or hoping. She told him she wanted to be included in major decisions, like moving to another continent or their child's religious upbringing. She told Joe she wished he'd share his mental steps and shifts that would affect their plans, even tentative and trivial daily fluctuations, because Alina was interested, she wanted to know, they were man and wife!

She didn't understand it when she started, but suddenly she was more wholly in the room. She could feel her own contours more clearly, and Joe's presence, and this insight strengthened her.

In that instant, she realized she was ready to leave with Joe, had been the whole time: she would be happy to move to another continent,

even permanently, if that's what he wanted. But Joe had to ask! Why
hadn't he? And she was suddenly embarrassed about how she'd used
her father as an excuse. But now, as she felt unfettered and whole, she
was prepared to admit even this. And she wanted to share her insight
with Joe, too, so he would know her a tiny bit better.

Then she noticed the girl sitting on the floor, listening and eating a
popsicle. When Alina had finished, the girl gave her a nod of approval.
Alina was surprised. The girl waved at her and walked out, first out
of the bedroom and then out the front door.

But Joe sighed, closed his eyes, and dug a thumb and forefinger into
his eyelids. 'You've changed.'

The lump formed in Alina's throat even before he started listing
the differences in her since the wedding and the baby: she was more
impatient, weepy, unenthusiastic, inconsiderate.

'I'm sure I have,' Alina shouted, devastated that he could not appreciate the flash of insight she'd just experienced and the big step she'd
taken. And his stony face and words reminded her of all the times Joe
hadn't noticed or guessed or bothered to know what she wanted, and
how each time she'd promised herself she wouldn't carry it around, but
now she pelted him with all of them, one by one, down to the very last.

She couldn't keep up with the twists and exhausting subplots of
the arduous, bitter discussion that ensued, or how it ended. After
they finished, she wasn't at all sure her husband grasped that she'd
experienced a moment of enlightenment. What she gathered was that,
before the conversation, Joe had wanted to leave Finland with Alina,
and now things were completely different.

Four days later, she came back to the emails. She'd been thinking
about them and come to the conclusion his reaction was justified: it
had been wrong for her to look at them. It wasn't her business who
sent the messages in Joe's inbox, and she wanted him to know that.

Reading someone else's email... that was like rifling through pockets,
rummaging through the garbage for receipts.

As she apologized, she noticed Joe's set jaw and hard eyes. Her
husband didn't have such hard eyes. She'd hoped to see Joe's sternness
gradually melt now, to feel some relief from it. And indeed the hard

stare had gone. But it wasn't the same old Joe there in their place; this was someone else.

He listened to her apology, as if from a distance. When she was finished, he nodded curtly, and said: 'Don't worry about it.'

Alina was washing the dishes when the girl reappeared by her side. The girl pointed at the living room, and Alina lowered the scrub brush to the sink.

Look, the girl's eyes said. They were full of compassion.

Alina followed the girl's gaze into the living room, where Joe was sitting on the sofa, browsing through his yearbook from Brown. He had shown it to Alina once. The pages were populated with identical headshots of young Americans in their funny graduation caps, their American smiles, against backgrounds in implausible colors. Pictures of teams playing American football or that mystifying form of netball, lacrosse.

Joe didn't realize they were watching him. How sad and vulnerable, how *small* he looked, Alina thought, as he browsed through the black-and-white images. The pictures were of his friends from college, who were now shaping the future of science and founding research centers as professors at the American universities Joe used to speak of like a first love, but which he no longer mentioned.

For a second, Alina thought he would start crying. He's become so broken, she thought. She glanced sideways and saw the girl looked sad, too.

Alina realized what had happened: Joe had applied for jobs and hadn't gotten anything. A wave of warmth surged through her.

'Joe,' she said softly.

He looked at her. Alina walked into the living room, sat down next to her husband, and touched his shoulder. For a moment something sparked in Joe's eyes, and then it was gone.

'Come here,' Alina said, spreading her arms to give him a hug.

But Joe shut the book, stood up wearily, and slowly carried it over to the desk drawer where it was kept. Alina had said it was the wrong size and shape for the bookshelf. He walked back over to her and stood there in front of her as if not knowing what to do.

Alina wrapped her arms around him. Joe hesitated for a moment but then relented. He was warm in her arms; she felt his shoulder blades under her fingers, the major and minor muscles, her lonely American husband.

'Joe,' Alina said, 'I'm sorry things turned out this way.'

'No, I'm sorry,' he said, and once again Alina was sure he would cry. She had never seen him cry before. Apparently he had when Samuel was born, but she had been so drained from effort, loss of blood, and relief that she barely registered the presence of Joe or the midwife.

Alina felt him cautiously stroking her hair and saying her name: *a-Leena*.

'I spoke with Jack.'

The name cracked like a whip, even though Joe was speaking so quietly she could barely make out the words.

None of this will become real if I don't let it in, she told herself.

Jack Demekis was from MIT, someone Joe spoke of in the same affectionate, reverential tones as he spoke of his grandfather.

I spoke with Jack.

She heard the ragged way he was breathing, the shuddering and gasping for breath, and remembered she had seen this once before: in the maternity ward, right after Samuel was born and the umbilical cord was severed.

That evening, Joe didn't take his book to bed. He lay on his back, looking sad. Alina felt a tightness in her chest, but she'd promised herself she wouldn't cry.

The whole day, she had felt as if she were wrapped in an invisible blanket. It was a peculiar, almost comforting sensation, similar perhaps to a drowning person when they finally stop struggling and let the sweet, warm exhaustion in. During the day, she'd felt tears suddenly streaming down her cheeks.

Joe's hand was on her shoulder, and she closed her eyes and felt the strap of her nightgown rise and then fall. Joe kissed her shoulder. *Baby*, he said. But his voice sounded apologetic. Joe was big and hard on top of her, and she realized it was happening now, now he wanted it. Alina could feel his weight on top of her, and had to strain to draw air into her lungs.

Her chest throbbed when Joe kissed her. She felt the blood rush to her face and fingers and toes. Joe looked serious, and she could feel his hands where they were supposed to be, where they and only they knew how to go. Alina's body throbbed: *don't cry, don't cry*.

She raised her arms straight up, her nightgown was gone, Joe yanked off her panties, her panties were gone, and she sensed what Joe tasted like. She had to put every ounce of energy into keeping the swelling wave of emotion at arm's length, and realized that this time everything would work, that whatever the source of the problem had been, she no longer had to fear it.

She stopped Joe's hand.

'Wait,' she said.

'What?' he asked.

She looked into the corner of the dark room, and out the window, where the cold lights of the parking lot glowed.

'What?' Joe asked again, trying to follow her gaze. But the girl wasn't at Joe's side, behind the curtains or outside the window. She was nowhere to be seen. Alina scanned the dark room for a long time before she believed the girl wasn't going to come to her aid.

'I don't know if I want to,' she finally said.

Her heart struck fast. Her hands were cold, and she thought, here they were: Samuel and Joe and her.

She had to say it once more, first to herself and then out loud, *I don't want to*, before she was sure it was true. She couldn't see Joe's face in the darkness and couldn't tell what he was thinking. The apartment was still, but in the dense silence she could distinctly hear the sound of something finally break.

MAGICICADAS

BALTIMORE, MD

From a distance, they looked like bees. The black, hardened body, the yellowish wing-stubs like an old man's toenails.

Joe scanned the article as he stepped out the doors of the library café and into the sun, heading for his office. Organic Nicaraguan fair trade coffee splashed from his overfilled paper cup to the back of his hand. Had it really been nearly two decades since the last time? The *New York Times* had dedicated three front-page columns to them, in which a professor from Berkeley speculated as to the impact of climate change on their distribution.

Magicicadas: before long they would blanket the lawns and the sidewalks; their quivering wings would cover trees, roads, and rooftops. They had spent almost twenty years germinating in the soil, but now they would dig their way out. Freshly molted, they looked like ghostly moths, red-eyed and translucent, surreally pale. Joe remembered the feel of the living carpet underfoot, the crunch of the nymphs' abandoned shells being crushed by every footfall.

Other front-page news included the long-awaited *iAm* device, which would apparently at long last hit the markets this fall, the tech bloggers' messianic expectations, the market's nervous twitches. And not a day without the smiling face of Freedom Media billionaire Ted Brown, this time in an article about CEO compensation, which had yet again risen to a record high.

It had rained during the night. The morning sky was clear, the temperature mild. Joe dodged a puddle on the pavers and crossed the lawn to Bloomberg Hall, where a couple of students sat outside, studying in the spring sunshine. A custodian was spreading wood chips the color of red wine in the planting strips fronting the brick walls.

The sharp, chemical-sweet scent of fertilizer wafted up from the soil.

Spring was divine in Maryland, warm and sunny, before the suffocating greenhouse summer. Joe walked down the stairs to the department and into the men's room. It was already a few minutes past the hour by the time he was washing his hands and his phone rang.

It was Daniella, of course: his daughter had started calling him in the middle of the day about all sorts of random things. There was something touching about it: his little girl whose every sentence stressed her independence but always called her Dad during passing period. Fifteen-year-old Rebecca never called anymore, even in direst need.

He'd call Daniella back as soon as he dried his hands. It was only after his phone stopped ringing that he suddenly remembered what he'd forgotten.

Shit.

Lisa.

Joe stood there, soapy hands in the sink. He was supposed to have submitted a request for Lisa to be enrolled as a PhD student for another year. Lisa was his best student, but she hadn't received a single job offer yet. Might she be doing something wrong? Did she sound overly apologetic, too sweet? Lisa's dissertation was basically finished, and it was superb, if not the most marketable. Still, Joe had been sure someone would hire her right away.

Under the circumstances, it would be better if she didn't graduate.

He'd promised Lisa to confirm things by yesterday; someone might cause a stink, because postponing graduation dragged down the department's statistics – meanwhile, he should have been in the seminar room four minutes ago, introducing guest lecturer Stan Lippman, who was no doubt already stroking his magnificent whiskers, gunning to run through his PowerPoint.

Joe was afraid Lisa would settle for adjunct: teaching introductory college courses, often at starvation wages. Commutes of hundreds of miles, eighteen-hour workdays without vacations. Or health insurance.

He was roused from his musing by his phone ringing again: *Twinkle twinkle little star*. He quickly rinsed and dried his hands. *Twinkle twinkle little star*. He would keep Lisa on as his TA, would recommend she postpone her doctoral defense no matter what Barb said. At least that way she'd keep her health insurance. And be a brand-new doctor during the next hiring cycle, not a last-year loser.

Joe pulled out his phone. 'Hello?'

The problem Lisa hadn't grasped was that after a year or two with no success in finding a job you got a reputation for being unhirable. There was no point upsetting students for no reason, but the job market was growing steadily more ruthless. And Lisa had so much potential.

'Joseph?' said the caller. 'Hi.'

Joe's heart skipped a beat.

'Alina?'

He had to step away from the hand-dryer, which, despite its apocalyptic wail, was astoundingly inefficient.

'Sorry to call out of the blue like this.'

The accent acted like a scent: Alina's voice carried him back through the years, like a fairy-tale trapdoor he fell through into a mirror-image world.

They fumbled between hellos and awkward how are yous. Alina spent a long time searching for words. Apart from the adorable intonation, Alina had always spoken English like a native when they were together, but now he could hear she no longer used it every day.

Joe realized she was approaching the real reason for her call when he heard her voice crack. 'I'm just calling because… Or I mean, I thought you ought to know.'

'What's wrong?'

'Samuel's over there somewhere. Maybe.'

Joe paused. 'Here? In Baltimore?'

'Well, um… In the States. That's all I know.'

'That's fantastic! Is he coming to see us? Or a friend?'

'No… not really. As a matter of fact, I'm not exactly sure what he's up to these days. Or, he's told me all sorts of things, but…'

When his ex-wife didn't continue, Joe asked: 'You gave him the number and address, didn't you? You have our new address, right, West Chestnut Parkway?'

Phone propped awkwardly between his chin and shoulder, Joe dried his hands on his trousers, grabbed his backpack, and hurried out of the bathroom. He was almost ten minutes late; the others would be wondering where he was.

'No, he's…' Alina said. 'I don't think he's planning… Or I mean, I don't know where he is at the moment. He originally went to the West Coast, to Eugene, but… yeah.'

Joe saw Kathy Liebgott wandering around the far end of the corridor, clearly looking for him. She started heading for the stairs. Joe covered the phone and tried to catch her attention: 'Kathy! I'm coming!... Listen, Alina, I really have to go. I'm already late. I have a lecturer to introduce.'

'Yeah,' she said. 'Sorry I called. This was a little... stupid anyway. I mean... I don't want to worry you.'

'It's really nice hearing from you. Let's talk more tomorrow. I'll call you back,' he said.

He remembered Alina always being thrown by this way of getting off the phone: *I'll call you back.* To her it sounded like, right away, as soon as possible. He'd had to explain that in the US that wasn't exactly what it meant. Like the *What's up?* Alina had taken as a conversation starter and to which she'd always offer a thorough reply, much to the listener's amusement.

Joe rushed to the lecture room, where Kathy stood at the door, frowning. He apologized for being late and introduced Stan Lippman, who was waiting his turn with a broad smile fixed in place.

Worry? Joe thought before the lecture began. Was that what Alina just said? After Stan Lippman got started, Joe's thoughts bounced back to Lisa: next year she would get a job offer and everything would work out for her, he was sure.

Snow and shame: the smell of Helsinki, twenty years ago.

Joe thought he could relate to how Monica Lewinsky must have felt, turning down autograph seekers at the airport: *I'm kind of known for something that's not so great to be known for.*

To his son, Joe must have represented one thing and one thing only. He was the father who had abandoned Samuel.

Joe remembered his own father's fork stopping halfway to his mouth when Joe told them he was moving to Finland. It was permanently tattooed on the folds of his brain, the way Dad had looked at him and said:

'*Finland?*'

Dad's tone meant Joe was intentionally throwing away his education, his future, and his family's values.

In Dad's defense, Joe had to admit that his father had asked questions
and listened carefully, eyes crinkled in concern, desperately scanning
Joe's face for some detail that would make his son's plans the least bit
comprehensible. Joe had insinuated that Mom and Dad were elitist and
stuck in their ways; that they thought Ivy League schools were the only
places in the world anyone was capable of accomplishing anything.

Finland was an unexpected but life-saving solution: he'd go there
instead of throwing himself into the rat race at some elite American
university, regardless of what Dad had assumed.

But Hannah: it was like an invisible fist clenching around his heart.
He had to tell them that now, too, that he wouldn't be marrying his
fiancée. Joe had sensed how happy, even relieved, Dad in particular
had been when he and Hannah started dating.

'But what is it *you* want?' Dad asked him then. 'What is it you really
want?'

Joe had wanted Alina; he'd wanted to be in Europe, he'd wanted a
life that their family and friends hadn't already lived and that wasn't
laid out in advance by his previous choices. He'd wanted a world where
you rode to work on a retro one-speed bicycle, cool and composed, he'd
wanted to flee George Bush Sr.'s oil-military-entertainment imperium,
and live instead in liberal, cultured, elegant Europe, where the Berlin
Wall had come down and the Soviet Union had fallen apart; Europe,
where people drank wine on terraces on linden-lined boulevards and
smoked cannabis openly at street-side cafcs, atc croissants with jam
for breakfast. Where African-Europeans weren't shut off in ghettos,
where turbo-charged financiers weren't allowed to take the government
hostage, where major corporations and banks weren't bailed out by
taxpayers, but where independent women were paid to take long,
cotton-soft maternity leave without having to worry about money. To
Europe, where people weren't religious to the point of imbecility, where
defending the Palestinians didn't mean you were self-hating. Where
evolution wasn't a matter of opinion, and where no one threatened
the lives of doctors who worked at abortion clinics.

That's what he'd wanted.

But *really*? What had he *really* wanted? Joe felt a pang.

'By all means, apply for work wherever seems best to you,' his dad
had told him. 'Your mother and I just want you to be happy.'

'But…' Joe said.

Dad looked at him. But what?

'But... You say *by all means apply*, *of course we want*, but you mean *but*.'

'It's your life,' Dad said, looking at him seriously. 'Do you understand? Your decision.'

'The question is, do you understand?' Joe said, and forced himself to look his father in the eye. He was startled to hear the words come out of his own mouth, and instantly saw the hurt he'd caused. Dad looked old, older than before.

Joe had the urge to apologize and ask what Dad thought, really thought; he could use some honest advice right now. But he already knew what Dad thought; it was exactly what Joe had decided to ignore, and then proceeded to, because the whole point of the plan was to prove that Mom and Dad were wrong.

Dad looked away and said, feeling the word out: '*Finland*.' He pursed his lips, trying to get a sense of how Finland tasted as an idea.

'The University of Helsinki has just founded a Center of Excellence,' Joe said, and could himself hear what this sounded like.

'Joe,' Dad said, and looked at him. 'Europeans might say things like that sometimes but...'

'They do research over there too, you know,' he said. 'Believe it or not. They have universities.'

'Joe,' Mom said. Her tone meant: don't speak to your father that way.

Dad opened his mouth to say something but left it unsaid. He appeared to wrestle with himself, then shook his head and started over: 'Let me get this straight. You've been offered a tenure-track position at UCLA, one of the best universities in the world, but you've decided to accept... *a year-long postdoc in Finland*?'

Joe's cheeks blazed.

'Helsinki collaborates with Stanford, Berkeley, and Oxford. They talk about innovation and networking a lot more than we do.'

'Joe.' Now Dad looked amused. 'Have you ever heard of anyone at Stanford needing to convince anyone how connected and innovative they are?'

'Dad, maybe you're not aware,' Joe said, 'what good work they're doing in Europe these days, even in the smaller countries. It's because of the quality public education and the free universities. Because half the population isn't sent out on the streets not knowing how to read, to sell drugs and mow each other down with Uzis. Besides, work isn't the only thing in life.'

'When you're young,' Dad said slowly, 'it may feel like all options are open to you. But later in life, you come to see that some decisions were critical.'

'Exactly,' Joe said.

He forced himself to look his father in the eye.

Dad looked at the tablecloth, evidently trying to digest the new information. He doesn't look angry, Joe thought, trying to breathe slowly as his heart hammered away.

Then his dad looked up at him and said quietly: 'Joseph. If you call right away – if you call today – I think it might still be possible…'

'Dad, I'm not calling UCLA. I already told them, I'm going somewhere else.'

From Joe's current vantage point, it was surprisingly difficult to relate to this self of twenty years ago. Had it seemed like a good idea simply to believe in the way he wished things were? To imagine that something would become true just because he wanted it?

In hindsight, it felt frighteningly probable that he had left the US to prove Dad wrong. During Joe's senior year of college, Dad had forbidden him from dropping out and founding a computer company with his buddy Zach; Dad hadn't bought the notion of the ever-shrinking computers sold to every household. Joe hadn't wanted to follow in his father's footsteps, fade like a wraith into the mists of theoretical knowledge.

But Dad had said: 'No way. You're going to graduate school.' At the age of fifty-one, Joe still had no idea if Dad had been absolutely right or totally wrong, but his unequivocal tone had made defiance impossible at the time. Instead, it had seemed like a good idea to get back at him six years later, in a way that had nothing to do with the original conflict and to which Dad never would have connected it. Joe would vehemently deny any link between the incidents, even to himself, but the reality was he was going to Europe because his dad thought it was a bad idea.

'What's Hannah going to do in Finland?' Dad asked after a long silence. 'Is she going to be able to find work as easily? She sounded pretty happy at Columbia.'

And when Joe didn't immediately respond, Mom came out from the kitchen, eyes wide, thinking she understood.

'Is Hannah pregnant?'

Joe coughed. He could feel Mom's and Dad's hopes and expectations weighing on him like a physical force.

It was too hard to look up, but he knew Mom stood frozen at the kitchen door, waiting for his reply. The silence seemed to last an eternity. He'd planned on telling Mom and Dad about Alina earlier: that he was going to marry a Finnish woman who was carrying his child, who was sensitive and intelligent and empathetic and lovely. But the glow of the setting sun was already staining the window-glass pink, and Mom had gone back into the kitchen to get the coffee, and he realized that Mom and Dad would have to meet Alina and see them together before they'd understand, and so he didn't say anything.

'I really liked Hannah,' Dad finally said.

And as Joe recalled this conversation, he suddenly had to take off his glasses and wipe his eyes.

He could hear his grandmother's voice in his mind: *Mentsch tracht, Gott lacht.* Man schemes, God scoffs.

Was anything good left of those nights he'd paced the dark Finnish apartment, bouncing a screaming baby at his shoulder, so Alina could get a moment's rest? Of the Finnish potato mash Alina pureed in the evenings and he spooned into Samuel's mouth?

He realized he'd been staring at the gray carpet in the seminar room too long when Kathy elbowed him: Everything OK? He flashed a smile at her, A-OK! and tried to shake off the feeling.

At the front of the room, the rev of ever-eager Stan Lippman's turbo-powered PowerPoint engine would have given ESPN's commentators a run for their money. He was their most interesting guest speaker this term, and Joe knew Lippman was particularly interested in hearing his reactions. Nevertheless, he had to make a concerted effort to keep from bolting out of the room.

As part of his presentation on the lateral connections between cat cortex areas V2 and V3, Lippman was asking the faculty and graduate students… what was the most hurtful thing they'd ever done to their parents? How would it feel to have an adult son you wouldn't recognize on the street? A son, your own flesh and blood, who spoke English with the same irresistible Scandinavian accent as Alina; used the definite article with the word *nature*, regularly confused the pronouns *he* and *she*?

The turquoise flame crackling from the commuter trains' electricity conductors, like welder's wands in the icy air; the blue-gray winter mornings; the fat flakes of snow falling softly in the gloom. The dry, Styrofoam sound of it squeaking underfoot in a hard freeze.

The warm light of the late-August sun with the Eläintarha playing field basking in it. The clank of the steel tracks under the number three tram. The soundless city, where he'd floated beyond the edge of the known world.

Helsinki looked so beautiful. From here, now.

The final scene at the airport: the satchel leaden over his shoulder, Alina's face, drawn with failure and disappointment. The way they looked at each other, their mutual unspoken, simultaneous apology: *I'm sorry, I didn't know this was the best I could do. I didn't know this about myself.*

The stirring, last-minute regret: *maybe there could still be a way.*

The little boy who'd just learned to walk, teetering unsteadily across the parquet at Helsinki-Vantaa International Airport, shrieking with joy.

'Samuel, come here, come tell Daddy... Samuel, let Daddy hold you. Hey, Samuel! Samuel. Daddy's going to leave soon and... Listen, you won't be able to... Samuel!'

The chortling one-year-old with his chubby cheeks. The ill-tempered squirm – *I don't wanna*! – and off again in another direction.

Then the awkward final goodbye. He'd planned to pick up his son one last time, tell him he loved him, give Alina a squeeze too, say out loud that it wasn't anyone's fault, let's be happy we had the courage to try, let's be happy we have Samuel.

But then – before the critical moment, before the parting words Joe was trying to formulate with a lump in his throat, the ones that would be Alina and Samuel's ultimate memory of him – he'd turned towards the line, to check if he needed to go yet. He'd only meant to glance.

But when he turned back around a second later, he saw Alina off in the distance, walking in tight, clipped steps towards the main doors, the one-year-old in her arms, their child, their shared life.

As if from behind a sheet of bullet-proof glass, Joe watched Stan Lippman present his favorite folds of cat V5 area like a tour guide making sure first-time visitors fully comprehended the value of local treasures.

Joe found himself considering stepping out of the lecture hall and calling Alina right back. Confess that he regretted not keeping in touch with Samuel. Admit that it broke his heart, but maintaining contact had just been too painful. Explain that the distance had been too great. He had no idea if his son was interested in having a relationship now, or if any attempts at contact from Joe at this late stage would just make the young man uncomfortable. Tell her that he hoped from the bottom of his heart Samuel would come visit them as soon as possible, so they could all meet. That would give Samuel a chance to get to know his American family properly; he could stay with them as long as he wanted.

Joe remembered how Alina had always wanted to take him day-hiking in Finland. Maybe Samuel's visit would be a good excuse to pack up the whole crew and go somewhere for a few days. A national park, the Nevada desert. They could take Samuel to Death Valley or the Great Basin. Or a baseball game.

The thought gradually calmed Joe. And when Stan Lippman came to his final slide, for the first time that day Joe heard what he was saying – that, in short, the cells in cat area V5 were like a Brooklyn bus driver: they pretended not to care, but when the shit hit the fan, would go out of their way to help anyone – and this sounded so interesting that Joe wished he'd heard something of the presentation itself.

Joe's phone burst out ringing on Sunday morning, while he was reviewing a lousy study submitted to a good journal.

He was alone in the house. Miriam was at a conference and Daniella was at the pool. Nobody could keep track of Rebecca's comings and goings. She flew off the handle if you tried to ask.

It was annoying how much time was wasted drafting even a cursory rejection of an article manuscript. Nor would Joe have had the time; work had piled up. As always, there wasn't anything you'd rather be doing with your free time, especially when you were swamped, than spending it on shoddy studies you wished had never been done in the first place.

As Joe wrote the review, he found his thoughts drifting to Ted Brown, Freedom Media and to whether the protest would do any good. Joe had been a key player in organizing a boycott of the media conglomerate's journals after it announced it was 'developing its academic publishing services.' Because the majority of academic publishers were controlled by Freedom Media, it could unilaterally dictate the terms for access to scientific information. Ted Brown now had the right to retroactively charge readers for work researchers had already done.

The problem was by no means new. Academic publishers had always extorted shameless subscription prices for their journals – even though the contents were produced by university-employed researchers, to a large extent on the taxpayer's dime. Researchers also wrote the peer reviews that ensured the studies were trustworthy, free of charge for the journals, including those in Brown's empire. But if a taxpayer wanted to read the results of a study they'd funded, access to a single article could cost as much as fifty dollars – and to form an understanding of the basics on a narrow topic, you needed to be able to browse dozens or hundreds.

The problem had recently come to a head when one of the biggest publishing houses had sold the academic side of its business to Freedom Media, who had already picked off its other competitors one by one and now held the majority of all academic publishing activity in its control, irrespective of field. The results of academic research, scientific information, was all in Freedom Media's hands. Joe himself had published dozens of papers in journals now owned by Freedom Media.

The conglomerate had then announced that, from now on, university libraries could either subscribe to Freedom Media's entire catalog or none of it. There wasn't a single university that could afford not to subscribe, assuming they wanted anyone to keep doing research, or even follow it; there wasn't a single academic who could get by without access to the published scientific literature. The same went for science journalists, doctors, nutritional biologists, urban planners, structural engineers, and environmental toxicologists – everyone.

Joe rose to answer the phone, astounded by the paper and its authors' lack of self-respect. He'd already rejected the same manuscript from Hartikainen, Kumpula, and Österman once before, when they'd submitted it to another journal, an even better one.

Everything about the study had been done wrong. The animals had been randomized into groups according to a bizarre logic, the statistical analyses conducted as if the analyst hadn't seen the research design. And why guinea pigs? These sorts of studies were typically done with cats, for a number of good reasons. Then the behavioral data had been scored incorrectly, rendering it useless, after which the loci of the neuronal lesions were used to make a circular argument regarding the supposed visual impairment the authors had failed to demonstrate. The study was not 'despite its deficiencies, interesting,' nor had it, 'certain methodological limitations notwithstanding, opened up new perspectives on the visual system,' as Hartikainen, Kumpula, and Österman claimed. The manuscript by Hartikainen et al. opened nothing on anything; it was utterly worthless, he wrote in his review, and should not be published in this or in any journal. Yes, the guinea pigs had gone blind and their brains had been damaged, but the study had been conducted so poorly that concluding anything from these changes was impossible.

But the same appalling disgrace of a study could always resurface with its definite conclusions in a toilet-paper publication like the *Journal of Neuroscience and Experimental Biology*, despite Joe's sacrificed Sunday. From there it would successfully dupe a first-year grad student into wasting energy on taking it seriously, and somewhere else a real researcher would cite it so carelessly that someone else would, without checking the reference, erroneously assume that Hartikainen, Kumpula, and Österman's conclusions made sense.

Part of Freedom Media's output – the *Journal of Neuroscience and Experimental Biology* was a prime example – was so scientifically inferior as to be considered a joke. There wasn't a university library in existence that would have voluntarily paid a single cent for it. These journals were nothing but a nuisance, because the studies published in them often bore a superficial semblance of credibility but hadn't been peer-reviewed rigorously as in respected journals. This meant the findings were rarely reliable. Even the best scientists make mistakes; that was why proper peer reviews were critical. That was the reason Joe and all his colleagues regularly sacrificed their personal time, free of charge, to reviewing and critiquing manuscripts submitted for publication.

But because the most prestigious publications were now in Freedom Media's hands, libraries had to – at the price dictated by Ted Brown – also order the bogus rags, the ones that were detrimental to science, humankind, perhaps even the planet.

Joe didn't realize how cranky he sounded until he pressed the green answer icon and growled a hello into his phone.

Alina! he suddenly remembered – he was supposed to call her back. After the lecture, the entire department had headed out to Sushi Hana with Stan Lippman, and Alina and the phone call had slipped Joe's mind.

Could it be Samuel on the phone right now, suddenly asking why Joe hadn't been involved in his life? It was almost Passover – wasn't Pesach the time, as Joe's mother would have said, when you welcomed strangers into your home with open arms?

But it wasn't Samuel on the phone, it was Lisa.

Shit, he hadn't taken care of that either! He needed four more hours in the day, perpetually.

'Joe,' she said, her tone unusually emphatic. 'You should get over here.'

'I'm sorry. My brain is such a sieve; I still haven't called Barb.'

'No, it's—'

'But let's just say you'll TA for me next year. We'll find you something. I promise.'

'*Joe.*' Something in Lisa's voice brought him up short. 'You need to get down here.'

He'd never heard her use this tone before.

'What's going on?'

'Just come in.'

His heart was racing all the way to campus, and as he pulled into the parking lot, he saw a police car. *What the hell*? An officer, with a blue uniform, a gun belt, the works, was talking to Rose, Joe's lab

assistant. Rose looked serious – sweet, ever-helpful Rose – and Joe
instantly realized—

No! Good God, no…

One of his students, one of the undergrads, who?

Chip Zukowski?

Someone had gone postal, pulled a Columbine – stalked into the
building in a long black leather coat with a semiautomatic pistol in
either hand, sending everyone screaming and scrambling under their
desks in a hailstorm of particle-board as bullets hammered through
cheap Scandi furniture. Joe practically ran to Bloomberg Hall, where
police officers were drawing cinematic yellow tape across the door.

Good God, who?

Now it had happened here, too, of course, why wouldn't it?

Please don't let it be Chip.

Please don't let it be any of mine.

Please let it be someone else, someone I don't know, please let him
have shot himself and no one else. We're insane, flashed through his
head, we've built a completely sick society: in Finland, or in any other
Western country, schoolkids don't go around assassinating their classmates. This was what shock meant: denial, not fully comprehending
the meaning of what had happened, because there was an aspect of
the catastrophe that bordered on the satisfying – he was horrified as
he followed the thought through to its conclusion – as if life had only
now become real, the world come to life.

This was what shock felt like.

This passing second felt like it had lasted hours, the entire morning
no longer than a second.

Joe reached for the door. A tall, mustached policeman raised his hand
and asked to see an ID. As if in a dream, Joe could hear someone inform
the officer that this was the head of the lab. *Sorry, Professor.* He was
allowed to pass; he saw the cream-colored break-room sofas, still clean,
the stylish table that had proved flimsy, the sleek plastic lines of the new
computers. All of it terrifyingly untouched, not blood-splattered, exactly
like before; it was horrifying, because that meant what had happened still
lay ahead, around the corner, beyond this still life, this surreal composition.

The dreamlike state didn't end until Joe saw Lisa, and time shuddered
forward again. He could tell from her face that no one had died; if
anything, she looked bored.

It was only now he realized how hard his heart was pounding. He had to steady himself against the table in the kitchenette.

'To be honest,' Lisa said, 'I've always thought it's just a matter of time. Before we have to deal with something like this.'

'What happened?'

She gestured for him to follow her down the hallway. The door to his office was flung wide.

The first thing Joe saw was the head of campus security, who said hello. The police officer next to him had his pen and notebook out, was jotting something down. Joe couldn't imagine either of them would look the way they did if someone had been shot.

'Professor Chayefski?' the officer said.

When he peered into his office, Joe froze. His computer's screen, hard drive, fan, and circuit boards had been smashed and strewn across the carpet. Black boot-prints stood out distinctly on the shards.

There were nicks in the walls, some deeply gouging the surface. The head of security speculated they were from the old, metal external hard drives – which Joe's team no longer used but had evidently been presumed to contain backups – being smashed against them. Ink had been spattered everywhere, something red and sticky smeared on his chair.

'Is anyone hurt?' he asked.

'Not to our knowledge,' the police officer said. For a fleeting moment, Joe thought he caught the officer studying his face intently.

'I don't think there was anyone here this morning except Rose and me,' Lisa said.

'So this happened last night?' Joe asked.

'We're looking into it,' the head of campus security said, playing the cool, blasé professional... showing off for the police officer? He was suddenly brimming over with the importance of his work, his entire life, as if he didn't have a cushy job at an elite private university where the most nefarious crime he had to deal with was shoplifting.

Joe eyed the gleaming reddish-brown pool on his chair. He nearly dipped in a finger out of curiosity, but then thought better of it.

'What is this?'

'Being tested as we speak.'

'Syrup, food coloring, and water? Am I in the ballpark?'

'You know anyone who might have a motive for doing something like this?' the police officer asked.

Joe frowned and stared at the carpet. The piles of gray flakes on the floor were evidently ash. What had they burned?

'How did they get in?' he asked.

As he asked the question, he turned towards the door, where a gash the size of a crowbar grinned in the jamb.

'Elegant work, I gotta say,' the policeman said, stroking his whiskers. The head of campus security chuckled. Too pointedly, Joe thought.

Splintered wood littered the floor. The door had been locked, but of course the average office door was easy enough to pop open with the right tools.

Joe noticed Lisa looking at him.

'Did you see the lab?'

Joe rushed into the other corridor, where big, black letters had been sprayed across the white wall:

VIVISECTION IS SCIENTIFIC FRAUD

Scientific fraud?
Joe's pulse leaped, and he was already sprinting for the animal units when Lisa grabbed his arm.

'Everything's fine.'

'Everything?'

'Yeah.'

'The B cages, too?'

'Everything.'

'Did you check the security logs?'

'Yes. No one even entered the corridor.'

But Joe had to check for himself. Even turning on the lights could interfere with the animals' circadian rhythms, potentially ruin someone's experiments. The security systems for the labs where the rats, cats, and monkeys were kept were so robust, especially for the monkeys, that the intruders hadn't been able to break in. There was no way an outsider could even tell in which corridor the animals were kept.

Someone had tried to wrench the heavy steel door open, apparently using the same crowbar. The lip of the door was warped, the paint chipped.

'Amateurs,' the head of security said to the police officer, a preteen trying to impress bigger boys. The policeman stroked his whiskers; to the security guard's patent disappointment, he didn't seem to have heard.

Joe's office was the only one that had been vandalized. The ash turned out to be committee statements from his paper archives. The intruders had burned the contents of certain files, the ones related to the institutional review board Joe had chaired for the last five years out of a sense of obligation.

The paper copies were meaningless, printed out as a formality. Perhaps the intruders had imagined they'd be hindering research, assumed that new applications would have to be sent in. But any permissions granted had already been sent electronically to any number of recipients, including the applicants.

Joe didn't store raw data on his computer, and his lab had double-backups of everything. But now he'd have to hunt down unfinished analyses, manuscript versions, already-commented drafts, recent literature. That would take time that could have been better spent elsewise.

The only thing that was lost for good were the photographs he'd transferred from his camera. Daniella and Rebecca in their Halloween costumes. Birthday cakes, graduate students after their defenses, Hans, Joe's German post-doc, hugging Lisa at his going-away party, Chad's tenure celebration.

The harassment had been going on for a while now. The previous incidents, as campus security called them, had been relatively innocuous, presumed the handiwork of juveniles.

Someone had scrawled graffiti on the external walls and windows of the laboratory wing, vulgar pictures and profanities in black marker. Even though it had happened on a couple of consecutive weekends, the vandalism didn't appear to follow a pattern, or to be particularly personal in nature.

Campus security had figured some drunk frat boys had been having a little fun. Young males displaying in front of females. They hadn't seemed particularly interested in the whole affair; Joe could recall the head of security's pompousness as he pontificated, in the patronizing tones of an experienced soldier, on *real* security threats, radical Muslims, what *terrorism* really meant.

When the first slip of paper appeared in Joe's departmental mailbox, it wasn't clear if it was related to the graffiti. The message was short, and unambiguous in tone:

If someone tortures for a living,
can they ever expect to be safe?

Campus security's reaction had been dramatically different from their response to the vulgarities the maintenance crew had scrubbed away with soap and water. The head of security had called Joe in to ask if he had any enemies (not to his knowledge), who, in his view, could have written such a threat (some fanatic?) and why Joe, specifically, had been targeted. (His mailbox was conveniently in the middle? His name had just been mentioned in the newspaper?) Joe'd been forced to promise that he'd inform them immediately if anything else out of the ordinary happened (absolutely, thanks for your help).

He hadn't taken the note very seriously himself. But now, in the aftermath of the break-in, the head of security urged him not to walk alone on campus after dark. Joe was startled.

Seriously?

Was he supposed to get himself a bodyguard now? Some muscle-bound ex-cop in dark glasses, wearing an earbud with a wire snaking out of it?

Joe hadn't wanted to bother anyone about the notes; something about them felt embarrassing, as if he were ultimately to blame. But this time, other people had been affected. If the vandals ever gained access to the animals, it could ruin, or at least delay, some promising PhD student's dissertation and career.

He called Barb Fleischmann on her mobile. Barb answered from a conference in Seattle. She was surprised; they weren't in the habit of calling each other on weekends.

Barb sounded tense, from which Joe realized her presentation must be about to begin. Barb was one of those people who never got the least bit nervous, even when giving a keynote in a cavernous hall. For goodness' sake, she gave presentations every week! In front of her most esteemed, most critical colleagues. And yet for some reason, in the weeks leading up to her conference talks the smallest things seemed to peeve Barb: that damned cupboard door is still off its hinges, why doesn't anyone around here ever take care of the common spaces!

Once she heard what happened, Barb was so shocked she momentarily forgot her presentation.

'Good God.'

'I know.'

'At our department?! I can understand why somewhere... you know, Parkingfield Inc. or whatever, those companies testing chemicals and detergents—'

'My thoughts exactly.'

'To a basic researcher?'

'That was the first thing that went through my mind, too.'

'Who are these people?' Barb said. 'Where do they come from?'

'This has happened elsewhere.'

'You mean that guy from UCLA? What was his name again?'

'Sipowitz.'

'Was that it?'

'Evidently he caved. Eventually. Changed fields.'

Barb was quiet for a moment. Then: 'Scientific *fraud*?'

'Yup.'

'What on earth does that mean?'

'I have no idea,' Joe said. 'But I kind of get why they didn't write: *People have strong and divergent views as to whether the use of animal models is justified, which is why it's crucial we as a society discuss the issue thoroughly and calmly, so everyone feels like their voice has been heard.*'

Barb's chuckle meant a lot to Joe.

At home, Miriam was wonderfully sympathetic, gave him a long, tender hug and poured him a big glass of wine. Maybe that was all that was needed, he thought.

'It's someone who got a D,' Joe said later that night. 'They'll be pissed off for a while and then they'll forget the whole thing.' Miriam was in her study, finishing something that couldn't wait. Nothing could, these days. Joe looked at his wife's focused face, glowing blue at the computer screen, at her slender, pretty fingers, which he had a sudden urge to reach out and touch.

'An A-minus,' she said to her laptop. 'They're the ones who flip out.'

The tap of nails against keyboard didn't slow.

There was something soothing about it not even occurring to her to take the incident too seriously. Miriam had an uncanny capacity to keep her cool while everyone else was losing theirs. She'd had to deal with all kinds of crises since being asked to chair the Department of Linguistics and Psychology the instant she got tenure. It was Miriam who handled the rare dismissals from the university; had a word with the younger faculty members who hadn't fully grasped the fine line between teacher and student. Miriam was also well-suited to being editor of the highest-impact journal in her field, the person whose role it was to sign the weekly *We regret to inform you*s and receive the email abuse that such decisions occasionally inspired.

It was this intelligence and capacity for rational thought that had appealed to Joe when they first met in D.C. This petite, fine-boned woman had quickly proven to be someone who could wallop him in a debate, who didn't start bleating when faced with a setback but organized practical matters with a deft hand. Joe had steeled himself for disappointment after their third date, when Miriam had agreed to come up for a nightcap. The sex would be cool and distant, at best competently mediocre. They were too compatible intellectually; their bodies would compensate by repelling each other. But from the first touch, it was clear his concerns had been groundless. It had seemed too good to be true.

Tonight, for some reason, Joe wished Miriam had taken a few hours off, but asking her to felt awkward. Other people's schedules wouldn't rearrange themselves just because he suddenly wanted to have some time alone with his spouse.

Their lives would go on.

He found himself lingering on the basement stairs without fully understanding why. The soft, dark smell of the cellar always made him think of childhood: the foosball table, the brick walls, the wall-to-wall carpeting.

Down in the basement, Saara was stuffing laundry from the hamper into the washing machine. She noticed Joe and looked up. For a moment, he felt like he was trespassing in his own home.

He asked Saara if she'd heard yet.

'Yeah,' she said, glancing at him in concern before pouring detergent into the washing machine. 'Miriam told me. Scary.'

Saara was Joe's pitiful attempt at maintaining some sort of connection to Finland. They had telephone-interviewed several au pair candidates. Miriam would have preferred a different girl, a Canadian, but had agreed to Saara at Joe's request.

But no special bond had formed with Saara, or through her with
Finland. Especially at the beginning, they'd invited her to join them
for dinner, or hang around when they had guests, but Saara wanted
nothing to do with them during her time off. It appeared to be a
matter of principle. She never engaged Joe or Miriam in conversation
or showed any interest in their work. She took care of the kids, the
meals, and the cleaning as agreed, but other than that kept to herself.
It was perplexing because she didn't seem to know anyone in town.
Saara had been with them for almost a year now.

Joe looked at the girls' clothes Saara was folding: pink tops emblazoned with slogans in silver glitter, black jeans, artfully distressed
and stained, underwear, knits, garments Joe didn't know what to call.
There were quite a few he didn't remember having ever seen before.
The baskets were constantly overflowing with Rebecca's clothes,
always new, always clean-looking. Daniella, on the other hand, had
to be coerced into turning over her dirty laundry, and she always wore
the same things until Miriam eventually dragged her off to the mall.

Joe reflected that he should ask his grad students if any undergrads
had been by lately to dispute half a mark, anyone who'd wanted to
raise a test score from an 86 to an 86.25.

But inevitably there would have been: the department was full of
them, nagging pre-meds whose acceptance to medical school and entire
future inevitably seemed always to hang on this particular quarter-point
on this particular test. Which, of course, it did.

The country code for Finland still came to Joe automatically. There
was something reassuring about the fact that it hadn't changed over
all these years. He found himself being cheered by the familiar, lucid,
Scandinavian note of the ring, which immediately let you know you
were calling abroad. The melody had something of the Finns' odd,
sing-song language to it, bright and foreign, lacking the aggressive
sounds of other European languages.

Occasionally Joe would find himself missing Finland, the gray and
black figures standing mournfully at the bus stops in the morning, as
if they'd just lost everything.

'Alina?'

Joe apologized for not returning her call sooner. He took a deep breath and then told her what had happened.

Even though he couldn't see Alina's face, from the long pauses and the cadence of her breathing, Joe could tell she was alarmed. He found himself downplaying the seriousness of the incident and leaving out details – such as it being his office specifically that had been targeted. Alina had sounded tired before he even began.

To change the subject, Joe asked where Samuel was at the moment. Alina wasn't sure, maybe Oregon.

'What's he up to these days, anyway?' Joe asked.

He recalled Samuel had graduated from high school – it must have been two, three years ago – at the top of his class. At the time, Alina had told him Samuel was interested in biology; Joe had been pleased.

Alina let out a small, nervous cough, the same one Joe remembered from twenty years earlier.

'Quite a lot has… happened… in his life,' she said. 'We had a little argument before he left. Or a pretty big one, actually.'

'Oh?'

'Well, I… I didn't want to burden you, since we don't talk that often. It seems silly only to call you with bad news. But Samuel went through a pretty rough period after high school.'

'Yeah?' Joe said.

He felt a pang of guilt: *since we don't talk that often.* He hadn't heard from Alina or Samuel in years.

'Yeah. And now he's joined this… or, well, the people he's hanging out with, I… argh! We didn't talk as much as we should have, either.'

'But is everything OK now?'

'Well, I… I'm not sure. He always bites off so much. There are so many things. He's very… He doesn't know how to protect himself.'

The same nervous cough again.

'What's he doing these days? Is he in school?'

'He had a job at this one company for a while.'

'A job?'

'Yeah. Some sort of… internship. I guess they were paying him, too. But then… Well, it's a long story, but he's in a little trouble now as a matter of fact. With the law, and…'

'What did he do?'

A long, uncomfortable silence. Joe wondered if Alina was wishing he hadn't asked. Then: 'There's been a lot of talk about it here. Yesterday there was even this... this thing on TV... it wasn't so nice – I mean, I don't even think all of what they were saying was true.'

'What sort of trouble is he in? Is there anything I can do?'

Alina sighed and went on, as if she hadn't heard Joe: 'Young people's lives seem so difficult these days. He carries the world on his shoulders somehow. Or maybe I'm the one who worries too much. He doesn't worry about anything. I don't think I— I should have been a better mother. We... I feel like all I ever talked about was what might go wrong and what he shouldn't do and – I went about things the wrong way. My husband, Henri, he and Samuel got into a fight, too.'

'A fight?' Joe asked, when Alina didn't continue.

'Yes,' she said. 'When our younger son, Ukko – he was found to have.... I mean he's been diagnosed with... a developmental disorder and... I don't know. I should have been... I didn't know how to...'

Joe waited for more, but it didn't come.

'You don't want to tell me more about it?'

'I... Let's talk later, if you don't mind. I can't... To be honest, it's just too much for me right now.'

Joe could hear the quiver in Alina's voice. A warm wave of concern washed through him. He wished he were in the same country so he could look her in the eye and tell her that everything was going to be fine.

'I'm happy to help out,' he said, hearing the hollow ring of the words. 'If there's anything I can do.'

A sniffle. A long silence. And then, in a small voice: 'OK.'

'Let him know he's welcome here,' Joe said. 'Give him my number and our address. And Mom still lives in New York. I'm sure she'd love to have Samuel stay with her if he's up that way. And if there's anything I can do, just...'

'Thanks.' Something in Alina's voice indicated there wasn't.

It was past nine by the time Joe got off the phone. He should have been at campus already. The tricky third section of the book, which he'd promised to the publisher last fall, had been waiting all term to be written. Yet here he was, still sitting in the kitchen.

An unknown creature from another world: that's what he must be to his son, an alien who for some incomprehensible reason sent him a card every fall that read:

שנה טובה

Shanah Tovah... Happy New Year!

Picking a card had been tough. *Shanah Tovah* felt phony.

When Daniella was born, the form at the hospital had asked for his religion. Joe had put down *quantum theory, for now*. His most vivid memory from Hebrew school was trying to touch tongues with Amy Davidson on the playground.

For people of his parents' generation, religion had been such a simple, straightforward matter. For obvious reasons. But when Daniella heard the word 'survivor,' the first thing to come to mind was, no doubt, a TV program.

As his mother never failed to remind him, Joe was his son's only link to his roots. And what kind of postcard would be any less phony – the President smiling in front of the Stars and Stripes? A humorous *Greetings from the United States* from a morbidly obese couple?

Anything coming from a father who didn't know his child was going to seem phony. Joe didn't have a clue what his son thought about him or about the US, or whether he wished Joe had stayed in touch.

Each fall when he sent the card, Joe would be reminded of how he'd represented one thing and one thing only to Finns, generally his nationality, and how everything he said and did was weighed against this. The mythical American-ness he represented, defined in some Finnish-Platonic heaven, was often diametrically opposed to his personal views. And then the Finns' absolution, even more hurtful than the stereotype: *But you're not* really *American, not that way.*

Finns viewed American-ness the same way Midwestern rednecks and Bible-Belt evangelicals did. Of course there were those in the US who didn't think of Joe and his friends, family, and coworkers as *real Americans* because they didn't watch Fox News, and didn't believe in carrying handguns, and opposed military crusades in the Middle East and Israel's excessive use of force. Living in Finland was sort of like living in Texas: you were alone with your convictions.

In a way, things had been easy for Joe in Finland, and yet often while he lived there it felt like there had only been enough room for one correct stance. Or maybe it just seemed that way because, as an outsider, he had a hard time recognizing nuances. But he'd surprised himself by wishing Finns wouldn't automatically assume he celebrated

Christmas. This reaction had felt strange. In the annual negotiation they had back home, Christmas almost always won out, and he had nothing against Christmas; as a matter of fact, he liked it. But it was still a choice. In New York, his cousins spent Christmas Day the traditional way: a movie and then out for Chinese. Joe had caught himself wishing that someone – just one person, anyone! – would give some indication that celebrating Christmas wasn't a foregone conclusion.

In the US, it had never occurred to him to display a mezuzah. Something about the custom felt awkward, but apparently his relation to it was more complex than he had imagined. In Finland, he'd always been more than willing to talk to Finns about his roots and his family if someone asked, but especially in a country where everyone's parents and parents' parents' parents' parents' parents were from Finland, trumpeting his exoticism by hanging a mezuzah would have felt doubly odd. Strangely, however, in Finland he'd started to notice the empty spot above the door staring back at him in a way it never had at home. The blank wall demanded conviction: you either hung it there or you didn't. There was no way for it to be seen in a certain light and with certain reservations, with the necessary footnotes, as would have been truthful.

Then it had dawned on Joe: was that in fact the point?

Getting to know Finns had proved challenging. Apart from the seminar room, which was lit like a greenhouse, the department was steeped in gloom. Apparently this was intentional: under cover of darkness, it was easier for everyone to slip into their offices without being spotted. The whole first month Joe was in Finland, he thought the university was closed. Or were Finns perpetually on strike, like the French?

Joe had gradually learned that if you sat still for a long time without making any sudden movements, you could catch the occasional glimpse of a Finn. In the wintertime, they would emerge soundlessly, especially in the morning dimness and the blue light of afternoon, to wander the corridors in solitude, mournful and mute. During the summer, the Finns would disappear to their cabins for months on end; the whole country could have been conquered without anyone noticing.

You could sometimes corner a Finn in the break room. These

lunchtime encounters did not, however, necessarily result in conversation. For those awkward two–three minutes you managed to chat
the Finn up, it would remain rigid and hold its breath as it offered
one-word responses, scanning the vicinity for an escape route, eyes
wide with fear.

Fortunately Wallenberg wouldn't flee when Joe stopped to chat. Joe
had asked him where the department's researchers met; they must
have a physical space where they collaborated. Was there a secret
meeting place somewhere Joe didn't know about? Where did they hold
departmental colloquia, guest lectures? Where did they discuss their
results, help each other develop their ideas?

'In the sauna,' Wallenberg had said.

For the life of him, Joe couldn't tell if the guy was serious.

In hindsight, Joe was amused to realize he'd advanced like a textbook
case through all the stages of culture shock.

The honeymoon had been followed by a crisis. The little things that
had initially struck him as cute started to bother him. Why couldn't
you get Mexican food anywhere? How come no one says hello? Why
doesn't anyone, especially men, introduce themselves or each other,
and why do they act as if they weren't in the same room? Isn't it
draining avoiding eye contact day in, day out – just so you don't have
to talk? Why is carrying a conversation a task relegated to women?
Why isn't anyone interested in what their colleagues are doing? Why
didn't anyone think it was rude not to show up at the faculty research
seminar he'd tried to start up? In any of his previous jobs, the withering
of scientific conversation would have signaled utter professional and
social collapse, wholesale surrender.

Were these people really *that* afraid of each other? So afraid
they'd rather do everything poorly by themselves than well together?
Wouldn't it be smarter to share their thoughts so they could refine
them as a team? But apparently it was more important for Finns to
do everything their own way, in solitude, without help, among old
friends. Finnish men in particular wanted to do everything alone, be
independent, tough, and brilliant, which is why offering feedback or
asking questions wasn't allowed, even those questions that would

have helped their work be even more brilliant. For the same reason, they didn't let girls play with them, except the most docile ones, in supporting roles. In the promised land of gender equality, women who were intelligent, educated, and too competent for their modest positions, were forced to the edge of the pitch, left at home for three, four years after giving birth, while everyone bragged about how much freedom of choice mothers had here. This was why Finns, in spite of their hard work and talent, hadn't succeeded in taking their companies global, Joe thought: because they didn't help each other, they just toiled away in solitude, and then when they failed, drank like teenagers and wallowed in shame.

Joe had decided not to get mixed up in university politics. But did Finns really think an alcoholic who had taken fifteen years to write his dissertation by himself in Helsinki was more competent than, say, a young woman who had just received her doctorate from Cambridge, when both of them were applying for the same temporary position?

Joe had tried to speak up on the woman's behalf, and in retrospect this seemed like the turning point after which it was hard to feel the same way about Finland. The woman had a bachelor's from NYU, a doctorate from Cambridge, and was interested in returning to Finland because she wanted to raise her child in her homeland. Joe had met her once at a conference; she seemed pleasant and had a sense of humor, and she had given talks that had garnered attention even in the US. She was an eloquent speaker, and her ideas had been well received, especially in the UK.

Joe had imagined the Finns would be drooling over her. She was even born in Finland, since apparently that mattered, blonde and Lutheran, a native Finnish speaker. Spoke Swedish fluently, too – Finland's second official language was not Russian – as was mandatory in Finland if you wanted a government job.

In the end, the three-year position was not awarded to the woman but the man: the one incapable of tending to his personal hygiene, the one who had spent ten years skulking around the department's corridors in his slippers. He hadn't published in years, and never in an international journal. Even so, Joe might not have intervened – the Finns had a few academic journals of their own that were unintelligible to the rest of the world – but then he learned that the job description had been rewritten at the last minute so the male applicant was the only one who qualified.

After recovering from his shock, he questioned how it could be possible that a clearly stronger female candidate had been deliberately excluded from the running. The response was dismissive shrugs: qualifications are so subjective. That's how these things go. No one was responsible for the decision, and above all, nothing could be done about it anymore. This is such a small country.

Joe had suggested a lawsuit be filed on the woman's behalf: Mr Slippers was so patently unqualified for the position. But the idea was met with horror; such activism was not in the woman's best interests, and certainly not in Joe's.

He'd been dumbfounded that no one protested, that they couldn't even *talk* about the decision – until he stumbled across the reason in a random comment used to describe the woman: the *outsider*.

The woman didn't appeal the decision. She told Joe she had no interest in working somewhere she wasn't wanted.

'Besides, I *am* an outsider,' she had said in an understanding tone, although to him there was nothing understandable about the whole situation: everyone lost.

The longer he worked there, the more incomprehensible Finland felt to him. Why did Finns talk incessantly about improving the quality of their universities when they fought against it tooth and nail? Why didn't they hire ambitious people from better schools and set them up with proper labs, give them real positions instead of ridiculous three-year pretend professorships? Instead, they renamed their universities at two-year intervals and established more and more Centers of Excellence and Expertise and Extraordinary Expertise, populated by the same figures as the earlier ones, doing the same things with equally insufficient resources and as isolated as ever. Then the latest Center of Super-Extraordinary Expertise would get a new director whose name or responsibilities no one could ever remember and who would spend a year drafting their job description before the funding ran out and they moved on.

The 'international connections' that played such a central role in advertising the department proved to be Wallenberg, who had attended Stanford twenty years earlier on a three-month stipend. The department did have an exchange program with Berkeley for master's students. A few had participated, Wallenberg assured Joe, but unfortunately he couldn't remember who or when. And Oxford: someone

from the department had done a postdoc there years ago, although
no one seemed to know what he was up to now.

As long as your own work was going well, the Finns' strange customs were nothing more than funny little curiosities. And the Finns'
tenacity, as navel-gazing as it was, was almost admirable in its own
way. When you were only visiting, you could collect funny anecdotes
about Finland like smooth stones at the seashore, polish them for
recounting at parties, and appear cosmopolitan.

Center of Excellence.

If he'd had a tenure-track position and even a small team to work
with, Joe could have stayed. There were so many good things about
Finland that he could have perhaps sacrificed his own ambitions,
dedicated himself to his family and the inherent satisfaction of his
work. Learned to ski in the coniferous forests, dazzled by the sun
bouncing off the February snow.

The longer the presentation went on, the more it seemed to fall apart.
Joe sipped his coffee and did his best to concentrate. He knew Raj had
high hopes for his experiments, and was even more eager than usual
to hear Joe's feedback.

The idea was interesting enough. Raj had lesioned selected pathways
in cat visual cortex that communicated with higher-level processing
areas. This was nothing new; it had been done thousands of times. But
Raj had been able to apply a recently developed method considerably
more precisely than those used in the past. In the first cat, the blinded
cortical neurons had appeared to rearrange themselves in a completely
unexpected pattern. Joe's entire team had been roused as if out of
a long hibernation. More often than not, their work was repetitive
drudgery, but all of the sudden they'd catch a flash of something that
made the dull days worthwhile.

Yet further experimentation hadn't generated consistent outcomes,
and when the cats were put down, the cellular-level results were
contradictory.

Once again, all that trouble for nothing. Not that it was ever for
nothing – it was often from your missteps and dead ends that you
learned the most.

Joe found his thoughts drifting. Organizing the Freedom Media boycott had turned out to be a challenge. Everyone wanted to focus on their work – understandably so – and avoid any extraneous commitments, especially time-consuming ones. Joe had initially approached potential participants via email and social media, but the response had been tepid, so in the end he'd been obliged to call most of them. Many sounded as if they were hearing about the whole thing for the first time. They all thought the situation was untenable and unfair, but very few wanted to add their name to a public list of boycotters. 'Reputation' and 'troublemaker' were words that frequently came up. As well as: *Thanks for doing such important work! Sorry I couldn't help out this time! Good luck!*

Most critically, no one was interested in resigning from the editorial boards; editing a prestigious publication was an academic merit. As long as researchers continued to submit manuscripts, work on editorial boards, and act as peer reviewers, the best journals would remain at the top of their fields. And as long as they remained at the top, researchers would continue to want to submit their manuscripts to Freedom Media, and libraries would be blackmailed into paying for a catalog of journals they didn't need.

Bringing about change was frustratingly slow, even in matters everyone agreed on.

Yet for the moment the boycott needed to be put on the back burner, until the fallout from the vandals' attack had been dealt with. They'd have to sift through the lab to figure out what had been destroyed, try to locate the missing data, draw up a list of the work that had been lost. What could be more frustrating? He was already behind with everything.

Facilities was supposed to come by to fix the door and install enhanced security systems. More surveillance cameras would be brought in, this time outside the labs. Until then, Joe would have to make do without an office. Great.

'Joe?'

He was startled to find everyone looking at him. Apparently they were expecting him to comment on something that had just been said. What had they been talking about?

He responded with some vague remark that didn't really have anything to do with anything and tried to remember what he'd been thinking at the start of the presentation, before his mind started to wander. But all he could think of was Roddy's response to the grumbling undergraduates lined up in the corridor: *you want credit for the course but you don't want to do anything for it.*

After the lab meeting, Raj stopped him in the hallway. Joe apologized for being so distracted and promised to offer more detailed comments on his results as soon as possible.

'Keep up the good work,' Joe said. 'We'll get something more solid soon.'

'That's not what I'm worried about,' Raj said. 'We just wanted to let you know that... if there's anything we can do.'

The others had gathered around behind him: Lisa, Sarah, Chen, Megan, Thando, Cheh-Han. Serious, silent, earnest.

'We're all happy to pitch in,' Sarah said. 'With the analyses or, say... If your office needs to be fixed up or something. Renovated.'

Raj's and the other PhD students' sympathy was like a ray of sunshine in the heart of winter. Joe realized that, this whole time, the break-in had felt more personal than he'd wanted to admit.

He wasn't in the habit of going for happy hour with his students the way some of the younger assistant professors did, but today he took the whole gang to PJ's for tacos and pitchers of beer. He felt an unexpected warmth inside as he looked around at his bright, socially adept, funny students, playing pool in the windowless basement bar and trashing the right wing of the Republican Party; suddenly he wished them well in a way that, despite his attempts, he couldn't describe.

More threats appeared in his departmental mailbox. At first occasionally, then every week. He was a Nazi, a concentration camp general, Goebbels, Mengele, *Todesengel*. Some of the notes made mention of Miriam and the girls.

Nazi.

Although Joe tried to take the harassment seriously, these attacks felt surreal. What good would it do to get upset? If he wanted reasons to be outraged, he didn't have to look far: across town, people were being murdered every day and drug debts were being repaid with firebombs. War was being waged in the Middle East, still. It was horrible – but what could you do? From this perspective, the vandalism was a relatively minor nuisance.

He forwarded the notes to campus security and reported them to the police. He didn't know what else to do, nor did he have the time. He couldn't leave his PhD students in the lurch. Pugilistic undergrads were lined up at his door, there were talks to prepare, papers to comment on. He would never forgive himself if he didn't finally finish the book this year, and he had to make it home every night by eight on the dot to relieve Saara. With Saara, punctuality was a must.

But his feelings changed after that Saturday night a brick hurtled through his office window. The tapes from the surveillance cameras showed a figure in dark clothing, average height, running straight towards Bloomberg from the upper quad, hurling the brick, and sprinting off. The assailant had a beanie pulled down over their face, and apparently even the police had no way if determining his or her identity.

It was all incredibly frustrating. Was it that hard for the police to find one vandal in Baltimore?

A departmental staff meeting was held where they discussed what action should be taken. In the end, the decision was unanimous: none. The police were investigating the matter. *But how actively?* Joe felt like asking. In nearly a month since the break-in, they'd turned up nothing.

A part of him wished someone would do something, no matter how trivial or pointless. Indicate that he wasn't the only one affected by the incident. That someone threatening his life and the lives of his family members, even as an empty gesture, wasn't a matter of no consequence.

After the meeting, Joe had wondered out loud why he was the one being targeted. What had he done that was so different from everyone else? Dozens if not hundreds of others were doing comparable research, thousands across the country, tens of thousands worldwide.

Barb Fleischmann immediately had the answer:

'You've been too successful.'

The National Science Award.

The year before, his name had appeared in all the media. Every paper reported the same details: extrastriatal refractive amblyopia, a previously unknown, unilateral visual impairment caused by a developmental disorder in the secondary areas of the visual cortex, was now, thanks to the research of Professor Joseph Chayefski, treatable in children. Professor Chayefski's work significantly increased the chances that, in the future, it would be possible to treat other forms of visual impairment, too, perhaps even some that currently led to blindness. He had been awarded a medal and prize money of half a million dollars.

The possibility of ending up a target for hate mail had never occurred to him. He'd been embarrassed by the prize money, since so many others were constantly producing equally good or even better work. It felt just as awkward to say he'd given half of the money to UNICEF. as to leave this intentionally unsaid. He remembered being amused by the reporters' implication that he had performed – and in the worst instances, through a single experiment – a Herculean feat, when the reality was it had been accomplished through the mundane work, the toil, put in by tens of thousands of people. No one accomplished anything alone: there wasn't a single experiment that meant anything in isolation, and all well-executed experiments benefited everyone. But no matter how hard Joe tried to emphasize the work of other researchers, without which he never would have come up with his idea, it was ignored in all the media.

The reporters were curious about blind children – how soon would they be able to see? In how many years? Can I put down three? You can't say? Hmm, whom could I ask? They were just doing their job, searching for a story about a specific disease and a lone hero. It was fiction, journalistic expertise.

But was that what he was being punished for now – for succeeding? They were attacking him because his work had been beneficial, because he hadn't sacrificed his animals in vain on useless experiments?

Why didn't they harass researchers who bungled their tests? Attack those who administered painful electric shocks to dogs but botched the design so that the results were inconclusive? Or forced rats to swim slowly to their death in basins with slippery sides, in order to produce yet another generic version of a drug with dozens of variants already on the market? He received such studies to review every week; they were appearing with accelerating frequency in new journals launched every month; they were being churned out across the globe faster than anyone could read them; they were published in increasingly mediocre journals without the tiniest iota of scientific rigor; they were supported by taxpayers in every Western country, because *it was important to conduct research*; they were produced in such numbers that wading through them was nothing but a hindrance.

That's what he felt like shouting at whoever vandalized his office: if anything was unfair to animals, wasn't it this, goddammit?

If being painted into a corner is frustrating, it's even more demoralizing to realize you did it to yourself.

He could still remember the evening he brought up the job in Berlin. The darkest time of year in Helsinki felt darker than he could ever have imagined. The snow had come late that year, which had meant an exceptionally dismal winter, even by Finnish standards. And once winter had rounded the final bend, it had been a torturous wait for the first signs of spring.

He wasn't sure what part childbirth, breastfeeding, lack of sleep, and maybe even hormones had played in Alina's stunned reaction. At least the guide for fathers he'd been given at the prenatal clinic talked a lot about mood swings among expecting women and new mothers. Was it healthy for Alina to be at home, with only the baby for company? She seemed to think it was her responsibility to stay home until Samuel was three; this appeared to be some standard for respectable motherhood in Finland. Joe's sister-in-law Marnie had spent a month at home, without pay, after Ben was born. But Alina interpreted the mere mention of this as criticism.

And his long days at work – was it true that all Finnish fathers packed up and went home at four P.M., no matter what? Even the prime minister? Joe thought he'd been incredibly flexible suggesting he take a couple of days off when Samuel was born, even though he'd just started at the university, but Alina's response had been one of disbelief. He thought he'd patiently explained why the hours between eight and eleven P.M. were especially valuable in terms of his work; nevertheless, she still seemed to cast pointed looks his way every time Samuel was down for the night and Joe opened his laptop.

It was surprisingly difficult to know what was expected of him. The arrival of a child brought changes to every father's life, but should he be comparing himself to fathers in academia back home? Who, it was true, worked ten-or twelve-hour days, even on weekends, but dedicated the rest of the time to their families? Were the rules different here?

How did scientists make it to the top of their field?

What about once they moved away from Finland? This was what he was trying to feel out, as delicately as possible, that black winter night he mentioned Berlin. But if he was correctly interpreting the look on Alina's face, they wouldn't be moving anywhere: it was as if he'd just told her about another woman, not a job in Germany.

Joe regretted his reaction. He should have controlled his temper, smoothed things over. But it had never occurred to him that their expectations for the future could diverge so drastically. Finland, his modest funding for a year-long postdoc, a couple of universities with a handful of positions being reserved for fifty-year-old Finns: had Alina really thought he'd permanently stay... *here*? To peck at the occasional crumb that *might* be tossed his way? She must have known the sort of life Joe envisioned for himself.

'Well, why the hell did we rent this apartment, then? If we're just going to turn around and move to the ends of earth!'

'To the ends of the earth? It's not that far to Germany.'

'Not that far?' Alina shouted. 'You have to *fly* there!'

'But—'

'Why the hell did I spend all this time and effort dragging in all these curtains and wallpaper and rugs and diaper tables? Why didn't you say anything?'

'I didn't realize you thought—'

'Just go then, goddammit! Go to Germany. I'm sure things are a lot nicer there. And then next year we can move to Ireland!'

In the end, he lost patience, too.

'Alina, I would never voluntarily trade this paradise for anything. Things are so fantastic here, with the parks full of bums pissing everywhere. And no one ever says hello... except when they're drunk, and then they hug like teenagers in love. But maybe, just maybe, there might be a *job* for me somewhere else when my funding here runs out.'

'I'm sure there is. So move!'

'I know, my expectations are so unreasonable... like being able to work. Doing the only work I know how to do. And that I'm actually pretty good at!'

'You'd never know it, considering how much you complain about it.'

'It's pretty easy to forget around here! Since it's impossible for me to do anything right!'

'Good! So that settles it then. You can take a job someplace else and get rid of your horrible wife and son at the same time!'

The next morning, in the bleak light of a Helsinki spring, Alina's puffy eyes, the conciliatory setting of the breakfast table. In a quiet voice his wife asked if he wanted coffee.

A truce, today, for a little while.

He couldn't do it.

He'd already dumped Hannah, made his mother cry, married Alina, uprooted himself to another continent and established a family there; he couldn't leave his wife and only child, ruin everything again.

He saw the tenderness with which Alina gazed at the baby in her arms; his son's crinkling face. Joe regretted everything, most of all his own stubbornness, but not Alina and not Samuel.

For their sakes, he had determined to become a totally different person: to give up on his academic ambitions and apply for a real job. They must have real jobs in Finland, right? he thought as he watched his little, chubby-cheeked son, who was trying to propel himself forward across the living-room floor but only succeeded in backing himself up underneath the sofa. An army of dust motes swam in the bright spring sunlight flooding through the windows.

With the help of a skeptical Alina, Joe had taken his wrinkled suit to the dry cleaners, made a list of likely employers – national and local research institutes and private companies – and dropped by in person to introduce himself. He wasn't going to give up, goddammit! If you had an education and were prepared to work your ass off, you would always find someone who'd hire you! If there was something an American knew how to do, it was to keep pushing on, to make a buck, even on the tundra.

Everywhere he went, the reception was mystified, even alarmed.

But what are you doing in Finland?

So why are you here if you don't have a job?

You don't speak Finnish, but... you're looking for work?

It was hard to know how to take this. Every foreigner couldn't be some mutant stepping out of a flying saucer, could they? It was the 1990s, for God's sakes!

It was like he thought he could learn to fly by flapping his arms: no wonder the locals were perplexed.

When his job search failed, he immediately registered with the

employment office, so he'd be able to find work the minute his grant
ended in August. But he was informed he was ineligible for unemployment benefits, because researchers were considered to be self-employed,
even when they weren't. At the advice of the employment adviser,
he enrolled in a Finnish course, where he studied the language's
agonizing consonant gradation with men from North Africa and
the former Soviet Union, in hopes that mastering it would get him a
job. The country had, of course, just descended into a depression of
historic proportions: banks had toppled and people had lost their jobs,
including those who spoke Finnish, Swedish, English, and German
without the need for any classes. But Joe wasn't going to give up,
goddammit: he knew he'd find some entry-level position somewhere,
at some international company, and gradually work his way up to
more meaningful tasks.

But an American passport and a PhD from the Massachusetts
Institute of Technology were not advantages in the eyes of Veikkola
Heritage Cheeses, Inc. They didn't open the door to an interview at the
Stockmann department store or for the position of director at a new
research center in the biosciences, because he had no work experience
– *in Finland*. The woman at the employment office couldn't care less
who in Boston or New York could recommend Joe or what sort of
networks he might have there; she asked if he could serve customers
in Swedish; did he have experience on the job in Finland.

'You're insane,' David told him, in a voice Joe had never heard his
brother use before.

Joe felt the lump in his throat as he thought about his little boy, who
had only recently learned to stand, and it took him a moment before
he could continue the call. At the sofa, Samuel kept pulling himself
up over and over, even though he'd plop to the floor each time after
swaying unsteadily on buckling knees – and suddenly Joe knew he
was incapable of doing the same.

Käsi – käsit? käseitä? No: kädet, käsiä. Ihmiseitten? No: ihmisten.
Over the course of the humiliating, incomprehensible Finnish class,
the rules of the game became clear to him: he was expected to put his
life on hold until he was able to play the role of native-born Finn. Until
that day – which would never come – his education, expertise, and
career would be shelved as immaterial, because he couldn't answer the
phone and say, without the tiniest hint of an accent: '*Rakennusyhtiö*

Ahlström hyvää huomenta. Pieni hetki, yhdistän.'

Ahlström Construction, good morning. Just a moment, I'll put you through.

Every week he received concerned calls from his mother, during which the topic of money was studiously avoided and cautious inquiries were made as to Joe's well-being, as if he were an old man whose mental faculties were starting to fail him. Mom listed open positions in Spain, Switzerland, and France. Have you heard of this research institute in Italy? Doesn't it sound like these Austrians are working on something similar to your doctorate? How many hours would it take to drive from Helsinki to Austria? I'm sure your father would love to come visit the Alps! His throat prickled as he forced himself to say: 'We're fine, Mom. You don't have to.'

But what hurt most was the letter Dad sent before Rosh Hashanah. Dad said that he'd come to accept that Joe's dreams were different from the ones he'd had for Joe; that he had a life and family in Finland now and it wasn't his ambition to become a leading academic in his field, even though he clearly had the aptitude for it. That if Joe felt like Dad hadn't given his full blessing to Joe's decisions, it was only because Dad hadn't been able to accept that Joe's dream of a good life was different than his. But now Dad understood. Joe had chosen his own path. Dad hoped Joe was happy and knew Dad loved him and respected Joe for having the courage to make his own choices.

Much love from home,
Dad

When Alina found Joe sitting on the edge of the bed, he was in tears.

It was the consonant gradation that saved him. Success had been made impossible, which was, perhaps, a good thing in the end. Otherwise he might have half-succeeded through tenacity: found a dead-end job at some Finnish research institute, learned to speak Finnish poorly, claimed moral victory and been bitter for the rest of his life.

Consonant gradation – he'd even remember the mile-long Finnish word for it until the day he died.

Asttevahtelu.

He almost burst into tears when the offer came over the phone. Samuel was walking unsteadily by now, without any help, and fall term was well underway without Joe. But out of the blue, after he had given up hope, Jack Demekis, his mentor at MIT, had arranged a position for him in Washington D.C. *Humiliating*, that was the word Demekis used to describe the contract. Demekis remembered the offer from UCLA Joe had received less than two years ago, was sorry he couldn't offer anything close to decent.

A second chance! A real lab! With the *necessary equipment*! Where people said hello, talked to each other! About what they were working on, even! Had fun and laughed! Where *American* wasn't a dirty word. Where you didn't hear jokes in which an entire nation was characterized by their predilection for being burned alive during WW II. And Holocaust jokes – so droll! – assumed added piquancy in the Nazi Germany-allied country of Finland, where an American basketball player had just been beaten up and his life threatened because of the color of his skin.

When Joe stopped in New York on his way to Washington, Mom fed and pampered him, did everything in her power to ensure he wouldn't come up with any other bright ideas for sending his life off the rails, impregnate any other beautiful women on the far side of the world.

Dad's gaze had been hard to take, because it was so full of warmth. 'Welcome back,' he had said, and gave Joe a big warm hug.

When Samuel was first supposed to come for a visit, Joe and Miriam were still living in Washington D.C.

Samuel had been six at the time. At first Miriam had reacted politely, even positively, to the idea, carefully avoided any hint of being opposed to it. But then there had been a fundamental change in circumstances: his second wife told him she was expecting a baby. It was only in hindsight Joe realized what a tough position Miriam must have felt she was in: having to welcome a boy she'd never met, from Joe's previous marriage, raised in another country, a complete stranger. And at the same time having to care for a newborn, with all the breastfeeding, crying, and long nights that entailed. Nevertheless, Joe didn't want to cancel the visit, and Miriam didn't outright demand he do so.

When they eventually settled on the dates, Joe spent several evenings trying to think of things to do with his son – movies, excursions. He'd hoped the visit would serve as a fresh start for them both, spark regular contact. Though of course there were certain hurdles to be jumped first, such as how they were going to communicate. Apparently Samuel was experiencing speech difficulties – had developed a bad stutter. Sometimes he would start to speak and stammer mid-word. Alina said that the boy would strain and tense every muscle in his body, fighting to continue.

Joe could hear the unspoken accusation. But if there had been anything he could have done to help Samuel get past his speech impediment, he would have done it. Besides, was the cause really that clear-cut? Samuel might have stuttered even if his father had stayed in Finland.

He hadn't dared ask Alina who was treating their son. She unfailingly interpreted such questions as criticism. In D.C., Joe would have immediately known where to turn for assistance, how to ensure that his son got the best help possible.

He recalled how insufferable Alina had sounded on the phone, spouting off psycho-medical lingo. She claimed that when people heard Samuel talk, they shot concerned glances at her, the mother.

Alina's way of playing the expert had been irritating, and Joe had been less supportive than he should have been. She, in turn, sensed this and took offense. The resorting to pseudo-medical jargon must have been Alina's strategy for staying sane, which Joe luckily realized before he said something lastingly hurtful.

Well before Samuel was supposed to arrive, Joe had read up on the latest research on stuttering. Apparently, it was frequently linked to significant life changes and stress, and generally passed on its own. In some cases, though, those in which the stammering appeared mid-word and involved muscle spasms, the prognosis was poor.

In addition to having problems communicating in his own language, the boy didn't speak any English. Alina had taught him key expressions for the trip – *yes*, *no*, *thank you*, *may I*, *telephone*. Joe had wanted to ask his son beforehand what he'd like to do on his trip, with Alina interpreting. But when Joe tried to suggest the Air and Space Museum, he was informed that his son was playing and could not come to the phone. He could picture the six-year-old stranger after his arrival, too intimidated to look up from the table, saying in a dejected voice: *yes, no, thank you, telephone*, waking up at four A.M. because of the time difference, padding around the dim house like a ghost, making long phone calls to Alina in Finland. In the evenings, Joe and Miriam would hear him sniffling in the guest room.

'It's going to be fine,' Miriam said, when she saw Joe staring at the bedroom wall at night. 'Maybe a little awkward at first – you two need to get to know each other.' The date of the visit had been set for December. Hanukkah would have just begun.

Joe's mom had announced she absolutely wanted to be there, too, to meet her grandchild, to light the candles with Samuel and sing 'Ma'oz Tzur.' The thought made Joe squirm. Was it a good idea to throw the kid into something so foreign right off the bat? OK, so the song was part of the family tradition, especially for Mom, but did they have to dump everything on Samuel first thing? Joe hoped his mom's grandmotherly instincts would have time to be spread more evenly among multiple victims by the time Samuel arrived, since Miriam would have already given birth.

Long before the trip, Mom had bought a little wooden dreidel to give to her grandson. She'd explain what the Hebrew letters painted on the sides meant, and he'd be able to play with it at Hanukkah every year, even back home in Finland. As Mom explained this over the phone – a month before the kid was scheduled to set foot on the plane – Joe realized she considered it her duty to instill every second of Samuel's stay with tradition, so some of it would stick to the shy Scandinavian boy.

Joe could still remember how uneasy Mom's plan made him. Yet now, looking back, the memory was accompanied by a hovering sense of guilt over how completely he had failed to pass on any sense of tradition or their cultural inheritance to his three children. At least with Rebecca and Daniella, he was able to share culpability with Miriam; they had been jointly inept in this new millennium in which there seemed to be no natural role for traditions, except the ones involving possessions and their acquisition, and those burdened with as little cultural-historical significance as possible.

Joe remembered Alina's trepidation about Samuel's long, solitary transatlantic flight. So young! On a plane, all by himself! He and Alina had had numerous lengthy, nearly identical telephone conversations about the flight and the fundamental safety of air travel, during which Joe would invariably and unconsciously adopt the stance that everything would work out fine. It must have had something to do with the unwavering Finnish skepticism Alina radiated, that nothing in this world could work, and that no one could survive, especially anything as complex and risky as a direct flight on the carrier advertised as the safest in the world, onto which her child would be escorted by hand and during every second of which he would presumably be magnitudes safer than, say, during his daily walk to preschool.

For Samuel, the flight would have probably been the highlight of the trip.

As the day approached, Joe consciously refused to cut Alina any more slack. Now they were going to stick to the agreement: they had made this decision together, the tickets were bought, let's not make things any more difficult for Samuel. Joe was prepared to promise to fly back early with his son, if Samuel wanted him to: that's how sure he was that everything would go smoothly. Miriam was right, Joe would say to himself after these nighttime phone calls, kids had no trouble adapting.

He could still remember the afternoon he was supposed to pick up Samuel at the airport: the pale winter sun in the cloudless sky; the dreidel lying untouched on his desk, where Mom had left it.

Alina said she'd left it up to Samuel. That even though he'd been amenable to the idea of seeing his father, even eager, he'd changed his mind at the last minute. He didn't want to go. Alina didn't know how to explain it any better than that.

He doesn't want to, get it? Joe could still hear the Finnish accent echo in his ears as he walked out of Bloomberg Hall into the mild spring evening, down the stairs, past the lower quad, and behind the building, where his car was parked.

The notion that a mother's hysteria wouldn't have seeped into a six-year-old's consciousness was absurd. What kid was going to fly alone to another continent when his mother let it be understood with every glance and gesture that it wasn't a good idea, maybe not even safe? Joe remembered what a hard time he'd had holding his tongue, and how Alina must have nonetheless picked up on it, and how difficult it had been to refrain from yet another conversation about how inflexible she was, how insanely rigid, and how, from this perspective, it maybe wasn't so surprising that their marriage had come to an end.

He doesn't want to, get it? That was when he'd lost any chance of getting to know his son, that summer.

Miriam was understanding, she even consoled him, despite being relieved in a subdued, guilt-tinged way.

Alina should have come, too, Joe realized later. It was the only way she'd feel sufficiently at ease not to spook Samuel. But this seemed like a tough proposition to present to Miriam. And what if his son really didn't want to come? A six-year-old pawn in a power struggle between his parents... the very thought was disgusting.

The following year, it occurred to Joe in February that if they wanted to schedule a new attempt for the summer, he was going to have to raise the issue now. But he remembered Alina's shrill voice, his own impotent anger and the bitterness that had permeated their home for weeks.

And Samuel: what if his son really didn't want to?

Joe hadn't had the heart to raise the matter. Spring came and went, then summer. Let's take a look a year from now, he remembered thinking. When the kid's a little older. Maybe Joe could travel to Finland.

A year from now.

Shanah Tovah.

Samuel's speech had, apparently, gradually returned to normal. Children were built to survive. Luckily.

Joe refused to shoulder all the blame for the divorce. Alina had ultimately refused to demonstrate the tiniest flexibility with regard to where they would live, although at first it looked like she would. As in the argument over Samuel's trip, Alina initially appeared more accommodating than she truly was. When it came time to make the final call, she slammed on the brakes.

Who knows? If they'd ever lived in the United States, they might still be together.

He felt some measure of gratification when, after winning the National Science Award and the smaller European prizes that automatically followed, he received official mail from Finland: an invitation to accept an honorary doctorate from the University of Helsinki. The letter was signed by the guy with the bad hygiene whose slippers Joe still vividly remembered. Evidently he was the head of the department these days. Joe had responded but forgot to mail his letter – which, to his chagrin, he only realized after it was far too late.

To make up for this, he had, on a whim, invited his former colleagues from Helsinki to join in a multi-university project he had just started up with some people from Princeton. Oxford was involved as well: Oxford, with whom the Center of Excellence already collaborated closely. Now that Joe could breathe freely again and his work was going well, it was easy to be generous. Who else was going to knock on the Finns' door and ask them to come out and play?

The proposal threw them into a tizzy. They discussed it in their steering groups and departmental committees, held meetings, asked for more time and consulted the views of the university council and the students. Six months later, when the project was in full swing and the roles for the summer workshop had almost all been assigned, the Finns announced their decision: unfortunately, they were going to have to 'prioritize their own research.' You see, they had their Center of Excellence in Helsinki, Dr Slippers explained via email, a world-class team that already collaborated closely with Stanford, Oxford, and UC Berkeley.

Joe had to leave campus by five, because he'd promised to help Daniella with her oral report.

On top of that, he and Miriam had argued over who was going to raise the other topic with their daughter again.

It had been two weeks now. Daniella hadn't heard him coming: the bathroom door had been open when Joe unsuspectingly crashed into what was happening upstairs. Daniella was standing in front of the mirror, her hair shower-wet, her milk-white, eleven-year-old body still in the steam's warm embrace. She was exactly halfway through puberty: at the stage when the small shoulder blades and round face are clearly those of a child, the budding breasts those of the woman to be.

When she saw her father, Daniella froze. Her lightning-fast attempt to hide something behind her back initially had Joe thinking, Here we go. My daughter has started smoking pot at the age of eleven. He

had two options open to him, both equally awkward: lie that he had
never smoked himself, or justify the premise that kids aren't allowed,
even though I've done it, too.

But it couldn't have been cannabis. As he stepped closer, Joe saw
what Daniella was holding behind her back was her mobile phone.
Apparently it had been aimed at the mirror when he walked in.

'What are you doing?' he asked.

'Nothing,' Daniella shot back, as if it were a casual question, but
her voice was trembling.

Joe stared at his daughter, and then it dawned on him. He realized
why, for a fraction of second, he'd imagined the person in the bathroom
was a stranger. The look on Daniella's face was one he'd never seen
before – it didn't belong to his daughter, it belonged to someone else.

She hadn't meant to do anything bad, she'd cried that evening, when
Joe and Miriam sat her down for a talk. She was just sending a picture
of herself to her boyfriend!

'*Your boyfriend*?' Miriam said.

'Why would you send him a picture of yourself – *naked*?' Joe asked.

Daniella was sobbing so hard she could barely get a word out. Joe
saw Miriam glance at him.

'So – you have some... boyfriend?' Miriam said. She looked as if
she'd just heard her child ate worms for lunch. '*Who*?'

'You guys don't know him.'

'What's his name?'

'Brock.'

'How long have you two been... dating?'

Daniella rolled her eyes. 'Mom.'

'What?'

'*Dating.*'

'Well, how am I supposed to say it? Together? How long have you
two...'

'Two weeks.'

'How old is this Brock?'

'Thirteen.'

'What do his parents do?'

'I dunno. Some kind of businessman, I guess. At least, his dad is.
Or... I dunno.'

'Let me see that picture again.'

Miriam handed the phone to Joe. He took a second look, although it was already etched into his memory. That expression, that stance, that pose, from an eleven-year-old.

It hadn't even occurred to his daughter there could be anything wrong with taking a picture of herself naked. Then again, based on how quickly she hid the phone when Joe came in, maybe it had.

But the boy had sent Daniella a picture of himself without his shirt on, too!

'She's *eleven*,' Miriam had said that evening as she pulled the bedspread off their bed. Joe felt like something was being demanded of him, but he wasn't sure what.

'They're probably just doing whatever they see grown-ups doing, too.'

'Do you know any grown-ups who do things like this?'

'You want to turn on the TV? Surf the internet a little?'

'OK.'

'Take a look at the music videos Rebecca watches on her phone?'

'OK, OK, I got it.' Then: 'Have you heard the way they talk about each other's pictures? Her and Joanna and Kyndra?'

'No.'

Miriam said she'd happened to catch the girls looking at each other's profile pictures on some social media site. *Kind of reserved, if you ask me. You don't really get, you know, that sort of authentic glow from this. I hate to say it, but do you really have that genuine spark? Your face is like cute and all... but – sorry to be so blunt – I'm not sure your nose really works in profile.*

They had confiscated Dani's phone until further notice, which had sparked a tearful storm of protest.

Joe wasn't familiar with the site where his daughter apparently spent most of her time these days. He'd known about a couple of the big teen sites – SocialU, Connect-ome, 4TeenZ – if such things even existed anymore. But during the talk with Daniella, it came out that both his daughters roamed around dozens of others he'd never heard of. Evidently some were meant for gaming, others were mobile apps, others something totally different – and all presumably outdated and abandoned now that he and Miriam had heard of them.

A quick browse of the bookstore at the mall revealed that plenty of advice was available. Doctor of Psychology Marianne Roberts's guide for tweens, preteens, and parents: *The Happy Preteen – How to Prevent*

Your Child's Facebook Depression. Facebook: such a wave of nostalgia. A second ago, everyone had been using it; the company had even gone public. Joe had read Colin Connor, PhD, MD,'s alarming book *How the Internet Permanently Changes the Way Your Teenager's Brain Works and What You Can Do about It* and decided to limit the amount of time the girls spent online. According to Connor, kids never learned to concentrate when their Messenger, SoMe and Instant windows were constantly open. Furthermore, services were increasingly trying to predict what users wanted, which led to limited input, information bubbles, and attention deficit disorders. But his and Miriam's attempt to cut back on screen time didn't last long; within a couple of days, both girls seemed to be losing their minds. Besides, apparently homework required the use of the internet these days. Since then, Joe had read Andrew Muir, PhD's book *The TechnoGenius Teen – Why the New Technology is Making our Children More Socially, Cognitively, and Linguistically Versatile* and felt guilty for keeping his children from developing skills critical to their future. On the whole, he didn't find Muir's arguments as scientifically persuasive as Connor's, but it was hard to say if there mightn't be some truth to them, or especially to come up with a practical solution to the problem. Which was why the girls were allowed to use the internet as much as they wanted to again, which meant that they really, really used it.

Perhaps in part because he wanted to postpone the unavoidable sexting talk with Daniella by even a few minutes, he stopped off at Eddie's on the way home to buy poppy-seed bagels. His throat tightened up when he thought about Daniella and Rebecca, the sites the girls might have already visited, his and Miriam's options as parents. On sleepless nights, he'd had nightmares in which the front page of the *Baltimore Sun* screamed about the child pornography that had been disseminated much more widely than the police had initially dared admit; of the entire state horrified by the eleven-year-old, whom everyone had seen naked. Dreams of his daughter coming home in tears, even after she'd changed schools. It used to be you only lost your reputation at your own school and among your own friends. Now you never knew where you'd bump into your youthful sexting shot: discovered by a boyfriend, at a job interview, dug up by a reporter, a sex-pic scandal at the Department of Defense. At this very moment, apparently, automatic web crawlers were scavenging the internet for pictures. Some of them were looking for material for kiddie-porn forums, from where it would be impossible to ever remove them.

His heart stung as he thought about the boy, this stranger, looking at a nude photo of Daniella, forwarding it to his friends – *check out this horny little bitch* –, grown men pleasuring themselves to her picture. His daughter was eleven, slept with a pink stuffed animal under her arm.

'Idiot,' Joe had heard Rebecca telling her little sister that evening, when she thought Joe and Miriam couldn't hear: 'You're supposed to crop out your face.'

When he got home, he found Daniella crying on the sofa. Saara was sitting next to her, looking helpless and holding a tablet. An image of an insect with big wings glowed on the screen.

'She says it's too late to finish it.'

Saara passed the tablet to Joe. Daniella bawled at her side, head buried in a throw pillow.

'It's too hard!'

Saara glanced at Joe. The look meant: when the head's stupid, the whole body suffers. Joe took the tablet and sat down. Saara got to her feet and tiptoed upstairs.

Joe drew Daniella into his arms and calmed her. He felt like saying 'Didn't I tell you to start on time?' but stifled the impulse. He'd reminded her about the oral report every night for two weeks, told her she shouldn't wait until the last minute. 'I know, I know,' Daniella had snapped. 'I'll do it tomorrow.'

Now the presentation was due the next day.

He gradually got his daughter to settle down. Daniella wiped away her tears and looked disconsolately at the insect site flickering on the screen and her notes.

'Are you supposed to do it on all cicadas or a specific species?'

'I don't know,' Daniella sniffled.

'Or just periodical cicadas?'

'I don't know!' Daniella shouted, and started crying again.

'Do you have the assignment somewhere?'

'It's not gonna help!'

Joe convinced his daughter to go get the paper that offered ideas on doing the report. He helped her pick a topic and scope it, and after that they started browsing together to see what they could find.

By nine o'clock, Daniella was bursting with enthusiasm. She had enough material for half of an hour-long lecture. Joe promised to listen to her do a run-through.

His daughter's authoritative, instructive tone caught him off guard. He'd witnessed the princess phase and the sports, the singing lessons and the giggling with friends, the glitter nail polish and the lip gloss, but never this odd teacherliness. Where did it come from? From Miriam? From him? From someone at school?

The periodical cicada spent most of its life, almost twenty years, underground in its juvenile stage, Daniella reported, until it was suddenly forced to grow up overnight, so it could dig its way to the surface for a few weeks.

Maybe children were taught to articulate and make eye contact in school these days, he thought. As Daniella spoke, he momentarily lost himself thinking about periodical cicadas, about how they knew to time their development so the entire generation would emerge at once. In most cicada species, the individual insects matured at different rates: a few would wake up every summer to buzz around while the rest of the brood stayed in the soil.

No one noticed them.

The mass of the generation that would be arriving this summer, Daniella said, would be almost double the weight of all Americans put together.

'Which, for an insect, is no small feat. Especially when you consider how overweight we are.'

Joe laughed, as was expected of the audience, and Daniella continued, looking satisfied. His little daughter, there she was, giving her oral report. Joe was touched and had to turn away. He remembered what he'd thought the first time he'd dropped Dani off at Miriam's parents for the night, how easily and confidently she'd stayed with her big sister, one-year-old Dani: life was full of moments whose purpose was to teach us to let go of our children. Every bedtime, day-care stay, school day, scarred knee, summer camp, vaccination, boyfriend. Daniella looked at him, concerned. She asked if everything was OK.

'Yeah,' Joe said, clearing his throat and sitting up straighter. 'Sorry.

Go ahead.'

'A few weeks after they emerge, the cicadas die,' Daniella continued. 'They leave behind over five hundred billion eggs – more than there are stars in the Milky Way. Thank you for your attention. You can find more information online at www so-and-so.'

'Bravo!' Joe clapped. 'You could come to San Francisco with me next week. Give a surprise presentation at the conference.'

Concern clouded Daniella's face.

Joe smiled. 'That was a joke.'

'Oh.'

Daniella scratched her back.

'What is it?'

'That thing about weight. At the end.'

'Yeah, what about it?'

'You think it's good? Talking about being fat.'

'Yes. It lends a nice concreteness. It helps people understand how many are coming. How many cicadas.'

'But what about Seth? He really is fat.'

'One of your classmates?'

'Yeah. His parents are fat, too.'

'He won't take it personally.'

'Any suggestions?' Daniella asked.

'It's really good, overall,' Joe said. 'The only thing that comes to mind is that I wouldn't say the twenty-year cycle protects them from predators.'

'What would you say?'

'It is thought to protect them.'

'What?'

'The twenty-year cycle is thought to protect them from predators.'

'That's what I just said.'

'You said it protects them.'

'Huh?'

'Protects is different than is thought to protect.'

Daniella looked like she was trying to bug her eyes out of their sockets.

'Hey, pleeeease.'

'We still don't know if it's true. That's why it's thought to protect them.'

Daniella rolled her eyes.

'You're so anal.'

'Researchers have to be.'

'Whatever.'

'It just occurred to me. Since you asked.'

Daniella sighed. She picked up her pen. 'So how did you put it?'

Joe's heart ached as he saw Daniella mark the spot in her file. Especially when he thought about his youngest child, it was hard for him to forget that someone, somewhere, wished them harm.

Alina had been convinced he was having an affair with one of his PhD students. Aleksandra was doe-eyed and warm, it was true, always ready to lend an ear, fawned over him and his problems. Sometimes Joe wondered how Aleksandra was doing these days.

She had cried when he had told her he was leaving Finland. They had hugged in the deserted university corridor, which was cast in the eternal gloom of a palliative care unit and where Joe no longer officially had an office. The way Aleksandra dug her fingers into his neck felt good and went slightly, but distinctly, too far.

Despite her stylish appearance, Aleksandra gave off an unmistakable air of insecurity, as if she were looking for someone to latch on to. She and Joe had met in the fall, when the maples blazed in the October sun as if aflame.

The day before, Joe had introduced himself to the students during the departmental orientation. During his little speech he'd played up the humor, in an only semi-deliberate protest against Finnish formality, a half-conscious choice to play the easy-going American. Lack of sleep had played an equally important role. He felt like he was perpetually in a state of inebriation; Samuel had just turned three weeks, and Joe hadn't slept more than an hour at a time since they'd brought him home from the maternity clinic. Yes, work could have gotten off to a smoother start in Finland, but Joe was brimming with optimism; the residual heat from his previous successes still powered the cogs.

Aleksandra had appeared at his door and, without introducing herself, asked what someone should do if they were interested in doing a dissertation.

'What on?' Joe asked.

She had eyed him for a few moments from under her brows – out of flirtatiousness or embarrassment, it was hard to say – and said, almost apologetically: 'The same thing you're working on.'

Joe hadn't taken her seriously at first. But Aleksandra had torn into her articles like a terrier. Criticism seemed to simply heighten her resolve; she reveled in doing more than expected.

This was what it was like, working with intelligent people who were hungry to learn. A bad argument never got past Aleksandra, and Joe had to learn to edit his words so as to avoid making statements that didn't hold up to scrutiny.

Alina couldn't stand Aleksandra. She'd brought Samuel by the department once when the girl was there, and Aleksandra, usually the picture of friendliness, had suddenly seemed bizarrely cold, hard. Joe had felt like leaving them to pull out each other's hair and ease the tension for all of them.

At home, he would silently formulate appropriate conversation starters, ones that presented Aleksandra in a positive light without overdoing it. But every segue felt wrong, every way of mentioning her proof positive that he had feelings for his student. Something inside Alina always went rigid at the mention of the department, the faculty, or students – anything remotely related to Aleksandra or Joe's work.

Skirting the topic had started feeling absurd. He wasn't even interested in her! Why was he tiptoeing around her existence?

Aleksandra was the one he'd ended up telling about Sandy Koufax, about the impact Koufax had had on his father. *No one else would have had the backbone*, Dad would say, and Grandpa would nod his head. No, they wouldn't.

Dad brought up Koufax's name any time someone engaged in immoral activity: when a senator was caught for financial improprieties, when Nixon and Watergate came to light. Dad hadn't been around to witness Enron or the subprime crisis, Lehman Brothers or Hurricane Katrina, but Joe was sure the name Sandy Koufax would have been mentioned if he had.

The second he stepped into the office, Aleksandra could tell something was bothering him.

'What is it?' she asked.

'Nothing,' Joe answered.

'Tell me,' she said softly.

Joe hadn't wanted to say anything at first. He wasn't going to make a mountain out of a molehill. He was a visitor in this peaceful, egalitarian Scandinavian country, where there weren't metal detectors in the schools and people didn't lose their homes if they needed back surgery. So many things were better here than they were in the States.

Since Alina took every comment or even question about Finland as criticism these days, Joe hadn't said anything at home about the joke. The person who'd told it was a researcher at the department, an energetic, pleasant woman, the one who led the break-time workout in the seminar room every Tuesday and Thursday. It had been Friday evening, a small group, a relaxed ambiance; people had been telling stories they wouldn't have dared tell in wider company, making caustic remarks about politicians, laughing loudly. It had been a genuinely fun evening. One of the people present – a research assistant, a nice, sociable young guy, openly gay – had told a gay joke. The joke clearly breached the bounds of good taste and was received raucously.

The energetic woman's joke must have had something to do with these circumstances, too, the fact that people were scoring points for stepping across the lines of political correctness. But no one laughed at hers.

Initially it had just fallen flat, as if the punchline was missing; Joe even remembered having smiled absent-mindedly. He would have overlooked the whole thing as no big deal – because that's exactly what it was – but the other foreigner present, Stefan, a German visiting Helsinki, had pulled him aside afterwards.

'Jesus,' Stefan said. 'Unbelievable.'

And later that night, Joe found himself thinking about Sandy Koufax.

Now, the Monday after, he found himself telling Aleksandra how Sandy Koufax had refused to pitch the first game of the 1965 World Series because it fell on Yom Kippur. Without Koufax, the Dodgers lost 8–2.

'No one else would have had the back—' Joe said, and then realized, to his mortification, that he was echoing his father word for word. He corrected himself: 'It was a really... unusual choice.'

He found himself recounting the whole legendary story to Aleksandra: how, after injuring himself, Koufax had played with his pitching arm blue from burst blood vessels, how the doctor had threatened amputation, how Koufax had promised he wouldn't touch a ball between games but practiced and played anyway, numbed himself with codeine and Butazolidin and capsaicin, and, after the games, had to plunge his arm into a tub full of ice.

He could hear himself telling how, after Yom Kippur, Koufax had returned to the mound and, despite the pain, pitched two shutouts for the Dodgers after their one loss. He led the Dodgers to the championship and won the Most Valuable Player award; that same year, he pitched a perfect game, which is a no-hitter in which none of the opposing batters reach base.

'I mean, who can do that?'

Aleksandra waited for Joe to go on. But first he would have had to explain to her what the World Series was, what a shutout was, what a no-hitter was, and how impossible it was to pitch a perfect game. And even then, Aleksandra wouldn't have heard the tremor in Dad's voice whenever he mentioned Sandy Koufax, wouldn't know that you didn't need to tell anyone from Dad's generation that Sandy Koufax was the youngest player ever inducted into the Baseball Hall of Fame.

'And this is all coming up now because…?'

They were standing in the courtyard of the university's handsome granite Jugendstil building, shivering in the frigid winter wind.

'I'm not sure.'

Joe looked down at the asphalt. Aleksandra seemed to be waiting for more. Finland was a peaceful, beautiful, steadfastly slow-paced country, but as exhausting as a two-year-old.

'I guess I just… wanted someone to know. Although of course no one can.'

It's not like telling Holocaust jokes wasn't allowed; they even told them in Joe's family. But those jokes were different.

He remembered smiling at the Finn's joke in vague disbelief. A little tightness in his gut, nothing more.

The experience had been so perplexing he still found it impossible to take offense. Back home, of course, it would have been intentional, malicious.

But here? Had he offended the woman somehow without realizing it?

He tried to think back to what he could have done to upset her, make her want to get back at him, but couldn't: they barely knew each other.

It wasn't until he recounted the story to Aleksandra that it dawned on him: it had never even occurred to the Finn that the joke could have anything to do with anyone who actually existed – and *was present*. She hadn't meant to cause offense. It was the only logical explanation.

This had to be the most peculiar form of anti-Semitism he'd ever come across: that to a woman like her Jewish people didn't exist.

Was this what it felt like to be gay? Everyone blithely and breezily assuming you're someone you're not.

But – the thought that everyone had the exact same background, the same roots, the same education, the same experiences, the exact same views? How bizarre, how odd it must feel to live in *such* a closed, small, shut-off world.

Finland's Nazi links were never discussed in Finland; there wasn't a Finn alive who seemed to feel the least compunction about the pact with Hitler. Nor did Finns, as former Nazis, seem the least bit uncomfortable criticizing Israel – because Finns saw themselves as having been part of a totally different narrative, a David and Goliath story where the Holocaust didn't feature, or any Jewish characters, either. In that story, the generation of the Finns' parents and grandparents was almost destroyed and swallowed up by the Soviet empire, but Finns survived through their own heroism, sacrificed themselves so their children could live in a free country.

It was a beautiful story.

Maybe everyone had to have their own.

Joe found himself wishing the world could tell a single, shared story instead. Even if it were messy and convoluted, imperfect and inconsistent, but one and the same. Aleksandra listened without commenting, let Joe sink into her big, kind, lovely eyes, the ones his wife despised.

Suddenly he realized what it must be like to come to Finland from somewhere totally different. After all, he shared a language and, in many respects, a cultural heritage with the Finns, partly even a common religious background. Yet for a moment, it had felt – seriously felt – as if the Finns had been laughing at his relatives' annihilation, wishing he'd be burned alive, too; now, today.

And as he explained this to Aleksandra, he realized he'd always imagined Europe as a gentler place than the United States, more humanistic, more environmentally friendly, more circumspect, more cosmopolitan, more peaceful, more in touch with reality, deeper, wiser.

To feel all this be turned irreversibly on its head was unnerving.

Aleksandra heard him out without her face betraying a single reaction. Yet Joe could tell she was recording every word and nuance, collecting every crumb of emotion to bear.

It wasn't long before Joe was the one who felt like consoling Aleksandra. After all, it was only one person, an anomaly. And one really bad joke.

Which it was, and which it was.

The tip was too small: he'd forgotten to stop at the ATM. The driver glanced at the bills and then at Joe, climbed back into his taxi, and sped off with an offended rev of the engine.

He sent the cab driver a silent apology and pulled his suitcase up to the front door. It was still light out, but for him the world appeared hazy because of the time change. He hadn't been gone long enough to adjust. He'd slept poorly for the grand total of three nights he'd spent in Switzerland, and probably had a sleepless night ahead of him tonight. He was returning from a research initiative kickoff held at an international institute in the neurosciences, the sort of meeting he had, for reasons vague to himself, recently started agreeing to.

In a way, the meta-level administration and politics were flattering, belonging to the inner circle, being invited. The thought of joining such groups used to make him uncomfortable. Not so much because of the gossip, power plays, and horse-trading – which were as common here as they were in Finland, only on a different scale – but because they gave off a whiff of surrender. The participants in these bodies had always been accomplished in their youth, generally done good, even superb, work, but they all seemed to have lost their keenest edge. Is that why they were sitting on these committees now, setting up projects and networks, coordinating institutions? So they could avoid the lab work, the frustration and the errors, the quagmire of the creative work proper? The work was ruthless, placed the Nobel winner and the novice on the same level, humiliated, punished, and rewarded at will. These program coordinators had always reminded Joe of Daniel

Dennett's metaphor of the marine invertebrate that, upon finding a suitable home, devoured its own brain as no longer necessary.

But after his stint in Finland, Joe had started valuing the efforts dedicated to advancing the interests of the community. It was important that they, the old folks whose step had slightly slowed, made sure the young hotheads had the opportunity to lay the groundwork for their careers when the time was ripe. Maybe that's why he'd also started getting involved in these projects, although they took up a lot of time.

Plus, he had to admit, his brain wasn't that of a twenty-year-old anymore – he could sense it himself. It was a relief to take the occasional day off from work, eat conference-room cookies, and think about things that weren't unbearably complex and too difficult, as every real research problem inevitably was.

Since Finland, he'd also come to realize, at least momentarily, that there was more to life than work. He no longer went in on Saturdays, only weekdays and Sundays, and came home early enough to see the girls before they went to bed. Miriam had made appreciative comments about how Joe, despite his career, did his part around the house. This had felt meaningful, and Joe was sure that without his misadventures in Finland, he would have made a much worse husband.

Joe lowered his suitcase to the porch, pulled out his keys, and opened the door. The house smelled familiar. He called out: 'Hey!'

A faint reply came from Miriam's office. Joe suppressed a mild feeling of disappointment that she didn't step away from her work to come say hello. But of course he'd only been gone a few nights.

Pumping plastic dance music echoed faintly from the basement: Rebecca was doing her nightly fitness program. It was Wednesday; Daniella was at dance. Joe dropped his coat onto his suitcase, opened a can of root beer from the fridge, and gulped it down. Air-conditioned travel seemed to have sucked all the moisture out of his body.

He wondered whether he ought to confront Rebecca about her nightly ab, thigh, and glute routine, or if it would only make things worse. He'd seen her eyeing her slim body at the mirror with a distressing frequency, brow furrowed in dissatisfaction, letting out sad sighs of disappointment as she pinched the fat-free skin at her ribs. If she caught him watching, she'd clench her jaw and widen her eyes: *What??!*

His daughter's weight was already at the low end of normal. Was she eating at school?

'Becca?' Joe called out. There was no answer.

He opened his suitcase, intending to unpack, but the very thought was exhausting. Right there on top was the digital music player he'd bought Rebecca at the Geneva airport. For Miriam, he had a scarf. Kind of a boring present, but luckily he was pretty sure about the color.

Please let Becca like it, please! He hadn't had the time to search and compare, make the obligatory confirmation call to Miriam. The player connected wirelessly to your phone and other devices, and let you listen to unlimited amounts of music, absolutely free of charge. This had sounded astonishing, even illegal, but the salesperson had explained the system was new, and the copyright organizations hadn't caught up yet because it completely bypassed the previous distribution channels.

Joe took out the player, closed the suitcase, and started towards the staircase, when he happened to notice something among the pillows on the couch: Rebecca's mobile phone, dented, pink. He could take it up to her room on his way.

As he climbed the stairs, he absent-mindedly reflected it was odd Becca hadn't been missing her phone. Incessant tapping was the soundtrack of their lives; his daughter would have rather given up one of her limbs than be without the phone. But now it had been abandoned on the sofa, and Armageddon had not arrived.

Joe stopped at the door to Becca's room.

There on the desk, in plain sight, was her purse. It was transparent plastic; the contents gleamed as if in a display window. He registered the bag as the handiwork of a famous designer. Even an out-of-it academic schmuck like Joe had heard the name.

Then he noticed the device.

It was inside the bag: sleek, rounded, bright and metallic, brazen, like a stylized vibrator. He couldn't see any buttons on its seamless surface, at least at first glance, nothing in the way of controls. Then he spotted the small wireless earbuds, separate but so similar to the ellipse in shape and color that they had to belong together. Is that what phones were like these days? This explained the discarding of the old one.

Who had paid for the new phone?

It was immediately apparent that the turbo-vibrator must have cost much more than an average phone. But how much? Hundreds of dollars, a thousand, maybe more? And where did his daughter get the money for such an expensive bag?

Music continued to carry faintly from the basement. Along with a textbook, makeup, scrunchies, and the new silver phone, Joe spied a small, cylindrical container. The colors and flashy striped logo glowed behind the purse's transparent plastic like a firefly.

ALTIUS!®

Something inside him balled up into a fist. Was his daughter taking a prescription he didn't know about? The packaging was too stylized to be aspirin. As far as he knew, Rebecca didn't suffer from any conditions that demanded regular medicating.

And then it sank in.

Birth control.

Rebecca was fifteen. She hadn't discussed this with her mother; Miriam would have told him.

'Becca!' he roared towards he stairs. 'Rebecca!'

The thumping beat continued. She couldn't hear; he was too far away. Joe glanced around the room. He would never snoop through his daughter's belongings, especially without her permission. But Rebecca's zumba aerobics session could last an hour or more. And she had purposely chosen a transparent bag.

Before receiving approval from the more skeptical layers of his mind, Joe had opened the bag and retrieved the container. So did this mean Rebecca was having sex regularly? With whom? He'd have to ask Miriam to talk to Rebecca; preventing pregnancy wasn't the only reason for using condoms. But why would a birth control pill be called ALTIUS?

> *Take once a day for pressure-induced interaction deficiencies,*
> *situational stress, and secondary social symptoms.*
> **ALTIUS!®**
> *Requires a doctor's prescription.*
> FOR RESEARCH PURPOSES ONLY.

Joe stared at the bottle. 'Pressure-induced interaction deficiencies'? 'Situational stress'? 'Secondary social symptoms'? Had his daughter started seeing a shrink who'd made up a bunch of problems to sell her drugs?

For research purposes only?

He scanned the bottle for information on the active ingredient. It was a chemical he'd never heard of.

The dance music kept pumping. Joe took the bottle and walked downstairs to Miriam's office. As he approached the doorway, he could hear her fingers racing across the keyboard like gazelles. She didn't appear to notice he was at the door.

'How was Switzerland?' she finally managed to say, while frowning at her screen. The gazelles continued to skitter.

'OK.'

'Good.'

Joe thought for a second and then asked: 'Where would Becca have gotten thousands of dollars of spending money?'

Miriam raised her eyebrows as if noting the question, but her uninterrupted, stony stare indicated she hadn't registered a single word of what Joe had just said. Standing there in the doorway, watching the cold light play across his wife's face, Joe experienced a flash of impotent fatigue in the face of the Western digital lifestyle, realized how it must feel to others when he spent every waking moment with his nose in a computer screen, until, half an hour before bed, he would 'relax' by browsing through the vital status updates of acquaintances.

'Did you hear me?' Joe said quietly.

'Mm-hmm,' Miriam said, her voice void of interest. 'I have to finish this for tomorrow.'

'Who's giving Becca psychoactive medication?'

Miriam finally tore her eyes from her laptop; now she looked irritated. It took a second before her fingers eased up.

'What?'

'Is Rebecca on some medication I'm not aware of?'

Joe held up the bottle. It was annoying, having to say everything twice these days: first to draw the other person's attention away from whatever screen they were gawking at, and then a second time once they were finally listening.

ALTIUS!®? Miriam was clearly oblivious. Joe asked if she'd given Rebecca money for a plastic bag designed by some Italian that must have cost hundreds of dollars. No. Lent Rebecca her credit card? No. Heard that Becca was taking prescription medication? No. Been aware that Becca had a new phone that might be doubling as a digital vibrator? No.

'Wait. Do you remember,' Miriam suddenly said slowly, 'me commenting on how Rebecca's hairstyle had changed overnight? A month ago, maybe?'

One day Rebecca had come home looking like a cheap copy of a Hollywood star. The one who'd been in a sitcom for years, the most popular of its cast of characters, who'd just divorced her second husband and had three children adopted from different countries. Becca had seemed years older, devoid of personality: it was hard to say if she was a young-looking twenty-five-year-old or a teenager styled to look like an adult.

Joe remembered Miriam remarking that although the change wasn't that dramatic – especially compared to the coal-black Goth dye-job from the previous spring – there was something about the haircut that struck her as affected, calculated, inappropriate for a fifteen-year-old. Joe had silently figured that Miriam was having a hard time seeing her little girl turn into a woman. Who could say what a teenager was supposed to look like these days? The styles and standards changed by the week, and nothing was the way it used to be.

'You know what else I saw?' Miriam said. 'From the window? A while ago. When Becca was going out one evening?'

After climbing into her friend's car, Rebecca had left the door open and, legs dangling, slipped out of her own jeans and into a designer pair that must have cost six or seven times as much as those Miriam had given her permission to put on her credit card. Then Rebecca had jumped out of the car and twirled around for the others, reveling in this display of forbidden fruit. It was the sneakiness that had caught Miriam's attention, and she'd kept an eye out for a while, but the jeans never appeared in the laundry hamper. Miriam had been meaning to raise the issue, but it had slipped her mind.

They listened: in the basement the workout pounded on. Miriam thought for a moment and then lowered her fingers to the keyboard.

'What was the name of that ingredient again?'

The unfamiliar drug turned out to be a chemical derivative of a compound originally used to treat autism. It had recently come out on the market and was now used to treat acute social disorders, such as extreme shyness. A quick search also brought up a discussion thread on a Yale University student organization website, where undergrads wrote that their status among their peers had improved after they'd started taking the drug. One said he might have survived finals at Princeton without **ALTIUS!®** , but never the social scene. Now he was one of the most popular guys on campus and his girlfriend was a model. The first page of search results was also plastered with personal profiles from the social media du jour: an Olympic swimmer confessed that he hadn't won a single league championship until he started using **ALTIUS!®**, because he'd suffered from a psychological block. It had been impossible to truly succeed without his friends' approval. *His body had been that of a champion, but his mind hadn't.*

Joe and Miriam exchanged glances and, without saying another word, went down to the basement, where Barbie music promising a perfect body and eternal perkiness was still pumping.

Rebecca swore she hadn't taken a single tablet of **ALTIUS!®**. How could they even suspect such a thing? And even if she had, it was none of their business! It kind of even seemed like they were forcing her to try it, the way they were acting. Yup, she was going to start taking them today, in protest against interrogations like this. The plastic purse was her personal property, and her parents didn't have any right to go through it, any more than they had the right to go into her room without her permission.

She hadn't done anything illegal, and her parents didn't have any right to accuse her, especially when they didn't have any proof!

'Becca, we just found thousands of dollars' worth of clothes, accessories, and electronics in your possession,' Joe said. 'So maybe we can agree that there is proof.'

'That you guys have acquired through totally fucking illegal means!'

'What is it we need to go into your room? A search warrant?'

Tears of fury glittered in Rebecca's eyes. Joe was obviously lying when he said he'd come into her room to drop off her thousand-year-old mobile phone – that doesn't even work! – supposedly out of the goodness of his heart. She found it impossible to believe that he, a renowned university professor, wouldn't have noticed she'd stopped using the two-year-old phone, which barely worked, ages ago. Besides, lying about it didn't change the fact that Joe had trespassed on private property without permission. As for where Rebecca had gotten her sleek, expensive new phone, which hadn't even appeared on the market yet – that was none of their business.

'Besides, *for your information*, it isn't a phone.' An offended huff.

'Well, what is it then?'

Rebecca paused, looked at them doubtfully, wondering whether it was worth tilting against windmills. Then she let out a sigh of apocalyptic despair.

'An *experience device*. If you must know.'

'An experience device? Is that some kind of joke?'

'Oooh, the company's trembling in its boots!' Rebecca spread her arms, eyes wide. 'World-famous technological innovator Joseph Chayefski isn't convinced.'

'Becca.'

'It's called an *iAm*.'

'I am?'

'Ooh, world-famous innovator Chayefski is also questioning the choice of name. The stock price is crashing! I can hear it from here.'

'Becca. Could you please kindly answer the question your mom asked.'

'As soon as my lawyer gets here.'

Rebecca had entrenched herself. In the end, Joe couldn't think of anything but to threaten to cut off her allowance (*go ahead*) and confiscate her credit card. (*who cares? I can't do anything with your stupid credit limit anyway.* A contemptuous glare.) Neither of her parents wanted to cut off Rebecca's allowance (*so don't*), but as they were responsible for her it was important for them to know where the drugs and the expensive things in her bag came from, and what she had done to get the money to buy them.

'You didn't even read me my Miranda rights,' Rebecca said, bugging out her eyes. Daniella sniggered in the living room. *Miranda rights.*

'Dani, go to your room,' Joe said. 'We're talking to Becca now.'

'Becky,' Miriam said. 'I find your tone—'

'As if I cared.'

'Don't talk to your mother that way.'

'Oh – but you guys can go through my stuff without permission, huh?' Rebecca stood and headed for the stairs, her face that of a misunderstood freedom fighter.

'Hey, Becca,' Joe called out, using a different tone. 'You know what I think?'

A glimmer of something darker below Rebecca's icy hauteur – a patch of meltwater? When he saw his hunch was right, Joe decided to continue, taking a new tack. Maybe his daughter still was an insecure teen who secretly wanted her parents to know what was going on in her life.

'I think,' he said, without the foggiest clue if he was on the right track, 'that you've gotten involved in something, and you're not sure what that something is.'

Rebecca glared at him from under her brows. Joe and Miriam waited. Rebecca swallowed, rubbed some imperceptible dirt from the ball of her thumb, and then, finally, little by little, proceeded to reveal at least part of what had happened.

A man and a woman from a major corporation had visited Becca's school: the same corporation that had underwritten the new wing of the gymnasium, which now bore the corporation's name. At times like these, Joe found himself yearning for Finland: the United States was fast developing into a place where the rich would be forced to retreat to palaces fenced off with barbwire. War was being waged with semiautomatic weapons on the streets of Baltimore; the city picked the sour fruits of income disparity every day. In this respect, Europe was wiser; here it was too late. Joe wished every American would have to spend a year living in Finland: it would make the country as a whole healthier.

In thanks for the cooperation of the school, the man and the woman had promised the students promotional gifts they could claim by becoming fans of the company in the social media everyone Rebecca's age had switched to this year. Rebecca had joined the fan base, and she'd received shampoo, conditioner, and hairspray in the mail.

'So? Then what?' Joe asked, sensing that his daughter was holding back on the most important part of the story.

'Nothing.'

'Did they send you that bag, too? And the drugs?'

Joe could see Rebecca retreating into her foxhole under the bombardment of questions. He was afraid this was the beginning of a war of attrition that could last days, even weeks.

'Did that company send everyone a bag that costs over four hundred dollars retail?'

'Of course not!' she snapped. 'Why would you want it then? If everyone had one.'

'So you're the only one who got one?'

Rebecca didn't answer.

'Did you have to do something to get it?'

Joe scanned her defenses for fractures or fissures, but didn't find the tiniest one.

'Becca, be honest. Did you use either of our credit cards without permission?'

'No! You guys start accusing me of being a fucking thief right away! I'm glad you trust me so much! Check your statements.'

'So what then? Are you selling drugs?'

Rebecca's eyes widened to plate-size, showed how incredibly, indescribably offensive it was to be accused of this, and Joe suddenly realized where her little sister Daniella had picked up her habit of bugging out her eyes.

'Becca, if you don't tell us, we're going to start imagining all sorts of things.'

But Rebecca was done confessing. Joe and Miriam confiscated the bag and the medication, as well as the new mobile phone and the designer jeans, everything they didn't know the origins of. *Go ahead, take it. See if I care.*

Eye-rolls, quivering lids. The superiority of a moral victory.

That night in their bedroom, Joe and Miriam could hear Rebecca sobbing upstairs. They looked at each other.

'She acts so tough – and then she starts bawling?' Joe wondered.

'You don't remember what it's like to be fifteen.'

'Were we too hard on her?'

'We'll talk to her tomorrow,' Miriam said, and turned off the light.

But Joe couldn't sleep. He tossed and turned in the sticky sheets, ruminating over the threats he'd received, the brick thrown through his office window, Daniella's sexting pic, which at this very moment could be circulating around digital networks, never to be deleted. What else had the girls done they didn't know about, what would pop out of the belly of the internet years down the line?

Joe turned over. He and Miriam had looked up Rebecca's device later that evening. The home page of the company that manufactured it, MinDesign, was taken up by an ad for the 'UI-free experience device' that was going to revolutionize the world as we know it. At the bottom of the screen, decreasing seconds counted down to the device launch, which was now six months away.

iAm.

Before bed, he'd tried to smooth over the conflict with his daughter by giving her the media player he'd bought her at the Geneva airport. But according to Rebecca, the thousand-year-old player, *not good for anything you'd ever want to do*, didn't change the fact that he had gone into her room, her private space, without permission. Besides, she found it hard to believe that he, acclaimed university professor that he was, wouldn't realize the eighteen-month-old device was completely incompatible with Rebecca's social media platforms. The fact that she could listen to unlimited music with it was useless, because she already had that as a premium service on her phone. Not to mention the idiotic UI, the piece of garbage didn't understand her friends' social media updates, and no one with a brain had used a device in the last hundred years where your friends couldn't see what music you were listening to. Joe had bought her a totally fucking useless piece of crap on purpose!

Nights when you lay awake could be so long.

Would air conditioning help? But that wasn't the cause of his insomnia. It wasn't so hot yet, even in Maryland.

When an hour and a half had passed and he still hadn't fallen asleep, Joe climbed out of bed and, on an impulse, turned on his computer.

After prolonged resistance, he had joined, as one of the last to do so, one of the major social media platforms of the early 2010s. It had tanked in popularity immediately afterwards – presumably because even people like him had finally signed up. The media imperium that had bought it for an astronomical sum just a year before lost its entire investment when subscribers canceled en masse. Nowadays it was the digital equivalent of a factory town where the people, the stores, and the banks had all decamped, but the empty industrial buildings and handful of disturbed souls wandering around continued to serve as reminders of a vanished way of life.

Joe had joined the latest social media platform, the one everyone was on now, at the request of the university's communications office. The university had its own social media service, but since no one ever visited it, they had stopped requiring its use. Now the communications office wanted researchers to write 'fun, light-hearted posts about life in the lab,' quirky little anecdotes that would 'give the public a glimpse into the researcher's personality' on this popular commercial site at least once a week. This would help the researcher build up his or her personal brand. Even if researchers arrogantly imagined otherwise, cross-channel communication was here to stay, and that went for academia as well. So announced the new head of the communications office, a twenty-five-year-old with a thick head of hair, who'd probably been trying to set a new kegstand record at his frat not more than a year ago.

The truth was, the kid explained at a mandatory information session, that everyone, including researchers and universities, built a personal brand, some just did it unsystematically and inefficiently, through old-fashioned, ineffective channels.

'The era of secrecy and stinginess has come to an end,' the kid proclaimed with the confidence of someone in their first leadership position. 'The way forward is through authenticity and openness, and through them, we'll thrive.'

Those who were stingy with their personal lives would *perish*, one by one, gradually, inexorably. The kid had spoken with particular enthusiasm about the upcoming *iAm* device; it would remove many of the artificial barriers we still faced today, take scientific communication to an entirely new level.

Joe had seen young researchers embrace the new branding opportunities enthusiastically. But would they help in the long run? Was it possible to talk about the neural pathways in the macaque area MT *authentically* and *informally*, showing a *sense of humor* and *personality*, and thus build your *persona into a brand*? The grad student in her twenties that the kid had talked about in admiring tones, the one who had thirty thousand followers: she was a good researcher, but you'd never know it from her social media site. What you did learn was that she worked on something related to synapses and had a beautiful smile, a slim waist, a fashionable new outfit every day, and undeniably amusing quips. Wasn't she worried that a future employer would start wondering if she was more interested in posing and picking retro-style digital filters for her selfies – which were inarguably stylish – than in recalibrating the ISI timing between stimuli, or redoing a botched experiment?

Joe probably just felt this way, he thought, because he was already too old and uncomfortable with emotionally charged, spontaneously personality-based, authentic multichannel communication, since he preferred intellectually grounded, guardedly fact-based, inauthentic single-channel communication. As a matter of fact, he didn't support any channel at all, he just wanted to get back into his lab, which was of course in and of itself old-fashioned, anti-branding and inauthentic. Was it possible that a life of constant surveillance felt completely natural for younger people? Maybe it felt more real than days in the lab, where no one could ever see you – and if they could, they couldn't be bothered to watch.

It was only now, sitting here at his computer in the middle of the night, that Joe realized that they were sending out constant reminders of themselves and their work through the new communications platforms – broadcasting everything to everyone, including those who wished them ill.

Those who followed them in order to do them harm.

They been watching his every move, he realized, had probably seen the two embarrassing updates he'd posted to the site at the request of the university's communications office. In one of them, he had mentioned Freedom Media and its strong-arm tactics, more appropriate for the mafia than an academic publisher.

Joe was also his daughter Rebecca's 'friend' in the new social media channel. He always wanted to put digital friendship in air quotes, like the neologism 'to friend.' His friend request to Daniella had been waiting months for approval, because she didn't have time to follow more than the four, five most important social media – the ones where she had happened to spot her crush of the day.

He felt a sudden, sinking mortification at the memory of what he'd done once he'd surrendered to digital networking – a shameful lapse in judgment. It had happened right after he joined the latest social

media service, when he'd had to click through his colleagues and
neighbors one by one to friend them. *Joe Chayefski would like to
be your friend.* The service had actively suggested them, too, as had
the people themselves: *Do you know Barbara Fleischmann? Barbara
Fleischmann would like to be your friend.* Some of the prompts were
peculiar; the system suggested he friend a Canadian internist he'd
never met. As far as Joe knew, his sole connection to the doctor was
an email he'd sent asking for a second opinion on a matter related to
a persistent cold of Rebecca's. Was the service accessing his emails
somehow? Was it possible he'd accepted something like this when he
ticked the terms and privacy policy in the 426-page legal text he hadn't
read? Someone at the department had just asked about Joe's winter
coat; it turned out that he was now publicly recommending this coat
with his name and face via social media, which he most definitely
hadn't intentionally allowed. The colleague guessed that someone had
probably uploaded a photo of Joe to the site without his knowledge,
where the automatic search functions had recognized his face and
the clothing brands he was wearing. Apparently he had to go in and
deactivate the functionality if he didn't want this information to be
turned over for marketing purposes. The terms of the service changed
every week, too.

The embarrassing lapse in judgment may have resulted from the
frenzy of sending and accepting dozens of friend requests within a few
days' time. Joe's bar for digital friendships had steadily lowered. He
had initially made a deal with himself that he would only approve his
closest colleagues as friends, because he intended on using the service
for work-related matters. He didn't even want competing research
groups to know the details of what was going on in his lab; they could
read the published articles like everyone else. But on the second day,
he was pinged by a pleasant acquaintance he'd sort of met through
work who didn't fulfill the original criteria but whose friend request
he accepted because it would have felt unnecessarily unfriendly not
to. It was simpler mentally to adjust the boundaries and purpose of
the media – maybe I won't post anything as personal as I originally
thought I would – than to give the impression that he wasn't interested
in maintaining normal contact with people he knew well. For every
request from a pleasant, semi-professional acquaintance, one arrived
from a completely non-professional context. It would have felt weirdly

impolite not to accept Rebecca's closest friend's mom, a nice woman. But in addition to requests from acquaintances who were close and likable, they gradually started appearing from those less close and less likable, and once he had started down this path, did he really want to tell some of these people, or this one in particular, whom he nevertheless knew perfectly well and saw on a regular basis, that *I'm more than happy to be friends with the parents of Rebecca's other classmates but not you, you goddamned cow.* It was just easier to accept every request.

After that, it felt most prudent to be fully visible on social media; to avoid being digitally marooned among semi- or wholly insignificant people he balanced things out by friending people he knew well, or didn't but wished he did. This meant that the bar in his own friend requests gradually and imperceptibly lowered, as well, perhaps in part because it was suddenly hard to think of many super-close people he hadn't already asked. And it seemed to make more and more sense, now that he was apparently doing this at the request of the university's communications office, to send a friend request to that one Finnish historian he'd chatted with once at that one conference but whose name proved quite the operation to locate. In the end, Joe found himself having wasted an entire evening in a peculiar, semi-addictive state, scooping up digital acquaintances like poker chips.

It was in this frame of mind that it happened. On a lark, he'd happened to check if a search would turn up a person named Samuel Chayefski. One, in Seattle, Washington, thirty-five years old. It wasn't until Joe saw the wrong Samuel that the wave of shame washed over him, an instant before he realized what his son's last name really was.

He'd found Samuel right away with Alina's surname. Click.

Send a friend request. Click.

Request sent.

Could this be the beginning of a new friendship? he remembered thinking. Even in air quotes?

He'd never gotten a response, and interpreted this as a clear message.

Joe was roused from his reverie by a familiar howl, Baltimore's nocturnal time signal: a police cruiser raced past, sirens wailings.

He dislodged thoughts of Samuel from his mind. Mistakes happened. His son could just say if he wasn't interested in hearing from Joe. Or, he supposed, it was also possible that Samuel never used that specific social media, hadn't even noticed the request.

Joe tapped in his user ID and password and entered his daughter-friend Rebecca's digital space. All previous thoughts were erased in the blink of an eye when her page popped open. Joe's heart skipped a beat.

sweet! i've never done this well on a test! hmmm, i wonder if it could it be because of my new friend A... :) it's easy to kick ass when your friends have your back... but no, for real... i did study... have an amazing weekend!!! stay in touch!! :) love you guys.

And yesterday:
*couldn't resist checking in before class to talk up this bag!!! ok so the price isn't so cute but... A REAL TRENTINO!!! I'M IN HEAVEN!! ^^*

And the day before yesterday:

is it just me or is A already making a difference with you know who...!! maybe i'm just imagining things?! anyway i saw him at passing period and it felt like the right words just popped into my mouth... even though A isn't supposed to affect that but...! :-) who cares when this is the end result! maybe we're soul mates and i just never knew it!! kisses kittycats!!!

Now Joe noticed a slew of things on Rebecca's page he wished he'd have paid attention to earlier. What fifteen-year-old has over four thousand friends? Who are these grown men and women? And companies?

All of his daughter's status updates revolved around the same themes: food and calories, clothes, shampoo brands, high-end shoes, designer jeans, the appearance of Hollywood actors.

Joe got momentarily sidetracked trying to imagine what his *zayde* would have said if he'd lived to see the sort of life they were living. 'I am that I am' no longer meant anything to their kids; *I am* was the name of a technological gadget.

Rebecca's updates also made regular mention of 'my little friend' or 'A' in conjunction with some positive event: boys, who noticed her in a different way than before, the looks of girls, more approving than before, better grades, being instantly aware when someone needed help.

It was only when it occurred to Joe to check Rebecca's friends list for the manufacturer of **ALTIUS!®** that the pieces started to click into place.

He'd been forced to restrain himself and wait until morning. He had gone and woken Miriam immediately, and they had browsed through their daughter's digital life together. But Miriam didn't see how getting Rebecca up in the middle of the night was going to do anyone any good.

At six o'clock on the dot, they planted her between them at breakfast table. Daniella, sensing that something juicy and potentially punishable was in the works, slipped up to the table as nimbly as a squirrel, carrying a bowl of cold cereal.

Rebecca looked frightened and was surprisingly open to answering their questions, perhaps in part because she wasn't exactly sure how much her parents knew.

The friendly, fashionable man and woman who'd visited the school had taken Rebecca out to eat. They'd explained that because she was a gifted young woman, who did well at school and was popular among her friends, Becca might qualify as a peer mentor for the company's **The Children Are The Future** campaign. Did Rebecca know that the average teen was in contact with only approximately 14.4 people a day, while for Rebecca the corresponding figure was 38.7?

Joe looked up information on the campaign later: **The Children Are The Future** wanted to 'grant every student the opportunity to succeed in school and the workplace regardless of socio-economic-cognitive background.' The children are the future! Click here to support **The Children Are The Future** campaign!

Thanks to the company, the school now had a **The Children Are The Future** drop-in center, a dedicated room where a specially trained individual, an approachable young woman, passed on information and tips about school, health, sports, and friends – everything a teen or a preteen needed to live a balanced life. Everyone that came by received a free **The Children Are The Future** backpack! (Size 55 l, colors navy and magenta.)

But best of all – as the school nurse explained when Joe contacted her – this didn't cost a dime! The campaign fully financed the drop-in center with its own funds. It was a win-win!

Did Rebecca like the gifts she'd received? the man and the woman wanted to know.

That was nice to hear. They also thought the shampoo and the hairspray were the best on the market, if not the most affordable. If Rebecca were interested in working with them, she could get a lot more gifts, better ones.

The man and the woman had heard from Rebecca's teachers that she was an exceptionally bright young woman. As a matter of fact, Rebecca had scored higher than 95 percent of her age-mates in the school district on standardized tests, and higher than 99.4 percent nationwide. The man and the woman wanted to be friends with everyone, but especially people like Rebecca, because Rebecca's behavior had a big impact on her peers. Peer-group impact accounted for as much as 95 percent of the personal consumption and lifestyle preferences of young people.

The man and the woman understood perfectly well why Rebecca was concerned about taking a drug that hadn't been prescribed by a doctor. They understood, although in their opinion, when it came to the ALTIUS!® molecule, it wasn't strictly accurate to speak of a drug. ALTIUS!® wasn't a medication; it was a *vmPFC-specific dendritic optimizer*.

Rebecca probably remembered from biology class that the vmPFC contained some of the brain's most critical structures when it came to social interaction. She didn't? What exactly were they teaching in school these days?

The ALTIUS!® molecule was unusual in that, whereas many drugs were discovered accidentally, ALTIUS!® had been developed based on the scientific understanding of how the brain worked. Over the past decade, a whole new world had opened up in the neurosciences, but as bright and well informed as Rebecca was, she probably already knew that. Scientists had developed this molecule into a super-precise fine-tuner for those specific receptor branches of those specific neurons of those specific areas of the brain that were known to choke during problems in interpersonal interaction. The abbreviation vmPFC came from the term *ventromedial prefrontal cortex*.

Because the new molecule was able to optimize dendritic functioning in those exact nuclei, those in the ventromedial prefrontal cortex, the first thing researchers had realized was that it could be applied in the treatment of numerous social interaction disorders – oh, Rebecca had heard of those, good! Perhaps there were students in Rebecca's school who suffered from problems related to social interaction? That would have gone completely untreated in the past? Yes, it was in principle the same molecule – or molecule family; there were various trademarks on the market.

ALTIUS!® had initially been conceived as a treatment for acute disorders. The real breakthrough had been realizing that, as a matter of fact, those who responded best to treatment were healthy individuals: bright, socially gifted, unusually good at making friends – just like Rebecca.

It had taken researchers a long time to understand how the brain worked.

As late as the early 2000s, the brain was still being described in terms of hardware and software.

But the brain was not a computer.

The brain's software was hardware, and it was all socially oriented: the brain was social hardware.

The brain had a built-in – if one insisted on using a poor, hopelessly outdated metaphor – wireless LAN card.

The brain was a sensitive, astronomically complex system of biomass that had been built to maintain contact with other brains.

For a long time, scientists hadn't understood this – and those legions of people who found themselves perpetually having trouble making and keeping friends hadn't gotten the help they needed.

That's why ALTIUS!® optimizers could do what others couldn't.

The issue was so complex that the normal pharmaceutical companies were lagging far behind.

It wasn't a drug; it was a fine-tuner.

Using it, the man and the woman said, Rebecca could finally and fully become the individual nature had intended her to be.

Did Rebecca want her life to be a moderate success? Or as successful as possible?

Did Rebecca want to be a faint shadow of her personality in the company of her friends – or the dazzling Rebecca she was deep down inside?

What they were talking about here was Rebecca's life.

What Rebecca wanted from life.

The important thing was to understand that ALTIUS!® didn't affect the natural function of neurons. ALTIUS!® simply—

The woman wanted Rebecca to look her in the eye now.

This was important.

The personality of a healthy young individual was in no way affected by the stabilizers. This was because the vmPFC stabilizers didn't change the natural functioning of the neurons, they simply protected the brain's natural biological ability to process information, boosted the brain's capacity to function the way nature had intended.

The *only thing* ALTIUS!® did was improve the neurons' natural signal-noise ratio.

Did Rebecca want to end up being outshined by other girls, even dumber, duller ones, when they were competing for boyfriends? Deficiencies in social reaction capacity hampered social communication, especially with members of the opposite sex. Rebecca didn't even want to *try* to see how fun and irresistible boys might find her?

Rebecca was probably aware that as much as 48 percent of observable sexual attractiveness was linked to self-confidence? Rebecca had perhaps noticed herself that when she felt funny, smart, and sexy, others felt it, too.

Did Rebecca want to try and see if heightened interaction skills would, through improved self-confidence and successes, boost her school performance, too?

It couldn't hurt to try, could it? After all, the SATs were approaching fast. As an intelligent young woman, Rebecca of course knew that SAT performance would have a decisive impact on which university she got into. And the university she got into would have a decisive impact on her income, her grad school opportunities, her friends, the caliber of her future spouse, her political orientation – the rest of Rebecca's life.

The woman had been lucky; she'd made it into a good university without optimizers, gone to medical school, and had a handsome husband, a lawyer, but – in retrospect, if she were totally honest with Rebecca – she wasn't sure if she'd dare take the risk of not trying an alternative like this if it were available to her.

Didn't Rebecca even want to try?

No, of course they understood.

Absolutely.

The man and the woman absolutely understood Rebecca's caution. Sometimes it was wise to take things slowly, think things over.

They understood that Rebecca had made her decision, at least for now. Of course the fine-tuners would give an edge to Rebecca's competitors who chose to use them – after all, that's what school was ultimately about, competition.

But of course having the courage to make your own decisions was much more important. The woman and the man admired Rebecca's ability to think for herself, to take ethical considerations into account when faced with a choice. The woman and the man wanted to respect this.

What was that? How did Rebecca know to ask such an intelligent question? Astonishing – she would clearly go far in life.

Yes, the studies the man and woman were citing had all been published in peer-reviewed journals. Rebecca's question was right on the mark. A robust peer-review process was necessary to ensure they were reliable. Here was one of the most recent ones, if Rebecca cared to have a look. Haxby, Svaboa, Lindstrom, and Colbs (2013), *Journal of Neuroscience and Experimental Biology*, 23, 212–257. This was a very well-regarded journal, in fact, largely funded by our own company. You see, the company's in-house journal was often months or even years faster than other journals, and a much more effective channel for disseminating the latest information. And it ensured they could pick the best experts for reviewers; people who would understand the quality and importance of the studies.

The *Journal of Neuroscience and Experimental Biology* was a top scientific journal. All the leading universities in the world subscribed to it: **Stanford, Columbia, MIT, Princeton, CalTech, Yale.** It was found in the libraries of every university, just like *Nature* and *Science*.

But Rebecca was correct: the molecule had not yet, as already noted, been officially approved for use by healthy young people; there was no question about that.

And absolutely, it was wisest not to take any of the numerous vmPFC optimizers the company manufactured – one of which, no doubt, would have a unique efficacy profile perfect for Rebecca – if she was completely satisfied with her sexual attractiveness, her status among her peer group, and her achievements at school and in life. Absolutely.

Why, in that case, Rebecca had no need for the optimizers. What a fantastic situation! The man and the woman wanted to congratulate Rebecca on such a happy state of affairs.

But the man and the woman still didn't want Rebecca to miss out on the lovely gifts.

Luckily there was also the option of choosing *casual friendship* as opposed to *full friendship*. Casual friends weren't required to take the **ALTIUS!®** tablets in peer-group situations publicly, the way full friends were. Of course a casual friend didn't receive all the same benefits as a full friend, either. Unfortunately. But Rebecca could choose the form of friendship that was the best fit for her.

Publicly take the tablets in peer-group situations? Good thing Rebecca asked; the man and the woman had clearly neglected to explain things properly. This simply meant that the **ALTIUS!®** had to be ingested in such a way that the man and the woman could verify that at least one other person had seen Rebecca having done so. As a matter of fact, it was often best to take it in the presence of one person at a time: this reinforced the sense of trust and belonging with the peer, which would increase the likelihood of the peer's being positively disposed to **ALTIUS!®**. But of course none of this applied to Rebecca, because Rebecca had decided not to try out the vmPFC-specific optimizers.

Had Rebecca ever seen a slightly unusual-looking bag like this? Wonderful! Rebecca was clearly up on the latest trends. So familiar with the line and even the model. It was nice to see an intelligent young woman who was also so hip. The man and the woman were glad Rebecca liked the bag. They thought Trentinos were luxurious, too, brought out the glow in Rebecca's flawless skin, now that they were looking at her here.

In order to be friends with them, all Rebecca needed to do was keep the Trentino with her all the time.

And the **ALTIUS!®** in the bag.

Would Rebecca be interested in carrying the Trentino bag with her wherever she went, even to school? And of course to parties, especially to parties. Could Rebecca go so far as to give the man and the woman her word that she would take the bag to parties with her? It would also be great if Rebecca could keep the bag nearby as much as possible, especially in situations where friends might be taking pictures. Of course there was no need to overdo it.

The man and the woman would also be more than happy to choose the contents of the bag. The first gift they'd like to give Rebecca was this mobile phone that was so new it wasn't even on the market yet. Isn't it cool? As a matter of fact, it's not really a phone, it's... well, Rebecca would find out when she tried it.

The mobile phone – that wasn't a phone, tee-hee! – would make a great addition to the **ALTIUS!®** she'd be carrying in her bag, as would any of the cosmetics and hair products Rebecca had already received in the mail. Now that she was a casual friend, the man and the woman could send Rebecca as much makeup and shampoo as she wanted – as long as they saw enough pictures of Rebecca and her bag on social media.

The phone was called an *iAm*.

And it wasn't a phone.

It *most definitely* wasn't a phone.

At first Joe didn't get why a company that manufactured hairsprays and deodorants wanted Rebecca to carry a drug originally developed to treat autism and a phone that looked like an astronaut's vibrator in her purse. After numerous clicks, he discovered that the American cosmetics company was owned by the same investment firm whose portfolio also included the manufacturers of several clothing brands popular among young people. But it was hard to find a connection for the other goods that had been pushed on Rebecca.

The Italian designer who had recently sold his business to a major apparel concern and whose legendary bag Rebecca was now carrying around didn't seem to have anything to do with the cosmetics industry or the manufacturer of the *iAm*. The American group that owned the pharma company marketing **ALTIUS!®** had recently merged with a British pharmaceuticals giant, but Joe didn't understand why any of these businesses would join forces to launch an assault on his daughter. It was clear, based on Rebecca's music files, that the mega-conglomerate that had swallowed up numerous British record and entertainment companies had, thanks to Rebecca's new friends, just opened itself a shortcut to showcasing its music to Rebecca's peers, but what did that have to do with shampoos and psychoactive drugs?

Who were the man and the woman who had visited the school?

Joe had spent the better part of the night looking up whatever he could find on **ALTIUS!®** and the *iAm*. It was only after several dead ends and a peripheral online forum sprouting inventive conspiracy theories that he had ended up at the website of a company called

Nudge. The company's client list brought him up short. It included MinDesign, the manufacturer of the *iAm* device. Nudge was also recommended in a personal testimonial by the familiar-sounding designer of an Italian bag:

> *Nudge completely changed my relationship to my work, its fruits, and the world. I no longer think of people as clients, I think of us all as one big entity. I don't think of marketing anymore – the concept has lost its meaning for me. If you're out there and you have a good business idea, there's only one thing I want to say on Nudge's behalf: try them.*

Nudge represented 'a completely new approach to products, consumers, and open, interpersonal collaboration.' According to Nudge, we were living in a revolutionary time, which meant revolutionary tools were needed. Nudge clearly wanted to provide these, but try as he might, Joe couldn't grasp what it was the company actually did. The website stated that Nudge clients would receive a *neuromarketing-based potentials analysis, penetrative tactics proposal, full-prism methodological palette, individually customized parallel integration*, and *precision-designed information targeting*, but nowhere did it explain what these things were.

At the fantastical conspiracy-theory website, Joe had come across the claim that Nudge was run by an enigmatic figure whose name didn't appear in the commercial register or any of the company's official paperwork. It was only when he connected the name and the news about a trial that it all started coming together. At the previous marketing company, the founder of Nudge, who had no official connection to Nudge, had, along with other key personnel, been repeatedly sued for illegal advertising, using indirect marketing methods prohibited in consumer protection laws, and putting consumers at risk. Proving a link between Nudge and the cases was difficult, because both the company and its personnel had changed. The only unifying factor seemed to be that mysterious figure, the CEO of the previous company, but in addition to fading so effectively behind the backdrop of Nudge as to be invisible, he had apparently changed his name.

Or so claimed the conspiracy-theory site. The site's credibility was called into question by some suspect allegations, however: according to its anonymous authors, Nudge made money by, for instance, programming the brain functions of individual consumers.

As he read about the lawsuits involving the company that had preceded Nudge, Joe broke out in a cold sweat. The company had established drop-in centers for health care, mental health, and daily exercise at schools and day cares and sponsored clubs for children. According to the conspiracy-theory site, the marketers had gotten the kids in a sports club in one Philadelphia school district hooked on an energy drink that had proved addictive. After the club pulled up stakes, many of the children had been unable to stop drinking it without the help of a substance-abuse clinic. The beverage contained a compound originally developed for the treatment of Alzheimer's disease that was eventually prohibited by law, but the teenage discussion boards were still full of instructions on how to make it with a combination of Grandma's Alzheimer's pills, ADHD medicine, caffeine, and five other illicit ingredients. Using a combination of theater, movie, and band clubs, the company had successfully increased North Dakota's plummeting smoking rates thirty-fold. And an informational campaign titled The Elderly, Exercise, and the Brain had gotten the residents of an entire chain of nursing homes addicted to certain sedatives; patients who tried to go off them suffered muscle spasms and strokes.

The company had, of course, been sued repeatedly. The damages it was ordered to pay sounded high – until you compared them to the product manufacturers' profits and the company's fees, which had skyrocketed.

According to the conspiracy-theory site, Nudge did exactly the same thing as the previous, demonstrably criminal company, only through new methods. Nudge had a dedicated line for legal damages in its budget. It was a profitable strategy.

It was hard to say how much of this was true, because the only source Joe could find was the conspiracy-theory website. In contrast, an article published by Freedom Media's largest media concern claimed that Nudge had 'brought us one small step closer to a happier world.'

Joe had been wondering why so many people he'd never heard of commented on the updates on Rebecca's profiles, and why they said the jeans they'd bought made their butt feel 'as if life were meant to be lived to the fullest' or gushed on consecutive days about the sensual shine of a new hair dye, mentioned by brand, that 'made you realize

life is for living now.' One of her friends mused if a watch that let
you **Keep Time in Luxury** would be suitable as **A Gift Idea. For Her.**

Regardless of how much the conspiracy-theory site said was true, one
thing seemed undeniable. Their daughter had sold off her entire life,
digital and real – inasmuch any of the latter was left – as advertising
space.

'You guys don't understand!' Rebecca wailed on the verge of tears, as
Joe and Miriam stared, slack-jawed, at the breakfast table. 'I'm the
one getting something out of this, not them! Otherwise I wouldn't
have done it! Besides, you guys can't stop me! They're my friends! You
can't tell me who I can and can't be friends with!'

You better believe I can, if it's the marketing department of a major
corporation, Joe thought, but he swallowed the words. There was no
way he was going to let his daughter sell her life to big business as
marketing material, and let her brain function be harnessed for their
purposes by the new miracle gadget. He didn't know what the device
was capable of, but whatever it was, it was not going to be done to
Rebecca.

He forced himself to calm down and asked her what she meant by
'getting something out of it.' Bags, makeup, facial wash, jeans? But
according to his daughter, it wasn't as much the things themselves, as
the fact that she was the first one to know when some new makeup or
article of clothing or band was about to become massive.

'Sometimes I get discounts on them. And even if I don't, I always
have them before everyone else.'

'You don't need a corporate sponsor,' Miriam said. 'We can get you
everything you need ourselves.'

Rebecca widened her eyes: yeah, right.

'Hey, look, a cat,' Daniella said, pointing out the window. She'd
been glued to the conversation, turning her face towards whomever
happened to be speaking at the moment. Joe glanced at his younger
daughter, who had moved over to the couch.

'But why would you want someone else, some *marketing director*,
to pick your clothes and taste in music?' he asked.

'They don't pick them.' Rebecca looked mortally offended. 'If I don't like them, I send them back.'

'To that man and woman?'

'But I've been the first one to try them. Everyone knows I always have the latest stuff, before anyone else has practically even heard of it. Especially if something blows up like that bag. I was the first one who had one. Everyone remembers that. And I can't do that without some help. I'm always on the verge of falling behind as it is! You guys don't get how hard, how stressful, life is these days!'

'If the pressure's so horrendous, wouldn't it be a relief to pull out of the race altogether?'

Rebecca glared at her father. The look meant: you're even dumber than I thought.

'But what do your friends think?' Miriam asked. 'Are they aware the thousands of pictures on your Facebook pages are actually product placement?'

'Mom, give me a break, no one's on Facebook anymore. Why don't you go back to 2011 where you came from?'

'Do they know?'

'You don't have to fucking shout. Of course they don't!'

'Aren't you afraid of what's going to happen when it comes out? That everything you do is an advertisement? That you don't have a will or personality of your own?'

'What are you talking about?' For the first time, a minuscule crack appeared to form in Rebecca's defenses. 'I don't see what the big difference is. If I buy the clothes or they do. I mean, OK, maybe when it's like a lame skirt I would never voluntarily wear but I get a message from them that right now it would be like super-extra-important for you to wear this as much as possible for the next couple of weeks. Would you please, honey?!! So that kind of makes me think a little. When it's not something I would wear. But I do favors for them, so they can do favors for me.'

Miriam and Joe exchanged dumbfounded looks.

'But what about the medication?' Miriam said. 'Aren't you worried about it?'

'I don't have to take it. They promised. All I have to do is keep it in my bag.'

'But everyone sees it.'

'Sooo?'

'Everyone reads what you post on social media.'

'Sooooo?'

'Claiming you took it. That it helps you with your friends, your math tests. That's what you've been saying.'

'Soooooooooooooooooooooo?'

'So they're going to figure it out sooner or later! Your friends! That you're playing them!'

Rebecca stared at Joe.

'Seriously, Dad, no one says "playing" anymore.'

'So substitute something better.'

A small but visible wrinkle had formed in Rebecca's brow. Joe placed all his hopes on it.

'How would they ever figure it out?'

'Come on, someone must know you well enough.'

'Like who?'

'You must have at least one real friend!'

His daughter looked so pensive it made Joe's heart ache.

He had been wondering how the marketing company gathered the information it needed from Rebecca. The answer had come out gradually, as he questioned his daughter.

Once Rebecca started using her *iAm*, the man and the woman would be able to monitor her social media activity to make sure the bag was showing up often enough. They needed to be able to check, so they could keep giving Rebecca the gifts she wanted. As a matter of fact, they would basically be able to see everything Rebecca saw – and a lot more, besides – as long as she didn't reconfigure certain default settings.

They wanted to be able to tip off Rebecca to the exact college she'd have the best time at, the exact boy she'd fall for hardest, the exact job she'd be most interested in, the exact news she'd want to read – and soon they'd be able to.

Thanks to the *iAm*.

The one thing she had to promise was to keep her new device on all the time. Which it would be, even when Rebecca was asleep, tee-hee! It would even register her dreams! The man and the woman would see to the rest. Rebecca wouldn't have to worry at all, because if she made the mistake of, say, putting something in the bag, saying something to her friends, sending her friends links – doing anything at all that wasn't appropriate for friends of **The Children Are The Future** campaign, that is, the man's and the woman's friends – they would be in touch. Or if something showed up in her closet or makeup bag that wasn't in the interests of a popular girl like Rebecca, their stylist would send her a helpful note. The stylist had a good idea of the kinds of trends that were fashionable among young people – and in particular, she knew what sorts of trends were in the pipeline. And that was often the important thing, wasn't it?

By the way, would Rebecca mind if the man and the woman sent her a check every week? Unfortunately the sum wouldn't be very large, but it would be enough to stock up on makeup and go to the movies. All Rebecca had to do was be sufficiently open to the suggestions of the stylist and the consumer advisers, the man and the woman's good friends. Of course she didn't have to agree to anything – it was Rebecca's life, after all, her style! Ha ha, that's all Rebecca needed, for the woman's friends to start dictating the shade of lipstick she wore. But if she wasn't the least bit open to suggestions, then... well, it might turn out that the friendship wasn't as mutually rewarding as it could be. All they were asking for was an open mind.

Would it be all right with Rebecca if the man and the woman sent Rebecca more gifts and discounts the more her friends started to use the same products as her? Of course Rebecca was under no obligation to tell her friends what items and clothes she liked. The man and the woman believed **friendship entails no obligations**.

Here was a list of companies and people Rebecca could, if she were so inclined, click as friends in that popular social media where the man and woman were already friends with Rebecca.

Or if it felt less complicated, she could just give the man and the woman the right to add people and companies as her friends. It did? Good. Then Rebecca wouldn't have to give think about the whole thing. The man and the woman would be happy to take care of it on her behalf.

And this was <u>friendship</u>, not a contract, so there was <u>no need</u> for Rebecca <u>to involve</u> her <u>parents</u>. For a contract, you obviously needed your legal guardian's permission, but for friendship, no. The man was well aware of this, because he was a lawyer by training.

As a matter of fact, it might be best if Rebecca didn't mention anything about the whole arrangement to her parents. Or to anyone else, for that matter. People who weren't as intelligent and privileged as Rebecca wouldn't necessarily understand. They would also want designer jeans and makeup for free, they would also want to be friends with the man and the woman, but unfortunately the man and the woman couldn't be friends with everyone. Everyone could be basic friends, though; there were <u>no restrictions on basic friendship</u>. You could get **basic friendship** now for a **special introductory offer** of $13.99 (+ sales tax). No obligation to buy! As a matter of fact, Rebecca could freely recommend basic friendship to anyone who was interested.

Rebecca obviously deserved better herself.

In honor of their new friendship, the man and the woman wanted to offer Rebecca a visit to the salon. They knew an amazing hairstylist who specialized in cutting hair for people Rebecca's age. Unfortunately the stylist was expensive, extremely expensive – oh? Rebecca had heard of the salon? All the kids Rebecca's age knew about it? But her parents would never pay that much for a haircut? Then this was perfect: the man and the woman were happy to offer Rebecca a visit to this studio. The stylist would give Rebecca's look a little lift. Rebecca would walk out with a chic new cut, one that was a perfect match for a luxurious Trentino bag.

Rebecca glared at the edge of the table, eyes narrowed in defiance. She didn't get what the problem was. She was the one who decided which products she'd use! And if she was a little casual with the truth on her blog now and again, out of mere friendship, it probably wasn't the end of the world.

'Someone's going to notice at some point,' Joe said. 'That it's all staged. And they're going to start thinking your entire life is a lie.'

'Boo-hoo.'

'Becca, you can fool all the people some of the time and some of the people all the time, but you can't fool all the people all the time.'

'Ooh, a quote from Abraham Lincoln!' Rebecca grabbed a hunk of hair in either fist. 'I'm shaking in my boots! I get it now, Dad knows best!'

'I'm serious! Aren't you worried people are going to start thinking you're a liar? A fraud without a soul? You'll become like those people Bubbie used to talk about, *Zayn vort zol sayn a brik, volt ikh…*'

'Dad, give it up.'

'... *moyre gehat aribertsugeyn.*'

'Was there a single real word in all that?'

'You know what it means?'

'Who gives?'

'Becky.'

'Sorry, Dad, I'm not buying your Yiddish shtick.'

'Nice, Becca,' Daniella sniped in an injured tone from under the table, 'no one says "who gives" anymore.'

'It means: if her words were a bridge, I wouldn't dare cross it.'

'Fascinating.'

'Aren't you afraid people are going to see you that way?'

'If I think they're starting to suspect, I'll just start taking the tablets. It's not that big a deal.'

Miriam and Joe stared at each other. For the two weeks Rebecca had been into Norwegian black metal, the church-burning variety, Joe had been afraid his daughter had sold her soul to Satan. But it was only now he realized how it would happen. Never mind that Jews didn't really believe in the devil.

But hey, he was the one who'd never hung up a mezuzah.

'*Look,*' Daniella said in an insistent voice. 'Cats don't have tails like that, do they?'

Rebecca let out a shrill shrick.

And then Miriam noticed it, too. 'What on earth...?'

Even Saara heard this. She emerged from the basement, where she'd been loading the dryer: 'What's wrong?'

She was already facing the right way. Her eyes widened, and she clapped a hand to her mouth.

When Joe saw Miriam's and Saara's expressions, he turned to look. He realized he'd vaguely wondered about the noise while he was waking up: it was like the sound of a bird hopping across the pavers, claws scratching against granite.

Standing outside his home in his robe, Joe's first thought, absurdly enough, was that Rebecca's new friends were getting back at her for squealing.

Followed by: did that fall off a garbage truck?

The rat had darted behind the house when he stepped out, but now it returned, having apparently decided that a middle-aged egghead didn't pose a threat. It was dining on the lawn, tail whipping back and forth as if claiming ownership of the lot.

Joe stepped closer. There was something biologically repugnant about the feral, omnivorous sewer rat. The beast had adjusted to our way of life too successfully, learned to eat everything we left behind, to sleep and breed in our sewage drains and dumps. Maybe that was worth celebrating.

When he finally grasped what the rat was gorging on there on the lawn, next to the plastic-wrapped morning newspaper, it felt like someone had punched him below the belt.

As his daughters would have said: hey, *please*.

Give me a break.

It had been dumped during the night without any of them waking up. A small mammal's carcass, or a significant part thereof, had been carried onto their property. Innards and body parts covered in sinewy membrane had been strewn around it, presumably for their shock value. The ribbons of intestine looked pitiful on the huge lawn, as if someone tripped while taking out the garbage. Apparently the indeterminate mass had been dragged across the grass.

The city and its sewers were teeming with rats. It wasn't particularly surprising for one to have found this buffet so soon.

Miriam came out, looking like she feared the worst. But, like Joe, her face morphed first into confusion and then disappointment.

'Is this the best they could come up with?'

'My thoughts exactly.'

'I woke up in the middle of the night and thought I heard something.'

'I guess it could be an accident.'

'Oh, come on, I don't buy that.'

'Fell off the back of a garbage truck. Compactor left open.'

'Into our yard?'

'Yeah, well. Maybe not.'

'Where's Saara?'

'She's keeping the girls in the house.'

They stood there for a moment in silence. Then Miriam asked: 'What kind of animal do you suppose that is?'

'A lamb?'

'Are lambs that big?'

'I don't know.'

Miriam shook her head, blew out between her lips – pffft, what a bunch of clowns – and went back inside.

It had to have been kids. Undergrads. A little mischief, stealing a couple of pounds of slaughterhouse remains to scare people. Of course, practical jokes were just what the parents of two adolescents needed most in their life.

But for the rest of the day, which he should have spent reading and editing Raj's manuscript and preparing a guest lecture to give at New York University, Joe felt his heart beating oddly out of time. The chapter commissioned for a textbook series was already a week late. There was a vague pressure in his chest, and when Lisa asked what was wrong, he couldn't describe it. His head was throbbing.

He wrote Raj a note and left, thinking he'd rest for a minute and then work from home.

The bass frequency booming from behind Rebecca's door pummeled Joe as he walked in the house; her stereo was shrieking as if it were the end of days. He recognized the thump as the hottest hit of the past few weeks. The artist was the latest nu R&B singer to be sold to Rebecca, the song a plea for oral sex.

This is it, there's a limit, he had a right to rest when he wasn't feeling well, he told himself as he bounded up the stairs. He yanked open the door – without knocking, which he remembered Rebecca having once melodramatically compared to a slap in the face – about to roar at his teenage daughter, couldn't he get a moment's peace in his own home, goddammit? And then he saw Rebecca's tear-stained face.

His hand was already reaching for the volume control, but now it paused.

'Just turn it off.'

Joe silenced the stereo; Rebecca wiped away her tears on her sleeve. The R&B artist's CD and a case of lip gloss lay on the desk, supposedly left there casually but evidently being uploaded to the digital network through the *iAm*'s tiny red eye for the whole world to see. On any other day – in any other year – Joe would have launched into a battle to remove product placement from his daughter's bedroom and, if possible, her life.

'What's wrong?'

Rebecca didn't answer.

'Tell me.'

She glanced at him from under the precisely drawn, professionally dyed brows that, in their adult attempt to please, were somehow more frightening than the Goth eyebrow piercings his daughter had preferred a couple months ago.

She looked down at her hands.

'Did you happen to go out into the yard?'

'You mean earlier today?'

Daniella and Rebecca had both seemed bewildered, but it never occurred to Joe that either of them would be traumatized by the practical joke. *Who did it?* Dani had asked, and all Joe could tell her was he didn't know.

The sanitation crew had come with their trucks that same morning, pretty quickly actually, and hauled off the remains; there was no longer any trace of them on the lawn. Rat poison had been scattered along the walls of the house. The men had also set out glue traps inside, which the rats' feet would stick to.

'Becca, don't let them bother you. They're angry people.'

'Whatever.'

'They're not worth worrying about.'

Suddenly his daughter looked at him.

'Are you sure?'

'What do you mean?'

'You don't do stuff like that if things are going your way.'

'I'm sure that's true.'

'Have you ever wondered why some people feel like things aren't going their way?'

Joe was startled. 'What do you mean?'

'This… society or whatever, it's totally sick! We live in this nice house and have two cars and a servant—'

'Au pair. The term is au pair.'

'Do you realize that two, three miles from here, there are ghettos where people are firebombing each other's apartment buildings? People who can't even read but can shoot an Uzi by the age of ten? Do you know what sorts of people live in this city? Do you realize what kind of world we fucking live in? And like Occupy, they were evicted from that park – even though they weren't doing anything illegal! What the hell are you supposed to do if you want things to change?'

It felt absurd, hearing this coming from a teenager who'd just sold herself off to commercial interests. As a matter of fact, at this moment she was wearing a shimmery top with silver letters emblazoned across the chest, the ironic phrase she and her sister seemed to drop into every sentence these days. Joe had seen them watching video-clips of clever, rebellious animation squirrels causing trouble and brushing it off with the quip. Joe didn't know what the slogan was being used to sell, but he'd start by wagering a small sum on vmPFC fine-tuners.

Rebecca was brimming with indignation, and Joe wasn't completely sure at whom it was targeted. Eventually, because he didn't know what else to do, he wrapped his daughter in his arms, and she seemed to allow this. Everything was so unfair, Rebecca wailed, uncontrollable, weird. Politicians were for sale, you couldn't trust anyone, one percent of the population owned ninety-nine percent of everything, and things were just getting worse even though that one percent was publicly demanding change, too.

Wasn't there anyone in the world who could do anything?

Joe tried to list examples of how positive political change had been brought about, but all those that came readily to mind were from the 1960s, and there was, he had to admit, something disconcerting about that.

The pivotal moment with Aleksandra came on the evening of her twenty-fourth birthday.

She'd stuttered and blushed when she invited Joe to the party: 'Just to drop by, even, I know you probably can't stay long.' He hadn't had the heart to say no, although the thought of spending the evening at a bar in the company of a bunch of young women made him uncomfortable.

Sitting at his computer that afternoon, thinking Aleksandra had gone for the day, he heard the clack of high heels through the open office door. When he saw her walking back from the ladies' in her pencil skirt and evening makeup, he realized how Everyday Aleksandra was the only version he'd met so far, and how long it had been since he and Alina had last touched.

And when she saw Joe, Aleksandra stopped in the corridor and looked him dead in the eye. She seemed to rise to her full height for the

first time; in her heels, she might have been taller than him. Although
she was standing at a distance, the space between them felt charged.

'How do I look?'

'Really nice.'

'Thanks.'

It was as if Aleksandra had finally given herself permission to smile
with her whole being. The heels clacked away. Joe heard the thunk of
the opening, then closing main door.

He went into the break room to make a pot of the French roast he
ordered from the United States. Finnish coffee was unfathomable to
him; it was like it had been intentionally left to stale in the cupboard
or unintentionally left unroasted. He caught himself feeling wistful,
as if he were watching a ship pull out of harbor. Some lucky Finnish
boy would get Aleksandra; they'd make love in a tiny European flat
and eat Brie together on the floor. Aleksandra didn't have a boyfriend
yet. She insisted she'd be alone for the rest of her life because she was
too picky.

He thought she had left, but apparently she'd just stepped out for
a smoke: when he went back to his office, he ran smack into a heavy,
cloying scent.

Aleksandra was at her desk, painting her nails. Her face went beet
red when she saw Joe.

'I'm sorry. I thought you left.'

'No, no, don't get up.'

When she was done with her nails, Aleksandra held out her hands
and blew on the polish.

'It's not too garish?'

'No.'

She looked at him.

'What?'

'Can I ask you something?'

'Shoot.'

Aleksandra hesitated for a fraction of a second. Did he want to head
to the party with her? Maybe stop somewhere on the way for a drink
before they joined the others.

She flushed down to her throat. Joe was on the verge of answering,
sure, why not, but the glint in Aleksandra's eyes, as if she were running
a fever or was high on coke, gave him pause.

'Oh? Um… Hmm.'

It was the first and only time Aleksandra ever made a move; she was too polite for it, too demure.

Joe lied that he had a conference abstract to finish before the end of the day.

'OK.' Now her voice was light-hearted, carefree. 'It was just an idea.'

Before she left, she said from the doorway: 'You don't have to come, you know.'

Aleksandra's scent filled the room long after she left. The conference abstract hadn't been due that day, but Joe had decided to sit in his office for an hour or two anyway, for reasons that now seemed unclear.

He closed his eyes, noticed his heart was pounding, and wished things weren't leading the direction they were.

He'd told Alina that the party was for the department's administrative assistant, a sixty-year-old woman. The whole department would be attending, supposedly. He was ashamed of his lie and wished that he'd at least told Alina the truth.

As he stepped through the doorway of the little restaurant not far from the center, he could hear from the raucous voices that Aleksandra and her friends were letting loose. There was something illicit in the way she pressed up against him when he hugged her in greeting.

'I'm glad you came.'

'Yeah. But I can't stay long.'

'I'm so glad you came anyway.'

A spot at Aleksandra's side had just opened up, and she insisted Joe take it.

Maybe he already knew as he was sitting down that before the night was out, Aleksandra would be in his lap, he'd be feeling the warm skin beneath her lacy blouse.

Aleksandra's friends were a group of fun, animated young women. In their shimmering, out-on-the-town dresses they talked about men too frankly, egged on by the presence of a solitary male. There was a performance element to the conversation, as if the women were putting themselves on display – *for* him although *not because* of him. It was more a case of feeding off each other's experiences and emotions: being women together, performing womanhood for a generic man. They seemed to take pleasure in it, perhaps for the same reason a group of big, brawny guys found it satisfying to be men together on a football team.

Joe had already decided he wasn't going to cheat on his wife. He wouldn't do to Alina what he had done to Hannah. He wouldn't be able to take it: the way he'd felt in the Italian hotel room with Alina, when Hannah was thousands of miles away yet present every second.

But he wasn't even halfway through his glass of wine before he was on fire.

Aleksandra mentioned something about Sandy Koufax and the perfect game – to show that she'd listened carefully.

Been a good pupil.

Or because she wanted to shut the others out.

Joe realized that he'd known since the moment Aleksandra appeared in his doorway that this was where they'd been headed.

He hadn't touched his wife in six months. Alina seemed to have decided they wouldn't be having sex, except perhaps to make another baby.

If Joe let it happen, less than an hour would pass before Aleksandra was giving him head in the bathroom there at the restaurant; riding him on the couch in her studio apartment.

Alina probably thought his tongue was all over Aleksandra at this instant.

So what difference did it make?

Aleksandra's cheeks were glowing as she related some story about Interrailing in southern Europe to her friends. Then: a fleeting touch, maybe an accident. How easily it happened: 'Oops, I'm sorry.' Aleksandra's fingers grazed his thigh, at first as if in passing, but then they returned.

It was unbearable; his lap was in flames. The women continued gabbing with each other. Didn't notice, or pretended not to. Or else it had all been so obvious to them from the get-go that they weren't interested.

In the end, he'd been forced to grab Aleksandra's hand. It was warm, radiated heat like live coals. She looked at him, eyes full of anticipation.

Joe thanked her, wished her a happy birthday, and pulled on his coat. Aleksandra cast him a long look. Was he sure he knew what he was doing, throwing away their only chance?

'I have to leave.'

'I'm glad you came.'

'Me, too. 'Bye now. You guys have a great evening!'

'You too!'

In the friends' farewells, Joe could hear the traces of the earlier flirtation jointly fanned on Aleksandra's behalf.

That evening was supposed to have been the end of it. Joe emailed Aleksandra, explaining that he really liked her as a friend and a student, which was why he wanted to keep their relationship strictly professional. For their sakes and the sake of his marriage. He said he understood if Aleksandra wanted to switch supervisors – as far as he was concerned, there was no need, but it might make sense, considering he wasn't sure how much longer he'd be working in Finland anyway.

Aleksandra replied immediately. *Here's the thing*, she wrote, which sounded so fluently American that it took Joe a second to realize she'd picked up the expression from his messages. Aleksandra seemed to absorb his expressions, opinions, and attitudes like a sponge. It was flattering, yet disconcerting at the same time.

Here's the thing: Aleksandra said she'd fallen in love with Joe the moment they met and knew from the start she'd get her heart broken...

Don't be silly; I'm not switching supervisors.

Aleksandra said she knew exactly what Joe meant. She didn't want things to change, either. Wished him and Alina nothing but the best.

The back-and-forth continued for several messages. It felt right and cleansing, as if a window had finally been opened onto a dank cellar. Joe also told Aleksandra about his difficulties with Alina; that he loved his wife, but it felt like they spent most of their time these days competing over whose life was harder.

For her part, Aleksandra revealed how many losers she'd been in pointless relationships with and how meeting Joe had, for the first time in years, sparked the hope that the right guy might be out there somewhere. She also seemed to understand his homesickness. Her family had lived in France when she was a teenager and she remembered how lonely the foreign objects in the grocery store could make her feel, the unfamiliar milk cartons unfriendly and cold.

The following Monday, Aleksandra hugged him the second they saw each other, and her touch was different, warmer, less expectant.

And Joe said that Aleksandra had pulled him up out of a chasm. 'No, you're the one who pulled me up,' she countered.

But the email exchange with her had upset Alina. She had read the messages behind Joe's back, maybe filled in the gaps, and, from what little she had seen, apparently been convinced that he and Aleksandra were having an affair. They had eventually cleared things up; at least on the surface. But Joe was painfully aware of his overreaction, the justified but outsized anger that clearly stemmed from a bad conscience about everything he'd told Aleksandra, and that he should have said to Alina instead.

In the end, it had all come crashing down at one of the university's public lectures.

The invitation to speak at it, in and of itself meaningless, had made Joe feel that at least someone was aware of his existence and believed he was still capable of something, even though in his heart of hearts he'd given up.

The woman was full-figured, voluptuous. Not beautiful but feminine, laughed loudly, wore earrings the size of dinner plates. What was her name again – Krista? Kristi? Kristiina? She'd introduced herself as a psychoanalyst, a Jungian. The distinction from Freudians had been important to her.

You're from America, Krista or Kristiina had said, looking hungry as she seated herself at Joe's table. You would never catch her in the United States, Krista immediately added: never, not even for a visit. I have absolutely no interest in going there, she announced. There were so many other countries in the world that were much more intriguing. Indonesia, for instance, which had terribly fascinating indigenous culture, dance, sculpture. Afghanistan, Bhutan. As well as many places in South America.

Joe had conceded this was true. He could feel the woman's eyes on him.

She changed the topic. Was he aware that, as an American, he consumed more natural resources per capita than anyone else on the planet?

'Painfully.'

'So why don't you do something about it?'

You: why don't you, as an individual, do something? Or you, you Americans, why don't you do something as a nation? He wasn't sure which the woman meant.

'Well, quite a few people are trying,' he began. 'But…'

'Is trying enough?'

It quickly became evident that Joe was responsible for his country's foreign policy; skewed domestic markets; overly rapid economic growth and deceleration; cotton subsidies, which were strangling the life out of developing countries; and history, above all history; the media's distorted representations of female beauty; and of course its stupid populace, *horribly stupid incredibly fat people*, and the bad movies made for them.

For some reason, Joe was not responsible for the American art-house films with little in the way of dialogue, which the woman seemed to love. In contrast, the fact that every Finnish novel was interpreted elsewhere as a depiction of alcoholism said nothing about Finns' concepts of art, humor, or culture, according to Kristiina, although she found the notion amusing. You see, Finns haD a unique sense of humor that demanded knowledge of their country and culture and language.

Krista asked why Americans didn't read newspapers, why they drove such big, polluting cars, why they were willing to start wars over Middle Eastern oil.

'If you read, say, Noam Chomsky,' Joe said, 'you'd understand that a lot of Americans have a pretty critical view of all that, too.'

But as far as Kristi was concerned, Noam Chomsky wasn't American, not really, not the way she meant. Nor had she read much Chomsky, Kristiina confessed. She read every night to broaden her perspectives. Jung… you could read Jung over and over and always find something new.

Finns drive a lot, too, Joe argued feebly, but for Krista that was different. Joe had just read an article that claimed Finland had more cars than people. Finland consumed unsustainable amounts of oil, too, didn't it? he asked. But according to Kristi, that wasn't the Finns' fault, because distances in her country were so vast Finns were only doing what was necessary. Joe listened and nodded.

He didn't say anything to Kristiina about what he'd heard from his historian friend: that at the outset of World War II, Finland

had refused to take in Jews fleeing Germany, because according to
the Finns they weren't refugees. You see, they had left Germany
voluntarily.

He never would have dreamed of blaming Kristiina for this, but
during the course of the lunch, he wondered more than once if he
ought to. It was hard to swallow the aggressive, willful taste of the
contempt Kristiina or Krista seemed to feel for him and the United
States. It was as if it carried a tinge of revenge, as if she'd had a chip
on her shoulder for decades, and now, at long last, the opportunity
had presented itself to give as good as she'd gotten.

And when Kristi criticized him for the Palestinians' present plight,
he tactfully refrained from mentioning that, although they might have
forgotten it, the Finns had supported Israel, seeing the Yom Kippur
War, when Soviet-backed Arab countries attacked a small, isolated
state, as an echo of their own Winter War.

'Why do you have to carry the guns?'

Kristi had to ask her question a second time before he understood.

'Should everyone have the right to carry the gun?'

'Hmm.'

'I don't think so. Especially handguns. Imagine if everyone in this
room had the pistol in their pocket. Would that make any sense?'

Joe said that, as a matter of fact, he didn't know anyone in the
United States who owned a gun. 'It's pretty rare that you need a gun
at an East Coast university.'

She didn't return his smile.

'On the other hand,' he said, 'in Finland I know Professor Wallenberg,
who owns a rifle, two shotguns, and a three-fifty-seven Magnum. He
just invited me to his cabin to go hunting. I'm not sure I dare.'

Krista eyed Joe like a tasty morsel.

'You have these school shootings,' she said, 'but you never learn the
lesson. Why not? Wouldn't it be best to outlaw the guns if everyone
is going around shooting them, even schoolchildren?'

Joe said that in his opinion it would be, but Krista didn't seem to be
listening. He then pointed out that there were quite a few firearms in
Finland, too, but Krista was already continuing: 'The death sentence
and the guns, that's why we will never understand each other, you
and us. You – and me.'

She jabbed a long fingernail first into Joe's chest and then her own, *you and me.* A soft hollow formed in her magnificent bosom, under the red silk blouse: you – and me.

The seminar continued after lunch, and it wasn't until his own presentation that Joe realized how pissed off he was. Don't these people have any manners? *You'll never catch me in the United States.* Seriously? You have no interest in ever visiting New York? Well, fuck you then, the capital of the world doesn't need you, you fucking hick. I'm sure Manhattan can't hold a candle to Helsinki. But you know that without ever having seen the place. So why don't you grab your blunderbuss and go watch your fucking Serbian movies in Hakaniemi?

Which, by the way, you'd have a much better chance of seeing in New York! The only thing you can find at the video rental here, you fucking philistines, is Schwarzenegger! Who happened to be born in Austria! You're the ones who created the Terminator, you goddamned Europeans!

At the end of the seminar Krista approached Joe and, with exaggerated friendliness, said she could take him to see the National Museum, if he were interested. Joe tried to formulate a polite way to decline, which seemed to amuse Krista.

'It has objects from Finnish history. Maybe they're not impressive enough for you. No Hollywood explosions. Boring everyday objects that show what the life was like. The real life of the people.'

'I find Finnish history extremely fascinating,' Joe said, and it was true. 'But I've already been there.'

He and Alina had gone to the museum right after he arrived. She had advised against it, but Joe had been eager to get to know his new homeland. He had tried to memorize the dates of Finland's wars; Alina had yawned and asked if they could go yet.

'The universal archetype can be seen in the history of the humanity,' Krista said. 'But maybe the humanity isn't so interesting to Americans.' She pulled a little mirror out of her purse and looked at herself from different angles, eyebrows raised.

When it was time for Joe to leave, Krista said they should share a cab, because she didn't live far away – which, as it later turned out, meant across the bay in Espoo. Krista wanted to stop for a drink, which Joe had no interest in doing, but the way she criticized American literature agitated him to the point that, before he knew it, he found himself in a gloomy Finnish bar drinking Kentucky bourbon straight up and listing all the ways Krista was wrong and why.

With an air of amusement, Krista or Kristiina adjusted the front of her silk blouse, which was taut against her breasts. Afternoon turned to evening, and Krista's plump lips curved up in a warm smile as she blamed Joe for JFK's infidelity and the way Americans had tolerated it… as well as the fact that they were incapable of approaching sex or nudity naturally. Her information about JFK was erroneous on any number of counts and rife with peculiar misconceptions, but in her view it was typical American arrogance to react patronizingly to the views of others. Joe was and the way he apparently did to everything he didn't know a thing about. Joe couldn't believe his ears; he decided he was going to have one last drink and explain once and for all how things *really* stood, after which he'd extricate himself from this appalling woman's company. But after knocking back that drink, he was still sitting at the same table, away from home, where he knew Alina was wallowing in self-pity and blaming him for not pulling his weight with the baby and working all the time even though he had a wife and a small child, and for wanting his life back, and for having an affair he wasn't having with a student.

Joe was roused from his reverie when he realized Krista had said something.

'A blow-up job,' she repeated, and looked at him intently like a cat.

It took him a moment to realize Krista meant oral sex.

'To do a blow-up job. I wonder what it feels like to do a blow-up job to the president of the most powerful country in the world? I think it feels the same as to do it to any man.'

'Krista, I think we've had enough to drink.'

'Men are all the same. Do you like to get the blow-up job, Joe?'

'Blow job, Krista.'

'What?'

'The right way to say it is "give a blow job." Blow job. Not "blow-up job."'

'What are you talking about?'

'That word you're using,' Joe said, and realized he didn't feel well when he momentarily closed his eyes. The room was swimming. 'It doesn't mean anything. There's no such word in English. The word is "blowjob."'

'I asked if you, Joe, if you like to do the blow… do the blow-up job.'

Krista's phonemes had started to slur during her previous (fourth?) gin-and-tonic, which Finns called *gin-tonics*. At lunch, Joe had noted that she only picked at a few carrots on her plate.

'Everyone likes to get the blow-up job. But what about doing? Do you, Joe, do you like to do the oral sex? I love the oral sex.'

'That's fantastic. Listen—'

'To do and get. Hmm?'

'I need to go home.'

'Control, control,' Krista said, smiling at him seductively and swirling a forefinger around the rim of her glass.

'Excuse me?'

'Always control. Hmm?'

'I'm sorry, but I'm not following.'

'You're a researcher, hmm?'

'So?'

'Maybe it's very frightening for you if you're spontaneous.'

'Listen,' Joe said. 'I've spent this whole afternoon and evening hearing about everything that's wrong with me and my country, and I'm sure you're right about everything, but I can't take back the Vietnam War or wipe American society off the face of the earth. And if you want to badmouth American literature, please read at least one novel written within the past thirty years and don't say *but it's not American that way*, the way you do about everything American you happen to approve of, because it *is* American, whether you like it or not. I'm not interested in discussing oral sex with you, either, if you don't mind, and I think you're so drunk that it's time for us to go.'

Krista was delighted: 'All right, yes! A reaction!'

Joe realized that everyone else in the bar had stopped talking and turned to look at them. Apparently Finns were familiar with the concept of oral sex shouted out loud in a bar, even in English. He asked the server for the check and grabbed his coat.

'I'll call us a cab,' Krista said, painting her lips. They were soft, too plump for such an irritating individual, the lips of a woman who lived life to the fullest. Joe involuntarily lingered on them a tenth of a second longer than he wanted to, as well as registering the thought that at least this woman was an adult, perhaps even a few years older than him, and most important of all she wasn't his student. Nor would he ever have to see her again.

'I'm not sure that's a good idea.'

'Two taxis. Makes no sense. Too expensive.'

It was raining outside: this is how he'd always pictured winter in the British Isles, not sunny and snowy but windy and wet. Krista opened her umbrella and, without asking, drew him under it. She was shorter than he was, and the umbrella kept jabbing Joe in the head. He could make out the pores and foundation on her face, smell the lipstick on her breath.

In the taxi, Krista studied him closely and at length, clearly at the wellsprings of a fresh thought. Her lips were parted.

'You're just there in the head.'

'Excuse me?'

'You. Researcher. You're always there in the head.'

'In my head?'

'In the intellect. Not in the emotion.'

'Oh, that's what you mean. I get it. You might be right.'

'Your culture is young. Immature.'

'And yours is old?'

'A reaction, a reaction! Good, Joe.'

'What year did the subway here open, anyway? In Boston it was put underground in 1897.'

'Joe, I hurt your feelings! Good! A reaction! Good.'

'Excuse me, but you didn't hurt my feelings.'

'You have so many Negroes there,' Krista said.

'*Negroes*?'

'The United States could never—'

'You've got to be kidding! That had to be a joke, right? Did you just use that word?'

'A Negro could never be President of the United States.'

'You guys have all this equality,' Joe said, 'but a woman could never be President of Finland.'

'That's different.'

'Really?'

Suddenly Krista stuck out her hand. It looked like she was going to poke him in the eye.

'Hey!'

He grabbed her arm.

'Wait. You have a... how do you say it in English? In your eye. This.'

'Oh. An eyelash.'

'Blow. You can make a wish.'

He blew. Krista suddenly looked at him more softly, almost tenderly, which caught him completely off guard.

'Did you make a wish?'

'Yes.'

She studied him and seemed to be expecting something, and, for some reason Joe could never explain to himself, even later, he gave her what she'd been waiting for for at least the past hour, already certain of victory. He pressed his lips to her broad mouth. It was both infuriating and a relief to finally give in, and contrary to all that was right and fair in the world, contrary to the way the world should have been, no kiss had ever felt so pleasurable. The world was insane, beautiful, there wasn't anything he wanted more than this, and this was the last thing in the world he wanted. They were drunk, but the talking was finally over; they stumbled, out of breath, into Krista's home in Espoo, Krista screamed loudly during sex and immediately announced after the act that she hadn't had an orgasm. Which was rare, she usually had no trouble coming, countless times and back to back, both by herself or with others, every time, men or women.

During the hungover ride home in another cab, Joe felt like a dirty paper towel on the floor of a Finnish train station bathroom. The sexual compatibility, if it had ever existed, had instantly evaporated in bed. You could learn from every experience in life, and what he walked away from this evening with was that making love could feel like sinking up to your ankles in late-autumn slush. After his protracted loneliness, the first touch had felt magical, but the pleasure had been limited to that one long kiss in the cab, and reflecting on it in hindsight, even a short kiss with Alina would have been a million times deeper and more fulfilling.

He thought about his three women and how, despite their abundance, he didn't seem to possess a single one, and how he'd cheated on his wife emotionally with Aleksandra and now physically with Kristiina, and he tried to think of a single aspect of his life he hadn't totally screwed up.

He tried to console himself later by thinking there was no way he could have saved his marriage, even if he'd done everything differently that evening, and that, conversely, it was unlikely anything would have

happened if things between him and Alina had been right. This didn't
justify his actions, of course, but it might still be true.

In retrospect, it seemed as if the whole period had been lived by a
totally different individual; once he got back to work and normal life
after his years of Finnish despair, it was impossible for him to imagine
he'd ever behaved this way.

Roughly a week after finding the carcass, the Chayefski family nearly
suffered a collective heart attack. At six in the morning, they were
woken by a blast from a foghorn, the kind that was sounded at ice
hockey games or Finnish May Day celebrations. The violent shriek
was followed by squealing, mid-frequency gibberish, like a robot at a
revival, squawking about finding religion.

Daniella started wailing, still half-asleep. Miriam jumped out of bed,
calm and authoritative, instantly evacuating her family. Down to the
basement now, girls, hurry! The hurricane is coming.

Joe threw on his robe and tiptoed downstairs, looked out the window
and saw five figures in gas masks and rubber overalls standing directly
across the lawn. One was shouting into a megaphone, as the others
repeated rhythmically: '*Shame on you! Shame on you!*' Then another
ear-splitting blast from the foghorn.

Joe stepped onto the cool, still-damp grass in his robe, unable to
believe his eyes. He scanned the gas masks for a face or even a pair of
eyes, but the figures had covered every square inch of their bodies so
thoroughly he couldn't even tell their hair or skin color. '*Shame on you!
Shame on you!*' When they saw him on the stairs, the figures seemed to
pause. One glanced at the others, and Joe thought he caught a faint,
stifled giggle. But then: '*Shame on you! Shame on you!*'

There was something so childish about it all that Joe had a fleeting
urge to chuck rocks at them, pull down his pants and stick out his butt.

He hesitated, said, 'Hey, listen, guys,' and started walking towards
the quintet.

There was a burst of laughter, a glance round at their comrades,
then they scattered. The robot yelling into the megaphone stayed the
longest – '*Shame on you!*' – but before long, all five of them were
hightailing it down West Chestnut Parkway. Joe saw them jump into a

van – light gray, or maybe white or dirty, he later told the police – and drive off. One last obnoxious blast of the foghorn. Then silence. The only trace of their visit were six big, sloppily scrawled signs erected in the yards of Joe and Miriam's nearest neighbors:

YOUR NEIGHBOR IS A MURDERER

Joe's name, address, and phone number were at the bottom, along with his passport photo, the one smiling on the departmental website.

When Daniella and Rebecca didn't think their parents could hear, Joe heard them pondering whether someone could get in the house if they wanted to.

'No,' he'd gone in to tell his daughters, completely sure of himself: 'They can't get in the house.'

But he could tell what the girls were thinking: if they can come onto our lawn while we're asleep, spread garbage around our yard, gather under our windows without any of us even waking up…

'Girls,' Joe said, looking each of them in the eye, 'I don't want you two worrying about this. Seriously. This is a problem for grown-ups to deal with. Those people are protesting in the wrong place; they don't understand this isn't the way to handle things.'

Daniella inhaled deeply, seemed to rise to her full height for the first time in ages. Adolescence hadn't yet shaken her eleven-year-old's faith in her parents; Dad still knew best. But Rebecca wasn't eleven anymore: when she eyed Joe cagily and he asked what she was thinking, she wouldn't say.

Rebecca went into her room and shut the door. Daniella had already flitted off down the stairs. Joe stood there at Rebecca's door, overcome with helplessness, as daily an occurrence for the parent of an adolescent as eating or sleeping, the constant shower of humiliation from the cornucopia of teenage tyranny.

But something about this experience was weightier than usual. For a second, Joe felt like nothing was in anyone's control, anywhere, that anything at all could happen at any moment. The sensation was new and oppressive. Downstairs, the television came on, droning with the periodical cicadas' deafening wall of sound.

BECAUSE DIFFICULT TOPICS ARE SILENCED TO DEATH

HELSINKI, FINLAND

It had been a chilly morning in the city; an icy drizzle had fallen when Alina walked up to the entrance of the YLE broadcasting building. But by afternoon the clouds had cleared, and now the sky was a dazzling blue.

She headed out to her car and opened the door. For the first time that year, the sun felt warm; it was beating down on the parking lot from a cloudless sky. Her worry that she'd be shivering indoors in her sleeveless dress had proved absurd; she'd been sweating under the glare of the studio's spots.

Alina checked the time on her phone. Was she late? The hospital was flexible, but she wanted to stick to their visiting hours, to make up in some small way for Dad's tantrum last week, when he squeezed a nurse's arm so badly it bruised. The week before, he had called a young female attendant a slut and pinched her backside.

Alina started up the car and let it crawl towards the gates. There was something comforting about the sunny city: the shy buds of the birches, the first blooms of coltsfoot in the road banks. Maybe spring would finally start now. The grimy mountains of gravel-packed snow had stubbornly lined the roadsides long into April: temperatures at the beginning of the month had seen record-breaking lows. After exiting the lot, Alina shifted into higher gear and wondered how the show would look to television viewers.

'In any case, it's a good thing we're talking about these issues now,' the appealing representative from the Social Democrats' youth organization, an idealistic twenty-year-old, had said into the camera towards the end of the discussion. Everyone nodded, Alina included.

That was why she had agreed to do it. And gladly: she had nothing against appearing on *Tough Talk* in an expert role and voicing the opinions expected of her. Presumably her perspective neatly rounded out the views of the representative from the refugee organization, the socially aware novelist, and the nation's number one racist. Although there was nothing new about her message, apparently someone needed to say it again out loud.

This was one of the things she'd learned since her first book was published: ideas didn't exist without faces to promote them. That's what they needed her for: to serve as the face that reminded Finns not every immigrant was an illiterate refugee from the conflict-ridden Horn of Africa; to be someone people could agree with or else oppose. No book by and of itself was going to do that.

This had come as a surprise to Alina initially. And she still thought there was something backwards about it, a book requiring someone to stand in for it – especially when you considered what an unremarkable figure she cut as a woman and an individual or how much more thoroughly you could present your arguments in a book. Wouldn't an actor have done a better job? Even if they read from a script?

But she had gradually come to relish the role. Take today's conversation, for instance: she felt she had succeeded in stating her case in a convincing tone and sufficiently succinctly – unlike, say, the chair of the youth organization, who kept trying the hosts' patience, arguing that there were many highly educated, intelligent, ambitious individuals who came to Finland from, for instance, Western Europe, the United States, and Asia, who never found their place here the way they did in other Western countries. By this point, she had her statistics down pat. The Vietnamese restaurant owner, the movie star known for his violent roles, the guy who maintained a xenophobic online forum: they all listened without interrupting as she explained how the majority of well-educated immigrants wanted – or at least theoretically could want – to settle permanently in Finland. And their reason was always the same: they had a Finnish wife. That there was no limit to what they were capable of or could accomplish, but they were excluded from the job markets through any manner of direct and indirect practices.

This was still largely the case, although so many things had changed in Finland in recent years. A gaudy new hockey arena had been erected by and named after a beverage bottler, and a shiny new soccer stadium in Töölö by the sponsoring telecommunications operator. Recently, a national electricity company had awarded its CEO tens of billions in options and a state-owned timber company its director millions (which had pissed many people off, because the company had just fired thousands of workers, and a banker millionaire was quoted bragging in the media that the liquidation of low-efficiency employees was in society's best interests). But although much had changed about Finland, its xenophobia had not.

The day after tomorrow, she would see which of her comments had made it into the broadcast. Alina still wasn't sure why people listened to her so politely, didn't start arguing with her. Of course she was seen as speaking on behalf of wealthy, white Christians – which wasn't, strictly speaking, true. Refugees from war-torn northern Africa always aroused the most emotions and friction. But the people Alina represented were glossed over harmoniously, as an aside of sorts.

How simple and straightforward everything was the second time around, she reflected as she pulled up to the traffic lights at the Helsinki Expo and Convention Center. She looked at the mud-spattered rear window of the station wagon in front of her, with its Baby on Board sticker, and realized she was thinking it for the umpteenth time: with Taisto and Ukko, she'd been a completely different mother, just like she'd been a completely different wife with Henri – surer, calmer. With him, she didn't have to be afraid that her husband would pick up and leave at any moment, say he'd never loved her in the first place.

Of course everything else had gone differently, too, ever since day care when smiling, rain-loving Leena, the teacher, welcomed the boys by immediately wrapping her arms around them and saying: 'We'll manage just fine! We always have.'

Alina still admired Leena's way of handling cantankerous children. Leena thought it was good they had a mind of their own and knew how to express their opinions and stick to their guns.

She must have been made for her job. If only Samuel had had a Leena, Alina thought.

'None of you have half as much fun at work as we do here every day,' Leena said at the first open house with a raucous cackle, which made tears well up in Alina's eyes. She almost felt she could fall in love with this woman.

The only things to slip past Leena were Ukko's problems; their source hadn't been discovered until preschool. Leena thought he was just a unique, sensitive, thoughtful boy – and still did, even after the diagnosis. Alina had told her about the tests when they had bumped into each other at the supermarket.

But the diagnosis probably didn't even exist back when Ukko was in day care. It was amazing how quickly medicine advanced.

Unlike when Samuel was born, Alina had clearly understood her role with Ukko and Taisto. And, oddly enough, this seemed somehow related to the fact that Henri was still feeling out his role as a father. For some reason, her partner's lack of experience reinforced Alina's belief in her own capabilities as a parent. The memory of her pettiness when Samuel was a baby felt like a surreal, shameful dream.

Samuel's childhood speech impediments, too, during which she had envisioned a lifelong downward spiral into marginalization and substance abuse for him, had perhaps been nothing more than a projection of her own anxieties. In the end, everything had worked itself out – despite the experts, who had instantly predicted permanent problems. Sometimes she wondered what would have happened if they had just been able to support her when she had needed it most.

The thought had occurred to her countless times: would it have been possible for her to have lived the same life, her life, without all the stress? Would everything have turned out just as well even if she hadn't been perpetually worried?

The only thing that warranted her concern now was Samuel's trial. Trials, Alina corrected herself: she had gotten used to thinking about the whole complicated mess in the singular, even though in reality every part of the troubling situation would be reviewed separately, and in more than one country.

But there wasn't anything anyone could do about any of that at the moment – least of all Alina, since she didn't know a thing about the law. Samuel had done what he could, the police were investigating the latest criminal reports lodged against him, and when it came to the earlier cases, the process was on hold and would continue in appellate court. And as for the most recent charges, worrying wasn't going to do any good. Especially now that Samuel was in the United States.

Invited to speak at a conference: her child was a trail-blazer. The pride she felt at that immediately mingled with a pang of conscience.

They said that, in moments of confusion, you should listen to your heart. But that was where the problem lay: her heart spoke with two voices. Which one was right?

It all depended on which one you listened to.

Alina stopped to let a young man pushing a stroller cross the road. As she waited, she opened the window and gazed out at the bare yards of the apartment buildings, the naked birches standing in them. Did Joe know what Samuel had gotten himself involved in? The question had been occurring to her with increasing frequency over the past few days.

You should have told Joe, a crow cawed from the roof of a nearby trash shed.

The way Samuel had always admired his father hurt Alina somewhere too deeply for her to be forthcoming with her ex-husband. She had meant to tell him what their son was up to these days, who he'd become, but hadn't been able to. It wasn't that there was anything strange or dangerous about it, of course. It would just be good for Joe to know.

After ending the call, she had stared, remote in hand, at the mute television she suddenly wasn't able to turn on. How many years had she been actively upset with Joe for not staying in touch with his son? The anger had developed into an internal routine. Whenever the headwinds had felt too strong, when things hadn't gone as planned, a reason for her disappointment had materialized of its own volition from the far side of the Atlantic. *Is it really* that *hard to call?* she had fumed at Joe as she hauled overloaded grocery bags in the rain. *Couldn't you have found* some *way of keeping in touch?* she yelled at Joe, when she and Samuel had argued about the expensive new soccer cleats he'd forgotten at the pitch, never to be seen again.

It wasn't until the phone call when she'd found herself incapable of saying anything to Joe that she finally started understanding things from his perspective: no, it wasn't necessarily that easy.

Teachers liked Samuel, they always had.

Alina remembered his biology teacher, who had, at an open house one evening, privately predicted that if anyone in Samuel's class would amount to anything, it would be Samuel. The teacher was an eccentric, antagonistic personality many found difficult. He was considered superior intellectually but socially inept. Samuel didn't talk much about school, but from the few words he said about this teacher, Alina had concluded that her son had formed a special bond with him.

It had only been that one other teacher in junior high who had claimed Samuel was dangerous. And all because the other kids in the class did whatever the man said whereas Samuel did not blindly obey. Alina needed to watch out for her son, she was told, make sure he learned to respect authority.

She duly nodded her agreement: of course he should. Meanwhile silently wondering: how? And: any authority, without question?

No teacher could manage a classroom if he didn't get Samuel on his side. Apparently he could control his fellow students, even when he was wrong.

As a young boy, Samuel was liable to forget how small he was and stick up for a kid he didn't know, being teased by much bigger boys on the playground. Alina had been proud of her son, but at the same time terrified by everything he would have to go through because of his temperament.

She remembered the disciplinarian teacher being upset with fifteen-year-old Samuel over a presentation he'd thrown together in a week, asserting he had used it to make a mockery of the teacher and the entire class. Samuel had been dumbfounded by the accusation. He said all he wanted to do was research what he'd been told to.

The assigned topic was 'How Each of Us Can Have an Impact.'

'So what was in the presentation, then?' Alina asked the teacher over the phone, her cheeks burning with shame. She was holding four-month-old Ukko in her lap, who at any moment would spit the nipple from his mouth and then start shrieking because the nipple wasn't in his mouth.

'It was… smart-alecky,' the teacher replied stiffly. 'He was trying to say to us: you're all pretty stupid. I'm not going to stoop to thinking about things like this.'

'I'm so sorry,' Alina said. She tried to sit stock-still, so the baby wouldn't begin crying before the phone call ended.

'He always wants to show off,' the teacher said huffily.

'I'll talk to him.'

'I thought I'd go ahead and call... Because with behavior like this, it doesn't matter how bright Samuel is, he's not going to... I just wanted you to be aware. It's for his own good that we set these assignments. We're not trying to *torture* him.'

'I'm sure that's true.'

'Mom!' two-year-old Taisto roared from the living room: *'Mo-o-om! I want a vi-de-o! Come turn on the vi-de-o!'*

'So if he could adjust that attitude a little...'

Balancing the phone between her cheek and shoulder, Alina teetered into the living room with the baby in her arms and clicked on the Moomin DVD.

'Yes, of course. Thank you for calling,' she said politely, thinking she didn't like this person she'd spent no more than five minutes talking to on the phone.

She had asked Samuel to show her the report once Taisto was down for his nap and Ukko was distracted, entranced by a rattle on the floor. The paper was on economics, a study of George Akerlof, Michael Spence, and Joseph Stiglitz's analyses of asymmetric information on markets. And some citations from a book by someone named Goleman. It wasn't until later that Alina learned that Akerlof, Spence, and Stiglitz had won the Nobel Prize for Economics.

'How do you know all this?' she asked her son.

'From the net.'

'You looked all this up yourself?'

'No, my English teacher helped me a little.'

'Why didn't you do it on the assigned topic?'

'I tried to! At first I put like don't buy normal clothes, buy ones made from organic cotton. But then – there was this thing on the news about T-shirts made from organic cotton, they're dyed with really toxic chemicals, too, and the toxins get into the water supply and the people who work with them are a hundred times more likely to suffer leukemia so I emailed Dad and said—'

'Joe?'

'Yes.'

'In America?'

Alina felt her pulse spike. Samuel stared at her, clearly trying to figure out what was going on.

'Where else would he be?'

Alina scanned the English-language article laying out the Nobelists' ideas on what sellers and buyers knew. She'd felt the tautness in her belly before it even came out that Samuel had gotten the article from Joe.

'Emailed?' Alina strove to sound normal, neutral. 'Really?'

'Is that not OK?'

'Of course it is. I just didn't—'

She felt a prick of conscience; she needed to be more relaxed about this in Samuel's presence. It would be good for her son to form some sort of relationship with his father: that's how she really felt, deep down inside.

'What does that look mean?'

'I just didn't know that... that you two were in touch.'

From the increasingly dissatisfied tone of Ukko's babbling, she could tell that she would have to go soon. Babies were wonderful, but after they were born, you had to take a ten-year break from all conversation.

'We're not,' Samuel said. 'I just... I couldn't think of anyone else to ask.'

'I'm here. What? Why are you looking at me like that?'

'Please, Mom.'

'What?'

'I'm sure you would have been a ton of help.'

Alina tried to not take offense.

'I know how to research things, too. But... you asked Joe?'

'Yes. And he said the problem is that there's asymmetric information about the markets.'

'Asymmetric?'

'That sellers know things that buyers don't.'

'Oh, like—'

'Like how the goods they're selling have been manufactured. What they've pumped into the river, how much mercury children have in their bloodstreams as a result of that specific factory being in that specific village.'

'But that's exactly why you have to be so careful about what you buy!' Alina was irritated that her son was giving his teacher a hard time, when for once he had the chance to use his talents on an assignment that clearly interested him. 'We consumers are the ones with the power,' she said. 'We shouldn't be so selfish and buy whatever we feel like, regardless.'

Samuel winced as if he'd been kicked. 'That's what everyone always says, but it's not true! We don't have the power, because we don't know how those goods have been made! That phone you just bought, it was reported that it was manufactured using – what was it called again? That stuff that made two hundred people sick at that factory? You just bought that phone! Because it looked like a good phone!'

Now the thud of tiny feet hitting the floor echoed from the children's room: Taisto was awake, too. Why couldn't he take proper naps like every other child?

'Yes, but I wouldn't buy it again,' Alina said. 'And neither would anyone else. Information travels fast these days. Anytime anything like that comes out, it turns into a scandal.'

'Maybe in one case out of a thousand. And even then, people just avoid one product and one manufacturer. The other nine hundred ninety-nine are just as bad. Everything is being made in countries where you can do whatever you want to the environment and your employees, because it's profitable.'

'So how can we know what to buy, then?'

'We can't! That's the whole point of the article. Asymmetric information. That's the reason why—'

'Hi there, Taisto,' Alina said to the toddler, who had appeared in the living room in his underpants. She tried not to lose track of what Samuel was saying. She had opened her mouth to ask him to continue, but now Taisto announced that he had a pee-pee. 'Yes, you do,' Alina said, trying to sound thrilled by his discovery.

Samuel waited patiently. Alina felt a pang of guilt. Every conversation with her eldest child ended in interruption. She'd have to try to do better.

'Information asymmetry,' she said in an encouraging tone.

'Yes. That's what keeps us from having an impact. Consumers can—'

'Taisto, are you hungry? I'm sorry, Samuel, go on.'

'… can supposedly have an impact, but because they don't know the kind and degree of impact they're having when they make purchases, the system is purely arbitrary. And that's why half the people in my class tell me, shut up, I don't care.'

'That's horrible. Everyone should take an active interest, at least to some extent.'

'You have a 'gina,' Taisto said.

'No, they shouldn't! We can't make it that hard for people! I just read…'

Taisto raised his voice to a roar: 'Mom, you have a 'gina.'

'… to make one kilogram of packaging glass…'

'That's true, Taisto, I do have a vagina.'

'… it takes six hundred fifty-nine different ingredients at various stages of the production process. Chrome, silver, krypton, isocyanates.'

'Normal glass?'

'You make glass by melting sand at a temperature of eleven hundred degrees,' Samuel said. 'But when you look at those thirteen primary processes used to turn sand into a jam jar, they're broken up into nineteen hundred fifty-nine smaller chains called unit processes. A normal glass jar. Almost two thousand separate unit processes, each one of which consists of hundreds of sub-processes. You need lye, for instance, and for that you need sodium chloride, limestone, ammoniac, fuel and electricity, and they have to be transported to the site.'

'I don't know how you've been dedicated enough to find all that out,' Alina said. She couldn't help keeping one eye on Taisto, who had toddled over to the shelf to pull out CDs one by one and drop them to the floor. She kept glancing back at Samuel, so he would feel like he had her full attention. The sound of cracking plastic echoed from the shelf as the CD cases clattered to the floor. The baby was still nursing in Alina's lap.

'During the process of manufacturing a glass jar, about a hundred different compounds end up in the water supply, maybe about fifty in the soil, and a good couple hundred in the air. I calculated that about twenty percent of the environmental impact of that glass jar, give or take, might come from the electricity, you know, that it takes to heat the furnace, but the impact depends on how that electricity has been produced.'

'You can't know that.'

'Of course I can't! And neither can anyone else, because it's so goddamned complicated. For once I tried to do something right. I tried to do a report that would explain how this system works. Since that was the assignment: 'How Each of Us Can Have an Impact.' Well, I tried to figure it out. But that's where the problem lies… that if you think about, for instance, health impacts, then in the manufacturing of that glass jar, some of the nastiest are the aromatic hydrocarbons, which are responsible for maybe an estimated seventy percent of the negative effects of that glass jar – if we're talking about cancer risks.'

'It's fantastic that you've looked into all that so carefully, but – Taisto!
Stop throwing those CDs this instant!'

'But what?'

'But your teacher probably wanted something…'

'Mom. No offense, but Mr Mäkelä isn't exactly the sharpest pencil
in the box.'

'Maybe he was looking for something a little more… like practical
advice. Taisto! Mommy's getting angry.'

'So recycle. Buy organic.'

'Probably something like that.'

'But it's all total bullshit!'

'Samuel!'

'We need to change the entire system, instead of robotically repeating
that we can have an impact when we really can't!'

'Recycling the things you buy is not bullshit. Taisto, Mommy's going
to come get you now.'

'Thanks, Mom. You want to teach me a little bit more about the
global economy and its complex links to the environment, health and
standards of living?'

'I don't like your tone.'

'Hey, you asked.'

Later that evening, after she had put Taisto and Ukko to bed, Alina
knocked on Samuel's door and asked if she could come in. Their
conversation had been bothering her.

'Likewise,' Samuel answered.

'I've just been thinking about… you emailing Joe.'

She saw her son instantly retreat into his shell. After some hesitation,
Alina worked up the nerve to ask what he remembered about his father.

Samuel looked stricken. Alina faltered as she recounted how little he
had been when his father left, and that his memories weren't necessarily
totally… Yeah, go on? Accurate? Every choice of words felt wrong
before it left her mouth.

'All I'm trying to say is that he might not be… as perfect as you
think he is.'

'What?'

Alina tried explain how, whenever Samuel talked about him, Joe was always so brilliant – an American professor and a symbol of intellectual superiority. Samuel had lowered his gaze to his feet.

'All I'm trying to say is… well, you don't really know him.'

Her son's tears came abruptly. Alina's cheeks were burning; she should have realized.

'And I'll never going to get to know him, either,' Samuel said, 'if I don't reach out to him.'

After this conversation Alina had called Joe for the first time in years. He told her that his son's email had been to the point, even formal. He had asked if buying a T-shirt made from organic cotton was more beneficial for the environment than buying a budget one. Joe had been flattered that he'd been the one Samuel had turned to.

He said that he didn't know anything about growing cotton. But he had wanted to help, so he had referred the question to an acquaintance, who explained that the issue was more complicated than it initially seemed. The acquaintance had sent Joe an article that described the Nobelists' research in lay persons' terms. Joe had passed it on to Samuel.

'I had no idea it would cause any trouble,' he said.

'Apparently at his school anything can.'

'So the kid had his teacher up against the wall, huh?' Joe laughed.

He sounded as if he were proud of his son. This irked Alina. Sending papers from the other side of the Atlantic was easy, but it was she who had to deal with the fallout from the teachers.

'His report wasn't on the assigned topic.'

'It sounds to me as if Samuel is growing up to be a man who knows how to think for himself.'

'His teacher would disagree.'

Joe thought Samuel was too smart. He means *for Finnish schools*, Alina thought. He was just being too circumspect to take the sentence to its conclusion.

'It'll be easier by grad school,' Joe said.

Alina didn't respond. She had no interest in initiating the conversation that would lead to Joe arguing how Samuel would get a better education in the United States. Finland had the best school system in the world, but Alina didn't feel like getting into this discussion.

'You do understand that as a member of my family, Samuel would get a free ride at my university?'

'Joe...'

'I'm just making sure you know.'

'Thanks for the concern. You've made sure. Thanks for being so thoughtful.'

'It would an incredible opportunity for him to do something. To become part of something.'

'To do something *there*. To become part of something *there*. To move his entire life *there*.'

'Alina, I know you didn't want to move from Finland, and no one is asking you to. But are you totally sure that—'

'I've told Samuel.'

'You have?'

'That he wouldn't have to pay tuition. Yes.'

'And he knows that means forty thousand dollars a year?'

'Joe, getting into the best American university possible isn't at the top of everyone's list of priorities.'

'Of course not, but—'

'Not everyone sees life as an academic rat race! There is value in other things than working all the time!'

'Liina, please. I don't have any ambitions for Samuel. I just want him to be aware of the opportunities available to him.'

'What did your grandfather always used to say you academic guys are? Weightlifters who train one muscle their entire lives? That's not what Samuel wants for himself!'

She could hear the cries of the jackdaws from outside, in two languages: *Mistä sinä sen tiedät?* How would you know? And: *Entä jos haluaakin?* What if he does?

She was so furious when she hung up that she swore out loud. As she was brushing her teeth that evening, she realized she was pressing down on the toothbrush so hard her gums ached. Joe was so America-obsessed and patronizing – why did she let it get under her skin? – but most of all she was infuriated by the fact that she was so small and vulnerable that she couldn't control her feelings. That a person whom she hadn't seen in God knows how many years could continue to elicit this sort of reaction from her, every time. Goddammit! If she didn't watch herself, something else would crawl out from under the irritation, and that something else she didn't have the energy to deal with now.

Even the next day, she was forced to calm herself at the playground as she pushed Taisto on the merry-go-round and Ukko napped in the stroller. She and Joe had their personal views, neither was right or wrong. They just saw things different ways. Samuel would decide for himself what he wanted to do with his life. And whatever that was, it would turn out well. Look how far he had come since the disastrous years immediately after Joe had abandoned them. It felt like a miracle: they made it after all, the two of them, even though for the longest time she had been alone and lost.

The weird thing was that once Joe left, life with a small child turned effortless overnight, even though she had more to do and deal with. If Joe hadn't pulled his weight when it came to helping out with the housework and the child, did it make it easier then to have to take care of everything by herself?

Oddly enough, it did.

She accepted everything as her responsibility, because there was no one else. She could focus on the laundry, the grocery shopping, and her sweet, serious child without arguments, disappointment, or bitterness over who was going to do what. Occasionally she wondered if she could have arrived at this point without driving her husband completely away.

Once Joe left, there wasn't enough money for anything, even though Alina and Samuel moved into a cheap one-bedroom miles from Töölö. And if the colorless, drizzly days at the edge of the wet sandbox had felt lonely as she waited for her husband to come home from work, after the divorce it felt like she had lost her final connection to the World and to Life, which for everyone else advanced along satisfactory, adult channels towards professional and personal realization. In the evenings, after she had gotten Samuel to sleep, the longing condensed and solidified into something urgent, something almost physical in the silent apartment; she blamed herself for Samuel's speech impediments and missed Joe so badly that it felt like something was trying to force its way out of her chest. Night after night, she had to stop herself from picking up the phone, so she wouldn't sob to her startled ex-husband on the other side of the Atlantic that she had made the biggest mistake in her life, that she could never love anyone else, that she would stop giving him a hard time, would buy flights for herself and Samuel first thing in the morning, if Joe would just take them back. I don't

care, we can live in an RV in your driveway! Take us back! On nights
like those, she had to bury her face deep in the pillow so her crying
wouldn't wake Samuel.

She had wanted to stay at home with her son until he was three. No
one in the outside world seemed to be missing her.

It was Julia who finally said it: 'You have to go to back to work or
you'll go crazy.'

Alina was offended by her friend's way of knowing what was best
for her. Julia's views felt particularly hurtful when Alina silently
repeated them to herself at night, alone in her queen-size bed, where
no single man would never make the mistake of straying again, and
that must have been officially designated a sex-free zone by now. Alina
had gotten the impression that Julia was secretly pleased that Alina's
marriage hadn't lasted. Not that it looked like Julia's would be lasting
long, either: in the spring, she had joined the urban explorers club
at her company, started wearing dark lipstick and dramatic shoes,
and 'sharing experiences' with her colleagues during weekend nights
out on the town that continued into the wee hours. A little later, she
had confessed to Alina that she'd been having a sexual affair with a
married man for some time now, her boss, whom she screwed regularly
on 'business trips' and, in her tawdriest moments, after work in the
back seat of his car.

'It's horrible,' Julia said, pinching the bridge of her nose between
her thumb and forefinger and shaking her head; she was a horrible
person and just thinking about what she had done made her sick to
her stomach, but she felt like a woman for the first time in her life.
Which of course made everything a thousand times more horrible
and arousing. Julia had let the man do things to her in bed (*and in his
car*, Alina thought) that she couldn't even suggest to Robert, simply
couldn't: no, even though she wanted them, and not just wanted,
needed, as a woman. Julia had to put a stop to it, had to, if only for
the children, first thing tomorrow, she knew that better than anyone.
Julia was so mixed up, didn't know if she had lost her mind... of
course she had, she could see it now in the way Alina was looking at
her, but she hadn't known life could feel like this!

The man was the best thing that had ever happened to her.

Julia's extra-marital relationship was an affront to Alina, as was the
fact that her friend seemed to have grown longer-limbed and slimmer,

her eyes more soulful, that she seemed to have found that inner radiance Alina had always been lacking. Every nocturnal groan of the pipes and nightly pop of the radiators announced that Alina would never find anyone ever again. No one would want a bitter, asexual woman like her, who drove every sensible man away – six thousand kilometers away! And meanwhile, Julia had two.

Alina hadn't wanted to see her for months after the confession, because the affair demonstrated that Julia hadn't understood a thing about what had happened in Alina's marriage, even though Julia was supposed to be her best friend. Nor did Alina want to hear any more about how she was 'shrivelling up like some martyr and denying herself everything,' and 'wasn't using any of her gifts and talents.' This was even more offensive than the thought of an overly red-lipped Julia awkwardly helping her married employer enter her in the back seat of his Benz.

Alina regretted that she had neglected all her other friendships during her time at home with Samuel. It had happened too easily, without her even trying. Aside from Julia, this stage of life hadn't come for Alina's friends until years later. Plus she had wanted to concentrate on Joe, to ensure he would settle into life in Finland.

The thought of going back to work contained a distinct enticement: a Get Out of the Muddy Sandbox Free card. There was nothing tempting about the Mercedes-Benz – the guy had kids, after all, two of them – but a gold-tone Moccamaster with two (!) pots – so many adults in one place! – the office coffee kitty, the older colleague who'd seen it all and griped that someone hadn't turned on the dishwasher again.

An office break room sounded like paradise.

Samuel's going to be two soon, Julia had said. He needs company his own age. *He needs company.*

After that, something hot seemed to be released inside Alina, and the next week, as she helped her whining two-year-old shovel wet sand into molds shaped like crabs and ships – it seemed to rain every single day that fall – she caught herself mentally formulating the serious talk when she would inform her solemn-faced son in his Mickey Mouse ears that life as he had known it was coming to an end.

Getting a job was, of course, mission impossible: everyone in the country had just been fired, including those people who knew how to do anything, and the rest would be getting the boot during the upcoming year, if there was any believing the evening news. The mark had been devalued, then cut loose to float freely, whatever that meant, and the reverberations of companies toppling one after the other and bank directors shooting themselves carried up to her politically and socially disconnected apartment. She had a university degree that was worthless, she didn't know how to do anything, she didn't have any work experience, and she only spoke six languages, two of them merely passably. The fact that she'd gotten a laudatory on her thesis, as Julia never failed to remind her, simply went to prove how arbitrary the university's grading systems were.

Attentive to details, she was, and conscientious – but who wasn't? There had to be tens of thousands of good little straight-A girls like her in Finland.

The fact that the job was actually offered to her felt like ultimate proof that the world was ruled by chance and caprice and that horrendous miscarriages of justice must have been a daily occurrence on the job market. Her degree didn't have anything to do with anything, especially not municipalities, pensions, or investing. At the job interview, she made it clear from the second she opened her mouth that it would be to the employer's advantage to hire anyone else they could get their hands on and was stunned into silence when the interviewer said, 'Why don't you start by telling us a little about yourself?' She told them that she wasn't sure if she wanted a job at all, let alone at the Municipal Pensions Fund, which she knew nothing about, and that, due to her education in the natural sciences, she would presumably be a poor fit for the work they were offering.

Or so she remembered after the fact. She'd been so nervous that once she made it downstairs and out the front door she realized her legs were shaking. She had no idea what she had said, but she was sure that anyone else would have done better.

When the phone rang, she was surprised. She had already put the interview out of her mind as a total failure, shameful evidence of how much better she would have to prepare the next time.

At the time she began working as a planner in the Research and Workplace Development team of the Competences and Coping Strategies unit of the Municipal Pensions Fund, the country's foreign exchange reserves had been depleted and municipal welfare budgets had been slashed by billions. She applied her mascara on dark winter mornings, absolutely positive that today would be the day her temporary position proved too good to be true; she would be told to find work in her own field, to go study, say, noradrenaline metabolism in fish at a research center whose discretionary funding had been terminated and that never would have hired her during the good times due to her lack of intellectual rigor. The locally owned clothing store where Alina tried to buy her first I'm an Adult, Take Me Seriously outfit for work, had gone under. The post office, photo studio, bookstore, and bank had all disappeared from the shopping center, and the walls of the vacantly grinning storefronts were now covered in the incomprehensible messages of adolescents that were apparently called graffiti. A dive bar whose name celebrated unemployment and being broke had opened where the bookstore used to be, selling pints of beer more cheaply than ever. On her way to work and the supermarket, Alina would note that the former owner of the sporting goods store, a mother of three who lived in stairwell B of her building, had begun parking herself at this pub starting first thing in the morning.

Capital had been unshackled to move freely, because it was to everyone's advantage, and the country had collapsed. Oil no longer flowed from the Soviet Union, and no one was interested in the icebreakers Finland used to build for the communists – or in Finnish shoes, shirts, or industrial machinery. That's why Painful Decisions were necessary. A current affairs show reported that the director of the SKOP bank had warned a decade ago that the national economy would suffer a staggering blow, because the financial institutions had started granting credit to securities traders and getting involved in the business themselves. But the same show featured another economist, who explained that the director's analysis was completely off the mark and ideologically biased and didn't have anything to do with anything. It was dangerous to start politicizing things during crises of this magnitude.

The spirit of the times seemed to be best crystallized in the reedy voice of the man who sang *it's a dog-eat-dog world* with a wonderful optimism, like a madman about to drive his car off a cliff, not knowing or caring what he was doing. People roared along with his song 'Armotonta menoa' at the dive bar in a rising state of inebriation every afternoon, and this was the image that always arose to Alina's mind, even years later, when she thought about the period after Joe left her and heard that Finns were known around the world for their capacity

for hard work. Hearing the sodden laughter of adults in the middle
of the day, Alina thought her head would explode.

How can we afford this? Wasn't the country in unprecedented financial straits? Wasn't this the moment when they needed the Spirit
of the Winter War?

Yet somehow Painful Decisions and the Spirit of the Winter War did
not require Alina's termination, which astonished her every passing
day. Cheeks throbbing with guilt, she would look away as the majority of fifty-year-olds dejectedly cleaned out their desks, hugged
their coworkers, and shut the door behind them without a glance at
their younger colleagues. Fifty-year-olds were *still young*, and *during
these difficult times it was important to remember that*: they had that
experience and valuable expertise, that *tacit knowledge* that would be
of *inestimable worth* when the country rose out of its plight. Every
exaggeration in the farewell speeches resonated with the collective
shame of those present; it was unlikely that any of those let go would
ever find work again.

But what were you going to do with fifty-year-olds? After all, they
already had one foot in the grave.

She had to wake Samuel up every morning while he was still fast
asleep and it was still dark outside. As she photocopied reports, she
found it difficult justifying her choices to herself: wouldn't it make
more sense for her to be at home with her little boy, especially since
the people for whom she photocopied the reports never read them?
But these flirtations with the thought of going back to being a stay-
at-home mom were based in the counterfactual assumption that she'd
be a stable role model for her child, energetic and brimming with new
ideas every day, dying fabric with natural materials or setting up soccer
skills courses out in the yard, or in case of rain, molding little animals
out of homemade Play-Doh with her son, humming all the while.
The truth was, that before she went back to work she had snapped at
Samuel with increasing peevishness, spent her nights brooding over
her failures as a woman, a mother, and member of society, and been
actively bitter with Julia, who was doing – in a car?! – the exact same
thing to her nice, reliable husband as Alina had been afraid Joe had
been doing to her.

Alina forced herself to not think about the hours Samuel spent at
day care, which regularly stretched beyond what she had promised

herself. An expert in early child education had just said on television that leaving a child at day care too long was the worst thing you could do to him or her. The discussion didn't say how many hours a day was too much, but regardless, Alina was sure Samuel ended up on the wrong side of the limit. And then, according to another expert, the most damaging thing you could do to a child was place them in day care too young, which the first expert felt was of no significance; this had been known for twenty years, apparently, but scientific facts were being confused for ideological purposes. Alina knew she had been too meek her whole life, and even now, most days she was incapable of more than keeping one eye on the ticking clock; the day care would be closing soon and here she was, still filling out mandatory paperwork for the members of the Working Life Development steering committee and the Public-Sector White-Collar Employees negotiating team that, because of meeting schedules, had to be sent out today. Day care group size limits had recently been abolished; what was needed now was the Spirit of the Winter War.

She still had a hard time remembering Samuel as a young child, because it immediately called up images of herself as an uptight, unhappy, insecure mother who made mistakes at one-minute intervals, and wasn't even able to get her defiant toddler into his rain suit without losing her temper. Every morning was forty minutes too short, and a two-year-old had no concept of time, being on time, or being late. When you raised your voice at a two-year-old, he would slam on the brakes for good. Every morning she was able to get Samuel to day care without tears and herself to the office on time was a victory. Things weren't made any easier by the day care staff's habit of reminding her that, *for his age, Samuel still had quite a number of developmental tasks to master* as well as *lapses in verbal fluency* which in all likelihood *seemed to be psychogenic in origin.*

'Psychogenic' was the professionals' nice–nasty way of saying that it was the mother's fault.

Samuel would in all likelihood be a special-needs child, one of the women had stated in a voice that seemed to lack the tiniest shred of humanity. What gave them the right to spout off like that? Alina wondered to herself later, and regretted not giving the woman a piece of her mind.

Her heart broke every time she saw her son, a year after his father left, carefully drawing leopards, cats, bulls, buses, and bulldozers, her three-year-old writing the word that she had to spell out for him: D, A, D. Her heart broke as looked at the mirror-image S in the boy's own name, which he had learned to write so he could sign the drawings he sent to his father. At one point there had been drawings to send every week, and in the end Alina discreetly stashed some in sealed envelopes in her desk drawers, because she wanted to protect Joe from the constant barrage, as much as she felt he deserved every ounce of guilt he was capable of feeling about the situation.

But that little boy's feelings: where would he stash them?

In hindsight, that period felt like a surreal nightmare.

Alina's coworkers also thought it was unfair that budget cuts were being targeted at children, seniors, and the mentally ill, but these conversations inevitably ended in head-shaking and sighs. That's just the way things were, evidently, in this economic situation. The country had to consider what it could afford.

She had a crushing, burning longing for Joe, the brazen, wonderful, unbearable American who would have immediately rolled up his sleeves if he were still here: Let's set up a little league baseball team for the kids! Let's start a weekly kids' book group! Run by the elderly! Let's found a theater group for the unemployed that performs at hospitals! Stop waiting for the municipality, the government, and God to rescue you, goddammit, you can see for yourself they're not coming! That's what Joe would have said, that was Joe's good side and bad side, he got frustrated, started doing things himself, immediately. Joe was impatient and couldn't stand things being done the way they always had if the outcome wasn't the best possible.

When she realized what he would have said, Alina started thinking: mightn't there be something they could actually do? Couldn't they, say, set up a day care for the kids themselves? She suggested it to her next-door neighbor, a hairdresser who had gone out of business, been trapped between mortgages, and now smoked on her balcony in the middle of the day, hair unwashed. Alina believed Samuel would have done better in a more free-form setting with other kids from the building than in municipal day care, where the adults seemed stressed out. There were a lot of neighbor kids that Samuel knew and got along with, and there were at least a dozen adults in the building who were unemployed. How do we want our children to spend their days? Let's agree on it, and that's the program for the day care. We can set up shifts and we all chip in what we can. Everyone participates, even an hour a week would be enough. Alina could easily watch the kids in the evenings or Saturdays.

The hairdresser took a tired drag of her cigarette, rubbed her make-up-free eyes and said, yeah, that might be nice, in a tone that meant it was never going to happen. Later that day, Alina saw her carrying home two big plastic bags of beer from the store.

Alina then remembered what Joe once said: 'The problem with you Finns is that you don't think anything is worth doing – except the things you've always done. And then you just adjust to it, even if it's the worst fucking deal in the world.'

She would have completely forgotten what life had been like in the years before Henri, Ukko, and Taisto and her first book if she hadn't kept a diary.

As a self-respecting divorcée, she had gone through a colorful series of lousy psychotherapists, sleazy lounge lizards, and – once she got to the 2000s – the bachelors skulking around online dating services, who wore sweater vests, painted miniature soldiers, and didn't look her in the eye during dates. She was told in the muffled home offices of therapists, downtown medical centers, strobe-lit discos, and the café of the Academic Bookstore, that her problem was an unprocessed relationship with her father, a neurochemical imbalance, chronic abandoned woman syndrome and a traumatic relationship to her own femininity. Each of these analyses was undoubtedly accurate, but it rarely felt as if acquiring this information had been worth the trouble of arranging a babysitter.

In order to get over her divorce and failure as a woman, mother, and citizen of the world, she allowed a doctor to write her a prescription for fluoxetine, which had apparently 'blown off the roof in America.' The enthusiastic doctor spoke of the 'legendary Prozac,' even though it wasn't called Prozac in Finland. Alina preferred not to have her neurochemistry tampered with, but because her resistance towards the legendary new Prozac that wasn't called Prozac appeared to offend the doctor, obediently took the pills for two weeks as a treatment for her divorce, threw up every single day, and left work early with a pounding headache. Going off the pills without consulting a doctor was not allowed, so Alina paid a second 356 marks plus 34.80 in office fees to inform the uncertainly smiling doctor that she had flushed the legendary Prozac down the toilet. She told the doctor, whose smile had grown stiff, that she had been pleased to discover that the dizziness and headaches stopped immediately, and as a matter of fact had come to the conclusion that she wasn't perhaps so seriously depressed as to require a prescription. The doctor was sorry in a way that let Alina know she had failed as a patient, and talked her into trying another medication, exactly the same but totally different, unbelievably effective, close to if not quite as roof-blowing as the previous one. It remained unclear to Alina how a drug could be more or less chemically identical yet different, but maybe she didn't need to understand. She accepted the prescription and on her control appointment smoothly assured the doctor that she had started the medication and was doing wonderfully. It certainly was a good and effective drug. After the fact, she was surprised by how naturally she had lied to his face. But she hadn't wanted to offend the doctor; he was doing his best. Alina just couldn't take a single more failure in her life. And the doctor seemed happy, because he'd been of some help after all. He promised that he'd be happy to help Alina in the future, too, if, down the road, she ever felt like a divorced single parent again, or that raising a child alone was difficult.

She had started falling for a considerate and well-dressed bisexual, who also seemed to like her. But on the third date he told her that he had come to realize that his bisexuality was a transitional identity. Now he understood, thanks to Alina, that by dating women he'd been trying to make his homosexuality more palatable to his parents. He was very grateful to her.

She was already on her knees in a one-bedroom apartment in Kerava that reeked of cigarette smoke, about to take the small and peculiarly shaped organ of a man named Just Call Me Jorma into her mouth – he had forced his way up to the same table at a cruise-ship-tacky disco and wouldn't leave – when at the last minute, luckily, she had the sense to tell Just Call Me Jorma, thanks, let's be in touch. She left in such a rush that she forgot her good spring coat, which irked her for years after.

For a full two years, she had squirmed in the offices of a pointy-nosed psychotherapist whose face vaguely resembled an angry hamster, trying to help the thearapist process his clearly unresolved feelings towards Jews. But no matter how hard Alina tried, at first delicately and in the end rather directly, she wasn't able to disabuse the therapist of his unshakable belief that she was interested in Joe in part or even primarily because he was Jewish. Again and again, every session came back around to Joe's Jewishness, the exoticism of a man from a foreign country, when what Alina wanted to understand was why she was so apologetic and dismissive of herself as a woman and a human being, and was there some way she could possibly rid herself of unnecessary insecurities, and if so, how? The therapist was also interested in Alina's experiences with other men: were they also immigrants? Did skin color make a difference to her? Had Alina ever thought that she could date, for instance, a Muslim? Had Alina ever thought why she, as a woman, sought out these sorts of relationships specifically? When the therapist didn't seem to be responding to their chats, Alina finally decided to end the treatment after a promising two-year start. Smiling rigidly, the therapist shook her hand, wished her luck, and mentioned in parting that quitting therapy was often a sign of permanent personality disorder.

But for the most part, the years passed with Samuel, at work, and alone, and those days were steadily exhausting, lonely, ordinary: she took Samuel to day care, kindergarten, and school, went to the office and the supermarket, made macaroni casserole, helped Samuel with his homework, scrubbed grass-stained sweatpants, scoured the remains of dried oatmeal from the pot, watched television, ate cinnamon roll dough straight from the freezer, and cried. She fretted about her boy, who month after month drew cheetahs for the father he would never meet. Maybe the boy knew it himself, because he would get stuck in the middle of every word, looking pained, before violently wrenching himself on to the next syllable. Alina had often thought that it was a miracle Samuel hadn't permanently lost his mind – not because of his own feelings, but because she was incapable of living a single moment without worrying.

She would never touch a child-rearing guide again for as long as she lived, but she knew with every fiber of her being that there was no way her relentless, apprehensive unhappiness could be anything but damaging to her boy.

But children survived. It was a miracle, pure and simple, like every green bud in the spring, every sprout thrusting through the soil. Nor was life pure suffering, of course: she had frequently thought that she and Samuel had grown so close because they had been forced to make their way through those years as a team.

Even though they hadn't seen as much of each other since the fall following Samuel's high-school graduation, things would eventually go back to normal. She knew it.

And luckily the years seemed to have formed a sufficient transitional rite to post-divorce middle age that when, at the age of thirty-six, Alina happened to meet Henri, who had broken up with his girlfriend three years before, it didn't even occur to her to pretend, try, or hope that the encounter would lead to anything. Their shared moment at the travel guide shelf at the library was natural and tender, even funny, in an unintentionally comic way, so when Henri asked Alina if she came to the library often, she started to, half-secretly from herself. And when they eventually, after far too long, bumped into each other again, delaying things felt pointless.

Henri was the embodiment of tolerance and compassion, the most considerate person Alina had ever met. She remembered wondering for the first two weeks if men like this really existed. Henri was incredibly calm, thoughtful, dared to face his own weaknesses and talk about them, didn't smoke or drink too much, had nothing against children or marriage, even for gays, didn't try to dress like a twenty-year-old, and didn't cultivate an 'ironic' mustache. Henri didn't have pinky rings or gold chains or crazy ex-girlfriends who screamed outside the window, jacked up on speed: 'Who the fuck is that bitch you have in there? I'm going to fucking kill her!' (Alina had known in the taxi line that she shouldn't have said yes when the personal trainer who'd just been fired had invited her over for a gin fizz, but sometimes the loneliness felt so unbearable, so suffocating, that she acted against her better instincts.)

Henri did his share, even more, with the boys. This wouldn't have been necessary – after her failed marriage, Alina had accepted the fact that men were not to be trusted in this regard – but suddenly she got more than she bargained for.

Alina was perfectly aware that Henri's air of accommodation, which some might have characterized as effeminate, wouldn't have necessarily sufficed as an erotic jackpot in all earlier stages of her life. If you wanted a big, growling brute in a leather jacket, who had no interest in the jabbering of women and swept you off your feet every single time, Henri was not the man for you. To her surprise, Alina found herself occasionally seeing this man, too, the one in the leather jacket, her personal secret, who didn't talk and whose coarse stubble chafed her skin when they kissed. Alina didn't see leather jacket guy often, but on the occasional lazy Sunday afternoon, when she was alone at home, often right after she'd woken up from a nap and everything still felt like a dream, the experience was so perfect that she wouldn't have given it up for anything. No doubt Henri had one too: a woman, young, moist-lipped, imaginary. Maybe Henri even met this moist-lipped woman on some of those evenings when the boys were snuffling in their beds, the lights were out, and Henri was moving inside Alina.

And as she reflected on this, Alina remembered the girl who had lain next to her in her marriage bed years ago. Alina understood that at some earlier point in her life she would have let the relationship with Henri fall apart over this; now she felt a simple, sheer sense of joy that she had the sense not to make life any more difficult for herself than it already was.

Another reason everything had gone more smoothly the second time around was she hadn't had to worry about money. The world could be a surprisingly different place for two employed adults than it was for a single parent.

What Alina did mourn in hindsight was not having been able to enjoy Samuel's childhood at all. It felt as if she had passed through a critical period of her son's life in some kind of haze. When she thought back to Taisto's infancy, she remembered the unhurried sunny afternoons when they would both wake from their naps and she'd lower her face towards his bald pate, inhale the warm scent of drowsy baby. They took long summertime walks in the park; she and Henri would kiss on the grass as Taisto slept in the stroller. When Ukko was a baby, the daily wordless conversations with her infant had been heart-stopping, the four-toothed grin and irresistibly chubby cheeks, the smile that tickled her brain. This is what it was like having children – your whole life filled with light.

From time to time she felt an inexplicable tinge of sorrow or loss, as if she were missing someone, but on the whole, those was the happiest days of her life to date.

Was infancy perfect and wonderful the second time around for everyone? When you knew how to take it easy?

With Ukko and Taisto, things had rolled along at their own momentum, despite Ukko's special problems and diagnosis. In contrast, her memories of Samuel's childhood, hazy and hole-ridden from sleeplessness, emanated nothing but stress and disappointment.

Yet it was hard to see how she could have been any stronger and more adult than she had been. At the time, there hadn't been even the tiniest glimmer of what lay ahead: an egalitarian relationship, a wonderfully complex blended family, and an interesting job. The angst caused by Joe's departure would have been eased by the knowledge that what awaited her was not bitter loneliness, but satisfying middle age, where she had permission to wear flowing orange caftans and big wooden beads, to feel like she had learned a thing or two about life and not think twice about how wide jean legs were supposed to be this year. And in which she knew herself and her body. She couldn't fathom having once envied those young, insecure women – children – who wandered the streets, bewildered, trying to hide their fear behind a tough attitude and clothes that were too tight.

When it came down to it, the divorce had been Joe's fault. She had needed support and intimacy that he had been incapable of giving her.

But what if you'd been different, too, roared a revving truck engine as she drove past a construction site, *than the person you are now? Would you still be together, would you have been happy, now that you're a different person, too?*

But she wasn't, and they weren't.

When she read the first interviews in the magazines, Alina looked at herself in astonishment, as if she were a different person. Was this really what she'd become?

These days, she had a hard time recalling the moment when she came up with the idea of interviewing women. It had seemed a daunting task – what made her think she knew how to write, for one? And where would the time come from? The boys were one and three, at the age where there was an overabundance of destructive energy and a distinct lack of sense. And yet for some reason, it was plain as day that she must start to write: if she didn't do this now, she would be giving up on everything, for the rest of her life. How enticing, how pleasurable, the thought still sounded! To stop struggling, to allow herself to go totally slack – to sink slowly beneath the surface, into full-blown mommyhood, into the mundane soup of evening glasses of white wine, mating-themed reality shows, and rare moments of unsatisfying sex, to perhaps learn to soften the keenest edge of disappointment with regular, progressively increasing doses of Xanax. Oh! How warm that embrace would be!

The thought simmered for some time without leading to action. Until eventually – as she kept running into presumably intelligent Finnish friends' remarkably dense thicket of anti-American prejudices – she'd had to admit to herself that the few years spent with an American spouse had changed her more than she'd admitted. Whether or not she wanted to, she saw Finland and Finns differently now.

Contrary to anything she could have imagined when she was married to Joe, she found herself defending Americans and their curious customs, even taking umbrage when they were misunderstood. Maybe it was impossible to be in such intimate, prolonged contact with another world without it changing your own.

For some time, she was held back by the notion that her personal experiences wouldn't be of interest to anyone. They were the experiences of one, solitary individual; we all have them. After the disappointment of a failed marriage had stopped hurting so much it drowned out everything else, she hadn't felt the need to prove anything to anyone. But one morning she had had less work than usual at the Municipal Pensions Fund, and that morning changed everything. There was something so utterly senseless and serendipitous about the whole thing that in hindsight it could even have seemed beautiful if it hadn't involved such profound shame.

She had gone to the break room on the second floor for a cup of coffee and picked up a glossy magazine from the previous fall that was lying on the table. On the cover, a TV journalist who had already broken up from her latest partner since the issue came out was still glowing with the bliss of new-found love.

Thumbing through the magazine, Alina came across an interview with a theologian concerned that people no longer understood what sanctity meant. According to him, and in contrast to what most people seemed to believe, sanctity had nothing to do with rigid moral strictures or resisting change, but acknowledging that something exists that is more important than an individual and their personal desires.

The first thing to come to mind then were the *I love me* ads she had seen around town, promoting some cosmetics-slash-jewelry expo, but then she remembered the church's online forum. It wasn't mentioned in the article, but Alina had just heard about it somewhere. The church had set up a website where you could log in to ask questions about religion.

She felt that something was missing from her life, something had always been off, and she couldn't explain it and didn't think any of her friends or coworkers would understand. For a long time, she had imagined the feeling was shame stemming from the divorce, longing for intimacy, and fear of growing old. The feeling had passed when she had met Henri, but later it crept back. She remembered how, when she became pregnant again, she had thought the baby would make life so full, so chaotic in a good way, that she'd forget the longing for good – who had time for existential crises when she was raising three children in a blended family? – and how disappointed she'd been when she hadn't after all. The younger boys had been one and three when she went back to work and sent them off to day care without the tiniest twinge of conscience; she'd already spent far too much time at home to feel guilty about needing a life of her own. But going back to work hadn't rid her of the feeling that somehow she was missing out on something. Maybe it was time for her to reach out to the church. Alina knew before she logged on that the church's forum had been created expressly for rotten churchgoers such as herself. But religion was a personal matter, after all, at least in Finland – what could be more suitable than to practice it through your data connection, from home, when it suited you best?

She read a few of the recent posts. They picked apart passages from the Bible in detail. One contributor was concerned that true Christianity was dying out: liberal women pastors wanted to destroy the apostolic tradition and homosexualize the population; you no longer heard the Word of the Living God at church. Another had cut and pasted dozens of newspaper headlines about bombings, terrorist attacks, and murders that proved Islam was a religion of violence and subjugation. Someone else suggested this had to do with the gay gas being pumped through the ventilation ducts at public swimming pools.

Alina hesitated for a moment but then thought: what could it hurt to try? This was a church forum; a serious question would surely elicit a serious response. She double-checked the instructions. Yes, this discussion board 'is a place for church employees to converse with all those who are interested.'

Ask anything you want about matters of the spirit.
Church staff will listen, discuss, and provide information on issues related to Christianity and the church.

Well...
It wasn't like she had anything to lose.
As a test, Alina wrote a brief message explaining her longing and wondering if it was religious in nature. She said she remembered her pastor from Conformation camp talking about mankind's longing for God.

It took her a long time to think of an alias, but because she couldn't come up with anything that felt natural, in the end she decided on her first name. It felt a little awkward but honest. Which, it crossed her mind, perhaps described who she was as a person.

The first reply came quickly:

So if you're hungry, does that have something to do with God, too?

She considered how she was supposed to interpret this response. Whoever wrote it was probably mocking her. It was someone who had never felt the same way, clearly. But Alina wanted to find someone to talk with, preferably a church employee, so she decided not to let this harassment get under her skin. If she responded politely, maybe someone else, someone thoughtful, would read it and reply.

Maybe, who knows...

Alina added a smiley at the end, to seem friendlier. The reply came in seconds, this time from a different name:

Wow... I gotta say, it sounds like your 'faith' is on a real firm footing there. Next time I stub my toe I'll wonder if Mickey Mouse had a hand in it. :)

Then a third person chimed in:

Why don't you religion lovers go tell your stories somewhere where they won't confuse the rest of us? Some people are gullible and might take your BS seriously.

Alina was stunned. Wasn't this supposed to be a church discussion board? Who were these people? The next reply had appeared, signed by **THE BODY OF THE LIVING CHRIST IS THE:**

For he saith, I have heard thee in a time accepted, and in the day of salvation have I succoured thee: behold, now is the accepted time; behold, now is the day of salvation. (2 Cor. 6:2)! Repeat the following prayer:
'Heavenly Father, I come to you in the name and blood of Christ. Forgive me my sins because of your grace, and Christ, dear Jesus, be Lord of my life. I turn away from sin and I want to live for you. I believe you died for my sins, to give me life. I accept you as the Lord of my heart and my personal savior! Amen.'
If you said this prayer with all your heart, then you have just been born again from above. Your sins have been forgiven! God is now your Father and you are His child. I proclaim you free of sin in the name of the work of Christ's work.
In the name of the Father, the Son, and the Holy Ghost, Amen.

Alina realized that coming to the site had been a huge mistake. There was no one here she had any connection to. She would just send one more quick post explaining why she was leaving the discussion:

Thank you for the advice, **THE BODY OF THE LIVING CHRIST IS THE,** *but I don't know if I'm quite there yet. I really just wanted to see what it's like here and maybe talk with someone who understands how I'm feeling. But it looks like I came to the wrong place. :) I hope you all have a nice day!*

She ended it with a smiley and hoped that no one would be offended by her leaving so rudely mid-conversation. She closed the browser and started looking up information for a report that she needed to finish before tomorrow.

But then she started to think.

What if someone else had replied? Someone serious? The pastor from her home parish wouldn't be monitoring the site, if he even worked for the church anymore. And yet she could see his bearded face as she re-opened the browser, and she remembered his heavy, coarse-looking wool sweater, navy blue, and how she had mentally snuggled up against its warmth alone in bed at night after she got home from camp. This time she remembered the website address by heart. She would just go have a quick peek.

Maybe one of the church employees would be like the pastor: fair, seemingly wise. Maybe they could even meet. Maybe she could talk with them face to face, get something out of religion she hadn't been ready for at the age of fifteen.

During Alina's absence, two more people had participated in the conversation, **Alina, I know** and **Sathityaeurus.**

Alina, I know
how you feel, because I've felt the same longing for heaven. At the time I was praying for my child, who was seriously ill, and she was healed. The doctors can't explain it, because it was a miracle. She had a serious illness, bone cancer, and now she's completely healthy.

Sathityaeurus
that's exactly how sick and stupid religious people are!! jesus christ, alina, have you also raised your kids to believe that all you have to do is pray and the lord jehovah nazarenus mormonius will heal you and you don't have to go to the hospital? what's so scary about

it? a blood transfusion? that would be awful! yuck, medicine!
scientifically researched knowledge that could even help! jesus
christ, i don't get your logic, you feel a tiny twinge and suddenly
you believe in tinkerbell. you're all so stupid you should be shot.

This was so far beyond the pale that Alina had written her reply
before she could think:

Excuse me, but I don't believe in miraculous healing or Tinkerbell.
You're talking about the experiences of a totally different person.
I find your tone offensive. Have a nice day.

She needed to get back to work, it was almost lunchtime, and before
that she needed to finalize a summary of the changes being proposed
to the laws governing pensions. But her heart was galloping and she
didn't want to close the browser, she wanted to see what **Sathityaeurus**
would come up with next. He responded almost immediately...

Sathityaeurus
Do you know what's offensive, Alina? What's offensive is mur-
dering hundreds of thousands of people in the name of religion.
What's offensive is not giving a burial plot to someone who has
worked and paid taxes his entire life without taking a single sick
day just because he doesn't belong to the church. What's offensive
is telling people fairy tales and pretending they're the truth. What's
offensive is feeding people someone's body and giving them his
blood to drink and teaching this cannibalistic ritual to children.
What's offensive is lying that someone has walked on water. What's
offensive is telling people that something that's pleasurable and
natural is a sin. If you came here looking for that kind of stuff,
there's no point calling someone offensive who argues logically
and justifies what he says. Go ahead and believe whatever shit
you want, but don't shove your crap down other people's throats.
Not everyone is as screwed up in the head as you are.

Come to me
all ye who believe, if ye ask, ye shall receive (pussy).
— layer on of hands

Below this there was a link Alina shouldn't have clicked, of course, which she didn't realize until it was too late, after she'd seen the screaming red close-ups of genital organs thrusting into each other on the monitor of the Municipal Pensions Fund's computer.

She spent almost an hour choosing the words for her reply to **Sathityaeurus**, who hadn't even existed for her before today. She had formed a clear mental image of him: an obese, bitter pensioner tapping away day and night with tobacco-stained fingers because his wife had left him and his kids hated his guts. She considered how best to take him down, which turns of phrase would hurt the intolerant **Sathityaeurus** deeply enough to jolt him out of his fog of incomprehension and into reality. After all, this wasn't only about her; it was about how other visitors to the site were being treated, too. It was to everyone's advantage that she talked a little sense into these sickos. She wrote her response and read it, added a few more piquant insults and took them out, then put them back in. In the end, she was satisfied with her polished reply, especially the bits that ruthlessly questioned **Sathityaeurus'** logic, and pointed out that, whether we like it or not, our lives are full of rituals, both those that derive from Christianity and those that don't, and above all Alina had not been shoving anything down anyone's throat and that **Sathityaeurus** had better wash his mouth out with soap and check his facts and take a good look in the mirror!

She posted the reply with a click and was pleased by how sharp it looked there on-screen. This was the best thing about the world these days, she realized, brimming with satisfaction: the meek and the cautious were no longer voiceless. She had always been one of those who came up with the snappiest replies when it was too late, after she had already lost and her opponent was long gone. Well, she wasn't going to lose anymore!

But **Sathityaeurus** never replied. *Well, where are you hiding?* Alina found herself writing. *Embarrassed by the gaps in your logic?*

Others had appeared in **Sathityaeurus'** place, though. **Awake, Whore of Babel!** pointed out that because Alina wasn't in the true faith and hadn't made a personal commitment to God, her soul would be damned. Alina needed to come to Yeshua of Nazareth, who was Lord of the Shabath. And then there was **Is This How…?**, who doubted the sincerity of her original post.

*So we're supposed to believe you came to this forum out of the
blue to sincerely ponder a theological cornerstones of Lutheran
revivalist doctrine... It just 'happened to pop into my head'...
Or might this be a theology student's morning devotional in
disguise... Is this how they're trying to force-feed the gospel
these days? Since the old tricks don't work anymore? There
aren't many people listening to the word at church, so you have
to come here... yawn!*

The liberal dyke woman pastors, to whom she clearly belonged,
had forced people to accept divorces and gay marriage, and bestiality
wasn't far behind. *What next, child molestation?* asked **Bow to Zion's
Bloody Bridegroom. HEADS OF THE CHURCH, WAKE UP!!** was
flabbergasted that Alina, this lesbian Lutheran pastor who had logged
in under a cowardly pseudonym, had even claimed to have an MSc.
Ha! You wouldn't find an MSc that stupid in a porn-mag fantasy!
What was wrong with Alina, anyway, why didn't she just come out
and say who she really was?

Alina missed lunch; she couldn't leave these astounding claims
about who she supposedly was uncorrected. And the 'global Muslim
conspiracy' to which she, Finland's largest newspaper, the Coca-Cola
company, and the Muslim Brotherhood allegedly belonged... were
there really people out there stupid enough to believe this stuff? And
as for telling her she didn't have an MSc... Well, she'd see about that.

She didn't have the sense to stop writing until she had revealed
that her children weren't Pentecostal, as **Pentecostalism is spiritual
violence** claimed; that her firstborn was barely even Christian, because
the boy's father wasn't Finnish. Alina didn't want to give away too
much, divulge details about herself that her attackers could use for
ammunition, but it was already too late. She realized that she had
sparked a completely new conversation: *Oh, so Alina had to get herself
some chocolate dick? :)* And: *Why aren't Finnish men good enough
for you? Too honest?* **Nonconformist** in particular seemed to get riled
up when Alina replied that her husband hadn't been any less honest
than anyone born in Finland, but it seemed like **Nonconformist** had
a few issues of his own he'd come online to process.

Muslim world domination was coming, he proclaimed, Multi-
culturalism meant multiplied social problems, even the prime minister

admitted that these days, and Finns had had enough of it, but thanks to foreigner-loving idiots like Alina tainted blood was still flowing into our country at an accelerating pace.

She gaped at her screen, dumbfounded. But the thread appeared to be continuing without any further input from her.

Nonconformist had no interest in offending. She seemed *like a decent, down-to-earth Finnish woman in other respects*, even though she'd *given in to the temptations of more exotic flesh*. It took a lot of hard work to find out things for yourself, continued **Trumpet of Truth**: you wouldn't find the truth in the newspapers, because difficult topics were silenced to death in them, since they didn't fit with the government's and the red-green media's official faggot-immigrant-lover worldview.

By now Alina was crying, even though she couldn't say why. Had it been **Nonconformist**'s last post?

These people mean nothing to me, she had to remind herself over and over: they're unfeeling monsters whose sole intent is to hurt. They had to be disappointed in their lives, marginalized, unhappy people who never left the house. It was better not to pay any attention to them, they didn't mean anything, there was no point in wasting tears on them.

Forgive them, she told herself in her office, as the tears streamed down her cheeks, for they know not what they do.

But she wasn't able to staunch the flow, and her coworkers asked what was wrong, and she went home hours before the workday ended.

Let me guess, Alina, began **Nonconformist** in his parting shot. *At first your husband was amazing and promised you the world but then he cheated on you and went back to where he came from. And you had to raise your mulatto brat by yourself. But he was so amazingly foreign!*

Who's laughing now, Alina?

Is he still amazing? Does your child still have an amazing father?

She would have dried her eyes when she got home and let the matter rest if she hadn't happened to watch a talk show during her lunch break the following day. A bishop was being interviewed about a school shooting that had taken place in Vihti a week earlier. A teenager – yet again – had taken a gun and killed his schoolmates, teachers, and then himself. The bishop said on television that it was important to support each other during this time of sorrow. The church even had an online forum, the bishop reminded the audience, a customer service channel where burdens could be shared. It was important to talk.

Alina's pulse accelerated, her palms started sweating, and she realized that she had risen from her chair in agitation.

That evening, she checked from her home computer: twenty-one new posts in the thread. She had decided in advance not to read them, any of them. She was surprised by how hard this was. She had to tear herself away, even though she knew reading them would cause her nothing but harm; it was as if something had taken her soul hostage.

It was fantastic that the church had a discussion forum. Everyone seemed to be in agreement about this – everyone except Alina. But she couldn't deny that ultimately, the forum had been of use to her, too. She had formally resigned from the church right after hearing the bishop's complacent, misleading words, and ever since mentally categorized her longing as existential loneliness in a postmodern society where people were too afraid to encounter each other.

The experience was so all-encompassing and absolute that upon resigning from the church she felt energized and invigorated, and the next morning, while the boys bawled, felt nothing but a lucid and present peace that felt almost spiritual. Since then, whenever she heard people talking about religion, she snorted and mentally spit in the direction of the church. After eating breakfast she called her highschool classmate Matti Hänninen whom she remembered having years earlier published a guide to picking berries and mushrooms, and asked what you were supposed to do if you weren't a writer but had come up with an idea for a nonfiction book.

After the workday, day care drop-offs and pickups, bedtime routines and tucking-ins, there wasn't a second left for writing, but she managed to steal a little by easing her Moomin DVD policies and putting every moment the children were asleep to use.

Julia had raised her eyebrows and scanned the ceiling as if searching it for an explanation when Alina told her about the book, commenting: 'That's pretty surprising.'

'How so?'

'I just never considered you the type to air her dirty laundry in public.'

Alina had refused to take offense. In the past she would have been incapable of doing so, but something about the divorce and life after Joe, the fact that she had survived, had changed the way she reacted to things. Not totally to anything, but a little to everything.

Due perhaps in part to her experiences on the church discussion board, she'd been afraid of becoming a target once the book came out. A researcher who studied attitudes about immigrants had said somewhere that she didn't always dare to discuss her research results publicly, because she had received so much hate mail. But unlike in the church discussion forum, Finland's craziest fundamentalists, radical atheists, and Islamo- and homophobes were not lining up in the bookstores waiting for Alina, brass knuckles at the ready. She had only one scare, when she received an email with a hostile-sounding subject. But as it turned out, the author wasn't angry with her for her red-green immigrant-loving attitudes but because she had only interviewed women.

The attention the book received, as paltry as it was, caught her off guard. No one, of course, recognized her on the street, nor did her name mean anything to almost anyone. But the book had been reviewed in the papers and talked about on radio. Three years had passed since then. A brief interview with her was even published in the country's biggest newspaper ('Immigrants are Individuals Too: Alina Heinonen, 43, examines multicultural marriage'). She'd shown up in a sweater at the first events she'd been invited to speak – an afternoon panel at the Multicultural Women's League, a TV talk show hosted by a female journalist – and later realized that she had looked like an insecure twenty-something and behaved apologetically, practically begging for someone to take her down. But it was at one of these events that it happened for the first time: out of the blue, one of the reporters, in an aside, called her an authority, and she was stunned to realize that she had arrived at a crossroads of sorts.

She was flabbergasted: was this how you became an authority?

'Finland's a pretty small country,' the journalist replied, when Alina tried to ask if there wasn't someone else who might have more to say, a researcher, or an activist from some NGO.

She still found it odd that journalists called and asked her what educated immigrants thought about university tuition, income tax rates, or getting rid of tax deductions for hiring help around the house. Shouldn't you be asking the immigrants themselves? Alina asked at first. She offered phone numbers, but the journalists said they weren't looking for a 'man-on-the-street's opinion' for this particular piece; they wanted a broader perspective. Or those who would have taken a phone number were offended that she didn't have a Zambian in her back pocket to offer them. She was just an amateur, she insisted: she was a neurobiologist who was a pencil pusher by trade because she didn't really know a thing about science. She had interviewed people for her book to amuse herself. To satisfy the need for a broader perspective, she tried to provide the contact information for a professor of sociology from the University of Pennsylvania, whom she had interviewed by phone and whose studies she had read by the towering stack, an individual who had spent years studying the experiences of highly educated immigrants in various societies, including all of the Nordic countries. There was another researcher in London, too, who knew all there was to know about the subject as a professional – a *real* researcher, unlike Alina, an amateur.

The journalists would sigh slightly at the other end of the line and then say, *hmm, thanks*, in a tone that immediately told you they wouldn't be calling Philadelphia, or London either.

'Do you happen to know any Finnish experts?' they'd ask.

'Do you know anyone in Finland I could interview?' they'd say.

'Do you suppose there's anyone at the University of Helsinki who could help?'

And: 'Could we come by with a photographer this afternoon?'

But that's exactly it, Julia explained to Alina that evening over a glass of wine, that's exactly why your book is so interesting: for once someone is saying something different from what those same three people have been droning on about for the past twenty years. Alina had forgiven her friend her initial dismissiveness. Julia's attitudes towards the book had changed markedly since it had been published and Alina was being interviewed by the press.

And she could choose this. If she wanted to, she could become an authority, which is what she, through some incomprehensible mechanism, already was in the eyes of some.

Evidently the only one who considered Alina a fraud was Alina herself.

The days seemed to have some meaning now, life a direction, no matter how arbitrarily selected. Her second book, *Puking in Pinstripes: Finns and Alcohol through the Eyes of Immigrants*, would be going to press soon. It had practically written itself from material left over from the previous one. According to the publisher, it was a sure-fire hit. The only thing that interested Finns even half as much as what the rest of the world thought of them was alcohol, and the book brought both of these topics together. The next book was already in the works, too. She was writing it in collaboration with a researcher from the university, an adjunct professor who had written her dissertation on the status of Russians in Finland and who was fortunately much more intelligent and educated than Alina. Being able to co-write was a relief, because the adjunct professor wouldn't let any idiocies slip into the book Alina would have to be ashamed of two years down the road. Besides, the adjunct professor would finally give the journalists the homegrown expert they were looking for.

As she turned onto the arterial, the thought suddenly occurred to her that she was – if she dared use the word, even silently – happy. The roadsides exposed by the melting snow still looked dirty, but the crocuses were already pushing up through the soil outside the apartment buildings. She had three sons, the first a content, independent adult and the younger two at a relatively easy stage. She was proud she had finished the book, although the idea had initially struck her as impossible. Life was busy – she still had a full-time job, now as a multicultural outreach planner at the Finnish Red Cross, and after work she had to go see her father – but maybe that was for the best, too. With Joe, it had felt like her husband's work was always robbing her of something; Henri's activities didn't seem to define her life unfairly in the same way.

She glanced at her watch. She would be with her dad in about fifteen minutes, right when visiting hours began.

THE CHILDREN ARE THE FUTURE

BALTIMORE, MD

No matter how many perspectives Joe tried to explain his situation from, Barb Fleischmann and Roddy didn't like the sound of the plan.

'I'm not misunderstanding you, am I, Joe?' Barb said in her departmental chair voice. 'Because if you're suggesting we start negotiating with vandals, with people who—'

'Barb, they're coming to my house!'

'Listen, Joe, I understand you may feel as if—'

'They're standing on my lawn, screaming into a megaphone at the crack of dawn on a weekend! They dumped a carcass in our yard!'

Roddy interjected, 'Wouldn't it be best to let campus security do their—'

'Like they have so far?'

Roddy shot him a look. The look meant: throwing a tantrum isn't going to help your cause.

'Joe, you're under a lot of stress now.'

'Which is only getting worse!'

'Joe, can we agree here and now that you won't—'

'No, we can't! My daughters are too scared to sleep at home! I can't concentrate on anything! And what are they going to come up with next? I have to do something.'

'Why don't we consider Barb taking over one of your courses and—'

'No! You're not going to take a single fucking course from me!'

Barb and Roddy exchanged lightning-fast, nearly telepathic glances. Suddenly Joe realized the way they were looking at him, the new caution with which they treated him. Barb took a deep breath and said, steadily and slowly, as if to a child: 'What is it you would like, Joe? What would help you?'

He raked his hands through his hair and tried to pull himself together. Barb and Roddy were his colleagues, not his enemies. There was no point taking it out on them.

'Well,' he said, trying to breathe calmly, 'I'd like to know who they are. What they want. That would help. To get a chance to tell them that this isn't how you go about changing things. To ask them if they really know what they're doing.'

'Joe, you have to understand…'

'Jesus,' he muttered.

'… that we cannot allow the department to get involved.'

'Huh? What do you mean?'

'In what you're suggesting.' Roddy glanced at Barb to make sure she had his back. She gave Roddy a curt nod: go on, I'm with you one hundred percent.

'What are you talking about? Of course you're involved, you already are! Or are you telling me you're going to fire me? All of us do work like this! This could have just as easily happened to you as to me!'

'Joe, we're going to leave this matter to the police and—'

'Roddy.' Joe's intonation finally brought him up short. 'After your office has been vandalized and you've been woken up at six in the morning by a foghorn and your neighbors have been told that you're a murderer, then we can talk about what *we're* going to do.'

Roddy looked at him, opened his mouth, and then closed it. It felt like, for the first time, he had finally heard what Joe was trying to say.

Barb looked at him and said: 'If you want to fly solo, I'm afraid you're on your own.'

He wrote the same message on every slip of paper. He left the notes everyplace he could think of: on the door to his office, at the entrance to the department, on the external walls of his house, at the front door.

Can we talk?

At the bottom of each, he carefully printed his name, phone number, email address, and home address.

'Are you sure that's a good idea?' Miriam asked that evening.

'There must be something they're trying to say,' Joe said.

'I wouldn't be so sure it's worth hearing.'

'Why else would they do something like this? Maybe it's something we can talk about.'

'Is that what you think?'

'If I even got a chance to find out who my disagreement is with. And over what, exactly.'

'But our address? I don't really like the thought of...' Miriam stopped herself and eyed the note, looking concerned.

'I'm pretty sure they already know it.'

It was the injured look on her face that made Joe realize it: this might end up coming between him and his wife.

'But now we have to get going. Dani!' he yelled. 'Are you ready?' He was proud of himself. Even though his home had been violated, his office trashed, he was so unperturbed he was going to take his daughter to a baseball game, because he had promised he would.

He calmly drove her downtown and purposely parked at a distance from the stadium. They walked through the Inner Harbor, past the tourist traps where retirees in white sneakers and ball caps padded from crab shack to souvenir shop. The sun was already low in the sky, it was pleasantly cool and not too humid. Maybe life wasn't over yet, after all, but here and now.

At Camden Yards, they sang 'Take Me Out To The Ball Game' during the seventh-inning stretch along with everyone else and watched the New York Yankees sock it to the Baltimore Orioles the way they always did. Everything would work itself out; everything would take a turn for the better. He would find those people, talk with them. Would discover what their beef with him was. They would stop, would be ashamed: like children. Next year would be normal again, good. *Shanah Tovah.*

Joe was sitting in his office, picturing his daughter giving her presentation in the school auditorium. Daniella's oral report had gone so well that she had been asked to give it again, this time to the entire school. That morning she had agonized over what to wear, and eventually asked her big sister for help.

Rebecca had lifted the hangers out one by one and eyed the tops and skirts.

'Seriously, Daniella?'

'I kno-ow!'

'You could have at least one outfit that's semi-wearable.'

'Tell me about it.'

'These are all… I mean… ewwww. Dani!'

'Stop reminding me.'

Joe wondered where Rebecca's stony, almost cruel gaze and manner came from. Had she inherited them from him? Or was it just adolescence, an inflexibility that would pass by itself within a few years? Joe knew he was too critical himself, too apt to comment on things he found nonsensical.

Miriam had been forced to go upstairs and cast pointed, reproachful looks Rebecca's way.

'Becky,' she said. 'Do you have to make things worse? Your little sister needs your support. She's nervous, can't you tell?'

'I was asked for my opinion. Excuse me for not bullshitting her to her face.'

'Becky.'

'*Mom*-my.'

In the end, Rebecca gave Daniella a top from her own closet. 'Here, that doesn't look totally lame.'

Daniella was already late for school, and Joe didn't have time to intervene. The shimmering top Dani was wearing when she left the house was one Rebecca's new friends had picked out for her. An ironic slogan was splashed across the front in silver letters. Communicating a casual, relaxed attitude and disparagement of the opinions of adults, it was the same slogan being digitally sown everywhere by clever animations that spread like viruses and that in one way or another contributed to building the brave new world of the *iAm* manufacturer or Ted Brown and Freedom Media. These clever animation figures also scampered through a feature-length movie made for three-to-ten-year-olds that Joe had just read about in the papers. According to the critics, the movie had a beautiful message and was the perfect feel-good flick for both children and adults.

That night over dinner, he tried to talk to Rebecca about why it wasn't a great idea to sell your life as advertising space, and how knowledge of everything she did carried down to her little sister. Was Rebecca sure she wanted to be advertising brain-altering chemicals whose long-term effects no one actually knew?

She responded with a grunt that sounded thoughtful. Her forehead was furrowed. For once she looked surprisingly attentive. Joe had already started imagining she was pondering his questions until he realized the source of her glassy gaze.

'Becca!'

Rebecca came out of her stupor and pulled the small silver buds out from under her hair. 'What?' she said in an injured tone.

'Did you hear anything I just said to you?'

'Stop fucking shouting! I'm watching a movie.'

'That is infuriating! I don't want you using that gadget in this house when there are others around! I can never tell if you're here or somewhere totally different.'

'You can't tell me what to do!'

'You don't see or hear anything these days. You're so engrossed in whatever's there.'

'Unlike you, when you're reading one of your scientific articles that are so fucking fascinating.'

The *iAm* device Rebecca had received as a gift from her 'friends,' the phone that wasn't a phone, was a mini 'UI-free' viewing device. The unit she had received was still a prototype, but an improved version would be coming to the market this fall.

You could use the device to browse the internet, watch videos, listen to music. But there was no user-interface to speak of, as the company explained in the user guide: the experiences were transmitted via a few small, stylishly designed electrodes directly to the sensory cortices. You still needed the terminals in the cortex but you didn't need the sensory receptors, the experiences but not the outside world – just the device.

Apparently the user experience was still a little choppy at times. According to Rebecca, things appeared in duplicate or disappeared completely pretty often, and the sound could randomly muffle in a weird way. But the feel was supposed to improve the more you used the device. Every detail – like where, what, and how she watched and the way her brain reacted to it – was apparently registered directly with the device's manufacturer. This meant the manufacturer could fix problems and upload new updates in real time. They could also automatically send Rebecca links, movies, and music customized just for her without any requests or unnecessary fiddling with the settings.

To say her new friends had been enthusiastic about the device was a gross understatement. For Rebecca, the coolest thing was being able to watch and listen to whatever she wanted even while she was in class or eating dinner. You didn't have to face any particular direction, like you did with a dedicated screen, because movies and written text appeared in front of your eyes when you focused on them. If you wanted to, you could also look right through them; it wasn't like the rest of the world went anywhere. So you could read your emails while you were strolling down the street, watch movies while you were jogging! Whatever you wanted, wherever you wanted! Without a screen or monitor. Within certain limitations, you could change programs and volume by power of thought. Calibrating the commands took some time and wasn't always perfect, a little like speech recognition in the early stages.

'What sense does that make?' Joe had asked. 'There's no way you can concentrate on what's going on here if you're watching a movie at the same time!'

Rebecca rolled her eyes. 'I'm sure I'm missing out on a ton.'

'Listen, Becca,' Joe said. 'About that medication. I believe you when you say you haven't taken it. But there's something about it I'd still like to…'

He considered how to continue. He didn't want to be too controlling or, on the other hand, frighten her too badly.

'I did a little looking into what's known about it.'

'Ooh, world-famous innovator Joseph Chayefski is on a mission to deconstruct. The stock price collapses!'

'It was developed to treat autism.'

'Hmm.'

'From what I can understand.'

'Uh-huh,' Rebecca said. She frowned at him as if she were deep in thought. The expression on her face encouraged Joe to continue.

'To be perfectly frank, I'm worried. I'm not convinced its long-term effects have been researched properly. Apparently it changes the way cell membranes work, and might affect transporters, too. How will that affect the brain? Tomorrow? Next year? Ten years from now?' He went on to say that he'd spent several days reading studies, trying to figure out what was known about the new neurochemical. But the studies that had been published were commissioned by a pharmaceutical company that was notorious for biasing their clinical trials, withholding research data, and leaving negative results unpublished.

Rebecca was staring straight ahead, looking thoughtful. Her smooth, perfect forehead was wrinkled. Joe felt a pang of tenderness. For once he had managed to hold his dear daughter's attention, for once his expertise meant something to his critical, intelligent girl – for once he got to be a dad, one his daughter found worthy of her undivided attention.

'We don't know,' he continued, more tenderly. 'We really don't. No one does. We would need proper, independently run studies, but they don't exist yet. Of course everything looks great in the pharma companies' own trials, because they purposely conceal all the problems. But that's not science, it's just marketing that looks like science.'

Rebecca looked at him for a long time. Just when he thought she wasn't listening, she nodded. Something about her expression was a little off.

'So could we make a deal that you won't take that chemical before you talk to us? Before we've had time to investigate what's known about it?'

From the look on Rebecca's face, which appeared to roam at the frontiers between confusion, uncertainty, and affection, Joe got the impression he was giving the pharma companies a drubbing.

'Your mom agrees with me,' he added. 'She's really worried about this, too.'

Rebecca stared at him as if she didn't understand what he was saying.

'So could we?'

'What?'

'So could we make a deal? Now. Shake on it.' He held out his hand.

'What?' Rebecca snapped and plucked the electrodes from her hair, looking irritated. Apparently she had put them back on without him noticing.

Oh, hell, no.

'What? *What?*'

'Did you have those electrodes on this entire time?'

'Excuse the fuck out of me.'

'Didn't you hear a damned word of what I just said? I've been talking for the last half hour!'

'I told you I was watching a movie!'

Hell, no. No!

'Besides, they're not fucking electrodes! They're called paws! And if you're done talking now, I'd like to finish watching this movie.'

Joe mentioned the device at the department in hopes of gaining some sympathy. The young assistant professors in particular were thrilled. Was the *iAm* really on the market? Finally! Was it as incredibly sexy as the rumors said? The new *iAm* didn't have anything directly to do with Apple. Their computers and phones were vestiges of last-millennium technology, the company itself on the brink of bankruptcy, for understandable reasons – how could it have overlooked how fleeting, how tenuous, its success would be? – but Steve Jobs, rest his soul, had still been one of the most important figures of the previous century, alongside Gandhi, Mother Teresa, and Dr King.

Could Joe bring the device in to the department, so they could at least see it?

Apparently it had to be calibrated separately for every brain, which meant they wouldn't be able to try it out, but could they maybe *touch* it?

Sometimes he felt all that was left of his daughter was a shell. And apparently he'd better get used to it. Joe had realized as he listened to his colleagues that before long that's all that would be left of anybody.

It's just a gadget, one of the older professors had pooh-poohed when he noted Joe's stupefaction. Just a gadget, that's all.

Yeah, someone else agreed: it's not like anyone's ever fully present today, anyway. Who didn't use their phone to check their email in the middle of a conversation, update their status while they were trying to set up a meeting, or surf the net during a conference presentation?

'I get that no one knows the long-term effects,' someone said. 'But no one knew them with television either. In the fifties, people were positive that watching TV would melt your brain.'

'And in a way they were right.'

Raj's quip was rewarded with laughter. Afterwards someone blurted: 'Oh yeah, of course! Congratulations, Joe! I just realized why they sent it to you!'

'Huh?'

'The *iAm*! It's partially yours!'

And when Joe didn't immediately understand, it was explained to him: such and such neural pathways, such and such connections in the MT area – hmm, I wonder who could have researched that? The control software and circuits for the new *iAm* device's visual stimuli had to be based on the prize-winning research conducted by Joe himself – not totally, of course, but in large part. Without his findings, it would never have been possible to develop the device.

Just enough time had passed since the publication of The Paper, Joe's main claim to fame, for an application prototype to have been developed.

Joe gulped.

It was true. He was so old – over fifty – and so out of it that he never would have made the connection. Without the work on vision that he and his research team had done, the device wouldn't exist. Except it would: someone else would have discovered the same things. Probably. Before long.

'Incredible,' someone said. 'I've never heard of a basic researcher being sent a thank-you present by a tech company. How cool is that? They finally understand that without basic research, applied research wouldn't exist!'

Joe never got a chance to explain that the device hadn't been sent to him, exactly, nor for very altruistic reasons. Cheh-Han patted him on the back. 'Good job, man. We're proud of you.' Someone went and ordered sushi and sodas for everyone to celebrate: 'This is so fantastic!' Joe listened to everyone's praise, let his group snap its suspenders, they had such amazing drive.

But after the sushi, he sat in his room for a long time, looking out the window as the sun gradually stained the lawn of the lower quad red.

Luckily the water was ice cold; Joe gulped thirstily from the drinking fountain. You could sense the sweltering summer was on its way. Some days, the sun shone ominously hot. After drinking his fill, he paused on his way down the corridor. Someone had tacked up a newspaper photo of Ted Brown's smiling face and written a quotation underneath about 'the statue of bigotry' and pissing on the hungry, the tired, the poor.

Joe was glad to see someone else in the department liked Lou Reed. The album *New York* in particular reminded Joe of his days as a graduate student at MIT. Reed's music had calmed him in the evenings during the final two-week cross-examination, when his voice was hoarse, his self-confidence shattered, and his university career, as he thought, forever lost.

Brown's picture had appeared on the bulletin board because of what had happened at the main library the week before, Joe realized. He felt a pang of guilt and tried to think the library workers' fate hadn't been his fault. Almost half the staff there had been fired – the less-educated ones, the ones who spoke English less fluently. Those lucky enough to hold on to their jobs would have to do the work of those fired, in addition to their own.

The firings had been the outcome of the library's attempt to negotiate terms with Freedom Media. Joe had been pressuring library management to do this for a long time. He had optimistically imagined that the bargaining would at least lead to a conversation. But Freedom Media had canceled the university's subscriptions to all scientific journals without warning.

There was no research without publications, so the library had no choice but to capitulate. The university's finances being what they were, this meant potential cuts to administration, instruction, and research, as well as raising the already-outrageous undergraduate tuition fees.

The Lou Reed song was 'Dirty Blvd'. In the lyrics, a New York landlord laughed until he wet his pants.

There hadn't been any contact with the animal rights activists for a while, and yet every night as he was turning in, it would cross Joe's mind: would his family's sleep be interrupted by a foghorn once again? But so far, nothing. Had the simple offer to engage in dialogue resolved the issue?

Since things seemed to have calmed down, he had time to pay a call at Rebecca's school. The visit had been on his mind for a while now.

The principal's polite assistant pointed him to a bench in the hallway. He waited his turn next to a chubby, frightened-looking thirteen-year-old boy who clenched a stack of books in his arms and looked like he was on the verge of bursting into tears. Joe was just about to ask the boy if everything was all right, when the door opened and the administrative assistant emerged to bat her eyelashes questioningly.

'Dr Chayefski?'

'Thanks,' he said, following her through the reception area to the principal's office.

She rose from behind her massive oak desk and circled around to shake Joe's hand. She was slim, sinewy, fiftyish. A marathon runner, he thought.

He asked the principal what company was preying on kids at the school.

'Excuse me?' the principal asked. Joe saw the change in her expression, so friendly just a moment ago. He had a hard time staying diplomatic. These people were supposed to be protecting children, not feeding them to the lions.

Joe took a deep breath, tried to smile, and calmly explain why he was there. Under the auspices of some campaign permitted at the school, his child had been sold neurochemicals whose effects on the brain Joe, at least, couldn't vouch for. Had the school been turned into a consumer interface for corporations?

The principal seemed surprised. She wasn't sure what Dr Chayefski was talking about. She explained that a day dedicated to 'promoting empathy' had, indeed, been held at the school. And she felt that the theme, ensuring equal opportunity for all, was important. But she knew nothing about marketing products to children, and she found it highly unlikely that anything of the sort would be happening. As for Nudge, the principal had never heard of the company. Was it possible that Dr Chayefski was mistaken?

'Are you aware,' Joe said, 'that "ensuring equal social opportunities for all" means the marketing of potentially harmful psychoactive chemical substances to teenagers for purposes that have not officially received approval from the FDA? And that children are being paid for this peer-to-peer marketing?'

'I beg your pardon,' the principal said, opening her eyes wide and shaking her head, 'but what on earth are you talking about?'

'My daughter had these pushed on her. The sales reps came to school for that express purpose.'

Joe showed her the package of **ALTIUS!®**. The principal didn't falter.

'Here,' she said, handing him a brochure printed in eye-catching colors, with an edgy layout. Joe scanned it.

The brochure claimed that the new vmPFC fine-tuners (ASK YOUR DOCTOR IF **ALTIUS!®** IS THE RIGHT MEDICATION FOR YOUR CHILD!) were effective at improving brain functioning in children suffering from problems with social interaction. And unlike the ancient psychoactives from the 1990s, they achieved this without interfering with the normal functioning of neurotransmitters throughout the brain's synapses and the body.

Joe felt like crumpling up the brochure and tossing it in the trash to show what he thought of it, but he restrained himself.

He told the principal that the brochure's claims came from the pharmaceutical company's marketing department. There wasn't necessarily an ounce of truth to them. Joe felt that it was the school's duty to stop these piranhas. The kids were defenseless under the marketing onslaught.

The principal apparently found such accusations outrageous; talk of 'predators' an affront to her professionalism. She didn't know where Dr Chayefski had gotten his so-called information, but it wasn't accurate. The school did have a campaign underway, and it was funded by private companies, but it dispensed advice and assistance on establishing social relationships, among other things, and did so for free – unlike the way things usually happened.

'It's covert marketing!' he yelled. 'I understand that it looks like science to you, but it may well be a complete crock!'

The principal calmly stated that for preteens and teens, problems with friends could be more damaging than learning disabilities. As a matter of fact – she dug into her file cabinet – here was a recent article indicating that surprising numbers of people suffered from pressure-induced deficiencies in social peer reactions. The problem often remained undiagnosed, despite the fact that many children would benefit significantly from vmPFC optimizers.

Was Dr Chayefski aware that the latest studies showed that even momentary <u>pressure-induced, socially based attention deficiencies could decrease decision-making agility by as much as forty-one percent</u>? This was, according to studies, <u>the most significant predictor of test success</u>.

The principal was not an expert in neurosciences like Dr Chayefski, it's true, nor was she an MD, but she could read with her own two eyes that this was a scientific study. Brain research was advancing; scientists were learning more and more about the brain and how to help people.

'You're missing the point,' Joe said, trying to calm down. He had also been completely ignorant of how brazenly the pharma companies had taken control of the scientific publishing business and the monitoring functions of the drug administration. He'd been shocked by what he'd found, once – provoked by Rebecca's new friends – he'd started looking into it. And he had probably just scratched the surface.

'They're happy to pretend we understand exactly how the brain works,' Joe said. 'But the reality is, all they have are ambiguous brain scans and inconclusive trial results that could be pure chance, or intentionally biased and partially reported.'

'Ah-ha,' the principal said, studying him closely.

'They're not devoted to science. They're pushing their own product.'

'I see.' The principal nodded. Joe could read what was running through her brain: pacify the madman.

'If I had to bet, I'm pretty sure you could get those same research results and brain scans by giving children cocaine. I have no doubt their enthusiasm would spike. I'm sure you'd see a difference in behavior. But is that exclusively a good thing? How do we know if a chemical like that optimizes something in the brain? It's pretty rare that a foreign substance does anything there other than mess things up.'

'Would you like to have a closer look at these?' the principal said, with exaggerated politeness.

She handed him the glossy printouts of the scientific studies.

'The pharmaceutical companies own a lot of the journals those studies are published in,' he tried to explain, more calmly. 'They fund, design, analyze, and interpret the tests for their own products. Does that sound impartial and reliable to you?'

'It says here that the first author is Harriet Warrington from Johns Hopkins—'

'She hasn't even necessarily seen the data. Companies ghostwrite those studies and then pay leading professors to present them at conferences as their own opinions. Just last winter, it came out that a professor from Emory had received two million dollars in lecture fees from a pharmaceutical company.'

Joe could hear himself. He sounded paranoid.

He tried to explain that publishing practices weren't in and of themselves faulty, but that they had been created for basic research. Big corporations, on the other hand, could afford to fund an infinite number of biased trials to achieve the desired outcome. That was why you could no longer believe everything these articles claimed at face value. But from the naïve responses of the principal, Joe understood that for her the system was too arcane to grasp. Science was constantly advancing; amazing new medications were coming to market at a steady clip. That had to be a good thing because the alternative was unthinkable.

'Let me know if there's ever anything else I can do for you,' the principal said in a controlled, overly friendly voice from behind her desk, as Joe slammed the door behind him.

After returning to his office, Joe called the company directly, and managed to reach the lead customer helper from customer service feedback division B. The customer helper oozed a moist, cotton-candyish obsequiousness that would have made a European instantly hang up, but when Joe asked about marketing to minors, the helper's voice cooled to Finno-Russian temperatures. The company adhered to all relevant laws and regulations. Yes, the company was participating in **The Children Are The Future** charity campaign, which distributed information about social inequality, prevented difficulties related to social interaction, and gathered funds for helping those in need. But the lead customer helper from feedback division B was unable to provide any further information on the campaign, unfortunately, because technically the campaign wasn't organized by the company, but by a nonprofit charitable association named **The Children Are The Future**, who were indeed in partnership with the company.

If Joe wanted to leave his contact information, someone would be in touch as soon as possible.

'No, the one who's going to be in touch as soon as possible is my lawyer,' he said, and hung up.

The cicadas, he realized later, as afternoon turned to evening: he'd forgotten to ask Daniella how her presentation to the school had gone.

Cicadas are a nightmare for wedding planners, he remembered Daniella having said during her report. And in conclusion: cicadas are, above all, a time machine.

'A cicada year leaves each of us with a memory that will last a lifetime. Whenever we think about the cicadas, we'll relive this year, this summer, these cicadas. After all, we have nearly twenty years to wait until the next time.'

'Good job, Dani,' Joe said out loud in his empty office, clapping at the setting sun. Maybe his daughter would sense his support, even from here, even after the fact.

He thought about his eleven-year-old and how anxious she'd been that morning; then about the ironic T-shirt Rebecca had lent her little sister. Joe had looked up the slogan online. Apparently, use of vmPFC optimizers was common among kids. They'd been marketed to healthy young people for some time now with the promise: become the personality, the brain, you're meant to be.

Joe had asked a psychiatrist colleague about this. Didn't breaking marketing laws land you in court? Of course it did, was the response. Not a week went by without a big pharma company shelling out a couple of million dollars to the family of a child who had died of a heart attack – while sales jumped by two billion, thanks to the illegal marketing.

The companies purported to follow all the laws and regulations. They always settled out of court and paid damages to the penny.

It turned out Dani had been advertising these dendritic optimizers during her presentation. To the entire school, in the most effective way possible, through between-the-lines flippancy and her own example, and Joe hadn't done a thing to prevent it. *And God saw all that he had made*, came to him from somewhere, *and behold it was very good*.

He would ask that evening how the presentation had gone and use the opportunity to explain why he didn't want Daniella or Rebecca wearing any more clothes stamped with that silver slogan.

That evening, Daniella wouldn't come down for dinner. Saara said that she'd returned from school in tears and lain in her room all evening refusing to talk or eat.

It was eight o'clock before Joe was finally able to convince his daughter to open the door.

'They say you torture them!' Daniella shouted at him. 'Animals!'

'What?'

'You torture animals! That you kill and torture animals!'

Joe couldn't believe his ears. It felt like he'd been slapped across the face.

'That you cut them up in pieces! That you sew kitten's eyelids shut so they end up cross-eyed for the rest of their lives! That you go into their brains and destroy their... brains!'

Everything seemed to be moving in slow motion; he could distinctly feel every second, how every one that passed was here and then gone. Joe held out a hand to Daniella where she lay on the bed, wished he could wrap his arms around her and comfort her, but she swatted him away.

'Is it true?' Daniella asked. Her face was red.

'Dani,' Joe began.

'NO! Is it true? Is it true!'

It felt like a knife was being twisted in his chest. It was true. Or no, it wasn't – *not the way you're thinking*. How are you supposed to explain this to a child?

'Is it true?'

Joe held his daughter's gaze for a long time.

'No.'

He was Abraham on the mountain, when Isaac asked where the sacrificial lamb was. He was Michael Corleone in *The Godfather*.

Daniella sniffled, rubbed her nose on her sleeve. 'Why are they saying it then?'

His daughter raised her tear-swollen eyes, and looked him in the face.

'They're people,' Joe said slowly, 'who don't understand what they're talking about. It's hard for people who don't do the kind of work we do to know what it's really like.'

Daniella's eyes were half accusing, half pleading. Joe could see she was hopeful, but couldn't yet decide if she believed him.

'Dani,' he said. 'Research is done so we can learn what the world is like and how things work. The more we know, the better we can do things like heal diseases and prevent people from dying.'

His heart went cold as he realized what he had just done – the very thing the reporters he looked down on did: he'd taught his daughter that knowledge had solely instrumental value.

Daniella listened and wiped away her tears, gradually calmed down. The presentation had gone well, she told him, until people had started catcalling her. The teacher had finally managed to silence the trouble-makers, but the damage was done. Joe saw that even though Daniella had settled down and was willing to talk to him, she still wasn't sure what to think.

Later that evening, when Rebecca came home smelling of beer and weed, Joe heard her say to Daniella: 'Sit down.'

'Why?'

And before Joe could sprint upstairs and order Rebecca to her room, she had batted her purple-stained eyelids twice with the self-confidence of an experienced, older woman: 'Dani. It's all true.'

Rebecca walked across the landing to her own room, a smile on her face. Of course there was no guarantee that the smile had anything to do with the situation at hand. She might have been watching a musician chosen by the shampoo-drug-clothing conglomerate on her UI-free experience device. The *iAm* didn't produce any external sound – obviously, since everything was reproduced directly on the cortex. The music did not consist of fluctuations in air pressure, but a series of synchronized nervous-system impulses in precise sequenc-es. Movies no longer needed to be projected on the screen; as with dreams, thoughts, and memories, the inner stage of the soul sufficed. The external world was an illusion, no longer necessary for anything. Which was amazing, of course, but you could never tell if a teenager was smirking at something her father said or simply watching a heart-warming comedy about the true meaning of life.

Joe watched from below as Daniella appeared at the top of the stairs and drilled into him with her eyes, which communicated disbelief, confusion, and something he'd never seen in them before. He knew he'd remember that look for as long as he lived.

Joe heard Daniella turn on her Blu-ray. The nu R&B singer recommended by the marketing company and, according to Rebecca, picked just for her, mewled for oral sex in a top with a familiar ironic slogan shimmering across it in silver letters.

That night, Joe lay in the dark and stared at the ceiling. No matter how he tried in his mind to reconfigure events, he still had a bad conscience about what he'd told Daniella about his work. We survive betrayal, he thought, but the first time is crushing, the first time you realize betrayal is even possible.

After lying awake for a while, he got up, quietly padded over to Daniella's door and slowly opened it. She was sleeping crosswise on her bed, one leg vertical against the wall. His daughter had kicked off her blankets the way she did every night. There was no longer any trace of her having cried herself to sleep for two hours. Her face was round, still a child's, forehead smooth again, like when she was little. There was nothing to be afraid of, nor ever any need to feel ashamed.

He wouldn't be in this situation, Joe realized, if he made slight adjustments to the way he worked. But he'd still be reliant on the results of the same animal models. Everyone used everyone else's results, even those who didn't have a single animal in their lab. The value of the experiments had nothing to do with who conducted them, or what his daughters felt about them.

Joe thought back to that childhood summer, to the breeze, hot as the steam of a Finnish sauna, as he stepped out of the synagogue, and how he'd asked his father where the clouds went after they traveled across the sky. He remembered his cousins and the clothes bought for the bar mitzvah, the verses he'd had to recite from the bimah and during which he'd been thinking not about his commitment and his values but the joint he and Barry had smoked before the ceremony and whether everyone could tell how stoned he was, followed by the record player he hoped he'd be getting from the relatives who would nevertheless bring something expensive and appropriate, like a gold-lettered work on the holy days by Rabbi Eliyahu Braverman. Except Uncle Adam, who would give him the new Rolling Stones album and assure Mom that one of the Stones was one-eighth Jewish.

His children were forming equally weighty memories now, the images that would make up their childhood, what they remembered life having been like. There was something poignant about the thought.

At her bat mitzvah, Rebecca had been given three smartphones.

Joe closed the door and tiptoed barefoot over to her room, where the walls were now plastered with photos of a popular electro musician. The other colors in the room had been picked to match this latest heartthrob's album cover. The R&B princess who sang about oral sex had been knocked from her pedestal and relinquished to Daniella for worship.

When Joe opened the door, Rebecca jumped. She was lying under the covers, utterly still, as if not wanting to give herself away.

'What?' came from under the blanket.

'Nothing,' Joe said. 'Go back to sleep.'

'Did something else happen?'

'No.'

Rebecca was quiet for a moment, and then said in a constricted voice: 'What I said to Dani...'

'Yeah?'

'Is that what you came in here to talk about?'

'No. I just missed you.'

Rebecca didn't immediately reply. Without her Hollywood hair and makeup, she looked younger, vulnerable. Like the girl Joe remembered.

'I'm sorry.'

'That's all right.'

'I don't know why I did it.'

'Maybe you thought she'd find out sooner or later anyway.'

'Yeah. Maybe. I don't know.'

Rebecca turned over and watched him from the darkness, blinking her eyes. As she rolled over, the covers fell away, revealing the lower-back tattoo she had gotten a year ago without Joe and Miriam's permission.

'I don't know what I was thinking,' Rebecca said again.

'I'll talk to her tomorrow.'

Joe gave her a kiss, turned, and pulled the door carefully shut behind him. His eldest daughter. His heart broke when he thought about the world and both his daughters.

SO, LIKE, YOU COULD BE THE LUCKY ONE

HELSINKI, FINLAND

Clichés are easier to laugh at when they're not crystallizations of your personal failures. You never know what you have until it's gone, and it wasn't until Samuel's two-year relationship with Kerttu Karoliina Lamminsuo had ended that it started looking like a paradise he should have guarded with his life.

The sun was shining yellow and bright as the InterCity train raced past the sheer red granite. The blue conifers standing stoutly on either side of the track fell back now and again, revealing shimmering silver lakes. Samuel sat in the restaurant car, gazing out the window at the intermittently emerging fields and willow-edged ponds. He drained his fourth cup of railway coffee, which, based on the shaking of his hands and hammering of his heart, hadn't been wise.

Despite numerous attempts, his mind was incapable of holding on to more than two alternating thoughts that aggressively repeated themselves, and interrupted each other like middle-aged drunks at a bar, in increasingly belligerent voices. One of the thoughts involved how perfect everything had been just a moment ago, in the spring, or even in the summer. His position in the world had felt as secure as Finnish bedrock, but in reality the entire edifice had been – as gradually became apparent – a full-size St Paul's Cathedral built of matchsticks without any glue. The fact that the tension had been incredibly delicate and perpetually susceptible to collapse, and that with the arrival of autumn had come crashing down as the result of few nearly random-seeming events, felt at the same time both unfair and so completely illogical that he began to suspect that the world had always been different than the way he imagined.

But the second thought, which threw its arm around the shoulders of the first in such a hearty embrace that it was impossible to squirm free, offered a faint possibility of correcting the situation. This would happen by starting from the clearest problem, the most critical matchstick; if he could force it back into place, the others might also settle back into their proper formations. The operation demanded solid confidence in his own abilities, but the better he believed his chances to be, the more likely he was to succeed. This had been proven on any number of occasions, with soccer, women, and math tests, which was why he'd promised himself that everything was going to work out for the best this time as well.

The fact that Kerttu was in Jyväskylä was a mistake that would be fixed.

Earlier that year, Samuel's more pressing problems had included Vilma Niittylä, an opportunity that had presented itself but that he'd had to leave unexplored, and his sole nine, in art, on a report card consisting otherwise of perfect tens. On the cusp of his final exams, the air had been filled with spring light and the fragrance of damp earth exposed by melting snow, and the mornings had dawned dazzlingly bright.

The morning the article appeared in *Finland Today*, he'd surprised Kerttu by bringing the magazine, a hot coffee, and a croissant to her in bed. He'd had to get up at six to make it to the convenience store and over to Kerttu's before she woke. The magazine had clattered through the mail slot the previous day in an envelope addressed to him.

'How come no one ever brings me breakfast in bed?' Kerttu's mom had said, impressed, still dressed in her robe when she opened the door.

'These are for you,' Samuel said in his sincerest voice.

Kerttu's mom waved her hand dismissively, yeah, right, and let him in. She always got a kick out of it when he flirted with her. Samuel got a kick out of it, too: his having formed this sort of relationship with a woman ten years his senior. He remembered someone having said that the best way to picture your girlfriend in middle age is to look at her mother, and in this regard he had no cause for complaint. Samuel kicked off his wet shoes in the entryway.

The familiar collection of empty wine and beer bottles eyed him blearily from the kitchen table. Kerttu's mom quickly cleared them away, humming in feigned nonchalance. Kerttu's stepdad's snores echoed from the bedroom, and her mom pulled the door shut with a movement Samuel wasn't supposed to notice.

'So this is it?' Kerttu's mom asked, reaching for the magazine.

'Yup.'

She opened the magazine and flipped to the right page. Samuel's heart was pounding. Kerttu's mom eyed the title in concern, and then glanced at him.

'I admire that brain of yours.'

'Well, I'm not sure it's that—'

'Promise me you won't get ruined?'

Samuel promised, even though he wasn't sure what sort of ruining Kerttu's mom had in mind. She handed the magazine back to him, telling him she'd buy a copy that afternoon and read it properly when she got home from work.

'Kerttu's probably awake by now,' she said, measuring coffee into the coffee maker.

A neutral male voice, steady and omniscient, flooded into the home from the radio: some research institute had predicted that the majority of jobs would disappear from Finland within the next ten years, but it would be even more catastrophic for the economy if they didn't.

Samuel was on his way up the stairs when Kerttu's mom called to him from the kitchen: 'That's the thing that's so great about you kids… you're not cynical about everything yet.'

Kerttu's room smelled of sleeping girl, unsullied dreams. Samuel waited next to the bed as Kerttu, in her nightshirt, read the magazine. The rays of the morning sun pushed their way in through the curtains.

She read it to the end without saying anything. Then she looked at Samuel with her bright blue eyes and nodded. 'I told you.'

'You did.'

'It's really goddamned good.'

'Thanks.'

Kerttu leaned in to hug him, her hair mussed from sleep. Suddenly Samuel was proud of his text in a new way, and remembered what it had been like meeting Kerttu for the first time, gathering up the courage to approach her.

Initially the essay had earned him a talking-to.

It was his fault, of course, writing about that topic in that way. The exact same thing would happen as in junior high. He might not get detention this time, but the message would be the same: it was important to be constructive, not take things too far. This was what he'd learned in junior high: you had to present teachers your thoughts in a format appropriate to their developmental level. You weren't allowed to say that the system was the problem. You had to say: remember to recycle. Separate your trash. Buy organic.

And leaving his essay in Mr Franzen's pigeonhole at school: that was begging for trouble. But when Samuel saw Mr Franzen in the hallway outside the music rooms, wearing his perpetual disappointed-in-the-youth-of-today face, the teacher had raised his chin and crooked a forefinger. Come here for a minute.

It was clear what Mr Franzen's *come here for a minute* meant: now listen here, snot nose, and let me teach you a thing or two about why things are much more complicated than you think. Mr Franzen would explain why the current catastrophe we're facing would just get worse if we did as Samuel proposed.

Mr Franzen taught biology but appeared to be better informed about societal issues than, for instance, Mr Liimatainen, the social studies teacher, who answered every question with an absent-minded *Hmm, good question, I'll bring you an answer next time*, but never did.

Mr Franzen had cast his weary gaze over Samuel and asked gravely: 'Am I to understand you wrote this, snot nose?'

The moment felt weighty. As Mr Franzen trained bloodshot eyes on him and the other students walked past on their way to class, Samuel had a sudden flash of the sorts of things he might accomplish during this lifetime.

That he, a snot nose, had written this preliminary essay on his own... Mr Franzen had a hard time believing it, and there was something particularly satisfying about this. Samuel had to dig into his bag and pull out the article summarizing the research of Akerlof, Spence, and Stiglitz, which luckily still traveled at the bottom with a bunch of other crumpled papers, the oldest from the year before last, together with Daniel Goleman's book.

Mr Franzen frowned, studied the article and the book, and asked again if Samuel had actually read them – and if so, *why*? After a thorough interrogation, Mr Franzen suddenly said: 'Let me borrow this,' and, without further explanation, left, taking Samuel's essay with him.

Subsequent to this exchange, Samuel's grade in biology had gone up a full grade point, even though he did worse on his tests than he had in the fall.

His father had emailed him the article on Akerlof, Spence, and Stiglitz a long time ago, back in junior high, for his report for National Environmental Awareness Day on 'How Each of Us Can Have an Impact.'

At first glance, the text had been as unintelligible as the words on the New Year's cards his father sent him every year. Samuel had parsed the precisely phrased sentences so many times that eventually he knew them by heart. And even though he hadn't seen his father since early childhood, as he slogged slowly through the ideas, it was hard not thinking that Dad just might be proud of him, respect how seriously he was taking the assignment. Despite its impenetrability, there was something so clearly momentous and valuable about the academic writing that it struck his adolescent soul as bordering on the sacred. After asking his teachers about various passages, he believed he had finally grasped the gist of the article, more or less. Even though he would never meet his father – Dad probably wouldn't have even remembered his existence if Samuel hadn't contacted him – it still felt important to prepare for the possibility that it might happen someday.

In junior high, the Nobelists' conclusions had opened the door to detention hall rather than to *Finland Today*. But in senior year, when the topics of the preliminary essays were announced, Samuel had immediately remembered the article on Akerlof, Spence, and Stiglitz.

He heard after the fact that, at Mr Franzen's request, the social studies and math teachers had also read his essay. Rumor had it that they agreed with Mr Franzen; Samuel ought to submit it for publication. But it was only when *Finland Today* called and asked for his tax card that it sank in: his words were actually going to appear in print.

And as for the facts that his text wasn't published with the other top essays from around the country, but as a separate feature, and that he was being paid two hundred and twenty euros for his thoughts on what it would take for the planet to survive: somehow it seemed like even Dad would be proud.

The article was, in essence, a summation of George Akerlof, Michael Spence, and Joseph Stiglitz's primary points combined with what Samuel had read of Daniel Goleman's book. He said to his teacher that he was embarrassed to be publishing a text that parroted the thoughts of others, to which Mr Franzen had replied that it was rare for even a Nobelist to have a completely original thought.

Finland Today had roped in a professor of economics, the chair of an environmental NGO, and one of the big shots from the Confederation of Finnish Industries to respond to his text. The moment Samuel opened the brown envelope, he had devoured these middle-aged blowhards' remarks. And, to a man, they had patronizingly considered his analysis, *despite its radical nature*, and *with certain reservations*, *worthy of discussion*.

Which meant the planet was doomed, at least if it were up to these old farts.

Despite the practical concerns raised, one of the comments noted, the bright, bold high-school graduate who wrote this essay was a member of that small group of thinkers on whose shoulders the future of the entire planet rested: thanks to young people like Samuel, there was still hope for the world.

The article in *Finland Today* had clearly made an impression on Mom and Henri. And that spring, the spring of Samuel's senior year, it became clear that the staff at his school read *Finland Today*, at least in situations like these. The language arts teacher copied the article for the whole senior class to read. Several teachers whom Samuel had never had made a point of coming up to him to say something about the article. Someone had even scanned it and uploaded it to the internet.

It was the scanning that reminded him of the possibility that had occurred to him earlier. He could translate the essay into English and publish it online; that way it would be accessible to non-Finns, too. His heart had pounded the moment the thought came to him. The fact that things would happen the way they eventually did never even crossed his mind.

Spring had passed slowly in anticipation of the graduation exams, in waiting, breast blazing, for real life to begin. He could still remember the way the weeks before dragged on, like the agonizing final hour of a five-day hike. While everyone else had long conversations with the guidance counselor, Samuel was dismissed with a wave: you can do whatever you want. As the others were retaking classes, he read comic books and played floor ball with the guys from the soccer team. When a valedictorian was needed to speak at graduation, no one even remembered to ask Samuel if he'd do it. The issue didn't come up until the week before, when the principal called to ask if he could hear some of the main points of Samuel's speech – it would be a formal event, after all, and they were expecting a pretty big crowd.

So that one hag had decided to give him a nine in art: she was fucking with him, of course, but it was harmless. Arbitrary was what they were, anyway, grades in artistic subjects. Nor did he have any intention of becoming an artist.

He knew he wouldn't be going for political science, although the social studies teacher Mr Liimatainen had suggested it, or anything from the humanities that the language arts and history teachers tried to foist off on him. Nor did he plan to *think carefully about the professional training each major prepared you for*, as Mom seemed to insist every time she opened her mouth. She kept asking Samuel to consider business school, med school, or law school, and when this didn't produce the desired result, she'd have a sudden urge to tell him yet again about her childhood friend Raija Tuomikoski, who had acquired a degree in theoretical philosophy and killed herself.

In the spring, the world had still been clear, sunny, and bright. The air smelled of fragrant, newly exposed black soil; coltsfoot thrust up from the damp earth. He studied in bed, under the blankets, first for his finals and then his university entrance exams, watched soccer from the cable box and knew he'd sail into the biology program on half as much effort as many who were left behind. And that was what happened, too.

Summer had also been warm and carefree, and for the most part he'd been able to forget the disappointment of his graduation party, since he'd had so much to do. The asphalt at the basketball court scorched the soles of his feet; the long picnics with his high-school classmates on the grass at Töölönlahti Bay seemed to promise a lifetime of liberation from adult responsibilities. He and Kerttu took her dog on long walks; the pooch trundled along, its compact body rocking from side to side, and sniffed the doings of fellow dogs on verges and lampposts. Occasionally – when Henri had evening appointments and Mom made the rounds of libraries and women's groups in the role of Author defending the free world from fanatics – he and Kerttu babysat his little brothers. His breast had swelled with pride as he skippered the pirate ship in the backyard. The four- and six-year-old great white sharks attacked, their little heads dripping with sweat, and Kerttu was tied to the mast to be rescued. In those rose-tinted moments, the graduation party didn't even cross his mind; for a long time afterwards it seemed as if those hot early-summer evenings when the smell of cut grass filled the air were the best thing that had ever happened to him.

Kerttu didn't pressure him to talk about the graduation party, either, not once the entire summer, and he was grateful to her for that. Because even though she didn't say anything, Samuel could tell from the way she looked at him and touched him that she understood.

And there was the smell of the July sun on Kerttu's skin, the lumpy ground under the sleeping pad as the mosquitoes whined in the tent at Nuuksio National Park, the lake that shimmered in the light-filled midsummer night, the campfire and the cold beer that tasted like his first ever: school was out, and they were finally in the game – through, for instance, essays that had been published in *Finland Today*. The world's problems had been caused by previous generations – thanks a lot, Mom and Dad, thanks a lot, grandparents – but now it was going to be their turn. Everything was possible! Life would go on as it had in high school, only freer, more fulfilling.

That summer, Kerttu had also, of course, talked about leaving.

She had tried to engage Samuel in serious conversations about the spot she'd been offered at the Department of Biological and Environmental Science at the University of Jyväskylä. Apparently it was home to the world's most prestigious degree program; nothing comparable existed in Helsinki, according to Kerttu. But whenever she brought up her plans to move to Jyväskylä, there had always been something going on, a floor ball match or an evening of beer tasting. Why did women always want to start deep conversations when something stellar was in the works?

Nor had it seemed a good idea to waste time worrying too much about things in advance. If Kerttu wanted to go off to Jyväskylä to study, that was what she should do. What did she mean, his opinion? It was her decision. If Kerttu didn't want a long-distance relationship, then maybe a long-distance relationship wasn't the best choice for her. Life was full of different phases. Tying yourself down with commitments was a bad idea, especially in a new situation where their lives would be changing completely. Both of them would be meeting dozens, hundreds, of new people that fall that they should feel free to get to know without any prior agreements or commitments – it would be smartest to take things one day at a time, right? Keep an eye on how things were going. How could they tell in advance the impact such massive changes would have on their relationship? After all, they'd been so young when they met, at such a tender age.

At these moments, he'd noticed a tinge of sadness appear in Kerttu's eyes, and sometimes the mood had hung hazily in the room all evening. Even Samuel had been semi-aware that the upcoming change might mean that something would actually *change*. And although he strongly disagreed with Kerttu's view that he'd started taking her for granted, in hindsight he'd been forced to admit that, at the time, he had, perhaps, been a little too focused on his own interests and activities. Nor was it inconceivable that the thought of Kerttu leaving might have also mingled with passing thoughts of the academic young women with whom he would be involved once the term started, perhaps intimately.

Be that as it may, the situation didn't fully dawn on him until he saw Kerttu in her corduroys, flowered sixties shirt, and flea market coat, carrying her winter clothes, yoga mat, and suitcase out the front door and climbing, tears in her eyes, into her mom's Volvo station wagon.

''Bye, Samuel.'

Kerttu waved her little hand out the car's passenger window. Her voice was thick and unsteady with emotion. It was September; some of the maples were already turning yellow, and the rowanberries burned bright red. Even though it wasn't cold, Kerttu was already wearing gloves, which suddenly struck Samuel as heart-rending: he was losing this, too. He was shivering; he'd run all the way from home in nothing but a T-shirt and jeans once he got the text message in which Kerttu suddenly informed him that today was the day she was leaving forever.

Kerttu was leaving today: that sort of explained why she had spent all night crying quietly to herself, pressed up against his back like a baby bird.

'Could we... You wanna go to a movie this weekend?' Samuel asked.

Kerttu's face melted into that blend of incredulity, disappointment, and bafflement that presaged divorces and influential feminist theories.

'Samuel!'

'You mean...' He gulped. 'Aren't you even coming home for the weekend?'

Kerttu closed her eyes and said in a quiet voice: 'This is kind of what I've been trying to tell you, all spring and summer.'

'But at some point, right?'

'I'm sure I'll come back at Christmas. For a little while.'

Samuel stared at her. 'Christmas?'

Was this what she'd wanted to talk about the night before last? When the Premier League match was just starting on TV, Man United vs. Man City?

Maybe he should have skipped it.

'Come here,' Kerttu said, her voice now tender.

She glanced apologetically at her mother, who was in the driver's seat, and reached out through the open window to touch Samuel's cheek. The touch was soft and familiar. *I never know what I have till it's gone*, flashed through his mind.

'Have a great fall, Samuel. And a fantastic freshman year. Let me know how everything goes.'

'Kerttu...'

'Samuel, both of us have all kinds of great stuff to look forward to.'

'Don't go, not yet. Hey. Let's talk, just for a sec, OK? I want to... Everything's up in the air between us. Come on, Kerde. Kerdenström. Please.'

But Kerttu turned towards the windshield and nodded at her mother, who had been listening tactfully while looking away – restraining her rage, as Samuel later learned, as much as she had always liked him. Kerttu's mom turned the key in the ignition, and the Volvo wagon chugged away too eagerly.

Samuel watched helplessly as the car turned out of the driveway and onto the street, towards Highway 4, Mäntsälä, and Lahti, the freeway to Jyväskylä, which might as well have been across the border in Russia, or on another continent.

He stood in the driveway for a long time, trudging off reluctantly when the old lady next door started giving him dirty looks from the window. In the garden of Kerttu Karoliina's former home, the apples glowed in the September sun, red-and-yellow, ripe.

The restaurant car had been empty when the train pulled out of Helsinki, but now almost every table was occupied. Everyone seemed to be doing the same thing at their coffee cups, hunching over and swiping at their digital screens.

Samuel looked at them and wished the engineer would press the gas or whatever it was you pressed in a train, because every minute that passed increased the probability that Kerttu would do something rash, something that wasn't in the interests of their relationship.

In the aftermath of this thought, he felt a nasty twinge somewhere in the vicinity of his gut, prompted by the possibility that he wouldn't be able to patch things up with her, that something had been irrevocably broken. But the thought was too big. He banished it from his mind and focused on staring out the window at the trackside willow-thickets that raced past too quickly.

The night before, he'd unexpectedly received a text message from Vilma Niittylä asking *What's up?* smiley and would Samuel wanna grab coffee someday smiley smiley, he didn't happen to be free right then by any chance smiley.

Vilma Niittylä was a cute girl from the same grade with whom Samuel had been stuck in an elevator and exchanged a few pleasurable, well-deserved French kisses after the lights had gone out. The situation had been complicated by the fact that Kerttu had also been in the same elevator and that the lights had come back on as unexpectedly as they had died. The elevator had been stalled for less than a minute, as Kerttu later reminded Samuel, repeatedly and without being asked: *less than sixty seconds*.

It had been prom night, and Kerttu had been in a bad mood from the get-go – maybe because Samuel had been two hours late. But it had meant a lot to *pappa* to see Samuel in his tux, so Samuel had dropped by the nursing home on the way. Whereas for Kerttu, it evidently would have meant a lot not to have had to wait alone, on a street corner, in vain, in the February sleet, all made up and hair done, wearing a heavy velvet skirt and the rest of her prom frippery – because Samuel simply hadn't remembered to fucking mention, as Kerttu put it, that the date they'd made no longer suited his majesty's schedule.

Which sounded inconsiderate, Samuel had to admit. But he hadn't remembered the date with Kerttu, set so long ago, until he made it to *pappa*'s nursing home, where the first thing he saw on the door was a sticker with a red diagonal line drawn through a picture of a mobile phone. This had also sparked an argument with her over how many old people's pace-makers would have actually exploded from a single text message, and might it have been worth sending one, goddammit, despite the risk. But *pappa* had made him swear to come on this occasion years before. Samuel wanted to visit his *pappa* as often as possible; his grandfather couldn't make it to the island anymore. And Samuel was sure he had mentioned dropping by *pappa*'s to Kerttu, or if, despite his intentions, he had neglected to, he was sincerely sorry.

The Vilma Niittylä incident had taken days to sort out. At first it seemed as if apologies and bouquets of fresh lilies wouldn't suffice to repair the damage. He was a so-and-so, he never did this or that, he had an unbelievable tendency to… and now on top of all that there was this incredible thoughtlessness, and Kerttu just didn't know if she saw any point anymore, since things had been like this from the very beginning, can you get that through your fucking skull? But the following Saturday afternoon, her stepdad had started shaking uncontrollably while carrying his bags of beer up the stairs, collapsed to the ground, and was taken to the hospital by ambulance and she was suddenly standing at Samuel's door on Sunday evening in tears, and had pushed her way into his arms as miserable and in need of consolation as if their quarrel had never existed.

That evening, Kerttu had felt warmer and better than ever next to him, and Samuel silently swore that he would never do anything to hurt her ever again. And yet even this happy ending compelled him to wonder fleetingly if kissing Vilma Niittylä in the elevator had been so catastrophic, after all; maybe sometimes it was possible to have your cake and eat it, too.

But the next morning, something felt distinctly different. Kerttu was pensive and distant, shut him out. Samuel hadn't interpreted this as stemming from anything other than her stepfather's close call.

Which it no doubt was, at least in part.

After finishing his coffee, Samuel left the restaurant car and returned to his seat. There, as the train rumbled along, he was privileged to listen the musings of two former au pairs on why your head itched when you talked about lice, but not when your scalp was teeming with them.

He still hadn't heard from Mom, oddly enough. Samuel had left a message on the table: *Take the motorheads to day care tomorrow, something came up, S.* He know Mom would be pissed, *some of us have JOBS, do you understand, you have to BE THERE at a certain time, you made a COMMITMENT to TAKE CARE of this, do you understand,* but it would do her good to have to haul the little pirates around for a few days: responsibility built character. After all, she was the one who brought them into the world. Besides, there was some guy with glasses and a carrot-colored beard hanging around the house, too, who had sired the motorheads and been like a father to them.

Henri wanted to be a sensitive father, willing to negotiate. But while a sensitive father negotiated, four-and six-year-olds were perfectly capable of, say, pumping five bottles of liquid soap onto the living-room rug, covering the armchairs with an even layer of sand carried in on little shovels, and cutting the kitchen mat into a pirate flag. On the nights Henri watched them, it seemed as if the little men often forgot to take their vitamin D, limits on television watching were ignored, and bedtimes were delayed, because Henri had to process some unusual emotional experience he'd encountered at his office or in life. As Henri didn't want to assume the role of authority figure while he was in an *affective state* – doing so was irresponsible – Ukko in particular would be cranky and bouncing off the walls the next day. Some might have perhaps interpreted this as proof that it was important to put the little men to bed on time instead of extensively processing your own emotions, but for Henri it demonstrated how dangerous it was to *engage in child-rearing tasks while in a state of affect.*

On these evenings, if you didn't have the presence of mind to come up with some excuse for getting out of the house, you got a chance to participate in Henri's reflection yourself, to listen to him explain how he wanted to be an emotional authority, to remain attuned to the boys' needs, and how it was important to process all of this. Henri was a competent psychotherapist, no doubt, despite or perhaps because of his continuous processing, which could be deduced from the constant shower of patient praise and gifts that he himself dismissed. Presumably those thousands of shelf-miles of tomes on compassionately treating psychoses and unstable personalities that filled the walls of their home had also been of use to him.

Since Mom was, with increasing frequency, out and about speaking on behalf of good causes and against bad ones, Samuel had thought it wisest to read a bedtime story to the little men whenever he happened to be at home and make sure they ate their bedtime snacks and didn't slip under the bed once the lights were out to play The Thrill of Adventure or Life on the Savanna. This gave Henri more time to concentrate on the kitchen chair, exchange places with it, tell off his invisible supervisor, and process.

But now they would have to manage without Samuel's help.

After Taisto was born, Mom had started treating Samuel like an embarrassing acquaintance who had overstayed his welcome. He would have gladly held the baby, learned to change diapers, and laid his pitifully wrinkled little half-brother down in his crib, but Mom seemed to get anxious the second he approached the baby. He never found out if it was because she didn't trust him with Taisto or because she couldn't bear to be parted from her little bundle of joy, even for a moment.

He'd been thirteen at the time. Once the baby came, Mom, who had always been particular about how she looked and what others could possibly think of her, had, literally overnight, transformed into a creature who wore baggy sweats and no makeup, smiled absent-mindedly at questions, and forgot to attend the open house at Samuel's school. She no longer talked to Julia over the phone about the meaninglessness of existence, but about breast pumps, sleep school, and how Taisto's stool had maybe grown a little firmer, finally! When Taisto whimpered in the middle of the night, Mom ordered a taxi and embarked on a nocturnal expedition to the emergency room at the Children's Clinic, the baby in her arms and Henri in tow.

'Guess what, Samuel,' Mom and Henri said, standing in the doorway of his room after their return, practically crying with relief. 'It looks like he might just have a cold.'

After the baby was born, Mom's entire being radiated purpose and contentment, which was, of course, a good thing. She even seemed to experience flashes of realization that her first child, the embarrassing adolescent leavings of her previous life, was in danger of being over-shadowed by her newborns. At such moments, she'd suggest, 'Let's rent a movie Friday night. That would be fun, wouldn't it?' Samuel could pick the movie and they'd watch it together. And that's what they did. Mom never made it past the first fifteen minutes. Two hours later, when the movie ended and Samuel turned off the television, she would start awake on the couch, where she'd been snoring, jaw slack.

'I'm sorry,' she'd say, wiping her mouth. 'I must have dozed off there at the end.'

It was understandable, of course: Mom had to get up in the middle of the night to bounce the baby back to sleep and again at five-thirty to put on the oatmeal.

In the years before Henri, Mom's life had revolved in a safe, un-changing orbit around work, television game shows, and candy bars devoured on the sly. When she retreated to her bedroom at night, Samuel could hear her crying softly to herself on the other side of the wall. On Sundays, Mom would make two-hour phone calls to Julia about how something just felt like it was missing, and reported in detail behind closed doors about the horrid stranger she'd picked up at a bar two months ago and practically had sex with, sighing to her friend about how dirty she still felt. Was this what life was supposed to be like? Was this it? Every week, Mom would elaborate to Julia about how she didn't know what she wanted to do with her life, which clearly was exactly what she wanted to do with it.

During these phone calls, she would berate Joe as a man, a father, and a human being. Samuel wondered about this. It had been years since the divorce, and Mom was still so angry? It also made him jealous: at least she had a real person to target her feelings on. It was Samuel's lot to miss an abstraction, to suffer from an absence, an empty, aching spot.

When he saw her tired face, he frequently had the impulse to hug her, to say something to cheer her up. And it always felt satisfying when he was able to get her to laugh. In order to spare his perpetually exhausted mother, he learned to load the dishwasher and get to his soccer games on his own.

It was impossible to say whether the hazy gray air of resignation floating around Mom was part of her personality or if – as Samuel had started to believe at some point – it was because Dad had left. Mom had never said or done anything in particular, didn't call in sick to work like Olivia's mom, didn't pop pills that made her speech slur and didn't drink every night until she passed out, like Kerttu's stepdad. But somehow, even after she had stopped crying herself to sleep and talking to Julia about something being missing, somehow Samuel still understood, from the furrows around Mom's mouth, from the way she poured her afternoon coffee at two on the dot, from the way she sighed as she settled into the armchair in front of the television: something about all this whispered it was all over for her.

Samuel had started hoping Mom would find someone, and it was worrisome when nothing happened. She wasn't staying single for his sake, was she? He'd been racking his brains for months, trying to think of the best way to raise the issue. He knew his mother might well be already at that developmental stage where sex and dating had started to interest her, but still felt elusive or embarrassing.

When the carrot-topped Henri appeared in their kitchen to stroke his beard empathetically, Mom's exhaustion had evaporated. Suddenly she didn't spend her evenings sprawled on the couch, munching resignedly on chocolate, but leaned forward, a glass of red wine in her hand, as she engaged in deep, adult conversations with her bespectacled admirer, whose nods imbued his surroundings with a therapeutic serenity.

Henri was Mom's age, handsome in his way, and apparently the first person in the world to understand Mom's endless self-examination and sense that something was missing. Or maybe Henri was just – as later occurred to Samuel – the country's most experienced professional when it came to looking thoughtful while he listened to hysterical women trapped in endless self-examination. At the beginning, Samuel had found it refreshing that Henri had been so interested in them – that intent, all-seeing gaze! Where did he get the energy? Henri was always interested in hearing their thoughts, weighed them thoroughly, asked clarifying questions, and was prepared to examine his own attitudes, even in the middle of the night.

He was a prominent figure of sorts in his field, served on the boards of many societies, and, due to his status, signed statements defending the rights of mental health patients and against increasing societal disparity. Every week, Henri gave lectures to large auditoriums packed with women with silk scarves and hyphenated last names, who wanted to grow as individuals and were forever fascinated by the impact a competitive society had on children and why it was so dangerous for parental figures to engage while in an affective state. Henri never got mad. Henri was never pissed off, nor did Henri ever behave unfairly. He simply slipped into an affective state on occasion. But if his heart was in the right place and Mom liked him, who was Samuel to judge?

There was only one thing about Mom that didn't seem to change, even after she met Henri. Whenever she talked about Dad, a tightness appeared in her voice that also made something in Samuel's chest constrict.

One time when he asked if she wished Dad had stayed, she answered: 'It wouldn't have changed anything.'

Samuel had also tried asking why they'd gotten divorced, and to this she said: 'Your father's priorities were pretty different than mine.'

And although Mom refused to say anything more about Dad or the divorce, Samuel had deduced that life in the United States was dissimilar to life in Finland: superficial, career-driven.

With Ukko, Mom and Henri no longer had a nervous breakdown every time he whimpered. This was reassuring: apparently even forty-somethings were capable of learning, at least under duress. Neither one went in to wake the baby during his naps anymore to make sure he was still breathing.

On some days, Mom's behavior was starting remotely to resemble the functioning of a healthy adult. For a brief while, Samuel thought that she would end up almost normal, that he'd be able to spend part of his late adolescence experiencing only the average amount of shame about his parents. But apparently this was an arena Mom felt a need to excel in as a parent. Once she went back to work, she came up with her grand project, perhaps specifically to surpass the limits of mortification she had already achieved.

It started with her hearing rumors at work that something called the internet had been invented. Mom's initial delight was followed by a period of equally irrational outrage. Why, anyone could write whatever they wanted there! When convincing the rest of the world to share in her moral indignation proved difficult, Mom muttered about the intolerance of Finns and then started spending her evenings at Henri's old laptop, tapping out something you weren't allowed to ask about and that provoked an irritated response if you interrupted. Nor did she, after the manic tapping stopped, turn into a mom you could feel the normal amount of shame about, but a Popular Author and Sought-after Panelist, who rested her chin on one hand and gazed dramatically into the camera in her headshots, lips freshly painted.

Everything adults did screamed obliviousness to the price their offspring would pay for their indiscretions on the pitiless asphalt of junior high playgrounds. By the time Mom's book came out, Samuel was in high school, where there was more room to breathe – but this was pure luck. Mom seemed to feel like she could pull whatever stunts she wanted, regardless of how it affected him.

Maybe Mom's outlandish transformations had played some role in that adolescent stage, Samuel reflected in hindsight, when he had pointedly huffed butane with the bad boys from the other homeroom and chucked rocks from the overpass where the metro trains lunged out of the tunnel and into the light. At school, when the teachers asked how he was doing, he pretended to think for a long time before responding in carefully considered detail that he had started cutting himself. He was curious to see if the Popular Author would turn back into Mom when she got a call from the school, and, to his delight, she did. He and his friends managed to hit a metro once, and the police had quickly nabbed them in the vicinity of the station. Fortunately, the incident had resulted in nothing more dangerous than a cracked windshield, but it had required a visit to the police station, a credible display of penitence, and damages, paid by Mom. It was reassuring to see that the Sought-after Panelist would not be participating in the evening of conversation at the local library that day. Apparently bringing Mom down from the stratosphere was possible; all it took was a little effort on his part.

Nowadays, the Sought-after Panelist and therapist-trainer Henri were more than happy to accept Samuel's assistance with the motorheads, unlike during Taisto's infancy. Not that he had anything against helping out: kicking around a soccer ball was nothing if not fun, and he was perfectly happy himself to read about the range of allosauruses and the mating rituals of hammerhead sharks. The best moments from high school he could remember in the shuddering train were the Sunday mornings in the yard with Kerttu and the little men, when Ukko shouted '*Thoot!*' every time he saw the ball and Taisto demonstrated his miracle save in slow motion.

Those moments had to have meant something to Kerttu, too, Samuel thought as the train approached Jyväskylä. Everything would be fine, once he got the chance to talk things out with her.

By the time he arrived that afternoon, Samuel himself realized he was too wound up. He hadn't slept all night, his heart was ticking in turbo, and the caffeine surging through his veins was making the little muscles in his face twitch uncontrollably. For some reason, Kerttu wasn't unreservedly overjoyed when he showed up at her dorm without warning. And for some reason, Samuel mocking her new hometown didn't seem to make matters any better. After all, Jyväskylä was known as the Athens of Finland, where one heard *Finnish in its purest form*, home to the country's *most prestigious university*, which was known for its *strong sense of national responsibility*. And even though Samuel was sure that, under the right circumstances, the ridiculousness of Jyväskylä's residents would have cracked Kerttu up, as it would anyone with half a brain, for some reason she wasn't laughing.

The fact that he demanded to stay and stayed, semi-coercively, on the floor of her dorm room didn't make Kerttu regret the decision she'd made, or at least not immediately. She flinched and edged away if he tried to touch her. And when he climbed in next to her at bedtime, she booted him to the floor with a painful karate kick.

Something about this was completely different than any of their past arguments. Kerttu had always been a hothead, flying off the handle at the tiniest provocation, like Samuel's kissing Marika Cederström at the beach, but if handled properly she always softened by the next day, or the following week at the latest.

Now Kerttu was calm and determined, not cold but unwavering, not unfeeling but direct. There was something frighteningly adult about her attitude, horrifyingly mature and inappropriate for a nineteen-year-old. Samuel wanted the teenaged girl back, the one who applied mascara in a crowded bus and couldn't help giggling in the library when he sang *ding-dong schlong, schlonga dinga ding dong*. But as became evident in that little dorm over the days that followed, convincing Kerttu to move back was impossible, because Kerttu had student orientation, a tour of the library, a freshman mixer at someplace called The Shack, coverall fittings at some goddamned shed, and in general far too many events and places to be that meant nothing to Samuel but sounded ominous.

He'd left in such a hurry that he didn't bring anything with him: no laptop, books, or clothes. Mom was trying to call him constantly now and texted at ten-minute intervals – she wondered, of course, where he was, was concerned – and also missed the servant who watched her kids so she could dedicate herself whole-heartedly to the roles of Red Cross expert and Sought-after Panelist. Samuel kept his phone on silent; sat in Kerttu's dorm room in the threadbare Napalm Death T-shirt and jeans he'd shown up in, because he hadn't brought a change of clothes. He ate chickpeas he found in the cupboard and tried every now and again to see if he could come up with the password for Kerttu's computer, which had evidently been changed. The fact that it wasn't *Samuel1*, *ILoveSamuel1*, or *Kerttu<3Samuel* was, in and of itself, disheartening.

Bored, he wandered this sinister city's rain-washed streets, which strangers marched up and down like robots. Anyone would have found the sight depressing, but it was enough to make Samuel want to throw himself down and beat his fists against the pavement.

He tried to talk to Kerttu about it that evening, but she didn't seem to relate to his pain.

'Shouldn't you be getting back to Helsinki?' was all she said.

'If you come with me.'

Kerttu sighed and didn't reply. She had only come home to jump in the shower, and now she was in her going-out makeup, fresher and lovelier than ever, spreading hummus on pita bread and popping slices of tofu in her mouth. Since her move, Kerttu had chopped bangs into her gorgeous long, blond hair; they looked sexy and alien. Whether it was the new haircut or new city or new life, something was making Kerttu's cheeks glow with a foreign, frightening confidence, an inner determination that Samuel had never seen in her before. To him it signaled irreversible catastrophe. A dark-blue braid had also been woven into her hair, and evidently its twin had appeared at the same time in the long locks of Möhis, Kerttu's tutor and plainly an influential figure, some sort of little Hitler, the leader of the local jugend squad.

If only I were as confident and persistent with women as my little brother Ukko, Samuel thought. Ukko loved four-year-old Helli Kyllikki and didn't hesitate to take the initiative.

'Isn't orientation starting for you guys, too?' Kerttu asked Samuel. 'How do you have the time to be hanging out here?' Her every gesture telegraphed that in a few moments she would be gone, and the thought saddened Samuel. 'Aren't you going to be bummed if you miss everything? You're only a freshman once.'

'It doesn't matter if I don't have you.'

'I'm pretty sure it does. I know we've had an amazing time here.'

'I'm thrilled for you.'

'You love this kind of stuff. And everyone loves you. That's the kind of guy you are. You'll have a thousand new friends in no time if you just haul your butt down there.'

'I don't want them, I want you.'

'How much you wanna bet some little biologist girl is going to kiss you the second the first elevator stops?'

'You're the only one I want to kiss.'

'Our dean just gave a welcome speech to the whole department, amazingly inspirational, in a good way... the way it ought to be at university. Like Aristotle, Newton, and now you. And since class has started, and the frosh fling is next week, and—'

'Kerttu, please. Come back to Helsinki with me?'

'Sam-u-el!'

'I'm just—'

'No, I already told you—'

'I know, I know. But—'

'So can you please believe me?'

'I just want to say that you can study biology and environmental science in Helsinki, too.'

'SAM-U-EL!'

'OK, OK.'

The door slammed, Kerttu took her pita bread and her bangs and went off to meet her new friends who didn't make her want to slam the door. Mom was trying to call, yet again; as soon as the phone stopped ringing the phone flashed, text message received, followed by the beep of a new voice mail.

He had kind of promised to take the rug rats to day care in the morning. But at the time, there was no way he could have known that a force majeure of this sort was imminent.

Samuel turned off his phone.

Towards the end of the week, an evening finally arrived when Kerttu wasn't out frolicking with her fellow students and she seemed to be in a slightly better mood when she came home. Maybe in part because Samuel had realized it was time to change strategies.

He had carried Kerttu's room mates' pizza boxes and reeking garbage out to the dumpsters, fixed the medicine-cabinet door that had fallen off its hinges, scrubbed the toilet and scoured the tub, bought an armful of red roses and an insanely expensive Argentinian Malbec, and prepared a meal for Kerttu that included vinegar-marinated mackerel – she ate fish now and again, although in principle she was vegetarian – cashew and bamboo-shoot salad, morning glory sautéed in garlic, roasted vegetables seasoned with mint and coriander, and tofu fried with ginger, lemon grass, coriander root, and chili and garnished with lime slices. He'd also had to buy a wok for the apartment, which seemed to have pleased Kerttu's roommates in particular.

Kerttu initially resisted, but after prolonged coaxing agreed to have a taste. To Samuel's joy, she was forced to admit that he knew how to marinate mackerel, even though he'd been a total shit as a boyfriend. As she ate, Kerttu forced Samuel to promise that he'd never pull a stunt like this again and that he'd leave soon for Helsinki, preferably tomorrow, because it was time for Kerttu to start getting used to her new life without him and that wasn't going to work if Samuel was sleeping on her bedroom floor. He immediately and gladly agreed. Thanks to the meal and the wine, which also included a nicely acidic Alsatian Riesling with the appetizers – he would have been screwed without his mom's Visa card – he gradually managed to distract Kerttu with amusing anecdotes about the good times they once shared, which smoothly but tactfully underlined the fact that no one in her brave new surroundings knew her the way Samuel did. *Nor was there any way they ever could*, he hoped Kerttu would silently add to herself.

Samuel also mentioned, as if it had just popped into his head, that no woman in the world had been as funny, smart, empathetic, affectionate, charming, discerning, stylish, beautiful, sexy, considerate, or as perfect for Samuel, both inwardly and outwardly, as Kerttu had. This was simply the impartial truth, and didn't of course mean that Kerttu shouldn't do with her life exactly as she saw fit and had already decided. But if – IF – she happened to come to the conclusion that maybe they shouldn't break up for good just yet, but continue their relationship in, for instance, one of the countless forms that existed between friendship and a long-distance and/or exclusive relationship, Samuel would be a completely different person than during their previous shared journey; he could promise that here and now. Although not much time had passed, he had learned more about himself and life since their split than he had over the past ten years put together. It had been clear to him that he loved Kerttu more than he could love any woman in the world, but it had still caught him off guard how perfectly, totally, absolutely he could fall in love with her over again, even after all these years. It was as if he'd learned to see his gorgeous girlfriend through new eyes and realized that he loved her many times more than he ever believed possible. He was able to say all this so calmly and without being overcome by emotion that he himself was surprised.

He thought he spied a small crack form in Kerttu's façade.

She said: 'Aren't you taking things a little far?'

'Just the opposite – words can't express a fraction of what I feel.'

'You're a mess.'

'That's what I'm trying to explain to you.'

'You just don't want to deal with this situation, but it will pass.'

'No, it won't.'

Samuel stared her in the eye. He could feel his cheeks blazing, as if he were developing a hundred-degree fever. He had only one goal in life; he could give up anything, but not Kerttu. He had decided – exactly thirty seconds ago – to take out a loan from the bank, buy a motorcycle, and ride it across South America, right now, tomorrow, and he demanded Kerttu join him. They would live in a tent, and earn money herding sheep and picking fruit, and make love in the wilds of Patagonia to the cries of the pampas cats in the night. He was kneeling in front of Kerttu in her dorm kitchen as he spoke and could feel his eyes getting wet: the only thing he wanted in life was to make her happy. If Kerttu would take him back, he would do anything to make sure she got everything she wanted out of life. She was the woman of his dreams. All she had to do was nod her head and he was hers to command.

Kerttu looked down at him from her chair.

'It might have been kind of nice if you'd done this back when we were still together.'

Nevertheless, Kerttu didn't pull her hand away from his, at least not yet.

'Of course! Absolutely. I guess I have to learn everything the hard way. I've learned so much about myself during the past few days that—'

She cut him off. 'Because, say, not calling when you promised to and not answering your phone because you're in Rymättylä with your friends having an extemporaneous ayahuasca party that's so intense you can't even send a single text message even though your girlfriend has left three hundred voice mails... that doesn't necessarily give the impression I'm the woman of your dreams and all I need to do is nod my head.'

'I already said I was sorry about Rymättylä.'

'And then there's that: how you think anything won't matter if you just say you're sorry... There's something about it that after the first ten thousand times isn't really that believable anymore.'

'No, I'm sure that's true.'

'How is it that you always remember your little brothers' stuff? That's what I don't get.'

'Their stuff—'

'How come you don't forget them at the entrance to the supermarket?'

'Their stuff just sticks in my head somehow. I have this... I dunno, somehow I just feel, like...' For some reason, the phrase that popped into his head felt shameful, so he made quotation marks in the air with his fingers. '"I'm responsible for them," or something.'

Kerttu's face was the picture of admiration. 'You know, that's really inspiring to hear.'

'You think?'

'Such a fantastic, super-responsible big brother.'

'Cool, because I've really done my best—'

It was only after she tossed half a glass of expensive Argentinian Malbec in his face that Samuel realized that she had been *talking ironic*, as four-year-old Ukko would have put it. 'I'm going to talk ironic now,' he announced in a serious tone whenever Henri listened to Eric Clapton at home. 'This music is *soooo* good.'

In a way, Kerttu's perspective was understandable.

The fact that Samuel was capable of caring for his little brothers might give the impression he'd purposely treated Kerttu, as she expressed it, like shit. That it hadn't had anything to do with overall irresponsibility and male chromosomes, as Kerttu had once believed, but her specifically, the girlfriend whose wishes and needs Samuel didn't give a flying fuck about.

Nevertheless, his stump speech had apparently had some impact, and perhaps Kerttu regretted throwing the wine in his face, because before long she apologized and dried it with a napkin, almost tenderly, he felt. And perhaps the fact that he was kneeling on the floor had played a role, too, as well as the fact that he hadn't budged, even after getting wine in his eyes, and perhaps it also helped that he continued to insist he had truly changed, he knew it, could feel it with every fiber of his being, and that of course the choice was Kerttu's to make, and this was about her happiness and that if she really wanted him to, he would leave immediately, this instant, and she would never have to lay eyes on him again for as long as she lived, even though it would break Samuel's heart.

Gradually, Kerttu, who clearly wanted to draw as firm a line as possible and milk the situation for all it was worth, was forced to let her expression melt a little. Samuel felt emboldened enough by this to lighten the mood with a few apt quips, which was risky, of course, but luckily they just cleared the bar, and Kerttu was amused in spite of herself. And when he dared to grow serious once again and place all his bets on one final card, look her dead in the eye and carefully take her hand, Kerttu didn't turn away but slowly, if with some initial reluctance, gave in and allowed herself to be pulled down to the floor, into Samuel's arms.

When one of her roommates came home and opened the front door, Kerttu's bare breasts were exposed not only to said roommate, who was standing in the doorway, but to the roommate's entire party of four. By this point, however, screwing on the kitchen floor had advanced to such a promising stage that it didn't seem necessary to allow the unexpected interruption to disturb them. The roommate also had the sense, after a few seconds of deathly silence, to slam the door and not return that night.

The next morning, however, Kerttu seemed subdued and didn't even want to take a shower together with Samuel. Instead of light-hearted banter, she heaved protracted sighs. And at some point between five to ten and ten on the dot, the possibility that had hovered in the air at the Helsinki railway station ticket-vending machine started to feel increasingly and troublingly likely: that what Samuel was dealing with was not necessarily a misunderstanding that could be easily remedied.

And the breakup sex that, for once, both of them had wanted just as fast, just as much, and at the same time, and that Samuel had, on the kitchen floor the night before, imagined was makeup sex, only seemed to make everything worse. It suddenly felt as if it would have been better to stay at home, participate in the activities for new students at his own university, and chase Kerttu out of all of those little nooks and crannies of his mind she had nestled into over the years along with her needs, accessories, mascara, and opinions. And during the next fifty milliseconds, which felt like a week of hell, Samuel realized subsequently and partly simultaneously that 1) Kerttu wasn't going to change her mind, which logically meant that 2) before long, the evening would come when she wouldn't be coming home but would be sharing the bed of some mustachioed Finnish Athenian who spoke the language in its purest form and would, no doubt, display a strong sense of national responsibility with his cock the second he was given the chance, and that 3) Samuel could take anything, but not this. And that 4) if he was going to have to face this situation, he would rather do it at home alone so he couldn't be sure if it had happened, which would, practically speaking, feel the same as if it really had happened, but for some reason would still be easier.

And so at twenty after four that afternoon, when Kerttu was at her study group for Introduction to Environmental Protection – a course in which, based on what Kerttu had told him, they taught a crock of the country's purest shit – he'd been forced to swallow his disappointment and drag himself to the train station, heartbroken. And at the station he even answered his phone when Henri tried to call three times in a row: he couldn't get hold of Mom and couldn't find Ukko's dragon outfit.

'It's hanging on the rack in the boys' room,' Samuel answered, trying to gulp down the lump in his throat, 'look underneath the other clothes. Yeah, I know, you can't see it, but it's still there, dig down underneath everything.'

He hung up and walked to the train. And so the other passengers wouldn't witness his sobbing, he hid in the freight car, the door to which had been left inexplicably unlocked. And there he sat, alone on the cold metal floor, listening to the thunk of the tracks until four hours later he arrived in Helsinki, where autumn was well underway.

In the days that followed, it started sinking in that Kerttu was the one who'd kept him from falling apart all summer.

Even though he had shut away his expectations for his graduation party and the resulting emotions in the deepest part of his mind, and even though they had nothing to do with Kerttu, for some reason it was impossible to keep them from breaking out now.

Kerttu was the only one he had told about the graduation party. Now he had to carry everything alone.

The memory was like a tiny, nasty electric shock. Beforehand, the thought of the party had been hot and electrifying; afterwards, Samuel could remember nothing but a disorienting fog, champagne, waves of relatives surging into their home, many of whom he didn't even know by name – *You look so handsome, Samuel* – the crushing pressure in his chest that was simultaneously the end of the world and its beginning.

To him, Dad's message had been unambiguous.

He no longer remembered the exact words. What he did remember was how his heart had raced after receiving the message and the fact that he had struggled to maintain a neutral expression in the presence of others for the rest of the day.

He couldn't bring himself to check Dad's message again, but he was sure that there was no other possible interpretation.

He didn't know what high-school graduations in the United States were like, but they couldn't be that different: Dad had to have understood the nature of the event in question. He knew Mom had sent Dad a message early that year, long before Samuel sent his own message informing Dad that he'd be matriculating soon.

The knowledge had been his companion all spring. Dad knew the graduation was coming and had promised to attend. Dad also must

have realized that it was an important day for Samuel, the most important in his life to date. He could still feel how the thought had burned
in his breast as he sat in the bus, how he curled up against it when he
went to bed. The other kids seemed to be nervous about the exams,
but he had no trouble taking them in stride, even relishing them; they
were a chance for him to demonstrate what he knew.

But: out of sight, out of mind. It wasn't anyone's fault. That's the
way life was.

There was no point moping about it.

Dad had his new, happy family and life in the United States.

Two weeks before his graduation, when Samuel learned he was valedictorian, by then at the latest it was clear Dad wouldn't be coming,
had never intended to. Samuel remembered the moment when he
finally understood how things were. He stood in the school's lobby
barely registering what the teachers who had come up to shake his
hand, congratulate him, were saying.

His father's visit had been all in his head.

At his graduation party, he smiled, relaxed and pleased, believed his
own voice, which spoke to the guests confidently and convincingly.
He celebrated over dinner and got drunk in town that night, as was
the custom, was carefree and good company as always. All he had to
do was swallow down the sensation of absolute loss that had, over
the course of the night, consumed him, though it was highly unlikely
that anyone else noticed.

Except Kerttu.

He could tell from her tentative glances at him during the after-party
that Kerttu knew exactly what he was thinking. Her fingers caressing
his hair; the unspoken condolences; the wordless understanding that
something in him had died.

Outside, fall was at its most brilliant. The lawns and gutters dozed
under blankets of bright yellow and fire-red maple leaves.

Because it was unclear to Samuel how his faith in women and life
would be restored, he found it most constructive to spend a few weeks
staring at a television program where viewers were encouraged to
guess what major national holiday Ind*p*nd*nc*_ Day might be. The

attractive hostess of this chat-based show wore a clinging swimsuit that accentuated her nipples so distinctly that if you squinted your eyes, you could imagine she was in the studio naked.

'So, like, you could be the lucky one who's gonna win up to two hundred euros right now! Can you guys imagine? What an amazing prize! So, like, seriously, guys, pick up that phone and give me a call and we'll answer, hey, what letter did you have in mind? And then we'll check and make sure it was the exact right one! So, like, seriously, give me a call, you don't even have to get up from the couch.'

Samuel could hear his brain cells melting, and there was something remarkably satisfying about this.

No one had ever dumped him before. There had always been something over-the-top and melodramatic about the tears of those who had been dumped. He'd had a hard time relating to the feeling, perhaps because he'd never experienced it before.

While there was still the minutest chance that Kerttu might change her mind and call, text, email, Messenger, FB, or friend him into some new digital community, it felt smartest to make waiting for this his primary activity. But the way the heavy, jagged lump of disappointment resulting from his dad and the graduation party weighed on his gut, it didn't feel like there'd be any good news soon.

He spent most of the day lying in bed without eating, except for the time he spent lying on the sofa. Mom desperately tried to figure out who this stubble-faced, television-watching, nineteen-year-old human trash bag was and what it had done with her lovely, independent, responsible, handsome, funny firstborn son. But in this condition, he felt like he had to exert enormous effort to squeeze out a single word from somewhere incredibly deep within. Which meant it was wisest to keep verbal communication with Mom constructive but minimal.

Like: 'Samuel, can we talk?'

'Just let me die in peace.'

Or: 'Samuel, is something bothering you?'

'Your face.'

It also felt reasonable to test the waters carefully by writing a series of increasingly lengthy professions of love on the public walls of Kerttu's various social media services. When these didn't elicit a response, something about the messages started feeling more and more embarrassing, for which reason it felt like a good idea to balance those out with sharp criticisms of Kerttu's life choices that even he noticed slipped into the needlessly personal at times and, to outsiders, might well have sounded worryingly bitter in places.

Mom voiced her suspicion that perhaps these weren't the most effective methods of improving Samuel's mood. But Mom was an old fart who didn't understand anything about love, and nothing was as infuriating as an old fart who was right.

The phone beeped from time to time, but it was never Kerttu. His friends asked him to the movies or wanted to know what was up, invited him to parties or skateboarding, begged him to take down Western turbo-charged capitalism. Answering the messages felt overwhelming. There wouldn't be anyone at the parties anyway, except women who were happy about the wrong things and men who didn't understand that promises were always broken and the planet was being destroyed. Let the young fight turbo-charged capitalism; he was too old, too jaded.

He wouldn't have even noticed his own nineteenth birthday if Taisto and Ukko hadn't sung 'Happy Birthday' to him and Mom hadn't given him a gift card for a sporting goods store. He would wake up spontaneously in the middle of the night, not knowing what to do with himself, or wouldn't fall asleep until five A.M., after having spent the entire night awake. On those few occasions when he left the house, he wandered the streets wearing the red hunting cap Kerttu had fished out for him from the tables at the flea market, sat on the benches at Tokoinranta Park, and envied the ducks their fellows and the drunks their bottles. He remembered having once wondered where the ducks from Töölönlahti Bay went in the wintertime, and now he knew: to the most sheltered, out-of-the-way corner of Tokoinranta Inlet. There they huddled together, warming themselves, occasionally casting a pitying duck-look his way.

Worried, Mom tried to shoo him out of the house for runs and to the doctor – *Thanks, Mom! I think I'll head out right now!* – and had, in a further alarming sign, completely stopped nagging him about the motorheads.

He had made himself unnecessary in his little brothers' lives as well: after a rough start, Henri and Mom seemed to have gradually grown into their responsibilities as the mother and father of a four- and a six-year-old, who actually had to schedule their clients' therapy sessions, advanced training for scarf-wearing women, and expertise on immigrant affairs, according to the boys' needs. Surely it was new and rewarding for them, responsibility built character, but the result was no one needed him anymore. Taisto had revealed the secret rocket route, Samuel's last trump card as king of walks to day care, to Henri, and Henri had shown them how to race through it at interstellar speed, which the little men now bragged about, eyes wide with awe. And if Mom and Henri let the motorheads watch television a little too long in the evenings and nowadays later and later, so they themselves could enjoy a moment's peace and quiet with their glasses of wine, perhaps the responsibility truly was theirs, as difficult as it was to believe.

'Hang in there, motorheads, it gets easier as you grow older,' Samuel said out loud before he realized he was lying. A bum on all fours, scrounging the shoreline for empty bottles, turned and gave him a quizzical look; he had heard Samuel talking to himself.

The impetus for change finally came one windy fall evening when clouds had gathered portending rain. Samuel was lying in bed at seven P.M., working up the willpower to drag himself out of bed for breakfast, when Henri knocked on his bedroom door and extended the offer of a serious, heart-to-heart conversation.

'I'm getting the strong impression that you could use someone to talk to.'

Henri's penetrating eyes looked at Samuel reassuringly from behind thin, metal-rimmed glasses. The sheer horror of this moment impelled Samuel to gather all his willpower right then and there and throw himself into his new degree program. Mom did her part by shoving him out the front door, afraid, evidently, that he felt responsible for the little men in a way that hindered his budding autonomy.

'We'll take care of them, seriously,' she said. 'Now go.'

'You sure?'

'They love you and love playing and spending time with you and of course look up to you like no one else, but you also have to live your own life.'

'Hmm.'

'You're the most socially gifted person I know,' said Mom, looking him in the eye. 'I don't know anyone who's as good with people as you are. Now go to that university and start your new life. Get everything you can out of it.'

She said she'd been thinking about things and realized that she'd been giving Samuel too much responsibility for his little brothers for a long time now. She was sorry; she'd been working too much and hadn't realized. According to Mom, she shouldn't have let him take the boys to day care regularly in his senior year. It wasn't fair to Samuel. It was good that he knew how to express himself so clearly now. Mom had learned her lesson. And besides, there was Henri to help her, too.

Nevertheless, Mom said she hoped that in the future Samuel would learn to communicate in a more constructive fashion, speak out when something was bothering him instead of crawling into bed in protest. She thought the time had come for him to take responsibility for his life.

Everything would turn for the better.

But it had been a month and a half since the other freshmen had started their studies. As he bounced around the lobbies of the university's remarkably confusing, anonymous buildings, it quickly became clear to Samuel that, for the others, life was rolling a long way off in the distance. The rounds of introductions and games were over; now people were building careers. Everyone had found their path and was moving onward, and always through the right doors. The scrawls in the bathroom stalls were rife with insider humor: ha ha, laughing was so much fun when you were one of the gang. Many of the fall lectures had already been held, and there were no smiling peer mentors around to explain to those who missed orientation what or where ViB1 was or what the hell these modules and points meant and how you accessed that fucking moodle, whatever it was, and why his user ID still didn't work. The trendy-looking students Samuel sat next to hopefully in the canteen acted as if he didn't exist and self-importantly discussed some proseminar they just had to get into that spring, and something about their tone was astoundingly demoralizing. Did they think he had the fucking plague?

Everything seemed to be going horribly, irreversibly awry, until he noticed the poster.

A gigantic, glossy ad had been tacked up to the bulletin board, inviting incoming biology students to the frosh fling in CAPITAL LETTERS and exclamation points. Wasn't the frosh fling some massive party for new students? Kerttu had been blabbering about hers, too. The jungle theme mentioned in the text and referenced in the layout struck Samuel as off-putting and childish, but then again CHEAP BOOZE! SMOKING! CROWDS! DESPAIR! sounded promising. Inspired by the poster, he visited the departmental website, where he learned that many of the tutors – one of whom had evidently been appointed to him, too – appeared to be attractive young women.

Maybe he shouldn't make things too difficult.

What if he just swallowed his past disappointments and threw himself whole-heartedly into everything that was still open to him? Maybe Kerttu hadn't been totally wrong after all. He'd still find his place.

After a lengthy search, he settled on a six-foot-tall tiger outfit from Helsinki's most expensive costume rental, which included an enormous mask and a bewilderingly long and tricky tail. He'd find some way of explaining the charges to Mom when the Visa bill arrived. The tiger costume made such a big impression at home, particularly on Ukko, that that alone seemed to justify the cost. It also felt oddly satisfying to hear both of the little men whining to Henri that they wanted to go to university, too.

When the big day came, Samuel showered, spent minutes at the mirror fixing his hair, patted the aftershave he had bought specifically for this event onto his cheeks, and demonstrated his sense of humor by standing in front of the mirror with Mom's eyeliner and painting on whiskers and coloring his nose black. He bought a ten-pack of beer and headed for the venue in good time. Would it have been better to be fashionably late, by, say, an hour? No, it was best to be on time; they might give instructions at the beginning or make introductions. He looked up the address three times to make sure he went to the right place and double-checked the bus schedules so he'd leave early enough to get there in time.

As he climbed the stately stone stairs of the University of Helsinki's old student union, he found himself coming up with the clever, self-deprecating quips he would post on various social media if he happened to get lucky tonight. Not to brag, of course, but it would be good for Kerttu to hear that he had left his previous relationship behind and was living a happy, independent, sexually healthy life. Maybe a private message to her, sufficiently loosely formulated, would be best, so there wouldn't be any misunderstandings regarding public boasting.

When Samuel made it to the right floor and burst into the granite-lined auditorium with his tiger costume and bag of beer, he was greeted with a pregnant silence that stopped him at the door cold. A crowd of senile-looking invalids in tuxedos, evening gowns, and medals was staring at him inquisitively from long tables covered in white tablecloths. Mom was a teenager compared to this bunch. Something about the men's gray beards and the women's bicycle-helmet-shaped hairdos, the flags and standards hanging from the walls, felt annihilating, and some ancient toad with a cane was croaking out a speech at the front of the room about a centennial celebration and the annual Porridge Party that had assumed its present form among the club's traditions in 1948.

With the eyes of the pensioners burning holes in his back, he slunk out of the auditorium in his tiger costume and over to the building where he had seen the poster advertising the frosh fling, even though he already had a hunch what he would find there. The party had been a week ago. The first thing to jump out at him from the poster, which for some reason hadn't been taken down yet, were the words THIS SATURDAY! BE THERE! The date was in much smaller print at the bottom.

At the same time, he spotted another announcement on the bulletin board, older than the frosh fling poster, already curling at the corners and partly covered by other flyers, and felt his heart drop ominously. The memo reminded him of something that had vaguely crossed his mind at some point and then been buried again beneath everything else.

All new students had to register by 15 September. Not registering meant losing your spot in the degree program.

That was a month ago.

He was standing in front of the bulletin board, still staring at the poster, when security came and informed him that, unfortunately, beer wasn't allowed inside the building.

The world had always been bound for destruction, of course, but never like it was now. There was over 400 ppm of carbon dioxide in the atmosphere, and the number was rising every minute. An island of plastic garbage the size of Texas was drifting across the Pacific Ocean and was impossible to clean up, because it wasn't an island but soup, Samuel would never meet anyone ever again, and there wasn't a single glass that was half-empty; they were all filled to the brim with piss.

If before he'd had a reason to get up from the couch twice a day – to

masturbate to the cute host of the chat-based television program –
now he couldn't even muster the energy to do that. His little brothers
looked at him, their childish faces grave with compassion. They clearly
wanted to help. But of course they had their own lives, relationships,
and busy day care careers to look after.

When he couldn't fall asleep at night, Samuel would read his *Finland
Today* article, overcome with shame. It was unbelievable how positively
his thoughts had been interpreted. *As our courageous high-school
senior Mr Heinonen indicates, there is still hope for the world.* It was
hard to say who was more naïve: the young writer who'd made a fool
of himself or the patronizing head-patters with their simpering replies.
Even terrifying things could be turned around, supposedly, if we all
just got down to work. Only an immature high schooler could live in
such a bubble. This whole time, his essay had preached catastrophe;
he just hadn't realized it. Its primary point was that, in contrast to
common belief, people couldn't make an impact with their consumer
choices, because they didn't know what they were doing.

He hadn't told Mom or Henri that he had accidentally given up
his spot at the university, but they sensed that things had gone awry.
Lying on his bed, he could hear through the door as Henri explained
to Taisto in the entryway: 'Samuel's not feeling very well right now.'

Ukko was thrilled. 'Is he barfing?' Ukko had had the stomach flu that
spring and had developed a deep fascination with the topic.

'No,' Henri said. 'Not feeling well in a different way.'

'Maybe he'll start feeling worse,' Ukko said hopefully.

Samuel could hear Taisto's footsteps stomping up to his door, as
resolutely as ever.

'I'm gonna ask him for some spit.'

'Please don't,' Henri said.

'But if he's sick…'

Taisto needed a sample of the patient's spit for his microscope.
He was interested in all manner of bugs, unlike Ukko, who was only
interested in those that caused vomiting. Our little generalist and
specialist, was what Henri told his colleagues.

'Please don't.'

'But if he's sick…'

'Now is not a good time, buddy.'

'But I want to look at it under the microscope.'

'Not now, Taisto.'

'Dad, guess what "lamb" is in pig Latin.'

'What?'

'Ambahambakamba.'

'Is that so.'

'Didja know, Dad? Didja know? I'm gonna ask Samuel if he knew.'

'Don't ask him.'

'I call the front seat.'

'No way, I do!'

The little men thundered out the front door with Henri, none of them remembering Samuel's existence.

The more time he had to surf online, the more he realized how fundamentally screwed up the world was. He'd spent the previous night investigating the astoundingly rapid advance of the present wave of extinction, the largest in the history of the world. It was mind-blowing to realize that all intents and purposes nothing was being done to stop this, and the longer you thought about it, the more incredible, frustrating, and infuriating it seemed.

He wished he could sleep all night, but it had become impossible for him to fall asleep before five A.M. And although he didn't have the energy to turn on his computer during the day, he had to find some way of killing time at night so he wouldn't totally lose his mind. During these long hours of darkness he had come across numerous websites calling attention to environmental problems, animal rights, and the catastrophic effects of the neoliberal economic system. He found himself spending more and more time on these sites and participating in the discussions. Hanging out online seemed only to increase his anxiety about the state of the world, but it helped him through the early-morning hours.

Enough time had passed since his father's message that there was no chance of any misunderstanding on that front.

Dad had not only said he'd be attending the party, he had also promised to comment on the article in *Finland Today* in greater detail when he had the time.

Translating the entire essay and the responses to it into English with the help of a dictionary had been a slow process, but Samuel had done it gladly, since he knew why he was doing it. At first he'd thought he'd publish the translation online. But because it was unlikely that Dad would stumble across it by accident, it had felt better to seal it in an envelope and mail it directly to him.

Now he could see how ridiculous that idea had been, too.

Dad had more interesting things going on in his life than a poorly translated essay written by a Finnish son who was a stranger to him.

Which one could also, of course, deduce from Dad's response to the diploma Samuel had sent him.

Samuel stared at the text. The letters glowed, ice hot, against the blue background of the computer screen.

The soles of his feet tingled. The pounding of his heart echoed in the dark bedroom. Outside, the evening was dark and rainy; the cold, wet trickles running down the windowpane promised November's freezing weather.

There was no question he should turn off the computer then and there. He should never have come back to this place. And yet there was never any question that he would. It was seven P.M., he had just woken up, and he had a long, lonely night ahead of him. After nagging for a few weeks, Mom had given up on trying to drag him out of bed in the mornings, presumably because it had proven hopeless.

Samuel had ended up in that part of the internet he should never have visited. Might it even be a crime? Apparently the police monitored these networks, too, these days, set traps for those who tried to hide in the gloom of these very corners. That was another reason he shouldn't have come here.

But the people on these websites knew about his father.

The on-screen text immediately caused his insides to heat up and burn, like a small, hot flame. He wasn't sure who maintained the site, but they were well informed not only about Dad's field of research, but also the methods he used, down to the species.

Samuel heard a car drive past outside; the sound receded and then disappeared.

He stared at the text. That's when it struck him for the first time, the act he realized he was capable of. But at that instant there was a knock at the door, and Samuel's heart leaped into his throat. The intruder had already started twisting the handle; he barely managed to dim the screen before the door was thrust open.

Mom stood there in the doorway, blinking at him and smiling uncertainly.

'Oh, you're awake,' she said brightly. It wasn't clear to Samuel what her point was, but it felt like pure fuckery.

'Have you noticed any...'

As she searched for the right words, Mom swayed on her feet, as if that would make it easier for him to guess what she meant.

'... effect? Any difference in the way you feel?'

She looked so phony-chipper that Samuel didn't feel like answering. She was referring to the medication, of course. In his moment of deepest despair, Samuel had made the mistake of letting Henri and Mom pressure him into seeing the nurse practitioner at the local health center. Samuel himself had been under the mistaken impression that he would be prescribed anti-depressants without any unnecessary chit-chat, be in and out in five minutes, prescription in hand. Weighing the matter in the waiting room, he'd forced himself to clear the psychological hurdles to taking psychoactive medication when he was basically a healthy young man. But in the end, admitting the severity of the situation was a relief. What made him think he was so emotionally sound that he didn't need medication? It wasn't likely that he was that much more balanced than everyone else his age. The very notion was narcissistic hubris, a delusion of grandeur, like trying to argue with his psych teacher at high school.

Besides, for the first time in the history of the world, mankind was destroying its living environment – wasn't taking antidepressants a totally justified reaction?

But it had been clear to the nurse practitioner that Samuel's early abandonment had wounded him deeply. The wounds caused by a father who rejected him simply hadn't been visible until now, at the challenging stage of becoming an independent adult.

'I think things have gone pretty well until now,' he protested.

The nurse practitioner looked at him critically. 'What do you mean by well?'

'Well, my grade point average is nine point nine, I got into the university on my first try, I've always had lots of friends, I was in a good relationship for a couple of years, I love my little brothers and they love me, my matriculation essay was published in *Finland Today*…'

He asked the nurse practitioner if he couldn't just have his serotonin levels tweaked so he could get on with his life. But only a doctor could do that. Besides, according to the nurse practitioner, serotonin theory didn't stand up to critical examination. But she thought it was perfectly possible that Samuel had been manic without realizing it.

'My whole life?'

'That's also possible.'

'Without noticing anything?'

'You wouldn't necessarily, it just feels good. A little hypomania.'

'So it feels good but it's bad?'

In addition to mania proper, current medicine also recognized bipolar II disorder, the nurse explained, which wasn't always easy to detect. A subclinical form that could be almost completely asymptomatic had just been added to the classification.

'If it's completely asymptomatic, why is it an illness?'

'It's a serious, life-threatening disease,' the nurse practitioner said, her voice quivering with affront. His role here was clearly to listen, not talk back to professionals who were trying to help.

It would take years of processing with an expensive expert, he needed to talk, talk, talktalktalk about his painful childhood experiences, and even then there were no guarantees his condition would improve. As a matter of fact, it often grew worse. Samuel clearly had a hereditary tendency to biological brain disease.

'So is there's some genetic test for it?'

The nurse practitioner paused, seeming to consider Samuel's question, but then looked at him in a totally different way and said: 'I wonder if you have a personality disorder?'

'What?'

'Since you're so argumentative.'

The nurse practitioner shook her head; an oppositional attitude didn't bode well. Luckily, they could start the medication immediately. It damaged the liver and thyroid glands and atrophied the brain, but in Samuel's situation it would be worth it. Besides, there were only a few trials indicating cerebral atrophy.

'That doesn't sound so good,' he said.

The nurse practitioner frowned. 'Psychotherapy's no picnic, either.'

'I wasn't exactly thinking—'

'Or as effective.' The nurse practitioner's mouth was set in a taut line. 'If that's what you're thinking. For many people, the symptoms only worsen during therapy.'

'I was actually more thinking along the lines of these worrying societal issues, climate change and… That maybe we should be doing something about them, but—'

'Untreated bi-po,' the nurse practitioner said, shaking her head. 'Nice prognosis.'

'But if there's no way you can tell a sick person from one who's completely healthy, then I don't think I'll—'

'Mmm-hmm.' The nurse practitioner inhaled the syllables and was already tapping furiously at her computer, classifying him in impartially disheartening terms.

When Samuel was at the door, she said: 'Good luck with that life of yours.'

Out in the hallway, he heard her sigh, evidently into the phone: 'You'd never believe what a sad case I just had in here. So young and so sick.'

Samuel roused himself from his reverie and realized Mom was still standing at the door to his room, waiting for an answer.

'Did you happen to notice that ad in the paper?' she asked, in a voice that was, if possible, even more phony-chipper than the one she'd been speaking in until this point.

Over the past few weeks, he had learned that the best way to deal with her in this mood was not to respond.

'Some company is looking for research assistants. Biosciences something.'

I can barely contain my excitement, Samuel thought.

'That could be fun, couldn't it?' Mom enthused. 'You could earn yourself some pocket money.'

For a long time Mom had tried to convince Samuel to attend his classes at the university and failed to understand why he refused. She hadn't been able to see how, by getting a degree, he would have been propping up academia's corrupt power structures that, in fact, needed to be dismantled, the way he had tried to explain to her. This had sounded so crazy to Mom that for a long time she refused even to talk about it, which was just fucking fine with Samuel. But after a little interrogation, she had finally squeezed a confession out of him about the embarrassing curtailment of his academic career.

Mom had approached the matter as a purely practical one and marched over to the phone, her Societally Influential Panelist-look on her face. It felt oddly satisfying to see her be bounced from one representative to another, continually asked to wait, and the expression on her face gradually shift from frustrated to deflated.

Upon understanding that his spot at the university truly was lost for good, she had apparently shifted strategies: she needed to get him to work. Even the prospect of the planet being destroyed was, in her view, fundamentally a product of Samuel having too little to do.

Mom kept blabbering; this company, Laajakoski Biosciences, sounded incredibly interesting to her. And she had clearly been expecting that upon hearing these magic words, this young man who was already starting to smell would rise immediately from his burial shroud and go out into the streets to praise life.

When he still didn't answer, Mom stared at him. 'You haven't started using drugs, have you, or I mean – experimentation is what I'm talking about, I guess, but you, you haven't, have you…?'

An agonizing wait. Why couldn't she leave him alone?

'It's just, I'm wondering what exactly is wrong with you. Can't you say something?'

It would be impossible to talk about the graduation party with Mom. The mere mention of Dad aged her ten years, made something cold, foreign appear in her eyes. And it wasn't her fault Dad couldn't give a flying fuck.

Over the past few weeks, Samuel had unintentionally stumbled upon a powerful weapon he hadn't known existed: simply by shutting his mouth and lying in bed, he could drive Mom to the brink of despair. Maybe it would have been worth trying earlier, in place of, for instance, chucking rocks at the metro and huffing butane.

When he still didn't show the slightest sign of answering, Mom said: 'Samuel, can I say one thing?'

'No.'

'But I'm getting the strong impression that there's something important going on here.'

Mom clearly interpreted his silence as permission to continue.

'Samuel, I'm getting the strong impression that you're at a place in your life where—'

'Have you ever noticed that that's what Henri always says?'

'What?'

Mom was clearly stunned that more than one word had passed her son's lips at a time.

'Every time Henri wants to express an opinion, he starts off by saying he's "getting the strong impression that." Mom, have you noticed that you never used to talk like that? Until you met Henri.'

From the look on her face, Mom was getting agitated.

'If you'll just listen to me for a minute, Samuel, and let me say what I have to say...'

'I'm getting the strong impression that I'm going to plug my ears.'

'What I want to say to you, Samuel, is this. I'm wondering if the time has come for you to start learning to take responsibility for yourself.'

'I wonder if there's going to come a time when you'll stop talking like a dickhead.'

'Samuel, I'm trying to help.'

'Yeah, well, it feels really fucking helpful.'

'Samuel...'

'Mom.'

Suddenly the door to Samuel's room flew open. In the doorway stood Ukko, his fine, carrot-colored, four-year-old's hair damp and curled with perspiration. He stared at Samuel, red-cheeked and dramatic.

'I'm gonna buy a cat with my potty money,' Ukko said.

'Aha,' Samuel forced himself to reply, in as enthusiastic a tone as he could.

A long time ago, *pappa* had started giving Ukko twenty-cent coins every time he used the potty. Ukko had faced some psychological hurdle to the procedure that adults found incomprehensible; but *pappa* had figured money might make it easier to clear. It was evident that Mom and Henri weren't convinced of the necessity, especially now, since the problem had disappeared ages ago. Every time they visited *pappa*, though, Ukko would dash straight from the front door to grunt in the bathroom, and almost always *pappa* managed to slip a coin into the kid's fist when Mom wasn't looking.

Ukko had already thudded back down the stairs. Samuel could sense Mom staring at him from the doorway, sick at heart and helpless. It

felt important to him to fix his eyes silently and impassively on a small,
uneven patch in the wall paint until Mom eventually left, which only
happened after a substantial delay and many maternal sighs of despair.

Samuel waited a long while after ringing the doorbell. He was starting
to think he'd gotten the time wrong when Matias suddenly materialized
in the doorway in his spiked-leather Goth gear.

'Faggot.'

'Dickhead.'

Matias turned and walked back inside as if it were all the same to
him whether or not Samuel followed. A wave of relief washed over
Samuel: it was as if a day hadn't gone by since they'd last met.

He followed Matias inside. They went down to the basement of his
parents' four-story house and plopped onto the couch where they'd
hung out countless nights over the years.

To Samuel's delight, there was no need for a pointless warm-up; within seconds they were right back where they'd left off. Their friendship
had been on such a solid footing for so long; they'd been through so
much together in the past. The timing of it had mattered, too: they'd
been best friends in junior high. It was evident in the way Matias poured
Samuel some homebrew and said: 'Latest batch from the home cellar.'

He handed over a glass of murky wine liquid with a blizzard of
particles swirling in it. The wine had *just finished* today. Technically it
still required filtering, but that would have taken an extra day or two.
Skipping the clarifying meant they could drink it right away.

What had Samuel been thinking, bitching about his problems to
that nurse practitioner? He wasn't sick; all you needed was friends to
keep you going.

After his hopes were dashed by the uptight nurse, Samuel had gone to
the doctor to ask if he could get on disability, like his classmate Mikko
Arpalainen. Mikko had a developmental neurological disorder, the
symptoms of which included feelings of loneliness and insignificance
and fantasies that life was transactional and everyone was selling
something, most of all selling out. That's why Mikko slept all day
and stayed up all night playing a computer game where combat took
place with swords and ancient magical powers.

But in the doctor's opinion, there was no indication of any permanent disability in Samuel's case. His problems were, according to her, normal everyday stuff that it was neither possible nor desirable to treat medically. Samuel had harbored some resentment towards the doctor over this. It was another reason it felt good hanging out with his friend, who understood him on a completely different level. Besides, what good would a prescription have done him? The very thought of antidepressants felt ridiculous to him now. If life was inherently empty, did it make sense to try and escape it through chemicals that screwed with the body's natural neurochemistry?

'Here,' Matias said, handing him an orange capsule.

'What's this?'

'Some new variation. I'm not totally sure.'

Samuel took the capsule and tossed it back with a swig of moonshine. Matias stood, turned on his gigantic television, and started playing a movie from his computer.

'Ballpark?'

'Can't remember. Good shit though. Should be.'

Back in high school, weekends had been rescued by a random Chinese web shop someone had stumbled across; word had spread quickly through their circle of friends. Various countries, including Finland, had their own stores within the shop. From the HEAVEN GOOD PLANT NUTRIENTS garden shop, you could order chemical modifications of cannabis, amphetamines, and ecstasy that the government hadn't gotten around to prohibiting yet because they hadn't existed until they were available for purchase. New substances appeared on the site every week, their names ranging from the straightforward (CANABBIS VARIATION, NEW – LEGAL!!) to the technical (aFRv-3-niH-CRyu) and the cryptic (Who Are The Phuong Phu Drang Police?) to the mystical (I am dancing at the feet of my lord, all is bliss, all is bliss). At the bottom of the page, there was a warning: *Only science use for research! Proffessionalism for customers! Not for recreation purpose!*

When a compound was prohibited as an illegal substance under a country's laws, it vanished from under the country's flag. Samuel and Matias had often ordered all kinds of weird stuff from the store for purposes of experimentation – partially because they knew that an interesting new novelty could disappear that same afternoon. No one should try these chemicals under any circumstances, a professor had said on television: the substances threw off the body's natural equilibrium and disturbed thousands of biological processes, with potentially serious consequences. If life felt empty, the answer was not medicating it with chemicals that interfered with the brain's neurochemistry.

'Wicked wine,' Samuel said, raising his glass. It tasted like boiled sock-juice spiked with urine and artificial apple flavoring. For homebrew, that was a strong showing.

'Thanks.'

'Nice alcohol content.'

'Yup.'

Matias could afford to buy wine, expensive imported stuff, from the state liquor store with his parents' dough, but doing so ran counter to his DIY philosophy. Making his own records from start to finish was appropriately punk, and the same went for the paint-thinner he drank. Or at least that's the way Matias explained it. People who didn't know him well often came away with the impression that he was from an impoverished or working-class family.

Samuel settled into the creaking sofa. Kerttu's absence still stung every second, even when he wasn't consciously thinking about it. Kerttu Karoliina Lamminsuo's long, sun-bleached hair, which now had now been chopped into alien, sexy bangs, Kerttu's perfect wide mouth, Kerttu's eyes, which would stop anyone in their tracks: they all etched tiny, painful cuts into his soul. The more exhaustively he pictured to himself the sleazy hipsters Kerttu could be kissing at this very moment, the more adult and mature a solution suicide by self-immolation started to seem.

He knew it was critical he thoroughly process the breakup and the emotions it had inspired with a close friend right then and there.

'It's actually a good thing we broke up.'

'Fewer complications.'

'Yeah. Can focus on what's important.'

'Tons of other chicks waiting out there.'

'Damn straight.'

Now that that was over, they could concentrate on the movie. A plumber had just rung the doorbell, and a young woman at a stove had teetered over in a hot-pink miniskirt and five-inch stilettos to answer. It looked to Samuel like the edges of the image had started curling in an impossible way. That could be because the movie had been downloaded as torrents from a sketchy peer-to-peer network whose members often amused themselves by secretly adding their own effects to the movies or editing out entire scenes. But the curling at the edges could also be because of the Chinese tablet, Samuel realized. Could he be feeling the effects this fast?

'Is this 'cid?' he asked.

'Could be.'

'It kind of feels like it.'

'I don't think I'm feeling it at all yet.'

'What was it called?'

'How Good Morning Are You. No one says "cid" anymore, by the way.'

'So what do they say?'

'Wouldn't you like to know, queerbait?'

'No one says "queerbait" anymore, by the way.'

'Yeah, they do.'

'Your mom, maybe.'

Matias had the house all to himself, because his mom was in Brussels, his dad in Vietnam, and his sister at the Aurora psychiatric facility: his mom was negotiating a bailout for the financial crisis, his dad subcontractors for a new factory, and his sister outdoor privileges.

The home had been completed a few years ago. Samuel thought back to the weekend-long housewarming party Matias had thrown without permission, and an unexpected wave of nostalgia washed over him. He remembered standing out on the steps, gazing at the shards of broken window in the fresh topsoil, when excited shouts had suddenly cut through the cacophony of voices and music. *Cops!* When he saw the police cruiser, Samuel had hastily stashed his drugs in the flowerbed, pleased with his hiding spot. And then a minute later, Jannika had burst through the front door and puked up half a bottle of Soave and half-digested saag paneer in the exact same spot, with a millimeter-perfect precision that entailed cosmic conspiracy.

He remembered thinking at the time that the aura of artificiality emanating from the house would gradually fade. But it had been two years since then. The graded yard still looked stark and incomplete; pine trees, ornamental shrubs, and large birches had been ripped out to

make room for the house's foundations, and nothing had appeared in
their place. A truckload of topsoil had been dumped on the property,
but for some reason a new lawn hadn't grown. The house had eight
bedrooms, a sauna, a swimming pool and hot tub, and an entire floor
for each child. It was built of wood and concrete with technology that
had only been used before a few times. Large, bright windows had
been punched into the walls, and a spacious atrium had been left at the
heart, where the snaking line of the massive spiral staircase could be
seen all the way from the entryway to the top floor. The dark concrete
and wood looked impossibly chic, the combination warmer than you
might imagine, but there was something about the overall effect that
left you restless. Perhaps because, Samuel thought, the house was so
much larger than you were used to seeing in Finland.

When no one was home, computer-controlled lights turned off and
on at random intervals so it looked like someone was inside.

In the basement, Matias had set up a home studio, where he stayed
up all night making demos for his band, drank energy drinks from
an enormous fridge dedicated solely to them, and used the massive
HD flat-screen TV to watch Japanese clips you couldn't find online
and where everything was authentic and performed by amateurs, not
actors the way they clearly were in the movie that was playing now.

'God, what a faker. That blonde.'

'She's pretty bad.'

'And not even that hot.'

'Yeah, well. If a chick like that came walking down the street, I think
both of us would think she was pretty fine—'

'But look at those fucking scars!'

'Where?'

'On her jugs.'

'Oh.'

'Check that shit out. That's one fucking botched boob job.'

'I didn't even notice.'

'But I'd fuck the brunette.'

'Which one?'

'Now *she* is hot. The one giving the blow job.'

'Oh, her. Yeah, why not?'

'At least if she knew how to moan a little more sincerely.'

'Yeah.'

'What a shitty faker. She doesn't fucking look like she wants it at all.'

'Nah, you're right.'

'I wonder how much she's getting fucking paid for this?'

Offended, Matias stood and went over to tap at the device wired to the giant screen.

'This one up is gonna go right up Steve Jobs' ass. Total piece of crap.'

Kerttu had loaned Samuel a book on gender and power once, and he'd been horrified to discover that he was exacerbating gender inequality with every thought that ran through his head. After finishing the book, he had promised himself and, most of all, the breasts of the women most affected, that from here on out he would treat breasts as neutral, not-to-be-sexualized body parts whose primary function was not to send him reproductive signals. If this task felt overpowering while he was studying alone for a math test, Matias' video wasn't exactly helpful. Samuel fleetingly wondered whether a movie in which a head-turning housewife and her busty friends offered themselves to an entire army of plumbers and policemen objectified women and tacitly supported sexist abuses of power. At one point, he had voiced this concern to Matias, who had answered: 'Yeah, well, it's not like I would pay anything for this.' Samuel would have considered boycotting porn for moral reasons, but then he'd heard a pop musician who gave up being vegetarian say that the most annoying thing in the world were moralists, people who set themselves above others with their condescending choices, and the last thing Samuel wanted to be was a moralist.

Matias poured more wine into Samuel's glass and smacked his lips.

'So you didn't go to college.'

'Hell, no.'

'What's that about?'

'I had better fucking things to do.'

But Matias, who should have joined in his jubilant chortle, frowned: 'Like what?'

'Well, I was thinking I'd kind of check things out.'

'Don't you get bored?'

'Nah, I gotta bunch of stuff going on,' Samuel said, finding himself shaking his head too long.

By the end of the summer, when the universities and other institutions of higher education had started posting the results of their entrance exams, Samuel's friends, even those who had done far worse than

him in school, had, one by one, squealed with joy on social media
about getting into the university of their dreams and whooped about
how *life is finally about the begin, yessss*! His classmates' excitement,
which hadn't roused the mildest reaction in him at the time, now felt
like a series of personal fuck yous. And by early fall, all anyone was
talking about on that social media that hadn't existed a year ago but
that everyone was on now were frosh flings and tutors and TAs and
cohorts. Each posting jolted him like an electric shock. The essence
of a university education appeared to consist of getting shit-faced
in coveralls and having drunken sex with uninhibited co-eds, which
it would have been amazing to disparage casually – from the inside.

Samuel had tried to convince himself that accidentally relinquishing
his spot at the university had actually been a semi-conscious protest
against the system. He'd follow in Matias' footsteps: they weren't going
to jump into the rat race the way everyone expected them to. There
were more pressing problems in life than maximizing your productivity
and consumption! The world needed to be saved from ecological
catastrophe, for instance. Besides, the ideology of perpetual financial
growth was insane. He and Matias would travel their own paths as free
men, make their own choices, ones they considered moral, because it
was your choices you had to live with for the rest of your lives.

Nevertheless, as he scanned his friends' non-stop updates, Samuel
felt pretty sure that saving the world would be easier if he had one
pointless, selfish, hazy booze and sex-filled freshman fall under his
belt. And then at most one more, as a counselor to the inductees, the
same sort of little Hitler as the one inducting Kerttu at the moment
in Jyväskylä. That would be enough.

But no booze- and sex-drenched frosh flings were in store for an
individual who followed his own path and accidentally gave up his
spot at the university. As the surging waves of dashes, bashes, hazing,
and fazing washed over him every day in social media, it eventually
felt wisest to drop that site completely and make a point of joining
the other one that was nice and quiet, because no one used it.

Had anyone noticed his departure? It was hard to say, because he
wasn't there to see.

Samuel had called Matias and suggested they get together precisely
because he could use some support in his aimless state. They had
grown apart over recent years, but perhaps the similarity of their

present circumstances would reunite them. Now, as the movie played, Samuel ridiculed his classmates' supposed future mastery of business administration and political science, which when it came down to it was nothing more than accommodating the expectations of their parents and the system. It wasn't independence; it was cowardice, pussyhood, the inability to do anything meaningful or bold with their lives.

Matias nodded at his side on the sofa, yeah, that's right. This felt comforting. Yet a pall was cast by the knowledge that Matias' situation wasn't perhaps completely comparable, in the end of all: just setting a time to get together for a homebrew tasting had proved surprisingly difficult. Matias was busy at the practice space, cutting an album with his post-extreme-metal band. The album was going to be even more extreme than the previous one, so extreme that maybe it wasn't even extreme or post-extreme metal at all. The critics could decide. But Matias' life at the moment seemed to be consumed day and night by the studio.

Emboldened by the wine, Samuel suggested that he could come hang out at the practice space someday, because he didn't have anything else going on at the moment. But the proposal put Matias' guard up. It was detrimental to the creative process to have outsiders present. Unfortunately. Making music was the channeling of a higher, mystical power in which the players were merely instruments. But if Samuel wanted to, he could participate in the process by joining their band's army of fans. And their latest song, 'Fuck you you fucking brainless consumer-polluter-whore!?', was available for download for ninety-nine cents from www.fuckyouyoufuckingbrainless-consumerpolluterwhore. com. Had Samuel already liked the band on all the social media he belonged to? If the band got enough likes, it could get a better price on ad services on a well-known search engine. Could Samuel recommend the band's link on his personal page in all his social media? If he personally recommended the band to at least a hundred of his friends, he'd get twenty-five percent off any order of mugs, T-shirts, underwear, and ball caps bearing the logo I DON'T GIVE A FUCKING FUCK ABOUT YOUR STUPID OPINIONS OR YOUR EMPTY CONSUMER LIFE from www.emptyconsumerlife.com/ shop. The band would also happily accept any ideas and suggestions for developing the site and its services. Samuel knew, didn't he, that if he wanted to become a member of the band's sales team by selling the band's products to his circle of friends, he'd be entitled to a fifteen percent discount on all SHUT YOUR FUCKING MOUTH YOU FUCKING BRAINLESS CONSUMER CUNT merchandise? And now, soldiers in the fan army could order exactly the same face paints, blood spatters, and skulls that the band themselves used!!! Ask for more details!!! Keep the faith!! Stay in touch!! ;–X \m/ ;-p }!!

And when Samuel tried to suggest to Matias – who, even when it was just the two of them, insisted on being called by his artist name, **Sathityaeurus** (Matias didn't want his fans to sense too much of a discrepancy between his private and professional identities; that wouldn't be authentic) – that they, say, go camping in Lapland, he didn't seem particularly enthusiastic. Matias would be on tour in Norway next week, and the band would be headed directly from there to host a black mass somewhere in Sweden where someone was planning on burning down a church. Not seriously, of course, but ironically. As Matias' band's home page proclaimed, old-school black-metal angst was so fucking corny – even though hopefully someone would really burn down the church!!!! March proudly, soldiers, and stay in touch! keep the faith!!! :) \m/ ;-p }].)

'OK,' Samuel said, trying to sound thrilled. 'Have a killer show.'

'Always.'

The intimate relationship between the buxom housewife and the plumber was taking deeper and more complex forms on the giant screen, but Samuel's thoughts were wandering. For some irrational reason, all he felt like talking about were Kerttu, his aborted education, and environmental destruction. But because both of the former had been thoroughly discussed and delving into the third wasn't going to do anyone any good, it didn't feel fair to further burden his friend with his cares.

Mom had finally lost patience with Samuel after he shot down all her suggestions for a sensible and productive lifestyle one by one. Nothing felt meaningful when you knew the planet was on the verge of destruction, if not already destroyed. The activist websites he buzzed around every night were full of examples, each ghastlier than the last.

'Well, do something else, then!' Mom said. 'If you don't like any of my suggestions!'

'Like what? What exactly am I supposed to do?'

'Anything!' she said. 'Do something about all those things you're always brooding over instead of just complaining about them!'

And for a moment, Samuel had considered Mom's advice. The likelihood of an oil spill in the Gulf of Finland was increasing every day. He'd remembered an NGO that was looking for volunteers to train as oil-spill responders, and initially the thought was inspiring. But was a bunch of nineteen-year-olds working by hand seriously the plan for preventing the damage from oil shipments that would soon exceed 200 million tonnes a year? Was it really possible that the only improvement to the frighteningly unsustainable time-bomb of a system was to have a couple of teenagers scrubbing birds drowning in the oil spillages of multinational corporations? Coming up with a new energy production, marine transport, and maritime safety infrastructure for the country, on the other hand, by himself, felt challenging. Besides, Samuel was already old at nineteen; in the scientific world, people made their major discoveries when they were young. Even the beautiful but aloof brunette at the local convenience store, the one who wore her hair up in a ponytail, looked through him as if he were air. If he couldn't get a convenience-store clerk to pay attention to him, how was he going to save the planet?

Samuel was also having a hard time focusing on his wine and the movie Matias had picked out because the thought of that job Mom had pointed out had been secretly gnawing at him. Just this morning on her way out the door, she had reminded him again about the ad she'd seen in the paper: Laajakoski Biosciences Inc. was looking for a research assistant. A high-school diploma was required, all other experience and expertise considered to the applicant's advantage.

Had he rejected the idea simply because it had been Mom's? He was disgusted with himself, couldn't explain why he was being such a dick to her. He had gradually transformed into a parasite, biting the only hand that still fed him. But something about Mom's way of babying and protecting him, an adult man, was impossible to accept, and he found himself torpedoing every single one of her suggestions, despite knowing that if the idea had been his, he might have already followed through on it.

As the movie played, Samuel tried to raise the topic by asking Matias if he should apply for a job at Laajakoski Biosciences like his mom kept telling him to.

'Why would you work at a place like that?' Matias asked.

'I don't know,' Samuel said. 'It might be... I dunno. Interesting.'

'That's how it starts,' Matias said.

'What?'

'Selling out.'

'True. But I'd be making money.'

Matias turned back to the screen without answering, end of conversation. For some reason this felt like a bigger disappointment than it should have.

Matias poured the final drops into Samuel's glass and put on a new movie: and now for something a little more authentic. Authentic meant a blurry image, inconsistent cuts, and overweight people, who started screaming alarmingly or behaving violently for no obvious reason.

Samuel had mentioned the job on his social media page a while back. At the time, Matias had sounded absent-mindedly supportive, figured that Samuel might find something cool to do there, meet new people. But Matias had been in a creative phase at the time; today he clearly didn't feel like talking. His new songs had been available via a global cloud service for days, and no one had listened to a single one, while hundreds of other bands had uploaded their songs, thousands a day, totallyfuckingcommercial shit. Nor had anyone downloaded Matias' band's Brutal Pagan app from the app store, even for a free thirty-day trial, although Matias had spent days of valuable working hours developing it, which was of course time away from his real profession, making music.

Samuel nodded, yeah, it must have sucked seeing your work go to waste. Matias answered that he didn't give a rat's ass about some idiotic cloud-service clowns or stupid app-market bullshit and that he never thought anyone would find anything authentic from that commercial shithole. Matias made music for the music itself, straight for his fans. Apps my ass!

And when he started to talk in a reedy voice about how important it was to express himself honestly and without compromises, Samuel realized that in the past he would have humored his friend, even thought he was right, despite the fact that Samuel hadn't found his own artistic medium yet. But now he caught both Matias and himself off guard by saying: 'I don't agree.'

Matias stared at Samuel, dumbstruck, as if he were someone so psychologically disturbed as to believe in the Christian God.

'I think some of us ought to do other stuff,' Samuel said. He wasn't sure himself what that meant, but for some reason the thought suddenly felt profoundly real.

'Like what?'

'I dunno. I figure there are a few problems in the world that haven't been solved yet.'

'Like climate change?'

'For instance.'

Samuel had found himself empathizing with the direct action the environmental activists talked about on their websites. One of the sites he'd been spending more and more time on lately was maintained by a group of Americans who fought for animal rights.

By any means necessary, if he had read between the lines correctly.

Direct action, it said in their posts, almost every single one. He hadn't agreed with the authors about everything, but the longer he read their arguments, the more convincing they sounded.

Matias smacked his lips: 'So I should break up my band?'

'Of course not.'

'That's going to get rid of emissions in China?'

'Of course not.'

'So?'

'So there must be something we can do.'

'We? Count a few more carbon footprints online?'

'That's not what I mean.'

'So what, then?'

There on Matias' creaking sofa with his glass of wine, Samuel could hear himself how accusatory and unfair he sounded. If he were in Matias' place, he would have hated what he was saying too; it must have sounded like he was deliberately trying to disagree. Yet at the same time, it felt like Matias was deliberately misunderstanding what he was trying to say.

As Matias fetched more wine and an angry Japanese guy on the screen wrapped a fat woman in chains that weren't supposed to feel good, Samuel regretted having come. They had drifted into a tense debate about the nature of authenticity, which oddly enough didn't seem to have anything to do with anything. As the conversation stalled, it gradually dawned on Samuel that he was seeing Matias in a totally new light. Literally: Matias seemed to be giving off a weird glow. A moment later, Samuel realized this was the effect of the Chinese web shop's How Good Morning Are You. And yet something about it still felt significant and real.

He had been most offended by what Matias said about his academic career coming to an end during his first weeks of freshman year. Samuel had come back to the topic, laughed that maybe it was a good thing he didn't get a chance to do what he wanted to right off the bat. As soon as the words left his mouth, he felt a pang in his chest: there wasn't a thing in the world he wanted more than to rewind his life to the early fall and do everything over again.

But Matias had nodded and grunted: 'It'll do you good.'

How so? he had felt like asking. What the fuck is that supposed to mean? He had a sudden vision of Matias lounging on his sofa, watching porn, as tidal waves surged across the continent.

'That's selling out, too, you know,' Samuel heard himself saying. His voice sounded more irritated than he'd imagined.

'Huh?'

'Playing in a band.'

'Really?' Matias said in the voice you used when something was so crazy that it became interesting. 'Because art created purely for one's own authentic self-expression is a form of selling out? Yeah, I can totally see that.' The expression on his face communicated the intensity with which he'd wrestled with this question throughout his lengthy artistic career.

'But you are trying to please someone else.'

'I am?'

'You need an audience for your music.'

'And your point is?'

'You also think about everything you do in terms of the genre and its expectations. You sweat balls worrying about what you're going to wear. So if you look at those album covers and T-shirt fonts and lyrics from that perspective, it doesn't seem so incredibly free and authentic to me. You're trying to sell them.'

Matias no longer looked so amused. He was breathing rapidly through his nose. He lowered the remote to the coffee table too calmly, and took a swig of beer before he responded.

The unnaturally white corpse paint Matias wore on his face during performances had to be exactly the right tint, his eyes lined and the bloodspatters painted just right; the pig heads displayed on the ends of spikes around the stage fresh and still bleeding because, Matias explained, the details were what mattered. Bands that had sold their souls tried to do exactly the same thing, too. It wasn't easy telling the real thing from a copy these days, but in the end authenticity would win out.

'Playing music is my job,' he said with a strained serenity.

'And conducting research isn't for Laajakoski's bioscientists? Why is it they're selling out when they put on a smart shirt to go to work but you're not when you put on your gear for a gig? Except they're making money and you're not?'

Matias emptied his glass. He looked stunned and disappointed in Samuel, who didn't grasp even the basics.

'It's a totally different thing.'

There were a thousand reasons why it was totally different. Matias was an artist. An artist was supposed to think about his appearance. And he didn't think about his appearance for his own sake, or an employer's, but for his audience's. Everything an artist did he did for his audience, in order to be able to offer it something flawlessly beautiful and authentic. Every artist entered into an unspoken agreement with his audience, and both parties had to keep their side of the bargain, otherwise it wouldn't work, he explained: when I get up on that stage, I promise to look and sound like a star, and you promise to worship me.

'Worship?'

'Yes.'

Samuel stared at him. Last time he'd been to one of Matias' shows, the audience had consisted of ten people, all friends of the band members, half of them underage. If there was anyone they worshipped, it was the bouncer who didn't ask for ID.

Matias shook his head and looked bored with the whole conversation. Samuel knew he should let up, but he couldn't stop himself.

'How is playing your job, anyway? You don't make any money off it.'

'Do too.'

'Ten euros a year.'

'More.'

'OK, so twenty. And you spend two grand on guitar supplies.'

'What's your point?'

'Doesn't that mean it's a hobby your rich parents are sponsoring?'

'Goddamn, you're such a fucking loser!'

'That might turn into a job someday?'

'Such a fucking loser.'

A long silence.

'So...'

The way Matias lowered his glass to the floor announced that, as far as he was concerned, the irritating conversation was over. He switched off the blurry amateur porn flick, pretty sucky actually, and turned on the music stream on his computer. What was that expression on Matias' face? Was he was intentionally looking for something to play that Samuel wouldn't like?

A classic song by a mega-brutal but unfortunately overlooked Norwegian band thundered from the speakers. It hurrahed at Christians, Jews, and Muslims having finally been gathered together to be tortured to death. In a growl that would have been unintelligible without the printed lyrics, the singer detailed how they were ritually slaughtered and then defecated on, their women gang-raped, heads ripped off with bare hands, the fetuses torn from their wombs to be fed to the priestesses of Satan, hearts still beating, and their bodies desecrated again after death as sacrifices to their Dark Lord, while rhythmically chanting children got to poke out the eyes of the Jews with long pagan sticks carved from chestnut branches at the darkest moment of the ancient ceremony of the new moon.

There was no denying the song had balls and, as Matias said, authentic warrior spirit, but something about it bothered Samuel. It probably did present keen societal criticism, sharp, understated humor and sophisticated between-the-lines irony, although Samuel hadn't been able to pinpoint where the irony and societal criticism were, exactly, when Mom had asked. Nor did the band's fans look the least bit self-deprecating in their black-and-white face paint, but that was probably because of the present post-artistic era, during which people were searching for questions, not prepackaged answers, artists were multilayered and complex, not moralizingly didactic, and messages were left intentionally ambiguous, leaving space for the listener's own interpretations. Nevertheless, Samuel had never had the nerve to come out and admit he had always been wussily disturbed by the part where the Christian female priest's pet poodle was captured, the pads of its paws seared in a bonfire and its claws removed one at a time, after which it was gutted and its viscera and internal organs were ripped out from the body cavity of the breathing animal and eaten in honor of Satan, and his priests laughed as the still-living beast howled and twitched on the altar, stomach spilling out. The bit about the dog took maybe twenty-five minutes of the forty-minute masterpiece. In Samuel's eyes as well as Matias', the song was absolutely a stratospheric moment in that specific subgenre of post-extreme metal (inasmuch as it was accurate to call the extreme metal that followed post-extreme metal post-extreme metal), one that specifically critiqued, at least according to Matias, the exploitation of animals for commercial purposes (if Samuel had a hard time finding support for this interpretation in the song itself), a musical onslaught unparalleled in its relentlessness, not to mention lyrics that were, impartially judged, *really fucking cool*, in Matias' summation of their thematic essence.

But something about this detailed account, as funny and sarcastic and subtly and effectively critical of institutionalized Christianity and people's hypocrisy as it might have been, still disturbed Samuel – which was, of course, the whole point of this subgenre of post-post-extreme metal, and in that sense the song was a total success, as was the band, which had managed to turn itself into what was perhaps the most significant work of post-extreme metal art. The lead singer had shot his band mate and later himself with a shotgun but not before he tortured his dog to death, apparently to dispel suspicions voiced on the most prominent extreme marginal websites that he wasn't serious about his hatred for animals and humankind. Mass murder would have crowned the band's reputation as the world's most popular post-extreme band. According to an adjunct professor from Rovaniemi who specialized in pop culture, the singer had been so extremely serious about his non-seriousness that through the performance of his life, he had admirably and successfully entered a space beyond extremism and existence not unlike the oeuvre of Martin Heidegger. (Nevertheless, the deaths were a shocking tragedy of the sort that ought to be prevented, the adjunct professor hurried to add.)

Samuel decided not to say anything. Music wasn't that important. Besides, after their preceding conversation, he didn't want to make things any more tense with Matias than they already were. But then he sensed something under his shirt. At first it felt like something crawling across his stomach – a tiny insect? Something warm, spreading.

He lifted up his shirt, probed the spot with his finger, and freaked out. Something wet.

He jumped up from the couch.

'I gotta take a piss.'

'You don't buy booze, you rent it,' Matias mumbled.

Samuel hurried into the bathroom, where chic dim lighting came on automatically and soundlessly in LED tracks and recesses concealed around the room. The bathroom was bigger than the apartment where he'd spent the bulk of his life before Mom met Henri.

He looked at his hand. It was bright red and wet.

When he pulled up his shirt, he saw it in the mirror. A small, pulsing black hole in his ribs. What the fuck? Relief surged over him like a wave when he remembered the Chinese tablet. It must have been a hallucinogen. But these were some pretty strong hallucinations. He licked his finger. He could clearly taste iron. And now the blood had formed a small splotch on his shirt. And on the floor, too, staining the dark granite tiles.

Blown away by the sight, he squatted down to watch the pool of blood spread. The puddle faded in and out of sight. The tiles were so dark, black, that both possibilities existed simultaneously. The world was incredible, amazing.

He opened the medicine cabinet and looked for a Band-Aid but couldn't find one. The walls were so glossy and the surfaces so smooth, matte, and elegantly detailed that you had to look for the cabinet by pressing and knocking the walls. The first time he'd been here, it had taken him fifteen minutes to figure out how to get water out of the tap.

The blood was still pumping out. He managed to make a plug out of toilet paper that seemed to staunch the worst of the flow. He taped the plug to his skin with a blister pad he found in the medicine cabinet and that he'd noticed once at the pharmacy cost almost ten euros apiece. It was the only thing in the medicine cabinet.

Whew. At least it wasn't getting any worse.

But when he came out of the bathroom, he heard that the forty-minute song was still playing and felt a fresh surge of heat at his ribs, which must have soaked the plug.

'Could we listen to something else?'

'Why?'

'Just because.'

'Why?'

'Anything else.'

'Is it making you uncomfortable?'

Matias stood and turned the music up.

'Seriously. Even some other track from this album.'

Matias shook his head, chuckled in disappointment, and clicked ahead to the next song. Suddenly he turned around. 'You're not that uptight, are you?'

'What?'

'About this song.'

'What about it?'

''Cause it has that part about Jews.'

'Um… what?'

'Yeah. I was just, like, if you don't have enough of a sense of humor…'

'But… don't they kill Christians and Muslims in it, too?'

'In a totally different way.'

'To be honest, I didn't even realize…'

'But you're Jewish.'

'My dad is. I went to Confirmation camp and—'

'I'm just saying, if that's why you don't see the humor in it.'

Matias' words sparked conflicting reverberations within Samuel. They resulted from something other than his having been baptized a member of the Lutheran church at Confirmation camp and having sung along, with the rest of the group and in his native language, *Lord I'm weary, lead me home*, and having climbed the rocks next to the church with the others to drink Koff beer from a yellow plastic Alepa bag and sing Juice Leskinen songs about how living was dying after which a couple of the girls cried, someone held on to Anniina's hair while she puked and everyone else had had the best Confirmation camp ever, seriously, you guys. Samuel had been under the impression that that was about as Finnish a Lutheran as you could get. It was true that when he turned eighteen he and Matias had immediately left the church, but maybe that was what a dyed-in-the-wool Finnish Lutheran did, too. But he couldn't remember Matias having ever referred to his paternal roots before. It smacked of a deliberate decision.

'No... I'm not... Go ahead and play it if you want. I wasn't trying to say you couldn't listen to it.'

Samuel could feel the wound continue to pulse, but apparently it had stopped bleeding.

It helped a little if you told yourself firmly that high-school graduation, a college education, and university degrees were only traditions. They were mere rituals whose primary function was to prop up existing institutions and power structures. Every individual could assign them as much value as they liked.

Which was why the most satisfying moment of that autumn was at hand.

Samuel was standing in the dark at Hietaniemi Beach, a lit joint in his mouth and a bottle of beer in his hand. What he needed was a solid counterpunch, an honest protest that would liberate him from the shit that had been raining down on him all fall. If he didn't express it properly, it would gnaw at him and rot his soul from the inside.

He'd already savored how amazing it was going to be watching the stream of urine drench his six laudaturs at the beach. 'I want a high-school diploma, too!' Ukko had shouted when Samuel told him about his plan. 'I wanna pee on a diploma, too!'

At first it looked like even piss would have no impact on the pompous stamps, official phrasing, and pretentiously heavy paper of the national matriculation board. For quite some time the diploma refused to be provoked; it serenely and maturely deflected the liquid onto the sand, which immediately sucked it up like a sponge. When the diploma refused to succumb, Samuel had been forced to take out another beer and gather up more liquid for a second attempt. This had the unpleasant consequence of prolonging the operation. And now, as he sat alone on the dark sands of Hietaniemi Beach, he realized that he would have to relive the entire spring while he waited, as if in punishment for his mistake.

When he was twelve, Samuel had fallen in front of the goal during a game, and a defender had jumped on his leg full-force, cracking the bone. For years after the cast was removed and the leg was pronounced officially healed, the pain would shoot up his spine if a ball happened to hit the right spot.

It was only now, in a mild cannabis-beer buzz, as he looked out at the city lights reflecting from the cold autumn sea that it dawned on him: like his leg, this spot would be sensitive for the rest of his life.

He shouldn't have expected anything.

Nor had he – or so he'd believed at the time.

He wouldn't have had the presumption to send his dad a copy of his diploma and final transcript if it hadn't been so outstanding. He had purposely let Mom remind him twice before he sent it. He'd savored how casually indifferent he'd seemed, dawdling with the diploma.

The congratulatory card that had come in reply was so brief that it could have been from the tax office.

He had buried the diploma and the card in the same mental closet as the graduation party and all the other things he'd never have to come back to again. But the card still stung, more sharply than he'd imagined. And something about the emotion that was now taking him over seemed to be gathering strength like a wave retreating.

Congratulations! Job well done! Best of luck in all your future endeavors from all of us.
Dad

He imagined remembering a voice: a deep note, flowing like water. It spoke his father's native tongue, and he understood it like thought.

He imagined remembering a presence like breath, or circulating blood. He'd seen his father's face in photographs, the beard that cast a shadow even when shorn, the chest, darker than the other daddies' in the apartment complex.

In one photograph, he was an infant in his mother's arms on the porch of *pappa*'s cabin, as the afternoon sun glinted off the pools in the rock-hollows. The cool sea breeze ruffled his father's hair as he looked skywards, mournful and all-knowing.

In most of the photographs, his father was completely absent. In those few where the dark male figure appeared, he stood at a slight distance from the others and blurry, as if already halfway gone.

Samuel took aim at the cold sands of Hietaniemi for a third time and let his body relax. His persistence was finally rewarded: the brightest symbol of the renowned Finnish educational system was ultimately forced to bend. The stiff, embossed surface of the high-school diploma soaked into a pitiful, limp rag and eventually tore down the middle.

The ritual could have been supremely satisfying, if he hadn't been compelled to execute it alone while a bone-chilling autumn wind scoured the deserted, nocturnal beach. Something about the fact that even this carefully planned climax didn't seem to generate greater pleasure was disheartening. In retrospect, going online to read the environmental positions of the political party that hoped to open a new coal-burning power plant and the mining company that had poisoned Lapland's waters with historic success hadn't been the best way of kicking off the evening. The Coal Party was *committed to leaving the earth to future generations in better condition than it is now.* The mining company *gave 101 percent to promoting the well-being of the environment, its employees, and mankind.*

On television the day before, the leader of one of the majority parties had been asked to tell consumers the most important thing they could do, at this very moment, on behalf of the environment.

Well, there are five million ways you can take action. Environmental consciousness isn't the exclusive province of any one political party. There are as many ways as there are people in Finland.

Give us one concrete example, the journalist said.

Well, the little things. Everyday things. They're the ways each of us can have an impact. And I know that most Finns already do them. As opportunity allows. Consumers are the ones who wield the greatest power. Whatever consumers want, companies will provide.

Give us one example. Just one way you personally have a positive impact on the environment.

Well, for instance, one easy way to conserve energy is to put the lid on the pot when you boil water. And buy environmentally friendly products, not ones that are most detrimental.

The words echoed through Samuel's head as he walked through the darkness to the bus stop.

People don't want change.

Activists said that if you told people something they already knew, they thanked you. If you told them something they didn't know, they got mad.

The night and the frigid, biting wind spoke of coming winter. Autumn's crystalline days were finally over, and as he walked Samuel realized that he hadn't enjoyed a single one. Crisp, sunny fall, his favorite season, had slipped by as if intentionally trying to sneak past him. The long, rainy, pitch-black winter stretched ahead of him.

The world had set a new record for carbon dioxide emissions over the past twelve months. He read online about an SUV dealership firebombed by the Earth Liberation Front.

'These misguided youngsters don't understand,' the car dealers' association representative said somberly in a televised interview, 'that real change takes place through democratic channels.'

As he walked alongside the cemetery wall, Samuel realized that apparently, by infinitesimal gradual increments, a person could be driven to the point where an arbitrary act intended solely to inflict damage started sounding acceptable. The weirdest thing was how it seemed to happen most effectively from trivial beginnings: a crappy conversation about principles with one's former best friend, a needlessly bitter headwind, the leader of a government party talking on television about pot lids when the amount of carbon dioxide in the atmosphere had exceeded anything remotely resembling safe limits long ago.

We need to stop whining and take action instead of reading online discussion boards, the websites said.

People don't want change, the websites said, what they want is someone to fix their broken toys.

The black trunks of the maples stood sentinel beyond the mossy wall of the cemetery, where the darkness was like a solid substance. Samuel was aware of the effort it took to keep himself together. It caught him off guard, this feeling he discovered inside himself: the more he tried to restrain it, the stronger it seemed to grow. Over the past few days, especially at night, his feelings for Kerttu had intensified into a burn he hadn't realized he was capable of feeling. And for some reason and by some logic that was wholly perverse and, thus, irrefutable, those feelings were inevitably intertwined with his dad. Kerttu had rejected him because he hadn't been good enough for his father and vice versa – and the most convincing evidence of this was that Kerttu and Dad had nothing to do with each other.

He told himself the fact that Kerttu didn't reply to any of his messages was unfair and humiliating, and the mortification was made worse by the knowledge that her unilateral radio silence was in fact anything but unfair; it resulted from a mature, adult decision to move on with her life. Dad hadn't come to the graduation ceremony even though he had promised, and this was exactly what Samuel deserved for being too enthusiastic about the prospect. He was the one being unfair here, and the awareness of this combined with the red-hot wave swelling within him made thoughts of Kerttu, his father, and everything else intolerable. He didn't consciously lump Kerttu and his father together as he trudged along the wet sidewalk from the deserted beach towards Mechelininkatu, but some part of him clearly made the association and resented them both equally.

He had waited for it for months, heart pounding, the email from his father containing the promised comments on his essay published in *Finland Today*. He'd been sure Dad would grasp the significance of the article. He'd been sure Dad would say something else, too, something that would bring them closer together, maybe: *Feel free to be in touch again.* Samuel had lived the entire spring for that email. It was the first thing on his mind every morning, every passing period as he checked his email, every evening as he calculated the time difference. Was it late enough on the East Coast that Dad might be headed home from work? Would now be a convenient moment for Dad perhaps to be reading his emails?

That email never came. Like Dad's casual undertaking to come to the graduation party – *Who knows? Maybe we'll see each other in the spring* – it hadn't meant anything. The only thing he ever heard from Dad was the New Year's card that arrived every fall, the familiar Hebrew letters he didn't know how to read.

The resentment became too much for him. In his room, he made one last-ditch effort to try and resist the still-swelling, overwhelming pressure to send Kerttu that ill-starred private message in which he briefly summarized what was wrong with women and parents and health-center nurse practitioners. Evidently some part of him thought it would make him feel better if he laid out in exacting detail why his life was empty and meaningless without Kerttu, why it wouldn't have been too much to ask for his father to in some way recognize the most important event of his life, and why, as he wrote this now, he suddenly hated Kerttu and her new life as a university student from the bottom of his heart.

Printed out, the message would have totaled well over ten pages in ten-point font. The second he pressed Send, he felt ashamed and, like absolutely everything else in his life, wished he could undo it. But it was only after he pressed Send that he realized that the Send button wasn't, as a matter of fact, the Send button, but the one that, if pressed, didn't communicate your message solely to Kerttu but, through her public profile, to the entire world.

Upon realizing this, he felt the full force of that hatred for the first time. It was an enormous, searing, flaming red mass that glowed white at its core. It took a physical effort to keep it from crushing him.

Because the still-swelling wave became too heavy to hold back, he had to switch strategies and focus all his willpower on the opposite tack: accepting things as they were, forgiving. His father hadn't known what he was doing. But this calved a completely new, iceberg-sized mass of stinging compassion Samuel had no room for. There remained a burning sense of injustice no one wanted to hear about, sheer helplessness, and a desire for vengeance targeted at his selfish father, who couldn't be bothered to realize he had ignored the most important event in his nineteen-year-old son's life.

Because it was impossible to do anything about any of it, in the end Samuel succumbed.

Lying in bed, he closed his eyes and finally let it happen, the thing he'd been holding back since the day of his graduation party: he allowed the burning, blinding wave to wash over him. At first it felt cold, like metal, but then he let it flow freely, and it scorched like fire. And when he allowed himself to remain at its core, without trying to escape, it eventually became almost pleasurable, the sensation of his soul going up in flames.

DIALOGUE BUILDS BRIDGES

BALTIMORE, MD

As he opened his study door in the darkened house, Joe felt a tingling in his fingertips and the soles of his feet.

It was a matter of professional responsibility. He had to keep up with the field, see what his colleagues were capable of these days. He pulled open the drawer.

There it was.

The device lay lifelessly, on top of the empty envelopes, sheets of stamps, and the step counter he had never used. Right where he'd flung it the night he'd finally lost patience with Rebecca. Moonlight was falling in between the curtains, and the device gleamed: brazen, sexy.

Rebecca hadn't been able to stay away from her *iAm*, even under threat of punishment. They had agreed that she could use the device two hours a day, max. But she had already been caught twice, sneaking back to get the *iAm* after the two hours was up and then attempting to spend the evening lying innocently in a nirvana of audio and visual stimuli, her cortex on fire. Joe had eventually been forced to lock the device in one of his desk drawers outside his daughter's permitted hours of use.

He had to admit that his curiosity had been piqued in part by the marketing event recently held on campus. The device seemed to be on everyone's lips these days.

The day before, he'd been headed from Bloomberg Hall to the library café to pick up a sandwich and coffee for lunch, when voices coming from the other side of the building caught his attention. He walked over to the stairs to see what was going on.

He was staggered by the size of the crowd; he couldn't remember having ever seen so many people on campus before. The TV crews were on the scene with their broadcast vans. Fat cables slithered across the lawn from the vans to the nearest building.

People were thronging below, where a large stage had been erected at the far end of the quad. The walls of the brick buildings surrounding it had been covered with gigantic banners advertising the MinDesign company. Behind the stage, a huge screen had been set up, blocking the main administration building all the way up to its bell tower. It took Joe a moment to realize that the preaching blaring from the enormous PA speakers and echoing from the walls of the buildings was coming from the short man in jeans pacing across the stage, microphone in hand.

So about these entertainment modules of ours that have been getting *a little attention lately*, he was saying into the microphone.

A murmur of amusement surged through the crowd. What a way he had with words!

Joe had learned later that the man on stage was the creative director of MinDesign. The company had offered to arrange the event at its own expense, and the university chancellor, the deans of the departments, and the communications office had welcomed it with open arms. Luring the general public to campus events was a nearly impossible task, but this time hordes of people had shown up.

Unlike the majority of the audience, who seemed to devour ravenously every morsel of information the director deigned to toss their way, Joe didn't understand most of what the man onstage was saying. Then he realized that the director was talking about the *iAm* device and the *neuroXperiences* it offered. The text projected on the screen above his head changed according to the topic at hand. Now it read:

CHARACTER DESIGN

I'd like to highlight a few of the positive aspects of the technology, the creative director said, growing serious. No one will be exploited. No one will be degraded. No one's rights will be trampled.

From his vantage point at the top of the stairs, Joe saw the crowd nod gravely.

You could finally enjoy your entertainment without reservations, the creative director explained, forehead furrowed like that of a man of consequence. MinDesign digitally constructed all of its characters from prototypes. They were calculated and compiled from the traits and characteristics of a large body of living models, it was true, but the final characters didn't feature the actual contours of real human models. No one was being objectified. No one was being forced to do anything.

The man in jeans gathered up every ounce of creative director charisma before his next roar, which boomed from the brick walls of the quad: No one will ever have to be alone again!

He was forced to wait before continuing, because people had burst out into spontaneous applause.

'Think about all those millions of lonely people who don't have anyone to keep them company!' his voice thundered from the speakers.

'Think about the multitudes who have been dumped!'

'Those who are too shy to face others in awkward, complicated situations, in line at the supermarket, on dates, in restaurants, those who find rejection more painful than most of us, those who can't stand to be rejected ever again!

'Well, have we got something for you!

'At long last, we have something for you, too!

'I have a message for you,' the creative director bellowed, simultaneously enraged by the cruelty of the world and moved by the nobility of his gospel.

'I have a message for you... You will no longer be alone!'

Joe didn't understand how an *iAm* device would save a lonely person who'd been dumped, but the crowd on the lawn kept clapping for minutes after the director stopped speaking. He stepped down from the stage; the rousing, victorious music was still blasting from the speakers.

Close-ups from the crowd were being shown on the screen: audience members enraptured by what they'd heard; a middle-aged woman wiping tears from her eyes. No one showed any sign of leaving. Quotes flashed across the screen, interspersed with emotional reactions from the crowd:

'Digital animation taken to a whole new level' – New York Times

'When it comes to new-millennium neurotechnology, MinDesign doesn't have a serious challenger in sight' – Time

'NeuroXperience will make you forget digital reality as you know it' – MSNBC

In the end the director had to appease the crowd; he took a few springing steps and bounded back up onstage. The clapping intensified into a storm of applause and cheers. The group ecstasy would have outshone a Christian fundamentalist rally.

Flowers and champagne were carried up to him.

The crowd was still clapping.

That same evening, the furiously applauding crowd from campus had been shown on national television, along with an interview with an expert on technology companies. According to the expert, the creative director of MinDesign, while perhaps a difficult personality, was a Bill Gates for the next millennium, a Gandhi for the new world.

Joe carefully avoided the creaking spots in the wooden floor and checked that the study door was closed. He couldn't make any noise; Rebecca's room was on the other side of the wall, and she might still be awake.

He placed the paws in his palm.

They were small and light, puny. These could be used to steer moving images and sound directly to sensory cortices? Ads for this device were being shown on TV at an accelerating pace; they appeared on your computer screen along with your email.

Would it actually feel real, without a screen or headphones?

He had to admire the device's streamlined allure; its curves communicated a pure desire to succumb to its user, to accommodate every wish.

Attaching the paws without the user guide proved challenging. Joe spent a long time trying to fix them, with little success, until it finally occurred to him to feel for the patch of bare scalp right behind the ear. The second it did, he remembered that was where he had seen Rebecca put the paws. He had to be on the right track.

It took him a long time to find the power button. It was so cleverly camouflaged that Joe was on the verge of aborting his attempt. But then his finger happened to graze the right spot. A tiny green light came on at the side of the device, and he felt a slight tickle as a silk-thin web of electric currents apparently thrust forth from the paw and started spreading across the skin of his scalp and temples. He had to hurry to attach the second paw in the right spot.

So they were capable of this: he found himself being impressed against his will. Five years ago, no one would have ever even dreamed of it. Just a moment ago, in research terms, it would have required some sort of full-head, helmet-like, magnetic-coil contraption – and even then it wouldn't have been possible.

The sound of the device starting up was so low that Joe more sensed it than heard it.

He waited.

At first nothing seemed to happen. Everything looked the same as before. He tried to press the small button that read TEST. He felt little pinches around his head, apparently at the spots where the tips of the net's current-filaments came in contact with his scalp. But nothing else happened. He took a deep breath. Was he supposed to calibrate the device somehow? Had Rebecca said something like that? Or was it—

He almost squealed out loud.

Right in front of him – in the air, seemingly hovering in the emptiness – glowed a big white screen.

Good God.

His heart was hammering. The screen was filled with text titled:

Getting Started: Calibrating Your *iAm* Experience Device

The user guide.

Joe stared at the screen. Was this how it worked?

Reading a user guide floating in mid-air felt peculiar. It also felt weird that he didn't need to move his eyes; the text automatically shifted to the middle of his field of vision, when he wanted it to. This clearly took some getting used to. Joe found himself constantly moving his eyes, trying to read traditional, printed text that stayed in place, but the device responded to movement by immediately shifting the entire screen a corresponding amount.

He also kept seeing the text in double vision, and occasionally it vanished completely mid-sentence. Before long, he became aware of a growing ache in the vicinity of his forehead. But the most awkward thing was that as soon as an association occurred to him, new images, screens, and documents opened up. The device appeared to be capable of typing at approximately the speed of thought. The text would appear in the white box at the top of his field of vision and, apparently based on his involuntary commands, the device would look up terms from both its own cloud-based memory as well as the World Wide Web. The verb 'calibrate' happened to remind Joe of the old tuner for Daniella's violin, long since fallen into disuse, which you could calibrate to the correct tuning. This spawned new menus, and he was instantly and unintentionally online, apparently, because the device opened ad windows for music stores, links to well-known violin concertos – one of which also began to play immediately; Joe got distracted admiring the young, incredibly skilled male violinist's fingers dance across the delicate neck of his instrument – and the *New Oxford American Dictionary*, which was already open at 'calibrate *tech*: to verify a scale of measurement, intervals, etc.'

He didn't know how to keep his thoughts from racing, and new windows and screens surged out in front of him, faster and faster. Finally, in the throes of a growing panic, he ripped the paws from his head and sat there for a long time, panting in the darkness.

He felt seasick. He marveled when he remembered that Rebecca had sat around for hours with the device attached to her brain. To some degree, she had even been capable of simultaneously concentrating on real-world events in the same room. After catching his breath, he returned the device to the drawer and locked it.

He went to bed in a state of agitation. It took him ages to fall asleep, and when he finally did, he had restless, surreal dreams.

Joe woke to the sound of his own snores and realized he had dozed off again.

He glanced around in the gloom, disoriented. He noticed a neuro-physiologist acquaintance shoot him a disapproving look. He hadn't gotten much sleep; he'd been up all night reading about animal activists.

About murders, arson, kidnappings.

Joe rubbed his eyes and tried to sit up straighter. The droning that had lulled him to sleep still carried from the front of the university's main auditorium. He was attending a mandatory training session for all faculty.

His thoughts kept jumping back to the articles he'd read during the night: he clearly hadn't been taking the animal activists seriously enough. He'd dismissed them as idealists, little girls looking for simple solutions to complex problems.

Like this Heather Miranda. She'd been caught in California in the parking lot of a major corporation, planting explosives under the

CEO's car. As the security company had summarized: a sick sadist who valued the lives of dogs over those of humans.

Joe had stayed up until the wee hours reading a detailed exposé on Heather Miranda and how she had brooded over her misanthropy in solitude for years, concocting ever-more elaborate revenge fantasies aimed at scientists conducting experiments with animals, until, under the influence of extremist groups, something finally snapped.

After reading the article, Joe's throat was like sandpaper and his stomach lining burned. He'd immediately sent stony-faced Frank Hackett, who answered for his family's safety, a question he'd never imagined asking: would a handgun, stored in a completely secure place that was definitely out of the reach of children, be excessive in their circumstances? The next morning he wondered who had sent the message: had he actually turned into someone who in all seriousness was considering – what, getting a handgun for a household with children in it?

Joe glanced up at the front of the amphitheater-shaped auditorium, where a woman in her forties was gesticulating on stage. This former CEO, who had never done a day of research in her life, had been lecturing for over an hour on the major themes shaping the research challenges of the future. She was wearing a dramatically cut cream-colored suit, heels, and minimalist platinum jewelry, and aspired to make those who'd made mediocre failures of their lives thrum with new possibilities. She currently worked as a freelance mindfulness trainer for corporate managers, and yet the dean's decision to invite her to speak was not based on her garden-themed mental exercises, but on the fact that in her previous, soulless life as a CEO she had accumulated a fortune of millions. Her main message seemed to be that life as you remember it had ended long ago.

Joe drowsily followed the smooth current of images the trainer was projecting onto the giant screen, where big goals, small successes, and future challenges alternated with cooperation, well-being, and responsibility, feeding into each other in a spiraling cycle. She looked ghostly in the darkness, her arms moving like a contemporary dancer's in the projector's cold glow.

Even though no one said so out loud, the training had been set up because the university was worried about funding streams drying up. In recent years, an ever-increasing slice of government support had been directed to competing universities. If this continued much longer, they were going to be left out of the loop.

Joe glanced at his watch: ten to. He was going crazy. After the woman's presentation, they would be treated to a persona workshop led by a gel-headed twenty-five-year-old, during which everyone would get the chance to customize an ideal scientific persona for him- or herself. Questions everyone ought to consider had been passed out beforehand:

Are there any extremely wealthy public figures (i.e. billionaires) who suffer from an illness that is in any way related to my research?

Are there any loved ones of an extremely wealthy public figure who are suffering or have suffered from a relevant disease/illness? (Remember the dead! A mother who has lost her child is worth her weight in gold!)

Is there a wealthy figure with a 'megalomaniacal' plan (time travel, contacting UFOs, cryo-preserving and reviving their body a thousand years from now, etc., NOTE! online task) they want to fund? How could my research play a part? (The group that comes up with the most far-fetched association wins!)

Am I on friendly terms with anyone extremely wealthy? Is there a natural way I could connect with them? (Suggest: lunch, a play, a tour of the university, come up with a shared hobby for your children – brainstorm as many ways as possible of taking the initiative!)

Research funding was continuously on the line; today, winners secured support from individual billionaires. The developer of the most popular social media had just donated a billion dollars to space research because he wanted to fly to Mars. The CEO of a major media house had pledged two billion dollars to founding an autism research unit at her alma mater; her son had been diagnosed with a disorder on the autistic spectrum and required new forms of treatment.

During the workshop, everyone would create a researcher persona who would engage with the outside world in a fresh, authentic way. This new persona bearing the researcher's name would glow in the digital void, a neon sign attracting the attention of lonely philanthropists who had billions to burn and important research questions to answer.

That afternoon, they would practice the natural nurturing of acquaintanceships. For the training, the university had hired professional actors to play the roles of the billionaires. Participants would rehearse talking about their field with the actors; the challenge was to keep the billionaires from feeling stupid or exploited.

Hell, no.

Joe grabbed his bag, pardoned himself to the person next to him, and stalked from the auditorium, down the hall, and out the doors of Bloomberg Hall, named for its billionaire donor.

Once outside, he blinked in the bright sunlight. On the playing field, the women's field hockey coach was yelling at her team. The fundraising training would be a waste for him anyway; he wouldn't have been able to concentrate. He might as well go home and try to do something useful.

Campus was growing lusher and greener by the day. As Joe crossed it to his car, his thoughts ricocheted from the persona workshop to the activists, what tack he should take. Plus there was the meeting of the boycott group. He wondered if he'd be able to get even half of those whose word counted most to attend. He'd spent the majority of the previous day calling them.

He unlocked the car with a click of his key. Even after opening the doors, he didn't notice anything out of the ordinary. It was only when he dropped his satchel in the back seat and climbed in behind the wheel that he realized something was wrong. His seat felt too close to the ground. A second later, he realized why: the wheels were as deflated as a young Finnish man's self-confidence.

Someone had slashed his tires.

A message had been scratched into the paint, and for a second Joe thought it was Ted Brown's reply to his Freedom Media library boycott:

no concessions

It took a moment for him to figure out it was a response to his own proposal: *Can we talk?*

And now the bad idea he'd come up with earlier felt like the only option he had left. There were no guarantees it would work, but maybe it was worth a try.

At first he tried to get one of the communications officers to arrange it. The university employed numerous people whose job it was to disseminate information on the research conducted in the institution's various departments.

Communications Officer Michelle Sedaris had reservations about Joe's proposal. Michelle was pleasant and sensible. She had interviewed him for the university newspaper when he won the prize.

Joe said that the university didn't really need to do anything. The debate could take place in one of the auditoria in Bloomberg Hall. He would handle all the arrangements himself. All he needed was for Michelle to post the invitation prominently on the university's website and send a press release to the media. Joe could draft the invitation and press release himself if she wanted him to.

But Michelle said: 'Hmm.' And then: 'That might get a little tricky. 'We don't have… the university doesn't have a clear communications strategy regarding this,' she tried to explain. 'Leo is still thinking about what he intends to propose. They have a meeting in two weeks. I'm sure we'll be wiser after.'

Joe was flummoxed. 'We can't stage one measly debate? I'd like to find these people and be able to talk with them.'

Michelle sighed. Joe felt like an old man the pharmacy staff were trying to keep calm until the police arrived.

'Leo isn't sure aggravating the situation is the right way to go.'

'A conversation is going to aggravate the situation? My tires were just slashed! In broad daylight!'

'I heard about that, Joe. I'm so sorry. That's terrible. I'm sure the police will catch them soon. But I think what Leo is going to propose at the meeting is that the university maintain as low a profile as possible on this in order to avoid attracting undue attention, because—'

'Leo? What does any of this have to do with him?'

'Dean of Arts and Sciences? Of course he has to have input.'

'His tires aren't the ones being slashed. It's easy for him to maintain a low profile.'

'I'm sorry, Joe. I truly am. I'd love to help.'

Joe canceled his lab meeting and left in the middle of the day. He went straight to Miriam's office and told her the university's communications officers didn't want to help and asked how she would feel if he organized the event in his own name.

They spoke for a long time. Miriam agreed with him: there was no point waiting any longer; it made more sense to take action. Unless they wanted to pull up stakes and move to another city.

'Or abroad? They'll find us if we stay in the country.'

'Maybe we don't have to go quite that far yet.'

Joe sighed and picked up his phone. He called information and asked for the number for the editor's desk at the *Baltimore Sun*. Then he called Lisa, who immediately agreed. The newspaper reacted the way he hoped they would, at first with reservations but an hour later enthusiastically.

It was only in hindsight that he understood the position he had put Lisa in. He called her again, but couldn't convince her to back down.

Police in riot gear funneled out of the van and onto the lawn of the lower quad. There had to be two dozen of them, in bulletproof vests and helmets.

Joe watched the police and felt an impotent irritation. Why now, why here? Why hadn't they been guarding his postdocs' animals, his laboratory when its doors were wrenched open with crowbars, his home when it was vandalized? Preventing mega-corporations from marketing psychoactive chemicals to children on the sly? Is this where police were most badly needed – in a public space where everyone was likely to be on their best behavior?

Spring was at its height, the sun shining warmly from a bright sky. The university had refused to help him set up the debate, but as soon as they got a call from the local newspaper, the communications office and the department were tripping over themselves to get involved. Joe eyed the banner hanging from the wall of Stanton Hall and decided he'd made a mistake.

But what was he supposed to do now that everything was in motion?

ANIMAL EXPERIMENTS – NEEDLESS CRUELTY OR USEFUL KNOWLEDGE?

DEBATE: PROF JOSEPH CHAYEFSKI VS. THE BLACK EARTH COLLECTIVE

After enduring demonstrations on his front lawn and death threats, Professor Sipowitz from UCLA had finally surrendered with the message: *you win*. A Molotov cocktail had been chucked onto the Sipowitzes' front steps – or actually the neighbors'– by accident. He'd moved out of town and changed fields after a public plea for his family to be left alone. Should Joe have done the same?

The event was officially sponsored by the paper because the university hadn't been able to decide its stance on it. Supposedly the university wanted to avoid drawing undue attention to itself, but now both Leo and Michelle were there on the lawn, smiling and speaking into the mic a television reporter was holding out while the cameras rolled. The news crew from another local station was stopping passersby outside the pastel-painted row houses on Charles Street, doing their damnedest to cook up a scandal.

Joe waited in front of the entrance to Stanton Hall, watching the young people clustered in their tribes on the far side of the quad: hippies, punks, politically affiliated, others less easy to characterize. Some were cheerfully erecting a tent and dishing up free lentil soup, Latin music played from big amplifiers and people were 'dancing against climate change.' One group appeared to be setting up a stand selling CDs, incense, and handmade soap.

An earnest-looking young woman of about twenty walked up to him.

'Excuse me, are you interested in biofuels?'

'Right now? Incredibly.'

The girl handed him a flyer. Joe wished he could go home, climb into bed, wake up in the morning, and realize he was breathing freely, allowed to do his work to the best of his abilities. It was the only thing he knew, the only thing he was good at, and now it was being taken away from him.

'I don't know what you make of all this.' The girl was brimming with energy and a dazzling, omnipotent optimism.

'I'm just frustrated,' he replied honestly.

'I felt the same way for a long time. It's such a complicated issue. But then I realized the only thing you can do is take action,' the girl said. 'Do what your heart tells you to.'

Under twenty. Had to be. She thrust a pamphlet at him.

'We agree that occasionally, *rarely*, under extremely *extremely* exceptional circumstances, animal testing can be useful.'

'Really?' Joe said, unable to conceal his bitterness but also somehow incapable of telling her who he was.

'We believe,' the girl said, repeating the name of her organization, 'that if someone's life is at risk and there's no way of conducting tests with tissue samples or cell cultures that would show which of two treatment methods is better, in that case it's acceptable.'

'I see.'

'Our website address is right here. Go check out our arguments. We believe that in that case, if that other method can save a human life and all cell cultures have been exhausted, down to the very last one, then animal testing is acceptable.'

'Even though the sick person would have been dead for twenty years by that time,' Joe said.

The girl didn't get it. Joe excused himself and stepped inside.

Dialogue – was it really such an unrealistic hope?

A pale boy in a long, black coat and a wide-brimmed hat spoke at length on behalf of one organization, a smug, ironic smile on his face. As he presented his counterarguments, the boy gazed at his black-rimmed fingernails; it seemed to Joe as if he weren't so much presenting views as repeating memorized turns of phrase.

For them, everything was theoretical. Absolute mercy and absolute suffering were set up in opposition to each other. In a monotone, the boy recited descriptions of experiments from the cruelest end of the methodological spectrum, but not their results. He listed alternative methods by which researchers had arrived at the same results, but not the fact that this happened twenty years after the fact, once they already knew what to look for.

Joe reflected that if these people understood anything about the daily work of a researcher, it would have been too mind-numbingly dull to oppose. He'd given a presentation on basic research and tried to explain what sort of questions animal models were used to answer. Lisa had looked at him encouragingly, but the activists appeared to be whispering and exchanging mocking glances while he spoke.

After Joe's presentation, a short, angry-looking girl had spent fifteen minutes talking about how it took a hundred thousand gallons of water to raise one kilo of beef. Now everyone was all ears while the pale boy smirked insolently at his toes and spoke in a raspy voice about how cattle ranchers in Canada illegally poisoned apex predators with pieces of Superlon hidden in chunks of meat, which blocked the wolves' digestive system and slowly killed them via internal bleeding.

'Listen,' Joe heard himself saying out loud, 'if I could just say something...' He saw the science reporter from the newspaper, who'd been chosen to moderate the debate, shoot him a cautionary glance. Up until now Joe had managed to restrain himself, but he found himself standing up. He had promised Miriam he would keep a handle on his nerves, breathe deeply and not lose his temper; remember that his anger would just give firepower to the other side. You're a wonderful, empathetic, considerate man and father, but in some situations you get worked up pretty easily, Miriam had warned, and I'm afraid that this is going to be one of those situations.

He took a deep breath and started over: 'Can we agree that we'll only talk about one topic at a time?'

The entire auditorium was staring at him.

'I don't get what poisoning wolves has to do with anything.'

'It's not the only thing you don't fucking get,' one of the young audience members called out, to boisterous applause.

Joe tried to steer the conversation to what he felt they were talking about: that experiments conducted with non-human beings were simply irreplaceably important for investigating the totality of human physiology, the nervous system and its diseases.

'Does it cause animals needless suffering?' he asked. 'No, not if the experiments are carried out properly.'

'Liar!' someone shouted. The others started to chant in a chorus: 'Liar! Liar!' The moderator had to quiet the crowd before Joe could continue.

'Let me finish, for God's sakes,' he appealed. 'I was saying that of course some of the tests cause animals suffering, and animals lose their lives. Absolutely. The point of some experiments is to cause pain. But is it needless? No. It buys us new knowledge.'

Joe looked out at the hostile faces surrounding him. His shirt was soaking at the armpits. He tried to remain calm and remember that he had finally been offered an opportunity to explain to these young people what was involved in scientific research – unlike in his lab, when he was just preaching to the choir.

'Is the suffering and death of animals too much of a sacrifice in the pursuit of knowledge?' he asked. 'I don't know. I seriously don't. If we think about it together and jointly come to the conclusion that it is, fine. Then we have to put a stop to it. That's what you're aiming for, of course. And, believe it or not, I respect that. I respect that you want to make the world a better place.'

He looked at the young people, their blank disdainful stares.

'But are you sure you're aware of all the things you're giving up? Are you positive you know what you're asking for? Are you positive you're not mistakenly thinking you can have your cake and eat it, too? Are you positive the majority agrees with you?'

'The majority agreed with Hitler,' someone shouted, to thunderous applause. The moderator nodded to a girl from a different organization.

'The problem, to be exact, lies in the fact that animal testing is based solely on established practice, not on it being demonstrably reliable,' she stated with the confidence of a seasoned speaker.

What?!? Joe felt like shouting.

'The majority of animal tests are never validated,' the girl continued. She was popular, and knew it. This girl was beautiful in the self-evident way of the young and healthy; she didn't need to try, she was radiant, and it was clear from looking at her that she thought she would stay that way forever, was God's chosen one solely because she was young.

Not validated? What the hell…?

'In other words, their reliability has not been officially confirmed at the level demanded of scientific methods.'

'What the hell?' Joe finally let slip, more loudly than he intended. '"Animal models haven't been validated"?'

Dead silence filled the entire auditorium. People were staring at him as if he were the devil. Joe found himself on his feet again.

'Excuse me, young lady, but what on earth are you talking about? 'Their reliability has not been officially confirmed?' What is that supposed to mean?'

'That their reliability has not been officially confirmed?' the girl said.

Now the whole auditorium burst out laughing and clapping for the beautiful girl. And she was beautiful, the one all the newspapers and TV channels would want to lead the coverage with. Suddenly everyone was shouting and talking at the same time, someone was pounding a fist against a desk and howling encouragement.

'Please remember to ask for the floor,' the moderator instructed.

Joe felt clammy. He was so exasperated that he was afraid he would physically attack someone if he weren't given the chance to explain to these people properly and thoroughly how things stood. He had tried his best, but the situation and the boy with the reedy voice and God's chosen one, the radiant girl, were too much for him. The entire debate was a basketball match without any rules, fouls weren't being called and no one was being sent to the showers even though hands were being whacked hard now, and on purpose. You didn't need an eye for the game or technique to win here, what you needed was an iron fist.

'There's far too little talk,' the girl said, batting her eyelashes, perfect even without mascara, 'about the fact that animal experiments could often be replaced with other methods if greater investments were made in developing alternatives.'

The girl started listing carefully memorized percentages of NIH research grants, how many millions of dollars had been awarded to laboratories that relied on experimental animals and how only pennies had been left over for 'alternative methods.'

Joe tried to ask for the floor, but the moderator turned it over to the pale boy. He started to talk about tissue and cell cultures that, if developed, could for all intents and purposes completely replace animal testing, but there wasn't the political will, because they were up against big corporations and rich private universities backed by millionaires.

'Those are used to test cosmetics!' Joe shouted. 'A particle accelerator would be of just as much use in researching the visual system! You don't understand a word of what you're saying. Do you hear me?'

'I'd appreciate it if the professor could refrain from interrupting me,' the pale boy said to his desk. 'In addition, one method that is extremely underused is computer modeling, which—'

'Goddammit!' Joe shouted. 'You're lecturing me on research methods, you eighteen-year-old dropout? What makes you think we don't already model absolutely everything we possibly can? We model our asses off! I have four PhD students and postdocs who do nothing but model! We model everything we can, absolutely everything, because the competition is so tough that otherwise we'd be wiped off the face of the earth!'

'I'd like to be able to finish,' the boy said to the moderator in a reedy, shrill voice.

The moderator said: 'I'd ask Professor Chayefski to remember that we're not discussing his research or a specific field of research but the problematics of animal experimentation in general.'

'There is no such thing!' Joe exclaimed. 'There are no general problematics! All research is specific and belongs to a specific field and investigates a specific question through a specific method! Please understand that you have to spend a little effort looking into the details if you plan on taking a stance!'

The boy continued holding forth on methods he had read about in books and that were used to investigate things he didn't know a thing about.

Joe tried to say make another point, but all he got in response were catcalls. Gradually he sank into his own thoughts. He felt drained, as if he'd been running in thick tar all day.

The anger he had experienced a moment ago had melted away somewhere; something painful and heavy had appeared in its place. The discussion flowed on outside him, off in the distance, among people who were interested in memorized numbers, witty slogans and lofty principals, the names of philosophers, a conversation where you could introduce clever comparisons you had practiced among your friends beforehand and everyone got to voice an opinion about everything and where every viewpoint was valuable.

Everyone had an opinion.

Dialogue was intrinsically important. It helped build bridges.

When the moderator asked Joe to express his views on fur ranching, he stood up and walked out. The young people booed at him all the way to the door. When he got home he discovered someone had spit on the back of his coat.

The only contribution that had been even close to constructive had been Lisa's. She talked about her own research. It was a bold move, through which she of course set herself up as a target. She described in detail what it was like working with laboratory animals, how they aroused feelings of tenderness and protectiveness, how you didn't want to cause them any suffering and did everything in your power to avoid it. Lisa wrapped up with a few good, quick examples of all the things that had been accomplished through animal models, what sorts of diseases had been eradicated, what medicines developed, how without animal experiments we would know basically nothing about the nervous system.

It was only when he was outside and saw all the young people with their identical devices, the immediate predecessors of the *iAm*, saw their tender, loving fingers stroking their little smart devices, it was only then that Joe realized what he should have said.

He poured himself a whisky. He had decided in advance that he wouldn't have a second, and since then had already drunk a third. He gazed out into the twilight of the spring evening, at the cardinal sitting in the raspberries, whistling its mating call.

It had been several days since the debate, but he still felt like he'd taken a drubbing. The beautiful girl's response kept pounding through his head, the one when Joe had listed the diseases that, unlike twenty years ago, could be treated thanks to research like his: *that could have been determined through other means.*

Sure, this twenty-year-old knew best, knew Joe's research, the studies he had designed, considering every element of every experiment over a period of eight years, checking them against the results of the pilots, making the same mistakes as everyone else thirty times, racking his brains with his colleagues, starting over again when everything went wrong. In the end, the solution had appeared, unsolicited and uninvited, like a teenager from Utah offering a Book of Mormon, but of course only because he had spent all those years trying. The solution had been a surprise to him, too, although in retrospect it had been the only possible one: the critical gene, which controlled an important peptide, affected the function of certain GABAergic interneurons in the secondary visual cortex – which had been completely obvious to everyone for fifteen years, except the interneurons were different ones than anyone had expected.

That could have been determined through other means?

And my views... on fur farming?

Everyone wanted to talk, but no one wanted to listen.

Joe had lambasted the students, the police, the media, and the whole world to Barb Fleischmann, who had answered his outburst uneasily while attending a conference in Barcelona. Barb was still able to do her work in peace, present her findings at conferences, because no one was attacking her – at least not yet. Which was a good thing, as Joe was forced to remind himself.

He also tried to take comfort in the fact that no one would be listening to Barb's presentation anyway: people were too busy reading their email and preparing their own presentations. What would conferences be like a few years down the road, when everyone had an *iAm*, when you wouldn't even need to pull out a laptop?

Barb said that she'd heard that a fur shop downtown had been forced to close its doors a while back. For over a year, demonstrators had gathered outside its front door with a megaphone chanting, *Shame on you! Shame on you!*, run past naked, broken the windows, and played sirens so loudly that the customers and employees had been forced to flee to save their hearing.

Joe nearly lost it. A fur shop? Furs were a luxury, a vanity product, there were alternatives to them.

Barb had sighed. 'They're fanatics. To them there's no difference. Listen, this is terrible, but my presentation is about to start. Take some time off. Go somewhere with Miriam. Martha's Vineyard for the weekend. I have to run.'

Rebecca had come up to Joe the day after the event to tell him she'd seen his performance. The whole thing? Joe hoped for a second, but no, Rebecca had only seen an extremely short clip published on the newspaper's website. It had been uploaded straight to her *iAm*, right to her brain. 'It was the weirdest feeling,' she said. 'I was just thinking, *I wonder how it went* – and boom, there it was! Without requesting it! I was watching the video that same second. In the car with Mom, at the stoplight! Dad, you have to try it. There's no going back from this technology.'

That girl was really convincing, Rebecca said, about how there wouldn't be any need for animal experiments but they just don't fund alternative methods. But you... Rebecca looked uncomfortable.

'It could have... gone a little better,' she said. Her eyes were full of compassion for him.

The website featured a ninety-second clip from the event that included two lines from Joe. In the first he was saying: '*Does it cause the animals unnecessary suffering? No.*' In the other he was roaring: '*What the hell are you talking about?*' The clip cut to the frightened face of a girl sitting in the audience. She looked twelve years old and hadn't said a word the entire event. Then it was the photogenic girl's line about alternative methods: the impartial opinion of a calm, dispassionate expert.

Rebecca couldn't help returning to the magical *iAm*. It never would have occurred to her to search for a clip like this – but now it appeared directly in her thoughts! It was true, then, what they promised: the manufacturer constantly registered everything she browsed, watched, and thought, and as a result knew how to offer directly and personally – already! after so little use! – content of specific interest to Rebecca. In addition to the clip of Joe, the device had shown comments, posts, and videos that pondered what sort of connections Professor Chayefski must have to the cosmetics industry, and fur farms and big-money corporations that had a vested interest in animal experiments, and how much chicken producers probably paid Professor Chayefski in invisible consultant fees.

'Did it show you my response?' Joe said. 'The one I sent in to the editorial pages?'

'No.'

'It's online, too. I can show you.'

'Oh. Now?'

'Yeah! I want to hear what you think about it.'

'You know, I think I'm kind of done. Not to be rude. I read so many articles and watched so many clips that I think my brain is kind of overloaded. I wonder if it does something to your brain if you leave it on all day long?'

'All day long? We agreed on two hours!'

'Oh, yeah. I guess we did. Mom must have forgotten to take it away from me.'

'Great.'

'In the end, I found myself watching a clip where someone was shaving their dog like Britney Spears circa 2007. For a second I thought the dog was here in the same room.'

'Fantastic.'

'I'm sorry, Dad,' his daughter had said, 'but I kind of agree with those people. It's not right. To the animals.'

And then: 'I love you, Dad, but I think what you're doing is wrong.'

Joe hadn't been able to do it. He hadn't been able to answer her.

Up until this point, he would have given anything for a chance to discuss the matter thoroughly, and there's no one he would have rather discussed it with than his intelligent daughter, but at that specific moment it felt like the floor had suddenly filled with tiny cracks. He was afraid he would collapse if he had to defend himself to one more person.

The ironic, amused aloofness, Joe remembered, with which the pale boy had skirted a question about the illegality of some animal activist tactics: at first he had simply said he understood that some people were prepared to go 'to pretty serious lengths' in order to achieve the necessary change. Even after being cornered, the boy had refused to elaborate, but he also refused to rule out any tactics.

'Do you support illegal methods as well?' the moderator asked.

'In my personal view and that of the organization I represent, the present situation is untenable and cannot continue,' the boy said to his palms.

'So in your opinion, is it justified to, for instance, break into the laboratory of a respected university professor and destroy computers and research equipment?'

'If we encouraged that, we would be guilty of inciting criminal activity.'

'But your website has a detailed list of researchers in this state who conduct animal experiments, along with their addresses,' the moderator countered.

After the debate, Joe had gone and checked out the site and the list. He had found not only his name and group there, but also a smiling headshot, the one published in the *New York Times* after he won the National Science Award. In addition to the researchers' names and home addresses, the list included the animal species in question and the street addresses of the research laboratories. In some instances the details were outdated, but the list was frighteningly comprehensive.

Joe's address was correct, down to the street and house number.

Every name on the list had been rated from one to five, based on the robustness of security systems. Parenthetical notes had been added ('Note! Hidden surveillance cameras at the entrances!'), as well the dates and results of previous acts of vandalism ('Hit 5.5.2004, 24 rats freed, cages broken, files and equipment destroyed').

At the bottom of the page, it read: *NOTE! Information not necessarily up to date! Always double-check your sources!*

'Wouldn't you say that publishing a list like this is, in practice, inciting vandalism?

'The information is completely public and was gathered from the official register of the Department of Agriculture, as well as mass-media sources.'

'But wouldn't you say you're implying something between the lines?'

'We publish neutral and unbiased information about animal rights on our website. We cannot be held responsible for the attitudes and incitements of the billions of people who use the internet.'

The moderator looked at the boy for a long time and then said: 'I think you're inciting people to commit crimes.'

The boy smiled at his troops. The expression meant: what did I tell you!

Further back, a girl stood up and read from a dictionary she had brought with her: 'To incite: to (try to) induce one or more people to take (often reprehensible) action through enthusiastic encouragement, persuasion, or by some other means; to spur, instigate, goad, foment, stir, agitate, provoke; *law* to (try to) induce someone to intentionally commit a crime.'

'The burden of proof,' the boy said in his reedy voice, 'lies with those who claim that our website enthusiastically encourages, persuades by some other means, or induces others to commit a crime.'

'Can you publicly state, here and now, that you do not approve of criminal activity?'

'We do not approve of criminal activity.'

'Can you publicly commit, here and now, to removing those lists from your website?'

'We publish neutral and unbiased information on animal rights on our website.'

'I'm sure you're perfectly aware the contradiction exists between the verbal condemnation of criminal activity and the publication of your list.'

'We have freedom of speech in this country that guarantees that a registered association can freely disseminate information that doesn't offend anyone's reputation, privacy, or religion.'

Joe's tumbler was empty again, even though he had just filled it. Night had fallen; everyone else was asleep.

The newspaper had published a little blurb reporting that animal activists had engaged in a debate with an animal experimenter. *An animal experimenter*. His personal view was that he studied the human visual system. Some people in his group conducted experiments on healthy participants, on humans, but who was interested in that? The four computer modelers in his group, the ones who in the young people's fantasies would save the world, weren't mentioned.

Everyone could make things look however they wanted.

Whereas before, Joe had received the occasional anonymous note, now the email flooded in. The senders were TV viewers, newspaper readers, each of whom had an opinion on the subject and the situation. Some of them were angry, furious – some on behalf of the animals, others on behalf of the young people. Some wanted to show their support for him and the fur farmers, and others thought it was scandalous that people's right to free enterprise was being stifled.

One writer had calculated how many thousands of laboratory animals had been poisoned to develop the latest vmPFC optimizers, and how many hundreds of thousands more would still be needed once competitors started copying the new craze and sought marketing permission for their me-too drugs.

A week to the day after the debate, the living-room window shattered and something thudded to the carpet so violently the couch shook. Saara, who had been watching TV alone downstairs, was startled and screamed so loudly that Daniella woke up and started crying. The time was a little past eleven P.M.

Joe and Miriam were called home in the middle of Roddy's sixtieth birthday party, where, for a moment, life had appeared tolerable again. When they climbed out of the cab in front of their house, a police car was parked outside their door, and a young female officer was recording Saara's account of events in her notebook.

The brick lay on the living-room floor like a hunk of petrified hatred. The carpet was covered in shards of glass that glittered a transparent, surreal blue.

That night they slept at a hotel.

None of them wanted to go home. *Dad, are you sure they're not going to come back?*

When they returned from the hotel, they had to spend a lot of time calming the girls down. On the first night, both made excuses to prolong their bedtime routines and whined about everyday things that were suddenly intolerable. When they finally got the girls to sleep, Joe felt like he had to stay downstairs to keep an eye on things, although it was unclear, even to him, what he was waiting for.

Miriam said good night and then walked upstairs without looking his way. As they dried the dishes after dinner, he had drawn her close, but she had seemed distracted and didn't respond to his overtures.

Joe sat in the living room late into the night, staring out into the darkness. The only thing he could see in the window was his own reflection, its contours soft, doubled, and blurry.

It was cold inside Bloomberg Hall; the air conditioning had been set so aggressively in anticipation of summer that you wanted to wear your coat at your desk. Almost like in Edinburgh, Joe thought. He'd been the keynote speaker at a seminar in Scotland once and shivered, his fingertips blue, for three days straight. It had been September and fifty degrees Fahrenheit inside the conference center.

Outside, the deserted lawn of the upper quad sprawled in the heat; the soccer-ball-kicking, textbook-studying undergrads were away for the summer. The grad students were quietly toiling away in their offices or discreetly stealing a day or two of vacation.

An outsider would have never known that animal activists had demolished the office just a few weeks ago. Joe's team had gotten used to the new furniture and already knew their way around the brand-new computers, despite the updated operating system. Even the freshly painted wall, its color a shade darker than the previous one, was finally starting to blend into its environment.

Joe had been annoyed to discover it would be impossible to get an exact match for the existing paint; if you knew where to look, you could tell that the recently painted wall reflected light differently than the others. He wished he could make the discrepancy disappear.

He tried to focus on Raj's manuscript, which he was supposed to be editing, but he was having a hard time concentrating. He'd had to make a call to Brad, his lawyer, earlier that day as a result of the catastrophic debate. A week after the event, a middle-aged woman who took in homeless cats contacted him and threatened to sue him for violating animal cruelty laws.

It was hard to say whether the lawsuit would end up being an un-
intentional farce or a nightmarish thriller. The cat lady had a good
chance of succeeding at both. Miriam had convinced him that there
was no point waiting for a summons to arrive; he may as well check
in with his lawyer regarding the wisest course of action.

'They don't have a case,' Brad had immediately said.

'I'm glad to hear that.'

'But it's a good thing you didn't waste any time calling me,' Brad
added.

It's a good thing you didn't waste any time: the words left a small,
nasty echo in Joe's mind, the possibility that something embarrassing,
unfair, and unreasonably difficult could still suddenly pop out of the
woodwork. But they hadn't heard any more out of the cat lady since,
and no summons had been delivered, at least not yet.

Nor could he stop thinking about Miriam; the brick incident seemed
to have taken more of a toll on her than the rest of them. Although
Saara and the girls had been scared, they appeared to have recovered
from their initial shock, at least as far as Joe could tell. But ever since
that evening Miriam had seemed muted and withdrawn.

Joe was frustrated that he'd spent the entire spring alone in the line
of fire. Whenever he'd wanted to talk, Miriam had grunted absent-
mindedly, her face glued to her smartphone. Apparently the banter
and news bites still flowed free and funny in social media, despite Joe's
snarl of woes. Now that she finally appeared to grasp that the problem
affected the rest of them, now when they finally could have joined
forces, his wife chose to close herself off in subtle, imperceptible ways.

He corralled his thoughts back to the manuscript. He heard voices
from the reception area – someone had a visitor – and did his best
to shut them out. He'd promised to get his comments to Raj today.
Early that year, Raj had measured reactions in the premotor areas of
the cat cortex that sparked interesting questions, and optimistically
wanted to interpret them as a sign of an important discovery. This
wasn't completely out of the question, but the younger the researcher,
the more likely he was to load results with too many expectations.
Raj's results absolutely deserved publication; however, at this stage in
the game it was hard to say what their significance was. Most of the
time, hopes were inadvertently set too high.

And yet: when you hustled enough, now and again you accidentally whacked the puck in, as a Finn might have put it. The critical thing wasn't being the most careful, the fastest, smartest, or strongest, but to learn to work the spots from where goals were made. Sometimes you didn't even realize you'd just slammed the puck into the net; Joe had considered one of his most significant finds a mere artifact for a long time. He also understood why Raj was in a hurry. If he were able to get the results published this fall, it would give him a leg up on the job market.

When Joe registered two sets of footsteps approaching his door, he expected a work-related matter. But when he looked up from the manuscript and saw the first man walk in, he realized this wasn't a business call.

There were two of them, both in dark suits. They looked exactly the way you'd expect them to: tall, square-jawed, distrustful. Lisa's worried face flashed past in the doorway behind them; apparently she had tried to help them.

The men walked right up to Joe's desk so he had to tilt back his head to look at them. He tried to think of a way to rid himself quickly and politely of these large men who were thrusting their hands towards him. He needed to finish these edits, so Raj could be the first to raise his flag, stake his claim on this virgin hillock. Joe was also in a hurry to get to a lab meeting, where they would be discussing inhibitor mechanisms in bipolar cells in a room where a guard from a private security company stood outside the door these days, because discussing interneuronal communication at the university was no longer safe – for him. Tens of thousands of others still did the same work, of course, carefree and happy.

'Professor Chayefski?'

'Yes?'

'Do you have a few minutes?'

'What is this about?'

One of the men flashed his badge. It looked exactly like the ones from the movies, the common cultural capital of the Western world, even for those who had never met a real-life agent. Joe registered Raj and Lisa lingering in the cybercafé, eavesdropping. He went and closed the door, shook the men's hands, asked them to sit, and offered them coffee, which they declined.

As he gave his name, the first man uttered the abbreviation embossed

on the badge, the one you heard in the movies, clipped, aggressive.
Joe started. Perhaps he hadn't really believed the FBI actually existed.
Maybe the fact that everything happened exactly the way you'd imagine
was what made the experience so absurd.

At the same time, he felt an unexpected hope rise up inside him. The
Federal Bureau of Investigation! Finally someone was doing something!

But his joy dwindled in the face of the men's low-pitched intonations
and curtly grunted answers. They were clearly reluctant to confirm
any of his suspicions as to what they were investigating or why. The
laboratory break-in and window-shattering brick they dismissed
outright as irrelevant. His initial joy that these men were on his side
darkened to vague concern about their reason for visiting him.

What the men wanted were answers; they skillfully sidestepped every
one of his questions. They wanted to know everything Joe knew. But
he didn't know anything. Even though they didn't say so out loud, the
men clearly had a hard time believing this. Joe found himself growing
increasingly uncomfortable and agitated, as he was forced to reply
over and over: I don't know. I have no idea. I can't say.

He had to consciously remind himself that he hadn't done anything
illegal. *This is a dream*, kept running through his head. *I'm in a dream
that has borrowed too liberally from cop shows on TV*.

But the dream didn't end when the men walked out the doors of
Bloomberg Hall. It continued in Lisa's gaze, in the pall of perplexed
circumspection that fell over the department.

He couldn't exactly remember word for word what the men had
asked, and how much he had filled in the blanks after the fact. He
came back to the episode over and over and could feel himself how
his recollections of the men's original questions gradually morphed
to correspond to his own interpretations and conclusions.

Did he have a son who was living in another country at the moment,
in Scandinavia?

Might this individual have something against him?

Not to his knowledge.

Was he aware of whom the boy was associating with these days?
What he was up to?

He didn't have a clue, except that he'd heard that the boy was in the
United States at present. He didn't even know his son. The boy had
a mother in Finland, and also a stepfather that he was close to. Last

Joe had heard, the boy had graduated from high school at the top of his class and was going off to university to study biology. He and his mother had had some sort of falling out, apparently, or maybe it was with the stepfather, but Joe didn't know the details. They ought to call his ex-wife in Finland; she would be able to give them more information.

Did he have any idea what the boy might have against him?

No. Like he just said, nothing as far as he was aware. To the best of Joe's knowledge the boy had no interest in him whatsoever. His son had not responded to attempts at contact.

'Contact?'

The men grew alert, exchanged glances. Joe was overcome by the irrational sensation that he'd just made a critical mistake. He explained to the men that he had tried to friend his son on a popular social media, but the boy had never answered.

'Never answered?'

The furrows in the men's foreheads deepened. Joe felt his armpits getting damp. The longer the conversation lasted, the more strongly he got the impression he was suspected of something. Which of course couldn't be the case.

The more often the question was asked, the more disturbing it started to sound: is it possible this individual has something against you?

Think carefully: what chip might he have on his shoulder?

Nothing, I don't think. At least nothing major. We haven't been very involved in each other's lives.

All the contact he remembered the boy having ever initiated had been positive. He had asked for help with school assignments, shared his report card, best in his class, sent an article that had been published in a magazine. Joe had done a poor job of maintaining contact with his son, and he regretted this, but he was still proud of how well Samuel had done. He'd been planning on attending his son's high-school graduation a couple of years earlier, but something had come up at work. From Alina's messages, he had read between the lines that his presence at the intimate family gathering wouldn't be missed. It had been a relief not to have to cancel the guest lecture in Florida, settled long before, to make the trip to Finland – but of course he would have done it for Samuel's high-school graduation, if the boy had wanted him to.

This continued to nag at Joe, even after the agents' departure: if

anything were amiss, he would have definitely heard about it from
Alina.

After the men left, he called Brad, who to Joe's surprise got angry.
Under no circumstances should Joe have spoken to federal agents
without an attorney present. The first thing he should have done was
call Brad! Besides, they didn't have the right to ask him questions
without his lawyer's presence.

'But I haven't done anything illegal,' he stammered.

'Listen carefully, Joe,' Brad said sternly, as if speaking to a child who
ran into the street when the light was red. 'Never tell an FBI agent
anything. Anything.'

'But they're on our side.'

'Joe, please.'

Joe waited for him to continue, but *please* seemed to cover the entire
message.

Then Brad said: 'There's one thing you can tell them.'

'The truth?'

'You can say one thing and one thing only: *excuse me, I'm going to
call my lawyer now*.'

But the worst thing happens at the end of April, when the cherries,
dogwoods, and magnolias are laden with pink and white blossoms and
their heavy, sweet scent permeates everything. The sun warms the back
of his shirt, the young men on the lacrosse team ooze testosterone as
they race across the field with their sticks, the bees buzz in the campus
flowerbeds.

Joe is with the rest of the department in the cybercafé, eating the
chocolate cake ordered in honor of Bob Lish's tenure, around the
time Daniella comes home from school. He is touched by the speech
in which Bob thanks him for his help, collaboration, and friendship.
From its personal tenor, Joe realizes that waiting for tenure has been
a lot harder on Bob than he imagined. He is happy for his friend and
colleague, happy with their easy-going cooperation, happy that they've
become a good team.

Maybe right about the same time as Daniella opens the mailbox, Joe
is thinking about Bob's dad, who is now dead; Bob's dad, diagnosed

with advanced Parkinson's at the same time Bob joined the department and began the arduous push for tenure, when he was required to work long days seven days a week while someone needed to be looking after his dad. At the moment when Daniella sees the package in the mailbox, Joe is, perhaps, thinking how impossible it had been for Bob to leave his dad in the big dilapidated house in the Midwest and how equally impossible it had been to convince his dad to move into a nursing home in a strange city hundreds of miles from the town where he'd spent his entire life.

While Daniella is thrilled by the sight of the package, Joe is, perhaps, thinking about his own dad, Daniella's grandfather, who lived at home and remained in surprisingly good health and his cantankerous old self until the end, always answering Joe's calls with: 'Haven't heard from you in a while.'

But now Dad is dead. Joe spoke at the funeral, overwhelmed by conflicting emotions, missing him, inconsolable, heart full of forgiveness; now Daniella has spent her day at school, and now the school day is over.

It is a divine spring day, the sun is shining gently, and the electric-blue indigo buntings are chattering in the trees outside the house. Daniella has gotten out of school early, earlier than she was supposed to, because her group meeting for National History Day was canceled. Saara hasn't picked up the mail from the mailbox the way she usually does, because she has gone to drop off some laundry at the dry cleaners.

The package is waiting in the mailbox with the bills and the blue flyers that appear every week, bearing the faces of missing four-year -olds: *have you seen me?*

The package is big. It's addressed to Daniella and Rebecca, and it's wrapped in orange gift-wrap and a bright red ribbon.

In hindsight, Joe can picture how it all unfolded: Daniella, his little daughter with the angelic curls, rushes up to the front door, the package in her arms, opens the door, drops her backpack to the hallway floor, starts impatiently tearing the stubborn tape from the cardboard with her delicate fingers… what is it whatisit!

In the end she is forced to give up and fetch the scissors from the kitchen. How come it's not opening? Daniella can't get the tape off even with the scissors, so she flips the package over. She rips it apart from the bottom, and this saves her life.

Inside there's a handmade wooden box.

Because the box is upside down, Daniella can't see the lid, which she would be able to lift off. She thinks for a moment and then starts to laboriously work the narrow side of the box off. When you have the box upside down, it looks like it was meant to be opened from the side – luckily.

Daniella manages to open the narrow side panel.

Needles cascade to the table. Their sharp, metallic smiles gleam in the sunlight streaming through the window.

There must be thousands of them in the box.

Daniella takes a step back. She calls her mom, who starts shouting before Daniella has even finished explaining: *Good God, Daniella!*

She is so startled by her mom's shouting that she drops the phone to the floor and starts to cry.

Don't touch it! Don't touch it, good God! DO YOU HEAR ME?

Daniella doesn't get why Mom is so mad at her.

Run outside this instant, run as far from the house as far as possible, and shut the door! Don't go anywhere! Stay there!

Daniella?

Daniella!

Do you hear me!

Are you still there!

Daniella?

DANIELLA!!!

Daniella is sitting on the kitchen floor crying when Miriam speeds into the driveway, stops the car, staggers out.

The front door is open.

The package is lying on the table, the gaily colored wrapping paper crumpled up next to it. Miriam's heart is pounding so fast her eyes go black, she stumbles in and snatches up her bawling daughter, hauls her out the door into the yard, half sits half falls to the lawn that smells of soil, coming summer, and fresh grass, she clutches her daughter to her chest, the birds are chirping in the big Japanese maple and for a moment she isn't sure if they're both still there, alive, she waits for the explosion but it doesn't come, her daughter is still crying and she has the presence of mind to slightly ease her grip and it feels like she hasn't lived a single day of her life until now.

THE LOVE SONG OF THOSE WHO WELCOME DEATH

BALTIMORE, MD

The bomb was not the work of a professional. According to the police, it was homemade, hand-assembled, and clumsy. Still, it would have probably gone off. The main problem was the box, which had been constructed and finished so carelessly that opening it from the side seemed logical.

The box contained a metal pipe, sealed at both ends, filled with potassium permanganate, sugar, and aluminum powder. A rudimentary, battery-powered detonator collated from basic parts from an electronics shop had been built into the lid.

The fact that the box was packed with needles led the police to believe that the intention had not been to cause material damage. Nor was it likely that the needles would have inflicted death.

The intent had been to cause as much pain as possible, the police decided: to disable and blind.

Daniella's and Rebecca's names had been printed prettily on the lid.

There is no more squabbling over chores and whose turn it is to take out the trash. New rules take their place:

We do not open packages or letters. If there is something in the mailbox, we wait for Mom and Dad to come home. If a package is delivered to the house, we do not touch it, we call the police immediately. If the package is delivered by car, we write down the license plate. We do not buy anything online. We buy books, clothes, and everything else we need directly from the store.

Neither one of the girls opens the mail. Any of it, especially letters addressed to them.

Neither one of the girls goes anywhere on her own.

If the girls go somewhere, bodyguards follow in a separate vehicle.

It's unfortunate that when Rebecca goes to parties, her friends will notice that two men are sitting outside all night in a car with tinted windows. But there's nothing that can be done about that.

If the doorbell rings, we do not answer. Friends are asked to call before they drop by.

If a stranger is seen in the vicinity of the house, we make a note of their identifying characteristics. If the same person is seen more than once, we take a picture with our mobile phone and show it to Mr Hackett, who comes by once a week to ask if there's anything to report.

A motion-triggered security, surveillance, and alarm system with a direct link to the security company is installed in the house.

The downstairs guest room is turned into a panic room with a steel safety door that is impossible to open from the outside when locked from the inside.

They practice getting down to the panic room as quickly as possible.

They practice opening the door to the panic room from the inside, because from now on, everyone in the family, including its youngest member, needs to know how to do it in their sleep.

They swear an oath that no one will go into the panic room alone or without cause, even if they're just playing around – ever.

They don't dream of using social media or posting pictures, not to mention checking in.

'You don't even breathe in a room where social media is being used,' Mr Hackett had said. He had looked Rebecca and Daniella dead in the eye, one by one. 'That goes for you two especially.'

The girls had nodded. Joe had never thought he'd see Rebecca look so small again, so compliant.

'Do you want me to be able to make sure you're safe? Good. Then stick to what I just told you.'

They consider getting a gun, but reject the idea, for many good reasons and many others that one could justifiably feel differently about.

They forget that anything like a personal life, career ambitions, or boycott against Freedom Media ever existed.

They practice how to gouge out someone's eyeballs, so the person is blinded for the rest of his life, probably, hopefully.

They try to believe what happened was real.

They cry, together and alone.

They work if they're able.

They go outside if they dare.

They sleep if they can.

They remember that neither of the girls opens the mail, especially letters addressed to them.

Neither of them – any mail.

They try to talk about something normal, at least once a week. It's important; they do their absolute best to remember what their lives used to be like.

Do something! Say you will not stand for this! Say this has to end, that we'll rip you apart with our bare hands, that we're going to buy a .410 shotgun, you can kiss your ass goodbye if you ever come around here again. Say you're on our side!

Joe pounds on Barb Fleischmann's door. He sends the dean messages in which he berates him as an administrator and a human being. He shouts at the provost in the administration offices. He spends lab meeting after lab meeting venting to the students, whose research results and dissertation projects remain unanalyzed and unsupervised.

The students cry, get mad, stay up all night, make cards for Joe, one drops her dissertation project during the final stretch and moves back in with her parents in Iowa. How is this possible? Isn't there anything anyone can do?

Barb Fleischmann is beside herself with shock, promises that action will be taken now. Roddy asks if Joe wants to spend the night at his place, and it isn't until afterwards that Joe wonders what the hell good that would do.

Lisa wraps her arms around him and presses herself against him, sweet Lisa, and at this Joe breaks down, too, for the first and only time, and isn't even sure himself why it happens just then.

The provost is apologetic and asks if Joe has spoken with the police. The burly security guard from administration comes by, pistol at his belt, to ask if everything's all right.

It's sweltering outside. Relentless gray clouds hang heavily over the city. It feels like a thunderstorm is perpetually coming, but it never does. The heat is so penetrating and hostile that it makes him want to give up.

Saara – who Joe has been afraid is thinking they deserved, if not exactly this, then something like it, because of their ruthlessly work-centered, competitive American-ness – throws her arms around them in tears and tells them she admires their courage, that she loves them and hopes they'll stay in touch, that they'll come visit her in Finland someday.

She tells them she's packing her bags immediately and going back home.

Rebecca refuses to go to school. Daniella doesn't understand why someone would want to do this to them.

Don't they understand that people can get better thanks to the experiments Dad does?

Miriam can't believe that anyone would be so sadistic. That anyone could do anything like this. Of course bad things happen in the world, every day, and even in this city, but they happen to other people, for understandable reasons, because they deal drugs or buy illegal weapons. Miriam had never believed that someone could be capable of being thoroughly, solely, and utterly evil, but now she understands.

She finally understands, and at the same time, she also understands how many things she has been wrong about in her life.

All of this Miriam says in Joe's presence, but as if in spite of his being there.

The mood at the department is funereal. People drop by to say a sympathetic word, to touch Joe's arm or shoulder when they see him sitting in the cybercafé.

Now, Joe thinks: now they finally understand.

But for some reason, the belated sense of gratification isn't comforting. It seems to Joe that the gestures of others seal him more and more hermetically in the alternate reality he's inhabited alone for some time now.

The university arranges an information session where at first the dean and then Roddy explain in solemn voices that one of their most renowned researchers has encountered a serious attempt at violence. Neither the university nor a single one of its representatives can approve of such actions, and they condemn them unequivocally.

Joe Chayefski is our good friend and our sympathies go out to his family, who have had to deal with inordinate stress and sorrow as a consequence of this unforgivable act.

Joe sits still and listens to their speeches as if he's running a high fever. For some reason he gets the impression that Roddy's voice isn't carrying in the auditorium. Roddy is doing a superb job of moving his lips, but his voice is inaudible. The dean looks solemn; he would have been a good candidate for a position in the Catholic Church, a cardinal to follow subserviently behind the Pope.

With his unruly hair and oversized clothes, Roddy looks like a lost little boy. Why isn't Barb Fleischmann here? he wonders. George Roediger isn't the department chair, Barb is. Not that it couldn't be any of them, the role of boss is an administrative joker that everyone ends up holding in their turn. Barb has stayed away today, Joe suddenly realizes, because her own research is too similar to his – even worse, arguably; Barb works with primates. Roddy thinks he's safe because he hasn't used animals in ten years: not because he thinks it's unethical, but because he's sixty, his fourth marriage is on the rocks, and he has gradually shifted into the class of researchers who hold lectures on the achievements of their youth, travel around administering national programs for the advancement of science education, write textbooks, and get their names in new publications primarily out of a sense of collegiality, old merits, and/or pity – no one is going to attack Roddy, Joe realizes, because Roddy is already out to pasture.

There's no guarantee, of course, that these terrorists understand that, Joe thinks. In their world, Roddy would probably be a top researcher again if his face were printed on the science pages of the newspaper next to the cortex of a macaque.

Maybe this is what a scientist should hope for most in life: never to discover anything in particular – or not at least to win any awards.

'I'd like to note,' Roddy continues, raising his face and suddenly sounding more emphatic than at any time to this point... and now something horrible is about to happen, for some reason Joe sees it coming.

Roddy would like to note that there are dozens of researchers in the Department of Neurosciences who do not do work with animal models but who use other approaches: these, these, and these.

What the fuck, Roddy? Joe nearly shouts. What the fuck, Roddy, what the fuck?

He stresses that comparatively little research conducted in their department relies on experiments with non-human animals and when it comes to primates, for instance, chimpanzees are not used in their department at all.

What the hell?

Joe feels as if his bloodstream is filling with bubbles that are about to reach his right ventricle.

The dean notes that experiments with non-human animals are by no means exclusive to their department, nor should their university be thought of as a research institution that particularly favors animal models. Many other universities conduct significantly more experimental work on animals than are conducted here.

The dean lists all the departments in the faculty and then all the schools and colleges in the university that have never conducted animal experiments: archaeology, cognitive sciences, communications, cultural and social anthropology... He might as well be reading a list of every soldier who has never shot at a living human being, every professor who has never failed a single student, every electronic device that has never been powered on, every surgeon who has never used a scalpel, every garbage truck driver with clean hands.

Joe gets out of his seat and walks halfway down the auditorium's central aisle. He stands there on the tricolor coat of arms embedded into the stone floor, where the Latin motto promises light and truth, that anyone who steps on – so undergraduates are told – will never graduate.

The dean stops, glances up and recognizes him, smiles encouragingly. Roddy, in contrast, looks like a schoolboy who has been caught in a fib.

Joe says: 'Roddy – what the fuck?'

Joe sits on a bench and breathes in the fresh, humid night air: the campus looks sad and beautiful in the darkness. He has been sitting in his office all night without doing anything, because he can't muster up the energy to go home.

The empty façades of brick buildings gleam in the light of the campus's bright halogens. The red-and-white bell tower of Whitton Hall stands tall and resolute against the night.

The rain starts that evening, arriving the way it often does on the East Coast, in a sudden, colossal deluge.

Joe lies in bed and listens to the rain that falls in spite of everything, indiscriminately, for everyone and everywhere. In less than thirty minutes, storm drains are overflowing and lawns are swimming; pools form in the yards and roads, downspouts spray like showerheads.

He climbs out of bed and goes to the window to look out at the street, now swollen like a river. A lone car bulldozes through the liquid mass, submerged nearly to its hood. He can barely make out the houses opposite, the rain is so impenetrable. When lightning flashes, thunder cracks almost simultaneously. The boom is deafening, and the alarms of the parked cars burst out wailing.

At Barb Fleischmann's recommendation he has turned over his lecture courses to his TAs, who have also promised to prepare and correct the exams. All he has to do is sign off on the paperwork.

It's been two weeks now since he has set foot in the department. Barb has sent his graduate students an email asking for their understanding – the circumstances are highly unusual – and encouraging them to offer each other peer support.

It's clear that, as soon as possible, life has to get back to normal, so normal it aches. But it's pretty hard to lead a normal life when you're not sure if it's safe to leave the house.

Dad, if we order a pizza, do you think someone might put something in it?

Yeah! They could do the same thing to us that they do to stray dogs. People put out chunks of meat and hide—

Becca, that's enough! Stop frightening your sister.

Joe, I'm going to take the girls and stay with Mom and Dad for a while, OK?

Joe, we need to go through these IRB approvals and get things up and running again.

NOTE! Information is not necessarily up to date! Always double-check your sources carefully!

VmPFC fine-tuners help you become your most perfect self.

Joe, the reviewers would like to see the revisions within two weeks.

Do you think…?

Dad, could someone try to send us another bomb?

We do not condone criminal activity.

Young people who took the **ALTIUS!®** optimizer reported feeling 76 percent freer and 65 percent more independent than those who took a normal enhancer.

The clip was sent straight to my *iAm*. I watched it at the stoplight, when I was in the car with Mom.

My personal view and the view of the organization I represent is that the current situation is unsustainable.

Animal experiments are based on established practice rather than any proof of validity.

That could have been determined through other means.

Occasionally, *rarely*, under *extremely* extenuating circumstances, animal testing can be useful.

Dad, I think what you're doing is wrong.

The next morning, after Miriam has packed the girls' clothes and belongings into five gym bags, the yard is crawling with them. The rain has softened the soil enough for the first few billion to burrow their way to the surface.

Joe heard the car-splitting racket from inside the house, but for some reason didn't make the connection. The chirping is shrill and frenzied; you instinctively want to cover your ears.

He picks his way through them as he rounds the corner of the house. Helping his wife haul the bags to the car, he tries not to see the exhaustion on Miriam's face. He pinches his lips, leaving a tiny slit to breathe through, while the cicadas careen through the air in swarms, crashing into his face, catching in his hair. He'll need to use an umbrella when he goes outside for the next couple of weeks, he realizes.

Because of them, he doesn't hear the phone at first. When he finally answers, they're shrieking in the background. They're singing so loudly it takes him a second to realize it's Hackett.

They make it so impossible for him to concentrate that he doesn't catch the reason for the security expert's call – they didn't have an appointment scheduled for today, did they?

They're dropping from the trees into his hair, which may be why he doesn't immediately get what Hackett means when he says someone named Simon Waters has successfully fished the requested data on his son. It feels like they're getting into his eyes and windpipe, which may be why it takes him so long to grasp the reason Hackett asks if he has a son who is currently living in Scandinavia. Because they're everywhere and in such preposterous numbers, they seem to demand his full concentration, and he thinks Hackett is mistaken when he tells him someone has been digging up information on his son in Finland.

He tells Hackett they'll have to get back to this later.

There are thousands and thousands per square foot, literally billions altogether. They've instantly covered trees, bushes, buildings, grass. Are there even more than last time? He's not sure. Maybe it feels equally surreal every cycle, since it's always been so long since the last. He opens the trunk, swatting the insects out of his face and hair. They haven't all molted yet; those still in the nymph stage scurry up tree-trunks and drop down, looking for a companion to mate with, billions of them at the same time, each singing its shrill, high-pitched mating call.

Joe turns his gaze upwards, and the air is black with them. Thousands upon thousands shower down from the sky, hurtle haphazardly through the air. In the streets, hordes of cicadas pop against windshields, smear into sticky clumps. People scream and panic, swerve into oncoming lanes, curbs, streetlamps. The insects get in your mouth and windpipe and you feel like you're gagging on them, and yet more keep flying from somewhere, while the constant, endless chirring fills your ears. It's like the trombone of the apocalypse, the stupendous, simultaneous, uninterrupted love song of millions of despairing insects living their first and only adolescence and welcoming their imminent death.

THE REST WILL TAKE CARE OF ITSELF

BALTIMORE, MD

Joe realizes his mistake once he's let the door slide halfway up. The entire garage has turned into a humming, seething black cloud. He should have gotten into the car first and then rolled up the door with the opener. But he's late, and has momentarily managed to forget the cicadas.

Maryland summer has arrived, gray and stinging hot. He notices it the second he steps into the garage, which is beyond reach of the AC. He's had to hang a big fan above the main staircase, because it's the only way he can coax the cool air to the upstairs bedrooms. Outside, the wet mist condenses on the skin in droplets in which air, sweat, and water are no longer distinguishable.

For the next three months, they will be moving from one air-conditioned indoor space to another in air-conditioned cars. The crowd at baseball games gets to guess the relative humidity from the scoreboard: one hundred, one hundred, or one hundred?

He tries to force himself to keep his eyes open as he swats his way to the car, but something about the haphazard barrage buzzing invasively in his eyes and nose is too much. He pinches his eyes shut and, holding his breath, fumbles for the door handle where he imagines it is. He feels like an idiot as he gropes the paint's smooth surface a palm's width too far to the rear. In the end he makes it into the car and slams the door.

He's late for the meeting with the Freedom Media boycott group. He's been preparing for this for weeks, devoted his Sunday evenings to convincing people this is important, invited and cajoled them into participating. Now he's angry that he has to waste time on this, too: he doesn't have room for such things in his life. And before the meeting, he needs to have a word with the person from the digital data security company.

He pulls his phone out of his pocket as he backs the car out of the garage. Of course he shouldn't talk on the phone while he's driving, but apparently the rules don't apply to anyone else on God's green earth, either, so...

Chief Data Security Consultant Simon Waters probably can't do much about what has already happened, Joe thinks as he brings up the number.

'Mr Waters?' he says, turning the car out of the drive.

The trees along the side of the road drip red-eyed, ghostly-winged insects like water during a rainstorm. A moment ago they didn't exist, and now they've swarmed the trees, covered every single millimeter of trunk.

After the needle bomb arrived, both Hackett and Brad recommended he immediately contact a digital security company. Apparently Digi-Hound was the best, hands-down, if not the most affordable. With the help of the right tools, professional staff, and customized services, Digi-Hound will find your bit-needle in the big-data haystack.

'I can almost guarantee you'll be surprised,' Simon Waters said during their first meeting. 'Every non-professional is.'

Waters, who has worked as a data security expert at, for instance, the National Security Agency, knows what kinds of back doors and holes have been built into home computers, social media services, email systems, internet browsers, webcams, and online banks over the years.

'So you break into people's computers?' Joe said in bafflement.

Waters had smiled at the question. Joe could see that the man was used to clients' technically inaccurate choice of words and moral mistrust, had learned to look mildly on their naïveté. The professionals at Digi-Hound, Inc. believe people have a right to keep their eyes open. The professionals at Digi-Hound, Inc. believe there's nothing wrong with knowing what sort of information is out there.

Wouldn't you like to get your hands on information that can be used to prevent violent attacks by, say, convicted criminals?

You don't have to ask twice.

In all earlier stages of his life, Joe would have scoffed at the service, sent off a letter to the editor or a criminal report to the police, but now there's nothing he wants more than this information. Of course he has always been among those liberal leftist idealists who want to limit police powers, spoil prisoners rotten. He still is, and he will come back around to defending all this actively, he promises himself – as soon as things are sorted out. But now, temporarily, civil rights and data protection have as much urgency for him as the feelings of an earthworm.

Welcome, police state, if that's what it takes to keep my brown-eyed daughters alive. And as Simon Waters says: we live in a society that operates this way regardless. You can choose whether you want the information or if you're going to let the mail-bomber use it.

'This is he.'

Waters' voice on the phone is all business; the accent suggests New York. Joe introduces himself and says: 'You promised to have some information for me by today.'

'Chayefski? Right – you were the ones who received the IED?'

The cicadas pop against the windshield.

'I already spoke with your wife.'

'That's right.'

'OK. If you could give me just a sec.'

From the sounds coming over the phone, Joe concludes that Simon is bringing up the correct file on his computer. The AC is on full blast, luckily; the car has cooled off in an instant.

At first Joe thought Waters' promises were so much hot air. But during a visit to the Digi-Hound, Inc. offices, he presented the information he had dug up on his client with permission: in twenty minutes, give or take, a stack as thick as a telephone book, Joe's life in its entirety down to the strength of his minus-lens eyeglass prescription, his mother's maiden name, the books he has ordered online, his friends' pets, conversations Joe believed were private, health insurance records.

Just the day before, Joe had, like the rest of the world, read about the latest state-snooping revelations. For years, it seems, the NSA has installed radio-frequency transponders on hundreds of thousands of home computers that can be used to monitor the doings of users who have never connected their computer to the internet. A year or two ago, such claims would have landed you in the asylum; now they were being reported on the front page of the *New York Times*.

The revelations had dumbfounded Joe – is this really the world we're living in? But when he mentioned the matter to Simon Waters,

Waters laughed.

'Oh, how innocent! How small-scale everything was back then!'

By the time an instrument becomes illegal, Waters has assured him, Digi-Hound, Inc. has already stopped using it. Five years is the rule of thumb: by the time the lawmakers have caught up enough that they know to prohibit the use of a certain tool, Digi-Hound, Inc. stopped using it five years earlier, on average. Generally for reasons of effectiveness. The contract Joe and Miriam signed expressly forbids the use of any and all illegal methods. Any legal risk is born exclusively by Digi-Hound, Inc. And Digi-Hound, Inc. is more than happy to bear it.

Of course this is also reflected in the price of their services.

Joe is roused from his reverie by the sound of Waters' voice on the phone.

'You have a son somewhere...'

'Yes, in Finland.'

'One more second, if you don't mind.'

A son in Finland.

Joe feels like he's sinking; of course they'll dig up anything to make money. Simon Waters' livelihood depends on whether he can come up with needles to look for in the haystack. Who's going to pay them to hunt unless they come up with a good reason for it?

But what if it's true?

Suddenly Joe remembers those serious, square-jawed men in black suits and feels a sharp spike in his pulse. Weren't they also asking questions about the same thing: his son who lives in Finland? He tries to calm down when he realizes he's passing other cars too aggressively. These are the very questions he wishes his wife didn't have to think about, a mother who's already frightened out of her wits. To Joe's surprise, Miriam has started speaking in positive terms about a Republican politician who promises to be tough on crime. It never would have occurred to her to vote for anyone of the sort in the past, but now for the first time it does.

That's exactly how those terrorists win! Joe let slip when Miriam mentioned the politician. Everything's lost if she allows herself to be ruled by her fears and forgets her values, Joe explained. She never would have looked twice at a populist like that before!

The way Miriam snapped back reminded him of the first hormone-hazy days after Rebecca's birth. He remembers his befuddlement at

Miriam's reaction to a trivial matter, as if his even-tempered wife had been switched for another one at the hospital.

Note to self: don't discuss politics until the girls are absolutely safe again. With anyone, but especially Miriam.

Now Simon has found what he's looking for, because he says: 'It doesn't look good. To be perfectly blunt.'

'For whom?'

'For anyone.'

Simon stresses that he and his team have been hunting for information that will help them form an overall view of the situation.

'So this doesn't mean that this would necessarily serve as actual evidence.'

'OK.'

'In court, for instance.'

'I understand.'

Simon explains that the information can help them track down more conclusive proof that could be used to, say, apply for a restraining order against Samuel or try to get the authorities to expel him from the country.

'Restraining order...? What exactly are we talking about?'

'Do you want to come by the office? Or do you have a minute right now?'

'I'm way too busy today. Just go ahead and tell me.'

'Well, this is what we have so far,' Simon says, and begins.

As Waters talks, Joe can feel his hands grow clammy gripping the steering wheel. The oncoming cars look fake, like something out of a computer game. He hasn't seen his son since the boy was less than a year old, and this is the person Simon Waters is talking about. As he listens to the information Waters itemizes, clearly and concisely, Joe silently wonders how rooted in fact all of this is. Mightn't some of it be over-interpretation?

Joe sways before the stream of words like a water-lily stalk. He grunts responses to Waters' questions as the signs of interchanges zoom past on I-695. He has successfully steered his car here, onto the freeway, apparently; he has no memory of having done so. And evidently the phone call is continuing. Joe tries to concentrate but Simon Waters' voice sounds eerily soft and far away. Somehow, while listening and peering through a windshield littered with broken insect casings,

Joe has managed to choose the right exit and make his way to his destination, even though everything around him seems to be bathed in a shimmering, wavering light.

After Joe parks, he opens the door and flinches as he feels the insects rebound from his face. For some reason he suddenly thinks of the billions of eggs from the cicadas' mating that will soon cover every inch of terrain. He climbs out of the car on stiff legs. For a moment it feels like he can't trust his balance, the earth lurches in the wrong direction.

He completely misses everything that happens during the meeting. He has prepared for this for weeks, months actually; this is what he has been aiming for all spring as chair of the boycott group; this is where he has personally invited these professors, deans, and library employees, called them at home in the evening, wheedled and bribed them, so that together they could form a sufficiently strong opposition. And now he spends the meeting in a state resembling an acid trip.

He listens to the others' statements as if they're speaking a foreign language, stares at their familiar faces as if they're mutants from Mars. One question pounds through his head. What is going on? But Alina isn't answering her phone. Joe has tried calling four times within the past half hour.

As chair, he doesn't have the audacity to step out of the room yet again. Everyone must be able to see it in his eyes: it's like he's just suffered a stroke, is losing his mind, has already lost it.

'Family crisis,' he says in a strained, lowered voice to the kind library employee who looks at him too warmly as they shake hands and asks if everything's OK.

All Alina has told him recently is: *Samuel's in a little trouble now.*

In fact, the main plot goes pretty much the way it always does in these cases, according to Simon Waters: an alienated young man, intelligent, even gifted, sadly throws away his potential due to lack of ambition or mental health issues, is dumped by his girlfriend and so bitter about it that he blames others and decides to take his revenge on society.

Samuel apparently had a good period after getting kicked out of the university – and this is what Alina has been telling Joe about. His son worked for a while at some company called Laajakoski, evidently with initial success, but slammed the door on his way out and became radicalized.

'What happened at Laaja... What was it again?' Joe finally remembered to ask Simon Waters. He feels like he's running a high fever. 'What happened there?'

'They conduct product safety tests. For corporations.'

'Safety...?'

'On animals.'

Joe feels dizzy.

His son – an animal activist? One of those who call him Hitler and spit on his back? Send bombs in the mail?

And he didn't even know?

The hazy, shapeless sunlight filters into the lecture hall through the dusty blinds. Joe's heart is hammering.

'You don't know the first thing about him,' Miriam said, voice quivering, when Joe called her from the corridor before the meeting. 'Not a thing.'

It has to be a misunderstanding, a few hastily drawn conclusions, an accumulation of unfortunate coincidences. But he can't get any clarity on the situation because he can't reach Alina. What the fuck is going on, why isn't she answering, he's been calling all day!

Miriam, on the other hand, is certain. Miriam tells him she's known this whole time deep down inside that something like this is going on. The ex-wife she's never met, the child raised in a foreign culture: something about this combination is sufficiently alien for Miriam to fill in the gaps with her own fears and catastrophic scenarios.

But she wasn't around to see when Samuel plopped onto the table at the Finnish maternity clinic, five wrinkled, purplish-red kilograms smelling of vernix. Miriam hasn't received Samuel's polite emails about school assignments and the letter containing a copy of his high- school diploma that begins 'Dear Joseph.'

Dear Joseph: something about that moves Joe so deeply that he has to lower his head.

This is all a misunderstanding.

Why isn't Alina answering? Five years is the rule of thumb. Always double-check your sources! What might the boy have against you? That could have been determined through other means.

It's true that he knows nothing about the boy – but not hearing any of this from Alina? Why didn't she keep them the least bit informed, goddammit? Joe is suddenly so enraged at his spineless, naïve ex-wife that he wants to strangle the gentle library employee sitting next to him, someone he has always liked. Eighteen-year-old experts who have pierced their lips with metal spikes and tattooed their arms with pseudo-Japanese characters have decided that laws no longer apply and have been coordinating his family's torture for nearly *two years* in the dark corners of the internet – and Alina hasn't bothered *to mention it*?

He suppresses the urge to leave the room and try her again.

The fragmentary words of Simon Waters' final report, the distinctive pseudo-impartiality that Joe urgently browsed in the car, neck hunched over the tiny screen of his mobile phone, skitter across his closed eyes like a swarm of cockroaches. Verbal abuse, traumatic breakup with his girlfriend. In his medical records, diagnoses of bipolar and oppositional-defiant disorders, treatment interrupted due to patient non-compliance. Direct indications of violence and its incitement. Disseminating hate speech online. Targets include the subject's father, Prof Chayefski.

'Hate speech?' Joe had marveled on the phone.

'There wasn't as much of it directed at you as at this girlfriend, but he wrote quite a lot about you, too.'

'What did it say?'

'Let's just say that… they weren't the words of a healthy man.'

Joe waited for Waters to continue. A moment later, he said: 'I don't get why the mother didn't force him into treatment… With these diagnoses from the health center and all. That makes you wonder.'

'What did he write?'

'Umm… that Joe Chayefski is a selfish person who doesn't care about anybody else's feelings… a typical example of a person who doesn't think about anything except his career and shows no interest in his closest relatives… etcetera etcetera. We can send you these documents if you want, of course.'

Joe still isn't sure if saying yes was a good idea. His throat goes dry.

Several court cases under review in Finland, all involving ecoterror-ism. Unwilling to cooperate, refuses to listen to anything contrary to his opinions. Recruited to militant animal rights organizations, apparently from the United States, most likely Oregon, gradually established contact with a terrorist cell in Great Britain. Arrested twice in England, released due to lack of evidence. Based on the totality of the data collected, can be considered the right hand of an anarchist operative named Tyler Burnham.

'So if you want my two cents, you'll need to keep this guy at a safe distance.'

Joe felt like he was falling from a great height.

But he would have heard from Alina, wouldn't he, if there were anything seriously wrong? At least something!

'Hey, I'm going to tell you this now and as plainly as possible,' Simon Waters said. 'There's no fooling around with these guys. Arson. Breaking and entering. Terrorism.'

'Arson?'

'Didn't you hear about the car dealership in Washington? These people burned it to the ground last year. Forty SUVs caught fire and their gas tanks exploded. It's a miracle dozens didn't die.'

'And Samuel was involved?'

'Excuse me?'

'Was Samuel involved in burning down that car dealership?'

Joe heard Simon inhale deeply, gather his patience.

'Can I say one thing, Professor Chayefski?'

'Joe.'

'Joe. You don't want to have anything to do with these people unless forced to in court.'

Even though Joe tries to breathe deeply in the dusty classroom, his lungs don't seem to fill. He remembers the article about Heather Miranda, the lonely dog-lover who brooded vengeance as a member of an activist group for years and eventually planted explosives under the car of the CEO of an animal research facility.

According to Waters, Samuel followed a similar developmental arc. At first he started harassing his employer, organizing all manner of disturbances, and in the end directly and violently assaulted those who worked with animals.

'I still don't understand,' Joe said to Waters. 'Why us?'

'My guess is because you're happy.'

'That can't be enough, can it?'

'You have everything he doesn't.'

'But—'

'To him that's wrong. Especially since he feels you're morally bankrupt.'

'But—'

'As far as he's concerned, you deserve to be treated the same way as those animals.'

'Did he write that somewhere?'

'You can check the exact wording from the files we send. But we've seen plenty of these extremist organizations. It's the way these people think. I'm sorry.'

Joe stares at the man in the gray blazer at the front of the room. He must be some agriculture professor from the University of Maryland Joe has invited, some smug prick who doesn't understand a thing about the real world and looks like an alien life form. The man starts up a PowerPoint. What his presentation is about, Joe doesn't have a clue.

When the library employee who looks like a friendly spaniel from a Disney movie touches Joe's arm and asks if he's feeling all right, Joe finally has to excuse himself and leave the room. He steps into the hall and brings up Alina's number, and there's still no response. He pounds the call button over and over; it has to go through sooner or later, by sheer force of will if nothing else.

The phone call from his ex-wife comes the next morning.

His pulse leaps: the country code for Finland. Finally.

He tried Alina again many times last night, after the meeting, but the calls went straight to voice mail.

'You called,' she says. Her voice sounds distorted, as if reaching him down an endless tunnel. Joe can't say whether it's because of his present state of mind or the actual distance involved.

'Sorry I didn't get a chance to call you back yesterday,' she continues. 'I've got these interviews and other obligations because of the new book.'

Alina sounds calm, even launching into an expansive, amused account of the journalist from a women's magazine who interviewed her about her book and how awkward she found it. It feels oddly satisfying to hear how abruptly she stops jabbering when Joe snarls at her.

'What's wrong?' Alina asks.

Joe realizes his hands are trembling. He's afraid his voice will crack. The only thing he's able to get out is: 'Samuel.'

But that's enough.

From Alina's effusive apologies, Joe can immediately tell that Miriam's worst fears are true, that Simon Waters' digital dogs are on the right track.

Alina's sorry; she's been meaning to tell him. Alina's sorry; she didn't know how to talk to him about it. Samuel does, it's true, have his... hmm, political activities, and Alina *has* been meaning to tell Joe about them. She called for that very reason earlier in the spring, doesn't Joe remember?

That was two months ago! Didn't it occur to her to try again? And how long has Samuel been nursing this hatred – for years? Joe spent the whole of last evening browsing through the emails, status updates, blog entries, and medical records he received from Simon Waters. The zip file is a seething nest of milk-white pestilence.

Hasn't Alina been to the website Samuel and his friends maintain?

Of course she has, and the language they use is harsh but...

But *what*? But *WHAT, ALINA*?!

She hadn't heard about Samuel's nocturnal online conversations with the recruiter from the American extremist organization; refuses to believe what Joe is telling her, even though he has it in black and white.

You can track the dates in Waters' package of files, follow the hate-mongering that continues night after night. From the choice of words and conclusions you can see how the constant fanning of the embers takes effect – Alina clearly hasn't had a clue where her marginalized son has been seeking solace and renewed self-confidence. And how painstaking, how informed, the recruiters are: they list Joe's laboratory and methods, know his CV by heart.

As the recruitment continues, the discussions with the recruiter decrease, eventually die out. They're followed by Samuel's regular, lengthy visits to locations where international extremist organizations operate, airplane tickets bought to activist training camps in the UK and the US.

Some of this Alina didn't know about; some of it she doesn't believe.

And the website Samuel founded, which encourages readers to attack researchers and their partners by any means necessary. *Hit 'em hard*, his son writes on the site. *The entire system needs to be toppled, but*

it won't happen as long as these people are in power. And you don't
wait for power to be given to you, you seize it.

Hit 'em hard.

And then, in the end, the logical culmination. An online conversation
with his former girlfriend. A conversation that was supposed to have
been private, encrypted using the same technology under shelter of
which, apparently, hard drugs, hitmen, and underage girls are, openly
and without any interference, bought and sold. A conversation that
took place a few days after the arrival of the needle bomb. A conversation that Simon Waters, thank God, has been able to fish out of the
dark net with his flashlights and hooks.

> *i think i did something really bad*
> *what?*
> *something*
> *[long pause]*
> *to who? him?*
> *[pause]*
> *yeah to my dad*
> *but he lives in the us*
> *that's where i am too*

Finally Alina's steady, unconcerned voice turns to muffled sobs, her
explanations grow panicked.

Joe forces himself to stifle his emotions. He can't afford to lose her
now, because Alina might be the only person through whom the police
can contact her son. In a strained, constricted voice, he tries to explain,
as if to a child or an imbecile, that the situation is much worse than she
has imagined. That for a period of almost two years Samuel has been
training with people to whom the law and human life mean nothing:
that he has become one of them. And that they must be stopped,
by force if necessary. Which is why Alina should make things easier
on everyone and let the police know Samuel's exact whereabouts. A
person like that needs to be expelled from the country or locked up
somewhere he's incapable of causing any more harm.

But Alina is horrified by what Joe is saying. It's hard to say how
convinced she is by her own performance: is it possible she has really
been this blind? And as the conversation continues, as Joe finds it harder

and harder not to lose his cool completely, Alina grows increasingly upset. Joe's heart floods with bitterness when he realizes that all of her energy is going into defending herself instead of dealing with the threat he and his family face. He has a hard time even pretending to listen as she launches into a bizarre despair- and guilt-tinged tirade on what a good, moral person her son is. During the call, it gradually dawns on him how distorted one's worldview can become, living in close proximity to a psychopath. Miriam's fears are justified; the boy is one of those who stroke your hair during the day, looking at you lovingly, and at night smother you with a pillow. Alina has no idea how badly she has been misled.

'Do you have any fucking idea what we've been going through?' he says.

'Of course I do!' she shouts. 'And I'm sorry! But what am I supposed to do about it?'

Joe is caught off guard by this outburst; he has never heard Alina shout like this before. But because she still seems incapable of grasping the reality of the current situation, he is more than happy to explain. Alina is the mother of a sick son. She has known for years what's going on in her family but has turned a blind eye to it because she can't handle the truth. It no longer occurs to Joe to try to ask or listen, he wants to lash out and inflict pain. Hearing Alina crying now doesn't do a thing to ease his plight, but he still revels in it; finally someone else is hurting, too, and this blackens his entire soul but also feels necessary and justified.

'I don't know everything he's up to!' Alina shouts. She has been worried about Samuel, too, but all she knows is what her son has told her. And Alina refuses to believe it. Samuel would never... he is nothing like the people who would do something like that.

Alina is proud of him.

Proud?

Yes, proud!

Proud of the son who, according to Finland's largest newspaper, heads the country's most dangerous extremist organization? Did Joe miss something, or didn't Samuel publicly order the terrorizing of researchers who use legal methods to conduct scientific research? *This* is the son she is proud of? The longer Alina talks, the more she agitated she grows, and the more outlandish her attempts at defending herself. Joe finally hurls the phone against the wall. It doesn't burst into shards the way it's supposed to but drops to the floor with a dull, impotent thud. He shouldn't have allowed the conversation to go on so long: Alina's grip on reality has loosened months or years before. She's fine with letting the world slide into anarchy because she can't relate to the fate of anyone outside her pampered little country where people don't understand the realities of life.

I think I did something really bad.

That thing inside Joe that, until now, has formed the core of his existence – a solid sense of purpose – has drained away. Something pitiless, metallic thrusts forth in its place.

He finds himself wandering slowly down the stairs and pushing the door open. A hot, sauna-like wave hits him immediately; the cicadas are susurrating like a chorus of chainsaws. For once, the sky is cloudless, blue.

That's exactly what Alina has always been like: gullible, easy to fool in her insecurities. Maybe he'd have a relationship with his son now, maybe none of this would have happened, if Alina hadn't implied that his presence at Samuel's graduation party two years ago wasn't necessary.

He stands there, barefoot, on the searing asphalt. He closes his eyes to the sun, which is beating down, implacable and white, high above the rooftops. He remembers what they said about the school shooting in Connecticut: it could have happened anywhere.

NO BIGGIE

HELSINKI, FINLAND

Alina stood in the hospital parking lot, phone in hand, and tried to get her breathing to steady. The air shimmered above the sun-warmed asphalt; the daffodils and tulips blazed in the planting beds of nearby buildings. Summer had just begun, and she was on her way to see her father, just like any other middle-aged woman whose surviving parent has fallen in love with a robot seal.

She had never before heard Joe speak to her like that.

She'd noticed he had tried to reach her the previous evening, but had been too busy to return the call; she'd figured she'd try in the morning. She'd left her phone on mute for the night and woken to the sight of six incoming calls, all from Joe. But it was midnight on the East Coast then; and in the afternoon, when she could have called, Alina had been scheduled to smile under silver umbrellas in the glare of flashes. She'd wondered several times that day what Joe's reason for calling might be, but then the journalist had wanted to hear about Alina's new book and her relationship to her body and how she maintained her weight and her motivation for wanting to speak out publicly on societal themes and if she had known as a child she was an exceptional individual and wow isn't that amazing. And this alone seemed to have sent Joe flying into a rage, the fact that Alina hadn't called earlier.

He had to have it all wrong. What he was claiming simply couldn't be true. Various isolated, unrelated incidents had occurred, unpleasant, even devastating incidents, and some of the pieces did fit too neatly together, but in real life things never clicked into place that way.

Her tears resulted more from Joe's aggressiveness than from anything he'd said. There was something frightening about the change in him; it was like he was a totally different person.

Alina had always considered her ex-husband, despite his many shortcomings and problems, fair-minded (if extremely driven and career-oriented), well-intentioned (if most sympathetic to what was in his own best interests), above all, a proper adult. As soon as she heard about the needle bomb, Alina had been one hundred percent on their side – of course! – genuinely sympathized with Joe's second family in their anguish.

But the lust for vengeance she'd picked up in his voice; the conclusions, drawn with horrific haste; Joe's desire to hurt others because they'd been hurt – a desire that clearly applied to Alina, too, who hadn't had anything to do with what happened – all of this was difficult for her to assimilate.

Suddenly, everything was either bad or good: everyone was either for Joe's family or against them.

Alina stared at the white brick building rising before her and the untended willow-brake stretching back behind it, the dozens of mute windows and impersonal entrances. That was where she had to go now: in through those doors. Face the raspy-voiced head nurse, who would yet again want to catalog whose bottom Dad had pinched this week or whom he had called a whore.

Joe was, of course, right in what he'd said about her.

What had happened in America was her fault.

Of course she was a failed parent! Of course she hadn't been able to collect brownie points with hand-pureed carrots, cloth diapers, and developmentally stimulating play like those women who actually had a husband. But whose fault was that, goddammit!

Fresh tears nearly welled up from the sheer unfairness of it all.

Alina walked in through the massive sliding doors of the hospital's main entrance. She had to collect all her willpower to banish her son from her mind and face her father.

It was true that her son and his friends had toppled a multinational corporation. Her son had driven the world's third-largest commercial enterprise that conducted animal experiments to the brink of bankruptcy, the one that had, hidden from the eyes of British animal activists, successfully established a subsidiary in Finland. Her son and his friends had brought down this giant without any funding, with a couple of computers from his own bedroom, *without doing anything against the law.*

As she waited for the hospital's sluggish elevator, Alina still found it hard to understand how this was possible, and if it was, why it wasn't news. Of course one could be of many minds about a company that poisoned, gassed, and dissected tens of thousands of animals a year. Of course there were a variety of opinions as to whether it made any sense for young people to sacrifice their time and energy, without compensation, to taking down this corporation. But wasn't it even newsworthy that a group of young people had felt it their moral responsibility to do so? And had succeeded?

This is what she had tried to explain to Joe. Of course she was Samuel's mother; of course she wasn't impartial! Of course she hadn't talked with the people who had lost their jobs, who were afraid when there was rioting in England.

The elevator chimed; the doors opened and Alina stepped in. Of course she wasn't personally acquainted with the CEO of Parkingfield Life Sciences International Inc., who couldn't buy himself peace of mind, even with his salary of millions, and apparently intended to move his family to Sri Lanka to escape the twenty-four-hour demonstrations outside his front door, the telephone harassment, and daily deluge of blacked-out paper that jammed the fax machines.

They have phones in Sri Lanka, too, Samuel pointed out when Alina asked what their plan was when the CEO moved to the other side of the globe.

Something Joe had snapped out to her during his harangue continued to nag at Alina but refused to take comprehensible form, even in the empty elevator. The deathly green numbers above the door changed as the elevator rose to the fourth floor.

The metal doors slid back soundlessly. When people talked about hospitals, they always mentioned the smell, but to Alina this place was associated with light: a thin grayness too dim for reading but too bright for sleeping. Nor was this a hospital, as she was reminded every time she visited. A nursing home that's indistinguishable from a hospital is a hospital, she thought. The head nurse with the alarming voice, big hands, and broad back didn't care for Alina, that was plain from every gesture and glance.

As she walked down the corridor towards the dementia unit, Alina dispelled the half-formed thoughts about what Joe had said and hoped that the nurses wouldn't notice her tear-stained face. She had used a wet Kleenex in the car to wipe the worst of the mascara from her cheeks, but her eyes were still puffy and red. She stepped in through the unit's glass door and saw her father in the living room.

Progress. Even Alina had to admit that.

Normally when she arrived, Dad was lying in his room, staring at the ceiling and ignoring the Spanish-language telenovela the nurses clicked on every afternoon, even though Alina had asked them to open the curtains and roll Dad out into the common area where the others were.

Dad was sitting in the room's most comfortable chair. He was hunched over, as if shielding the small creature huddled in his lap, soft white fur rising and falling steadily. Alina's first, automatic impression was that it was 'breathing' – the perception was nearly impossible to shake. Dad coddled the creature like a baby.

The head nurse had told Alina that after evening tea, Dad would retreat to his room and wanted to be alone with his pet. In the past, he had kicked and screamed when led back to his room. There was a surprising amount of strength left in the old man's withered muscles; he had inflicted green-and-blue bruises on the arm of a nurse named Pirjo. Occasionally the nurses had to call up three brawny orderlies from downstairs to haul Dad to his room. And every time they did Alina felt like they were blaming her, because it was her father causing the trouble.

There was something similar between this feeling and the way she'd felt when Samuel had started day care: she made him come here because she couldn't deal with him anymore.

Alina stood at the doorway to the living room and waited for Dad to notice her. With its bookshelves, old-fashioned rugs, and pots of baby's tears, the living room of the hospital that wasn't a hospital could have been mistaken for a cozy space if it weren't for the permeating reek of loneliness, shame, urine-soaked diapers, and human misery being swept under the rug. And this strange flat light, Alina thought. Why couldn't they just get some normal lamps?

'Dad,' she said. 'How are you? It's Alina,' she added. She wasn't sure if her dad was connecting her face to the right person.

He shot her a quick glance and said: 'Hi.' Then pressed his nose to the seal's snout and crooned: 'Are you hungry yet?'

My father is in love with a robot animal, she thought, while my son is trying to save the original.

'Have you been outside at all today?' she said to her father, and sensed the hostile glances around her. The head nurse had shown Alina the weekly schedule, explained why the residents only went outside on Friday mornings – if the weather was nice; in Finland, it almost never was. She lowered her hands to Dad's hunched back, where the shoulder blades and vertebrae formed bony lumps beneath her fingers. Every time she touched her father, it felt like someone was tugging at her heart.

'Does he like that, when you pet him?'

'It's a machine,' Dad growled.

Alina had to remind herself then that an electric motor hummed beneath the pelt of plastic and artificial fibers, along with mechanical joints and metal limbs that didn't feel anything. If a Finnish company's plans came to fruition, it wouldn't be long before they were being assembled on mass-production lines in a Chinese factory.

Everyone was enamored of the seals.

Why not just take pleasure in the fact that he's excited about something, an old man?

At least he has company now.

And look how happy it's made him.

I suppose an animal is better than nothing.

Hanna the Healing Seal was a gift from an IT company that wanted to sell one to every ward of every nursing home in Finland. The editorial board of Finland's largest daily was also thrilled about the seals, hoped that an innovation like this would serve as an engine to drive the Finnish technology industry. Discussions of the seal inevitably entailed mention of Nokia, the Fallen Mobile Phone Empire: could this be the nation's new hope, an industry that wouldn't abandon us this time?

Only a few hundred Hanna the Healing Seals had been sold, to an American mental hospital, but hopes were high. In the States, the empathetic machines had quickly soothed the insane. The gadgets could soon be comforting the elderly who had lost a loved one, one of the paper's editorials envisioned. The robot seals would teach social skills to people with behavioral disorders and offer children who had no adults in their lives a sense of security.

A machine? Alina wondered. A machine is going to teach children social skills?

'It's probably better than pumping them full of mind-numbing drugs,' said the office worker the TV news plucked from the street to represent the views of the common man, an opinion that prompted a professor to write a letter to the editor* the following day.

A robot seal didn't poop on the floor. A robot seal didn't suffer if you didn't care for it properly. A robot seal didn't die if you forgot to feed it. A robot seal could listen to you forever. A robot seal could sit in any lap, even that of an old man everyone else avoided. A robot seal produced purrs of satisfaction when you petted it, completely realistic ones. And if you mistreated it, a robot seal squealed as if in pain, although it was impossible to hurt it for real.

---

* A TOY CANNOT PROVIDE HUMAN COMPANIONSHIP

On 12 June, YLE Public Broadcasting published a news story on artificial seals being considered as an alternative treatment method for mental health problems and loneliness. The program contained some inaccuracies that, in the interests of preventing misunderstandings, I feel compelled to correct. As the leading expert in vmPFC optimizers, I interpreted the gratuitous comments of office worker Nelli Neuvonen as referring to this new class of targeted treatments, about which I have written numerous successful works for the layperson. And although it is important that both medicines and seals be discussed critically, I find the caliber of discussion YLE has provoked to be unfortunate.

Although toy seals may, apparently, be used in some instances to complement neurodendritic optimization proper, it is irresponsible to speak of 'pumping [old people] full of mind-numbing drugs' and to compare a toy to scientifically validated medical treatment. Unfortunately, a toy seal cannot permanently improve interpersonal relationships, prevent a violent man from beating his wife black and blue, or provide the warmth of human companionship.

Office worker Nelli Neuvonen's stance is not constructive; there is no cause to exacerbate non-existent conflicts between seals and dendritic optimizers. What we humans require more than anything is a warm, understanding companion, not allegations and slander.

Hannes Meriläinen,
Professor of Neurodendritic Optimization, Turku

Alina's mouth curved into a smile every time she remembered what her intelligent, fun, adult son Samuel had once observed.

All the traits every online dater says they're looking for, Alina remembered as she stroked the back of the father no one could stand to live with anymore.

It was on seeing the white blossom on the rowan trees that Alina finally realized what Joe had been referring to with his taunt. She paused outside the hospital's sliding doors. It had been exactly two years since then: the same time of year, the same delicate, pale-green early summer.

Samuel's graduation party.

The party she had spent two months preparing for. She had picked out the napkins, defrosted the freezer, washed the windows, rented a steam cleaner for the couch, bought the flowers, ordered the mandatory sandwich cakes no one liked, hauled home cream, strawberries, and bottles of wine in a taxi, her bra straps damp with sweat and her hair gritty with street-dust. And booked the invalid taxi in time for Dad, because if she waited until the last minute it would be too late; she had been certain until the end that she would forget.

It had been exactly two years since then. The missing cake server, fetched from the neighbors in a panic, the sparkling wine that sprayed onto the rug in the entryway, the glasses she was afraid would run out but didn't prove to be a problem after all, the mountain of dishes in the kitchen, Julia's easy-going niece lending a hand. The leaves of the birches that had just thrust forth a crinkled, shy mint-green from their buds, now vigorous and full-grown in the noonday sun.

Dad had seemed hopelessly old and sick, even though in hindsight he had still been not too badly affected. Capable of moving about, with assistance, had even behaved himself, although he didn't necessarily remember names anymore. And, oh, how he had beamed from the moment he was helped through the door. When had this special connection between Samuel and his *pappa* formed? Dad had never looked at Alina with such tenderness, never greeted her with such touching, whole-hearted joy; how come he had never granted all this to her, his only child? It was as if during her childhood he'd been forced to stint on love, and now with Samuel radiated nothing but acceptance and admiration.

And the long, exuberant squeeze Samuel gave his *pappa* – it was like a complete story of its own, with a beginning, a middle, and an end. Until she witnessed it, Alina hadn't realized how much this day meant to her dad.

But as she stared at the brick wall of the hospital, she felt a sudden sinking sensation. Was it possible it might have meant a lot to Joe too if he had been there?

The way Joe had just claimed a moment ago on the phone.

It was true that he had, in an email early the year of his son's graduation, asked what sort of occasion it was going to be – would there be a lot of guests? And of course Alina had immediately known what Joe was getting at: indirectly inquiring if his presence was required. True to character, he didn't have the guts to ask her directly. She could still remember how Joe's attitude had made her want to explode with rage. The all-permeating sense of obligation. Joe obviously didn't give a shit, and he was asking Alina to give him a pass via email.

He wanted her blessing on his spinelessness on an important event like this!

The engine of a car starting up in the hospital parking lot made Alina start. The car crawled past slowly, headed for the exit.

It wasn't Joe's attitude, the car's tires said as they crackled over the loose gravel. *It was yours*, the engine grumbled as it accelerated onto the street.

Was this true?

What if Joe really would have come if she'd told him to, had even wanted to?

The possibility hadn't once occurred to her until now, standing paralyzed in the sunny parking lot.

She had had no idea Joe had told Samuel he might come.

Only a couple of close relatives will be there, Alina had written to her ex-husband at the time. *No biggie.*

And Joe! Joe, who had known her for years, knew the darkest, most tortured recesses of her heart: of course he had read her implied message accurately. Had immediately understood. Joe had replied with a brief message, asking her to give his warmest congratulations to Samuel.

Alina squeezed her eyes shut, opened them again, and stared at the asphalt in front of her. Could it be possible this alternative scenario was true? A rare chance for her son to see his father – and she had sabotaged it?

It felt hard to believe that she could have misinterpreted the entire episode so badly. But the hot, snarling coil in her breast told her that was precisely what had happened.

After his conversation with Alina, oddly enough, Joe doesn't feel anything. The rage and the bitterness seem to have been wrung out of him. All that's left is numbness.

Miriam has turned away from him recently. He calls to let her know what Alina just said. Gradually, during the difficult call, Joe realizes that his attempts at consolation and reassurance aren't doing any good; it's as if his wife is in retreat, iron-clad against any accidental moment of empathy between them.

The call ends in a mutual antipathy Joe doesn't remember ever before experiencing with his wife. Afterwards, he can't stop thinking about Alina and the things Miriam just said about her. Miriam's way of judging his ex-wife, whom she has never met, strikes him as offensive – which is bewildering given how harsh he himself was with Alina.

That evening Joe tries to watch television. How trivial it all seems – all the things the reporters consider significant.

As he stares at the bleak stream of news from the Middle East, Joe doesn't see mutilated bodies at the side of the road; he thinks about Alina and what they both now know. Next the newscasters give airtime to a placebo researcher from Harvard who says he's gotten his hands on trial data indicating that, with long-term use, the vmPFC optimizers that have already been prescribed to millions of children cause symptoms resembling alcohol-induced dementia and liver damage. According to the researcher, the pharma company has suppressed a mountain of research demonstrating that, over the long term, optimizers do not make children more socially skilled, but passive and susceptible to mood disorders.

Via a press release, the company reiterates its belief that the drugs are effective and safe. On a normal weeknight, Joe would have been riveted by all this; now he stares at the researcher and wonders where he gets the energy.

In the heart of the purplish-black night, Joe finally understands why Alina can't admit to what happened. Deep down, she must know it's true.

Alina can't, because all this springs from her.

Something

... really bad.

Everything Samuel has written about Joe in that rancorous tirade, about his selfishness, his workaholic ethos, his American-ness, his preoccupation with his own career...

It's all Alina.

It's from Alina that Samuel has heard everything he spreads about his father online. Not directly, but in the most effective possible way: between the lines, straight into the vein, the distillation of loneliness suckled with Alina's breast milk, starting from that very first night at the maternity hospital.

Despite his being mentally ill – as is his mother, perhaps – Samuel is still the repository of Alina's genuine, hidden feelings. He is Alina's disappointment, Alina's revenge, her ancient jealousy, Alina's twenty-year-old loneliness made flesh.

That's why Alina must know; that's why it's impossible for her to admit it.

Joe suddenly realizes no one else will understand, probably not even the boy himself. Only Joe and Alina can see where this comes from – because it springs from them.

On television, the newscasters have moved on from Gaza and prescription medication via Syria to injections to make lips plumper than Botox does. Joe stares at the flickering images and remembers what they said about the school shooter in Connecticut on the radio: even if we knew every last thing about the perpetrator, it still wouldn't make his actions any more comprehensible.

To the rest of you. That's what they meant: *to the rest of you.*

Heavy metal bars gleamed at the windows. Even though the store was open for business, you had to buzz to get in.

The wind had been propelling huge masses of charcoal-colored clouds across the sky since morning; they swept past as if in a hurry. The breeze eased the burden of the heat, but the sweaty humidity remained relentless.

'Welcome! Welcome!'

The gun merchant was of Asian descent, fat, and spoke a mile a minute, like a real estate agent jacked up on speed. His accent was Southern born and bred. From Arkansas maybe or Georgia. The shop owner just wanted y'all to feel comfortable with whatever gun you chose. Which gun y'all ended up with made no difference to the shop owner, because whatever y'all ended up choosing, that model was going to be the right one. You had simplicity on the one hand, recoil on the other: any of these handguns could be the right one for y'all.

He didn't want y'all to like the gun you bought; he wanted y'all to *love* it.

The wood paneling and moose heads on the wall created the impression of a prison tricked out to look like a Finnish summer cabin. Price-tagged rifles in dozens of calibers and lengths were racked side by side in handy holders, conveniently within reach if, say, a buck happened to drop by. A huge assortment of professional equipment was tidily arrayed under the glass countertop. And next to the cash register stood a framed replica of a one-dollar bill with a semiautomatic pistol in the middle and the slogan 'The Right to Bear Arms' in a screaming font at the bottom.

There were four types of handgun that the owner, bouncing from one end of the shop to the other, wanted to show y'all real quick. Ultimately the choice came down to the main purpose of the gun. Was the intent concealed carry or to keep it on the nightstand?

Experience was the best teacher. The shop owner underscored this message with a frightening anecdote about a hunting trip where everything went awry. He guessed that two weapon types in particular would be most appropriate in their situation. He would show them the models designed to be easy for people such as themselves. *Concealed carry*, Joe thought. Something about the term struck him as childish, scary, or sick, maybe all three at once.

The last time he had come by the house, Hackett had asked Joe and Miriam to step away from the girls.

'Listen, I'm not sure what you think about – um—'

And even before Hackett continued, Joe had known what he was going to say.

'Handguns?'

'Yes, I never recommend bringing a gun into a household where there are children, and in general I'm not a whole-hearted firearms supporter myself, but—'

'Me either.'

'But in your situation, if we don't catch this person in time…' Hackett took a moment to choose his next words. 'If we're not able to bring him in in a controlled fashion, as might be the case due to lack of evidence, it might be worth remembering that there's something you can do if you want…'

Joe had zero interest in helping Hackett out on this one.

'… to feel totally safe,' the security expert finally said.

Joe was the one who'd asked Hackett about it in the first place. With every day, every moment that passed, it felt as if something important inside him died.

There still wasn't any definitive information on Samuel's whereabouts. Or if there was, it wasn't being passed on to them. All they were told was that the police had taken action. Alina had apparently communicated to Samuel the request to turn himself him in to the authorities and return to Finland, but it was unclear if the message had had any effect.

Bumping up their home surveillance had caused strife. Joe felt the cameras already had created an atmosphere of fear. When he said so Miriam had given him a look that made him wonder if this was how marriages ended.

'An atmosphere of fear?' his wife asked. 'In a household where a former cop is teaching an eleven-year-old how to gouge out an adult man's eyeballs?'

And then there was the recent conversation he'd made the mistake of engaging in on an anti-activist discussion board.

He threw a brick through your window, but you haven't acquired any means of defending yourselves? He's on the loose, and you're not doing anything about it?

He mailed a bomb to your house, but you're not going to spend two hundred bucks on a pistol to defend your wife and kids?

After the arrival of the needle bomb, Joe hadn't even considered opposing a security-system upgrade. He had looked on, almost tearing up with gratitude, as the guy in coveralls climbed their ladders and attached brand-new surveillance cameras in strategic spots to the inner and outer walls of the house, ensuring coverage of the remaining dead corners. Now a one-legged, revolving, humming eye watched from every angle day and night while they stepped in and out of the house, made dinner, went to bed. The new enhanced surveillance made him uncomfortable, but this concern belonged to another reality, maybe the same one where you could ponder questions like whether numbers really existed.

Buying a gun was in a different league, though.

In recent weeks he'd been forced to re-evaluate his worldview, but this was one line he had no intention of crossing.

But because Hackett had started from the premise that a quick visit to a gun store wasn't going to hurt anyone, no one was going to have to commit to anything, and because he'd already set up a time, Joe hadn't been fast enough to come up with a polite refusal. And the gratitude with which Miriam had accepted Hackett's solicitude – of course we'll be there, wonderful, thank you so much, what time on Thursday? – made Joe wary. Tense moments seemed to arise with Miriam for no reason at all these days. Which was why he had reluctantly followed her inside when Hackett met them at the gun store he recommended, rang the ADHD-afflicted Asian-American shop owner's buzzer, and opened the triple-locked, barred door.

Yes, the shop owner was saying. This one doesn't have a safety. You're absolutely right about that, ma'am. Do you know where the safety actually is, ma'am?

'The most important safety is here.' The gun merchant raised a forefinger to his temple. He looked at each of them in turn to make sure they understood the profundity of the lesson he was imparting. 'Nothing can replace the safety here.'

This was a line he had used thousands of times, Joe realized. Maybe it was a spiel they taught you when you were earning your gun-sale MBA, or during weekend seminars sponsored by gun manufacturers where they served venison sandwiches, bear soup, and beer during the breaks.

He glanced at Miriam out of the corner of his eye, but she didn't respond to his *What have gotten ourselves into?* look; she just kept listening to the heavy-set shopkeeper, nodding submissively, lips lightly parted, emanating unreserved female approval for everything he said. As he witnessed this, Joe felt a pang of jealousy.

His wife had consistently avoided meeting his gaze since the moment she stepped out of her car. Something about her had changed, Joe had thought, as he watched her walk towards him in her sunglasses and heels. Something about her was harder, sharper than before.

He had hoped they'd be able to patch things up today.

'I have some simple advice for y'all,' the gun merchant said, still staring at Miriam and leaning over the counter as if he wanted to leap across it and into her arms. 'Don't press the trigger unless you intend to shoot.'

Miriam frowned and nodded slowly, as if there were some profound life lesson here. The shop owner looked at her for a long time as if to make sure that the message truly sank in, and then nimbly twirled a metallic gray revolver with a classic, round barrel up from the counter and into his hand.

'I'd recommend this model in particular for folks who don't have prior experience with weapons,' he said. He looked back and forth between the gun in his hand and Miriam's eyes.

Then he took the gun by the barrel and handed it to Joe, who started. It looked to him like the prototype of all handguns.

'This would be my number one recommendation for y'all if you haven't grown up around guns.' The shop owner was already retrieving the bullets from the cupboard. He recommended this model because it was idiot-proof.

Point and shoot: just like a digital camera.

'The rest will take care of itself,' he added.

Contrary to his best intentions, Joe found himself grabbing the grip the shop owner held out to him.

The revolver was heavy. It had been formed to fit the palm perfectly.

'What caliber is it?' Miriam asked in her most convincing Quality-Conscious Consumer voice.

The shop owner was delighted by the question. Joe tried to wipe away droplets of the man's saliva from his face as discreetly as possible while the shop owner enthusiastically explained, 'Ma'am, it's important for y'all to understand that the caliber of the bullet isn't the most critical factor in a gun's usefulness.'

'Really?' Miriam nodded, frowning. 'So what is, then?'

'Placement,' the shop owner said.

Placement: which circulatory organs you were able to pierce and how effectively. This didn't mean, the man rushed to explain, that caliber didn't matter. A forty-four leaves a pretty different kinda hole than a twenty-two. Here the shop owner glanced meaningfully at Hackett. Yeah. Hackett was pleased; now he was being invited to participate: a twenty-two will do the trick, it'll just take a coupla weeks, ha ha. The shop owner remembered Miriam and Joe again, the prissy academics, and instantly grew serious. 'It's a thirty-eight,' he told them.

'Right.' Miriam nodded importantly, chin raised as if the number meant anything to her.

She looked so small to Joe, so very small.

As he walked to the parking lot and his baking car, Joe wondered why it was that holding a gun in your hand, even an unloaded one, immediately changed your perspective on the world and your place within it. He couldn't pinpoint how, exactly, but he could feel the blood rushing in his ears for a long time after he handed the gun back.

Miriam was tossing clothes and other necessities into two big suitcases. She had come by without the girls to replenish supplies.

Joe sat on the bed in his elder daughter's room and watched Miriam's delicate hands, which appeared to find the right garments from the various cupboards swiftly and unerringly. Miriam went through Rebecca's underthings, pants, skirts, shirts and knits, and organized them into two piles without the slightest vacillation, the necessary ones into the suitcases and the rest back into the closet. Joe admired his wife's methodical technique: first Daniella's clothes, then Rebecca's, both one category at a time.

Miriam's eyes looked tired.

'How have you been holding up?' she asked in a quiet voice, as if she'd sensed Joe's gaze on her.

'Fine.'

'Are you getting any enough sleep?'

'Some nights are better than others.'

Miriam nodded. When she didn't take the conversation any further, he said: 'It's hard getting anything done.'

'It is,' she agreed.

Silence again.

As he watched her pack, Joe knew both of them were thinking about the second argument at the gun shop. Or maybe the first. The more time that passed, the more difficult it seemed to clear them up.

Joe wished they could agree on a consistent *iAm* policy. Apparently the *iAm* suffered from similar privacy vulnerabilities as social media, which had been forbidden to the whole family. In their present situation, Joe had a hard time attaching too much importance to the issue – so what if some advertiser tried to target something specifically at him? They had bigger things to worry about. But he had cited privacy protection and data security issues while justifying to Rebecca his decision to keep the experience device locked permanently in his desk drawer; he couldn't very well allow his daughter to defy Hackett's explicit instructions. It would be good for Miriam to be aware of this, so they could present a unified front in face of any adolescent blitzkriegs. But raising the topic with her was hard for as long as what happened after the trip to the gun shop continued to come between them.

Miriam didn't even know that Raj had, to everyone's surprise and joy, managed to wheedle three sample *iAm* devices for the lab. This was exactly the sort of thing Joe would have normally told his wife about the same evening. Raj had gone and given a presentation to the nerds at MinDesign about Joe's paper and spoken passionately about its fundamental relevance to neuroXperience, which the *iAm* clearly relied on in many of its features. Raj's passion had apparently flustered them enough that they'd decided the easiest solution would be to give him a few devices on the condition they be given the right to mention in any printed material that Joe's entire group used it. Raj had agreed to the arrangement on the spot, which in other life circumstances would have prompted Joe to sit him down for a serious talk.

Apparently the group's research data, manuscripts, and images could be gradually moved to an *iAm*-compatible storage cloud. Joe hadn't had the energy to oppose the plan once he saw how thrilled the others had been with it. Everything would be faster, everything would be easier, they would rid themselves of pointless wires and screens and workspaces! And above all: they would get the device months before anyone else.

To Joe's surprise, he had been infected by the enthusiasm of Raj and the others: later that same day, he had unexpectedly found himself trying out the device for a second time, just for the hell of it – after all, it wasn't like Rebecca had any use for it anymore.

He watched Miriam stuff the last pairs of underwear and socks from Rebecca's dresser into the suitcase. In a minute, his wife would be wrapping up, lugging the suitcases downstairs, and driving off to her parents' across the state line. Joe had the sudden urge to ask her if he could fix her a drink. He'd picked up some fresh mint on a whim. He could blend the mint, ice, and lime with chilled vodka and they could sit in the living room for a minute and take a load off, like two adults who had been through an unnecessarily rough spring. Miriam could stretch out on the sofa and Joe could rub his wife's feet. Together they could have a laugh over how insane everything was. Or a cry.

'You want a drink?' he asked. 'I could make us one.'

'No, thanks,' Miriam said. The answer came so quickly she couldn't have even considered it.

What was the source of the conflict, anyway? It wasn't like either of them wanted a gun, let alone to use one.

And yet here they were.

As had become plain during the second argument at the gun shop, Miriam wasn't prepared to leave her children defenseless, in the event that a threat presented itself. But this was one compromise Joe was not willing to make. Miriam had seemed to reconcile herself to this after the argument, evidently having seen there was no room for negotiation. But the difference of opinion had remained hanging over them like an invisible net.

Joe followed her into their bedroom where she moved on to her own closet. He watched her fold her wool knits and skirts into the suitcase and jam tightly rolled hose into the gaps. Miriam's hands moved rapidly, her expression was tense. Joe had noticed the grooves in her forehead years ago, when they first appeared. They looked even deeper now. He wished he could tell his wife that after the arrival of the bomb, something about her had changed – something other than what affected all of them. But he didn't know how.

'The principal finally promised they could stay,' Miriam announced.

'Doug and Mike?'

'Yeah.'

At first the school had fussed about the burly men from the security company who followed Rebecca and Daniella from morning till night. During school hours, a black car with tinted windows always parked at the corner outside the school.

Neither one of the girls was to walk a single yard outside alone, ever. The first one to get out of class, usually Daniella, had to wait for her sister inside the building. Miriam or one of her parents would pick them up and drive them home, with Doug or Mike, whichever was on duty, following in his own vehicle. Miriam's parents lived across the border in Virginia, a two-hour drive during rush hour. The girls were now sitting in traffic four hours a day on their way to and from school.

One of the bodyguards stood watch in their car every night wherever the girls happened to be sleeping.

They'd wanted the children to have a normal life.

'The principal said the two of you had had some sort of conflict,' Miriam said to Joe.

'I just went to ask if direct marketing of psychoactive drugs to healthy children on school property was OK with her.'

'And was it?'

'Absolutely.'

Miriam's chuckle was an unexpected ray of light. Joe realized that, for some reason, he'd imagined she had switched sides on this issue as well.

'You have your button, don't you?' he said, even though he knew there was no need to ask

Miriam pulled it out of her pocket and showed it to him without saying a word.

The button was bright red and set in the middle of a white plastic cube. It looked like a toy. Joe checked for the thousandth time to make sure he also had his in his pocket. The smooth, plastic surface felt reassuring.

The red buttons marked his hard-bargained victory over his wife's wishes. Without these devices, their house would now contain a gleaming gun with a snub nose, brown grip, and room for six bullets in its cylinder. The one that didn't require anything more than point and shoot, and the rest would take care of itself.

Instead a red button was to be carried everywhere. This would be drilled into the heads of the girls; Miriam's parents had each been given their own button as well.

Pressing the button would bring Doug or Mike running, around the clock. An LED came on when you pressed the button, and if there was no response from the other end, it kept burning to indicate that the device would stay transmitting the signal for as long as the batteries held up.

The downside of the alarm – which Joe had momentarily feared would lead to the inevitable arrival of the Adorable Handgun – was range. The technology had been designed for hospitals and office buildings and had a range of under a few miles. On the other hand, the bodyguards always sat within shouting distance of the girls; the button was meant as a last resort in the unlikely event that someone managed to break in without Doug or Mike noticing.

The primitive technology had sounded unbelievable to Joe. Was it possible that, in this age of wireless data networks, subcutaneous computers, and GPS locators, there wasn't a better personal security device than a silly-looking analog cube with lousy range and no memory?

Just the opposite, Hackett had said. Computers were dependent on the data network, they slowed down and malfunctioned; wireless networks acted up; digital messages could be blocked. When you wanted certainty, you used robust technology that the police and the army had relied on for decades.

'If I had to bet my life on either this or this,' Doug had said, holding the red button in one hand and his mobile phone in the other, 'I'd chuck the phone in a heartbeat.'

Miriam roused Joe from his reverie by clicking the locks of the second suitcase shut. Joe wanted to prolong his wife's visit for another moment, but was so flustered he couldn't think of anything to ask except how things were at work.

'Well,' she said, 'I can't say I've been giving it my best.'

Joe realized that he didn't have the foggiest idea what Miriam had going on professionally. Normally she shared what she was working on.

Miriam heaved the suitcases up onto their wheels and lifted them over the threshold.

'Let me give you a hand.'

'Thanks, I got it.'

Joe asked when she thought she'd be able to come home with the girls. Miriam seemed to interpret this as criticism.

Of course you don't know. Of course you can't. I would never ask that, of course not. Yes, absolutely, the only thing that mattered to him too was that the girls were safe.

Joe refused to be hurt by what Miriam had said. He'd been guilty of the same, taking things out on people who had played no part in his plight. On Barb, on Roddy, on his students, on that person from the IRB who unsuspectingly asked about the ethical permissions for the latest experiments.

You want me to tell you where you can shove your ethical permissions, goddammit? Joe had felt like shouting. Why don't you ask whoever sent my daughter a box full of needles?

He'd also taken it out on the lab animals: his group had started a new series of experiments that Joe had repeatedly rejected in the past as too painful for the cats. The research question was logical and the results would in all likelihood generate numerous publications, but in the past he'd been loath to do it – especially after hearing his daughters' views. Yet now, to get back at his tormentors, who would never even hear about the experiments, he had ordered his mousiest second-year grad student to start them – the student who had told him that she'd rather work on something else and whose career would for years or decades be inseparably entwined with this specific painful methodology, just because Joe said so. This clearly wasn't right, but he forbade himself from thinking about the matter, because the most important thing now was defending scientific integrity. Why scientific integrity needed to be defended so rigidly and through these specific means, Joe was unable to say and had no intention of trying to.

He had also avenged himself on the employee from the digital reputation management company to whom he had turned and who was only trying to help. He had allowed bitter disdain to ooze from every sentence he spoke as he sat in the company's offices, watching that competent, courteous thirty-year-old, with blond highlights in her sleek, stylish hair, check the exact terms used to describe him as an inhumane, unscientific, unfeeling perpetrator of crimes against animals, a Nazi general, and how 'controversial' his 'status in the scientific community' had supposedly become. He needed this woman's help, because apparently someone had replied to these animals who propagated their filth in the internet's darkest alleyways. It could have been one of his students, presumably with the best intentions, but whoever it was had, through this counterstrike, spawned long threads of messages, entire hate forums dedicated to Joe's work, which in terms of sheer volume alone increased the probability that they would pop up first in search results.

The worst mistake had, of course, been the public debate, because it had been covered in the media, which the search engine prioritized. One of Freedom Media's television stations seemed to be misrepresenting it with such abandon that one would have thought some journalistic monitoring body would have stepped in and put a stop to the worst of the hyperbole. Joe didn't think he should have to pay a digital reputation management company four thousand dollars because people were intentionally trying to misconstrue him. But as long as an online search of his name brought up *Joseph Chayefski animal molester*, *Chayefski's research results fabricated*, and *Joseph Chayefski's 'science' is fraud* at the top of the search results, he needed this woman's help. She had her ways, she claimed, of cramming the worst of the garbage down in the search results. Making it completely disappear was, of course, impossible.

No one imagined it was possible to silence the screamers; instead you had to shout more loudly.

Millions and millions of searches. Evidently it would gradually help. Even page two or three on the most popular search engine would be enough. Nearly all of the clicks happened on the first page of results. If they removed the worst of the crud from the main page, hopefully the university administration would forget about it.

This is what he was paying this woman four thousand dollars for. For starters. Plus five hundred dollars a week for as long as she had to continue.

Simon Waters had recommended Joe unplug himself from the internet, immediately, on all devices. The woman with pearl earrings and blond highlights, on the other hand, wanted him to set up a personal blog and post there as often as possible. Preferably at least once a day, so they could get the blog up on page one of the search results. The more furiously he wrote, the higher the position he would command in the search results.

It didn't matter what he wrote, as long as he posted it online.

The woman suggested that Joe, for instance, post a brief update as to where he was and what he was doing. Every few hours. Nowadays there were good applications that would automatically publish your current whereabouts.

Simon Waters told him this would be signing his own death warrant.

Joe had asked Roddy if the university couldn't take it upon itself to remove the inaccuracies; they had resources at their disposal. But Roddy informed him that the university had already done so. It was paying a much higher sum to remove the same things from its own search results.

To remove him.

In the past, the university had wanted his name to appear on its first page of search results.

Joe had tried to turn to Brad for help, too: Freedom Media needed to be sued or threatened with a lawsuit. He would have previously scoffed at any claim that a major media company would systematically attack a private individual. But on consecutive days this week, one of the Freedom Media tabloids had printed a series of 'expert opinions' that questioned Joe's research methods and scientific status. All reputable researchers would of course simply laugh at such talk, but internet searches awkwardly brought them up among the first results. That morning, Joe had called the newspaper and asked on what basis they had selected as their 'expert' the very colleague to whom Joe had denied tenure ten years earlier, and who had since made it the purpose of his life to disprove every result Joe reported during his career, with pathetic determination.

Joe had come to suspect that Freedom Media had launched a coordinated campaign in its print outlets and television stations, along with their websites and discussion boards, to tarnish his reputation. If his boycott were the least bit effective, it could endanger Freedom Media's academic publishing business or at least put a dent in it. They, the researchers, held all the power; the reality was that academic publishers were no longer necessary. Perhaps someone at Freedom Media had noticed that Joe was the one evangelizing most zealously about this.

But Brad didn't believe in the lawsuit. Brad thought it would be difficult if not impossible to prove that editorial boards independent of each other, at least on paper, would have taken it upon themselves to stain the reputation of a solitary researcher.

Joe could tell from his lawyer's voice that Brad thought he was paranoid. Which he no doubt was.

Joe had probably been calling him too often. There was nothing more his lawyer could do for him. His life had fallen apart, but that wasn't Brad's fault.

Meanwhile, a key figure in the boycott, Joe's friend from grad school, now a professor at Princeton and the scientific editor of the best journal in the field, had, to Joe's disappointment, pulled out. He said he didn't want a corporation with as much influence as Freedom Media after him. He had heard they kept a list of names.

This wasn't necessarily mere paranoia: Joe remembered that the last time he'd talked about the boycott, he'd seen a clean-cut man he didn't recognize in the back row, who seemed to be taking notes.

'Talk to you later,' Miriam said tiredly at the top of the stairs. Joe repeated his offer to carry the suitcases, but she still wanted to do it herself.

Joe watched his petite, dark-haired wife of sixteen years laboriously haul her cases down the winding staircase.

Miriam stopped halfway and turned to look at him as if she wanted to say something. For a moment, her expression was almost tender. It crossed his mind to wonder: would she say she wanted to set aside their quarrel – quarrels?

'What's wrong with you?' he had retorted when Miriam, after leaving the gun store, had burst into an out-of-left-field tirade about his behavior. According to her, he didn't take her seriously as an adult with just as much right to defend herself as any man. It hadn't even occurred to him to pass the gun to her to try: was she so utterly trivial, so negligible in his eyes, was his wife's safety inconsequential, her capacity for self-defense non-existent?

Joe hadn't liked the way Miriam looked at him at that moment. He didn't like the fact that he'd been married for sixteen years to someone who reacted this way, in this situation.

'What's wrong *with me*?'

Miriam thought he was spineless, gutless. He should be hitting back at people who thought they could use violence to shape the world to suit their own ideas. Whereas Joe just wanted to withdraw into his shell, let the terrorists win.

But he'd been less stunned by his wife's fury than by his own reply. He had never used that word before during an argument with her.

'You should have asked to hold the motherfucking gun in the shop if it meant so goddamned much to you! And do you think you could let some things just fucking slide, chalk them up to a stressful period of our lives, be a little more fucking generous?'

Everything that happened recently had contributed to this outburst: the stress, the injustice of it all, his concern about the future, his guilt about the work he had neglected, and of course his own vague worry about the possibility that Miriam was right. He was startled to hear his next words, sounding as if they came straight out of their adolescent daughter's mouth.

'What the fuck are you lecturing me for?'

For the first time, Joe thought he understood what it must feel like to be a teenager. When life was unbearably uncertain, the last thing you needed to hear was moralizing. Besides, why was Miriam acting as if it were her life and career that were on the line here? What right did she have to start playing the martyr? He was the one with death threats and lawsuits raining down on him! He was the one who was hated by his estranged son!

And when he should have had the sense to keep his mouth shut, Joe said: 'If there's anyone in this family who's had it easy, it's been you.'

After this, Miriam had been right about everything. Joe had agreed with her unquestioningly. He had apologized over the phone, and Miriam had said she forgave him. Yet the moment tasted of failure, of permanent damage. Something in the way she said quietly that maybe it would be best to continue this conversation later, something in her tone, told him there would be no coming back to it. Nor had there been.

As for trying to set up a meeting with Samuel: Joe had suggested this after they received the red buttons from Doug's and Mike's company. It sounded tricky to him, too, but sensible, and he'd been proud of coming up with the idea. Miriam had listened, brow furrowed, a smile of disbelief on her lips. The idea was to clear the air, Joe had tried to explain. To intervene in a situation that seemed to be growing increasingly out of hand.

But Miriam had just said: 'Are you kidding me?'

Joe stared at her. 'How so?'

They'd been standing on the sidewalk in front of the security compa-ny's offices. People had walked past, quickly turning away when they realized that they had wandered into a family squabble. Miriam stared at the concrete sidewalk and then blinked twice in rapid succession: 'Do I need to explain?'

'What? Explain what?' he pressed.

Miriam looked up at him. 'How do you picture this playing out, Joe? That we'll just give him a call? Invite him over?'

'Sure!'

'You're still hoping it isn't him, aren't you? For everything to be fine.'

'No, that's just it! If it is him – wouldn't it make it harder for him to think of us as some sort of... I don't know, targets, if he met us? If he saw how wonderful our daughters are, and how... normal we are?'

An unamused laugh, and then Miriam shook her head.

'He's a psychopath, Joe. Incapable of understanding the feelings of another living being.'

'He probably is.'

'No, you don't understand! He has practiced completely shutting out what it feels like to be a sentient, suffering being. He has no interest in understanding what it feels like when he inflicts pain.'

'Still,' Joe said. 'Or maybe for that very reason. Then at least we'd know what we're dealing with.'

He'd felt his voice quivering at the memory of what it said in the newspaper's in-depth profile of the young Norwegian man, about the same age as Joe's Finnish son, who'd stepped into the courtroom with a Nazi salute, who'd shot a hundred of his age-mates, who wanted to make the world a better place. According to the story, the guy had trained himself to develop the serenity required: using Buddhist meditation techniques, he'd learned to silence his compassion for those living beings who would be forced to give up their lives in the service of his personal project, which only a handful of other people in the world even pretended to understand.

Miriam's voice had cracked when she finally said: 'Besides being dangerous, that is an utterly, absolutely idiotic idea.'

Joe understood, but at the same time he didn't understand at all.

'What could he do to us? We have bodyguards!'

'Joe, I don't understand how you—'

'Two professional killers! Who can snuff the life out of a man with their bare hands in thirty seconds! What could he do in their presence?'

'Joe, I have to say, you're scaring me now.'

'Press the red button and they'll rush in and snap his neck. Who would be in the greater danger?'

'I'm being totally serious, Joe. I don't understand what you're talking about anymore.'

'We can meet him at a coffee house with the whole city watching. We might be able to talk things out! At least some things!'

But Miriam was done listening. Miriam couldn't fathom how mentally unstable her husband had become. Miriam walked away, heels clacking, and left him standing in the scorching sun in front of the security company's offices. After thinking for a moment, Joe chased after her.

When he caught up to her, Miriam was digging through her purse for the car keys, hands trembling.

'So this is better?' he asked. 'Living in constant fear and uncertainty? Growing harder and sicker by the day?'

Like you, he meant. And when Miriam stopped, lowered her purse and turned towards him, he could tell from the way she looked at him that she knew it.

Hackett had agreed with her, of course. Hackett was paid to guard them from the outside world, to prevent anyone from approaching them. Joe's suggestion drowned under the drone of the periodical cicadas in the hot, gray Maryland haze, calcified in Miriam's turned back. Of course Simon Waters had agreed with her, too. And the police... the police went so far as to downright forbid them from contacting Samuel: they would handle the investigation; by no means should Joe take matters into his own hands, they said.

On the sidewalk in front of the security company, Miriam's injured eyes hadn't blazed with victory but exhaustion that was akin to Joe's and yet different, and he felt that his wife's disappointment had something to do with him specifically.

Miriam reaches the final curve of the stairs and carries the suitcases down.

She steps from the final tread to the hardwood floor, the one Joe spent a whole week installing seven years ago. He can still remember how satisfying it was to feel the pieces snap perfectly into place, maybe because some part of him had doubted until the very last second that they would.

Miriam has said everything she intends to. Joe still tries to come up with something conciliatory, something to show that he wants to fix everything. But because he isn't sure what conciliatory gestures might make things worse, he can't come up with the words quickly enough. Besides, he has already apologized, Miriam forgiven him. She checks her red button one last time and twists the doorknob. Up until the moment the front door closes behind her, Joe considers rushing after her and saying something, grabbing her shoulders, the soft warmth and narrow bones he knows so well. He feels like kissing his wife, and also feels like it's important to do so now.

He remains mute and immobile. A moment later he hears the cheerful thrum of her hybrid Accord starting up.

I COULD HAVE SWORN I JUST HEARD YOU SAY I'M SORRY

HELSINKI, FINLAND

Alina fits the key into the lock, leans into the door the way she always does, and steps in. Everything is totally normal. The house smells familiar, but with a whiff of something unidentifiable.

An hour to go before she has to pick up the kids. The day care and school are sponsoring a joint information session on developmental challenges in social interaction and their treatment. The goal is to teach children to keep an eye out for potential problems so that intervention can take place as early as possible. To this end, the school has established a new drop-in center where professionals offer children and parents advice on interaction disorders and their treatment. It's a relief to hear kids are getting the help they need. Apparently dozens of children in the past few months alone have been prescribed vmPFC dendritic optimizers, which evidently can be used to accurately fine-tune cell functioning in the orbitofrontal cortex. The campaign has an inspiring name, too: **The Children Are The Future**.

Alina hangs her coat in the entryway and realizes she's expecting the hospital to call at any moment. But the call never comes – it's all the same to them if she shows up during visiting hours or not. They're no doubt relieved she isn't there, casting critical glances their way. The only one at the hospital who might miss her presence is Dad, but for him every day lasts an eternity and eternity lasts a day. Dad doesn't remember that it's Thursday, or that she visits on Tuesdays, Thursdays, and Sundays. Dad doesn't have a calendar, and Alina's sure they don't remind him she is coming. Besides, every time he sees her, Dad says: 'So you decided to show up for once.'

But she just wasn't up to it, not today. It feels like everything Joe said during their last phone call is still ringing in her head.

She managed to avoid thinking about it for a full two days – because she was so certain it couldn't be true.

They say there's no doubt.

'I'm sorry,' she finds herself saying out loud, but to whom?

'What did you say?'

Alina is so startled by Henri's materialization from the bedroom that she almost drops her purse. It feels like she's been caught doing something shameful.

Everything is totally normal.

'Oh, hi,' she says, unable to meet his eyes. 'I didn't realize you were here.'

'Our workshop was canceled,' Henri says.

'I see.'

Henri looks at her for a long time. He is holding one of his psycho-therapy books, one of those in which the therapist has the right answers and every case has a satisfying beginning, middle, and end. No one commits suicide – or if they do, the therapist learns a life lesson and grows from the experience.

He asks: 'What did you just say?'

'Did I say something?'

Alina feels her cheeks growing hot. She's the worst liar she knows.

'I could have sworn I just heard you say "I'm sorry."'

'Oh.'

'So you didn't?'

'Not that I know of.'

'Strange.'

Alina walks into the kitchen to move the dishes around so she won't have to meet Henri's gaze. Her heart is beating too fast, even though there's no reason for this: everything is totally normal. Henri mutters something, goes back into the bedroom with a grunt, and assumes his reading position: on his back, with the pillow doubled up against the wall.

That morning, Alina listened to a talk show on YLE about school shootings. She was thrown to realize she'd unconsciously mistaken the Finnish show for American NPR; just the day before, she had listened to the same conversation, nearly verbatim, from the United States. The only differences were the names of places and people: Connecticut is now Nurmijärvi, Daniel Zyslewinski is Hannes Vihinen.

The tone was also identical. Both the Finnish newspaper reporter who has investigated the story and the host are capable of measured conversation. The fact that it's possible to discuss things this way, in calm voices and in a soundproofed studio, enunciating carefully – *What could we do to prevent such tragedies from happening in the future, Hannes Vihinen?* – something about this all-permeating moderation, this absolute control, strikes Alina as morbid. In addition to the reporter Hannes Vihinen, who has written a book about the school shooting, the host was joined in the studio by some serious-sounding psychologist or psychiatrist, who said all the things Alina knew he would say.

A twenty-year-old-boy, whom no one had singled out as violent, took his mother's life and then drove to his former elementary school, where he shot and killed twenty first-graders and six adults.

If these things are going to be discussed, Alina wants them discussed at a hysterical roar. She wants author and expert Hannes Vihinen and that velvet-voiced woman to run out into the street naked and smash things, not indulge themselves in long, weighty pauses and displays of professional gravitas.

'Even if we knew everything about this boy,' the journalist intones, 'we still wouldn't understand.'

'Could you explain what you mean, please, Hannes Vihinen?'

'I think that an act such as this is, simply put, beyond our comprehension.'

Suddenly Henri's voice carries from the bedroom, as if from a different reality: 'Didn't you go see your dad today?'

Alina stares at the gleaming metal sink.

This is what we have collectively decided to do about this, she thinks: talk about it in dispassionate voices on the radio. *Reflect* on what we could do. *Ask* every year, *what could we do*, Dr So-and-So, Therapist So-and-So, to prevent such tragedies occurring in the future?

This is how we intend to prevent this in the future, the next time: by asking on the radio, on television, and in the papers, what could we do?

Alina picks up a dirty plate from the counter. Everything is totally normal.

He told someone he did it.

He said it himself.

Told who, supposedly? she screams silently, still certain that Joe is mistaken, has jumped to conclusions in his desire to find some arbitrary target for his own vindictiveness. Suddenly she is so furious she wants to hurl the plate against the wall.

The program host has another question for the journalist. 'You interviewed the boy's father several times for your article. What do you think was the father's key message for your readers?'

'He wanted everyone to be afraid.'

'Afraid?'

'He was emphatic about it. "What I want is for everyone to understand to be afraid. To be afraid that this could happen to anyone."'

'Weren't you supposed to go see your dad?' Henri asks again, evidently closer now, because his voice is louder, clearer. Do you have to shout? someone inside Alina snaps at him.

Some Kerttu. Does the name Kerttu Lamminsuo mean anything to you?

Alina remembers Kerttu well, her favorite of Samuel's girlfriends. Samuel has told Kerttu that he sent the package to the girls, Joe said. According to Joe, their conversation was vacuumed up from the internet using some sort of spyware.

Alina stares at a dirty plate and remembers the day from the chaotic fall following Samuel's graduation when he announced he'd been offered a job at Laajakoski. Alina had nearly burst with relief. It felt like the answer to the silent prayers her heart had been offering up all autumn long. Samuel had been so happy about the job, and it had seemed like the perfect fit for him.

And these are not merely her interpretations. No, she hadn't imagined Samuel's enthusiasm, the way his voice grew deeper when he talked about the research. The look on Samuel's face spoke of the satisfaction that a certain, identifiable type of individual – male, someone inside Alina adds – experiences when focused on an operation demanding precision and skill, like a woodpecker on the repetitive trajectory of its beak.

Alina realizes she's been staring at the spaghetti pot soaking in the sink. She starts mechanically loading the plates crusted with remnants of yesterday's pasta into the dishwasher. She remembers how she'd been at home in the middle of the day, atypically so, preparing a speech for an immigrant women's association event, when Samuel came home.

She'd been surprised to hear the key turn in the lock, imagined it was Henri, and immediately thought something must have happened to Taisto or Ukko.

That moment when the door opened: the way her child looked, her adult son, standing there in the entryway, Alina can still remember the sensation of free-fall, the premonitory shock.

Samuel came in and said he'd walked off the job.

Alina was stunned. She had risen to her feet, still at the table.

Why?

Without taking off his shoes, Samuel walked into the living room and sat down on the sofa. Why? Alina asked again. Samuel's voice was thick with stifled emotion: because I had to.

Alina remembers feeling like the world had started spinning in the wrong direction, her own middle-aged impotence in the face of this. She remembers trying to ask what happened, to talk her son into changing his mind, even though she didn't properly grasp what he had decided and why.

Her son had made his decision, had no intention of allowing himself to be persuaded otherwise. If there had been a period of deliberation, it was over.

At one point during the subsequent tortuous, incomprehensible conversation, Samuel said he knew what he had to do. Alina remembered thinking, Do you really? And being afraid, because Samuel looked exactly the same as before, and yet so utterly different. Nothing about the way he was dressed, his face, his gestures or expressions had changed but there was something about the transformation in him, which must have happened within the past week, that was horrific, unnatural.

Over that week, Samuel's eyes had aged fifteen years. Alina had a hard time forgiving – herself or the world, she wasn't sure – the fact that something so meaningful had been lost during such a short space. And since then, every time she has seen Samuel, every time she has talked with him, every time she has thought about him, Alina has wondered the same thing: who has her son become?

As she fills the dishwasher, she realizes as if for the first time that nobody can see into the soul of another person. How can anyone be expected to do that? The thought is so overwhelming and impossible that she has to silence the voice that, against her will, struggles to emerge from somewhere within her.

She remembers the helplessness she felt when Samuel was a curly-haired, chubby-cheeked toddler and she dropped off her defenseless little boy, who had no say in the decisions of important people, at day care. She remembers being afraid that, in her absence, in the emotionally distant hands of the wrong, inattentive people, her son would change without her noticing.

'Alina?'

Henri appears in the kitchen. Only now does she realize that the groan she just heard has apparently come from her. It must have been plainly audible: Henri has heard it in the bedroom.

'What's wrong?' he asks, a large, soft-contoured presence at the periphery of Alina's field of vision.

She stares at the dishwasher. She has finished filling the half-empty racks before she realizes that the citrus press is strangely shiny, too chalky-dry to be dirty. She looks at the gray utensil rack, where at this point it's impossible to distinguish dirty from clean.

'Hey,' Henri says. 'Hey.'

Alina feels him touch her back. She has doubled over. Maybe Henri's wondering what's going on, but it's only because she needs air. Why doesn't he open the window? Her heart is beating so fast that it has exceeded some risk limit; her pulse almost feels slow. At the least she needs to fish out the obviously clean things and put them away, but how? At this point, it's impossible to tell them apart.

They were clean, she tries to say out loud, but what emerges from her mouth is something between a coughing human and a choking bird. Alina no longer sees the dishes nor the open metal door of the dishwasher, but some sort of center, an oval where she could focus all her willpower if she wanted, but it's spinning... why?

'Breathe,' Henri says in a worried voice. 'Take a long, deep breath.'

There's something she needs to tell him, something important, but that something has rippled out of reach. She hears the panic in Henri's voice, the professional resolve that quickly replaces it. She has tried to get the citrus press in her hand to stop shaking for some time now, but it won't obey. They need to leave soon to pick up the boys. *Hannes Vihinen, what could we do to prevent such tragedies in the future?* The harder she squeezes, the faster and more jagged the movement becomes. In some indefinable way, this is also connected to the gasping, which has accelerated… is that really her breathing? But someone is holding her in a massive, constricting bear hug now. 'It's OK,' Henri whispers, too calmly, and she needs to break free or she'll suffocate, she needs air, the boys need to be picked up, she's about to faint. And she could take everything else, but somehow the citrus press is on the floor now. Alina squirms against Henri's embrace with all her strength. Why can't he see? They're all mixed up in there, the clean with the dirty.

I CAN JUST PICTURE HIM

BALTIMORE, MD

When word of the FBI raid gets out, their arrest of a group of known extremist activists in Eugene, Oregon, it seems to epitomize this entire lunatic spring: an absurd dream that has turned from an implausible comedy into a thriller.

The weather is hot and getting hotter, the humidity like a wet rug spread over the city. Alina has spoken with Samuel on the phone. She has asked him to return to Finland, but he won't. Joe believes Alina when she says she did everything in her power to persuade her son.

When word of the arrests arrives, Joe heads straight home from campus, repeatedly reminding himself that it's all over now. The knowledge of the mass arrest is an incredible relief, which is why it's so weird that it doesn't seem to make a lick of difference. As he drives past the artificial playing field and the verdant Japanese maples dripping with clusters of summer green, the observatory surrounded by ancient oaks, he realizes that the fireball inside him is smoldering still, and even hotter than before.

When word arrives, the caller from the FBI or the prosecutor's office – Joe isn't sure which, after the fact – reels off the list of charges to him in a steady, dispassionate voice, like a Finnish newscaster reading the sports results.

Breaking and entering.

Felony vandalism.

Conspiracy.

Telecommunications harassment.

Use of a destructive device.

The public servant continues reading in his public-servant voice, as uninterested in Joe's thoughts as only a public servant can be.

'You are under no obligation,' the man at the other end of the phone line reads from his script, 'but as a victim of the crimes, the court grants you the opportunity, should you so desire, to bring to the court's attention factors that in your view the court should take into consideration.' The guy sounds bored to tears.

Why doesn't this feel like anything? It's all over.

Among the individuals apprehended by the police is a foreign activist, Samuel Heinonen, who will be charged with possession of a destructive device and its attempted use.

I think I did something really bad.

This is what it feels like when his son is arrested: nothing. When word of the FBI raid arrives, its core message is this: it makes no difference who sent the bomb. Joe is merely the latest victim of a formless, amorphous rage that is directed indiscriminately and, thus, is ultimately pointless. He has stopped sending Roddy, Lisa, Sarah, Raj, and Barb Fleischmann daily links to news stories about ecoterrorists and the latest incredible research results achieved using animal models, because he has gradually come to realize the message is turning against itself. He cannot shift his feelings to them. Their sympathies are directed elsewhere; his braying has grown tiresome. He can see them thinking they'd deal with this better than he has. Every single one of them imagines they'd stay sane, unlike him, whose classes have been canceled and lab meetings devolved into forums for diatribes. He has seen with his own eyes how uncomfortable or else amused the students are – some up in arms, others complaining to the dean. He has been following the online group Stand Up! for weeks, their plans for preemptive retaliatory strikes against the most nefarious activist cells – to go in there with baseball bats and hunting rifles and stop a couple of crimes from happening for a change. But theirs is a totally different crew, made up not of nerdy researchers but deer hunters, fur farmers, slaughterhouse owners; Joe envies them their capacity to act, to do something, it would make him feel better, too, but the very thought of allying himself with these gun-lovers and meat-cutters exacerbates his sense of being alone. Joe feels ashamed and sad about the young graduate student forced to begin the new, painful experiments on cats, and wishes he could take back his childish, sadistic decision, but it's too late, the damage is already done.

When word of the arrests arrives, tears well up in Miriam's eyes, but

she doesn't throw herself into Joe's arms the way he's been waiting
for her to all spring; instead she looks gray, wan, thin.

She walks into the house without looking at him, her face set in determination. She marches up to the lockable antique china cabinet Joe
has inherited from his grandmother and that, up until now, has served
as a repository for the girls' birth certificates, insurance documents,
and newspaper clippings selected according to a peculiar, consistently
inconsistent logic.

The girls are at school, and Joe realizes Miriam has chosen the timing
specifically so she won't have to explain to them why she's driving two
hours to the house to see Dad without bringing them along. Miriam
unlocks the door, clicks open her purse, and pulls out a metallic,
snub-nosed object with a brown grip that is, for some reason, called
special. The one recommended for those with no experience to speak
of and who don't need concealed carry.

Joe doesn't try to stop Miriam, who also pulls out a small box. She
opens this and plucks out six gleaming shells, one by one. Miriam
slides them into the cylinder. Joe is surprised to see she knows how
to do this.

This petite woman in a well-cut skirt and heels stands in the living
room, loading a revolver with slender, delicate fingers. Light glints off
her glossy black hair, which curls at her nape. For a fleeting moment,
Joe sees his wife through wholly new eyes, and the combination of
the safe familiar Miriam and this revolver-loading stranger makes him
want her the way he did when they were young.

The force of his desire catches him off guard. They haven't had sex
in months. For years their intimacy has been tender, warm, calm,
egalitarian, unexcited, risk-averse; burning desires and needs seem to
have been left behind on the far side of thirty. The very thought of sex
while dealing with pressures of work and the girls and everyday life
has felt onerous, obligatory – even before this new life, when they go
to bed in an agitated state, when every phone call might mean another
maiming, the tiniest rustle a murderer in the house.

In a fraction of a second, the flash of desire morphs into sadness.

It's only after this that he realizes something else.

'You went back to the store.'

'Yup.'

'Before you heard or after?'

Joe hears how strained, how constricted, his voice sounds.

Miriam replies: 'Right afterwards.'

She turns and looks him in the eye. She's wearing plum-colored lipstick and her lips are parted. Joe believes he more or less understands what the look on Miriam's face means. *And if you have anything to say about it, you can go fuck yourself.*

He feels like giving back as good as he's getting, but he has the sense to stem the urge in time. You'd be so young, so beautiful, he thinks, without that look on your face. He watches from the other side of the room as Miriam lowers the loaded revolver into the cupboard. He hears the heavy, dull thud as it hits the wooden shelf. Miriam closes the door, locks it, and lifts the key between forefinger and thumb.

'There are two keys. We'll keep one here,' she says, slipping the key into the zippered pocket in the lining of her purse. 'And we'll keep the other one here.'

She walks into the kitchen and places the second key in the cobalt blue Finnish vase Saara brought, that lives on top of the fridge. And then Miriam looks at her husband to make sure he understands.

They have to do something to celebrate. It's all over, but they won't be able to believe that unless they mark it somehow.

Nothing has been resolved, but this moment is as good as any other for celebrating. If they wait for the trial to run its course, they'll be waiting for months, even years. There will be appearances, hearings, pre-trial motions, and appeals, Kafkaesque twists during which perpetrators might become victims, formalities become results, and nothing ever necessarily resolved. That's why they have to decide it's all over now.

It's as true as anything else.

And beforehand, it's a spectacular idea: Mexican food! The girls are more excited than Joe dared hope. It will be wonderful having them back in the house for the first time in ages. Knowledge of the loaded snub-nosed revolver in his grandmother's antique china cupboard throbs somewhere in the back of his mind. He has to get rid of the gun, and soon: the girls must never know it was brought into the house. But they'll talk about that once Miriam has had a chance to calm down, stopped thinking he wants to pick a fight.

There's no better night for a party.

On the other hand, Joe hasn't thought out what it will feel like to raise his glass in a toast when he still has the acidic burn in his stomach lining. What it will feel like to mark the day when no one's promising anything is going to change.

What it will feel like to sit next to Miriam again at the dinner table.

His wife makes a point of verifying over the phone: 'Is it still there?'

Joe groans. 'Hey, come on.'

'I don't have any way of checking from here.'

If he wanted a proper power struggle, it would be easy to take the revolver from the antique cupboard and return it to the shop. Or drive to the marina at night and toss it in the harbor somewhere between the Bubba Gump Shrimp Company and the World Trade Center Institute, listen to it splash into the dark, diesel-scented waters of Chesapeake Bay.

Joe isn't sure what irritates him most: the fact that Miriam suspects him of having done so, the fact that it isn't true, or the fact that it could be.

'Miriam, it's over now,' he says. 'Samuel was arrested. Along with his friends.'

'Is it there or not?'

'Doug and Mike will be sitting in their cars right outside the door!'

'This is not a trivial matter for me, Joe.' Miriam's voice trembles; he can hear how shaky she still is. This mingles with his suppressed anger over the way she went behind his back to buy the gun.

'I haven't touched it,' he finally admits. 'It's there in the cupboard.'

Miriam knows the terrorists may never go to jail. Anything can happen during a trial; rapist-murderers are freed every day on technicalities. Brad has reminded him of this, too: there are no guarantees about what will happen in court. But even Brad believes they can cautiously assume the situation will be brought under control.

Miriam tells Joe she tried to get the police to drive by now and again.

'They haven't lifted a finger yet,' he says. 'You think they're going to show up, sirens howling, now that... those people have been arrested?'

We live in a city where gangs mow each other down with submachine guns every day, Joe counters this. Firebomb the competition with Molotov cocktails.

'Exactly,' Miriam says, and this quickly the atmosphere becomes tense.

What he meant was that perhaps the police have better things to do than patrol an area with a relatively low crime rate. What Miriam, in contrast, meant was that here again we see proof of the laxness of the police and politicians: the criminals should have been brought to justice long ago. This sparks a desire in Joe to remind her of the consequences of such attitudes: just last month, an ordinary Baltimore resident shot dead an unarmed teenager because the kid made the mistake of taking a shortcut through the man's yard. That the kid had been wearing a hoodie and had his hands in his pockets had spawned much debate in the papers.

None of this needs to be said out loud; a mutually bitter sense of being misconstrued arises in each of them without further encouragement.

But tonight, everything will be fine.

The girls and Miriam will be coming home; he'll cook and make everything up to his daughters, remind them and himself of what's most important in life: family and a sense of belonging, love – none of which a single terrorist can take from them.

He has, however, had to suppress slight irritation that that he's going to have to remove the *iAm* for an entire evening. In no time flat, the device has become a hit at the department. Those lucky enough to have gotten one have started analyzing their results and writing their manuscripts on them. From the speed of the transition and the postdocs' enthusiasm, Joe realizes that this is one innovation it will be impossible to ignore.

At first Joe tried to resist the change. He turned down the *iAm* intended for him, much to the delight of Sarah, who, as the student next in line in terms of seniority, immediately took the device for herself. He did, however, blurt out something about its lousy usability. Raj, who had been champing at the bit for the *iAm* to appear on the market since the previous fall, replied that the experience improved exponentially with use; you ought to use it five or ten times before drawing any conclusions. The hundred billion neurons in the brain formed a complex and, above all, extremely plastic whole.

But the double and disappearing images surprised him: 'That's only supposed to happen if you use it after someone else.'

'Really?' Of course that's what had happened in Joe's case: the device's circuitry had already adapted to Rebecca's neural pathways.

'So you finally tried using it, then?' Raj asked. 'Someone else's?'

'No... no,' Joe said, clearing his throat. Raj gave him a curious look. 'I just heard... an... acquaintance told me.'

'I see,' Raj said.

Joe could feel his cheeks growing hot.

But Raj also gave him a useful link to tips that would help to fine-tune the *iAm* experience.

'If your acquaintance happens to be interested.'

'I'll let him know,' Joe said, leaving the room too fast.

Some functions, like automatic saccadic motion monitoring, could be disabled if desired. It was also possible to limit the number of screens – which in the blogs and guides were called *mimages*, for mental images – if you felt like you were drowning under the surging stimuli.

Applying these tips led to a completely different experience on Joe's third try. It was clearly easier to control the automatically launching *mimages* when you deactivated the distracting eye-motion function. And if you stayed cool-headed under the waves of information, you could slip into the stream of opening screens, calmly fix your gaze up ahead, and swim in the direction you wanted in spite of the cross-currents. The more relaxed you stayed, the more pleasurable the experience was. Focusing your attention didn't always work, but you accumulated skills rapidly when you used the device every day, which was oddly satisfying.

Joe was not going to become a genuine *iAm* user for data security reasons alone, but he was happy to play around with Rebecca's unused device, to keep up with the latest technological developments in a strictly professional capacity. And the device was surprisingly handy. For instance, while cleaning the house in preparation for the girls' arrival, it would be ultra-convenient to check his email at the same time. Using the device in the girls' presence didn't seem feasible now that he had forbidden Rebecca from doing so, so when the girls moved back in, he'd only be able to use it at work.

But as he followed the thought through to its conclusion, he was surprised at himself: had it really come to this? Removing the paws for one evening felt like a sacrifice? And then he realized how onerous the thought of separate computers, televisions, and phones had grown in less than a month. To have to press buttons – using muscles! – and wait for a device to react? It all felt like something from the Stone Age.

He'd promised himself he wouldn't buy any premium experience modules – they cost hundreds of dollars apiece and were of no interest to him. Oh, he might have tried the odd free module once or twice at night, to take the edge off the stress. But there was no way he'd go any further; why, he didn't have the time.

However, the night before, something about the mind-numbing, straightforward idiocy of race-car driving suited his restless frame of mind, during which proper concentration was impossible. Another three key people had dropped out of the Freedom Media boycott group. One received direct hints that political activism was not in her professional interests; the other two begged off due to lack of time. And maybe because of this late-night news, sheer frustration, exhaustion, and maybe also because the device knew to offer it at just the right moment, Joe became momentarily lost while staring at the distractingly loud and incredibly convincing trailer for the Formula 1 Grand Prix car sports module that opened in front of him. As he watched, he felt that in this life situation, in this state of undeserved near-ruin, he was entitled to indulge whims that under normal circumstances he would have absolutely disregarded as a waste of time. And would have disregarded now, too, if selecting them had required anything so arduous as a single muscle movement.

Apparently the device was controlled by eye motion, or maybe even predicting it. The mere press of a forefinger would have sufficed to deter Joe: if one genuine muscle movement had been required, he never would have tried out the Formula One module. But no touch was required before he felt the multiple seat-belt straps pressing into his ribs. Somehow – from some activation of subcortical circuitry? – the device could tell that his mind had selected this, and the mighty rumble of the carbon-fiber-composite Scuderia Ferrari F14-T's turbo engine shook the seat with such muscular, primal force – with such manliness! – that Joe caught himself being thrilled because he feared for his life.

Three Grand Prix track alternatives floated before him in the darkness as his ears locked up from the roar. A rush of adrenaline, and nothing was as real as this. If they were giving him half an hour for free, was he really such a stick-in-the-mud that he was going to turn up his nose at a gift? What else did he have to do that was so pressing at one in the morning? Especially now that they had caught the terrorists? He

was blown away by the heavy reek of the fuel, the oily track glistening
in the sun, the sound of rubber burning against asphalt, the genuine
panic as he slid sideways into the tire barrier at three hundred miles
an hour. The sensation of speed was difficult to describe; you had to
experience the terrific g-force compression at the curves yourself. He
was surprised to find himself pulling out his credit card so he could
finish the race. The world was sliding deeper into chaos by the day, and
his chest throbbed with guilt over the mousy doctoral student forced
to conduct the painful cat experiments – he never would have guessed
that in this life situation it would occur to him to spend his nights
in a Formula 1 simulator. But oddly enough, it was the only thing to
do. What a release, what liberating pleasure! He was the last person
in the world to waste time on computer games, and this was the last
moment when anyone would – but to be able to concentrate this fully,
this intensely, on something so utterly pointless as tires screaming at
chicanes – he was alive again, for the first time in ages, if only for a
moment – and forget the odious dung heap his life had become.

Afterwards, he felt simultaneously gorged and hungry, super-alert
and unable to concentrate. A migraine-like nausea seemed to follow
every *iAm* session. The return to three-dimensional, material reality
was inevitably unsettling, which might have resulted from the fact that
every session was longer than the one before.

Which hadn't been his intention, of course.

He wasn't getting enough sleep as it was.

But, boy, was it worth it!

Searching for articles was light-years faster with the *iAm*; shuttling
between traditional media functions so easy that even sending email
was a pleasure. It was a joy dodging between social media while out
running, searching for reference articles over a chicken-breast dinner
while simultaneously keeping an eye on the news in the tiny corner of
his field of vision where it so conveniently and automatically appeared.
He saved tons of time. And because the device executed his wishes
lightning-fast and without the slightest friction, he was never alone
with his thoughts anymore. Reading was effortless, too. He could order
any work he wanted from the neuron-pathway library the second it
occurred to him; the opportunities for education were limitless. Joe
had ordered more books for the device than he'd initially imagined
– even a few novels.

Besides – and he was proud of this: he had been so wise, so adult, or perhaps his testosterone levels had simply lowered sufficiently with age – he'd already figured out what else he needed to do. Days ago, after his first experience sinking in digital quicksand, he was smart enough to consult the section of the printed user's guide that explained how to deactivate the entertainment modules.

Since that first misstep, he has – unlike nine out of ten test users – shut down the most frivolous Xperience modules, the neuro-libraries' vast adult entertainment and gossip collections. Another reason why he has some moral currency saved up – to waste on, say, virtual motor sports, which, after all, was a relatively harmless form of escapism.

The earlier module was a pure accident. Someone should have warned him.

Joe takes comfort in the fact that something similar has happened to nine out of ten *iAm* users during their first session. At least that's what it said in the technology-site article featuring interviews with a hundred *iAm* test users. And – unlike him – many of them were badly addicted. The new technology demanded practice, which was completely natural. That being the case, the concerns some users were voicing were, in the company's view, exaggerated.

After getting a basic grasp of how the device works, Joe had browsed its various standard menus: Internet, News, Phone, Movies, Series, Entertainment, Tasks, Experiences. There was nothing new about this. The device did everything you could do before, too, only faster, more efficiently, and without the need for separate devices.

But that was what made it tricky: not a single association was the same after you had wired your cortex into the *iAm*. As a menu was offering itself, anything at all might come to mind. You might, for instance, involuntarily think that a category called Entertainment probably didn't contain anything uplifting. That it had to be the one category no one would admit to browsing but that would immediately get the highest numbers of users. The one advertisers would be fighting tooth and nail to get into, and as a result of which there would be less and less room for science, culture, and investigative journalism.

Before he had finished the thought, the contents of the Entertainment menu shimmered in his darkened study like a ghostly, transparent mirror.

This was the menu he didn't want to enter.

This was the menu he mentally resisted before he even knew what
it contained. But now the Entertainment menu was already selected,
evidently. Somehow – how? From the activation of neural pathways
in the frontal insula? – the device could tell his resistance contained a
wicked trace of curiosity.

The instant the menu opened – when it was already too late – he
realized he was seeing the final item in the submenu more distinctly
than the others. And just like a moment ago, the selection didn't
require a conscious decision on his part, a click – or even a thought.

Celebrities
Gossip
Chat
Naughty but Nice
Adults Only (18+)

It was more seeing than choosing. The letters of the last category
seemed to glow in sharper relief than the others; the eyes may have
sought it out because of the parentheses and the numbers, too.

But he didn't have time to realize any of this before the Adults Only
section had already opened.

His introductory courses included a lecture on those long-ago discovered neurons in the premotor cortex whose activation patterns could
be used to predict where a test subject would move his or her hand.
The decision was visible in the neurons slightly prior to the sensation
of deciding; the neurons reacted a bit before the test subject felt they'd
made up their mind. There was something disconcerting about the
experience: the participants in the experiments got upset if they were
shown the direction of movement the neurons had predicted, because
to their minds they hadn't been ready to decide yet.

Were these the neurons the device was able to monitor? Joe wondered.
Or the ones these received input from? The device saw that this was
where he wanted to come, deep down inside, because he didn't want
to, and it was able to execute the commands faster than he could
retract them.

But what now?

Joe stared ahead, heart pounding. Something had appeared in the
dark room. A hand floated about three feet in front of him, a woman's

hand that seemed to be sketching something in the air. Words.

The hand drew tidy stick figures somewhere at the height of the desk lamp. The graphics were more believable than Joe ever would have believed: the letters automatically corrected from white to black as they crossed the white wall.

He had no idea how they'd been capable of this. The glowing hand was now writing three choices under the Adults Only (18+) submenu of the *iAm* device's screenless screen, and they remained floating in the darkness before him.

Men
Women
Both, please!

His eyes must have stopped at Women, apparently, because the other alternatives had vanished. He was breathing faster.

This hadn't been his intention.

This was what he got: this was what Raj had meant by the experience improving exponentially with use.

He was too stunned to look directly at a single face. He tried to turn away, but they stayed right in front of him. They appeared to take pleasure in his gaze, but they couldn't see anything – could they? They had to be images, computer-modified videos of some sort. There was nothing to be afraid of; they were just bitstream.

This was simply too much for him. Joe's hands felt clammy and cold.

The device was following his choices so quickly now that he had a tough time keeping up. For some reason, his mind must have wandered to one of his introductory-course students, about the same age as the girl whose assertive eyes were now confronting him in his study.

Over the years, he had learned to shrug off the attentions of female students. He was proud of how skillfully he'd learned to dodge the occasional, inevitable schoolgirl crush. He ran into it every five years or so: a certain type of woman, still testing her wings, looking for an older man like him. In the best case, it was combined with an intellectual curiosity he could respond to genuinely, safely allow the first experience of a personal teacher-student relationship. This was what had gone wrong with Aleksandra in Finland all those years ago. He'd been too young and inexperienced, confused by his own frustration and unhappiness, to head off her obvious attraction to him. But he'd learned from the experience. It had been remarkably satisfying, learning how to avoid the pitfalls that the younger Joe would have rushed into headlong.

But now in his dark study, a lightning-fast barrage of advancing, changing menus revolved before him, and all he could make out was the odd word here and there: Edit, Clothes, Accessories, Accept. And now this cute, petite, sweater-wearing stranger in front of him – whom he had, apparently, by some incomprehensible mechanism, chosen from among the others, faster than the speed of thought – looked at him earnestly, hungrily, in the shadowy study. Dark, straight, nearly black hair cascaded softly over her bare, narrow shoulders. But Joe was less awed by her gaze than by how the encounter felt: it seemed real.

And long before, heart pounding, he indicated acceptance, the girl was unbuttoning her sheer sweater. Nor did she stop, even though now Joe tried consciously to think: Pause. Stop. Exit. What was he supposed to say to the device? He had to be able to interrupt the function somehow – but how? The sweater fell back to reveal a sleeveless white top through which he could make out the girl's breasts and big, brown areolae. Joe didn't even realize he was giving his approval to what the girl asked with her eyes, as she slowly raised her arms and drew her shirt over her head. Nor did he have time to think anything beyond that he needed to turn off the device – but how? – before she was reaching one arm behind her back and releasing the clasp of her bra.

She was scandalously young. For a man his age, there was something fundamentally shocking about the experience reflected in the feigned innocence of her gaze, especially since he'd made it a rule for himself not to give in to this with a single student. She stood there before him, arms folded in front of her, the unclasped bra covering her café-au-lait breasts. She looked at him and waited, not so much out of consideration for him, as it felt at the moment, but, as Joe later realized, as a result of the designers' careful calculation: so he would have time to take in the view before the bra dropped to the floor.

When the girl said her first words, his heart pounded in shock: he hadn't meant for this to happen.

He was a pulsating, burning bundle of nerves.

Who was this girl? And why did none of this feel artificial? None of it was real, but his heart was still galloping hard, and of course it was wrong, but the application didn't stop. He should have read how to reject an experience in the 436-page *iAm* guidebook, which was easy to find online. But the girl had to be real, because if she wasn't, nothing was, and a fraction of a second before Joe had time to select or want, the girl slowly turned around. Apparently the only thing he could do was hold out his hand, his real biological right hand, and reach for the device to turn off the power, but it felt like a physical impossibility: did he even have limbs? When the girl steadied herself against the wall and leaned forward, the short skirt covering her round buttocks hiked up. Her frank, open gaze over her shoulder said one thing only.

Come.

The girl was wearing a skirt and thigh-high black stockings, but she was not wearing panties, and this wasn't right, in any number of ways, in any way, and who was this girl, she was legal, wasn't she, was she being paid for this, and had she definitely agreed to this, to be the object of his gaze, of anyone's gaze? And where did all of this come from – the standard fantasies of some men's site?

For some reason, one imagined touch would remain the last bastion, impossible to simulate. Touch was the most inalienable form of humanity, the one that would finally reveal the truth. And that's why, simply to prove to himself they couldn't do it yet, that by now at the latest the lie would be exposed, he slowly reached out and tentatively, as if afraid he would burn himself, grazed the girl's back with his fingertips.

Of course touch was just like the other senses. Of course you could make anyone feel anything by stimulating the cortex with electricity; there was nothing magical about that.

But to realize that touch can be a lie…

… yet isn't.

None of this was real; a mad scientist's dream out of a philosophy textbook.

The girl's sigh startled him; nevertheless, she responded softly to his touch. His whole palm was resting on her slender lower back now; she was alive and warm, silken. This was real. The girl's ribs rose and fell in time with her breathing. She had closed her eyes. Beneath his fingers, Joe could feel the fast, taut heartbeats, and this was real, and blood must have been circulating inside her warm body. He tried to close his eyes, but the girl was still standing there before him.

It was only then that it occurred to him to move his limbs. He didn't know where he got the impulse to start from his feet, but they proved easier than his hands. The sense of movement in his own – real – extremities instantly muted the *iAm* sensations enough for some vestige of control to return. Locating his hands demanded every ounce of willpower he still had, because they felt like they didn't belong to his body – the real ones were over there, in front of him, on the girl's warm breasts – but when he finally succeeded, the *iAm* reality faded to an unconvincing translucency.

There was something embarrassing about it. Just a second ago, he'd imagined a shimmering beam of light was a living person?

He managed to locate the device itself by fumbling around. It was on the desk in front of him, right where he left it, and once he pressed and held the power button, the entire screen finally whimpered and died.

Whew.

This was sick, unbelievable.

This is what we can do; this is how far we've come.

He suddenly remembered the marketing event held on campus last spring, a subsequent television program featuring interviews with the model hopefuls. The developers of the *iAm* were said to have gathered photographs from thousands of models, facial features and body parts from women and men of all ages. This is what those people had wanted, to become parts of these experiences.

The body parts of a select few hopefuls had been amassed into a prototype bank, organized by continuums of features based on algorithm-calculated averages. Every user could then adapt these to create visual perceptions that corresponded to their personal wishes. As Joe had, apparently, just done without realizing it – because the device followed his selections so rapidly that he didn't have time to make them consciously.

The technology still had its limits, he read later on a well-known technology blog. Compiling all of one's desired traits into a virtual character was evidently still a relatively clumsy process. And yet ten years from now it would be impossible to tell these artificially constructed perceptions from real ones, the blogger wrote.

A handful of the thousands of starry-eyed youth desperately competing to become *iAm* image-bank models had been interviewed on television. MinDesign only picked the best of the best; the competition wasn't fair, and no one ever said it would be. But if you wanted your dreams to come true, it was worth a shot. They would live forever in people's experiences as *iAm* characters, the young interviewees pointed out.

'I want my life to have meaning,' one explained.

'I don't get why I should settle for anything less,' said another.

The youngest were Daniella's age. For those under fifteen in particular, it was important to be able to build a career from home. Not all of them could make the rounds of photo shoots and modeling agencies due to school or curfews. But every single one of them had a computer at home, and a webcam on it. All you had to do was to go to the legal agreement on their webpage and click Accept.

'You just have to focus on being your natural, authentic self,' said Cindy Markingson, 16, from Bloomington, IN. 'And be ready to do a hell of a lot of work.'

'That's the whole point, the *iAm* doesn't lie,' said a boy who, based on his appearance, had fallen into a vat of hair gel as a baby. 'If you see your profile getting hits, you know those people picked you. Or some part of you. With the *iAm*, your brain picks what you really want.'

'I don't have any problem admitting it,' said a middle-aged woman, who according to the reporter's intro had had her nose, eyelids, and cheeks done, her forehead smoothed, her breasts enlarged, and her vocal cords shaved to make it as an *iAm* model. 'I want approval just as bad as anyone. So, like, I don't get what's so wrong with it.'

Of course *iAm* models raked in the dough, the interviewees asserted in turn; of course making it as a model afforded you a certain status that was otherwise impossible to achieve; of course it was a calling card that ensured access to the right circles. But all this was just material, superficial. It doesn't guarantee happiness, they said.

'Why are you here?'

The reporter thrust her microphone hopefully in the direction of a pudgy Midwesterner standing in the winding, half-mile line. Getting people to embarrass themselves wasn't hard; what set an ace reporter apart was her ability to sniff out that one person in a hundred who would make herself a laughing stock in as memorable a way as possible.

'Well, for a lot of reasons,' the woman replied, and you could immediately hear from her earnest tone that the reporter had struck pay dirt. It was plain from the woman's brassy curls and buck teeth that she had little chance of making it into the *iAm* image banks; she was a reporter's dream. Without needing a second to reflect, the woman said: 'But most of all, I signed up because this is, like, a path to immortality.'

It might be best not to use the device at night, as appropriate as his usage had been since that one mistake. Maybe reading would be easier from real paper, too, instead of the screenless screen, where thousands of digital *mimages* and Formula 1 experience modules were lunging at you every second. Was it really that great to be constantly interrupted by news, email, and ads for experience modules?

Joe hasn't read a single one of the novels – *prose-form neuro-narrative Xperiences* – he bought for the device, at least not yet. He started one, a couple of times, actually. But by the second page, something more pertinent has always appeared: with wizardly precision, the device offers enticing content of every description. In particular, articles about crimes committed by animal rights activists, which the device has learned to pluck from the other stories in Joe's news feed, seem to appear with increasing frequency on his screenless screen. Is he just imagining it or have they also grown more sensationalistic? And of course there are an infinite number of other useful functions that can be accessed with the device equally quickly: informative, social, emotionally engaging, shocking, dramatic, newsworthy, cultural.

All afternoon, as Joe waits for Miriam and the girls, the device jeers at him like a tiny, malicious witch. After so many days of using it, it's surprisingly hard going cold turkey. It announces itself every few seconds, as if by some remote mechanism: Joe is constantly thinking, Why don't I put on the paws after all? Just for a second, while I still have time? I could check the charges being brought against the activists and read my emails while I'm vacuuming. Or find out what sort of shenanigans the alcoholic former baseball star everyone's talking about got up to yesterday. And while I'm grilling the chicken, I could watch Act I of *King Lear*, the production by that legendary London theater company. I mean, grilling is going to take more than a couple of minutes, what am I going to do with myself in the meantime?

The incessant inner chirring continues until evening and comes to a head when he goes to the bathroom, which in its slowness and aimless sitting around is intolerable. He has to generate every thought and impression by himself from beginning to end. How onerous! And worst of all, not a single thought seems to lead anywhere – unless he puts active effort into it. No menus open, nothing reacts to his wishes, nor does concentrating on any object bring it to life in a series of increasingly specific choices.

A momentary panic stirs. How is he going to make it through an entire evening without the diversion of the *iAm*? Is this clamorous inner heckling seriously what his own, normal thoughts have started feeling like? Is it really impossible for him to take a shit in peace?

Apparently a forced fifteen-minute separation from the device does wonders.

Joe channels his self-loathing into a massive cleaning operation – vacuuming, scouring the kitchen and the bathroom – and promises to mend his ways, to stop himself from slipping any further down the road he has unintentionally ended up on. He's so furious about his unexpected experience-device addiction that for a few minutes he's able to huff and puff out his frustration without remembering the package the girls received, his estranged psychopath son, or the FBI raid.

And in part thanks to this, it feels important to him to offer the girls a nourishing, balanced, lovingly prepared meal, to prove that he's still capable of functioning in physical reality.

Their ordeal is over.

The perpetrators have been caught.

Defying the cicadas, he sets up the grill before the girls' arrival, so they won't have to wait while he cooks the chicken breasts. And no, he's not going to check his email while he does it, as convenient as that would be. Ever since she was a little girl, Rebecca has loved grilled food. For once, Joe makes the guacamole himself; Rebecca is always complaining that the store-bought versions are nothing but chemicals and additives. And no, he's not going to take a peek at the news headlines.

He also goes down to the basement and brings up two bottles of Sol to chill in the fridge. He's made a deal with himself that he's going to offer Rebecca half a glass with a slice of lime in honor of their having survived the ordeal.

He can already picture the gesture coming as a complete surprise to Rebecca, the joy with which she accepts. Maybe after that, both of them will see each other in a slightly different light, more adult, more equal. His fifteen-year-old is growing into an adult and within a few years will slip out of reach.

When Miriam appears at the door with the girls, Joe says 'Hi' and kisses her on the cheek.

Miriam turns her head in a way that makes him feel uneasy.

'What's in your eyes?' Daniella asks.

'My eyes?'

'They're all red,' Miriam agrees, studying his face.

'It must be… Maybe it's allergies,' he says.

The women stare at him doubtfully.

'You've never had them before,' Miriam points out.

The truth is he was up until three in the morning, wired into the *iAm*, because it would have been frustrating and absurd to quit after the first, unfair instance of driving off the track in the Monaco Grand Prix, now that he had paid for the entire experience module.

'What stinks in here?' Rebecca asks.

Her tone towards him is the opposite of the reception Joe has been imagining, and her body language indicates that it's a struggle for her to force herself across the threshold. It is only now that he realizes his notions of Rebecca's favorite food may be months, if not years, out of date. What would she eat if she were allowed to choose? Suddenly he has no clue. In the space of a year, a fifteen-year-old changes her hair, her wardrobe, her taste in music, her vocabulary, her hobbies, her circle of friends, her ethical convictions, and her relationship status a dozen times.

'Is my *ammer* still here?' Rebecca asks, after shedding a pair of new-looking shoes in the entryway.

'Your what?'

'My account has been hacked.'

'Your what has been what?'

Rebecca rolls her eyes. 'My *iAm* experience device, Professor Chayefski,' she says, over-articulating as if talking to someone with a developmental disability. 'Is it still being kept on the premises?'

'It's upstairs in the drawer.'

'Are you sure?' Miriam asks, looking him dead in the eye.

'No one has touched it, as far as I know,' Joe says, clearing his throat.

He hurries out from under his wife's and daughter's gazes and into the entryway to tidy up the shoes, which are already in perfect order.

'Great,' Rebecca says in her know-it-all voice. 'That means it's been hacked.' She pulls out her phone and starts tapping out the news to her friends.

'I told you, Becky,' says Miriam, who is still standing in the entryway with her shoes on, as if weighing whether or not to come in.

'Yeah, I know, I know.'

'You need to be more careful with your passwords. If I can guess two out of three of them, then—'

'I know, I know.'

'Remember that site I showed you? About passwords?'

'I know, I KNOW!'

Now that the *iAm* and social media have been forbidden, Rebecca has, after a period of raging, gone back to her incessant texting with her friends. Joe is afraid she'll end up running into a light post or getting scoliosis as she walks through life, shoulders hunched, face glued to her screen. And then there's the constant monitoring: according to Miriam, Rebecca has been caught on social media again, broadcasting to the entire world whose party she's going to on Saturday night, as if she hadn't learned a thing from Hackett's warnings.

Miriam takes off her shoes and walks into the living room. She surveys her surroundings as if she's in a stranger's home.

'So what has been hacked?' Joe asks his wife.

Miriam doesn't have time to respond before Rebecca sighs and reluctantly tears her eyes from her phone.

'My *iAm* account has been charged for dozens of hours of some news service, email connections, and God knows what else. And some fucking Formula One races. Almost a thousand dollars.'

Joe is stunned: 'Huh?'

Miriam nods at him. 'Last night. Becky just checked this morning.'

Tap tap. Once again Rebecca's eyes are nailed to her tiny screen from the couch, where she has collapsed with her phone.

'And fucking porn,' she says.

'Really?' Miriam asks, and looks up from the orchids she's inspecting on the windowsill: Joe has been given detailed instructions for their care, which he has consistently neglected. 'I hadn't heard that.'

'Yeah. Some sex modules.'

Joe's cheeks are burning. This can't be happening. He specifically paid for the modules with his own credit card.

He suddenly remembers having heard that the device automatically sends its manufacturer and programmers information about the user's location, somatic nervous system reactions, selected *mimages*, mass activations of neuron populations, even the nervous-system impulses of lone neurons. Apparently it's partially unclear, even to experts in the field, who this data might be delivered to.

'Don't they...' He gulps as he sets the kitchen table. 'If someone buys them... then don't they have to pay for them themselves, with a credit card or...? I mean... how did you get the information?'

'There's a per-minute fee.'

'Oh, so...?'

'Yeah. That comes on top of the credit-card bill.'

'Is that so?' He hopes he doesn't sound as horrified as he feels.

Joe can feel Rebecca's eyes studying the back of his neck. Based on the pause in her tapping, he deduces she has even lowered the phone to her lap. The thought flashes through his mind then: I should have taken my own *iAm* when it was offered.

'They withdraw it from your account,' Rebecca says. 'The fee depends on how many minutes are included in your package.'

The silence that follows feels like it's directed at him personally. He doesn't know what to do with himself. No more *iAm*, Joe thinks: not even on campus. His use of the device ends here and now.

Then he remembers Miriam's and the girls' bags.

'Should I got get your things from the car?' Joe asks his wife, who is standing at the living-room window, arms folded across her chest.

'We, um, well...' Miriam says, and hesitates before she adds, 'That's everything.'

He stares at her. 'What?'

'Let's talk about this later, shall we?' Miriam says when she sees Daniella, who comes out of the bathroom and clearly also wants to hear *what*.

'I can see *everything* on my account statements,' Rebecca says in a voice that means *everything* is something disgusting.

'Everything what?' Daniella asks, copying Rebecca's position on the sofa down to the millimeter.

'All the stuff that guy's been doing. What kinds of things and with what kind of woman,' Rebecca says.

'How can you see all that?' Joe asks, before he has the sense to stop himself.

For a second, Rebecca looks perplexed by the horror in his voice.

'There are different prices for different senses.'

'Aha,' Joe says, trying to keep the pounding of his heart from being audible in his voice.

'Like, sounds are probably always included in the entry-level packages. And some basic characters.'

'What's a basic character?' Daniella asks.

'Maybe you don't need to know all the details, Dani,' Joe says, opening a can of salsa and pulling the plastic wrap off the guacamole.

As he calls Miriam and the girls to the table, he feels like a throbbing ruin of a man. He's hot and sweaty down to his internal organs; his perversity shines from his face, wheezes in his breathing.

Daniella sits at the dining table, but Rebecca remains standing behind the back of her chair as if she's about to make a speech. To have something to do, Joe clicks on the radio. Every second without eye contact with one of his family members is an oasis of relief.

'I can just picture him,' Rebecca says, picking at her nails.

'Becky, that's enough,' Miriam says.

'What's he like?'

'Dani, you too. Both of you, sit down.'

'Spends all day sleeping and stays up all night alone at his computer, too scared to talk to anyone,' Rebecca says. 'All the times in the usage log are from evening to early morning.'

'It's some poor guy stuck in a semi-developmentally disabled stage,' Miriam says.

Everyone takes their usual seats, but the table seems to have bizarrely changed shape. Joe's headache seems to be getting worse.

'But they'll catch him, won't they?' Daniella says.

'Of course. We can get his EnEfPee,' Rebecca says. 'You have to request it in writing. It costs a little bit, but—'

'EnEf...?'

'NFP. Neural fingerprint. It's kind of like a fingerprint of the central nervous system.'

'How?' Joe asks, even though he doesn't mean to. 'Isn't it... the device is registered to you, isn't it?'

'Yeah, but every nervous system has its own.'

'Really?'

'The *ammer* retrieves it the first time you use it and saves it in the settings. It can store like two hundred of them.'

'Wow.'

Joe's heart is racing. It's wonderful being a neuroscientist at the top of his field, someone people can turn to with questions about brain function.

'Dad, can I get an *ammer*, too?' Daniella says in the nagging tone she uses when she knows she's not going to win.

'No.'

'Waaahhh, why not?'

Joe waits for everyone to start eating, but someone always has something more pressing to swipe at on their phone screen.

'I'm just going to send a quick note to work to say that I'm unavailable for the rest of the day,' Miriam says, and taps out the message on her phone.

Even the most burning desire for a beer apparently can't get a bottle of Sol to move from the fridge into Joe's hand of its own volition; he has promised himself he won't open it until everyone is ready to eat. Besides, he wants to save the moment, to savor it with Rebecca in honor of their new, adult father-daughter relationship. But now Daniella has pulled out her phone, too. Every time the rest of the family is finally ready, one of them has grabbed their phone again during the wait.

'Could we eat soon, please?' he says, his eyes on the bowl of iceberg lettuce he's carrying to the table. 'Excuse me, Miriam, could I ask you to get the sour cream?'

She frowns at her phone, swipes the screen and smiles attentively at someone else somewhere else. The phone rotates a little when she starts tapping out her response, and from the color of the screen Joe can tell she isn't sending a message to work, but is chatting with someone on a private messaging service. A pattering sound comes from the living-room windows, as the magicicadas crash into the glass.

'How do you have sex using an *iAm*?'

'As if, Dani. There's no way I'm telling you. You're eleven, for God's sakes.'

Joe is forced to repeat his question to his wife before Miriam starts and raises her eyes.

'OK,' she says, and puts her phone back in her purse with a snap. 'Let's eat. Dad has prepared a lovely meal for us.'

'I'm sorry,' Miriam says to Joe privately, while Daniella is loading up her plate with chicken. 'I promised Jill I'd send her comments on our nature-nurture material for the colloquium next week.'

Joe nods and looks at her for so long that she grows uneasy and coughs.

Take some more! Eat up, guys. Have some more! I'm so happy to have you all here again – it's been so long.

'It's some PEDOPHILE,' Daniella says. 'Let's report him to the Neighborhood Sex Offender Watch.'

'Hey, yeah,' Rebecca says, and looks at her sister, inspired by this sudden insight. 'He is so busted.'

'Could we drop this already!'

Everyone appears startled by Joe's outburst. It's undeniably at odds with the homecoming vibe.

The conversation moves on to other topics for a moment: to Daniella's swimming, the clothes Rebecca wants to buy. Joe notices that she hasn't eaten anything yet.

'The only good thing about him is that he's an animal activist,' she says to her phone.

'Huh?' slips from Joe's mouth.

'He reads all the animal activist sites,' Rebecca says. 'Every night. He'd have to be an animal activist to be that into it.'

'Do you think it's…'

Daniella's thought remains unfinished, because she only realizes mid-sentence what she's saying.

Suddenly the room is deadly still. The others have realized, too.

Joe sees the fear on Rebecca's face.

'I am so calling the cops,' she says.

'Are you sure that's necessary?' he says.

They all gape at him.

'How can you say that?' Miriam asks.

The gradually intensifying headache is hammering Joe's skull to tiny shards of bone. Hopefully it isn't a migraine. Worst-case scenario, he'll have to lie in the dark for the rest of the evening. Which doesn't sound like such a bad alternative, actually.

Rebecca frowns.

'What do you mean, is it necessary?'

'Well… maybe we can sort this out… some other way,' he says, not understanding himself what he's talking about.

Rebecca stares at him.

'Some other way? My account has been hacked.'

'Yeah, I got that, but… what I'm trying to say is – let's just think about it for a minute.'

Rebecca gapes at him, slack-jawed.

'Why?'

'I'm getting seriously worried about you,' Miriam says to Joe.

He prays, Dear God, let this headache be a migraine; pleads for a heart attack, preferably fatal, a stroke, anything, so he can slip from the world smoothly and as soon as possible.

Miriam has pulled out her phone in response to a beep. Whomever she was smiling at has replied.

But now, Joe realizes, and a wave of relief washes over him, it's a ridiculously small thing but even so a life saver: beer. He retrieves the bottles from the fridge. The condensation that has beaded up on the glass makes his fingers wet.

Yet Rebecca responds to his carefully planned offer of beer casually, without looking up: 'No, thanks.'

Joe is so surprised by the response that he just stands there at the table, brow furrowed. She didn't even glance at the bottle.

'Beer?' he says. 'It's Mexican.'

Miriam lowers her phone to her lap – mid-message! – and her tortilla to her plate and turns to look at him. Joe suddenly realizes what it must feel like for the younger members of the psycholinguistics faculty when they end up in Miriam's crosshairs. At the same time, he realizes that during their entire sixteen yeas of marriage, up until this spring, he has never been in this position with his wife.

'Excuse me?' she says.

Rebecca is also staring at Joe, eyes cartoonishly round, mouth halfway open in disbelief.

'It's good with lime,' Joe says. 'I cut some slices.'

The only thing he can do is continue down his chosen path. A parent must be, above all, consistent in his decisions.

'I don't want it! Are you deaf?'

Joe turns away from the others. He downs half of the bottle of Sol he has been saving for Rebecca in one swig and feels anger threading through his throbbing migraine. When he closes his eyes, poison-green patterns dance in that upper fourth of his field of vision, in the place where the search commands for the *iAm*'s non-screen write themselves.

'Excuse me,' Miriam repeats. 'Did you just offer our fifteen-year-old daughter beer?'

'Rebecca, could you please put your phone away while we eat?' Joe says. 'That's always been kind of the rule in this household.'

'You used yours last time,' she mutters, unaware of what's going on.

'Yes, I did,' Joe says to Miriam, who is staring at him. 'Sue me.'

It's so great seeing you guys again! I'm so glad you're here! The chicken breasts Joe has grilled outside, shirt plastered to his back – the temperature has passed the hundred-degree mark today, with a relative humidity of one hundred percent – are still lying almost untouched on the serving dish. They're too charred for Daniella after all; they've just been learning about carcinogens at school.

Even though they used to avoid red meat and were eating vegetables more and more often, ever since the package arrived in the mailbox, it goes without saying that meat is served at every meal. Veal, which Joe never used to touch for ethical reasons, is now a staple.

Rebecca moves a small piece of chicken around on her plate and occasionally cuts it into even smaller pieces. It's a familiar routine: the chicken will end up in the trash. Rebecca isn't fooling anyone with her dismemberment routine, but on the other hand, they won't let her not take any. Maybe this is the outcome all child-rearing principles naturally strive towards and, in spite of the arguments, end at: an arbitrary, logically indefensible ritual no one would consciously pick but that allows them to avoid the most violent clashes.

'This is really good.' Miriam smiles bravely, and Joe's heart breaks.

His wife is leaving him; he has known it since the moment he saw her in the entryway without her bags.

He manages to scrape and cut pieces of chicken until they're white enough for Daniella.

But the chicken isn't the only tortilla filling Rebecca has a problem with. The sour cream isn't fat-free, the avocados are basically pure fat, the beans are hard on the digestive system, same goes for the onion, and because Joe has grilled the peppers and zucchini in oil, Rebecca's going to pass this time, thanks, next time try to keep an eye on how many gallons of oil you drown them in.

In the end, she sits silently at the table and stuffs her tortilla with nothing but lettuce. Joe watches this operation, struggles not to say anything and most of all to stop himself from imagining neural fingerprints in public pedophile registers. Miriam has excused herself to go to the bathroom but has remained standing in the hall between the bathroom and the kitchen to tap at her screen, where the arriving messages clearly contain something irresistible and amusing.

And then it happens: Joe's eyes light on the jar of salsa, and he unwittingly asks Becca if she won't try some of that at least. And because even the salsa isn't acceptable, Joe, in a burst of exhausted, migraine-induced irritation – alleviated by the beer to the point that he immediately followed it with another, which he has already finished, and is now battling a burning desire to crack a third – asks why.

'What the hell is wrong with *that*?'

And this, along with a few more well-chosen lines, develops into a ferocious fight revolving solely around tomato salsa, which Miriam, after a slight delay, also returns to participate in and that for all four of them will, perhaps, remain a more profound and permanent memory than any other family-defining experience. Daniella, who usually chatters on obliviously even if full-blown nuclear war is raging around her, stares silently at her plate, eyes wide, and then slips off to her room.

At first Joe refuses to go back to the store simply because the salsa he grabbed at random and in a hurry from the shelf at Whole Foods contains sugar.

'How much sugar is actually in there?' Joe asks.

'Read the fucking label!' Rebecca shouts.

'That's nothing but tomato and vinegar!'

'Joe, I'm not sure that's the most constructive approach,' Miriam says, going so far as to lower her phone for a moment.

'There is a TON OF SUGAR in it!'

It rapidly becomes plain how impossible it is to force a nearly full-grown woman to eat if she has decided otherwise. Rebecca raises a scene that beats any reality TV show for decibel levels and includes, in addition to melodramatic expressions and a tearful tantrum, the throwing of objects, the slamming of doors, and in the end the refusal of all contact.

Now they can't even beat a whole-wheat tortilla into her body.

'Nice work, Joe,' Miriam says.

The cicadas cover the trees, lawns, and rooftops in an unbroken, red-eyed carpet that has become a natural part of the landscape. As he walks, they're crushed under the soles of his shoes, but it no longer feels like anything; they've turned into a kind of gravel. He nods at the parked vehicle occupied by one of the two men who take turns looking out for his daughters' safety, but because of the tinted windows, he cannot tell which.

Every time he sees the SUV, he remembers to check that his red safety button is still in his pocket. On a few occasions, he's left it in his other trousers.

Is it time to give up the button?

It's all over. Besides, there's a loaded revolver in his grandmother's antique china cupboard that will kill any intruder.

Point and shoot. The rest will take care of itself.

Maybe that's the reason he shouldn't give up the button yet.

He swats away the most annoying insects buzzing in his eyes, unlocks the car with the press of a button, and jumps in. He speeds aggressively back to Whole Foods and parks illegally on the sidewalk out of sheer revenge. He spends fifteen minutes in the store inspecting the ingredients printed in a minuscule font on the jars of salsa. He's about to pay for the lone No Added Sugar salsa he could find when his phone starts ringing.

Even before he sees the name on the screen, he guesses that it's Brad calling. It's been a while since the activists' first appearance in court. Or was it called a hearing? Joe isn't sure anymore. Apparently there might be several. Before the trial proper, battles would be fought with weapons known as pre-trial motions that Joe still doesn't fully grasp, even after Brad's whirlwind explanations. In any event, some powwow – the second, and like the first, procedurally routine, at least for the moment – occurred today. That must be what Brad is calling about.

His lawyer's voice is sharp, all business: 'Are you sitting down?'

'What?'

'You might want to sit down.'

'Umm well… you caught me at the supermarket.'

Joe tries to balance the phone between his cheek and his shoulder as he taps his debit card PIN code into the payment terminal. He remembers Raj having said that you can program your card into the *iAm* so the device can connect to payment terminals using nothing more than your NFP.

'How are you guys holding up?'

Brad's voice sounds surprisingly casual.

'Fine. I mean, considering,' Joe adds, feeling a pang of guilt about the blatant lie.

'Good,' Brad says. 'But listen. The deal is this…'

For a second Joe thinks there's a problem with the line, because Brad stops talking for such a long time.

'Yes?' Joe says.

'He's missing.'

'Excuse me?'

'Yeah. It's looking like he's not around. May even be outside the state. And I'm not necessarily saying he's anywhere near you guys, but—'

'Heyyyyy… hey, slow down a little. Who are we talking about? *Samuel*?'

'Yes.'

At this information, Joe's heart thumps two heavy beats.

'Free?'

'I don't want to worry you for no reason,' Brad says, too quickly. 'And there's no cause for panic, but—'

'Wait… what happened?'

'He didn't show up at court today.'

Joe is at a loss for words.

'It's perfectly conceivable that he just didn't get the information about the new date. It was pushed up.'

'But how is this possible? Isn't he in jail?'

The silence that follows is like a huge fist that grabs Joe's heart and squeezes.

Brad says: 'Didn't Susan call you?'

'Huh? Who? No.'

'Seriously? Susan. My assistant.'

'No.'

'That is weird. She promised to call that same day. You haven't received any calls from an unidentified number?'

Joe winces. Of course he has. But they're always telemarketers. He never returns calls to numbers he doesn't recognize.

'Susan must have tried multiple times,' Brad says. 'Have you been reachable this whole time?'

Joe's stomach lurches. It's always possible that the phone has remained unanswered because he's been perpetually connected to the *iAm* whenever he's been at home. And when you're hooked up, you don't feel like being interrupted unless absolutely necessary.

Joe realizes he's holding up the checkout line, shoves his card back into his wallet, grabs the jar of salsa, and walks out into the soupy summer air.

'I was thinking I'd wait to call you personally,' Brad says, 'until after today, so I'd have a better idea of what the deal is. But, yeah, he didn't show up—'

Joe breaks in: 'But what would she have told me? Susan.'

'That he was released.'

'Huh? During those first proceedings?'

'They weren't proceedings. And the charges of telephone harassment and conspiracy stand.'

'OK,' Joe says. He doesn't have the slightest idea what this means or doesn't mean.

'But like I said beforehand,' Brad hurriedly continues, as if afraid Joe is going to lose it, 'we have a quite a few options for how to proceed.'

'But didn't you say that we might be able to use the destructive device to – or that you could try—'

'It was thrown out. Susan was supposed to tell you right away. I don't understand how she never reached you.'

'Thrown out?'

'Insufficient evidence.'

Destructive device: the attempted precision of the term still strikes Joe as ridiculous. Destructive device – how is a television not one? Or an *iAm*?

A lot of charges brought against other activists arrested at the same time were thrown out as well, Brad continues.

'So he didn't do it?' Joe asks. He doesn't have the patience to wait for Brad to get to the end of one of his long-winded circumlocutions.

'Joe,' Brad says. 'What has happened and what the court decides—'

'Yeah, I get it, two totally different things. But someone must have said something there, right?'

But Brad is too well trained, too experienced; this is a line he wouldn't cross in his sleep. He explains in detail and with a lawyer's precision how, in this case, the court saw, and that as a lawyer, Brad can partially understand, in this situation it isn't perhaps technically most natural for the court to, and none of this in any way affects, and now we just have to look at things from the perspective that...

He says: 'I wouldn't have called otherwise, but when Samuel didn't show up in court, I... But there probably isn't any real cause for concern.'

Brad's tone as he says this sends something dark flowing through Joe's body. He watches with unseeing eyes as a woman in a chic suit and incredible jewelry sails her boat of a car into the parking lot, as majestic as a goddess.

Joe has to go back and tell Miriam, who is going to leave him, that *he* is free; apparently has been for some time.

That there was insufficient evidence for his involvement with the destructive device.

He's surrounded by a normal East Coast afternoon, people going about their business. Somewhere in the background, quietly, as if behind a rushing mass of water, Brad speaks in his stultifying voice about the legal motions they'll use to respond.

'So there's no point getting discouraged,' he winds up. 'We still have a lot of aces up our sleeve.'

Joe stares ahead, dumb. He has no idea what Brad just said.

'How long has he been free?'

'A week.'

'A week!'

'I figured he wasn't going to go anywhere, since he had to be back in court today. And I thought you knew. I'm really sorry, Joe.'

'Yeah.'

Brad politely waits a moment longer, but when Joe clearly doesn't have anything else to say, the lawyer continues giving advice.

'If he gets in touch with you, try to record the phone calls. And Joe – you guys have something at home, don't you?'

'What?'

'That you can use to defend yourself. If necessary.'

The sliding doors of the wine shop across the parking lot glide soundlessly open and then close again. Joe is overwhelmed by a sudden urge to get wasted. Immediately and intentionally, to drown all hundred million of his neurons in perfect anesthesia.

He needs to tell Miriam as soon as he gets home.

Home.

The girls! His wife!

It would be hard for a bystander to believe how quickly a man his age, build, and with his history of exercise, can rush to his car, peel out of the lot, tires screeching, and race home like a madman.

He wrenches the front door open so violently that the knob slams into the wall.

Rebecca stares at him from the living room, where she's watching television. Miriam has been loading the dishwasher; she emerges from the kitchen with a surprised look on her face.

'Is… everything all right?' he pants from the door.

His daughter's expression asks, Have you lost your marbles?

'Huh?'

'You – you guys have been OK here?'

'Why wouldn't we be?' Miriam asks.

Rebecca rolls her eyes.

'Where's Dani?'

'How the fuck do I know?' replies Rebecca.

'Don't talk that way.'

'You're one to talk.'

Joe feels something cold flow through him. He walks over in front of the screen.

'What's that supposed to mean?' he asks softly.

'What the fuck are you lecturing me for?'

A lightning-fast glance at Miriam, who doesn't have time to conceal her expression, is enough. Joe's inference is correct.

You're one to talk, what the fuck are you lecturing me for? What Rebecca means is his conversation with Miriam outside the security company offices.

Joe takes a deep breath.

He looks at his wife, who turns away.

Miriam has told Rebecca her own version behind his back. For some reason this feels like a bigger betrayal than getting a handgun, maybe in part because a gun, unlike an adolescent's disrespectful attitude, is something that can be disposed of.

Joe feels like shouting at his wife and his daughter, Don't you fucking understand that our lives are in danger here, goddammit! We're at war! And you're ganging up on me behind my back instead of us trying to support each other! He has already opened his mouth to shout at his daughter, to pronounce some unreasonable sentence on her, the nature and justification of which he will come up with later.

But at that instant, they all notice it. Miriam shrieks; Joe feels his blood freeze. Someone is standing at the door, against the hot-pink light of the setting sun.

A large male figure in black clothes.

Joe is already lunging to protect his daughter – in hindsight it feels oddly unclear exactly how he thought he would serve as her shield – before he realizes it's Doug, one of the two bodyguards who sit in a vehicle outside the house. Doug and Mike, two brawny men capable of killing a person with their bare hands in less than thirty seconds – as specifically laid out in the security service's contract – who sit in their SUVs watching the girls around the clock, day in, day out.

'Everything OK here?'

Doug studies them from the doorway. His massive size, his unflappable presence, the unnatural dimensions to which he's swollen himself with anabolic steroids, feel incredibly reassuring.

'Everything OK?'

'Yeah.'

'You just rushed in so fast I thought...'

'I was in... kind of a hurry,' Joe says, and coughs.

'OK. I just figured I'd check.'

'Thanks,' Joe says, too embarrassed to look at Doug's face, which has seen it all.

'OK, cool,' Doug says, glances around one last time, rotates his muscle-bound bodybuilder's frame, and exits. Joe watches as the door closes behind him.

Joe looks at his daughter. Rebecca looks so small crouched on the sofa, her birdlike shoulder blades frail. After standing there for a moment, he realizes he's still holding the jar of sugar-free salsa. He lowers it to the table. What he needs to do now is spend the next half hour begging his older daughter to come back to the table, and he no longer has the energy. But to his surprise, Rebecca rises on her own initiative and walks to the table without saying a word. Joe squeezes her on the way, from the side, with Rebecca's shoulder pressing into his chest. This his daughter seems to allow.

Joe watches as Rebecca, out of courtesy, dribbles a milliliter of sugar-free salsa on her lettuce. NO ADDED SUGAR! The girl will die of a deficiency disease, but some completely different father, in some completely different circumstances, is needed to fight this fight.

'I'm sorry,' he says.

Rebecca glances at him, and her face is that of a child.

'For getting mad,' he says. 'I've been a little stressed out.'

Rebecca doesn't lift her eyes from her plate but her eyelashes quiver, and sometime later her slender shoulders start to shake. The movement is barely perceptible but unmistakable. He lowers a hand to her arm, and this she permits.

He draws Rebecca into an embrace. He feels her tears, warm against his neck. As Rebecca sobs Joe is happy that he can hold her again like this.

'Everything's going to be fine, Becca.'

'Yeah.'

His daughter wipes mascara away on her sleeve, gets to her feet without looking at him, and walks upstairs. She has eaten less than half of her lettuce-filled tortilla.

When it's just the two of them, Miriam perches on the side of an armchair, as if she's in a stranger's home. She seems to summon up all her willpower before she looks Joe in the eye and begins to talk.

HOMICIDE, BCPD

BALTIMORE, MD

When Samuel appeared that evening, he was able to walk up to the house without anyone stopping him, and ring the bell.

In retrospect, the Baltimore City Police Department is unable to say which is more surprising: the fact that Samuel was walking down West Chestnut Parkway just as Miriam was stepping out the front door, or the fact that no one recognized him. A copy of Samuel's high-school graduation photo had been distributed to all patrol officers; the photo was studied carefully weeks ago.

At the time, two armed bodyguards, whose sole task was to prevent this very thing from happening, were sitting outside the house. The thought makes the oldest, biggest, most paunchy detective from the Baltimore PD homicide team lower a pen to his messy desk and pinch his closed eyelids between his thumb and forefinger. Two hired bodyguards, the mother and the younger daughter outside, all of them aware of the boy's release – and the kid is allowed to stroll casually onto the property.

When the police question her, Miriam says she doesn't think it possible that she would have seen Samuel. The homicide unit calculates that Miriam must have been standing less than a hundred yards from him.

Shortly after nine P.M. on Saturday night, Miriam stepped out the front door with Daniella and climbed into the car to drive Rebecca to a party. It was evening, but the street was well lit. During his reconstruction of events, the paunchy detective determines that when Samuel was walking down the gentle slope from the direction of the One World vegetarian restaurant and Ben's Deli, Miriam was most likely standing in front of the garage, which had a direct view of the street. The evening shift worker at Ben's Deli remembers Samuel because he stopped in to buy a bottle of wine. The time is marked on the register receipt: *9:09 P.M., Have a nice day!*

The conclusion the police come to is this: Miriam saw Samuel, but didn't consider what she saw significant. The Homewood campus is nearby; students Samuel's age are a constant presence in the vicinity. Nothing about his appearance called attention to itself.

Miriam absolutely refuses to believe the investigators' theory. The paunchy detective finds this understandable.

To him, the bigger mystery is the fact that Michael Badecker, one of the bodyguards, didn't see anyone from his car either. The paunchy detective can comprehend the obliviousness of an untrained middle-aged woman, but when it comes to Badecker, the detective finds it odd. The evening Samuel walks – apparently all the way from the Haines Street Greyhound station, which is miles away – up to the Chayefski residence without anyone stopping him, the armed, experienced, and well-trained Mike Badecker is sitting in his vehicle, with its nose pointed in the direction of Samuel's approach.

Security professional Mike Badecker also finds the scenario described by the detective odd. Badecker would have definitely seen the target. There's absolutely no way Samuel could have been walking down West Chestnut Parkway at the time indicated. Mike has been doing this work for fifteen years, get it?

Sure.

The paunchy detective gets it. He's more than familiar with Mike's employment history, since the two are former colleagues from the BCPD. They still run into each other in professional settings now and again.

Due to the nature of the work, the agitated Mike explains to the paunchy detective, you end up developing a 'personal radar.' A professional is constantly scanning his surroundings, even when he's not consciously doing so.

This might well be true. The paunchy detective doesn't want their chat to grow any more strained than it already is.

It's the log files from Mike's phone that reveal why he didn't see Samuel. The paunchy detective is rewarded for this breakthrough at O'Shaughnessy's that Friday; Captain Stanley Harper of the homicide unit buys his detective a shot of rye with a Natty Boh chaser when he hears about the files fished out of Mike's phone's memory.

As Samuel walked towards and, apparently, initially past the Chayefski residence, security professional Mike Badecker was hunched over his phone. The device's memory, which the paunchy detective acquires a warrant to inspect, indicates that Mike Badecker spent four minutes browsing for information on the Orioles matchup against the Red Sox, followed by three minutes trying to buy tickets for the next Orioles game. Because Mike wasn't successful in this endeavor, he spent a further seven minutes looking for tickets at an online reseller. This period covers the projected time of Samuel's arrival by a wide margin.

Doug, on the other hand, got a good look at Samuel from his vantage point in his vehicle. Douglas Krapotkin tells the paunchy detective at the East Fayette Street police station that he remembers glancing up from his paper and seeing a lanky guy with curly hair ambling casually down the street. Doug remembers thinking, That's a good-looking kid, fit, broad shoulders. But Doug's car was already running, they were about to leave, and it was his responsibility to wait for Ms Goldberg Chayefski's hybrid Accord to start up and then follow it. Doug doesn't remember thinking that the individual walking down the street could cause any trouble; what Doug does remember wondering was whether he'd have time to wash his SUV before his shift ended.

Mike Badecker and Doug Krapotkin's performance as the professionals responsible for ensuring the safety of the Chayefski family arouses derision among the detectives from the homicide unit. Gathered around the bar at O'Shaughnessy's that Friday, they calculate the total amount the Chayefski family has shelled out for security experts to sit around in their cars all spring and then, at the critical moment, be browsing baseball scores and thinking about waxing their car.

Everyone on the homicide team knows Krapotkin and Badecker; they're former BCPD. Working private is always thought to be better paid than it actually is. Perhaps it's from this fertile ground that a tiny but irrepressible germ of schadenfreude sprouts. Every one of those small-paycheck, small-dick basic police stuck in his job is secretly delighted to see a former colleague who was too good for cop work piss all over his fancy private-sector dress shoes.

Nevertheless, by far the heartiest Irish-Polish-Baltimorean guffaw at O'Shaughnessy's is triggered by the fact that, although Doug and Mike normally took turns, at the critical moment they were both on the clock. When Samuel showed up, both of them were present, which is a detail so delicious it even elicits an amused grunt from Captain Harper, who always heads home early and never indulges in more than one drink.

Slightly before midnight, when three shots – two in rapid succession, the third a moment later – echo from the brick walls of 505 West Chestnut Parkway, the Chayefski residence, security expert Douglas Krapotkin, who was hired to ensure the family's safety, is sitting in his vehicle on the other side of town. At 11:35 P.M. (estimated), the time the shots were fired, security professional Douglas Krapotkin was, according to his account, eating a chicken burger in front of a home where his clients' daughter Ms Rebecca Chayefski was consuming cannabis products (in small amounts) and champagne (in significant amounts). According to Ms Chayefski, the most dramatic event to take place at this address was an argument that developed with her best friend Ms Amanda Greenwald on the topic of Rihanna's Fashion Against AIDS clothing line.

The report drafted by the paunchy detective makes no mention of what twenty-one-year-old Samuel Heinonen, bearer of a Finnish passport, did during the fifteen minutes between his being seen on West Chestnut Parkway by the clerk working the evening shift at Ben's Deli and Doug the security guard, and the moment he rang the doorbell. Maybe he wasn't sure of the address and went to the wrong place at first. Maybe he had second thoughts and walked around to reconsider. Maybe he wanted to be sure that the car leaving the driveway, which was followed by two larger vehicles with tinted windows, made it far enough. Maybe Heinonen scouted out the house before he walked up to the door.

But this is all speculation. The paunchy detective from the homicide team isn't in the habit of including information in reports that cannot be substantiated with facts.

Nor does the paunchy detective from the Baltimore PD homicide unit say so to the survivors, because he doesn't want to add to their guilt, but it's plain to him that things would have turned out differently if, at the critical moment, Mike Badecker and Doug Krapotkin had been posted outside 505 West Chestnut Parkway, where the Chayefskis lived.

SPECIAL PRICE, JUST FOR YOU

BALTIMORE, MD

When the doorbell rang, Joe had been feeling all night like something was wrong. It was hard to say why; after all, he'd spent every evening in recent weeks the same way: at home, alone.

It was weird, in a way, hiring bodyguards just for the girls. He and Miriam would have been equally helpless if something happened. But paying for four people would have been absurd, not to mention financially unfeasible. Things had still felt ordinary and under control when Miriam drove off with their daughters. It had been clear that she would be the one to go: Rebecca needed to be driven to her party, and if Daniella went along, Miriam and both of the girls would have a bodyguard protecting them the whole time.

Rebecca had expressed disdain for the party, but Joe had registered the buzz surrounding it for weeks. The boy throwing it was a couple of years older than Rebecca and a topic of endless fascination to the female students in his elder daughter's class. The details weren't divulged to Joe, of course, but he'd noticed that every time the Only Boy Who Mattered came up in conversation, Rebecca's and her friends' voices rose an octave or dropped to a whisper.

Things had felt utterly ordinary when Rebecca had drifted downstairs in a cloud of sweet perfume half an hour after the departure time she herself had decreed. The party had started two hours earlier, but Rebecca had erupted at the suggestion that she arrive then. It was important to show you didn't care as much as you did.

Rebecca's eyes had been meticulously lined, and she had sprayed her long, beautiful hair into a gummy hive on top of her head. Her face was pale. Joe, who was reading on the sofa, felt a pang in his chest. How hard she tried! And how hopeless it was, trying to get someone to like you. And how effortless it would be for Rebecca with those with whom it was meant to happen. This is what he'd suddenly wanted to express to his daughter. All the cold embraces that lay ahead, all the genuine, life-altering encounters.

Miriam was in the hall and had already opened the front door. Rebecca and Daniella were putting on their shoes as Joe looked on, moved by the future joys and disappointments his girls had no inkling of as yet. How their hearts would break in the years to come!

He hugged his daughters despite Rebecca's resistance, and reflected that he and Miriam weren't the only married couple in the world to get divorced. It wasn't like he was losing the girls.

It could have been a lot worse. He and Miriam had discussed things calmly, as adults. Now that they'd made the decision to split, maybe they could treat each other respectfully again.

It was hard to say why, but as Joe watched his family in the entryway, it suddenly seemed obvious to him that everything would work itself out. Regardless of whether or not one of the criminals who had attacked them had been released, they would survive. They already had.

But then the front door closed, and Miriam and the girls were gone.

The second Joe was alone, the strange sensation crept up on him.

He didn't believe in premonitions, but once his family had left, he could tell something was wrong; he just wasn't able to put his finger on what. He decided it was the result of stress and fatigue. And last night's conversation with Miriam, the decision to separate: no wonder he felt weird.

Miriam didn't have anyone else; she just wanted to think things out. Well, there was someone, she finally admitted, a guy Joe supposedly hadn't met. He instantly knew who she meant, a colleague of hers. They'd been introduced to each other at a party once and Joe had noticed the way the guy had spoken to Miriam. He was the one she had been smiling at through her phone screen at the dinner table.

The guy had nothing to do with her decision, though. Miriam wasn't involved with him, sexually or otherwise, nor did she have any intention of getting involved with him. At least not for now.

Miriam wanted time to think. Her own space.

The separation felt like such a natural decision that Joe hadn't even felt hurt. Maybe he just didn't realize what had happened yet. It would strike him later, out of the blue, when he saw Miriam on the guy's arm for the first time.

But something was awry. Something else. Joe was eating a tuna sandwich in the kitchen when he was overcome by an irrational impulse to get out of the house. The fan was humming loudly above the stairs; the humid darkness outside the windows suddenly gave off something irrevocable.

He never should have let the thought enter his mind.

The fact that he couldn't see anything in the windows except his own reflection meant, of course, that someone in dark clothes could be out there, motionless, watching him.

He forced himself to gulp down the rest of his sandwich and browse the editorial pages of the *New York Times*. He considered turning off the lights so no one outside could see in. But sitting alone in the darkness didn't exactly sound appealing.

He was just tossing the empty tuna-fish can in the trash and putting the mayonnaise back in the fridge when the doorbell rang. He froze. It was evening, and he wasn't expecting anyone.

He could feel the hammering of his heart throughout his body.

Someone had tried to blind his daughters and the perpetrators were on the loose, but there was still someone totally normal at the door. A neighbor wanting to borrow a cup of sugar. A girl scout selling cookies.

His palms were clammy. His thoughts raced to the front door; he had locked it, hadn't he? The girls had been the last to step out, but Joe had remained inside. They normally didn't turn the bolt until they went to bed. Anyone with any skill could pick the first lock in a heartbeat.

None of their neighbors had borrowed sugar in the past three years. No girl scout had ever knocked on their door.

He had been lurking out there in the darkness, waiting until Joe was alone. A cold spike pierced his heart when he realized how it would happen.

That's what he was going to do to Joe.

That's what these people wanted, to give them a taste of their own medicine. Joe suddenly remembered what he'd read in a Fight For Freedom! post: by popular vote, one of the terrorist cells had chosen exsanguination as the preferred method of eliminating Joe and his colleagues. The kid would be calm, composed, but his smile would be that of a madman, and he would want to take his time, watch Joe bleed dry. Exsanguination, the killing of a living laboratory animal through bloodletting. Recommended particularly in cases when you don't want to leave traces of lethal chemicals in the tissue.

This is what it had been about the whole time: the package had been sent to him because, by being addressed to the girls, it would hurt Joe more than anything they could do to him personally. And now it was his turn.

The doorbell rang again.

He had already pressed the red button in his pocket three times – it was useless; Mike and Doug were miles out of range – when three separate thoughts flashed across Joe's mind nearly simultaneously. The possibility of survival ran through his body like an electric current: the basement door. And the phone.

And above all: the china cupboard.

He thought through the three alternatives in fractions of a second. From the basement, he'd be able to make it out the back door, and he could slip out to the street that way. He'd have to sprint as fast as he could, hope that he'd be able to outrun the killer. The biggest problem was the gate. The basement gave onto the back yard, and he wouldn't be able to make it out of there without going through the gate, which was just to the right of the front door.

He had no interest in racing a twenty-year-old whose veins were pumping with a lifetime's worth of adrenaline.

The doorbell rang again, twice, demandingly.

He tiptoed towards the antique cupboard. He'd have to open it first. And then – was he really capable of shooting someone? Of course. Absolutely. But he wouldn't do it unless forced to. Unless the killer broke down the door, crawled in through the window. The phone: he needed to call 911, wait for the patrol to arrive, and hope the kid wouldn't break down the door in the meantime, smash the windows.

Joe's heart was galloping; the room felt like it was spinning. Where the hell was his phone? His hands shook as he groped at the hall console, which was littered with dried-out ballpoint pens, rumpled receipts, and coins. This would be the end of him: not remembering, thanks to creeping senility, where he'd left his phone.

The kitchen table.

He lunged from the hallway into the kitchen, dripping with sweat, and it didn't even occur to him that this lifesaver was also about to be yanked out of his reach. He saw the phone and started reaching for it. He almost squealed when it suddenly burst out ringing. The phone shimmied across the table; its ringing resonated in the echo chamber formed by the tabletop, the walls, and bottom of the cupboards. Under the ringtone proper, the vibration growled like a Doberman.

Joe stared at the phone. The boy had decided to block the line by calling it himself.

Joe had only one option left. And as he fumbled the key out of the blue Finnish vase on top of the fridge, he started bargaining. While the phone rang, he offered death everything he had: he would give up his work if he were allowed to live. He would give up his marriage and any possibility of future companionship. He would give Miriam her own life, her new friend who made her smile, her unanticipated, ill-advised career in politics. He would give everything he owned if he were allowed to live. He would start speaking out to his colleagues on behalf of animal rights; he would devote his life to pondering questions that could be answered without sacrificing a single living creature.

There was only one thing he wouldn't agree to.

There was only one thing he would keep beyond the reach of Death's icy claws.

And as soon as he refused – he had known the whole time that the final offer was coming, known that everything that preceded this was nothing but a warm-up, small talk, drinking tea at Death's bazaar – he knew the game was up. Because this was what Death wanted. There was only one thing Death had ever wanted. Only Rebecca and Daniella would do.

His door was not marked with blood, nor did he have a firstborn son to offer, and he had to give his daughters. And for the symmetry to be perfect, the one who had come to claim his daughters was the firstborn son he didn't have.

The phone had stopped ringing.

Joe didn't panic; he knew it would ring again a second later. As it did, right after he walked over to his grandmother's antique cupboard and unlocked it. The terror of a moment ago was gone; the key slid effortlessly into the lock. The phone started ringing again just as Joe was retrieving the ponderous, snub-nosed, loaded revolver from the cabinet. It felt heavy, fit his palm better than he remembered.

Gun in hand, he walked back into the kitchen and picked up the phone still grumbling on the table.

The bargaining had ended. He might as well answer.

As he pressed the button, he could picture with remarkable clarity all the things he would accomplish with the years left to him, if he were allowed to go on. Why had he spent almost his entire adult life cloistered in the confines of that department? He could have been doing whatever he wanted. Instead he'd wasted his life at a computer, drafting papers that were buried among millions of others just like them. Not a single one of the research results made a bit of difference.

'Hello?' he said into the phone.

There was no response. Joe found himself wholly at peace; there was no sensation of dread, no sense of finality. He was simply disappointed that this was how it was all going to end.

And then he heard a deep male voice replying: 'Hello?'

Something about it was different from what Joe had been expecting.

'Joseph Chayefski?'

'Yes, this is he.'

'Hi. This is…'

He doesn't catch the name at first, due to the accent, the peculiar Scandinavian way of pronouncing each vowel distinctly and one at a time, as if respecting them as independent entities. How painstaking he and Alina had been, trying to think of a name that would work in both languages!

His heart is pounding; this is how it will end. Joe hears the male voice falter slightly. Samuel must have decided further explanation is in order.

'Alina Heinonen is my mother.'

Something about this isn't the way Joe expected it to be. The young man's tone, the way he introduces himself: confident, substantial, used to taking charge.

'Could you come open the door, please?'

'Excuse me?' Joe manages to groan.

'I'm at your door.'

And something in that voice's self-evident authority, its frank forthrightness, compels Joe to do as he's told. As in a dream, he walks to the front door, the loaded revolver still in one hand. When he gets there, Joseph Chayefski voluntarily frees the lock and opens the door to the son he abandoned, who has now come to take his life.

THIS IS BAWLMER, HON

BALTIMORE, MD

He never thought that when the door opened he'd be looking down the barrel of a loaded revolver.

Samuel's heart had been pounding since that afternoon, when he rolled into Haines Street, Baltimore's dirty-white concrete bus station. Suddenly he would have given anything to stay in the Greyhound's sweltering embrace. When you spent enough time on the bus, you stopped wanting to get off; the uncomfortable seat turned into a safe, cozy nest. He wanted to keep traveling southwards, back west, to California, anywhere.

But Baltimore was the end of the line. He was going to have to jump to the asphalt on his numb legs and venture into the little station, which reeked of inequality and unfulfilled dreams. American poverty looked different than the Finnish variety: there was something deeper, more unfair, more final about it. And at the grimy station that cloudy evening, it, too, seemed to saying he shouldn't have come.

The trial in Oregon had turned out to be a peculiar blend of etiquette and informality. The judge and the lawyers knew each other and clearly met regularly under similar circumstances; the only thing that changed were the names and the details on the paperwork. For these people, it was like being at the dentist's. There was something reassuring about it, but it also made him nervous. These people wouldn't take the foulest abscess personally. They would break for lunch, even when there was nothing that could be done.

The judge in particular was surprisingly relaxed and casual. She seemed intelligent, competent, and weary of crime, a woman who knew her articles and clauses and didn't bother putting up a front.

When the destructive device charge came up, the judge looked at the prosecutor like a mother who's seen it all and is caught off guard for once. Samuel felt the shivers running up and down in his spine: they were going to let him go. The judge said to the prosecutor: 'You must be kidding.'

Samuel felt the guilt blazing from his face like neon paint. The prosecutor was looking at him, too: I know you did it. Before the judge even concluded her final statement – which ended with 'and that sort of thing' – the lawyers were gathering up their papers. Everyone in the courtroom had already mentally moved on to the next case, the next wife beater, the next teen shooter.

The look the prosecutor shot Samuel from the courtroom door wasn't the one he'd been expecting, that of a bully who'd been humiliated on the playground: *just you wait until the teacher isn't looking.* Instead, the prosecutor was chatting breezily with a colleague, glanced back absent-mindedly.

Luckily animal rights activists were nearly always released OR: on their own recognizance. Even low bail would have been a catastrophe. Samuel had been living off Tyler's frugal inheritance for the past three months, which was starting to grate on their friendship. He was always worrying about whether he was pulling his weight. Was this arrangement fair? He remembered walking into the hotel restaurant that morning in Portland without it occurring to him that breakfast wasn't necessarily included; he hadn't even had enough cash on him for the cheapest item on the menu, cornflakes. If he'd been capable of thinking about anything except the knot inside him – good God, what had he done? – he'd have been embarrassed when he'd had to excuse himself from the silken smooth tablecloth and leather-bound menus while the waiter looked on in surprise.

One night in jail had been enough to instill a healthy sense of proportion in Samuel. Money was just money.

When the guy in the next cell started groaning in the middle of the night, Samuel was positive they were the moans of a dying man. The fat black guy lying across from him, with inflamed needle-tracks in his arm and repulsively swollen legs, the stories of excrement-filled milk cartons tossed into cells, the routine rapes, the guards who smuggled in drugs and guns to gang leaders, all of this brought Samuel to the rapid realization that he'd never dedicated a moment's thought to the sorts of conditions prisoners were forced to live in – and that doing so would have been in his interests.

The trial felt surreal, thanks to everything he'd witnessed in the cell, the adrenaline coursing through his veins, and lack of sleep. And the queasiness that had come on during the night and intensified in the courtroom hadn't passed, even in the Greyhound bus, despite the fact that he'd slept like a log for the first twelve hours of the bumpy, uncomfortable ride, head against the window.

Once he got out of jail, he'd popped into an internet café to check what was being written about him in Finland. Nothing, for the most part. An activist was no longer interesting once he was beyond Finland's borders. Maybe if someone shot him, Samuel reflected. He thought back to what had been written about him when the latest investigation against him had been opened, for securities crimes, after he wrote in his blog that the stock price of Parkingfield was in a free-fall and the company was on the verge of collapse.

He'd been charged with trying to manipulate stock prices. According to the newspapers, Tyler was using him: oh, how he loved the reporters from the mainstream papers, the all-knowing intelligentsia from whom not a single secret motive remained hidden; not a single social injustice unaddressed.

Luckily he was able to do something; otherwise he would have gone crazy. Reading *War and Peace*, the paperback Volume I he'd bought for the long bus ride, he'd identified strongly with one of the main characters who was so fed up with socialites and balls that he felt going off to war was a relief.

Walking to and out the main doors of the Baltimore bus station, Samuel felt like he had a poisonous cactus growing in his stomach. The humid greenhouse heat slapped him across the face, like a wet rag. The station was located a little outside the center of town; for locals, the area probably wasn't particularly unsafe, but something about it and the rumble of the twilight city pulsing in the distance struck him as disconsolate. Before long, it would be dark.

He saw the yellow American taxis lined up at the edge of the deserted parking lot and remembered the wrinkled ten-dollar bill in his front pocket; he'd been saving it there so he wouldn't accidentally spend it on food. The bus ticket to Baltimore, along with the granola bars, fruit, and odd sandwich he'd bought on the road, had gobbled up the last of his funds.

How easy so many things would be if he had even a little money.

It was hard not to think about what lay ahead. The further he had progressed on his multi-day, three-bus journey, the more powerfully the waves of memories about Dad had crashed against him. Over the course of the uncomfortable, jolting ride through the tornado zone of the Midwest and past the shimmering silver Great Lakes towards the East Coast, the pressure had gradually climbed up from his stomach, from his chest.

When he finally disembarked, legs stiff and neck aching, before the final leg of the journey, he could clearly feel the lump had risen to his throat. He thought about the jungle scenes, the lions and leopards he'd stumbled across as an adult, on the top shelf of the closet, where Mom had hidden them. He'd scrawled them for his dad at the age of four. There were sheaves of sheets, carefully filled to the edges. He'd even known how to write DAD at the top of each one, the second D flipped in a mirror image of the first.

The fact that Mom had taught him the letters but had never sent the pictures had initially struck Samuel as confusing and sad, then understandable, then incomprehensible, and ultimately all of the above.

After transferring to the last bus, which left amazing, unfathomable New York City behind and raced southwards through industrial parks built in squalid fields, headed down the New Jersey Turnpike towards Pennsylvania, he had a distinct feeling that coming had been a mistake.

For the remainder of the trip, he'd succeeded in burying his misgivings under practical concerns – Where can I find a map? Where will the bus stop in Baltimore? – but now, as he stood in the filthy parking lot of the bus station, the premonition returned, more pressing than ever. This was going to end badly.

The hot summer afternoon was turning to evening; the sun's tea-colored rays cast long shadows across the asphalt.

He closed his eyes.

He couldn't turn back.

He realized he'd had this feeling before: that life was utterly unpredictable, that nothing he'd striven for had any meaning. It was the feeling he got whenever something momentous, something he'd been readying himself for thoroughly, was finally happening.

The same feeling had nearly tilted the ground out from under his feet prior to the meeting with the director of Steveson, Briar & Gates.

Why the hell did I get myself into this, spend so much time preparing for this? he had wondered at the time. Is this really what I'm devoting my life to, maybe even going to jail for? Why? As he stepped into the gleaming Manhattan high-rise in the suit he'd just bought, after all the endless practice interviews and background research, it had suddenly been plain as day to Samuel that it was all pointless.

No one had ever believed they'd win.

The idea of victory had never occurred to Samuel, even after Steveson, Briar & Gates had requested a meeting. The goalposts had been moved so many times only one shot remained – and it was inconceivable that they might actually hit it home.

On the morning of the meeting, the New York sky had been a clear, dazzling blue. The sun had shone between the skyscrapers; off in the distance, Samuel spotted a plane making its approach into La Guardia. Something had made him think of the light board opposite the Helsinki railway station, the one with share prices running across it in red letters. He wasn't sure it was there anymore, but its purpose continued to confound him. Investors were hardly going to wander down to Railway Square to check stock prices. Why were they displayed there, above everything? It wasn't like you could actually follow them, outside and so high up.

It was only when he and Tyler stepped out of the cab that morning in Manhattan that he realized why they were there: for the same reason as the cross on a steeple. Tyler patted him on the shoulder and wished him luck – give 'em hell – and stayed on the sidewalk to wait.

It had gone without saying that Samuel would be the one to attend the meeting. After all, his beagle pictures had started everything, and the message from the bank indicated they were expressly expecting him. By this time, he knew the organizational chart of Steveson, Briar & Gates by heart, but he'd had to hustle to get a suit from the flea market. He reflected after the fact that if he'd known he was going to win, he would have gone in in a hoodie.

As he rode the elevator to the top of the glass high-rise, dressed in his wrinkled suit, Samuel silently went over his group's core demands, the ones they'd agreed on during the emergency meeting that had lasted

all night. He went through his opening remarks at lightning speed
a final time, as well as the rules they'd set for playing with the bank
directors. Last of all, he reminded himself of the minimum negotiating
outcome they'd collectively settled not to compromise on.

His heart was hammering as he was led by two guards past the plate-
glass doors and introduced to the bank director he'd never met but
whom he would have recognized in his sleep. The man was fortyish,
thick-haired, and polite, shorter than Samuel would have guessed based
on his photograph. There was a doughiness to him; Samuel mused that
his pasty skin would burn in the sun in a matter of minutes.

The other side held all the trump cards. As he returned the banker's
firm handshake, Samuel was still at heart a deferential teen. He had no
more than a high-school education; his understanding of the corporate
world had been non-existent until a couple of years ago. He was
wearing frayed sneakers and didn't have enough money in his bank
account for the plane ticket home. He tried not to project inevitable
loss as he followed the expensive creak of the banker's hand-tooled
leather shoes across the parquet, into the room where billions were
transferred at the press of a button and where it would be made plain
to the interloper who held the power in Western democracies.

But when the soft, doughy, aftershave-scented banker folded his hands
on the hardwood negotiating table, took a deep breath, and flashed a
tentative smile at Samuel, he suddenly realized that they would win,
that they already had.

'From our perspective, the situation is more or less this,' the banker
said.

They didn't want to negotiate, criticize, bargain, or justify – they
just wanted to be left in peace.

Samuel still remembered the moment as one of the most rewarding
of his life. He saw the banker's cufflinks gleaming in the soft morning
light that flooded in through the wall-sized window. It felt as if power
had been poured into Samuel's body. He had no problem patiently
listening to the man's meandering speech, giving him a friendly smile.

Just two months earlier, Steveson, Briar & Gates had refused any
contact with Samuel's group.

In a televised interview that night, the CEO of Parkingfield Life
Sciences International had said there was only one word for what the
ecoterrorists practiced: *pure evil*.

'Pure evil,' Tyler said, as they watched from the battered armchairs in his living room. 'Isn't that two words?'

Their phones had started to ring that same evening: people were calling from all over Oregon, across Washington, the Midwest, the West Coast, Europe, Brazil. They hadn't even updated the website yet, but everyone had heard. The news spread more quickly than anything they'd drummed out during earlier campaigns. Everyone wanted to let them know they'd heard, and was it true, is this really happening, what the hell, guys, you did it! We did it! We actually did it!

It was only then that they believed it themselves.

From the spontaneous applause and elated shouts, from the people who came to Tyler's house and threw their arms around Samuel's neck before they even said anything, from the full bottle of champagne Kaitlin poured over his head in the entryway and let gurgle until it was empty – something about all this told him that this sensation of fulfillment and belonging was something a person felt perhaps once in his lifetime. Samuel had realized it the moment he saw the crowd waiting outside Tyler's house, their expressions uncertain, eager – was it really true? His heart still leaped when he thought about it. He had never experienced anything like it, and probably never would again.

There are so many of us, he'd thought. They can't put all of us in jail.

There was still a lot of heavy lifting to do, but after that, every phone call, every visit, and every message, ratcheted up the enthusiasm. Parkingfield couldn't borrow money anymore. Even banks like Steveson, Briar & Gates had dropped Parkingfield, so that they wouldn't have to deal with Samuel and Tyler anymore.

This was power; this was how you seized it.

From then on, everything was easy. Steveson, Briar & Gates was the biggest operation. During the tightest two-week push, the three of them – Samuel, Tyler, Kaitlin – didn't step away from their laptops or set foot out of the house for longer than thirty minutes at a time. On Saturday night, when the rest of the world was out having fun, when most of their group was partying – we won! – the three of them were updating online action bulletins, coordinating phone campaigns against the next banks and securities traders, pink sheets and the

OTCBB; there was no reason to stop there. They set up a month's worth of events in Washington, California, New York, Pennsylvania, Britain, Finland. There was still an Antarctic ice sheet of work they were chipping away at with teaspoons, toothpicks, nails worn to stubs, and they always had to do it today or this week so they'd have time to hit the next target before some random counterstrike brought them down. They had to keep their cool, they couldn't look down: if they made the mistake of allowing the amount of work or their opponents' clout to get to them, the strength would drain from their limbs.

Samuel knew he'd never forget the night during the most intense spurt when finally, at two A.M., after no one had had time to eat anything but carrots for dinner and didn't take any breaks except to go to the bathroom, Kaitlin slammed her laptop shut, threw herself back onto the bed, and burst into tears. They were scared something had happened: someone died, fallen ill, something.

Just sheer exhaustion, as it turned out.

'What a fucking life!'

'Tell me about it.'

'I can't take it anymore! I'm too tired.'

'Go to bed.'

'No, I really have to finish this page, because everyone's going to start looking first thing in the morning to see where they're supposed to—'

'Kaitlin! Go to bed!'

'It'll be over soon. A few more weeks.'

'Exactly. We need you. *Alive*. Go to bed.'

During the battle's final, most brutal surge, no one had to say anything to get the others to crack up. Lack of sleep led them to the brink of hysteria; people, thoughts, and feelings no longer existed, only the campaign, the goal, each minute, which they could either put to use or waste, let the other side win.

If someone had just paid them, even half the minimum wage: that would have bought them macaroni.

It was Kaitlin who said it first: that they would never be forgiven for the fact that their campaign had worked. Samuel had thought she was being paranoid. Like he'd said to Tyler: they couldn't imprison thousands of activists around the world to stop the campaign.

Tyler had looked at him: 'They don't have to.'

'What do you mean?'

'All it takes is a few.'

Samuel didn't remember the conversation until the afternoon when the boots of the FBI SWAT team thundered on the porch and their computers, papers, and books were packed into boxes and carried out to the law enforcement officers' vehicles. It was only then that he fully understood what Kaitlin had meant. *They* would never be forgiven, the three of them.

One thing you learn as an activist is that the goalposts move.

The first time it happened, you didn't know what hit you. Then you got angry, depressed, tried to bargain.

The same stages as grief.

Which was what it was.

Power also means this: the right to decide the position of the goalposts. Discovering this comes as a surprise, because no one ever says it out loud.

This was how the goalposts moved: at first, demonstrating peacefully was legal. At first, they could freely distribute flyers outside the fence of the Laajakoski research center – even talk about what was going on inside. They could leave their signs up from dawn till dusk. But the days passed; the footage Samuel shot circulated online. More young people joined the demonstration, some of them loud, some angry, others bringing a canister of moonshine. They were all mystified: wasn't the message getting through?

This was how the goalposts moved. The police don't use a spray made from chili peppers on peaceful protesters. The police will always ensure public safety first and foremost by offering assistance, advice, and guidance. And the police did their best to assist, advise, and guide Samuel and his fellow protesters. They were instructed to clear the area in the interests of public safety.

But why?

From a public space where they had every right to be? They weren't on private property, nor were they creating a disturbance. Samuel was more than happy to go over this ad infinitum with the police as well as the media, who finally showed up the second week.

People worked here! Real jobs were at stake. Valuable foreign investments. This was explained to the demonstrators again and again.

But this was exactly what they were protesting against.

The situation grew increasingly embarrassing for the CEO of Laajakoski Biosciences Inc. Why couldn't the police, with their assistance and guidance free the area from demonstrators? Reporters called the CEO: 'You *still* have those kids squatting at your gates?' And the delicious sign, that ended up on the insert on the nightly news: '*Laajakoski PseudoSciences, Inc.*' Now the CEO had to make more calls to the government politicians he'd supported during the elections – completely legally and openly. There was nothing illicit about contributing to election campaigns, as the CEO was compelled to reiterate to reporters, to his own mounting discomfort.

This was how the goalposts moved: the CEO was concerned. He was particularly concerned about the safety of the young people. Things might get out of hand. Before long, someone was going to overreact. It was the health of the demonstrators that was at risk. Most were well behaved, but a few seemed aggressive. The reporters, on the other hand, loved the images of police in riot gear; big, humiliated robots faced down by the roars of the callow crowd.

The police didn't have the resources to keep this up for weeks on end, did they?

Maybe for these reasons, Samuel guessed, or maybe for some that were never aired, the police were eventually compelled to exercise their *right to, under exceptional conditions, use necessary force in the line of duty*. As the police superintendent reminded Finland during a press conference, the police are charged with maintaining public order and preventing possible crimes. Accordingly, to maintain public order, they had attempted to remove certain particularly disruptive individuals from the site.

Even after all the reports and internal investigations, it remained unclear to Samuel if the supervisor, who so stonily and competently assumed responsibility for events, knew how Officers Korhonen and Virtanen had decided to resolve the situation late on that long, restless Sunday. Police command stressed how inebriated some of the demonstrators had been. The threat of public disturbance had been apparent; they hadn't wanted to risk accidents or bodily injury. And as the superintendent kept reiterating, the majority of demonstrators had obediently dispersed when ordered to by the police – any and all ambiguity involved these three individuals alone, who deliberately defied police orders to clear the area.

The demonstration was legal, Samuel kept reiterating to the police officers who wrenched his arm and tried to stop him from handcuffing himself to the bike rack. They were on public property.

No one tried to deny this after the fact.

Pepper spray is manufactured from capsaicin, a chili pepper extract. Samuel doubted that many of his former classmates, now busy and successful in their university studies, would have remained there, wrists locked to the metal bike rack, after hearing the angry hiss of the pepper spray at eye level. He remembered feeling rough, gloved hands grabbing his jaw and forcing his eyelids open.

But above all, he remembered the enormous white-capped cumulus clouds rising in the blue sky above the Laajakoski research center, the last thing he saw before squeezing his eyes shut. Even after he closed them, he had gazed on the clouds and mused they were like snow: enormous, inaccessible snowbanks.

What was pain? Nothing but intercellular communication along certain pathways of the central nervous system. You could observe it like clouds in the sky, without identifying with it, without panicking.

That's how they must do it, too, he had realized as he felt the cool liquid seeping under his eyelids, the cold substance gradually crawling across the senseless whites towards the center. As he waited for the burn that would begin within the second, he realized that this was also how the researchers experimenting with animals must do it, how they must harden themselves so they could do their jobs.

We're all the same. We all do the same things, just for opposite reasons, he reflected, and then concentrated on thinking about enormous white mountains of clouds.

Samuel walked into the waiting room of the bus station, where a kid his age was dozing in a wheelchair. The kid was holding a cardboard sign scribbled with black marker. He had flipped it over to hide the text – panhandling was forbidden inside the station – but as he shifted in his seat, Samuel caught a glimpse of it:

Iraq war vet
Hungry
Please help

Samuel stared at the sign and thought about the police officers: the one who'd forced his eyes open, and the one who'd squirted the pepper spray. He thought about those hundreds of people writing in the online forums, who hadn't participated in the demonstration but knew for a fact that in Finland the police never used pepper spray without cause. These online individuals, who had never met Samuel, also knew that pepper spray hadn't been used in this case either, as well as Samuel's reasons for lying about it.

Samuel would still have been curious to learn what crime had been prevented by spraying his eyes with a combination of chili pepper extract and ethanol, the only purpose of which was to inflict as much pain as possible without causing permanent damage.

One of the officers had eventually been released; the other had received a small fine. Samuel could still remember the police supervisor civil-servant voice in the news clip: solemn, responsibility-shouldering. The officers' use of force had been justified, if excessive, he maintained.

Both the legs of the kid in the wheelchair had been amputated at the knee. He was wearing a red Veterans' Association baseball cap, and it suddenly reminded Samuel of his hunting cap, which he had worn the same way, bill to the back. Where the cap was now, he didn't have the faintest idea, and somehow this felt tragic.

He spent a moment figuring out how far West Chestnut Parkway was from the bus station and what the cheapest way of getting there was.

He'd traveled here, all the way from Oregon, three thousand kilometers by bus across ten states to face the person he didn't want to face and to confront the thing he would finally have to confront.

He sat for a moment on the fake-leather benches, next to tired African-American families making for Virginia, the Carolinas, Georgia, or Tennessee with their suitcases and sundry poorly secured bundles. Samuel looked at them and envied them their normal, exhaustingly mundane journeys.

Realizing he was staring rudely, he turned his gaze to the muted television bolted to the ceiling. A female journalist in a canary-yellow suit was interviewing a serious, bearded middle-aged man, who spoke profusely and at length. At the bottom of the screen, text was running across a blue background:

HARVARD RESEARCHER: VMPFC OPTIMIZERS CAUSE DEPENDENCY AND DEMENTIA

PHARMA COMPANY ADMITS: VMPFC OPTIMIZERS CHEMICALLY MODIFIED ALCOHOL

Samuel stared blankly at the screen and then closed his eyes.

All the way here from Oregon, the same distance as Helsinki to Lisbon.

Who do you think you are? a voice inside him suddenly asked. *What do you think you're going to accomplish here?* He'd been preparing for this his whole life, and following through wasn't going to do any good. *It doesn't make any sense*, he told himself.

Nothing I've done has ever made any sense.

When night fell, Baltimore was a wounded dog itching for a fight: not immediately dangerous but unpredictable. Cold signage glared in the dusk, advertising alcohol and bail bonds. As he walked the streets of the unfamiliar city, Samuel gazed at the row houses painted in pastel colors and the way they turned into slums on the next block; the posters from the elite university that advertised free substance-abuse treatment for volunteer test subjects. There was an artlessness to the tangled power lines, rusted trash cans, and garbage bags tossed to the sidewalks in the mean, narrow side streets, but after the sun went down, no one appeared to venture off the main roads. It was impossible to guess what was going through the heads of the people sitting on stoops in their shirt-sleeves as gleaming cars the size of tanks slid past slowly in the hot summer night, a slow low-frequency beat thumping behind their impenetrable windows.

As he arrived at West Chestnut Parkway, Samuel realized what he'd forgotten. Luckily there was a dog-walker he could ask. She knew a little deli not too far away, next to a cute-looking vegetarian restaurant.

After he stepped out of the deli, Samuel had to stop for a moment to think: was he really ready for this?

He walked down the quiet street lined with stately hardwoods, past the impressive homes. The sun had set; a damp darkness lay over the city, heavy as a blanket. The street was poorly lit. He advanced slowly, peering into the shadows for the right number.

When he finally found the place, his heart skipped a beat. The house looked new, painted off-white, more normal, more modest than he'd imagined. Rhododendrons grew on either side of the porch, their dull leaves fake-looking in the gloom.

A light burned in the window.

After he realized he'd involuntarily stopped walking, paralyzed, Samuel forced himself to march up to the dark porch of his father's American house. Upon reaching the door, he pressed the bell as fast and hard as possible, so he wouldn't have time to think.

At first he thought no one was home.

He had rung the doorbell many times now. The wrought-iron numbers on the house were the right ones, and the copper doorplate read 'Chayefski.' The warm summer evening was laden with the cloying odor of rot; the dark, soot-edged clouds hung low but refused to rain. He pressed the round white button in the wall one last time. Once again, the tinkling, plastic melody carried through from the other side of the wall, muffled but unmistakable.

The lights appeared to be on inside.

In the end, he forced himself to pull his phone out of his pocket. There wasn't much left of his pre-paid American talk time; he'd been specifically saving it for a situation like this. And now he would have to call his father for the first time in his life, which felt harder than taking down an international conglomerate.

The phone rang for a long time. After a few rings, he stopped expecting anyone to pick up. But the call didn't go to voice mail: when he finally heard a male American voice say hello at the other end, he was so stunned that initially he couldn't speak.

There he was, on the phone, finally.

Samuel had a hard time breathing as, stammering for the first time in years, he tried to explain who he was. Speaking English suddenly felt like an impossibility, even though he'd just given a speech in the language to an audience of three hundred. Every grammatical mistake it was possible to make within the space of a few sentences, he made. Now, as the encounter threatened to take place, it felt so utterly desperate and pathetic that he would have called off the whole thing if he could have. At some remote frontier of his consciousness, he registered that his dad sounded a bit peculiar. Then again, what did he know about the way his father usually sounded?

But as they spoke, he realized he could hear the voice on the phone and also coming from somewhere else.

His father had to be nearby, inside the house.

Dad was inside but he wasn't opening the door? Samuel was so perplexed by this that his verbal clumsiness increased exponentially. In the end, he managed to communicate that he was standing at the front door. It was happening; it was really happening.

After hanging up, he stood and waited. He grew agitated as the seconds passed, started wondering if his dad had really said he would come and open the door or had he just imagined it? He couldn't recall the exact contents of the call, the critical final words.

He'd imagined this moment thousands of times over the years: what it would feel like when the front door of 505 West Chestnut Parkway opened and it finally happened.

There were countless variations on the theme. They changed with the seasons, his age, and life circumstances. In most of them, Dad lived in an old two-story wooden house, the same one as the luscious young women in the television series who'd inherited magical powers from their mother. Sometimes Dad was a deathly ill old man, who could no longer rise from his bed and croaked there unintelligibly, one withered hand raised. Sometimes a tuxedoed Dad was strutting on a meticulously shaven lawn, leading a hundred guests in an overly formal toast at a magnificent garden party he was throwing in his own honor, for some reason in period costume in the grounds of a Central European estate.

But one thing never varied. Every time Samuel rang the doorbell, he'd accomplished something significant, generally invented something that would save the world. In that sense, his timing fit the script astonishingly well: after all, they had won. Parkingfield had been driven from the New York Stock Exchange.

But this particular scene had never been among those variations he'd involuntarily scripted in his mind: the door to his father's home being opened by a short, middle-aged man in glasses, pointing a gun at Samuel's face.

One glance was enough to tell him that this middle-aged man brandishing a revolver on the doormat could not be the same person he'd engaged in countless internal battles with; this was somebody totally different. Even though he'd heard from Mom that things were chaotic for Dad at the moment, even though he'd heard her appeals for her son to return to Finland, presented in states of rising hysteria, Mom still seemed to have underestimated the gravity of the situation.

Samuel had just returned from Portland to Eugene when Mom last called him. She'd been crying, panicked, suddenly sure that everything they were saying about him was true.

The worst thing was, of course, that it was. The memory of what he'd done crackled in his mind like an electric shock. But he'd protected Mom, because this was an unfair burden to place on her. He'd spent twenty minutes reassuring her: 'It's all lies, I promised, don't you remember? Nothing illegal. Ever. Why would we suddenly start compromising on that, especially now?'

That had calmed her down. When he got off the call, he felt like he was about to explode. Mom believed he was moral, good; the thought was heartbreaking.

Good God, after what he had done.

And the worst part of it was how easy it had been.

Neither of them dared to move.

This was Samuel's father.

The North American songbird that a moment ago had joyously twittered a foreign tune into the darkness had fallen silent. Samuel stared at the man before him, squinting in disbelief.

This was his father.

This was his father.

This was his father.

'Uh, hi,' he said, feeling like an idiot. 'Is this a bad time?'

'I'll shoot.' The man was gripping the gun awkwardly and harder than Samuel would have wished. 'I swear,' he continued feebly, 'I'll shoot if I have to.'

Samuel believed him. But this had to be a joke. This was his father?

Samuel slowly raised his arms and hoped the gesture would ease the tension. 'Can we just… take it easy?'

The man looked like he might empty the entire cylinder into Samuel out of sheer rage, or just as likely, slide to the ground and burst into tears.

What he'd been expecting, he couldn't say. But not this, Joe realized. He was ashamed of how his hands shook as, heart racing, he aimed the revolver at the tall, curly-haired young man, standing looking stunned in his doorway.

The experience was so bewildering that he completely missed some of what Samuel said. He hadn't been prepared for this.

The kid slowly raised his arms. He seemed surprisingly calm.

'Don't come any closer,' Joe heard his own voice saying.

'OK, I won't.'

'I'll shoot,' Joe said.

The boy – the man – didn't move a muscle, but his presence seemed to retreat. Joe realized he was just as afraid as his grown terrorist son that he would pull the trigger even though he didn't want to. To see if he could, to prove that he could.

It felt unfair to have to kill a man. It would be self-defense, but still.

The young man waited apprehensively, arms still raised.

Joe needed to do something now. Was it too late to call the police? But all his energy was directed into reconciling himself to the realization that this was his son. The dark, bearded man – whom Joe had been imagining as a boy this whole time – had to be… what? A little over twenty? He looked older, ageless, anything between twenty and thirty.

Standing at his door was not that little boy he remembered, still shy of two, or the insecure, misunderstood, deranged teen Joe had been afraid of all spring, but a big, charismatic paratroop commander. This was a man who tossed himself on his bunk and let his muscles relax after doing his forty nightly pull-ups, a man who lifted a hand at a stadium and inspired a hundred thousand people to carry out his will. One look into this man's confidence-inspiring eyes and the idea of calling the police was absurd.

That's why the boy had been capable of doing all those things. All the things he'd done to Joe and his family and the things he'd done to others, too, like terrorizing an apparently legal, billion-dollar company off the stock exchange. Even its bankers didn't dare oppose the hatemongers anymore.

'Is there any chance you could put that away?' The young man frowned and nodded at the gleaming metal object that seemed heavier and more unsteady in Joe's hand. His son didn't look like evil incarnate, but what would that look like? It wasn't like he'd grow a pair of horns, even if he'd sold his soul.

Joe stared at him.

He wanted to toss the gun aside and shout at the kid to go to hell. But now something about the entire scene was off... what? Joe had to think before he could pinpoint where the sense of surreal familiarity, of being hoodwinked, was coming from. And then he realized.

Zayde.

He was going to have to shoot his grandfather. The boy was a dead ringer for his grandfather, or what Joe's grandfather had looked like as a young man. Joe's grandfather, but with Joe's brother David's features, a young Bruce Springsteen lookalike in a beanie: that's who'd been waging war on them. And still something behind it all was oddly reminiscent of the blond, blue-eyed Alina.

Here, before him, stood what had come from him, from him and Alina.

And maybe it was due precisely to this sense of mingled familiarity and alienation, this surprising sensation of his own family's unexpected presence, that Joe, to his own shock, finally did as the psychopath standing on his doorstep urged in increasingly confident tones: he allowed the hand holding the snub-nosed revolver to drop gradually to his side.

It was like a hypnotist's suggestion: in the end, it was a relief to give in. Maybe he wanted to die, deep down inside, he thought in exhaustion.

'Thanks. Fantastic. That's great,' the young man repeated in a steady voice, as if talking to a lunatic. 'Do you think you could... put that on the ground?'

He towered head and shoulders over Joe. His broad shoulders, his physical dominance, seemed to fill the hall. Something about this young man, the son he didn't know, the criminal, commanded Joe's immediate respect. The idea that he could feel this way about someone who wanted to maim his daughters, kill them… life never ceased to amaze. And that voice, the foreign yet strangely familiar tones – for a split second, Joe could imagine his own voice coming from this young man's mouth, only in a Finnish accent. But then the impression faded; Joe's voice was nowhere near as deep, nor did his presence radiate such command.

It was as if the young man before him made the moment fill with light. He irresistibly drew you to him; maybe this was what it felt like to be a moth at a campfire.

An anarchist: that's what he'd expected, he realized, someone angrier. An aggressively pierced punk rocker in intentionally ripped clothes, red and black – like the young men who spit on his back at the debate sponsored by the *Baltimore Sun*. And above all smaller, adolescent-seeming, narrow-shouldered. There was no evidence in this visitor of the hostility, the incitement to violence, emitted by the bitter, scrawny man-children at the debate. But neither was there anything apologetic, none of that harmless frumpiness that had stamped the other half of the activist crowd.

Miriam is never going to understand this, Joe thought impotently, obeying his son as if spellbound. But he wasn't going to shoot anyone; he could see that now. And by some peculiar logic, it also seemed to him that he deserved what he had coming. What else had his fatherhood been for any of his three children but a random pattern of survival and drifting, good intentions and accidents, desperate rescue attempts, hopeless bailing?

He slowly crouched down and did as he was asked, lowered the revolver to the floor. The red doormat muffled the sound into a heavy thunk. Joe kept staring at the mat. He'd never realized it didn't read *Welcome* above the big, smiling, clawed crayfish the way he'd always thought, but *This is Bawlmer, hon.*

'Why don't I go ahead and take this?' Samuel said.

He gave Joe a questioning look. Shivers ran up and down Joe's spine when he saw Samuel bend down to pick up the revolver. Am I getting a fever? he wondered. It was surprising to notice that it was only once he had let go of the gun that he was able to breathe freely.

The boy stared at the weapon in his hand. He stood there for a long time, as if he couldn't believe what it was.

For a moment Joe was sure he'd made a mistake. The kid wasn't a psychopath who wanted to toy with him, to play cat and mouse. Maybe this whole thing was a series of convoluted misunderstandings, he thought, and then his heart skipped a beat.

The revolver was steady in the Samuel's hands as he raised it and pointed it between Joe's eyes. Everything he'd learned at the group Lab Animals Keep Us Safe and Healthy flashed through his mind: that psychopaths win you over with sweet smiles, make you fall in love with them, invite your trust. That psychopaths are by no means stupid but razor-sharp, never openly unhinged but skilled at friendship, lovable, hug you warmly — and only once they've made it into your confidence, slit your throat with a practiced hand.

The young man looked him dead in the eye, and that gaze was so utterly spent, so bitter, that there was no longer any misunderstanding anything.

Samuel clearly remembered the rainy, lightless morning the phone call came. It had been a week before Easter. November seemed to have started early that fall and never ended: even though the days were long, the sky remained a flat, unbroken gray. Colorless trees stood sentry along rain-slicked roads; Helsinki looked black and white, permanently so.

Of course it had been a sum of coincidences: that the courier had left the package on the wrong floor, that Samuel just happened to be the one who picked up the phone. But the strangest thing was that it had never occurred to him to wonder, and he'd been working in the building for months. By the time the phone rang, the morning sleet had faded to a normal Helsinki drizzle. Outside the windows, a cantankerous wind tore at coat-hems and flipped umbrellas inside out as hunched figures plowed doggedly through puddles. Samuel was sitting in his office, so focused on what he was doing that he was reluctant to answer; the phone buzzing on his desk meant an unnecessary interruption. He finally lifted the receiver and grunted a distracted hello. The parameters he'd spent the last fifteen minutes trying to fit together in his model were still spinning in his mind like tops when the voice on the line asked someone named Tomppa to bring a box of supplies to BeeTwo. Samuel had never heard of Tomppa, the box of supplies, or BeeAnything.

'Hold up, I'll check.'

He opened the door and glanced into the corridor.

That had to be it. A medium-sized cardboard box neatly wrapped in packing tape had been left next to the door. He'd already passed it three times that day without noticing.

'Is it this one with Degerström Laboratory Supplies on it?'

'Whew! That's it. I was starting to get scared.' The man paused for a moment before continuing: 'There's no way I could get you to…'

'Sure, no problem,' Samuel said. 'I'll bring it down.'

He picked up the package, whistled his way to the elevator and downstairs, glad that he could help the caller out. He'd be back at his models in five minutes.

The air underground was moist, cooler than in the corridors upstairs. He'd never had any reason to come to the basement before, the floor marked with a letter-number combination indicating two stories below street level.

After the fact, he couldn't remember what had been going through his head when he pressed the buzzer and reached for the cold metal handle of the fire door that read B2 – Laboratories and Contagion Risk – Unauthorized Access Strictly Prohibited. The door gave onto on a brick hallway with testing supplies stacked against the walls, and empty metal cages evidently intended for transporting animals.

The caller had told him to come to B202 and knock. For the caller, what took place there had to be so banal, so mundane, that it hadn't crossed his mind to prepare Samuel for what he'd see when the door opened.

It happened exactly the way they said it did. Why everything changed only once you saw it with your own eyes – that was troublingly hard to explain to yourself.

In many ways it was a shame Samuel had to leave Laajakoski.

The position as a research assistant at Laajakoski Biosciences Inc. felt like it had been custom-made for him. During his very first week at the staid, credible office building, Samuel realized how much it was possible to learn in life if you just made it into the right surroundings. The insight was so sudden and terrifying that he almost forgot to breathe. Blizzard-blinded and buffeted by the north wind, he had stumbled upon a five-star hotel, where, as luck would have it: Congratulations, you're our millionth customer! You just won a private suite and free drinks for the rest of your life.

The work itself was more interesting than he would have imagined, and the more dedication he brought to his tasks, the more responsibility he was given. The plush wall-to-wall carpeting and light filtering in through the venetian blinds seemed to underscore the black, white, and chrome-gray adultness of the premises as he walked in every day.

The fall after Samuel's high-school graduation, his life had been irrefutably and irreparably ruined. It was only in retrospect that he was able to see how deeply the breakup with Kerttu had hurt. He wasn't a sixteen-year-old anymore, whose broken heart would mend overnight. It was clear to him it would take time to get back on his feet. But that the process could last an eternity – several *weeks!* – had been unbearable.

But that one phone call had fixed everything. When the position as a research assistant at Laajakoski Biosciences Inc. was offered to him, it was bizarre, feeling his mental health being restored to him, literally during the course of one telephone conversation. He could almost hear the resuscitated rush of the healing synapses in his central nervous system when he was told that the position had been offered to him first, apparently, out of a field of sixty good applicants. He'd already mentally steeled himself for the fuck you email, *unfortunately we've decided to go with someone else this time*, that would end in an overly detailed description of what a well-educated, experienced, charismatic, and superior individual had been selected instead. But he was informed during the phone call that his article in *Finland Today* had made a big impression on everyone at Laajakoski. After an autumn of wandering through a post-high-school wilderness, the call finally seemed like a guarantee that things would slip naturally into their proper place for him. And so they had.

At Laajakoski his gaze was met in a friendly, pleased sort of way that reminded him of the year his school soccer team won the league championship. The fact that he hadn't studied economics – so you just browse through Stiglitz for fun, is that it? – earned him points he'd thought lost for good. The women in particular included him in their sushi debates, were eager to hear his opinion on the things adults spent their days wrestling with.

This was exactly what he'd been missing.

And these thirty-year-old adults in glasses and sober clothing: how healthy they looked, how balanced and capable of putting things in perspective. As he observed them, Samuel felt ashamed. This whole time, people this sensible and calm had been doing constructive, ambitious work on behalf of science instead of drunkenly pissing apart their high-school diploma at Hietaniemi Beach. While some people had been wallowing in the swill of online discussions, fanning misanthropy on discussion boards, and ogling the tits of TV chat hosts, these people had been conducting research. While he'd been lying at home pretending to be mentally ill, the director of research and his colleagues had published a book on endocrinology and toxicology that Samuel had never heard of but that he ordered online that same day, using his mother's credit card.

The most remarkable thing was, Samuel realized as he chuckled along with everyone at the director of research's sailing-themed anecdote during coffee break, that the tiniest impulse to go over to the dark side had vanished without the least effort: the entire ideology of evil he had just irreversibly aligned himself with no longer existed. The office chairs alone were so comfortably soft and beautifully shaped, the building so bright, clean, and adult, that there was clearly no longer any need to worry about the state of the world.

Which was interesting in that, in spite of Samuel's new job, climate change had not been wholly stopped. The soup of plastic trash continued to bob in the middle of the Pacific Ocean, and it was unlikely that new marine safety infrastructure been built for the Baltic Sea. But clearly more significant in terms of the environment than these minor deficiencies were the facts that he got to sit here, moving numbers around Excel tables on a brand-new, super-powerful computer that no high-school student could afford, and that, according to that beautiful woman with a university degree, it was super-cool having him around. He could be part of something again, do something constructive, not necessarily for the environment but definitely for science, and in the grand scheme of things that was the same, or at least as valuable.

And what was this about the planet already being destroyed? How so? Everything was still salvageable; all they had to do was get to work. He was going to sign up for the volunteer oil-spill cleanup crew that very evening: it wasn't going to be on him, at least, if action wasn't taken against a potential spill!

Samuel gazed admiringly at his boss, Adjunct Professor Veera Hakkarainen, who carried her brain from one meeting room to another in a rangy frame reminiscent of a human body, with which she maintained a coolly polite, disinterested relationship. Seeing this aroused a heartfelt desire in Samuel that, like these individuals, he would grow up to be a harmlessly smiling adult, who wanted nothing more out of life than successful fertility treatments, hellish trips to the supermarket, a station wagon, a golden retriever, and an endless cycle of children's ear infections. These grown-ups didn't know how easy it was to drop unintentionally out of the world of office buildings and coffee breaks. These fortunate souls had no idea how ruthless the world was, how safe their meeting rooms. In the mornings, just the thought of going into work made something inside Samuel melt with relief.

Over the course of the winter, it felt increasingly certain that no nineteen-year-old would bother expressing his contempt for humanity at the beach, penis in his hand, if he were surrounded by women with a sense of humor, with whom he could leave the planet unsaved and concentrate on something interesting. Nor would he be ranting online if a balding, credible director of research, who wore the clean dress shirts favored by forty-somethings, wanted to hear what he, as a young man with good judgment, thought about the colors used in these new layouts for the Laajakoski website: he wouldn't have time.

Samuel's role as a research assistant was to input figures from forms into the computer and mechanically clean up files as instructed: coffee-making, but in Excel.

He approached his coffee-making with the diligence only accessible to those experiencing the residual terror of annihilation and despair. He made it a point of pride to be the first one at work every morning. He was going to be the one who remembered to replenish the coffee supply even though it wasn't his job; he was going to be the one to throw himself into every one of his duties more conscientiously, more quickly, and more thoroughly than expected. It was rewarding, being allowed to do simple tasks without the potential for failure, when you knew it was in the service of meaningful scientific research. His breast burned as he smiled at the lousy jokes of his thirty-something colleagues during coffee breaks. He knew that if it hadn't been for the catastrophic autumn he wouldn't have recognized it as such, but the experience resembled something one could tentatively think of as happiness.

It was inspirational, seeing the sum that appeared in his account on the final banking day of the month. After his fall of scraping by the figure was substantial. He was earning his own money! He was capable of doing something useful!

Besides, the beautiful, snotty girl with the ponytail who worked at the convenience store and could never tear herself away from her fingernails long enough to pay attention to him, even when ringing up his bus pass, had started flirting with him. Her flirtations had swiftly developed to such a state of single-mindedness that before he knew it, Samuel found himself at her house, in her bedroom, drinking cider and making out. In her girl-scented, figure-skating themed sanctuary, it came out that the girl, Viivi, had thought Samuel was many years older than she was, which was oddly encouraging for a failure who'd been kicked out of college, as were her breasts, which Viivi allowed him to fondle freely in a sexualized, non-gender-neutral fashion. And then it gradually dawned on Samuel why Viivi had so persistently ignored him and lifted her pert nose in the other direction with a sniff every time she loaded money onto his bus pass. It had never occurred to him to interpret her disdain as a blanket she warmed herself in after too many rejections and cold embraces. It had never occurred to him that Viivi had, of course, expected that the tall, good-looking older boy would make the first move if he were the least bit interested. And when Viivi revealed this to him on her stuffed-animal-edged bed, it dawned on Samuel that even an exceptionally beautiful woman's hard, crushing arrogance might be nothing more than insecurity.

And the evening of his first payday, as he kissed Viivi's silken lower belly and coltish hip-bones after she'd stripped down to her panties, he was no longer in a hurry to get anywhere, nor was he striving towards anything. All his bets had been placed on the spring entrance exams, for which he had pulled out his books months before the others. Not dedicating any particular thought to Kerttu's frigid autumnal declaration of autonomy, he found it hard to resist taking pleasure in

Viivi's soft tongue as it began its slow exploration of the particulars of his body. It was hard to see what needed to be fixed or changed in the world as Viivi rocked in his arms, ponytail undone. Samuel could hear the television and the mundane sounds of her parents moving around downstairs; the bedroom door was unlocked.

One might think that the decision that had determined the entire future course of his life had been complicated, difficult. And yet the choice had been straightforward and easy: simply put, there had been no choice for him.

Why did they have to be beagles: the gentlest, friendliest creatures in the world?

By the time the call about the cardboard box came that one morning, Samuel had managed to carve out a satisfactory ecological niche for himself at Laajakoski Biosciences Ltd.

Something about the math he got to apply when analyzing data and modeling results was a natural fit for him. And something specific about the math that posed no problems for him, seemed to generate significant headaches for many authentic, astute researchers. This surprised Samuel. Up until now, he'd only had his peers to compare himself to.

When, after protracted nagging, the adjunct professor agreed to assign him his first research challenges as a test, Samuel had felt the sweat bead up on his brow. He'd looked at the research results spread across the adjunct professor's desk, which he was supposed to construct his model with – now that he'd boasted about his long-form mathematics and the adjunct professor's introductory-level textbook, which he'd stupidly gone and read without being asked. If he solved the problem, he could advance from coffee-maker to ball boy, but when he saw the figures before him, he'd realized, to his horror, that his brain had melted to uselessness. It had happened imperceptibly over the fall as a result of an unvaried diet and lack of mental activity; he'd spent too long in his mother's presence, which would have atrophied the brain of a child prodigy.

But to the surprise of both Adjunct Professor Hakkarainen and Samuel himself, the opposite had proven true.

Even though it hadn't had much practice recently, apparently his brain was still agile. After overcoming his initial apprehension, he felt a satisfying mental hum as his neurons immediately and effortlessly revved out of their rest cycle whenever a mathematical conundrum of sufficient complexity was presented to him, and he realized he was allowed to stretch his abilities to the limit and see how far they would take him.

It was a relief to get onto the court immediately, bypassing the university, to be able to hit the ball as hard as he could, without limitations.

His job settled into helping with the processing, analyzing, and modeling of data with the adjunct professor's assistance. It took some time for him to grasp the rules, but gradually he was able to answer the easiest lobs semi-independently on her behalf. And through curiosity and sheer tenacity, he soon found himself returning mathematical balls that would only recently have seemed unattainable.

Even though his performance exceeded expectations, the new job title and raise announced by the director of research that spring caught Samuel off guard. The chance to do such interesting work already felt unfair; being paid to do it was outrageous. The director of research hugged Samuel too tightly at the restaurant one Friday night and magnanimously gave him a bottle of whisky worth three hundred euros, which the director then drank himself and sloshed on the floor of the bar at the tail end of the night, not long before he was carried out to a cab by six sweating employees. As Samuel walked, still dumbfounded, down the dark streets towards the railway station, he thought that Laajakoski Biosciences Inc. was both the best and most natural thing that could have ever happened to him: a lottery win that had been tailored just for him.

When he answered the call about the package the courier had left on the wrong floor, Samuel had already decided he would keep working at Laajakoski and not even try to get into the university. Now that he had successfully made it through the back door and onto the court where the tournament was just heating up, calling everything off so he could attend the mandatory introductory courses and get shit-faced in funny coveralls held little appeal for him. But Adjunct Professor Veera Hakkarainen gently coaxed him into changing his mind: he could always earn his degree while he worked, and for someone as gifted as Samuel it would be a cinch.

When the caller asked for Tomppa and the missing dog swing, Mom had just the Sunday before asked Samuel if he'd started growing again. Henri's interest in Laajakoski stroked Samuel's ego, although what he did seemed to go over Henri's head.

Describing his work to Henri and Mom, Samuel realized he'd learned more over the past few months at Laajakoski than during his whole time at high school. His worldview had expanded so rapidly he could hear the seams splitting. Every day felt unique, weighty; he could go anywhere, learn anything.

As he explained this, he noticed Mom suppressing a sigh and looking away.

'What?'

Alina took a deep breath and then looked at him: 'Sometimes you sound so much like your father it's scary.'

Afterwards, he kept thinking that his knees had given way, but the truth was he'd remained standing and behaved normally. The man who opened the fireproofed, reinforced door on floor B2 of Laajakoski Biosciences Inc. probably hadn't even noticed there was anything wrong.

And as the man thanked him, Samuel didn't feel anything but a tiny, imperceptible undercurrent where one hadn't existed a moment ago. It was like a faint bodily background noise as he handed over the cardboard box, irksome, but in a way that didn't demand attention.

He hadn't known – and yet at the same time of course he had.

Nor had he immediately known how to react to what he saw. But as he handed the package to the man on B2, he suddenly realized what the package was and what it was going to be used for.

They were on the other side of the window, clearly visible to the man's rear left. The curtain that looked like it was normally pulled across the glass had been left open for some reason. The moment was similar to how he'd always imagined the rending of the veil in the temple, although there was no thunderclap.

This was what he had brought.

For that, for what happened on the other side of that window.

When the door closed, he was suddenly aware of the powerful hum of the air conditioning. It must have been audible the whole time. The mathematical model he was working on upstairs, from data gathered by his boss, crossed his mind as if testing whether it was all right to come in.

This was what he had voluntarily participated in over the past few months.

Behind that window was where the raw material for his work came from. The material that, up until now, had been nothing but a series of interesting brainteasers, mere numbers, abstractions: that was all he'd been working with. Of course he'd always made the connection to the relay batons and anchors of living creatures' hormonal systems. But still: it had never occurred to him to think through how the numbers were acquired.

Like this.

Here.

He turned around and tried to pick up mentally where he'd left off, but it felt like he'd left his office ten dark, oppressive years ago. He walked to the end of the hall on unsteady legs and pressed the button that released the corridor's electronic lock. He felt high.

For the rest of the day, he drifted in a hazy state of indifference reminiscent of physical numbness. Every person, object, thought, question, or feeling he tried to focus on had retreated behind an alien, weblike veil. He was surprised afterwards that no one had noticed. At least no one said anything.

Of course, hammered through his head that evening when his little brothers jumped on his back and head in their leopard and lion costumes.

'Come on, Samuel, let's play pet store, come on!'

'Hey, so this is the cheetah cub and he comes in to buy it, 'kay? And it knows how to talk, 'kay? 'Kay?'

Samuel! Samuel! Samuel!!

He played pet store like someone with brain damage, mechanically discussed the alternatives with the six-year-old salesperson who was also one of the two animals for sale, swiped an air credit card to pay the two-euro charge, and then carried the sleeping beasts home, into the boy's bedroom, in his arms, like the living carrying the dead.

This is what we're capable of, hammered through his head.

This is our goal, this is what's important to us: this is what we want.

Only semi-present, he tried to acknowledge Ukko and Taisto's deluge of concerns, each so important that it had to be expressed at a shout and at the same time as his brother's. At day care we read a book that had swear words in it and guess what, guesswhat, Darf Vayder has a black helmet with bars in front of his mouth, that's why his breathing sounds so funny, guess what, Helli Kyllikki asked me and Arttu to marry her but I think she might change her mind when she's a grown-up and guess what we're building at day care, guess what – a time machine.

He watched with unseeing eyes as his mother fixed dinner for his little brothers, soothed Taisto, who was shrieking and throwing a tantrum on the floor because his slice of ham was the wrong shape. He only half-registered his surroundings as he watched her gently lead Ukko to the table, even though Ukko couldn't eat because his cars were busy watching the moon.

'How was work today?' Henri asked from across the table, helping himself to the salad and olive oil.

Henri, as ready as ever to listen, to nod his carrot-topped head earnestly, to support his co-conversationalist in those specific developmental tasks and challenges in emotional growth he or she wanted to face at that moment.

'Fine.'

Luckily Henri didn't dig any deeper; instead, he launched into an account of the training he'd led that day, of which Samuel heard nothing.

'You seem a little preoccupied,' Mom observed.

'I'm just tired,' Samuel said.

He had to concentrate extra hard even to pretend he was listening.

He thought it was just the initial shock, but the surreal feeling didn't pass the next day, either.

He couldn't stop thinking about how methodical everything that happened behind the glass wall was: every single one of those leashes, pieces of plastic, pairs of tongs, and tubes so ingeniously designed, with such engineered precision.

This is done in our name.

He must have known that all along.

And he had.

In a way.

For the week that followed, he sat at work without seeing anything. All his energy and willpower went into trying to get used to the idea that this was the way the world was: that we wanted it this way.

That it was for our common good, that it was best for everyone this way. And, above all, that it had been decided democratically, and was done in accordance with all the rules.

That once more it was a question of what Mom had talked about last fall: time for him to grow up.

That he'd always known, that nothing had changed, that he'd only seen what he'd always known.

That this was what the world was like; he just had to accept it.

He tried his hardest.

The sense that he had to do something about it didn't come until later – the first time he told another person what he'd seen.

'Hello?' the voice answered, after numerous rings.

'It's Samuel,' he said. 'Did I catch you at a bad time?'

He wasn't sure if calling was allowed. He heard how normal, even casual, his own voice sounded through the nightmarish thumping of his heart. It was the first time they'd spoken on the phone since the breakup.

A wave of relief washed over him when he heard the sincerity in Kerttu's voice. Samuel apologized for what had happened last fall and how things had ended.

But Kerttu navigated through the embarrassing events of the past mercifully and without exacting a pound of flesh. It had happened in the interim, the miracle, like bird-cherry blossoms in the spring: Kerttu had forgiven him.

He had been so young.

'How's everything going?' she asked, and this was what he'd never been able to resist. Even though Samuel couldn't see her patient, all-understanding eyes over the phone, he could feel her waiting. She could tell from his tone that something was wrong.

'I saw something at work a little while ago,' he said, his voice thick like a rope, 'that I don't think I'm ever going to forget.'

This was the reason the doors in the basement were triple-locked and monitored with security systems. This was the reason why what took place in the basement was spoken about the way it was. This was the reason why scientific articles were written the way they were. He'd known that, too, in a way, and yet he hadn't understood that the purpose of words is also always to conceal.

The photographs in the lab's brochures were always shiny and bright, the model beagles healthy and happy. Every animal looked cooperative, eager to expand the range of scientific knowledge. Even animal rights groups weren't allowed to disseminate realistic images: people would be shocked.

This was what he'd participated in. This was what his model equations involved. And he'd known the whole time, too, and was that why he was crying as he told Kerttu over the phone. Or was it because, of all animals, they had to be beagles?

As he stared at the loaded revolver in his stranger-son's hand, Joe realized that he'd made an irreversible mistake thinking they could talk things out. Suddenly he understood what Miriam had been trying to say this whole time. That someone could be so bitter, so fanatical, so disappointed by life, so absolute in their belief that their opinions gave them the right to terrorize, torture, kill – well, he wasn't going to stand for it. This son of his had no way of forcing Joe to accept his thoughts. And the realization of this, the anger it sparked, and the accompanying knowledge of his own impending death, filled Joe with a certainty that swept away any trace of fear.

'I'm sure you have your personal thoughts and experiences that mean a lot to you,' he said, looking his son in the eye.

He wondered if he could wrench the gun from Samuel's hand if he did it quickly, suddenly, and confidently enough.

'Things probably seem to you the way you think they are. And I'm sure you have your reasons, ones that seem important to you. But you should understand, that doesn't make your perspective the only right one.'

The boy looked taken aback. His eyes narrowed to slits. He slowly opened his mouth and said: 'Right back at you.'

Joe buried his face in his hands. This is the reason he'd be shot: because they saw him as a fanatic. All spring he'd been hoping to have a dialogue with one of them. That hadn't happened.

'What are you laughing at?' Samuel asked.

'I'm not laughing.'

'You chuckled.'

'Oh.'

'Just a little.'

'Yeah. Well. Maybe,' Joe said. He was tired. Would he be shot if he sat down? He tried to prepare himself for what it would feel like... would it hurt? Or would it go more easily than he imagined?

'What was so funny?'

The young man looked interested. Maybe he was hoping for a chance to argue, or get the final impetus for his act of bloodshed.

Joe thought for a moment.

'Well,' he said, 'I was at this one debate last spring.'

He glanced at his son. Samuel was still aiming the gun at him. Talking would feel more natural, it occurred to him, if the other party weren't aiming a loaded revolver at his head.

'And?'

'No one there seemed to be interested in how things really are.'

'Is that how it seemed to you?'

The boy's voice sounded bitter.

'You might find it hard to believe,' Joe said slowly, 'but things don't become true just because they're reported in the newspapers. Those fanatics had already such fixed opinions there was no room for discussion. No one wanted to hear anything that contradicted their view. No one was interested in how things really are.'

It seemed as if something inside the boy had boiled over. His voice was clogged, and the hand holding the gun trembled as he said: 'Right back at you.'

Joe couldn't restrain his laughter. 'They had no idea what they were talking about! They were mixing up a hundred different issues, and it felt like they were doing it on purpose.'

'Is that how it felt?'

'Nothing they said,' Joe said tiredly, 'had anything to do with what

I do.'

Samuel looked at him: 'Why would you think everything is about you?'

Joe was stunned: 'What?'

'That debate,' Samuel said. 'I watched it online.'

Joe listened to how weary his own voice sounded as he said: 'That five-minute clip isn't exactly the whole story. But you people aren't interested in that.'

'You people?'

'You and those friends of yours.'

'In the first place,' the boy said, 'you don't know the first thing about what my friends are interested in. You don't even know who they are. In the second place, I watched it online.'

'Listen to me! I said, that five-minute—'

'The whole thing.'

Joe was floored. Now his son was looking him dead in the eye.

'It lasted an hour and a half,' Joe said. A hairline fracture appeared in his confidence.

Samuel nodded. 'One twenty-six. I watched it from start to finish.'

Joe felt a pang of shame. Samuel was right, of course: you should never assume you knew what you didn't. But of course that was how these guys operated: tirelessly sniffed out trivia that would help them fan the flames of hatred.

'Well,' he said, 'I'm sure it made for pleasurable viewing.'

'It was a lynching.'

Joe raised his face. His son's expression was difficult to interpret.

'You were alone, and for once there were a lot of them,' Samuel said. 'They came there to lynch you publicly.'

Joe was surprised to feel something warm rising within him. He forced it down. Just when he thought that the boy had partially understood something, Samuel let the corners of his mouth turn down and said: 'You were wrong about everything.'

'What?'

'About everything you said there.'

Joe sighed. 'You people would know.'

'You were talking about things,' Samuel said, 'you don't comprehend. And could you stop saying "you people" when I'm the only one you're talking to?'

Joe felt the familiar anger rising in him. 'Oh, so I don't know? I don't know a thing about my own work?'

'That's the key phrase,' Samuel said, nodding. *"My own work."'*

Samuel seemed surprisingly calm as he eyed Joe. And what his son said next seemed like the essence of something, although he wasn't sure what: that because Joe thought about everything from the perspective of his own work, he didn't see the irrevocable damage his words and deeds caused.

He didn't know what he was doing, Samuel said.

Joe lost it then. 'But that's the whole reason you're here, too! Unfortunately, my work is what we're talking about! You people started this, and now we're here fighting about it, goddammit!'

Samuel stared at him, face white. Joe was sure he would shoot now. 'Is that what you think?' he shouted. 'That I'm here because of some experiments of yours?

'Well, why else then?' Joe shouted back. 'You break into my lab, smash my living-room windows, scream into a megaphone, make death threats! Why the hell do you think we have a handgun in the house now? A gun none of us wanted? Why the fuck are you going on and on, beating around the fucking bush! Shoot me now, goddammit, or put that gun away, I can't take it anymore! Do what you came to do!'

Samuel looked as if he'd been whacked in the face with a shovel. 'Is that what you think? That I'm going to shoot you?'

Joe was momentarily speechless. 'That's... sort of the impression anyone might get,' he said finally.

He couldn't keep his eyes from skimming across the gun Samuel was pointing at him. When he noticed this, Samuel also glanced at the gun. He seemed startled that it was still in his hand. For some reason, Joe wasn't surprised when he let the gun drop.

'Right back at you,' his son said softly.

Joe gulped. It was true, of course. He'd been aiming the same weapon just a moment ago. But that was different.

'I... live here,' he said. And then stuttered something about wanting to protect his family.

After a long silence, Samuel said quietly: 'Could we clear up one thing before we talk about anything else?' The gun was pointing at the floor now. 'I don't have anything to do with those people who have been tormenting you. With the exception of one message.'

Joe stared at the doormat before him. He glanced at the gun by Samuel's side. Now that he couldn't see the young man's face and wasn't focusing on the choppy Finnish accent, Joe could clearly hear his brother David's baritone in that voice.

'Or the ones at the debate who tried to explain what they were interested in, and who you yelled at that *your* work and *your* career and *your* experiments and *your* methods were more important than anything they wanted to talk about or knew about. You were yelling at them, saying they didn't understand anything, even though they'd just been trying to tell you what they felt was more important than your experiments or any individual's needs and desires. You yelled at them that they needed to know every detail of your work before they could say any of those thousands of things that they think about every day and that you know nothing about. But I still don't have anything to do with them.'

Joe didn't understand why, but it felt like his body was on fire. Samuel said that when you see what's sacred to you offended enough times, it becomes harder and harder to understand why people don't want to respect it, or even try to.

I have a fever, Joe thought.

If someone has something important they've tried to say over and over but no one hears it, it's easy to feel like their whole life is being dismissed, Samuel said. The one in a position of power has to take the first step. The bigger one has to listen to the smaller one, not vice versa.

Joe had no interest in his son's didactic diatribe, but he stood there as if paralyzed. His limbs had been sapped of strength. He'd been wronged, and even if it wasn't the impartial truth, it was still the truth, maybe his alone and no one else's, but still true. He didn't know why, but the more he resisted the kid's accusations, the hotter the fire inside him burned.

'Say what you will,' Joe said. He knew his legs would give way soon if he weren't allowed to sit. 'People who send children needle bombs to prove some obscure point of their own are sick. Evil through and through. Say what you will, but in this matter there is only one, absolute truth. No matter what their justifications are, I'm going to do everything in my power to ensure that a single animal rights activist isn't able to spread his gospel of hatred as long as I live. I will

do everything in my power to ensure that you can practice a legal
profession without having to fear for your well-being.'

And at this, Samuel appeared to lose it. Joe's field of vision had
contracted to a flat gray oval; he felt pressure in his chest.

'Are you kidding me?' the boy said.

And then Samuel asked the question over and over: did Joe really
think animal rights activists would send his daughter a bomb?

The boy looked so genuinely bewildered that Joe didn't even know
what they were talking about anymore.

It had just felt like too much. To have someone greet you by pointing
a loaded revolver at you: who was this person?

The whole bus ride, he'd consciously kept the swirling vortex at
a distance, but when he saw the gun in his father's hand, Samuel
couldn't avoid it anymore: the red-hot, iron-flavored wave he'd finally
succumbed to two years earlier, that night after the beach. And out of
somewhere rose a parade of images of his father in the most prestigious
newspapers, always carefree, smiling, respected, telling the whole world
how animal research would save it.

When he saw the gun on the floor, he'd initially reached for it to set
it at a safe distance. But as he looked at it, he'd had a flash of comprehension of what it was, what the sole purpose for its manufacture
was, and what the father he didn't know had just intended to do to
him. He'd seen it on his father's face: he had really decided to do it.
And when he thought about all he'd been forced to bear because of his
father over the years, what he'd had to go through without any help
from his father – on top of that, it didn't feel fucking fair to have a
loaded weapon aimed between his eyes! He'd been overwhelmed then
by an unexpected, irresistible desire to show his father what it felt like:
was it fun having the barrel of a gun pointed in your face?

As he explained this out loud, he saw the doubt play over Joe's face,
the justifiable skepticism that wasn't likely to pass any time soon.

But as Samuel spoke, he realized it hadn't been revenge or merely
fear motivating him. It crossed his mind that maybe, without realizing
it, he'd even thought he could get back at the police officer who'd
sprayed chili extract in his eyes.

Maybe the right word was *power*, he realized as he tried to find a euphemism for the impulse, something that would mask its true nature. The urge had surprised him; he hadn't realized he'd find it so strong within him.

To do that to someone just because you suddenly could: he was ashamed.

Dad was still sitting on the floor. Dad's nose was running, and his bald crown looked frail and defenseless. The sight hurt Samuel, and he was forced to turn away. He wasn't sure if the American father he didn't know would listen to anything Samuel planned on telling him, imprecisely and awkwardly in a foreign language, but this would be the only chance he'd ever get to explain what he'd done. There was nothing he was less eager to do, but he would have to try now.

He'd never felt anything like what he felt that night when he came home from Hietaniemi Beach. As he, in a state of rising inebriation, pissed his high-school diploma to tatters in a personal protest that went unnoticed by the world, he'd had a vital insight. He'd never realized that it was possible to be so wholly, so utterly disappointed in life and its most allegedly meaningful aspects. Later that night, when he'd allowed the bright red, long-smoldering coals to blaze into flame, he'd realized that what he'd been waiting for was never going to happen.

Suddenly something Kerttu had asked many times with a tactful delicacy and that he'd always ignored as irrelevant clicked into place. Suddenly something Mom had repeatedly telegraphed in concerned glances and protracted sighs but he hadn't understood unfolded from a new angle. Suddenly the thing the rest of the world had understood all along but that he'd refused to believe crystallized in the exhaustion that followed the red vortex. The thing he'd sought most in life, the hope that had lent him the strength to achieve everything he'd accomplished thus far, had no basis in reality.

This whole time, it had existed only in his head. Dad would never contact him, never notice who he was, never know anything about him. With the same irrefutable logic that unerringly drew connections between completely unrelated things, he understood that night that there was nothing he'd ever be able to do on behalf of the planet:

there was no way he could have any impact on the climate, prevent the current wave of extinctions, or do anything about any of those millions of other problems that were growing worse by the day.

The next morning, he felt like he'd been bled dry. Not knowing what to do with himself and not wanting to deal with Henri and Mom, he'd set out to wander the city aimlessly. It had been a chilly day and the sky like asphalt, with unchanging light the color of windswept granite. He numbly rode the number three tram, walked around the Market Square and Eira, boarded a bus at the railway station without looking at the number. By evening he'd walked himself into such weariness that he was forced to rest at a bus stop in a neighborhood that had drawn him to it all day, even though there was nothing for him there, or anywhere else.

Darkness had fallen some time ago and it had started to rain. He sat there looking out at the familiar terrain, only to run up against the same thing over and over: that nothing he hoped for, waited for, and yearned for was true.

Just as he was thinking there wasn't a single creature in the world he meant anything to, anyone who could see what had happened to him, he noticed something familiar about the hot-pink rubber boots ambling lazily on the other side of the street. And the worn leather leash that made a sharp click when it locked, the four furry feet, the tail that dragged along the ground. And when he realized that the toes of the rubber boots had turned towards him a few moments ago, he reluctantly raised his head to meet Kerttu's mom's gaze from across the street.

Kerttu's mom was no doubt right in her opinion of him. He had broken her daughter's heart, without even realizing what he was doing. She had every reason to look down on him and think men, especially the ones Samuel's age, were pigs, because it was true.

He wished from the bottom of his heart that Kerttu's mom would leave, go home to Kerttu's stepdad, who about this time of day would start staggering around the kitchen with a bottle, eager to talk about his youth and his zest for life, which at the age of fifty hadn't gone anywhere, do you hear me, anywhere!

But Kerttu's mom crossed the street. Samuel heard the rubber soles of her boots slap against the road and saw the shadows cast by the yellowish streetlamps. He kept his eyes turned towards the ground, but he couldn't avoid the rain-soaked dog that nosed its head between Samuel's knees and pricked up its ears absent-mindedly. The dog wagged two lethargic sweeps of greeting with its tail.

'What's wrong?' Kerttu's mom asked. Samuel caught a glimpse of the concern on her face, although he studiously avoided eye contact. If there had been any judgment there initially, it had melted away.

Samuel shook his head, but couldn't tell himself if this signaled *nothing* or that he didn't want to explain.

Kerttu's mom asked: 'Is everything OK?'

Samuel shook his head.

Kerttu's mom tried to ask the same thing once more, phrased slightly differently. Samuel didn't want to be impolite, but it would be impossible for him to say a single word without everything gushing out. There was nothing he could do about anything, so there was no point talking about it, either – the only thing he was capable of was vomiting his disappointment, sense of injustice, self-loathing, anger, and shame all over Kerttu's mother, who didn't deserve it.

But the dog: it was happy to see him. The wagging tail slapped rhythmically against the post supporting the roof of the bus stop. His blood sugar was low after not eating all day, and Samuel wasn't sure he had the strength to rise from the cold plastic seat. But from his position, he couldn't avoid seeing the dog, its doleful expression. The dog nosed its way deeper into his lap.

And even though he'd decided he would never think about it again, memory now forced it back into his mind, the incident that had haunted him for a decade and a half now, when Mom had asked him if he wanted to go by himself to the United States for two weeks to visit his father. He remembered being dazzled by the opportunity Mom was presenting, so earth-shattering for a six-year-old that at first he'd had a hard time believing it. Boarding an airplane alone was far and away the best offer that had ever been made to him. Besides, the United States meant the page in his animal book about the bald eagle, and that was another reason he'd wanted to go, whole-heartedly, absolutely.

The decision had been his: Mom really was going to let him go.

When she had suddenly started talking about how he might feel scared on the long, lonely journey, start crying or having regrets – Mom probably hadn't said the last of these out loud, but in his memory, the message written across her face had been, literally, this – he remembered being confused. Him? *Regretting flying on an airplane?*

How do you feel about it, Samuel?

Samuel?

Do you want to go see your daddy?

Or not?

You'll have to speak English there, you know.

Samuel, now are you telling me how you really feel, deep down inside? What would be best for you?

From Mom's questions, he understood that, by boarding the plane, he would also have to meet his father. A lump had risen in his throat, a fluttering in his chest, as he tried to recall the bearded, shadowy man in question. But all the memories were like blurry, bleached photographs. He stood there, heart pounding, as if staring at the gleaming black watery surface without being able to see what lay beneath. At the same time, he realized what the choice would entail. The whole time he was in the airplane, Mom would be alone. There was no way he could go, he realized. Mom didn't have any other friends; she would never last two weeks without him. But the hardest thing was the finality of the decision: he hadn't understood that in making this choice, he'd also chosen never to see his father for the rest of his life, never to fill that empty, aching hole in his chest, that void where everyone else had something, no matter how broken, alcoholic, violent, embarrassing, or flawed: *something.* He hadn't simply chosen to stay at home, but permanent, utter estrangement from his father, and he'd chosen it himself, no matter how small and ignorant he had been, and if he had chosen differently, his entire life might have changed, and – well, he'd never be able to forgive himself that.

And although Samuel knew the beagle well, the way it happened still came as a surprise. It was warm, and he could feel its heartbeat through the smooth brown-and-white coat. He knew he shouldn't, but as he petted the soft, wet, muddy-smelling dog, it felt so warm and floppy-eared and trusting in his lap, its white feet so gentle, its lips so slack. He took in the way it looked at him with its dog eyes, the way it let everything be, the way it had no explanations, names, or solutions, the way it didn't find anything remarkable – human concerns belonged solely to humans. Here was its warm muzzle and it didn't occur to the dog to spoil everything by talking.

Standing there with her rubber boots on and her umbrella, Kerttu's mom, whose face he luckily couldn't see, could tell it was happening, and he couldn't help it anymore, and finally the misery came pouring out. And the dog didn't care; it just looked at him, brow furrowed in concern, and kept pressing its warm nose into Samuel's lap.

He had no idea how many nights, weekends, and months he'd spent as a teenager looking up information on his dad; it had gradually turned into a part-time job. But that's when it came to an end, that night at the rainy bus stop with Kerttu's mom and the dog. After that, he stopped expecting anything from his father.

Over the weeks that followed, he pored over every morsel of information he'd gleaned about Joe Chayefski from Mom and the World Wide Web and mourned them, one by one. The random anecdotes, the photographs, the home address, the phone number, the girls' photos – he swept them up in his mind and tossed them out, one by one, as well as those tiny, nonsensical crumbs gathered from the web's most random corners (ANNOUNCEMENT: Neuroscience undergraduates only allowed 2.5 credits during Intersession will be able to earn 3 credits per Dr Chayefski's adjustment at the end of Intersession!). All the irreplaceable lifelines he had secreted away in his heart and secretly studied in his bedroom at night… he cut up every single one of them individually over the days and weeks that followed and destroyed them. Had he really placed so much trust and hope on a complete stranger, on a man who probably didn't even remember his existence?

Mom had observed him from a distance, uncertainly, not understanding what was happening inside him, not wanting to make matters worse, not knowing how to help. He saw how worried she was, and he no doubt seemed like someone drowning in depression, someone who'd scorched his soul, who was verging on suicide.

How incomprehensible, how infuriatingly frustrating, how *fucking* unfair, he remembered thinking during those weeks: to have to mourn so goddamned much for someone he'd barely known – and who was alive and well, carefree. He was stunned by the perfect, all-encompassing sorrow he felt, something totally novel for a nineteen-year-old. He felt he was trapped in a wash of frigid blue water, numbing and disabling him – a precise antithesis to that burning tidal wave he'd experienced at Hietaniemi Beach.

Without that experience, he would have done everything wrong. In hindsight there was no question in his mind; without that labor, without those cool blue weeks, he never would have been capable of doing right by the beagles. He didn't know what would have happened or where he would have ended up, but the motivation would have been of the wrong kind.

At a library in Helsinki he had heard a Buddhist monk talk about love. You could recognize love, the monk said, by the way it didn't present alternatives or demands, didn't weigh costs. You could recognize love, the monk said, by the way it filled the heart with light. You could recognize love, the monk said, by the way it shifted attention away from one's self and one's own desires. Love, the monk said, instantly knew what to do.

It wasn't until he talked to Kerttu that Samuel gradually started understanding what had happened to him once he opened the door on floor B2 of Laajakoski Biosciences Inc. It wasn't until after he talked to Kerttu and weighed his options that he realized this was a *kairos* moment, not many of which are granted to us but that determine who we become.

Something about the experience was so fundamentally different from that metallic-tasting despair he'd been forced to face the night he came home from Hietaniemi Beach that another thing dawned on him, too: that without either of these experiences, he wouldn't be here now, or not at least like this. He wouldn't be who he was without every detail he'd been forced to mentally transfer from important to trivial, every dream he'd been forced to bury, without those weeks that had passed as if in a blue-black storm cloud, without that hollow the experience left behind, without that hole that still ached if someone prodded it, and always would. Without Kerttu's mom and dog and without Kerttu's voice on the phone, he wouldn't have been able to tell love from hate.

Without them, he would have done something for the beagles similar to what he did that night after coming home from Hietaniemi Beach, something exactly the opposite of what he ought to have done, something he would still regret.

With the exception of that one incident, that happened after he came home from Hietaniemi Beach, everything had gone the way it should have.

What he'd done for the beagles at the Laajakoski Biosciences Inc. research center could still, was even likely to, land him in jail, but that was the price of his decision. He hadn't had a choice. The only thing necessary for the triumph of evil is for good men to do nothing.

But that night he came home from Hietaniemi Beach, Samuel had done the very thing his father was now accusing all of them of, including those he'd never met.

Samuel watched Joe laboriously haul himself up from the doormat in the entryway, where the shoes and clothes of teenage girls were strewn across the coat and shoe racks. He was ashamed by how he'd barged uninvited into his stranger-father's life, and how he'd allowed his own fright to throw him into such a rage. Of course they were on edge here. After everything that had happened to them – he should have been more generous.

How difficult it was to put yourself in another's shoes, he thought, even after everything he'd been through.

'Forgive me,' he said to his father.

It was only when he heard the tremor in his own voice that he realized what a deep place the request came from. Joe didn't answer. Samuel stepped towards him, concerned. Perhaps it would be wisest for him to leave.

'Forgive me. That was a horrible thing for me to do. You just startled me,' he said, holding the gun out to Joe. His father looked at it as if not comprehending what it was. Joe closed his eyes, waved the gun away, and went into the living room where he sat down on the couch. Samuel looked at the gleaming revolver in his own hand. He felt a wave of nausea as he thought about what he'd just done with it.

'Should we put this away somewhere?' he asked.

Joe rubbed his head and didn't respond. He looked pale, and beads of sweat had formed on his brow. Samuel was concerned. Had he done serious damage? Men that age had heart attacks.

He lowered the gun between the claws of the grinning red crayfish on the doormat. *This is Bawlmer, hon.*

'Are you OK?'

Joe waved his hand impatiently. Apparently that meant yes. Or would you get out of here already.

Samuel was standing in the entryway, feeling helpless. The fan was humming loudly somewhere further inside. What should he do now? Samuel didn't want their one and only encounter to end this way.

'Dad?'

At this, Joe appeared to start. Now he looked at Samuel with glistening eyes, as if suddenly remembering who they were to each other.

'I'm sorry for showing up like this out of the blue. It clearly wasn't the best time.'

Joe gazed at the floor, didn't speak.

Samuel interpreted this as permission to continue. 'Can I come in? Just for a minute. I'd like to talk some more.'

Joe kept staring at the floor. Without saying anything, he finally nodded.

Samuel's English was easy-sounding, but foreign; Joe realized his son had had to learn the language the same way as every other Finn – at school. So this was Samuel: sparkling black eyes and heavy black stubble, reluctant long curls poking out from under an oversized beanie. Young people were remarkable, so ready to risk their lives: a beanie in Baltimore in the summertime.

Feeling pressure in his chest, Joe listened to Samuel, who was looking around in curiosity and complimenting him on the house. And when his son sat down on his living-room couch as naturally as if it were something he did every day, Joe realized why this man hadn't come here to kill him – why that was an utter impossibility.

Whatever it was that people who committed horrendous acts had in common, clearly didn't exist in this man. That feeling of being ultimately misunderstood, of being victimized by the whole world, was completely alien to this man. He was too comfortable in his own skin, his eyes were too inquisitive; he radiated calm assurance that no matter what he set his mind to do, he'd succeed.

Apparently what had just transpired truly had been nothing but a reflex on Samuel's part. Joe had a hard time believing this – until he reflected that the same was true of him.

Samuel studied him with concern, even compassion – no doubt because he was sitting, paralyzed, on the couch, unable to speak.

'You... came.'

This much Joe was finally able to cough out.

'I'm sorry I didn't let you know beforehand,' Samuel said. 'Or actually I tried to call a couple of times, but no one ever answered.'

In order to say something, Joe heard himself fumbling at increasingly awkward attempts at small talk: 'Where did you come from?'

'Federal prison. Most recently. Since you ask.'

Joe swallowed. Samuel seemed to register his fright and corrected himself: 'Or I mean, Oregon. Eugene. Portland.'

Eugene, Oregon, Joe managed to fish out of the aching folds of his brain, anarchist capital of the United States. Where violent, head-line-grabbing demonstrations against capitalism had been coordinated, where various eco-extremist movements were headquartered. Every ecoterrorist had traveled through Eugene at some point in their lives, someone had said in the Stand Up For Your Research Rights! discussion forum.

'Oregon?' Joe said, wondering if he'd be able to recognize a heart attack if he were having one. 'You have friends there?'

'Yup. I was invited to speak at this one event,' Samuel said. 'A seminar in Portland.'

The Society for the Ethical Treatment of Animals, Samuel explained. Thanks to the research he'd conducted during the past few months, Joe was familiar with it: a militant organization whose members believed he was wrong, a seminar where they discussed how best to destroy his career and his work.

Something in the demeanor of this stranger, this young *zayde* – his son – radiated such confidence that it seemed it had always been clear that today would be the day he'd show up, without warning, from Oregon. But the young *zayde* also seemed troubled: something was bothering him. Joe was incapable of being more than semi-aware of this, all of his energy still directed to telling himself that he didn't need to be afraid of this person after all.

'Nice to meet you,' Samuel said. Then his expression changed, and suddenly he stood up. He went into the entryway, where he'd left a grubby unbleached canvas bag and bent over to rummage through it.

Samuel said: 'I brought you this.'

For a split second, a fresh wave of panic washed over Joe, as his son drew a heavy, dark object out of the bag.

Joe blinked.

A bottle of wine.

'I hope you like it. It was all I could afford. I bought if from that deli.'

If it hadn't been for his own experience with Freedom Media, Joe might not have been as willing to believe what Samuel told him.

It was, evidently, true that during that difficult fall two years ago, Samuel had expressed his thoughts in writing. It was also true that he hadn't been particularly diplomatic as he described his feelings. It was true that he'd posted his opinions about his ex-girlfriend and Joe in a public forum, and it was true that one could read a certain hostility into these diary entries, intended to be private and written at his weakest moment.

And according to Samuel the health-center staff had been forced to choose some diagnosis based on his two fifteen-minute visits – protocol demanded a pertinent diagnosis for every consultation. The harried nurse, who'd had to enter something in the system, had made a stab at the combination that seemed most accurate to her. The diagnoses didn't matter, she had perhaps thought – if they turned out to be inaccurate, they would be corrected later, when Samuel returned for treatment. Of course no one was supposed to be able to access the secure medical records without authorization, but it looked like Simon Waters really knew what he was doing.

Evidently Samuel genuinely had joined forces with an environmental activist named Tyler Burnham, but only much later, after seeing the beagles being experimented on and realizing that all the demonstrations held outside the fence of the Laajakoski research center accomplished, aside from momentary media attention, were eyefuls of pepper spray and the tightening of the center's security systems – even though the entire country felt that what Samuel had exposed taking place there was outrageous.

According to Samuel, Tyler was one of the most compassionate, considerate, and intelligent people he knew. In Samuel's view, he had just been too successful. Hearing this, Joe felt bitterness and a sense of being misunderstood beading up in every one of his cells again.

'So that's how it goes?' he said sarcastically. 'When you gain enough influence, they start calling you a terrorist?'

Samuel thought for a moment and then said: 'You try waging a campaign against a really big company. One that has more money than God.'

Joe felt a nasty twinge inside.

His son continued: 'Do it so well that it actually starts to affect their market share. Try to drive them off the stock market, for instance. And do it in such a way that the whole world can see online that it was only you and your two best friends who were behind it all. Do that and see what happens to you.'

Joe tried to gulp down the foul-tasting sensation in his chest. He didn't like this; the boy had misunderstood everything. Society wasn't like this, this wasn't the sort of country, of world, he lived in, this wasn't what Western democracies were like, the boy didn't know what he was talking about.

But for some reason, Joe couldn't stop himself from asking: 'What happens?'

Samuel looked at him: 'The goalposts move.'

That much Joe had apparently understood correctly; Samuel and his friends had really taken down an international, publicly listed corporation, terrorized it until it was unable to function. And although Joe immediately remembered the well-groomed, friendly woman from the DRM company whom he was still paying every week for robot-powered online searches, and even though he also remembered his colleagues who had bowed out of the boycott because they'd heard Freedom Media would start to smear the reputations of any who tried to stand in their way, even then, he refused to tolerate this. The persistent burning in his stomach lining told him that his son was wrong, that you couldn't deal with the world this way.

'Wait.'

Samuel went to get his phone, fiddled with it for a second, and then thrust it out. On the screen was a picture of the front page of a highly regarded financial newspaper printed on pink paper. The news itself was in a mid-sized column:

'Parkingfield LS Suspended from NYSE'

Samuel zoomed in by spreading his thumb and forefinger.

'"According to blah blah blah from the blah blah blah,"' he read quickly, and then slowed down: '"The Parkingfield Life Sciences International Inc. no longer meets the NYSE's continuing listing criteria. Market capitalization blah blah... fallen below $50 million."'

Samuel looked proud. Joe no longer had the energy to get mad or explain to his son why what he'd done was wrong. This was precisely what was so odd about the world we lived in: it was acceptable to demonize a lawfully functioning company this way. Whatever you thought of them, their operations were still legal. You couldn't start threatening people, smashing places up.

'The methods you people use,' Joe said, feeling a hundred and fifty years old. They wouldn't be able to come to any sort of understanding after all. 'The bricks, the baseball bats, the bombs...'

Samuel stared at him in disbelief.

'What are you talking about?' he asked. 'How many times do we have to have this same conversation?'

'So what did you use to scare them, then?'

'Telephones.'

'What?'

'And we didn't really even scare them. And they weren't the ones we called.'

'You used your phones? But you didn't call them?'

'Exactly. It didn't take us long to realize it wasn't worth it.'

According to Samuel, the strategy was similar to the one used against the apartheid regime in South Africa: you politely ask associated companies if they, in the interests of their international reputation, might not want to consider shifting their business elsewhere. It was pretty hard to continue animal testing if no one would sell you supplies, if no one would transport your animals from the airport, if animal foodstuff couriers refused to work with you, if you couldn't get a missing bolt mailed to you.

When ten thousand young people around the world called the same bank director every day to politely ask if he was certain his bank wanted to be the one to extend credit to this specific company – say, everyone just once an hour, that added up to eighty thousand calls during one workday – the strategy started having an impact.

'In our experience, within a couple of months they come up with other places to invest their money. Ones they don't need to answer a single phone call about. We haven't frightened, threatened, or terrorized anyone.'

Joe stared at Samuel. According to the company and the authorities, key personnel had been attacked with baseball bats and bombs. But Samuel maintained the whole campaign had been conducted via a couple of laptops from the bedroom of a suburban home. Joe suddenly realized that all his information had come from sources selected and recommended by the *iAm*. He was ashamed. Why hadn't he – supposedly a critical, independent thinker – thought to seek out alternate opinions, more impartial information?

He'd been misled, either without any particular intention or, in the worst-case scenario, deliberately.

Joe had to breathe in deeply. It sounded like quite the achievement: his son and his friends driving a billion-dollar enterprise from the New York Stock Exchange without resorting to violence, without doing anything illegal.

'I saw online that you were involved in a sort of similar effort, in a slightly different sector,' Samuel said. 'Feel free to use our strategy if you like the model. We won't charge a finder's fee.' A tiny smile twitched at the corners of Samuel's mouth, but he had the sense to smother it. 'I noticed you succeeded in getting them on your case, but not much else.'

Joe could feel the ire rising within him. He hadn't been able to stifle completely his reluctant admiration for what his son had accomplished. He couldn't help it: he respected the protesters' ingenuity, determination, understanding of monetary flow. (Not could he help the tiny, unfair, inappropriate thought: the boy hadn't turned out to be a Finn – but an American!) And yet this admiration galled Joe so badly that he was gritting his molars.

There were a million reasons why what they'd done was wrong, no matter how clever and determined they were. Joe understood why Parkingfield Life Sciences International – which also owned Laajakoski Biosciences Inc. – had sued them for coordinating these campaigns. It served them right. It was of course wrong of Parkingfield LS if, as the boy claimed, they had really put the full force of their billions of dollars into having articles and blog entries written about Samuel and his friends that made them sound like terrorists. And at that instant, everything that was being said about Joe himself in Freedom Media's tabloids and TV stations and websites flashed through his mind. But it didn't change the fact that attacking someone for arbitrary reasons was unacceptable.

We haven't terrorized anyone. The boy had no idea what it felt like to be on the receiving end of constant harassment.

'But that's what it is!' Joe squawked, and felt ancient, sick, and for some reason tearful as well. 'Tele-terrorism. Eighty thousand phone calls a day to a person who's trying to make a livelihood by legal means, support his family?'

'Yeah, well,' Samuel said. 'We call it lobbying. To us, terrorism is endangering someone's life or health. Or threatening to. But let's not get hung up on that. This is civil disobedience, and of course we accept any and all punishments mandated by law.'

'You people don't understand what lobbying is.'

'Or do we?' Samuel said. 'We'd rather do it above board, too, buy enough politicians with campaign funding. We just didn't have the money.'

'Some of you are prepared to go to any lengths.'

The mention of the infamous and dangerous activist Heather Miranda brought a tired smile to Samuel's lips. He shook his head. Variations of the article sponsored by the security company had been published in nearly two dozen newspapers and circulated in online forums, punctuated by exclamation points and horrified commentary.

According to Samuel, the story of the real Heather Miranda went as follows: two representatives from a private security company had infiltrated a group of animal rights activists and spent two years trying to convince dozens of people to carry out a violent strike. Because no one had agreed, they'd eventually been forced to recruit an individual who'd used heroin for years, done prison time for violent crime, and also happened to sign a petition on behalf of animal rights. Initially the security company reps couldn't convince Miranda to carry out the strike they wanted, even though she was seething with hatred for the system, humankind, and big business. In the end, after a year of hounding, Miranda finally caved. The men from the security company had had to acquire the explosives, make the bomb, transport it to the company parking lot in their own van, hide it in the agreed spot, and then pick up Heather Miranda at home, drive her to the same parking lot, and leave her there alone – so the security company could 'happen' to show up and apprehend her on suspicion of ecoterrorism.

It was true, Samuel explained, that Miranda had agreed to be driven to the scene. But she hadn't carried out a violent attack. It was conceivable that she would have carried it out as promised – but that hadn't, in fact, happened.

Heather Miranda had received ten years in prison for her complicity, while the security company reps were now prominent anti-ecoterrorist consultants. They were paid thousands of dollars to teach infiltration methods to the authorities, private security service providers, and corporations.

'There's probably no way I'll ever get you to believe,' Joe said, 'that some of you people are genuinely dangerous.'

Samuel looked impatient: 'I really love that "you people."'

'So replace it with something better,' Joe snapped. 'Animal rights activists... environmentalists.' This hairsplitting was getting exhausting. But Samuel succeeded in presenting a few – if very selective – examples drawn from among Joe's colleagues, their methodologies and public statements, and Joe felt a twinge of embarrassment. Maybe there really was something to what Samuel was saying; every group was made up of all sorts of people.

And although the boy opposed the work Joe was doing and felt that the millions spent on it would have been better directed to more urgent needs – for instance, saving children dying of malnutrition, providing health care for all Americans, slowing climate change, and so on – he still viewed Joe's work differently than the work of those whom he and his friends had decided to stop. According to him, Parkingfield Life Sciences would do anything to any creature for any reason, as long as they were paid. According to Samuel, most of the tests were conducted to meet corporations' unique legal needs, cover up real research results, or, at their most beneficial, to create a new artificial sweetener, even though over thirty already existed on the market. Millions of animals a year for tests that were, in practical terms, unnecessary.

Joe refused to believe this; the system couldn't function this poorly. Nevertheless, Samuel got him to concede that he wasn't familiar with every aspect of the system, and didn't know what percentage of research results a company might leave unpublished in order to protect their business.

'Don't you think it might be a good idea for people like you to know? Wouldn't it be a good idea if you looked into it a little?' Samuel asked. 'You have a much better chance of wielding influence than, say, we do.'

The fact that Joe could, in his own work – at least theoretically – consider methodologies independently for each research question, sounded important to the boy. But to his mind, Samuel said, the most important thing was what he'd understood only after he and his friends had broken into Laajakoski's data archives.

'If you're interested…'

He left the sentence hanging while he retrieved something else from his bag. A heavy-looking gray box. A hard drive.

'There are a few research results here. Have a look if you'd like to.'

Joe studied his son. By now he had to admit to himself that the boy might actually know something he didn't. Samuel held the hard drive out to him, and Joe realized that if he accepted it, he might end up on a slope that would send him sliding somewhere deeper than he was prepared to go.

'Is that what you stole from them?'

Samuel nodded. 'When we realized what was on it, we asked for a little help.'

'What kind of help?'

There were programs, Samuel explained, that crawled along predetermined digital routes like insects, collecting everything they came across.

'Their business secrets?' Joe asked.

'Yes.'

'But that's a crime.'

'Yes, it is.'

'Of course I'm not going to touch them.'

Samuel looked at him and then at the hard drive in his own hand, and thought for a long time.

'I think there are things here that we should all see. And I mean all of us.'

Joe stared at him. He felt like he was facing a decisive fork in the road but had no idea where either route would lead him.

'This is what you were defending at that debate,' Samuel said to Joe, holding up the hard drive. 'Among other things.'

More than anything else, this was what he and Tyler had wanted to stop.

'We live in a Western democracy governed by elected politicians, not corporations,' Joe said. 'If there's something wrong with the system, it needs to be fixed through political, democratic means. You people are living in some imaginary dystopia that exists solely in your heads.'

Samuel met his eye without flinching. He nodded at the hard drive in his hand. 'If you open these files, you'll learn something about how our democratic political system functions. I think there are things here you didn't know. And I think that when you do see them, you might be frightened.'

Samuel said that in the past, he also would have thought someone claiming stuff like this was crazy. But he'd seen the contents of the hard drive.

'That was acquired through criminal means,' Joe insisted.

Samuel extended the hard drive closer. 'Is what is criminal always morally unjustified? Open these and tell me if you change your mind.'

But just when Joe thought he would have to make the critical decision – either be complicit in a crime or disappoint his son – Samuel's expression abruptly changed. He frowned and let the hard drive fall to his lap, as if accepting that Joe was not going to take it. He seemed to be searching for words.

When Samuel began to speak again, Joe could see how hard he was finding this.

The first time his son said it, Joe thought he misheard.

'What?' he asked.

'The package.'

Joe stared at Samuel.

'That was sent to your daughters,' he said.

'Yes?'

'I'm to blame.'

His young face suddenly expressed fathomless remorse.

It had been a mistake. That's what he'd finally made it seem, after sufficient retroactive rearranging of the details in his mind: a minor slip. For nearly two years, he'd managed to put the incident out of his mind. Now and then it resurfaced, nipped at him, and slipped out of sight again. He'd spent countless nights rationalizing to himself that his actions hadn't necessarily led to anything.

But after he heard about the needle bomb in the package, he'd realized that he'd have to accept responsibility for what he'd done. Even though the trip to Baltimore was partly inspired by curiosity, the desire finally to meet this Joseph Chayefski, maybe even ask for his help with the hard drive, the primary motive for Samuel's visit had been the package.

He'd seen a news report about it while he was in Eugene, sitting in Tyler's kitchen.

The sun had been shining through the windows and the warblers singing in the bushes when Samuel came down to breakfast. He'd just returned from Los Angeles the previous night. He'd been afraid he couldn't make the trip, but in the end they'd promised to pay his way. He felt tired but re-energized. For a brief moment, things looked good. The trip had gone well, and the audience appeared to have heard what he had to say. Evil and injustice had been temporarily repelled, balance restored, people still open to common sense.

But right before Tyler raised his tablet and said, *You hear about this? Some brain researcher on the East Coast*, right before Samuel had time to register Tyler's words, before Samuel saw the headline on *Resist!*, the online magazine, before Tyler had time to read his father's statement out loud, before any of this, Samuel somehow knew already what the consequences of his actions had been.

He'd squeezed his eyes shut and taken a deep breath. When the ocean rages, the waves only crash on the surface; below the water is calm. It's not the facts that defeat us, but how we react to them.

He'd had to travel to a conference in Portland that same day, and he'd been freezing despite the warm spring sun; the chill seemed only to intensify in the four-star conference hotel where he was put up, he, who didn't even have money for a cab from the airport.

Calm down, he'd tried to tell himself for the duration of the conference, although he knew it was pointless.

Before his speech, he gave his signature to a shy hippie-girl activist. Her eyes had lit up when she saw him: *But aren't you…?* Samuel had obediently played his part as she reached for her notebook and pen, hands trembling, and held them out to him like a meek baby bird.

He remembered having managed to shoot a little broken smile in her direction. But the pressure inside him didn't ease up, even when he forgot about it.

For Sandy, Samuel had written. Beneath it he had added a quote from Martin Luther King, a favorite he used all the time, a choice that now seemed so shameful and hypocritical he felt like tearing up the paper the instant the pen rose from it.

As he climbed up in front of a crowd of four hundred in the packed auditorium, force of habit luckily came to the rescue. He'd already said the same things in so many places that he could naturally assume the mask he'd come to represent The Issue in. The first few times, he'd been afraid he wouldn't know how to choose the right words, that he'd stumble over the complexity of it all, the overabundance of details.

'You don't have to do anything,' Tyler had said then. 'It's been given to you as a gift. Don't do anything in particular. Just stay out there, and it will come to you.'

And that's what Samuel had learned to do. In Portland, too, the words had come of their own volition, partly from memory, partly in fresh new bouquets that surprised even him. There's no way I could have summarized that so neatly. Did I really come up with that?

He'd spoken about how the threat of ecoterrorism and violent acts committed by environmental activists had started to be represented in the official statistics. But then he'd shown his Portland audience, one slide at a time, that if you got your hands on the statistics and looked at what lay behind the out-of-control numbers, it turned out that 'acts and attempted acts of serious violence' almost exclusively entailed legal demonstrations. The authorities were including marches, writing on the street with chalk, throwing a cake in a CEO's face in front of the TV cameras. This was what he'd spoken about: power meant that you could title the columns in an Excel table however you chose without ever having to account for your choices. This was what he'd spoken about: that activists who acted out of compassion towards living creatures weren't likely to be the first ones going around threatening anyone's life or well-being.

He felt rotten to the core as he spoke, and afterwards when he heard people say it had been the best speech ever. The steady, crushing pressure inside him hadn't let up for a single second, even during the thunderous applause. Later that afternoon, as he was vomiting in the men's room, he could hear the little, bird-boned hippie girl reciting the MLK quote to one of her friends on the other side of the wall, in the women's restroom, explaining who'd dedicated it to her. As he stood doubled over the toilet bowl, he could hear the girls browsing through his social media pages to find out if he had a girlfriend, and then he realized what he should have done a long time ago: that a person like him could never say another word about compassion or morals.

Nor had he.

He'd committed a single act of terrorism during his lifetime, an act motivated by sheer, unmitigated hatred, the desire to hurt another living being – he, who spent his life preaching the exact opposite.

When he heard about the bomb in the package, he'd instantly known what sort of moment was at hand. He'd experienced his first *kairos* moment in the basement of Laajakoski Biosciences Inc.; this was his second. And in June, when the heavy boots of the FBI SWAT team finally thundered against the porch-planks, he simply thought: I deserve this. He heard the others' exclamations of disbelief, the stunned amusement, Zaia's fearful wail: *They're packing submachine guns and Kevlar? Because we have a website where we tell people to pick up the phone?* And while the SWAT team storming the house in full combat gear performed its finely honed choreography with its MP5 submachine guns and precisely assigned roles – it was like ballet – he realized that the rhythmic sound he'd been hearing for a while now had to be a helicopter.

Tyler had said more than once that they'd be showing up soon. That you didn't take down an international corporation without consequences, that retaliation was inevitable. It was like the morning dew that indiscriminately blanketed everything. You might as well accept it if this was the life you chose. It had been clear to Tyler from the start that no matter what they accomplished, the goalposts would be moved. They'd be moved so the same thing would never happen again.

Samuel had witnessed in disbelief the concerted campaign to discredit their actions: the press articles saying that the photographs and videos he had shot on floor B2 of the Laajakoski Biosciences Inc. research center weren't real, but fabricated and spread with malicious intent by a dangerous, uncooperative individual. The op eds saying that justifiable questions about research methods were

no longer relevant criticism, but instead a threat to the health of
citizens and would bring medical advances to a halt. Similarly a legal
demonstration viewed through this prism became illegal, unnecessary
force became necessary, the concealing of research results scientific
self-criticism, the swindling of money 'in the public interest.' The
procedures shown in his photographs, of which no one ostensibly
approved, somehow demonstrated that Laajakoski/Parkingfield was
a profoundly moral actor that wanted the best for humankind,
animalkind, and the environment.

But that the exposing of these lies was terrorism: that was a surprise,
even to Tyler.

Samuel had never accepted it. In his view, only sore losers moved
the goalposts. But as he lay spread-eagled on the wooden floor that
morning, as the trained, gloved hands of the FBI SWAT officer patted
him down, searching for hidden weapons, he accepted his lot, because
he deserved it. With practiced efficiency, they loaded Tyler's books,
papers, and computer into big boxes and carried them out to their
vehicles. This day had always been coming, at last he was getting what
he deserved.

When the story began, Joe knew he didn't want to hear it. Samuel's
contorted face indicated that he was deadly serious; he was saying
he really had done it, though a minute before Joe never would have
believed it of him.

He tried to ask his son to spare him the telling, but it seemed to be
important for Samuel to voice what he had done.

As he opened his eyes in the bedroom that evening two years ago,
after coming home from Hietaniemi Beach, he wasn't sure if it was
day or night. Apparently he'd fallen asleep.

In the wake of the tidal wave, he felt unreal, washed clean. It felt
as if he'd been sleepwalking through life and had finally woken up.
He could still taste the metal in his mouth; it was a relief that he no
longer had to struggle against the feeling.

I must cultivate the ability to accept what I cannot change.

The world is what it is.

We all share responsibility.

He climbed out of bed on stiff limbs. The house was dark. Mom and Henri were asleep. The autumn wind was playing outside in the bare birches; they scratched against the window like bony, hooked fingers.

Samuel seated himself at his desk and powered up his computer. It whirred on. He could hear the Chinese components click as they warmed up; a tiny fan hummed somewhere inside the metal shell. At some fringe of his consciousness, he realized that his red hunting cap, the one Kerttu had bought him at the flea market, had fallen from the back of his chair. He kicked it into the corner, where Mom would come and pick it up two months later without his knowledge and hang it in the entryway closet, where he would never think to look for it.

When he saw the right website load on the screen, something flowed through his body like cold liquid.

He'd once visited a site that listed the names and addresses of laboratories and researchers who conducted animal experiments. He'd also seen a picture of the young men who maintained the site. They wore black, struck dramatic, defiant poses on a misty heath right before daybreak.

He'd promised himself he wouldn't come back to this site; he knew that if he did, he wouldn't act out of compassion, but out of an impulse he shouldn't feed.

Yet the site maintained by the boys in black came to mind whenever he thought about his father. It made its presence known whenever he thought about everything that was wrong with the world.

How easy it would be to have an impact in this one, trivial instance.

That night two years ago, when he came home, exhausted and humbled, from the deserted, windswept beach, and saw his father's jubilant smile on the website of a major American newspaper, he returned to the listing site.

Of course his father's name was on it. But the address was wrong.

It seemed Dad's info was years out of date.

Samuel's hand trembled as he reached for the mouse.

In the newspaper articles where his smiling father explained that animal research would save the world. The narrative never wavered. Exceptional individual Joseph Chayefski had saved the vision of the children of the world. The sentient beings at whose expense Dad had accomplished the heroic feats in his career were not mentioned in this article, because they weren't part of the feel-good story.

How different the winner's achievements would have looked if they'd been shown alongside the collateral of scientific victory, the suffering on which it was built; if those who had no words, and who hadn't given their consent, were also allowed to bear witness.

Of course, their story was never told.

That was why he did it, that night.

He had to go to a lot of trouble to find two other researchers whose information was also incorrect; informing on his father alone would have been too transparent. After finally locating the other two, unknown to him, in whose protective tarp he could wrap his father, he contacted the group through the data network that operated outside the official internet and through which he would be impossible to trace.

Some inner voice told him what he was doing was wrong, unquestionably so, but he'd decided in advance not to listen to it. The instant the thought had popped into his head, he realized he couldn't vacillate.

hey, i just happened to notice some info on your site looks outdated. check these three, i think the contact info below is correct.

No one answered, which was difficult to accept. He'd sacrificed his soul to put them on the tail of a significant international researcher, a future Nobelist perhaps. These nobodies who hadn't done a thing to deserve his help and whose setup was completely lacking in credibility – these jokers had the gall not to reply.

But when he visited the group's site a week later, he felt a rush of adrenaline.

The information had been corrected.

His heart raced when he noticed that the names and information of the three updated entries had been highlighted. At the bottom of the page, there was a note that new information for those three had been received. Always double-check your sources, the site administrators encouraged.

His palms were sweating.

What had he done?

It didn't mean anything, an inner voice quickly whispered: it didn't matter. No one visited sites like this, the whole group was sketchy.

He told himself the same thing when he went to bed, fingers clammy and back sweaty. Nothing would happen as a result of the updated information. Besides, they would have updated it themselves before long. What lunatic was going to search for his victims randomly online anyway? Attacking people just because their name and address had been written in a bright color on a website? Yeah, right. His agitation was an overreaction, just like any time Dad was involved. It was as Kerttu said: when it came to his father, Samuel lost all sense of proportion.

He'd imagined this was activism. In spite of the guilt, he'd imagined he'd done his part, no matter how small. He found it hard to forgive himself that later.

It was months after, when he knew Tyler, that he'd mentioned something about the site.

Tyler had been annoyed.

That site and the people who maintained it were counterproductive. What were they trying to accomplish by frightening people? Embittering them, encouraging them to buy handguns? Besides, attacking individual researchers was inefficient – a bit like trying to take down an apartheid government by breaking the windows of a random Johannesburg homeowner. And inciting people to violence, Tyler continued: how was this any different from terrorism? It would be pretty hard to claim you'd acted out of compassion. Flirting with violence only led to its increase, he said.

Samuel had stared at Tyler, paralyzed.

Swinging baseball bats around appealed to a certain type of young man, Tyler said. But that had nothing to do with societal change.

Shame had prevented Samuel from saying anything else.

He'd never been able to confess to Tyler what he'd done.

Guilt throbbed within him for a long time, but a single address didn't amount to much. After that conversation, he monitored the situation daily, tried to prove to himself he hadn't done anything serious. And luckily there had never been any news from Baltimore.

Until last April.

The memory of what he'd done struck like a bolt of lightning when he'd watched the boys in blacks' video of Dad's public lynching at the campus debate. They'd come to butcher him unfairly, a thousand against one. It was Samuel's fault, as wrong as Dad was in his lack of comprehension and narrowness of perspective.

Dad always and only thought about things through the lens of his own work, didn't understand the sort of organized crime he was unwittingly defending with his words, or how childish and harsh his arguments sounded to the ears of those who had seen the beagles. After watching the video on the sly in Eugene, it occurred to Samuel to check if someone had taken action against his dad. And almost immediately he'd come across the communiqués about the laboratory break-in, the brick, and the demonstration in the Chayefskis' yard.

And none of this would have happened, Samuel realized to his horror, staring at his laptop in the guest room of Tyler's creaking wooden house in the middle of the night, if he hadn't done what he had.

His son's tears caught Joe off guard. Samuel was leaning forward, elbows on thighs, palms covering his face.

From his spot on the old blue IKEA sofa, Joe stared at this stranger, this Samuel, sitting across from him, unable to get another word out. He started when the overly bright fluorescent light above the kitchen counter flickered three times, as if in supernatural signal. Samuel pulled a crumpled tissue out his pocket and blew his nose. Joe wanted to say something, but he'd already been forced to reverse his beliefs and perceptions about his son and the entire world so often tonight that he didn't know where to start.

Through the misty veil of his astonishment, Joe heard Samuel's voice, thick with emotion, saying he didn't expect to be forgiven. He understood that, and he hadn't come here seeking absolution, only to confess, to find peace.

Was that it?

Joe was too dumbfounded to reply. This was what the boy had done: emailed his father's address to someone? This was his abominable terrorist act? This was what Samuel had borne two years of crushing guilt over – sending an address? One they could have found anywhere with a couple of clicks?

He was forced to check with Samuel one last time – had he understood correctly? It was the fresh surge of tears that finally convinced him.

Joe stared at this stranger, his son. It felt as if only now was he starting to grasp who he was.

A gentle summer rain had begun falling. The drops pattered against the roof like the drumming of tiny fingertips. Outside the living-room windows, a streetlamp glowed, solitary in the darkness. A poor man's Statue of Liberty, Joe thought.

Samuel wasn't around in October to hear his friends Tyler Burnham and Kaitlin O'Shea be sentenced to prison without parole for tele-communications harassment and conspiracy. The court found that the perpetrators' website, used to mobilize thousands of young people in the United States, Canada, Europe, and South America to call bank directors, stockbrokers, airlines and laboratory supply manufacturers, with the aim of toppling a private company, was illegal.

Samuel wasn't around two weeks before Christmas to hear a pair of animal rights activists who called themselves Fight Back be convicted of breaking into Professor Joseph Chayefski's test animal laboratory, and trespassing and vandalism at his home.

Samuel wasn't around to hear all his suspected connections to the crimes committed against the Chayefski family be disproven.

Two weeks after Samuel appeared on his father's doorstep in Baltimore, the FBI located the man who had mailed the explosive device to Daniella and Rebecca Chayefski, thanks to a neighbor's tip. The neighbor had noticed him moving large amounts of agricultural supplies into his basement, even though he lived in the middle of the city and worked for the postal service.

In the man's home, the police found guns, fertilizers suitable for the manufacture of explosives, and supplies for almost ten needle bombs exactly like those received by the Chayefski family. Some of the packages had already been assembled.

All the police needed to do was ask why. The man confessed straight away. He wanted a chance to explain, had wanted one for twenty years.

The registrar's office at Columbia University confirmed that the man had studied in the same graduate cohort as Miriam Chayefski née Goldberg. According to his transcripts, he had dropped out after one year. The man told the police that he hadn't known what he wanted from life. Papers discovered in his home indicated that he'd apparently been writing a play he never completed and that he had gradually withdrawn from all social contact.

The 557-page manifesto he'd published online was characterized as misogynistic and right-wing extremist. The man emphasized that he supported animal experimentation and in no way wanted his actions to be interpreted as a condemnation of Joseph Chayefski's work. Animal research saved millions of lives, he later stated during his trial.

The man told the police that he sent the package so Miriam would finally, years after intentionally avoiding him when they were students, notice him.

Miriam wasn't sure she had any idea who he was.

By the time they stepped outside, the rain had stopped. The dark, cracked bark of the huge linden glistened; the light falling from the porch gleamed in the droplets on the raspberries.

Samuel walked down the rain-washed steps and waited for Joe, who said he had to go back in to get the car keys. The dark-leaved rhododendron, which had looked so sinister upon Samuel's arrival, seemed to have shrunk.

He had the same feeling he'd had as a teenager when Mom picked him up from the police station, after he'd been caught throwing rocks at the metro. He'd heard one of the police officers mention to a colleague that the kid's father wasn't in the picture. From his insinuating tone, Samuel understood that this made his juvenile delinquency understandable but also more reprehensible. For the entirety of that long evening he spent waiting at the police station, only one thing had worried him, to which any potential fines, talking-tos, or criminal records were minor footnotes: what Mom would say.

It was only when she hugged him that he knew they'd get through everything, even this. And walking home from the bus stop that evening, he could feel how Mom was holding his hand, always would, no matter what.

And now, as he stood with the father he didn't know on a warm, wet evening in Baltimore, he felt cleansed, new. He could sense his limbs more distinctly than before, every muscle and joint. This is me. The air smelled of rain and summer night, and everything was possible again. He would return to Finland and go to prison for pictures he wasn't allowed to take and information he wasn't allowed to distribute because people needed to be protected from the truth. But remarkably, none of this carried the urgent significance it had in the past. He filled his lungs with the fresh, grass-scented air.

Joe appeared on the porch: 'The car's in the garage.'

'I don't mind walking.'

'Don't be silly.'

Joe had promised to take him to a hotel for the night. Apparently there was a decent one across from campus. Joe wanted to see him again the next morning, for them to spend some time together. During his journey here, it hadn't even occurred to Samuel that this was how things could end up.

'You know, don't you,' Joe said, eyeing him, 'that we're in a particularly dangerous part of Baltimore?'

Samuel was surprised. Wasn't it just the opposite? 'Where?'

'Baltimore.'

Samuel only got the joke when he saw his dad's expression. Joe turned around to lock the door and then walked down the steps. Samuel waited on the gravel driveway and wondered whether he'd have guessed what his dad was going to say, whether he'd be sick to death by now of his dad's sense of humor, if he'd grown up with him.

This American neighborhood felt tranquil, sleepy: the crime and violence inundating the city beyond had been successfully confined elsewhere. It was all so idyllic, the roads lined by large beech and maple trees, the houses surrounded by manicured lawns.

'This must be a nice area to live,' he said.

'We picked it for the schools.' Apparently many of the city's schools weren't the kind you dared send your kids to. 'We also wanted to live in a neighborhood with sidewalks.'

It had never occurred to Samuel that there might be some other kind. As he looked around, he reflected that this was the life he would be leading if he and his mom had returned to the United States when Joe did. Not this exact house maybe, but another one, comparable to it, in a different city maybe.

When Joe turned the key in the garage lock and the motorized door slowly hummed upwards, Samuel felt something start flowing through him, and realized his old life was over. It blew through him like a wind: suddenly he was free to do whatever he wanted. The path he'd followed for the past two years didn't need to dictate the rest of his life.

There was something incredibly moving about this. He could do whatever he wanted.

Joe saw his son staring down at the gravel. 'Is everything OK?'

'Yeah,' Samuel replied. And when he raised his gaze, he saw his father's brown eyes and thought, for the first time, that he'd like to learn to know who and what sort of person his father was.

The garage door was halfway up when Joe seemed suddenly to remember something. 'Wait a sec. I'll be right back. There's something I have to take care of that can't wait,' he added, and bounded back to the porch and into the house.

Samuel stood there watching his father. It was amazing, having this opportunity. For a fleeting moment, he was almost grateful to the anonymous sadist who sent his half-sister the package. Without that, he wouldn't have come here, wouldn't have wanted to be a bother.

And luckily nothing had happened to her. Would he be meeting them tomorrow, too, maybe? The thought made his heart leap. Might they even become friends?

From somewhere beyond the fence he heard a sinuous, flute-like whistle. It sounded like a blackbird, Samuel thought, but it might be some other species, American. And that made him suddenly think about this year, this summer, these particular weeks: one of the people in Eugene had reminded him about them, when Samuel had vaguely mentioned heading back east before he returned to Finland.

'The cicadas,' someone had immediately said. 'Now is the time.'

'That's right,' someone else had added. 'You'll probably just catch the tail end of them.'

He had barely started wondering where they were – was it too dark? Did he know what to look for? – when the sound of a car approaching at astonishing speed caught his attention. The engine-gunning driver had to be confused about where he was, the night was so still. Some kid who just got his license, Samuel thought, thinking back to his high-school classmate Matias, who had raced through the warm Finnish summer nights like a madman.

While Samuel was hearing the car in Baltimore, Alina was in Helsinki, waking up to the digital drumming of her phone's alarm clock. She quickly silenced it so it wouldn't wake Henri and the boys. After opening the kitchen curtains to the summer sun, she remembered her demented father, how she hadn't been present enough in his life. And then she remembered her son, who'd been arrested by the FBI and whom she hadn't been able to prevent from traveling to see his own father, Alina's American ex-husband, for the first time in his life and at the worst possible moment.

When Samuel was standing in front of the rising garage door and listening to the approaching car and Alina was pulling back the kitchen curtains in Helsinki, Joe was opening the antique china cupboard and taking out the box of bullets.

He emptied the revolver's cylinder. The sound of the tapering, metal-skinned shells clunking to the table was dark and heavy, inspired confidence. He packed the gun and the ammunition into a beige canvas bag bought ten years earlier at an art museum in Washington D.C. The gun wasn't going to stay in his home for another second, no matter what Miriam said. He would take it to whatever police station was still open, throw it into Chesapeake Bay if he had to, but he was getting rid of it tonight.

At that instant, a sensation like an electric shock shot through his body: the red button! He'd forgotten all about it. He'd pressed it earlier that evening – an entire lifetime ago. He quickly pulled out his phone and brought up Doug's number; he needed to let them know it was a false alarm, otherwise they'd think his life was in danger when they were back in range. As the phone rang, Joe thought about his son, who was yawning outside in the summer night, stretching his long, young limbs in the yellow lamplight. In their yard, Joe thought, feeling his breast swell with pride.

Luckily Doug answered right away: 'Yeah?'

Joe blurted out why he was calling: he had pressed the button but there was no danger. Doug calmly heard him out, explained that he was in his vehicle at the moment, watching a house the size of a castle in whose vaults Rebecca was slow dancing and vainly trying to catch the attention of the Only Boy Who Mattered. Mike, on the other hand, had followed Miriam and Daniella's car and would no doubt be returning to the Chayefski residence soon. Apparently they'd stopped along the way for a bite.

Doug promised to pass the message on to Mike.

'Thanks,' Joe said. 'Can you call right away? Just so there isn't any misunderstanding.'

'Yeah, of course.'

Doug's deep, reliable growl was reassuring, and Joe felt his pulse instantly slow. He had just thrown the bag over his shoulder and was walking towards the hallway when he heard a large passenger vehicle approaching their property, engine howling. He was bewildered to hear the change in its pitch as the tires suddenly chomped into soft grass.

Samuel was absent-mindedly eyeing the surveillance cameras installed outside the house and thinking they looked new when he saw the car's headlights dip and flash as it slalomed onto West Chestnut Parkway. The speeding vehicle was a big SUV with tinted windows; a drug courier, flashed through his mind. When the SUV drew level with Samuel, the driver suddenly wrenched the wheel so the vehicle popped the curb and slewed across the lawn, making straight for him. Samuel was sure he was going to be run over. This was Baltimore, he suddenly realized: a city where eight-year-olds shot each other with Uzis over drug debts. Dad's joke was funny because it was true.

As Samuel watched the car lunging towards him, Alina was taking off the robe she had put on not long before. The sun was shining from a cloudless sky; the building was still warm. As she measured the oats into her bowl, Alina thought about the FBI, and how if someone had told her that one day her son would be arrested by them, she never would have believed it.

She remembered the last time Samuel had visited her, how she had inhaled her son's scent and thought that she wouldn't change a second of her life if it meant giving up this moment. Samuel had looked nonchalant, but Alina could feel nothing but concern for him. She felt it now, in her breathing, in her posture, in her heart, which leaped into her throat every time the phone rang. She couldn't help it; she was perpetually on edge. Alina knew that Samuel was forced to present himself as totally cool, independent, and fearless, for his mother's sake, so she wouldn't lose it.

Suddenly Alina was ashamed of how she'd been never been capable of being wholly on her son's side. She was embarrassed by how she had always been so hung up on legality and consequences And she remembered the question Samuel had surprised her with that one summer they hadn't made it to the cabin after all. Adolescence hadn't arrived; Samuel had been a mild-mannered preteen, with no sign yet of the gangly, slouching adolescent or the tall, broad-shouldered adult yet to emerge. The plan had been to go to the island with *pappa* for at least a week, atypically the three of them, but that week a bloom of blue-green algae had traveled into the little bay where the sauna and cabin were. It was disgusting, of course, and problematic: they couldn't wash dishes, go to the sauna, bathe. Alina remembered standing on the shore with her son and her father, still in relatively good shape at the time, and gazing out over the vivid poison-green soup shimmering in the shallows as far as the eye could see. They'd been forced to turn around and go back home. That had never happened before.

As the sea sprayed into the boat on the way back, Samuel had suddenly looked at her.

'Mom?'

'Yes?'

'What does sacred mean to you?'

Alina hadn't known how to respond.

She still didn't know. *Or didn't dare?* screeched an early-rising crow malevolently from the birch outside the window. *There's no such thing as sacred*, the crow jeered. All Alina knew how to do was feel guilty about raising her child into a world where, if anything sacred still existed, she hadn't been able to safeguard it – or even tell him what it was.

As she dribbled water into her oat flakes, Alina remembered her sadness about the ambivalence of everything; that she was incapable of being simply and solely happy about anything, even her son and his victory over Parkingfield Inc.

Alina turned on the microwave. She didn't want to close the curtains, even though the morning sun was making her squint. As she spooned the grounds into the coffee maker, she reflected that she had wasted three-quarters of her life worrying. It only made things worse.

She waited for the coffee maker to finish burbling. As she watched the coffee drip, she suddenly felt, distinctly and clearly, that she should have been a better support to her son and his friends. After all, at least they had tried, tackled something in a meaningful way. *Unlike you*, a chaffinch whistled in a bright, tinkling soprano, *you haven't done anything, not a single thing, about anything – that's why these children sacrifice themselves.* As she listened to the chaffinch, Alina wished she could have been wholly on her son's side, even for a moment. And now, on this June morning right before Ukko and Taisto woke up, she finally was.

Samuel bounded off when he heard a male voice snarl something at him. There was insecurity behind the anger, and Samuel had time to register the impression that the person yelling at him had failed at something important. It all happened in a split second: he had a momentary impulse to get a look at the gang member so he'd be able to describe him to the police, but dropped the idea; it was more important to take cover on the other side of the hedge. But – Dad! – he couldn't leave his father to the mercies of a drug dealer; Dad was a small guy, feeble, had just practically had a heart attack. Samuel would have to turn back. But before he could, he heard two shots.

The cracks were sharp and came in such rapid succession that they melted into one. It was only when he turned around to look that Samuel was perplexed: he was falling, about to hit the gravel. The echo of the third shot spattered from the walls of the night-shrouded houses a few seconds later. For some reason, he only felt the bite now. He realized he'd just been hit. In the ribs. But the first two, where...? He saw the purplish-black sky directly overhead, and it was high – how could it be so high? – and felt the night around him, soft as velvet.

He heard footsteps approaching; a large man with a gun was racing towards him. The man held his semiautomatic pistol in both hands, arms extended, but had let his hands drop to the right, as if aiming at a carefully chosen point at his feet. Samuel heard the sound of the SUV; the engine was still running. At the same time, he heard a mobile phone start ringing somewhere within the gunman's clothes. Samuel drew his hand to his lower back and sensed something start flowing from the effort. His hand felt wet, sticky. The mild American night felt like water on his skin. But it was as if he had just seen the night sky for the first time: how high it was, how inaccessible. And he was surprised by the wind, the tireless wind, which he sensed as a delicate tremor on his flesh although it blew across the entire Atlantic, from the East Coast of the United States over the Gulf of Finland, to Helsinki.

As he flung open his front door, Joe saw the SUV with its engine still running and a hulking silhouette in the darkness, in the stance of a trained professional. A mobile phone could be heard ringing faintly in Mike's jacket. He looked apprehensive as he stepped cautiously towards the dark figure sprawled on the ground, to kick away the gun the intruder must have on him somewhere, to make sure the close call was actually over. Mike's face didn't reflect any of what he would come to say later: *If the guy's intentions weren't bad, why did he run? Why did he have a beanie pulled down over his face? Why was he checking out the security systems?*

Samuel felt the wet-smelling grass against his cheek and heard the metallic, sinuous song. He thought about his father; now he was lying here, was the gang member going to get his dad? But Dad was standing over there, at the door, perfectly calm. Dad was fine, that was the main thing. Samuel scrabbled at the gravel to push himself up, but during the space of a single second it felt impossible and then unnecessary, he was fine down here on the ground. His hands struck on something coarse, like ears of barley, perhaps. Dad looked so worried... don't worry, Samuel felt like saying, everything's going to be fine. He glanced at his hands and realized what he had thought were ears of grain were dead insects, or their shells. He let his hands sink, they could stay where they were, nothing above him but the night sky, remote, unfathomable.

Joe would come to relive that evening over and over.

Before he went back inside to get the gun, it occurred to him that this was what he'd meant when he'd written his address on the slip of paper, along with the question, *Can we talk?* This was what he'd meant when he'd proposed the debate to the *Baltimore Sun*. Those efforts had failed, but now his belief in humanity was restored. As he turned from the garage to get the gun and the bullets so he could drive his son to the hotel, he felt pride in what had happened and that he'd believed in the possibility of dialogue. He was pleased that he'd trusted his intuition, and pleased above all that his son was the one who had granted him this opportunity. He wondered what the boy would think of the sisters he'd never met.

When he reached the porch, he glanced at his adult son standing by the garage: young, healthy, long-limbed. The Baltimore night was warm and humid, the air rain-washed, clean.

This didn't exist in Finland. It was another thing his son had unexpectedly reminded him of: the Finnish summer night was pale, flawlessly beautiful, but proud, inaccessibly cool, always kept its distance. Joe remembered how during his first year in Finland he'd anticipated nights like this all through May, when the weather started to warm up; had waited for summer proper to start. But by the beginning of August the wind had blown chill off the sea; no real summer – American summer – ever came. The chorus of crickets, the warm, dark evenings, the Fourth of July fireworks, the deep, fragrant, silken violet night: American summer.

And he thought about the crickets, how he couldn't hear their soft, familiar murmur the way he could on normal summer nights. And that was what made him realize it as he opened the front door: from the peace that had fallen over the porch, fuller than before. It was only then that he remembered, after thinking it might still be too early for crickets: the cicadas.

That was why he'd been feeling so weird all evening. That was why he'd imagined something portentous was about to happen: the cicadas had stopped screaming.

And even though he'd stepped outside a few moments ago, it was only now that he understood what he'd known from his first footfall – something had crunched under the sole of his shoe, and he wondered how he could have missed them even in the darkness. Incredible. The porch and street were covered in shells. The lawns were blanketed in the empty, dead husks of insects. The cicadas were gone.

He drew the fresh, humid summer night deeper into his lungs. Everything was wrong with the world, but he could stand here, see his son outside his home: momentarily grasp that this was the only instant, the only night, the only summer. He saw the rhododendrons in the darkness, the raindrops glittering on their leaves in the light of the streetlamps, and the small dogwoods along the road that had flowered pink that spring, like tufts of cotton candy.

Before Joe stepped back in, he reflected that this was the way to show a Baltimore summer: at night, in silence, when it was easy to breathe. He felt an unexpected, tender surge of happiness. This was exactly what he'd hoped his Finnish son would see when he finally came to stay.

ACKNOWLEDGEMENTS

I am greatly indebted to my American friends, whose help has been invaluable in writing this novel. For their time, help, discussions and, most of all, their friendship, I want to thank Josh Connor, Lisa Davidson and David Goldberg in particular. I also want to thank Lila Corwin Berman from Temple University, to whom I was introduced by Lisa.

I want to thank my agent Elina Ahlbäck and her team, my translator Kristian London, and Alyson Coombes, Lynn Curtis, Becky Kraemer, Juliet Mabey, Paul Nash, Mark Swan, Margot Weale and all the wonderful people at Oneworld I have been lucky to work with.

I would also like to thank Selja Ahava, Jukka Appelqvist, Hanne Appelqvist, Laura Arpalahti, Anna Heinämaa, Jussi Hermunen, Elina Hirvonen, Tuomas Juntunen, Inderjit Kaur Khalsa, Vera Kiiskinen, Juhana Kokkonen, Lasse Koskela, Pekka Lund, Piia Posti and Janne Sarvikivi for their careful reading, useful comments, discussions and friendship. It would take many fewer drafts than the number read by Tuomas and Anna to make most people lose their minds. Piia's sharp, detailed comments were of enormous help.

Huge thanks also to Hannu Harju, and a particular thank you to my editor Petra Maisonen. I admire Petra's patience and professionalism in reading, editing and commenting on endless new drafts while humoring a madman. A massive thank you also for Heini Kantala's close reading.

I am very grateful to Marianne Connor, Andy Walker and Colin Muir, who jumbled my thoughts in an instructive and useful way. I would like to thank Ben Norris for the literary discussions, brilliant reading suggestions and support, as well as Antti Ritvanen, Tuuve Aro, Nina Gimishanova and all the members of Nobelistiklubi.

I would like to thank Marcia Angell, Ben Goldacre, David Healy, Irving Kirsch, Ingrid Newkirk and Robert Whitaker for the journals,

books and articles that influenced this novel. One of my fictional
characters reads Daniel Goleman's book *Ecological Intelligence* in
particular detail and actively draws from its information on cotton
farming, glass production and environmental problems. The metaphor
of the love song and the time machine is from Iver Peterson's article
17-Year Cicadas Answer Cue With a Crunch Across the East in the
New York Times. I also borrowed thoughts from Douglas Rushkoff's
book *Life Inc.*, and Sherry Turkle's book *Alone Together*, which
considers the relationship of humans and robots in a fascinating
way. I am particularly grateful for Will Potter's illuminating book on
environmental activism, *Green Is the New Red*, which has been a key
influence on this novel. I recommend all the aforementioned authors
and works to the reader as well.

Regardless of all the help and advice I received, responsibility for
every factual error and implausible or illogical detail in the novel is
my own.

A huge thank you to Aarni and Anna, Laura and Matti, Mum and
Dad.

And the biggest thanks of all to Emilia, for everything.

ABOUT THE AUTHOR

© Markko Taina

Jussi Valtonen is an author and psychologist from Helsinki. He studied neuropsychology in the United States and screenwriting in the UK. His previous works include two novels and a short story collection. He currently lives in New York.

ABOUT THE TRANSLATOR

Kristian London is an American translator who divides his time between Seattle and Helsinki.

Oneworld, Many Voices

Bringing you exceptional writing from around the world

The Sky Over Lima by Juan Gómez Bárcena (Spanish)
Translated by Andrea Rosenberg

A Very Special Year by Thomas Montasser (German)
Translated by Jamie Bulloch

Umami by Laia Jufresa (Spanish)
Translated by Sophie Hughes

The Hermit by Thomas Rydahl (Danish)
Translated by K.E. Semmel

The Peculiar Life of a Lonely Postman by Denis Thériault
(French) Translated by Liedewy Hawke

Three Envelopes by Nir Hezroni (Hebrew)
Translated by Steven Cohen

Fever Dream by Samanta Schweblin (Spanish)
Translated by Megan McDowell

The Postman's Fiancée by Denis Thériault (French)
Translated by John Cullen

Frankenstein in Baghdad by Ahmed Saadawi (Arabic)
Translated by Jonathan Wright

The Invisible Life of Euridice Gusmao by Martha Batalha
(Brazilian Portuguese) Translated by Eric M. B. Becker

The Temptation to Be Happy by Lorenzo Marone
(Italian) Translated by Shaun Whiteside

Sweet Bean Paste by Durian Sukegawa (Japanese)
Translated by Alison Watts

They Know Not What They Do by Jussi Valtonen (Finnish)
Translated by Kristian London

The Tiger and the Acrobat by Susanna Tamaro (Italian)
Translated by Nicoleugenia Prezzavento and Vicki Satlow

The Woman at 1,000 Degrees by Hallgrímur Helgason
(Icelandic) Translated by Brian FitzGibbon

Frankenstein in Baghdad by Ahmed Saadawi (Arabic)
Translated by Jonathan Wright

Back Up by Paul Colize (French)
Translated by Louise Rogers Lalaurie

Damnation by Peter Beck (German)
Translated by Jamie Bulloch

Oneiron by Laura Lindstedt (Finnish)
Translated by Owen Witesman

The Boy Who Belonged to the Sea by Denis Thériault
(French) Translated by Liedewy Hawke

The Baghdad Clock by Shahad Al Rawi (Arabic)
Translated by Luke Leafgren

The Aviator by Eugene Vodolazkin (Russian)
Translated by Lisa C. Hayden

Lala by Jacek Dehnel (Polish)
Translated by Antonia Lloyd-Jones